AN EPIDEMIC ANTHOLOGY

*A Fiction Collection of All Manner of Plagues, Pandemics &
Disease*

EDGAR ALLAN POE   DANIEL DEFOE   MARY SHELLEY
JACK LONDON

CONTENTS

MASQUE OF THE RED DEATH

EDGAR ALLAN POE

THE MASQUE OF THE RED DEATH

THE "RED DEATH" had long devastated the country. No pestilence had ever been so fatal, or so hideous. Blood was its Avatar and its seal—the redness and the horror of blood. There were sharp pains, and sudden dizziness, and then profuse bleeding at the pores, with dissolution. The scarlet stains upon the body and especially upon the face of the victim, were the pest ban which shut him out from the aid and from the sympathy of his fellow-men. And the whole seizure, progress and termination of the disease, were the incidents of half an hour.

But the Prince Prospero was happy and dauntless and sagacious. When his dominions were half depopulated, he summoned to his presence a thousand hale and light-hearted friends from among the knights and dames of his court, and with these retired to the deep seclusion of one of his castellated abbeys. This was an extensive and magnificent structure, the creation of the prince's own eccentric yet august taste. A strong and lofty wall girdled it in. This wall had gates of iron. The courtiers, having entered, brought furnaces and massy hammers and welded the bolts. They resolved to leave means neither of ingress or egress to the sudden impulses of despair or of frenzy from within. The abbey was amply provisioned. With such precautions the courtiers might bid defiance to contagion. The external world could take care of itself. In the meantime it was folly to grieve, or to think. The prince had provided all the appliances of pleasure. There were buffoons, there were improvisatori, there were ballet-dancers, there were musicians, there was Beauty, there was wine. All these and security were within. Without was the "Red Death."

It was toward the close of the fifth or sixth month of his seclusion, and while the pestilence raged most furiously abroad, that the Prince Prospero entertained his thousand friends at a masked ball of the most unusual magnificence.

It was a voluptuous scene, that masquerade. But first let me tell of the rooms in which it was held. There were seven—an imperial suite. In many palaces, however, such suites form a long and straight vista, while the folding doors slide back nearly to the walls on either hand, so that the view of the whole extent is scarcely impeded. Here the case was very different; as might have been expected from the duke's love of the bizarre. The apartments were so irregularly disposed that the vision embraced but little more than one at a time. There was a sharp turn at every twenty or thirty yards, and at each turn a novel effect. To the right and left, in the middle of each wall, a tall and narrow Gothic window looked out upon a closed corridor which pursued the windings of the suite. These windows were of stained glass whose color varied in accordance with the prevailing hue of the decorations of the chamber into which it opened. That at the eastern extremity was hung, for example, in blue—and vividly blue were its windows. The second chamber was purple in its ornaments and tapestries, and here the panes were purple. The third was green throughout, and so were the casements. The fourth was furnished and lighted with orange—the fifth with white—the sixth with violet. The seventh apartment was closely shrouded in black velvet tapestries that hung all over the ceiling and down the walls, falling in heavy folds upon a carpet of the same material and hue. But in this chamber only, the color of the windows failed to correspond with the decorations. The panes here were scarlet—a deep blood color. Now in no one of the seven apartments was there any lamp or candelabrum, amid the profusion of golden ornaments that lay scattered to and fro or depended from the roof. There was no light of any kind emanating from lamp or candle within the suite of chambers. But in the corridors that followed the suite, there stood, opposite to each window, a heavy tripod, bearing a brazier of fire that projected its rays through the tinted glass and so glaringly illumined the room. And thus were produced a multitude of gaudy and fantastic appearances. But in the western or black chamber the effect of the fire-light that streamed upon the dark hangings through the blood-tinted panes, was ghastly in the extreme, and produced so wild a look upon the countenances of those who entered, that there were few of the company bold enough to set foot within its precincts at all.

It was in this apartment, also, that there stood against the western wall, a gigantic clock of ebony. Its pendulum swung to and fro with a dull, heavy, monotonous clang; and when the minute-hand made the circuit of the face, and the hour was to be stricken, there came from the brazen lungs of the clock a sound which was clear and loud and deep and exceedingly musical, but of so peculiar a note and emphasis that, at each lapse of an hour, the musicians of the orchestra were constrained to pause, momentarily, in their performance, to hearken to the sound; and thus the waltzers perforce ceased their evolutions; and there was a brief disconcert of the whole gay company; and, while the chimes of the clock yet rang, it was observed that the giddiest grew pale, and the more aged and sedate passed their hands over their brows as if in confused reverie or meditation. But when the echoes had fully ceased, a light laughter at once pervaded the assembly; the musicians looked at each other and smiled as if at their own nervousness and folly, and made whispering vows, each to the other, that the next chiming of the clock should produce in them no similar emotion; and then, after the lapse of sixty minutes, (which embrace three thousand and six hundred seconds of the Time that flies,) there came yet another chiming of the clock, and then were the same disconcert and tremulousness and meditation as before.

But, in spite of these things, it was a gay and magnificent revel. The tastes of the duke were peculiar. He had a fine eye for colors and effects. He disregarded the decora of mere fashion. His plans were bold and fiery, and his conceptions glowed with barbaric lustre. There are some who would have thought him mad. His followers felt that he was not. It was necessary to hear and see and touch him to be sure that he was not.

He had directed, in great part, the moveable embellishments of the seven chambers, upon occasion of this great fete; and it was his own guiding taste which had given character to the masqueraders. Be sure they were grotesque. There were much glare and glitter and piquancy and phantasm—much of what has been since seen in "Hernani." There were arabesque figures with unsuited limbs and appointments. There were delirious fancies such as the madman fashions. There was much of the beautiful, much of the wanton, much of the bizarre, something of the terrible, and not a little of that which might have excited disgust. To and fro in the seven chambers there stalked, in fact, a multitude of dreams. And these—the dreams—writhed in and about, taking hue from the rooms, and causing the wild music of the orchestra to seem as the echo of their steps. And, anon, there strikes the ebony clock which stands in the hall of the velvet. And then, for a moment, all is still, and all is silent save the voice of the clock. The dreams are stiff-frozen as they stand. But the echoes of the chime die away—they have endured but an instant—and a light, half-subdued laughter floats after them as they depart. And now again the music swells, and the dreams live, and writhe to and fro more merrily than ever, taking hue from the many-tinted windows through which stream the rays from the tripods. But to the chamber which lies most westwardly of the seven, there are now none of the maskers who venture; for the night is waning away; and there flows a ruddier light through the blood-colored panes; and the blackness of the sable drapery appals; and to him whose foot falls upon the sable carpet, there comes from the near clock of ebony a muffled peal more solemnly emphatic than any which reaches their ears who indulge in the more remote gaieties of the other apartments.

But these other apartments were densely crowded, and in them beat feverishly the heart of life. And the revel went whirlingly on, until at length there commenced the sounding of midnight upon the clock. And then the music ceased, as I have told; and the evolutions of the waltzers were quieted; and there was an uneasy cessation of all things as before. But now there were twelve strokes to be sounded by the bell of the clock; and thus it happened, perhaps, that more of thought crept, with more of time, into the meditations of the thoughtful among those who revelled. And thus, too, it happened, perhaps, that before the last echoes of the last chime had utterly sunk into silence, there were many individuals in the crowd who had found leisure to become aware of the presence of a masked figure which had arrested the attention of no single individual before. And the rumor of this new presence having spread itself whisperingly around, there arose at length from the whole company a buzz, or murmur, expressive of disapprobation and surprise—then, finally, of terror, of horror, and of disgust.

In an assembly of phantasms such as I have painted, it may well be supposed that no ordinary appearance could have excited such sensation. In truth the masquerade license of the night was nearly unlimited; but the figure in question had out-Heroded Herod, and gone beyond the bounds of even the prince's indefinite decorum. There are chords in the hearts of the most reckless which cannot be touched without emotion. Even with the utterly lost, to whom life and death are equally jests, there are matters of which no jest can be made. The whole company, indeed, seemed now deeply to feel that in the costume and bearing of the stranger neither wit nor propriety existed. The figure was tall and gaunt, and shrouded from head to foot in the habiliments of the grave. The mask which concealed the visage was made so nearly to resemble the countenance of a stiffened corpse that the closest scrutiny must have had difficulty in detecting the cheat. And yet all this might have been endured, if not approved, by the mad revellers around. But the mummer had gone so far as to assume the type of the Red Death. His vesture was dabbled in blood—and his broad brow, with all the features of the face, was besprinkled with the scarlet horror.

When the eyes of Prince Prospero fell upon this spectral image (which with a slow and solemn movement, as if more fully to sustain its role, stalked to and fro among the waltzers) he was seen to be convulsed, in the first moment with a strong shudder either of terror or distaste; but, in the next, his brow reddened with rage.

"Who dares?" he demanded hoarsely of the courtiers who stood near him—"who dares insult us with this blasphemous mockery? Seize him and unmask him—that we may know whom we have to hang at sunrise, from the battlements!"

It was in the eastern or blue chamber in which stood the Prince Prospero as he uttered these words. They rang throughout the seven rooms loudly and clearly—for the prince was a bold and robust man, and the music had become hushed at the waving of his hand.

It was in the blue room where stood the prince, with a group of pale courtiers by his side. At first, as he spoke, there was a slight rushing movement of this group in the direction of the intruder, who at the moment was also near at hand, and now, with deliberate and stately step, made closer approach to the speaker. But from a certain nameless awe with which the mad assumptions of the mummer had inspired the whole party, there were found none who put forth hand to seize him; so that, unimpeded, he passed within a yard of the prince's person; and, while the vast assembly, as if with one impulse, shrank from the centres of the rooms to the walls, he made his way uninterruptedly, but with the same solemn and measured step which had distinguished him from the first, through the blue chamber to the purple—through the purple to the green—through the green to the orange—through this again to the white— and even thence to the violet, ere a decided movement had been made to arrest him. It was then, however, that the Prince Prospero, maddening with rage and the shame of his own momentary cowardice, rushed hurriedly through the six chambers, while none followed him on account of a deadly terror that had seized upon all. He bore aloft a drawn dagger, and had approached, in rapid impetuosity, to within three or four feet of the retreating figure, when the latter, having attained the extremity of the velvet apartment, turned suddenly and confronted his pursuer. There was a sharp cry—and the dagger dropped gleaming upon the sable carpet, upon which, instantly afterwards, fell prostrate in death the Prince Prospero. Then, summoning the wild courage of despair, a throng of the revellers at once threw themselves into the black apartment, and, seizing the mummer, whose tall figure stood erect and motionless within the shadow of the ebony clock, gasped in unutterable horror at finding the grave-cerements and corpse-like mask which they handled with so violent a rudeness, untenanted by any tangible form.

And now was acknowledged the presence of the Red Death. He had come like a thief in the night. And one by one dropped the revellers in the blood-bedewed halls of their revel, and died each in the despairing posture of his fall. And the life of the ebony clock went out with that of the last of the gay. And the flames of the tripods expired. And Darkness and Decay and the Red Death held illimitable dominion over all.

A JOURNAL OF THE PLAGUE YEAR

DANIEL DEFOE

A JOURNAL OF THE PLAGUE YEAR

BEING OBSERVATIONS OR MEMORIALS OF THE MOST REMARKABLE OCCURRENCES, AS WELL PUBLIC AS PRIVATE, WHICH HAPPENED IN LONDON DURING THE LAST GREAT VISITATION IN 1665. WRITTEN BY A CITIZEN WHO CONTINUED ALL THE WHILE IN LONDON. NEVER MADE PUBLIC BEFORE

It was about the beginning of September, 1664, that I, among the rest of my neighbours, heard in ordinary discourse that the plague was returned again in Holland; for it had been very violent there, and particularly at Amsterdam and Rotterdam, in the year 1663, whither, they say, it was brought, some said from Italy, others from the Levant, among some goods which were brought home by their Turkey fleet; others said it was brought from Candia; others from Cyprus. It mattered not from whence it came; but all agreed it was come into Holland again.

We had no such thing as printed newspapers in those days to spread rumours and reports of things, and to improve them by the invention of men, as I have lived to see practised since. But such things as these were gathered from the letters of merchants and others who corresponded abroad, and from them was handed about by word of mouth only; so that things did not spread instantly over the whole nation, as they do now. But it seems that the Government had a true account of it, and several councils were held about ways to prevent its coming over; but all was kept very private. Hence it was that this rumour died off again, and people began to forget it as a thing we were very little concerned in, and that we hoped was not true; till the latter end of November or the beginning of December 1664 when two men, said to be Frenchmen, died of the plague in Long Acre, or rather at the upper end of Drury Lane. The family they were in endeavoured to conceal it as much as possible, but as it had gotten some vent in the discourse of the neighbourhood, the Secretaries of State got knowledge of it; and concerning themselves to inquire about it, in order to be certain of the truth, two physicians and a surgeon were ordered to go to the house and make inspection. This they did; and finding evident tokens of the sickness upon both the bodies that were dead, they gave their opinions publicly that they died of the plague. Whereupon it was given in to the parish clerk, and he also returned them to the Hall; and it was printed in the weekly bill of mortality in the usual manner, thus—

Plague, 2. Parishes infected, 1.

The people showed a great concern at this, and began to be alarmed all over the town, and the more, because in the last week in December 1664 another man died in the same house, and of the same distemper. And then we were easy again for about six weeks, when none having died with any marks of infection, it was said the distemper was gone; but after that, I think it was about the 12th of February, another died in another house, but in the same parish and in the same manner.

This turned the people's eyes pretty much towards that end of the town, and the weekly bills showing an increase of burials in St Giles's parish more than usual, it began to be suspected that the plague was among the people at that end of the town, and that many had died of it, though they had taken care to keep it as much from the knowledge of the public as possible. This possessed the heads of the people very much, and few cared to go through Drury Lane, or the other streets suspected, unless they had extraordinary business that obliged them to it

This increase of the bills stood thus: the usual number of burials in a week, in the parishes of St Giles-in-the-Fields and St Andrew's, Holborn, were from twelve to seventeen or nineteen each, few more or less; but from the time that the plague first began in St Giles's parish, it was observed that the ordinary burials increased in number considerably. For example:—

> *From December 27 to January 3 { St Giles's 16*
> *" " { St Andrew's 17*
> *From January 3 to January 10 { St Giles's 12*
> *" " { St Andrew's 25*
> *From January 10 to January 17 { St Giles's 18*
> *" " { St Andrew's 28*
> *From January 17 to January 24 { St Giles's 23*
> *" " { St Andrew's 16*
> *From January 24 to January 31 { St Giles's 24*
> *" "{ St Andrew's 15*
> *From January 30 to February 7 { St Giles's 21*
> *" " { St Andrew's 23*
> *From February 7 to February 14 { St Giles's 24*

The like increase of the bills was observed in the parishes of St Bride's, adjoining on one side of Holborn parish, and in the parish of St James, Clerkenwell, adjoining on the other side of Holborn; in both which parishes the usual numbers that died weekly were from four to six or eight, whereas at that time they were increased as follows:—

> *From December 20 to December 27 { St Bride's 0*
> *" " { St James's 8*
> *From December 27 to January 3 { St Bride's 6*
> *" " { St James's 9*
> *From January 3 to January 10 { St Bride's 11*
> *" " { St James's 7*
> *From January 10 to January 17 { St Bride's 12*
> *" " { St James's 9*
> *From January 17 to January 24 { St Bride's 9*
> *" " { St James's 15*
> *From January 24 to January 31 { St Bride's 8*
> *" " { St James's 12*

From January 31 to February 7 { St Bride's 13
" " { St James's 5
From February 7 to February 14 { St Bride's 12
" " { St James's 6

Besides this, it was observed with great uneasiness by the people that the weekly bills in general increased very much during these weeks, although it was at a time of the year when usually the bills are very moderate.

The usual number of burials within the bills of mortality for a week was from about 240 or thereabouts to 300. The last was esteemed a pretty high bill; but after this we found the bills successively increasing as follows:—

	Buried.	Increased.
December the 20th to the 27th:	291	
December the 27th to the 3rd January:	349	58
January the 3rd to the 10th:	394	45
January the 10th to the 17th:	415	21
January the 17th to the 24th:	474	59

This last bill was really frightful, being a higher number than had been known to have been buried in one week since the preceding visitation of 1656.

However, all this went off again, and the weather proving cold, and the frost, which began in December, still continuing very severe even till near the end of February, attended with sharp though moderate winds, the bills decreased again, and the city grew healthy, and everybody began to look upon the danger as good as over; only that still the burials in St Giles's continued high. From the beginning of April especially they stood at twenty-five each week, till the week from the 18th to the 25th, when there was buried in St Giles's parish thirty, whereof two of the plague and eight of the spotted-fever, which was looked upon as the same thing; likewise the number that died of the spotted-fever in the whole increased, being eight the week before, and twelve the week above-named.

This alarmed us all again, and terrible apprehensions were among the people, especially the weather being now changed and growing warm, and the summer being at hand. However, the next week there seemed to be some hopes again; the bills were low, the number of the dead in all was but 388, there was none of the plague, and but four of the spotted-fever.

But the following week it returned again, and the distemper was spread into two or three other parishes, viz., St Andrew's, Holborn; St Clement Danes; and, to the great affliction of the city, one died within the walls, in the parish of St Mary Woolchurch, that is to say, in Bearbinder Lane, near Stocks Market; in all there were nine of the plague and six of the spotted-fever. It was, however, upon inquiry found that this Frenchman who died in Bearbinder Lane was one who, having lived in Long Acre, near the infected houses, had removed for fear of the distemper, not knowing that he was already infected.

This was the beginning of May, yet the weather was temperate, variable, and cool enough, and people had still some hopes. That which encouraged them was that the city was healthy: the whole ninety-seven parishes buried but fifty-four, and we began to hope that, as it was chiefly among the people at that end of the town, it might go no farther; and the rather, because the next week, which was from the 9th of May to the 16th, there died but three, of which not one within the whole city or liberties; and St Andrew's buried but fifteen, which was very low. 'Tis true St Giles's buried two-and-thirty, but still, as there was but one of the plague, people began to be easy. The whole bill also was very low, for the week before the bill was but 347, and the week above mentioned but 343. We continued in these hopes for a few days, but it was but for a few, for the people were no more to be deceived thus; they searched the houses and found that the plague was really spread every way, and that many died of it every day. So that now all our extenuations abated, and it was no more to be concealed; nay, it quickly appeared that the infection had spread itself beyond all hopes of abatement. That in the parish of St Giles it was gotten into several streets, and several families lay all sick together; and, accordingly, in the weekly bill for the next week the thing began to show itself. There was indeed but fourteen set down of the plague, but this was all knavery and collusion, for in St Giles's parish they buried forty in all, whereof it was certain most of them died of the plague, though they were set down of other distempers; and though the number of all the burials were not increased above thirty-two, and the whole bill being but 385, yet there was fourteen of the spotted-fever, as well as fourteen of the plague; and we took it for granted upon the whole that there were fifty died that week of the plague.

The next bill was from the 23rd of May to the 30th, when the number of the plague was seventeen. But the burials in St Giles's were fifty-three—a frightful number!—of whom they set down but nine of the plague; but on an examination more strictly by the justices of peace, and at the Lord Mayor's request, it was found there were twenty more who were really dead of the plague in that parish, but had been set down of the spotted-fever or other distempers, besides others concealed.

But those were trifling things to what followed immediately after; for now the weather set in hot, and from the first week in June the infection spread in a dreadful manner, and the bills rose high; the articles of the fever, spotted-fever, and teeth began to swell; for all that could conceal their distempers did it, to prevent their neighbours shunning and refusing to converse with them, and also to prevent authority shutting up their houses; which, though it was not yet practised, yet was threatened, and people were extremely terrified at the thoughts of it.

The second week in June, the parish of St Giles, where still the weight of the infection lay, buried 120, whereof though the bills said but sixty-eight of the plague, everybody said there had been 100 at least, calculating it from the usual number of funerals in that parish, as above.

Till this week the city continued free, there having never any died, except that one Frenchman whom I mentioned before, within the whole ninety-seven parishes. Now there died four within the city, one in Wood Street, one in Fenchurch Street, and two in Crooked Lane. Southwark was entirely free, having not one yet died on that side of the water.

I lived without Aldgate, about midway between Aldgate Church and Whitechappel Bars, on the left hand or north side of the street; and as the distemper had not reached to that side of the city, our neighbourhood continued very easy. But at the other end of the town their consternation was very great: and the richer sort of people, especially the nobility and gentry from the west part of the city, thronged out of town with their families and servants in an unusual manner; and this was more particularly seen in Whitechappel; that is to say, the Broad Street where I lived; indeed, nothing was to be seen but waggons and carts, with goods, women, servants, children, &c.; coaches filled with people of the better sort and horsemen attending them, and all hurrying away; then empty waggons and carts appeared, and spare horses with servants, who, it was apparent, were returning or sent from the countries to fetch more people; besides innumerable numbers of men on horseback, some alone, others with servants, and, generally speaking, all loaded with baggage and fitted out for travelling, as anyone might perceive by their appearance.

This was a very terrible and melancholy thing to see, and as it was a sight which I could not but look on from morning to night (for indeed there was nothing else of moment to be seen), it filled me with very serious thoughts of the misery that was coming upon the city, and the unhappy condition of those that would be left in it.

This hurry of the people was such for some weeks that there was no getting at the Lord Mayor's door without exceeding difficulty; there were such pressing and crowding there to get passes and certificates of health for such as travelled abroad, for without these there was no being admitted to pass through the towns upon the road, or to lodge in any inn. Now, as there had none died in the city for all this time, my Lord Mayor gave certificates of health without any difficulty to all those who lived in the ninety-seven parishes, and to those within the liberties too for a while.

This hurry, I say, continued some weeks, that is to say, all the month of May and June, and the more because it was rumoured that an order of the Government was to be issued out to place turnpikes and barriers on the road to prevent people travelling, and that the towns on the road would not suffer people from London to pass for fear of bringing the infection along with them, though neither of these rumours had any foundation but in the imagination, especially at-first.

I now began to consider seriously with myself concerning my own case, and how I should dispose of myself; that is to say, whether I should resolve to stay in London or shut up my house and flee, as many of my neighbours did. I have set this particular down so fully, because I know not but it may be of moment to those who come after me, if they come to be brought to the same distress, and to the same manner of making their choice; and therefore I desire this account may pass with them rather for a direction to themselves to act by than a history of my actings, seeing it may not be of one farthing value to them to note what became of me.

I had two important things before me: the one was the carrying on my business and shop, which was considerable, and in which was embarked all my effects in the world; and the other was the preservation of my life in so dismal a calamity as I saw apparently was coming upon the whole city, and which, however great it was, my fears perhaps, as well as other people's, represented to be much greater than it could be.

The first consideration was of great moment to me; my trade was a saddler, and as my dealings were chiefly not by a shop or chance trade, but among the merchants trading to the English colonies in America, so my effects lay very much in the hands of such. I was a single man, 'tis true, but I had a family of servants whom I kept at my business; had a house, shop, and warehouses filled with goods; and, in short, to leave them all as things in such a case must be left (that is to say, without any overseer or person fit to be trusted with them), had been to hazard the loss not only of my trade, but of my goods, and indeed of all I had in the world.

I had an elder brother at the same time in London, and not many years before come over from Portugal: and advising with him, his answer was in three words, the same that was given in another case quite different, viz., 'Master, save thyself.' In a word, he was for my retiring into the country, as he resolved to do himself with his family; telling me what he had, it seems, heard abroad, that the best preparation for the plague was to run away from it. As to my argument of losing my trade, my goods, or debts, he quite confuted me. He told me the same thing which I argued for my staying, viz., that I would trust God with my safety and health, was the strongest repulse to my pretensions of losing my trade and my goods; 'for', says he, 'is it not as reasonable that you should trust God with the chance or risk of losing your trade, as that you should stay in so eminent a point of danger, and trust Him with your life?'

I could not argue that I was in any strait as to a place where to go, having several friends and relations in Northamptonshire, whence our family first came from; and particularly, I had an only sister in Lincolnshire, very willing to receive and entertain me.

My brother, who had already sent his wife and two children into Bedfordshire, and resolved to follow them, pressed my going very earnestly; and I had once resolved to comply with his desires, but at that time could get no horse; for though it is true all the people did not go out of the city of London, yet I may venture to say that in a manner all the horses did; for there was hardly a horse to be bought or hired in the whole city for some weeks. Once I resolved to travel on foot with one servant, and, as many did, lie at no inn, but carry a soldier's tent with us, and so lie in the fields, the weather being very warm, and no danger from taking cold. I say, as many did, because several did so at last, especially those who had been in the armies in the war which had not been many years past; and I must needs say that, speaking of second causes, had most of the people that travelled done so, the plague had not been carried into so many country towns and houses as it was, to the great damage, and indeed to the ruin, of abundance of people.

But then my servant, whom I had intended to take down with me, deceived me; and being frighted at the increase of the distemper, and not knowing when I should go, he took other measures, and left me, so I was put off for that time; and, one way or other, I always found that to appoint to go away was always crossed by some accident or other, so as to disappoint and put it off again; and this brings in a story which otherwise might be thought a needless digression, viz., about these disappointments being from Heaven.

I mention this story also as the best method I can advise any person to take in such a case, especially if he be one that makes conscience of his duty, and would be directed what to do in it, namely, that he should keep his eye upon the particular providences which occur at that time, and look upon them complexly, as they regard one another, and as all together regard the question before him: and then, I think, he may safely take them for intimations from Heaven of what is his unquestioned duty to do in such a case; I mean as to going away from or staying in the place where we dwell, when visited with an infectious distemper.

It came very warmly into my mind one morning, as I was musing on this particular thing, that as nothing attended us without the direction or permission of Divine Power, so these disappointments must have something in them extraordinary; and I ought to consider whether it did not evidently point out, or intimate to me, that it was the will of Heaven I should not go. It immediately followed in my thoughts, that if it really was from God that I should stay, He was able effectually to preserve me in the midst of all the death and danger that would surround me; and that if I attempted to secure myself by fleeing from my habitation, and acted contrary to these intimations, which I believe to be Divine, it was a kind of flying from God, and that He could cause His justice to overtake me when and where He thought fit.

These thoughts quite turned my resolutions again, and when I came to discourse with my brother again I told him that I inclined to stay and take my lot in that station in which God had placed me, and that it seemed to be made more especially my duty, on the account of what I have said.

My brother, though a very religious man himself, laughed at all I had suggested about its being an intimation from Heaven, and told me several stories of such foolhardy people, as he called them, as I was; that I ought indeed to submit to it as a work of Heaven if I had been any way disabled by distempers or diseases, and that then not being able to go, I ought to acquiesce in the direction of Him, who, having been my Maker, had an undisputed right of sovereignty in disposing of me, and that then there had been no difficulty to determine which was the call of His providence and which was not; but that I should take it as an intimation from Heaven that I should not go out of town, only because I could not hire a horse to go, or my fellow was run away that was to attend me, was ridiculous, since at the time I had my health and limbs, and other servants, and might with ease travel a day or two on foot, and having a good certificate of being in perfect health, might either hire a horse or take post on the road, as I thought fit.

Then he proceeded to tell me of the mischievous consequences which attended the presumption of the Turks and Mahometans in Asia and in other places where he had been (for my brother, being a merchant, was a few years before, as I have already observed, returned from abroad, coming last from Lisbon), and how, presuming upon their professed predestinating notions, and of every man's end being predetermined and unalterably beforehand decreed, they would go unconcerned into infected places and converse with infected persons, by which means they died at the rate of ten or fifteen thousand a week, whereas the Europeans or Christian merchants, who kept themselves retired and reserved, generally escaped the contagion.

Upon these arguments my brother changed my resolutions again, and I began to resolve to go, and accordingly made all things ready; for, in short, the infection increased round me, and the bills were risen to almost seven hundred a week, and my brother told me he would venture to stay no longer. I desired him to let me consider of it but till the next day, and I would resolve: and as I had already prepared everything as well as I could as to MY business, and whom to entrust my affairs with, I had little to do but to resolve.

I went home that evening greatly oppressed in my mind, irresolute, and not knowing what to do. I had set the evening wholly—apart to consider seriously about it, and was all alone; for already people had, as it were by a general consent, taken up the custom of not going out of doors after sunset; the reasons I shall have occasion to say more of by-and-by.

In the retirement of this evening I endeavoured to resolve, first, what was my duty to do, and I stated the arguments with which my brother had pressed me to go into the country, and I set, against them the strong impressions which I had on my mind for staying; the visible call I seemed to have from the particular circumstance of my calling, and the care due from me for the preservation of my effects, which were, as I might say, my estate; also the intimations which I thought I had from Heaven, that to me signified a kind of direction to venture; and it occurred to me that if I had what I might call a direction to stay, I ought to suppose it contained a promise of being preserved if I obeyed.

This lay close to me, and my mind seemed more and more encouraged to stay than ever, and supported with a secret satisfaction that I should be kept. Add to this, that, turning over the Bible which lay before me, and while my thoughts were more than ordinarily serious upon the question, I cried out, 'Well, I know not what to do; Lord, direct me !' and the like; and at that juncture I happened to stop turning over the book at the ninety-first Psalm, and casting my eye on the second verse, I read on to the seventh verse exclusive, and after that included the tenth, as follows: 'I will say of the Lord, He is my refuge and my fortress: my God, in Him will I trust. Surely He shall deliver thee from the snare of the fowler, and from the noisome pestilence. He shall cover thee with His feathers, and under His wings shalt thou trust: His truth shall be thy shield and buckler. Thou shalt not be afraid for the terror by night; nor for the arrow that flieth by day; nor for the pestilence that walketh in darkness; nor for the destruction that wasteth at noonday. A thousand shall fall at thy side, and ten thousand at thy right hand; but it shall not come nigh thee. Only with thine eyes shalt thou behold and see the reward of the wicked. Because thou hast made the Lord, which is my refuge, even the most High, thy habitation; there shall no evil befall thee, neither shall any plague come nigh thy dwelling,' &C.

I scarce need tell the reader that from that moment I resolved that I would stay in the town, and casting myself entirely upon the goodness and protection of the Almighty, would not seek any other shelter whatever; and that, as my times were in His hands, He was as able to keep me in a time of the infection as in a time of health; and if He did not think fit to deliver me, still I was in His hands, and it was meet He should do with me as should seem good to Him.

With this resolution I went to bed; and I was further confirmed in it the next day by the woman being taken ill with whom I had intended to entrust my house and all my affairs. But I had a further obligation laid on me on the same side, for the next day I found myself very much out of order also, so that if I would have gone away, I could not, and I continued ill three or four days, and this entirely determined my stay; so I took my leave of my brother, who went away to Dorking, in Surrey, and afterwards fetched a round farther into Buckinghamshire or Bedfordshire, to a retreat he had found out there for his family.

It was a very ill time to be sick in, for if any one complained, it was immediately said he had the plague; and though I had indeed no symptom of that distemper, yet being very ill, both in my head and in my stomach, I was not without apprehension that I really was infected; but in about three days I grew better; the third night I rested well, sweated a little, and was much refreshed. The apprehensions of its being the infection went also quite away with my illness, and I went about my business as usual.

These things, however, put off all my thoughts of going into the country; and my brother also being gone, I had no more debate either with him or with myself on that subject.

It was now mid-July, and the plague, which had chiefly raged at the other end of the town, and, as I said before, in the parishes of St Giles, St Andrew's, Holborn, and towards Westminster, began to now come eastward towards the part where I lived. It was to be observed, indeed, that it did not come straight on towards us; for the city, that is to say, within the walls, was indifferently healthy still; nor was it got then very much over the water into Southwark; for though there died that week 1268 of all distempers, whereof it might be supposed above 600 died of the plague, yet there was but twenty-eight in the whole city, within the walls, and but nineteen in Southwark, Lambeth parish included; whereas in the parishes of St Giles and St Martin-in-the-Fields alone there died 421.

But we perceived the infection kept chiefly in the out-parishes, which being very populous, and fuller also of poor, the distemper found more to prey upon than in the city, as I shall observe afterwards. We perceived, I say, the distemper to draw our way, viz., by the parishes of Clarkenwell, Cripplegate, Shoreditch, and Bishopsgate; which last two parishes joining to Aldgate, Whitechappel, and Stepney, the infection came at length to spread its utmost rage and violence in those parts, even when it abated at the western parishes where it began.

It was very strange to observe that in this particular week, from the 4th to the 11th of July, when, as I have observed, there died near 400 of the plague in the two parishes of St Martin and St Giles-in-the-Fields only, there died in the parish of Aldgate but four, in the parish of Whitechappel three, in the parish of Stepney but one.

Likewise in the next week, from the 11th of July to the 18th, when the week's bill was 1761, yet there died no more of the plague, on the whole Southwark side of the water, than sixteen. But this face of things soon changed, and it began to thicken in Cripplegate parish especially, and in Clarkenwell; so that by the second week in August, Cripplegate parish alone buried 886, and Clarkenwell 155. Of the first, 850 might well be reckoned to die of the plague; and of the last, the bill itself said 145 were of the plague.

During the month of July, and while, as I have observed, our part of the town seemed to be spared in comparison of the west part, I went ordinarily about the streets, as my business required, and particularly went generally once in a day, or in two days, into the city, to my brother's house, which he had given me charge of, and to see if it was safe; and having the key in my pocket, I used to go into the house, and over most of the rooms, to see that all was well; for though it be something wonderful to tell, that any should have hearts so hardened in the midst of such a calamity as to rob and steal, yet certain it is that all sorts of villainies, and even levities and debaucheries, were then practised in the town as openly as ever—I will not say quite as frequently, because the numbers of people were many ways lessened.

But the city itself began now to be visited too, I mean within the walls; but the number of people there were indeed extremely lessened by so great a multitude having been gone into the country; and even all this month of July they continued to flee, though not in such multitudes as formerly. In August, indeed, they fled in such a manner that I began to think there would be really none but magistrates and servants left in the city.

As they fled now out of the city, so I should observe that the Court removed early, viz., in the month of June, and went to Oxford, where it pleased God to preserve them; and the distemper did not, as I heard of, so much as touch them, for which I cannot say that I ever saw they showed any great token of thankfulness, and hardly anything of reformation, though they did not want being told that their crying vices might without breach of charity be said to have gone far in bringing that terrible judgement upon the whole nation.

The face of London was—now indeed strangely altered: I mean the whole mass of buildings, city, liberties, suburbs, Westminster, Southwark, and altogether; for as to the particular part called the city, or within the walls, that was not yet much infected. But in the whole the face of things, I say, was much altered; sorrow and sadness sat upon every face; and though some parts were not yet overwhelmed, yet all looked deeply concerned; and, as we saw it apparently coming on, so every one looked on himself and his family as in the utmost danger. Were it possible to represent those times exactly to those that did not see them, and give the reader due ideas of the horror 'that everywhere presented itself, it must make just impressions upon their minds and fill them with surprise. London might well be said to be all in tears; the mourners did not go about the streets indeed, for nobody put on black or made a formal dress of mourning for their nearest friends; but the voice of mourners was truly heard in the streets. The shrieks of women and children at the windows and doors of their houses, where their dearest relations were perhaps dying, or just dead, were so frequent to be heard as we passed the streets, that it was enough to pierce the stoutest heart in the world to hear them. Tears and lamentations were seen almost in every house, especially in the first part of the visitation; for towards the latter end men's hearts were hardened, and death was so always before their eyes, that they did not so much concern themselves for the loss of their friends, expecting that themselves should be summoned the next hour.

Business led me out sometimes to the other end of the town, even when the sickness was chiefly there; and as the thing was new to me, as well as to everybody else, it was a most surprising thing to see those streets which were usually so thronged now grown desolate, and so few people to be seen in them, that if I had been a stranger and at a loss for my way, I might sometimes have gone the length of a whole street (I mean of the by-streets), and seen nobody to direct me except watchmen set at the doors of such houses as were shut up, of which I shall speak presently.

One day, being at that part of the town on some special business, curiosity led me to observe things more than usually, and indeed I walked a great way where I had no business. I went up Holborn, and there the street was full of people, but they walked in the middle of the great street, neither on one side or other, because, as I suppose, they would not mingle with anybody that came out of houses, or meet with smells and scent from houses that might be infected.

The Inns of Court were all shut up; nor were very many of the lawyers in the Temple, or Lincoln's Inn, or Gray's Inn, to be seen there. Everybody was at peace; there was no occasion for lawyers; besides, it being in the time of the vacation too, they were generally gone into the country. Whole rows of houses in some places were shut close up, the inhabitants all fled, and only a watchman or two left.

When I speak of rows of houses being shut up, I do not mean shut up by the magistrates, but that great numbers of persons followed the Court, by the necessity of their employments and other dependences; and as others retired, really frighted with the distemper, it was a mere desolating of some of the streets. But the fright was not yet near so great in the city, abstractly so called, and particularly because, though they were at first in a most inexpressible consternation, yet as I have observed that the distemper intermitted often at first, so they were, as it were, alarmed and unalarmed again, and this several times, till it began to be familiar to them; and that even when it appeared violent, yet seeing it did not presently spread into the city, or the east and south parts, the people began to take courage, and to be, as I may say, a little hardened. It is true a vast many people fled, as I have observed, yet they were chiefly from the west end of the town, and from that we call the heart of the city: that is to say, among the wealthiest of the people, and such people as were unencumbered with trades and business. But of the rest, the generality stayed, and seemed to abide the worst; so that in the place we call the Liberties, and in the suburbs, in Southwark, and in the east part, such as Wapping, Ratcliff, Stepney, Rotherhithe, and the like, the people generally stayed, except here and there a few wealthy families, who, as above, did not depend upon their business.

It must not be forgot here that the city and suburbs were prodigiously full of people at the time of this visitation, I mean at the time that it began; for though I have lived to see a further increase, and mighty throngs of people settling in London more than ever, yet we had always a notion that the numbers of people which, the wars being over, the armies disbanded, and the royal family and the monarchy being restored, had flocked to London to settle in business, or to depend upon and attend the Court for rewards of services, preferments, and the like, was such that the town was computed to have in it above a hundred thousand people more than ever it held before; nay, some took upon them to say it had twice as many, because all the ruined families of the royal party flocked hither. All the old soldiers set up trades here, and abundance of families settled here. Again, the Court brought with them a great flux of pride, and new fashions. All people were grown gay and luxurious, and the joy of the Restoration had brought a vast many families to London.

I often thought that as Jerusalem was besieged by the Romans when the Jews were assembled together to celebrate the Passover—by which means an incredible number of people were surprised there who would otherwise have been in other countries—so the plague entered London when an incredible increase of people had happened occasionally, by the particular circumstances above-named. As this conflux of the people to a youthful and gay Court made a great trade in the city, especially in everything that belonged to fashion and finery, so it drew by consequence a great number of workmen, manufacturers, and the like, being mostly poor people who depended upon their labour. And I remember in particular that in a representation to my Lord Mayor of the condition of the poor, it was estimated that there were no less than an hundred thousand riband-weavers in and about the city, the chiefest number of whom lived then in the parishes of Shoreditch, Stepney, Whitechappel, and Bishopsgate, that, namely, about Spitalfields; that is to say, as Spitalfields was then, for it was not so large as now by one fifth part.

By this, however, the number of people in the whole may be judged of; and, indeed, I often wondered that, after the prodigious numbers of people that went away at first, there was yet so great a multitude left as it appeared there was.

But I must go back again to the beginning of this surprising time. While the fears of the people were young, they were increased strangely by several odd accidents which, put altogether, it was really a wonder the whole body of the people did not rise as one man and abandon their dwellings, leaving the place as a space of ground designed by Heaven for an Akeldama, doomed to be destroyed from the face of the earth, and that all that would be found in it would perish with it. I shall name but a few of these things; but sure they were so many, and so many wizards and cunning people propagating them, that I have often wondered there was any (women especially) left behind.

In the first place, a blazing star or comet appeared for several months before the plague, as there did the year after another, a little before the fire. The old women and the phlegmatic hypochondriac part of the other sex, whom I could almost call old women too, remarked (especially afterward, though not till both those judgements were over) that those two comets passed directly over the city, and that so very near the houses that it was plain they imported something peculiar to the city alone; that the comet before the pestilence was of a faint, dull, languid colour, and its motion very heavy, Solemn, and slow; but that the comet before the fire was bright and sparkling, or, as others said, flaming, and its motion swift and furious; and that, accordingly, one foretold a heavy judgement, slow but severe, terrible and frightful, as was the plague; but the other foretold a stroke, sudden, swift, and fiery as the conflagration. Nay, so particular some people were, that as they looked upon that comet preceding the fire, they fancied that they not only saw it pass swiftly and fiercely, and could perceive the motion with their eye, but even they heard it; that it made a rushing, mighty noise, fierce and terrible, though at a distance, and but just perceivable.

I saw both these stars, and, I must confess, had so much of the common notion of such things in my head, that I was apt to look upon them as the forerunners and warnings of God's judgements; and especially when, after the plague had followed the first, I yet saw another of the like kind, I could not but say God had not yet sufficiently scourged the city.

But I could not at the same time carry these things to the height that others did, knowing, too, that natural causes are assigned by the astronomers for such things, and that their motions and even their revolutions are calculated, or pretended to be calculated, so that they cannot be so perfectly called the forerunners or foretellers, much less the procurers, of such events as pestilence, war, fire, and the like.

But let my thoughts and the thoughts of the philosophers be, or have been, what they will, these things had a more than ordinary influence upon the minds of the common people, and they had almost universal melancholy apprehensions of some dreadful calamity and judgement coming upon the city; and this principally from the sight of this comet, and the little alarm that was given in December by two people dying at St Giles's, as above.

The apprehensions of the people were likewise strangely increased by the error of the times; in which, I think, the people, from what principle I cannot imagine, were more addicted to prophecies and astrological conjurations, dreams, and old wives' tales than ever they were before or since. Whether this unhappy temper was originally raised by the follies of some people who got money by it—that is to say, by printing predictions and prognostications—I know not; but certain it is, books frighted them terribly, such as Lilly's Almanack, Gadbury's Astrological Predictions, Poor Robin's Almanack, and the like; also several pretended religious books, one entitled, Come out of her, my People, lest you be Partaker of her Plagues; another called, Fair Warning; another, Britain's Remembrancer; and many such, all, or most part of which, foretold, directly or covertly, the ruin of the city. Nay, some were so enthusiastically bold as to run about the streets with their oral predictions, pretending they were sent to preach to the city; and one in particular, who, like Jonah to Nineveh, cried in the streets, 'Yet forty days, and London shall be destroyed.' I will not be positive whether he said yet forty days or yet a few days. Another ran about naked, except a pair of drawers about his waist, crying day and night, like a man that Josephus mentions, who cried, 'Woe to Jerusalem!' a little before the destruction of that city. So this poor naked creature cried, 'Oh, the great and the dreadful God!' and said no more, but repeated those words continually, with a voice and countenance full of horror, a swift pace; and nobody could ever find him to stop or rest, or take any sustenance, at least that ever I could hear of. I met this poor creature several times in the streets, and would have spoken to him, but he would not enter into speech with me or any one else, but held on his dismal cries continually.

These things terrified the people to the last degree, and especially when two or three times, as I have mentioned already, they found one or two in the bills dead of the plague at St Giles's.

Next to these public things were the dreams of old women, or, I should say, the interpretation of old women upon other people's dreams; and these put abundance of people even out of their wits. Some heard voices warning them to be gone, for that there would be such a plague in London, so that the living would not be able to bury the dead. Others saw apparitions in the air; and I must be allowed to say of both, I hope without breach of charity, that they heard voices that never spake, and saw sights that never appeared; but the imagination of the people was really turned wayward and possessed. And no wonder, if they who were poring continually at the clouds saw shapes and figures, representations and appearances, which had nothing in them but air, and vapour. Here they told us they saw a flaming sword held in a hand coming out of a cloud, with a point hanging directly over the city; there they saw hearses and coffins in the air carrying to be buried; and there again, heaps of dead bodies lying unburied, and the like, just as the imagination of the poor terrified people furnished them with matter to work upon. So hypochondriac fancies represent Ships, armies, battles in the firmament; Till steady eyes the exhalations solve, And all to its first matter, cloud, resolve.

I could fill this account with the strange relations such people gave every day of what they had seen; and every one was so positive of their having seen what they pretended to see, that there was no contradicting them without breach of friendship, or being accounted rude and unmannerly on the one hand, and profane and impenetrable on the other. One time before the plague was begun (otherwise than as I have said in St Giles's), I think it was in March, seeing a crowd of people in the street, I joined with them to satisfy my curiosity, and found them all staring up into the air to see what a woman told them appeared plain to her, which was an angel clothed in white, with a fiery sword in his hand, waving it or brandishing it over his head. She described every part of the figure to the life, showed them the motion and the form, and the poor people came into it so eagerly, and with so much readiness; 'Yes, I see it all plainly,' says one; 'there's the sword as plain as can be.' Another saw the angel. One saw his very face, and cried out what a glorious creature he was! One saw one thing, and one another. I looked as earnestly as the rest, but perhaps not with so much willingness to be imposed upon; and I said, indeed, that I could see nothing but a white cloud, bright on one side by the shining of the sun upon the other part. The woman endeavoured to show it me, but could not make me confess that I saw it, which, indeed, if I had I must have lied. But the woman, turning upon me, looked in my face, and fancied I laughed, in which her imagination deceived her too, for I really did not laugh, but was very seriously reflecting how the poor people were terrified by the force of their own imagination. However, she turned from me, called me profane fellow, and a scoffer; told me that it was a time of God's anger, and dreadful judgements were approaching, and that despisers such as I should wander and perish.

The people about her seemed disgusted as well as she; and I found there was no persuading them that I did not laugh at them, and that I should be rather mobbed by them than be able to undeceive them. So I left them; and this appearance passed for as real as the blazing star itself.

Another encounter I had in the open day also; and this was in going through a narrow passage from Petty France into Bishopsgate Churchyard, by a row of alms-houses. There are two churchyards to Bishopsgate church or parish; one we go over to pass from the place called Petty France into Bishopsgate Street, coming out just by the church door; the other is on the side of the narrow passage where the alms-houses are on the left; and a dwarf-wall with a palisado on it on the right hand, and the city wall on the other side more to the right.

In this narrow passage stands a man looking through between the palisadoes into the burying-place, and as many people as the narrowness of the passage would admit to stop, without hindering the passage of others, and he was talking mightily eagerly to them, and pointing now to one place, then to another, and affirming that he saw a ghost walking upon such a gravestone there. He described the shape, the posture, and the movement of it so exactly that it was the greatest matter of amazement to him in the world that everybody did not see it as well as he. On a sudden he would cry, 'There it is; now it comes this way.' Then, 'Tis turned back'; till at length he persuaded the people into so firm a belief of it, that one fancied he saw it, and another fancied he saw it; and thus he came every day making a strange hubbub, considering it was in so narrow a passage, till Bishopsgate clock struck eleven, and then the ghost would seem to start, and, as if he were called away, disappeared on a sudden.

I looked earnestly every way, and at the very moment that this man directed, but could not see the least appearance of anything; but so positive was this poor man, that he gave the people the vapours in abundance, and sent them away trembling and frighted, till at length few people that knew of it cared to go through that passage, and hardly anybody by night on any account whatever.

This ghost, as the poor man affirmed, made signs to the houses, and to the ground, and to the people, plainly intimating, or else they so understanding it, that abundance of the people should come to be buried in that churchyard, as indeed happened; but that he saw such aspects I must acknowledge I never believed, nor could I see anything of it myself, though I looked most earnestly to see it, if possible.

These things serve to show how far the people were really overcome with delusions; and as they had a notion of the approach of a visitation, all their predictions ran upon a most dreadful plague, which should lay the whole city, and even the kingdom, waste, and should destroy almost all the nation, both man and beast.

To this, as I said before, the astrologers added stories of the conjunctions of planets in a malignant manner and with a mischievous influence, one of which conjunctions was to happen, and did happen, in October, and the other in November; and they filled the people's heads with predictions on these signs of the heavens, intimating that those conjunctions foretold drought, famine, and pestilence. In the two first of them, however, they were entirely mistaken, for we had no droughty season, but in the beginning of the year a hard frost, which lasted from December almost to March, and after that moderate weather, rather warm than hot, with refreshing winds, and, in short, very seasonable weather, and also several very great rains.

Some endeavours were used to suppress the printing of such books as terrified the people, and to frighten the dispersers of them, some of whom were taken up; but nothing was done in it, as I am informed, the Government being unwilling to exasperate the people, who were, as I may say, all out of their wits already.

Neither can I acquit those ministers that in their sermons rather sank than lifted up the hearts of their hearers. Many of them no doubt did it for the strengthening the resolution of the people, and especially for quickening them to repentance, but it certainly answered not their end, at least not in proportion to the injury it did another way; and indeed, as God Himself through the whole Scriptures rather draws to Him by invitations and calls to turn to Him and live, than drives us by terror and amazement, so I must confess I thought the ministers should have done also, imitating our blessed Lord and Master in this, that His whole Gospel is full of declarations from heaven of God's mercy, and His readiness to receive penitents and forgive them, complaining, 'Ye will not come unto Me that ye may have life', and that therefore His Gospel is called the Gospel of Peace and the Gospel of Grace.

But we had some good men, and that of all persuasions and opinions, whose discourses were full of terror, who spoke nothing but dismal things; and as they brought the people together with a kind of horror, sent them away in tears, prophesying nothing but evil tidings, terrifying the people with the apprehensions of being utterly destroyed, not guiding them, at least not enough, to cry to heaven for mercy.

It was, indeed, a time of very unhappy breaches among us in matters of religion. Innumerable sects and divisions and separate opinions prevailed among the people. The Church of England was restored, indeed, with the restoration of the monarchy, about four years before; but the ministers and preachers of the Presbyterians and Independents, and of all the other sorts of professions, had begun to gather separate societies and erect altar against altar, and all those had their meetings for worship apart, as they have now, but not so many then, the Dissenters being not thoroughly formed into a body as they are since; and those congregations which were thus gathered together were yet but few. And even those that were, the Government did not allow, but endeavoured to suppress them and shut up their meetings.

But the visitation reconciled them again, at least for a time, and many of the best and most valuable ministers and preachers of the Dissenters were suffered to go into the churches where the incumbents were fled away, as many were, not being able to stand it; and the people flocked without distinction to hear them preach, not much inquiring who or what opinion they were of. But after the sickness was over, that spirit of charity abated; and every church being again supplied with their own ministers, or others presented where the minister was dead, things returned to their old channel again.

One mischief always introduces another. These terrors and apprehensions of the people led them into a thousand weak, foolish, and wicked things, which they wanted not a sort of people really wicked to encourage them to: and this was running about to fortune-tellers, cunning-men, and astrologers to know their fortune, or, as it is vulgarly expressed, to have their fortunes told them, their nativities calculated, and the like; and this folly presently made the town swarm with a wicked generation of pretenders to magic, to the black art, as they called it, and I know not what; nay, to a thousand worse dealings with the devil than they were really guilty of. And this trade grew so open and so generally practised that it became common to have signs and inscriptions set up at doors: 'Here lives a fortune-teller', 'Here lives an astrologer', 'Here you may have your nativity calculated', and the like; and Friar Bacon's brazen-head, which was the usual sign of these people's dwellings, was to be seen almost in every street, or else the sign of Mother Shipton, or of Merlin's head, and the like.

With what blind, absurd, and ridiculous stuff these oracles of the devil pleased and satisfied the people I really know not, but certain it is that innumerable attendants crowded about their doors every day. And if but a grave fellow in a velvet jacket, a band, and a black coat, which was the habit those quack-conjurers generally went in, was but seen in the streets the people would follow them in crowds, and ask them questions as they went along.

I need not mention what a horrid delusion this was, or what it tended to; but there was no remedy for it till the plague itself put an end to it all—and, I suppose, cleared the town of most of those calculators themselves. One mischief was, that if the poor people asked these mock astrologers whether there would be a plague or no, they all agreed in general to answer 'Yes', for that kept up their trade. And had the people not been kept in a fright about that, the wizards would presently have been rendered useless, and their craft had been at an end. But they always talked to them of such-and-such influences of the stars, of the conjunctions of such-and-such planets, which must necessarily bring sickness and distempers, and consequently the plague. And some had the assurance to tell them the plague was begun already, which was too true, though they that said so knew nothing of the matter.

The ministers, to do them justice, and preachers of most sorts that were serious and understanding persons, thundered against these and other wicked practices, and exposed the folly as well as the wickedness of them together, and the most sober and judicious people despised and abhorred them. But it was impossible to make any impression upon the middling people and the working labouring poor. Their fears were predominant over all their passions, and they threw away their money in a most distracted manner upon those whimsies. Maid-servants especially, and men-servants, were the chief of their customers, and their question generally was, after the first demand of 'Will there be a plague?' I say, the next question was, 'Oh, sir I for the Lord's sake, what will become of me? Will my mistress keep me, or will she turn me off? Will she stay here, or will she go into the country? And if she goes into the country, will she take me with her, or leave me here to be starved and undone?' And the like of menservants.

The truth is, the case of poor servants was very dismal, as I shall have occasion to mention again by-and-by, for it was apparent a prodigious number of them would be turned away, and it was so. And of them abundance perished, and particularly of those that these false prophets had flattered with hopes that they should be continued in their services, and carried with their masters and mistresses into the country; and had not public charity provided for these poor creatures, whose number was exceeding great and in all cases of this nature must be so, they would have been in the worst condition of any people in the city.

These things agitated the minds of the common people for many months, while the first apprehensions were upon them, and while the plague was not, as I may say, yet broken out. But I must also not forget that the more serious part of the inhabitants behaved after another manner. The Government encouraged their devotion, and appointed public prayers and days of fasting and humiliation, to make public confession of sin and implore the mercy of God to avert the dreadful judgement which hung over their heads; and it is not to be expressed with what alacrity the people of all persuasions embraced the occasion; how they flocked to the churches and meetings, and they were all so thronged that there was often no coming near, no, not to the very doors of the largest churches. Also there were daily prayers appointed morning and evening at several churches, and days of private praying at other places; at all which the people attended, I say, with an uncommon devotion. Several private families also, as well of one opinion as of another, kept family fasts, to which they admitted their near relations only. So that, in a word, those people who were really serious and religious applied themselves in a truly Christian manner to the proper work of repentance and humiliation, as a Christian people ought to do.

Again, the public showed that they would bear their share in these things; the very Court, which was then gay and luxurious, put on a face of just concern for the public danger. All the plays and interludes which, after the manner of the French Court, had been set up, and began to increase among us, were forbid to act; the gaming-tables, public dancing-rooms, and music-houses, which multiplied and began to debauch the manners of the people, were shut up and suppressed; and the jack-puddings, merry-andrews, puppet-shows, rope-dancers, and such-like doings, which had bewitched the poor common people, shut up their shops, finding indeed no trade; for the minds of the people were agitated with other things, and a kind of sadness and horror at these things sat upon the countenances even of the common people. Death was before their eyes, and everybody began to think of their graves, not of mirth and diversions.

But even those wholesome reflections—which, rightly managed, would have most happily led the people to fall upon their knees, make confession of their sins, and look up to their merciful Saviour for pardon, imploring His compassion on them in such a time of their distress, by which we might have been as a second Nineveh—had a quite contrary extreme in the common people, who, ignorant and stupid in their reflections as they were brutishly wicked and thoughtless before, were now led by their fright to extremes of folly; and, as I have said before, that they ran to conjurers and witches, and all sorts of deceivers, to know what should become of them (who fed their fears, and kept them always alarmed and awake on purpose to delude them and pick their pockets), so they were as mad upon their running after quacks and mountebanks, and every practising old woman, for medicines and remedies; storing themselves with such multitudes of pills, potions, and preservatives, as they were called, that they not only spent their money but even poisoned themselves beforehand for fear of the poison of the infection; and prepared their bodies for the plague, instead of preserving them against it. On the other hand it is incredible and scarce to be imagined, how the posts of houses and corners of streets were plastered over with doctors' bills and papers of ignorant fellows, quacking and tampering in physic, and inviting the people to come to them for remedies, which was generally set off with such flourishes as these, viz.: 'Infallible preventive pills against the plague.' 'Neverfailing preservatives against the infection.' 'Sovereign cordials against the corruption of the air.' 'Exact regulations for the conduct of the body in case of an infection.' 'Anti-pestilential pills.' 'Incomparable drink against the plague, never found out before.' 'An universal remedy for the plague.' 'The only true plague water.' 'The royal antidote against all kinds of infection';—and such a number more that I cannot reckon up; and if I could, would fill a book of themselves to set them down.

Others set up bills to summon people to their lodgings for directions and advice in the case of infection. These had specious titles also, such as these:—

'An eminent High Dutch physician, newly come over from Holland, where he resided during all the time of the great plague last year in Amsterdam, and cured multitudes of people that actually had the plague upon them.'

'An Italian gentlewoman just arrived from Naples, having a choice secret to prevent infection, which she found out by her great experience, and did wonderful cures with it in the late plague there, wherein there died 20,000 in one day.'

'An ancient gentlewoman, having practised with great success in the late plague in this city, anno 1636, gives her advice only to the female sex. To be spoken with,' &c.

'An experienced physician, who has long studied the doctrine of antidotes against all sorts of poison and infection, has, after forty years' practice, arrived to such skill as may, with God's blessing, direct persons how to prevent their being touched by any contagious distemper whatsoever. He directs the poor gratis.'

I take notice of these by way of specimen. I could give you two or three dozen of the like and yet have abundance left behind. 'Tis sufficient from these to apprise any one of the humour of those times, and how a set of thieves and pickpockets not only robbed and cheated the poor people of their money, but poisoned their bodies with odious and fatal preparations; some with mercury, and some with other things as bad, perfectly remote from the thing pretended to, and rather hurtful than serviceable to the body in case an infection followed.

I cannot omit a subtility of one of those quack operators, with which he gulled the poor people to crowd about him, but did nothing for them without money. He had, it seems, added to his bills, which he gave about the streets, this advertisement in capital letters, viz., 'He gives advice to the poor for nothing.'

Abundance of poor people came to him accordingly, to whom he made a great many fine speeches, examined them of the state of their health and of the constitution of their bodies, and told them many good things for them to do, which were of no great moment. But the issue and conclusion of all was, that he had a preparation which if they took such a quantity of every morning, he would pawn his life they should never have the plague; no, though they lived in the house with people that were infected. This made the people all resolve to have it; but then the price of that was so much, I think 'twas half-a-crown. 'But, sir,' says one poor woman, 'I am a poor almswoman and am kept by the parish, and your bills say you give the poor your help for nothing.' 'Ay, good woman,' says the doctor, 'so I do, as I published there. I give my advice to the poor for nothing, but not my physic.' 'Alas, sir!' says she, 'that is a snare laid for the poor, then; for you give them advice for nothing; that is to say, you advise them gratis, to buy your physic for their money; so does every shop-keeper with his wares.' Here the woman began to give him ill words, and stood at his door all that day, telling her tale to all the people that came, till the doctor finding she turned away his customers, was obliged to call her upstairs again, and give her his box of physic for nothing, which perhaps, too, was good for nothing when she had it.

But to return to the people, whose confusions fitted them to be imposed upon by all sorts of pretenders and by every mountebank. There is no doubt but these quacking sort of fellows raised great gains out of the miserable people, for we daily found the crowds that ran after them were infinitely greater, and their doors were more thronged than those of Dr Brooks, Dr Upton, Dr Hodges, Dr Berwick, or any, though the most famous men of the time. And I was told that some of them got five pounds a day by their physic.

But there was still another madness beyond all this, which may serve to give an idea of the distracted humour of the poor people at that time: and this was their following a worse sort of deceivers than any of these; for these petty thieves only deluded them to pick their pockets and get their money, in which their wickedness, whatever it was, lay chiefly on the side of the deceivers, not upon the deceived. But in this part I am going to mention, it lay chiefly in the people deceived, or equally in both; and this was in wearing charms, philtres, exorcisms, amulets, and I know not what preparations, to fortify the body with them against the plague; as if the plague was not the hand of God, but a kind of possession of an evil spirit, and that it was to be kept off with crossings, signs of the zodiac, papers tied up with so many knots, and certain words or figures written on them, as particularly the word Abracadabra, formed in triangle or pyramid, thus:—

ABRACADABRA
ABRACADABR
ABRACADAB
ABRACADA
ABRACAD
ABRACA
ABRAC
ABRA
ABR
AB
A

Others had the Jesuits'
mark in a cross:
I H
S.
Others nothing but this
mark, thus:
* *
{*}

I might spend a great deal of time in my exclamations against the follies, and indeed the wickedness, of those things, in a time of such danger, in a matter of such consequences as this, of a national infection. But my memorandums of these things relate rather to take notice only of the fact, and mention only that it was so. How the poor people found the insufficiency of those things, and how many of them were afterwards carried away in the dead-carts and thrown into the common graves of every parish with these hellish charms and trumpery hanging about their necks, remains to be spoken of as we go along.

All this was the effect of the hurry the people were in, after the first notion of the plague being at hand was among them, and which may be said to be from about Michaelmas 1664, but more particularly after the two men died in St Giles's in the beginning of December; and again, after another alarm in February. For when the plague evidently spread itself, they soon began to see the folly of trusting to those unperforming creatures who had gulled them of their money; and then their fears worked another way, namely, to amazement and stupidity, not knowing what course to take or what to do either to help or relieve themselves. But they ran about from one neighbour's house to another, and even in the streets from one door to another, with repeated cries of, 'Lord, have mercy upon us! What shall we do?'

Indeed, the poor people were to be pitied in one particular thing in which they had little or no relief, and which I desire to mention with a serious awe and reflection, which perhaps every one that reads this may not relish; namely, that whereas death now began not, as we may say, to hover over every one's head only, but to look into their houses and chambers and stare in their faces. Though there might be some stupidity and dulness of the mind (and there was so, a great deal), yet there was a great deal of just alarm sounded into the very inmost soul, if I may so say, of others. Many consciences were awakened; many hard hearts melted into tears; many a penitent confession was made of crimes long concealed. It would wound the soul of any Christian to have heard the dying groans of many a despairing creature, and none durst come near to comfort them. Many a robbery, many a murder, was then confessed aloud, and nobody surviving to record the accounts of it. People might be heard, even into the streets as we passed along, calling upon God for mercy through Jesus Christ, and saying, 'I have been a thief, 'I have been an adulterer', 'I have been a murderer', and the like, and none durst stop to make the least inquiry into such things or to administer comfort to the poor creatures that in the anguish both of soul and body thus cried out. Some of the ministers did visit the sick at first and for a little while, but it was not to be done. It would have been present death to have gone into some houses. The very buriers of the dead, who were the hardenedest creatures in town, were sometimes beaten back and so terrified that they durst not go into houses where the whole families were swept away together, and where the circumstances were more particularly horrible, as some were; but this was, indeed, at the first heat of the distemper.

Time inured them to it all, and they ventured everywhere afterwards without hesitation, as I shall have occasion to mention at large hereafter.

I am supposing now the plague to be begun, as I have said, and that the magistrates began to take the condition of the people into their serious consideration. What they did as to the regulation of the inhabitants and of infected families, I shall speak to by itself; but as to the affair of health, it is proper to mention it here that, having seen the foolish humour of the people in running after quacks and mountebanks, wizards and fortune-tellers, which they did as above, even to madness, the Lord Mayor, a very sober and religious gentleman, appointed physicians and surgeons for relief of the poor—I mean the diseased poor and in particular ordered the College of Physicians to publish directions for cheap remedies for the poor, in all the circumstances of the distemper. This, indeed, was one of the most charitable and judicious things that could be done at that time, for this drove the people from haunting the doors of every disperser of bills, and from taking down blindly and without consideration poison for physic and death instead of life.

This direction of the physicians was done by a consultation of the whole College; and, as it was particularly calculated for the use of the poor and for cheap medicines, it was made public, so that everybody might see it, and copies were given gratis to all that desired it. But as it is public, and to be seen on all occasions, I need not give the reader of this the trouble of it.

I shall not be supposed to lessen the authority or capacity of the physicians when I say that the violence of the distemper, when it came to its extremity, was like the fire the next year. The fire, which consumed what the plague could not touch, defied all the application of remedies; the fire-engines were broken, the buckets thrown away, and the power of man was baffled and brought to an end. So the Plague defied all medicines; the very physicians were seized with it, with their preservatives in their mouths; and men went about prescribing to others and telling them what to do till the tokens were upon them, and they dropped down dead, destroyed by that very enemy they directed others to oppose. This was the case of several physicians, even some of them the most eminent, and of several of the most skilful surgeons. Abundance of quacks too died, who had the folly to trust to their own medicines, which they must needs be conscious to themselves were good for nothing, and who rather ought, like other sorts of thieves, to have run away, sensible of their guilt, from the justice that they could not but expect should punish them as they knew they had deserved.

Not that it is any derogation from the labour or application of the physicians to say they fell in the common calamity; nor is it so intended by me; it rather is to their praise that they ventured their lives so far as even to lose them in the service of mankind. They endeavoured to do good, and to save the lives of others. But we were not to expect that the physicians could stop God's judgements, or prevent a distemper eminently armed from heaven from executing the errand it was sent about.

Doubtless, the physicians assisted many by their skill, and by their prudence and applications, to the saving of their lives and restoring their health. But it is not lessening their character or their skill, to say they could not cure those that had the tokens upon them, or those who were mortally infected before the physicians were sent for, as was frequently the case.

It remains to mention now what public measures were taken by the magistrates for the general safety, and to prevent the spreading of the distemper, when it first broke out. I shall have frequent occasion to speak of the prudence of the magistrates, their charity, their vigilance for the poor, and for preserving good order, furnishing provisions, and the like, when the plague was increased, as it afterwards was. But I am now upon the order and regulations they published for the government of infected families.

I mentioned above shutting of houses up; and it is needful to say something particularly to that, for this part of the history of the plague is very melancholy, but the most grievous story must be told.

About June the Lord Mayor of London and the Court of Aldermen, as I have said, began more particularly to concern themselves for the regulation of the city.

The justices of Peace for Middlesex, by direction of the Secretary of State, had begun to shut up houses in the parishes of St Giles-in-the-Fields, St Martin, St Clement Danes, &c., and it was with good success; for in several streets where the plague broke out, upon strict guarding the houses that were infected, and taking care to bury those that died immediately after they were known to be dead, the plague ceased in those streets. It was also observed that the plague decreased sooner in those parishes after they had been visited to the full than it did in the parishes of Bishopsgate, Shoreditch, Aldgate, Whitechappel, Stepney, and others; the early care taken in that manner being a great means to the putting a check to it.

This shutting up of houses was a method first taken, as I understand, in the plague which happened in 1603, at the coming of King James the First to the crown; and the power of shutting people up in their own houses was granted by Act of Parliament, entitled, 'An Act for the charitable Relief and Ordering of Persons infected with the Plague'; on which Act of Parliament the Lord Mayor and aldermen of the city of London founded the order they made at this time, and which took place the 1st of July 1665, when the numbers infected within the city were but few, the last bill for the ninety-two parishes being but four; and some houses having been shut up in the city, and some people being removed to the pest-house beyond Bunhill Fields, in the way to Islington,—I say, by these means, when there died near one thousand a week in the whole, the number in the city was but twenty-eight, and the city was preserved more healthy in proportion than any other place all the time of the infection.

These orders of my Lord Mayor's were published, as I have said, the latter end of June, and took place from the 1st of July, and were as follows, viz.:—

ORDERS CONCEIVED AND PUBLISHED BY THE LORD MAYOR AND ALDERMEN OF THE CITY OF LONDON CONCERNING THE INFECTION OF THE PLAGUE, 1665.

'WHEREAS in the reign of our late Sovereign King James, of happy memory, an Act was made for the charitable relief and ordering of persons infected with the plague, whereby authority was given to justices of the peace, mayors, bailiffs, and other head-officers to appoint within their several limits examiners, searchers, watchmen, keepers, and buriers for the persons and places infected, and to minister unto them oaths for the performance of their offices. And the same statute did also authorise the giving of other directions, as unto them for the present necessity should seem good in their directions. It is now, upon special consideration, thought very expedient for preventing and avoiding of infection of sickness (if it shall so please Almighty God) that these officers following be appointed, and these orders hereafter duly observed.

Examiners to be appointed in every Parish.

'First, it is thought requisite, and so ordered, that in every parish there be one, two, or more persons of good sort and credit chosen and appointed by the alderman, his deputy, and common council of every ward, by the name of examiners, to continue in that office the space of two months at least. And if any fit person so appointed shall refuse to undertake the same, the said parties so refusing to be committed to prison until they shall conform themselves accordingly.

The Examiner's Office.

'That these examiners be sworn by the aldermen to inquire and learn from time to time what houses in every parish be visited, and what persons be sick, and of what diseases, as near as they can inform themselves; and upon doubt in that case, to command restraint of access until it appear what the disease shall prove. And if they find any person sick of the infection, to give order to the constable that the house be shut up; and if the constable shall be found remiss or negligent, to give present notice thereof to the alderman of the ward.

Watchmen.

'That to every infected house there be appointed two watchmen, one for every day, and the other for the night; and that these watchmen have a special care that no person go in or out of such infected houses whereof they have the charge, upon pain of severe punishment. And the said watchmen to do such further offices as the sick house shall need and require: and if the watchman be sent upon any business, to lock up the house and take the key with him; and the watchman by day to attend until ten of the clock at night, and the watchman by night until six in the morning.

Searchers.

'That there be a special care to appoint women searchers in every parish, such as are of honest reputation, and of the best sort as can be got in this kind; and these to be sworn to make due search and true report to the utmost of their knowledge whether the persons whose bodies they are appointed to search do die of the infection, or of what other diseases, as near as they can. And that the physicians who shall be appointed for cure and prevention of the infection do call before them the said searchers who are, or shall be, appointed for the several parishes under their respective cares, to the end they may consider whether they are fitly qualified for that employment, and charge them from time to time as they shall see cause, if they appear defective in their duties.

'That no searcher during this time of visitation be permitted to use any public work or employment, or keep any shop or stall, or be employed as a laundress, or in any other common employment whatsoever.

Chirurgeons.

'For better assistance of the searchers, forasmuch as there hath been heretofore great abuse in misreporting the disease, to the further spreading of the infection, it is therefore ordered that there be chosen and appointed able and discreet chirurgeons, besides those that do already belong to the pest-house, amongst whom the city and Liberties to be quartered as the places lie most apt and convenient; and every of these to have one quarter for his limit; and the said chirurgeons in every of their limits to join with the searchers for the view of the body, to the end there may be a true report made of the disease.

'And further, that the said chirurgeons shall visit and search such-like persons as shall either send for them or be named and directed unto them by the examiners of every parish, and inform themselves of the disease of the said parties.

'And forasmuch as the said chirurgeons are to be sequestered from all other cures, and kept only to this disease of the infection, it is ordered that every of the said chirurgeons shall have twelve-pence a body searched by them, to be paid out of the goods of the party searched, if he be able, or otherwise by the parish.

Nurse-keepers.

'If any nurse-keeper shall remove herself out of any infected house before twenty-eight days after the decease of any person dying of the infection, the house to which the said nurse-keeper doth so remove herself shall be shut up until the said twenty-eight days be expired.'

ORDERS CONCERNING INFECTED HOUSES AND PERSONS SICK OF THE PLAGUE.

Notice to be given of the Sickness.

'The master of every house, as soon as any one in his house complaineth, either of blotch or purple, or swelling in any part of his body, or falleth otherwise dangerously sick, without apparent cause of some other disease, shall give knowledge thereof to the examiner of health within two hours after the said sign shall appear.

Sequestration of the Sick.

'As soon as any man shall be found by this examiner, chirurgeon, or searcher to be sick of the plague, he shall the same night be sequestered in the same house; and in case he be so sequestered, then though he afterwards die not, the house wherein he sickened should be shut up for a month, after the use of the due preservatives taken by the rest.

Airing the Stuff.

'For sequestration of the goods and stuff of the infection, their bedding and apparel and hangings of chambers must be well aired with fire and such perfumes as are requisite within the infected house before they be taken again to use. This to be done by the appointment of an examiner.

Shutting up of the House.

'If any person shall have visited any man known to be infected of the plague, or entered willingly into any known infected house, being not allowed, the house wherein he inhabiteth shall be shut up for certain days by the examiner's direction.

None to be removed out of infected Houses, but, &C.

'Item, that none be removed out of the house where he falleth sick of the infection into any other house in the city (except it be to the pest-house or a tent, or unto some such house which the owner of the said visited house holdeth in his own hands and occupieth by his own servants); and so as security be given to the parish whither such remove is made, that the attendance and charge about the said visited persons shall be observed and charged in all the particularities before expressed, without any cost of that parish to which any such remove shall happen to be made, and this remove to be done by night. And it shall be lawful to any person that hath two houses to remove either his sound or his infected people to his spare house at his choice, so as, if he send away first his sound, he not after send thither his sick, nor again unto the sick the sound; and that the same which he sendeth be for one week at the least shut up and secluded from company, for fear of some infection at the first not appearing.

Burial of the Dead.

'That the burial of the dead by this visitation be at most convenient hours, always either before sun-rising or after sun-setting, with the privity of the churchwardens or constable, and not otherwise; and that no neighbours nor friends be suffered to accompany the corpse to church, or to enter the house visited, upon pain of having his house shut up or be imprisoned.

'And that no corpse dying of infection shall be buried, or remain in any church in time of common prayer, sermon, or lecture. And that no children be suffered at time of burial of any corpse in any church, churchyard, or burying-place to come near the corpse, coffin, or grave. And that all the graves shall be at least six feet deep.

'And further, all public assemblies at other burials are to be foreborne during the continuance of this visitation.

No infected Stuff to be uttered.

'That no clothes, stuff, bedding, or garments be suffered to be carried or conveyed out of any infected houses, and that the criers and carriers abroad of bedding or old apparel to be sold or pawned be utterly prohibited and restrained, and no brokers of bedding or old apparel be permitted to make any outward show, or hang forth on their stalls, shop-boards, or windows, towards any street, lane, common way, or passage, any old bedding or apparel to be sold, upon pain of imprisonment. And if any broker or other person shall buy any bedding, apparel, or other stuff out of any infected house within two months after the infection hath been there, his house shall be shut up as infected, and so shall continue shut up twenty days at the least.

No Person to be conveyed out of any infected House.

'If any person visited do fortune, by negligent looking unto, or by any other means, to come or be conveyed from a place infected to any other place, the parish from whence such party hath come or been conveyed, upon notice thereof given, shall at their charge cause the said party so visited and escaped to be carried and brought back again by night, and the parties in this case offending to be punished at the direction of the alderman of the ward, and the house of the receiver of such visited person to be shut up for twenty days.

Every visited House to be marked.

'That every house visited be marked with a red cross of a foot long in the middle of the door, evident to be seen, and with these usual printed words, that is to say, "Lord, have mercy upon us," to be set close over the same cross, there to continue until lawful opening of the same house.

Every visited House to be watched.

'That the constables see every house shut up, and to be attended with watchmen, which may keep them in, and minister necessaries unto them at their own charges, if they be able, or at the common charge, if they are unable; the shutting up to be for the space of four weeks after all be whole.

'That precise order to be taken that the searchers, chirurgeons, keepers, and buriers are not to pass the streets without holding a red rod or wand of three feet in length in their hands, open and evident to be seen, and are not to go into any other house than into their own, or into that whereunto they are directed or sent for; but to forbear and abstain from company, especially when they have been lately used in any such business or attendance.

Inmates.

'That where several inmates are in one and the same house, and any person in that house happens to be infected, no other person or family of such house shall be suffered to remove him or themselves without a certificate from the examiners of health of that parish; or in default thereof, the house whither he or they so remove shall be shut up as in case of visitation.

Hackney-Coaches.

'That care be taken of hackney-coachmen, that they may not (as some of them have been observed to do after carrying of infected persons to the pest-house and other places) be admitted to common use till their coaches be well aired, and have stood unemployed by the space of five or six days after such service.'

ORDERS FOR CLEANSING AND KEEPING OF THE STREETS SWEPT.

The Streets to be kept Clean.

'First, it is thought necessary, and so ordered, that every householder do cause the street to be daily prepared before his door, and so to keep it clean swept all the week long.

That Rakers take it from out the Houses.

'That the sweeping and filth of houses be daily carried away by the rakers, and that the raker shall give notice of his coming by the blowing of a horn, as hitherto hath been done.

Laystalls to be made far off from the City.

'That the laystalls be removed as far as may be out of the city and common passages, and that no nightman or other be suffered to empty a vault into any garden near about the city.

Care to be had of unwholesome Fish or Flesh, and of musty Corn.

'That special care be taken that no stinking fish, or unwholesome flesh, or musty corn, or other corrupt fruits of what sort soever, be suffered to be sold about the city, or any part of the same.

'That the brewers and tippling-houses be looked into for musty and unwholesome casks.

'That no hogs, dogs, or cats, or tame pigeons, or ponies, be suffered to be kept within any part of the city, or any swine to be or stray in the streets or lanes, but that such swine be impounded by the beadle or any other officer, and the owner punished according to Act of Common Council, and that the dogs be killed by the dog-killers appointed for that purpose.'

ORDERS CONCERNING LOOSE PERSONS AND IDLE ASSEMBLIES.

Beggars.

'Forasmuch as nothing is more complained of than the multitude of rogues and wandering beggars that swarm in every place about the city, being a great cause of the spreading of the infection, and will not be avoided, notwithstanding any orders that have been given to the contrary: It is therefore now ordered, that such constables, and others whom this matter may any way concern, take special care that no wandering beggars be suffered in the streets of this city in any fashion or manner whatsoever, upon the penalty provided by the law, to be duly and severely executed upon them.

Plays.

'That all plays, bear-baitings, games, singing of ballads, buckler-play, or such-like causes of assemblies of people be utterly prohibited, and the parties offending severely punished by every alderman in his ward.

Feasting prohibited.

'That all public feasting, and particularly by the companies of this city, and dinners at taverns, ale-houses, and other places of common entertainment, be forborne till further order and allowance; and that the money thereby spared be preserved and employed for the benefit and relief of the poor visited with the infection.

Tippling-houses.

'That disorderly tippling in taverns, ale-houses, coffee-houses, and cellars be severely looked unto, as the common sin of this time and greatest occasion of dispersing the plague. And that no company or person be suffered to remain or come into any tavern, ale-house, or coffee-house to drink after nine of the clock in the evening, according to the ancient law and custom of this city, upon the penalties ordained in that behalf.

'And for the better execution of these orders, and such other rules and directions as, upon further consideration, shall be found needful: It is ordered and enjoined that the aldermen, deputies, and common councilmen shall meet together weekly, once, twice, thrice or oftener (as cause shall require), at some one general place accustomed in their respective wards (being clear from infection of the plague), to consult how the said orders may be duly put in execution; not intending that any dwelling in or near places infected shall come to the said meeting while their coming may be doubtful. And the said aldermen, and deputies, and common councilmen in their several wards may put in execution any other good orders that by them at their said meetings shall be conceived and devised for preservation of his Majesty's subjects from the infection.

'SIR JOHN LAWRENCE, Lord Mayor.
SIR GEORGE WATERMAN
SIR CHARLES DOE, Sheriffs.'

I need not say that these orders extended only to such places as were within the Lord Mayor's jurisdiction, so it is requisite to observe that the justices of Peace within those parishes and places as were called the Hamlets and out-parts took the same method. As I remember, the orders for shutting up of houses did not take Place so soon on our side, because, as I said before, the plague did not reach to these eastern parts of the town at least, nor begin to be very violent, till the beginning of August. For example, the whole bill from the 11th to the 18th of July was 1761, yet there died but 71 of the plague in all those parishes we call the Tower Hamlets, and they were as follows:—

Aldgate... 14
Stepney... 33
Whitechappel... 21
St Katherine, Tower... 2
Trinities, Minories... 1
Total... 71

The next week was thus:
Aldgate... 34
Stepney... 58
Whitechappel... 48
St Katherine, Tower... 4
Trinity, Minories... 1
Total... 145

And to the 1st of Aug. thus:
Aldgate... 65
Stepney... 76
Whitechappel... 79
St Katherine, Tower... 4
Trinity, Minories... 4
Total... 228

It was indeed coming on amain, for the burials that same week were in the next adjoining parishes thus:—

St Leonard's, Shoreditch... 64
St Botolph's, Bishopsgate... 65
St. Giles, Cripplegate... 213
Total... 342

The next week prodigiously increased, as:
St Leonard's, Shoreditch... 84
St Botolph's, Bishopsgate... 105
St. Giles, Cripplegate... 421
Total... 610

And to the 1st of Aug. thus:
St Leonard's, Shoreditch... 110
St Botolph's, Bishopsgate... 116
St. Giles, Cripplegate... 554
Total... 780

This shutting up of houses was at first counted a very cruel and unchristian method, and the poor people so confined made bitter lamentations. Complaints of the severity of it were also daily brought to my Lord Mayor, of houses causelessly (and some maliciously) shut up. I cannot say; but upon inquiry many that complained so loudly were found in a condition to be continued; and others again, inspection being made upon the sick person, and the sickness not appearing infectious, or if uncertain, yet on his being content to be carried to the pest-house, were released.

It is true that the locking up the doors of people's houses, and setting a watchman there night and day to prevent their stirring out or any coming to them, when perhaps the sound people in the family might have escaped if they had been removed from the sick, looked very hard and cruel; and many people perished in these miserable confinements which, 'tis reasonable to believe, would not have been distempered if they had had liberty, though the plague was in the house; at which the people were very clamorous and uneasy at first, and several violences were committed and injuries offered to the men who were set to watch the houses so shut up; also several people broke out by force in many places, as I shall observe by-and-by. But it was a public good that justified the private mischief, and there was no obtaining the least mitigation by any application to magistrates or government at that time, at least not that I heard of. This put the people upon all manner of stratagem in order, if possible, to get out; and it would fill a little volume to set down the arts used by the people of such houses to shut the eyes of the watchmen who were employed, to deceive them, and to escape or break out from them, in which frequent scuffles and some mischief happened; of which by itself.

As I went along Houndsditch one morning about eight o'clock there was a great noise. It is true, indeed, there was not much crowd, because people were not very free to gather together, or to stay long together when they were there; nor did I stay long there. But the outcry was loud enough to prompt my curiosity, and I called to one that looked out of a window, and asked what was the matter.

A watchman, it seems, had been employed to keep his post at the door of a house which was infected, or said to be infected, and was shut up. He had been there all night for two nights together, as he told his story, and the day-watchman had been there one day, and was now come to relieve him. All this while no noise had been heard in the house, no light had been seen; they called for nothing, sent him of no errands, which used to be the chief business of the watchmen; neither had they given him any disturbance, as he said, from the Monday afternoon, when he heard great crying and screaming in the house, which, as he supposed, was occasioned by some of the family dying just at that time. It seems, the night before, the dead-cart, as it was called, had been stopped there, and a servant-maid had been brought down to the door dead, and the buriers or bearers, as they were called, put her into the cart, wrapt only in a green rug, and carried her away.

The watchman had knocked at the door, it seems, when he heard that noise and crying, as above, and nobody answered a great while; but at last one looked out and said with an angry, quick tone, and yet a kind of crying voice, or a voice of one that was crying, 'What d'ye want, that ye make such a knocking?' He answered, 'I am the watchman! How do you do? What is the matter?' The person answered, 'What is that to you? Stop the dead-cart.' This, it seems, was about one o'clock. Soon after, as the fellow said, he stopped the dead-cart, and then knocked again, but nobody answered. He continued knocking, and the bellman called out several times, 'Bring out your dead'; but nobody answered, till the man that drove the cart, being called to other houses, would stay no longer, and drove away.

The watchman knew not what to make of all this, so he let them alone till the morning-man or day-watchman, as they called him, came to relieve him. Giving him an account of the particulars, they knocked at the door a great while, but nobody answered; and they observed that the window or casement at which the person had looked out who had answered before continued open, being up two pair of stairs.

Upon this the two men, to satisfy their curiosity, got a long ladder, and one of them went up to the window and looked into the room, where he saw a woman lying dead upon the floor in a dismal manner, having no clothes on her but her shift. But though he called aloud, and putting in his long staff, knocked hard on the floor, yet nobody stirred or answered; neither could he hear any noise in the house.

He came down again upon this, and acquainted his fellow, who went up also; and finding it just so, they resolved to acquaint either the Lord Mayor or some other magistrate of it, but did not offer to go in at the window. The magistrate, it seems, upon the information of the two men, ordered the house to be broke open, a constable and other persons being appointed to be present, that nothing might be plundered; and accordingly it was so done, when nobody was found in the house but that young woman, who having been infected and past recovery, the rest had left her to die by herself, and were every one gone, having found some way to delude the watchman, and to get open the door, or get out at some back-door, or over the tops of the houses, so that he knew nothing of it; and as to those cries and shrieks which he heard, it was supposed they were the passionate cries of the family at the bitter parting, which, to be sure, it was to them all, this being the sister to the mistress of the family. The man of the house, his wife, several children, and servants, being all gone and fled, whether sick or sound, that I could never learn; nor, indeed, did I make much inquiry after it.

Many such escapes were made out of infected houses, as particularly when the watchman was sent of some errand; for it was his business to go of any errand that the family sent him of; that is to say, for necessaries, such as food and physic; to fetch physicians, if they would come, or surgeons, or nurses, or to order the dead-cart, and the like; but with this condition, too, that when he went he was to lock up the outer door of the house and take the key away with him, To evade this, and cheat the watchmen, people got two or three keys made to their locks, or they found ways to unscrew the locks such as were screwed on, and so take off the lock, being in the inside of the house, and while they sent away the watchman to the market, to the bakehouse, or for one trifle or another, open the door and go out as often as they pleased. But this being found out, the officers afterwards had orders to padlock up the doors on the outside, and place bolts on them as they thought fit.

At another house, as I was informed, in the street next within Aldgate, a whole family was shut up and locked in because the maid-servant was taken sick. The master of the house had complained by his friends to the next alderman and to the Lord Mayor, and had consented to have the maid carried to the pest-house, but was refused; so the door was marked with a red cross, a padlock on the outside, as above, and a watchman set to keep the door, according to public order.

After the master of the house found there was no remedy, but that he, his wife, and his children were to be locked up with this poor distempered servant, he called to the watchman, and told him he must go then and fetch a nurse for them to attend this poor girl, for that it would be certain death to them all to oblige them to nurse her; and told him plainly that if he would not do this, the maid must perish either of the distemper or be starved for want of food, for he was resolved none of his family should go near her; and she lay in the garret four storey high, where she could not cry out, or call to anybody for help.

The watchman consented to that, and went and fetched a nurse, as he was appointed, and brought her to them the same evening. During this interval the master of the house took his opportunity to break a large hole through his shop into a bulk or stall, where formerly a cobbler had sat, before or under his shop-window; but the tenant, as may be supposed at such a dismal time as that, was dead or removed, and so he had the key in his own keeping. Having made his way into this stall, which he could not have done if the man had been at the door, the noise he was obliged to make being such as would have alarmed the watchman; I say, having made his way into this stall, he sat still till the watchman returned with the nurse, and all the next day also. But the night following, having contrived to send the watchman of another trifling errand, which, as I take it, was to an apothecary's for a plaister for the maid, which he was to stay for the making up, or some other such errand that might secure his staying some time; in that time he conveyed himself and all his family out of the house, and left the nurse and the watchman to bury the poor wench—that is, throw her into the cart—and take care of the house.

I could give a great many such stories as these, diverting enough, which in the long course of that dismal year I met with—that is, heard of—and which are very certain to be true, or very near the truth; that is to say, true in the general: for no man could at such a time learn all the particulars. There was likewise violence used with the watchmen, as was reported, in abundance of places; and I believe that from the beginning of the visitation to the end, there was not less than eighteen or twenty of them killed, or so wounded as to be taken up for dead, which was supposed to be done by the people in the infected houses which were shut up, and where they attempted to come out and were opposed.

Nor, indeed, could less be expected, for here were so many prisons in the town as there were houses shut up; and as the people shut up or imprisoned so were guilty of no crime, only shut up because miserable, it was really the more intolerable to them.

It had also this difference, that every prison, as we may call it, had but one jailer, and as he had the whole house to guard, and that many houses were so situated as that they had several ways out, some more, some less, and some into several streets, it was impossible for one man so to guard all the passages as to prevent the escape of people made desperate by the fright of their circumstances, by the resentment of their usage, or by the raging of the distemper itself; so that they would talk to the watchman on one side of the house, while the family made their escape at another.

For example, in Coleman Street there are abundance of alleys, as appears still. A house was shut up in that they call White's Alley; and this house had a back-window, not a door, into a court which had a passage into Bell Alley. A watchman was set by the constable at the door of this house, and there he stood, or his comrade, night and day, while the family went all away in the evening out at that window into the court, and left the poor fellows warding and watching for near a fortnight.

Not far from the same place they blew up a watchman with gunpowder, and burned the poor fellow dreadfully; and while he made hideous cries, and nobody would venture to come near to help him, the whole family that were able to stir got out at the windows one storey high, two that were left sick calling out for help. Care was taken to give them nurses to look after them, but the persons fled were never found, till after the plague was abated they returned; but as nothing could be proved, so nothing could be done to them.

It is to be considered, too, that as these were prisons without bars and bolts, which our common prisons are furnished with, so the people let themselves down out of their windows, even in the face of the watchman, bringing swords or pistols in their hands, and threatening the poor wretch to shoot him if he stirred or called for help.

In other cases, some had gardens, and walls or pales, between them and their neighbours, or yards and back-houses; and these, by friendship and entreaties, would get leave to get over those walls or pales, and so go out at their neighbours' doors; or, by giving money to their servants, get them to let them through in the night; so that in short, the shutting up of houses was in no wise to be depended upon. Neither did it answer the end at all, serving more to make the people desperate, and drive them to such extremities as that they would break out at all adventures.

And that which was still worse, those that did thus break out spread the infection farther by their wandering about with the distemper upon them, in their desperate circumstances, than they would otherwise have done; for whoever considers all the particulars in such cases must acknowledge, and we cannot doubt but the severity of those confinements made many people desperate, and made them run out of their houses at all hazards, and with the plague visibly upon them, not knowing either whither to go or what to do, or, indeed, what they did; and many that did so were driven to dreadful exigencies and extremities, and perished in the streets or fields for mere want, or dropped down by the raging violence of the fever upon them. Others wandered into the country, and went forward any way, as their desperation guided them, not knowing whither they went or would go: till, faint and tired, and not getting any relief, the houses and villages on the road refusing to admit them to lodge whether infected or no, they have perished by the roadside or gotten into barns and died there, none daring to come to them or relieve them, though perhaps not infected, for nobody would believe them.

On the other hand, when the plague at first seized a family that is to say, when any body of the family had gone out and unwarily or otherwise catched the distemper and brought it home —it was certainly known by the family before it was known to the officers, who, as you will see by the order, were appointed to examine into the circumstances of all sick persons when they heard of their being sick.

In this interval, between their being taken sick and the examiners coming, the master of the house had leisure and liberty to remove himself or all his family, if he knew whither to go, and many did so. But the great disaster was that many did thus after they were really infected themselves, and so carried the disease into the houses of those who were so hospitable as to receive them; which, it must be confessed, was very cruel and ungrateful.

And this was in part the reason of the general notion, or scandal rather, which went about of the temper of people infected: namely, that they did not take the least care or make any scruple of infecting others, though I cannot say but there might be some truth in it too, but not so general as was reported. What natural reason could be given for so wicked a thing at a time when they might conclude themselves just going to appear at the bar of Divine justice I know not. I am very well satisfied that it cannot be reconciled to religion and principle any more than it can be to generosity and Humanity, but I may speak of that again.

I am speaking now of people made desperate by the apprehensions of their being shut up, and their breaking out by stratagem or force, either before or after they were shut up, whose misery was not lessened when they were out, but sadly increased. On the other hand, many that thus got away had retreats to go to and other houses, where they locked themselves up and kept hid till the plague was over; and many families, foreseeing the approach of the distemper, laid up stores of provisions sufficient for their whole families, and shut themselves up, and that so entirely that they were neither seen or heard of till the infection was quite ceased, and then came abroad sound and well. I might recollect several such as these, and give you the particulars of their management; for doubtless it was the most effectual secure step that could be taken for such whose circumstances would not admit them to remove, or who had not retreats abroad proper for the case; for in being thus shut up they were as if they had been a hundred miles off. Nor do I remember that any one of those families miscarried. Among these, several Dutch merchants were particularly remarkable, who kept their houses like little garrisons besieged suffering none to go in or out or come near them, particularly one in a court in Throgmorton Street whose house looked into Draper's Garden.

But I come back to the case of families infected and shut up by the magistrates. The misery of those families is not to be expressed; and it was generally in such houses that we heard the most dismal shrieks and outcries of the poor people, terrified and even frighted to death by the sight of the condition of their dearest relations, and by the terror of being imprisoned as they were.

I remember, and while I am writing this story I think I hear the very sound of it, a certain lady had an only daughter, a young maiden about nineteen years old, and who was possessed of a very considerable fortune. They were only lodgers in the house where they were. The young woman, her mother, and the maid had been abroad on some occasion, I do not remember what, for the house was not shut up; but about two hours after they came home the young lady complained she was not well; in a quarter of an hour more she vomited and had a violent pain in her head. 'Pray God', says her mother, in a terrible fright, 'my child has not the distemper!' The pain in her head increasing, her mother ordered the bed to be warmed, and resolved to put her to bed, and prepared to give her things to sweat, which was the ordinary remedy to be taken when the first apprehensions of the distemper began.

While the bed was airing the mother undressed the young woman, and just as she was laid down in the bed, she, looking upon her body with a candle, immediately discovered the fatal tokens on the inside of her thighs. Her mother, not being able to contain herself, threw down her candle and shrieked out in such a frightful manner that it was enough to place horror upon the stoutest heart in the world; nor was it one scream or one cry, but the fright having seized her spirits, she—fainted first, then recovered, then ran all over the house, up the stairs and down the stairs, like one distracted, and indeed really was distracted, and continued screeching and crying out for several hours void of all sense, or at least government of her senses, and, as I was told, never came thoroughly to herself again. As to the young maiden, she was a dead corpse from that moment, for the gangrene which occasions the spots had spread [over] her whole body, and she died in less than two hours. But still the mother continued crying out, not knowing anything more of her child, several hours after she was dead. It is so long ago that I am not certain, but I think the mother never recovered, but died in two or three weeks after.

This was an extraordinary case, and I am therefore the more particular in it, because I came so much to the knowledge of it; but there were innumerable such-like cases, and it was seldom that the weekly bill came in but there were two or three put in, 'frighted'; that is, that may well be called frighted to death. But besides those who were so frighted as to die upon the spot, there were great numbers frighted to other extremes, some frighted out of their senses, some out of their memory, and some out of their understanding. But I return to the shutting up of houses.

As several people, I say, got out of their houses by stratagem after they were shut up, so others got out by bribing the watchmen, and giving them money to let them go privately out in the night. I must confess I thought it at that time the most innocent corruption or bribery that any man could be guilty of, and therefore could not but pity the poor men, and think it was hard when three of those watchmen were publicly whipped through the streets for suffering people to go out of houses shut up.

But notwithstanding that severity, money prevailed with the poor men, and many families found means to make sallies out, and escape that way after they had been shut up; but these were generally such as had some places to retire to; and though there was no easy passing the roads any whither after the 1st of August, yet there were many ways of retreat, and particularly, as I hinted, some got tents and set them up in the fields, carrying beds or straw to lie on, and provisions to eat, and so lived in them as hermits in a cell, for nobody would venture to come near them; and several stories were told of such, some comical, some tragical, some who lived like wandering pilgrims in the deserts, and escaped by making themselves exiles in such a manner as is scarce to be credited, and who yet enjoyed more liberty than was to be expected in such cases.

I have by me a story of two brothers and their kinsman, who being single men, but that had stayed in the city too long to get away, and indeed not knowing where to go to have any retreat, nor having wherewith to travel far, took a course for their own preservation, which though in itself at first desperate, yet was so natural that it may be wondered that no more did so at that time. They were but of mean condition, and yet not so very poor as that they could not furnish themselves with some little conveniences such as might serve to keep life and soul together; and finding the distemper increasing in a terrible manner, they resolved to shift as well as they could, and to be gone.

One of them had been a soldier in the late wars, and before that in the Low Countries, and having been bred to no particular employment but his arms, and besides being wounded, and not able to work very hard, had for some time been employed at a baker's of sea-biscuit in Wapping.

The brother of this man was a seaman too, but somehow or other had been hurt of one leg, that he could not go to sea, but had worked for his living at a sailmaker's in Wapping, or thereabouts; and being a good husband, had laid up some money, and was the richest of the three.

The third man was a joiner or carpenter by trade, a handy fellow, and he had no wealth but his box or basket of tools, with the help of which he could at any time get his living, such a time as this excepted, wherever he went—and he lived near Shadwell.

They all lived in Stepney parish, which, as I have said, being the last that was infected, or at least violently, they stayed there till they evidently saw the plague was abating at the west part of the town, and coming towards the east, where they lived.

The story of those three men, if the reader will be content to have me give it in their own persons, without taking upon me to either vouch the particulars or answer for any mistakes, I shall give as distinctly as I can, believing the history will be a very good pattern for any poor man to follow, in case the like public desolation should happen here; and if there may be no such occasion, which God of His infinite mercy grant us, still the story may have its uses so many ways as that it will, I hope, never be said that the relating has been unprofitable.

I say all this previous to the history, having yet, for the present, much more to say before I quit my own part.

I went all the first part of the time freely about the streets, though not so freely as to run myself into apparent danger, except when they dug the great pit in the churchyard of our parish of Aldgate. A terrible pit it was, and I could not resist my curiosity to go and see it. As near as I may judge, it was about forty feet in length, and about fifteen or sixteen feet broad, and at the time I first looked at it, about nine feet deep; but it was said they dug it near twenty feet deep afterwards in one part of it, till they could go no deeper for the water; for they had, it seems, dug several large pits before this. For though the plague was long a-coming to our parish, yet, when it did come, there was no parish in or about London where it raged with such violence as in the two parishes of Aldgate and Whitechappel.

I say they had dug several pits in another ground, when the distemper began to spread in our parish, and especially when the dead-carts began to go about, which was not, in our parish, till the beginning of August. Into these pits they had put perhaps fifty or sixty bodies each; then they made larger holes wherein they buried all that the cart brought in a week, which, by the middle to the end of August, came to from 200 to 400 a week; and they could not well dig them larger, because of the order of the magistrates confining them to leave no bodies within six feet of the surface; and the water coming on at about seventeen or eighteen feet, they could not well, I say, put more in one pit. But now, at the beginning of September, the plague raging in a dreadful manner, and the number of burials in our parish increasing to more than was ever buried in any parish about London of no larger extent, they ordered this dreadful gulf to be dug—for such it was, rather than a pit.

They had supposed this pit would have supplied them for a month or more when they dug it, and some blamed the churchwardens for suffering such a frightful thing, telling them they were making preparations to bury the whole parish, and the like; but time made it appear the churchwardens knew the condition of the parish better than they did: for, the pit being finished the 4th of September, I think, they began to bury in it the 6th, and by the 20th, which was just two weeks, they had thrown into it 1114 bodies when they were obliged to fill it up, the bodies being then come to lie within six feet of the surface. I doubt not but there may be some ancient persons alive in the parish who can justify the fact of this, and are able to show even in what place of the churchyard the pit lay better than I can. The mark of it also was many years to be seen in the churchyard on the surface, lying in length parallel with the passage which goes by the west wall of the churchyard out of Houndsditch, and turns east again into Whitechappel, coming out near the Three Nuns' Inn.

It was about the 10th of September that my curiosity led, or rather drove, me to go and see this pit again, when there had been near 400 people buried in it; and I was not content to see it in the day-time, as I had done before, for then there would have been nothing to have been seen but the loose earth; for all the bodies that were thrown in were immediately covered with earth by those they called the buriers, which at other times were called bearers; but I resolved to go in the night and see some of them thrown in.

There was a strict order to prevent people coming to those pits, and that was only to prevent infection. But after some time that order was more necessary, for people that were infected and near their end, and delirious also, would run to those pits, wrapt in blankets or rugs, and throw themselves in, and, as they said, bury themselves. I cannot say that the officers suffered any willingly to lie there; but I have heard that in a great pit in Finsbury, in the parish of Cripplegate, it lying open then to the fields, for it was not then walled about, [many] came and threw themselves in, and expired there, before they threw any earth upon them; and that when they came to bury others and found them there, they were quite dead, though not cold.

This may serve a little to describe the dreadful condition of that day, though it is impossible to say anything that is able to give a true idea of it to those who did not see it, other than this, that it was indeed very, very, very dreadful, and such as no tongue can express.

I got admittance into the churchyard by being acquainted with the sexton who attended; who, though he did not refuse me at all, yet earnestly persuaded me not to go, telling me very seriously (for he was a good, religious, and sensible man) that it was indeed their business and duty to venture, and to run all hazards, and that in it they might hope to be preserved; but that I had no apparent call to it but my own curiosity, which, he said, he believed I would not pretend was sufficient to justify my running that hazard. I told him I had been pressed in my mind to go, and that perhaps it might be an instructing sight, that might not be without its uses. 'Nay,' says the good man, 'if you will venture upon that score, name of God go in; for, depend upon it, 'twill be a sermon to you, it may be, the best that ever you heard in your life. 'Tis a speaking sight,' says he, 'and has a voice with it, and a loud one, to call us all to repentance'; and with that he opened the door and said, 'Go, if you will.'

His discourse had shocked my resolution a little, and I stood wavering for a good while, but just at that interval I saw two links come over from the end of the Minories, and heard the bellman, and then appeared a dead-cart, as they called it, coming over the streets; so I could no longer resist my desire of seeing it, and went in. There was nobody, as I could perceive at first, in the churchyard, or going into it, but the buriers and the fellow that drove the cart, or rather led the horse and cart; but when they came up to the pit they saw a man go to and again, muffled up in a brown Cloak, and making motions with his hands under his cloak, as if he was in great agony, and the buriers immediately gathered about him, supposing he was one of those poor delirious or desperate creatures that used to pretend, as I have said, to bury themselves. He said nothing as he walked about, but two or three times groaned very deeply and loud, and sighed as he would break his heart.

When the buriers came up to him they soon found he was neither a person infected and desperate, as I have observed above, or a person distempered—in mind, but one oppressed with a dreadful weight of grief indeed, having his wife and several of his children all in the cart that was just come in with him, and he followed in an agony and excess of sorrow. He mourned heartily, as it was easy to see, but with a kind of masculine grief that could not give itself vent by tears; and calmly defying the buriers to let him alone, said he would only see the bodies thrown in and go away, so they left importuning him. But no sooner was the cart turned round and the bodies shot into the pit promiscuously, which was a surprise to him, for he at least expected they would have been decently laid in, though indeed he was afterwards convinced that was impracticable; I say, no sooner did he see the sight but he cried out aloud, unable to contain himself. I could not hear what he said, but he went backward two or three steps and fell down in a swoon. The buriers ran to him and took him up, and in a little while he came to himself, and they led him away to the Pie Tavern over against the end of Houndsditch, where, it seems, the man was known, and where they took care of him. He looked into the pit again as he went away, but the buriers had covered the bodies so immediately with throwing in earth, that though there was light enough, for there were lanterns, and candles in them, placed all night round the sides of the pit, upon heaps of earth, seven or eight, or perhaps more, yet nothing could be seen.

This was a mournful scene indeed, and affected me almost as much as the rest; but the other was awful and full of terror. The cart had in it sixteen or seventeen bodies; some were wrapt up in linen sheets, some in rags, some little other than naked, or so loose that what covering they had fell from them in the shooting out of the cart, and they fell quite naked among the rest; but the matter was not much to them, or the indecency much to any one else, seeing they were all dead, and were to be huddled together into the common grave of mankind, as we may call it, for here was no difference made, but poor and rich went together; there was no other way of burials, neither was it possible there should, for coffins were not to be had for the prodigious numbers that fell in such a calamity as this.

It was reported by way of scandal upon the buriers, that if any corpse was delivered to them decently wound up, as we called it then, in a winding-sheet tied over the head and feet, which some did, and which was generally of good linen; I say, it was reported that the buriers were so wicked as to strip them in the cart and carry them quite naked to the ground. But as I cannot easily credit anything so vile among Christians, and at a time so filled with terrors as that was, I can only relate it and leave it undetermined.

Innumerable stories also went about of the cruel behaviours and practices of nurses who tended the sick, and of their hastening on the fate of those they tended in their sickness. But I shall say more of this in its place.

I was indeed shocked with this sight; it almost overwhelmed me, and I went away with my heart most afflicted, and full of the afflicting thoughts, such as I cannot describe just at my going out of the church, and turning up the street towards my own house, I saw another cart with links, and a bellman going before, coming out of Harrow Alley in the Butcher Row, on the other side of the way, and being, as I perceived, very full of dead bodies, it went directly over the street also toward the church. I stood a while, but I had no stomach to go back again to see the same dismal scene over again, so I went directly home, where I could not but consider with thankfulness the risk I had run, believing I had gotten no injury, as indeed I had not.

Here the poor unhappy gentleman's grief came into my head again, and indeed I could not but shed tears in the reflection upon it, perhaps more than he did himself; but his case lay so heavy upon my mind that I could not prevail with myself, but that I must go out again into the street, and go to the Pie Tavern, resolving to inquire what became of him.

It was by this time one o'clock in the morning, and yet the poor gentleman was there. The truth was, the people of the house, knowing him, had entertained him, and kept him there all the night, notwithstanding the danger of being infected by him, though it appeared the man was perfectly sound himself.

It is with regret that I take notice of this tavern. The people were civil, mannerly, and an obliging sort of folks enough, and had till this time kept their house open and their trade going on, though not so very publicly as formerly: but there was a dreadful set of fellows that used their house, and who, in the middle of all this horror, met there every night, behaved with all the revelling and roaring extravagances as is usual for such people to do at other times, and, indeed, to such an offensive degree that the very master and mistress of the house grew first ashamed and then terrified at them.

They sat generally in a room next the street, and as they always kept late hours, so when the dead-cart came across the street-end to go into Houndsditch, which was in view of the tavern windows, they would frequently open the windows as soon as they heard the bell and look out at them; and as they might often hear sad lamentations of people in the streets or at their windows as the carts went along, they would make their impudent mocks and jeers at them, especially if they heard the poor people call upon God to have mercy upon them, as many would do at those times in their ordinary passing along the streets.

These gentlemen, being something disturbed with the clutter of bringing the poor gentleman into the house, as above, were first angry and very high with the master of the house for suffering such a fellow, as they called him, to be brought out of the grave into their house; but being answered that the man was a neighbour, and that he was sound, but overwhelmed with the calamity of his family, and the like, they turned their anger into ridiculing the man and his sorrow for his wife and children, taunted him with want of courage to leap into the great pit and go to heaven, as they jeeringly expressed it, along with them, adding some very profane and even blasphemous expressions.

They were at this vile work when I came back to the house, and, as far as I could see, though the man sat still, mute and disconsolate, and their affronts could not divert his sorrow, yet he was both grieved and offended at their discourse. Upon this I gently reproved them, being well enough acquainted with their characters, and not unknown in person to two of them.

They immediately fell upon me with ill language and oaths, asked me what I did out of my grave at such a time when so many honester men were carried into the churchyard, and why I was not at home saying my prayers against the dead-cart came for me, and the like.

I was indeed astonished at the impudence of the men, though not at all discomposed at their treatment of me. However, I kept my temper. I told them that though I defied them or any man in the world to tax me with any dishonesty, yet I acknowledged that in this terrible judgement of God many better than I were swept away and carried to their grave. But to answer their question directly, the case was, that I was mercifully preserved by that great God whose name they had blasphemed and taken in vain by cursing and swearing in a dreadful manner, and that I believed I was preserved in particular, among other ends of His goodness, that I might reprove them for their audacious boldness in behaving in such a manner and in such an awful time as this was, especially for their jeering and mocking at an honest gentleman and a neighbour (for some of them knew him), who, they saw, was overwhelmed with sorrow for the breaches which it had pleased God to make upon his family.

I cannot call exactly to mind the hellish, abominable raillery which was the return they made to that talk of mine: being provoked, it seems, that I was not at all afraid to be free with them; nor, if I could remember, would I fill my account with any of the words, the horrid oaths, curses, and vile expressions, such as, at that time of the day, even the worst and ordinariest people in the street would not use; for, except such hardened creatures as these, the most wicked wretches that could be found had at that time some terror upon their minds of the hand of that Power which could thus in a moment destroy them.

But that which was the worst in all their devilish language was, that they were not afraid to blaspheme God and talk atheistically, making a jest of my calling the plague the hand of God; mocking, and even laughing, at the word judgement, as if the providence of God had no concern in the inflicting such a desolating stroke; and that the people calling upon God as they saw the carts carrying away the dead bodies was all enthusiastic, absurd, and impertinent.

I made them some reply, such as I thought proper, but which I found was so far from putting a check to their horrid way of speaking that it made them rail the more, so that I confess it filled me with horror and a kind of rage, and I came away, as I told them, lest the hand of that judgement which had visited the whole city should glorify His vengeance upon them, and all that were near them.

They received all reproof with the utmost contempt, and made the greatest mockery that was possible for them to do at me, giving me all the opprobrious, insolent scoffs that they could think of for preaching to them, as they called it, which indeed grieved me, rather than angered me; and I went away, blessing God, however, in my mind that I had not spared them, though they had insulted me so much.

They continued this wretched course three or four days after this, continually mocking and jeering at all that showed themselves religious or serious, or that were any way touched with the sense of the terrible judgement of God upon us; and I was informed they flouted in the same manner at the good people who, notwithstanding the contagion, met at the church, fasted, and prayed to God to remove His hand from them.

I say, they continued this dreadful course three or four days—I think it was no more—when one of them, particularly he who asked the poor gentleman what he did out of his grave, was struck from Heaven with the plague, and died in a most deplorable manner; and, in a word, they were every one of them carried into the great pit which I have mentioned above, before it was quite filled up, which was not above a fortnight or thereabout.

These men were guilty of many extravagances, such as one would think human nature should have trembled at the thoughts of at such a time of general terror as was then upon us, and particularly scoffing and mocking at everything which they happened to see that was religious among the people, especially at their thronging zealously to the place of public worship to implore mercy from Heaven in such a time of distress; and this tavern where they held their club being within view of the church-door, they had the more particular occasion for their atheistical profane mirth.

But this began to abate a little with them before the accident which I have related happened, for the infection increased so violently at this part of the town now, that people began to be afraid to come to the church; at least such numbers did not resort thither as was usual. Many of the clergymen likewise were dead, and others gone into the country; for it really required a steady courage and a strong faith for a man not only to venture being in town at such a time as this, but likewise to venture to come to church and perform the office of a minister to a congregation, of whom he had reason to believe many of them were actually infected with the plague, and to do this every day, or twice a day, as in some places was done.

It is true the people showed an extraordinary zeal in these religious exercises, and as the church-doors were always open, people would go in single at all times, whether the minister was officiating or no, and locking themselves into separate pews, would be praying to God with great fervency and devotion.

Others assembled at meeting-houses, every one as their different opinions in such things guided, but all were promiscuously the subject of these men's drollery, especially at the beginning of the visitation.

It seems they had been checked for their open insulting religion in this manner by several good people of every persuasion, and that, and the violent raging of the infection, I suppose, was the occasion that they had abated much of their rudeness for some time before, and were only roused by the spirit of ribaldry and atheism at the clamour which was made when the gentleman was first brought in there, and perhaps were agitated by the same devil, when I took upon me to reprove them; though I did it at first with all the calmness, temper, and good manners that I could, which for a while they insulted me the more for thinking it had been in fear of their resentment, though afterwards they found the contrary.

I went home, indeed, grieved and afflicted in my mind at the abominable wickedness of those men, not doubting, however, that they would be made dreadful examples of God's justice; for I looked upon this dismal time to be a particular season of Divine vengeance, and that God would on this occasion single out the proper objects of His displeasure in a more especial and remarkable manner than at another time; and that though I did believe that many good people would, and did, fall in the common calamity, and that it was no certain rule to judge of the eternal state of any one by their being distinguished in such a time of general destruction neither one way or other; yet, I say, it could not but seem reasonable to believe that God would not think fit to spare by His mercy such open declared enemies, that should insult His name and Being, defy His vengeance, and mock at His worship and worshippers at such a time; no, not though His mercy had thought fit to bear with and spare them at other times; that this was a day of visitation, a day of God's anger, and those words came into my thought, Jer. v. 9: 'Shall I not visit for these things? saith the Lord: and shall not My soul be avenged of such a nation as this?'

These things, I say, lay upon my mind, and I went home very much grieved and oppressed with the horror of these men's wickedness, and to think that anything could be so vile, so hardened, and notoriously wicked as to insult God, and His servants, and His worship in such a manner, and at such a time as this was, when He had, as it were, His sword drawn in His hand on purpose to take vengeance not on them only, but on the whole nation.

I had, indeed, been in some passion at first with them—though it was really raised, not by any affront they had offered me personally, but by the horror their blaspheming tongues filled me with. However, I was doubtful in my thoughts whether the resentment I retained was not all upon my own private account, for they had given me a great deal of ill language too—I mean personally; but after some pause, and having a weight of grief upon my mind, I retired myself as soon as I came home, for I slept not that night; and giving God most humble thanks for my preservation in the eminent danger I had been in, I set my mind seriously and with the utmost earnestness to pray for those desperate wretches, that God would pardon them, open their eyes, and effectually humble them.

By this I not only did my duty, namely, to pray for those who despitefully used me, but I fully tried my own heart, to my full satisfaction, that it was not filled with any spirit of resentment as they had offended me in particular; and I humbly recommend the method to all those that would know, or be certain, how to distinguish between their zeal for the honour of God and the effects of their private passions and resentment.

But I must go back here to the particular incidents which occur to my thoughts of the time of the visitation, and particularly to the time of their shutting up houses in the first part of their sickness; for before the sickness was come to its height people had more room to make their observations than they had afterward; but when it was in the extremity there was no such thing as communication with one another, as before.

During the shutting up of houses, as I have said, some violence was offered to the watchmen. As to soldiers, there were none to be found. The few guards which the king then had, which were nothing like the number entertained since, were dispersed, either at Oxford with the Court, or in quarters in the remoter parts of the country, small detachments excepted, who did duty at the Tower and at Whitehall, and these but very few. Neither am I positive that there was any other guard at the Tower than the warders, as they called them, who stand at the gate with gowns and caps, the same as the yeomen of the guard, except the ordinary gunners, who were twenty-four, and the officers appointed to look after the magazine, who were called armourers. As to trained bands, there was no possibility of raising any; neither, if the Lieutenancy, either of London or Middlesex, had ordered the drums to beat for the militia, would any of the companies, I believe, have drawn together, whatever risk they had run.

This made the watchmen be the less regarded, and perhaps occasioned the greater violence to be used against them. I mention it on this score to observe that the setting watchmen thus to keep the people in was, first of all, not effectual, but that the people broke out, whether by force or by stratagem, even almost as often as they pleased; and, second, that those that did thus break out were generally people infected who, in their desperation, running about from one place to another, valued not whom they injured: and which perhaps, as I have said, might give birth to report that it was natural to the infected people to desire to infect others, which report was really false.

And I know it so well, and in so many several cases, that I could give several relations of good, pious, and religious people who, when they have had the distemper, have been so far from being forward to infect others that they have forbid their own family to come near them, in hopes of their being preserved, and have even died without seeing their nearest relations lest they should be instrumental to give them the distemper, and infect or endanger them. If, then, there were cases wherein the infected people were careless of the injury they did to others, this was certainly one of them, if not the chief, namely, when people who had the distemper had broken out from houses which were so shut up, and having been driven to extremities for provision or for entertainment, had endeavoured to conceal their condition, and have been thereby instrumental involuntarily to infect others who have been ignorant and unwary.

This is one of the reasons why I believed then, and do believe still, that the shutting up houses thus by force, and restraining, or rather imprisoning, people in their own houses, as I said above, was of little or no service in the whole. Nay, I am of opinion it was rather hurtful, having forced those desperate people to wander abroad with the plague upon them, who would otherwise have died quietly in their beds.

I remember one citizen who, having thus broken out of his house in Aldersgate Street or thereabout, went along the road to Islington; he attempted to have gone in at the Angel Inn, and after that the White Horse, two inns known still by the same signs, but was refused; after which he came to the Pied Bull, an inn also still continuing the same sign. He asked them for lodging for one night only, pretending to be going into Lincolnshire, and assuring them of his being very sound and free from the infection, which also at that time had not reached much that way.

They told him they had no lodging that they could spare but one bed up in the garret, and that they could spare that bed for one night, some drovers being expected the next day with cattle; so, if he would accept of that lodging, he might have it, which he did. So a servant was sent up with a candle with him to show him the room. He was very well dressed, and looked like a person not used to lie in a garret; and when he came to the room he fetched a deep sigh, and said to the servant, 'I have seldom lain in such a lodging as this. 'However, the servant assuring him again that they had no better, 'Well,' says he, 'I must make shift; this is a dreadful time; but it is but for one night.' So he sat down upon the bedside, and bade the maid, I think it was, fetch him up a pint of warm ale. Accordingly the servant went for the ale, but some hurry in the house, which perhaps employed her other ways, put it out of her head, and she went up no more to him.

The next morning, seeing no appearance of the gentleman, somebody in the house asked the servant that had showed him upstairs what was become of him. She started. 'Alas I,' says she, 'I never thought more of him. He bade me carry him some warm ale, but I forgot.' Upon which, not the maid, but some other person was sent up to see after him, who, coming into the room, found him stark dead and almost cold, stretched out across the bed. His clothes were pulled off, his jaw fallen, his eyes open in a most frightful posture, the rug of the bed being grasped hard in one of his hands, so that it was plain he died soon after the maid left him; and 'tis probable, had she gone up with the ale, she had found him dead in a few minutes after he sat down upon the bed. The alarm was great in the house, as anyone may suppose, they having been free from the distemper till that disaster, which, bringing the infection to the house, spread it immediately to other houses round about it. I do not remember how many died in the house itself, but I think the maid-servant who went up first with him fell presently ill by the fright, and several others; for, whereas there died but two in Islington of the plague the week before, there died seventeen the week after, whereof fourteen were of the plague. This was in the week from the 11th of July to the 18th.

There was one shift that some families had, and that not a few, when their houses happened to be infected, and that was this: the families who, in the first breaking-out of the distemper, fled away into the country and had retreats among their friends, generally found some or other of their neighbours or relations to commit the charge of those houses to for the safety of the goods and the like. Some houses were, indeed, entirely locked up, the doors padlocked, the windows and doors having deal boards nailed over them, and only the inspection of them committed to the ordinary watchmen and parish officers; but these were but few.

It was thought that there were not less than 10,000 houses forsaken of the inhabitants in the city and suburbs, including what was in the out-parishes and in Surrey, or the side of the water they called Southwark. This was besides the numbers of lodgers, and of particular persons who were fled out of other families; so that in all it was computed that about 200,000 people were fled and gone. But of this I shall speak again. But I mention it here on this account, namely, that it was a rule with those who had thus two houses in their keeping or care, that if anybody was taken sick in a family, before the master of the family let the examiners or any other officer know of it, he immediately would send all the rest of his family, whether children or servants, as it fell out to be, to such other house which he had so in charge, and then giving notice of the sick person to the examiner, have a nurse or nurses appointed, and have another person to be shut up in the house with them (which many for money would do), so to take charge of the house in case the person should die.

This was, in many cases, the saving a whole family, who, if they had been shut up with the sick person, would inevitably have perished. But, on the other hand, this was another of the inconveniences of shutting up houses; for the apprehensions and terror of being shut up made many run away with the rest of the family, who, though it was not publicly known, and they were not quite sick, had yet the distemper upon them; and who, by having an uninterrupted liberty to go about, but being obliged still to conceal their circumstances, or perhaps not knowing it themselves, gave the distemper to others, and spread the infection in a dreadful manner, as I shall explain further hereafter.

And here I may be able to make an observation or two of my own, which may be of use hereafter to those into whose hands these may come, if they should ever see the like dreadful visitation. (1) The infection generally came into the houses of the citizens by the means of their servants, whom they were obliged to send up and down the streets for necessaries; that is to say, for food or physic, to bakehouses, brew-houses, shops, &c.; and who going necessarily through the streets into shops, markets, and the like, it was impossible but that they should, one way or other, meet with distempered people, who conveyed the fatal breath into them, and they brought it home to the families to which they belonged. (2) It was a great mistake that such a great city as this had but one pest-house; for had there been, instead of one pest-house—viz., beyond Bunhill Fields, where, at most, they could receive, perhaps, two hundred or three hundred people—I say, had there, instead of that one, been several pest-houses, every one able to contain a thousand people, without lying two in a bed, or two beds in a room; and had every master of a family, as soon as any servant especially had been taken sick in his house, been obliged to send them to the next pest-house, if they were willing, as many were, and had the examiners done the like among the poor people when any had been stricken with the infection; I say, had this been done where the people were willing (not otherwise), and the houses not been shut, I am persuaded, and was all the while of that opinion, that not so many, by several thousands, had died; for it was observed, and I could give several instances within the compass of my own knowledge, where a servant had been taken sick, and the family had either time to send him out or retire from the house and leave the sick person, as I have said above, they had all been preserved; whereas when, upon one or more sickening in a family, the house has been shut up, the whole family have perished, and the bearers been obliged to go in to fetch out the dead bodies, not being able to bring them to the door, and at last none left to do it.

(3) This put it out of question to me, that the calamity was spread by infection; that is to say, by some certain steams or fumes, which the physicians call effluvia, by the breath, or by the sweat, or by the stench of the sores of the sick persons, or some other way, perhaps, beyond even the reach of the physicians themselves, which effluvia affected the sound who came within certain distances of the sick, immediately penetrating the vital parts of the said sound persons, putting their blood into an immediate ferment, and agitating their spirits to that degree which it was found they were agitated; and so those newly infected persons communicated it in the same manner to others. And this I shall give some instances of, that cannot but convince those who seriously consider it; and I cannot but with some wonder find some people, now the contagion is over, talk of its being an immediate stroke from Heaven, without the agency of means, having commission to strike this and that particular person, and none other—which I look upon with contempt as the effect of manifest ignorance and enthusiasm; likewise the opinion of others, who talk of infection being carried on by the air only, by carrying with it vast numbers of insects and invisible creatures, who enter into the body with the breath, or even at the pores with the air, and there generate or emit most acute poisons, or poisonous ovae or eggs, which mingle themselves with the blood, and so infect the body: a discourse full of learned simplicity, and manifested to be so by universal experience; but I shall say more to this case in its order.

I must here take further notice that nothing was more fatal to the inhabitants of this city than the supine negligence of the people themselves, who, during the long notice or warning they had of the visitation, made no provision for it by laying in store of provisions, or of other necessaries, by which they might have lived retired and within their own houses, as I have observed others did, and who were in a great measure preserved by that caution; nor were they, after they were a little hardened to it, so shy of conversing with one another, when actually infected, as they were at first: no, though they knew it.

I acknowledge I was one of those thoughtless ones that had made so little provision that my servants were obliged to go out of doors to buy every trifle by penny and halfpenny, just as before it began, even till my experience showing me the folly, I began to be wiser so late that I had scarce time to store myself sufficient for our common subsistence for a month.

I had in family only an ancient woman that managed the house, a maid-servant, two apprentices, and myself; and the plague beginning to increase about us, I had many sad thoughts about what course I should take, and how I should act. The many dismal objects which happened everywhere as I went about the streets, had filled my mind with a great deal of horror for fear of the distemper, which was indeed very horrible in itself, and in some more than in others. The swellings, which were generally in the neck or groin, when they grew hard and would not break, grew so painful that it was equal to the most exquisite torture; and some, not able to bear the torment, threw themselves out at windows or shot themselves, or otherwise made themselves away, and I saw several dismal objects of that kind. Others, unable to contain themselves, vented their pain by incessant roarings, and such loud and lamentable cries were to be heard as we walked along the streets that would pierce the very heart to think of, especially when it was to be considered that the same dreadful scourge might be expected every moment to seize upon ourselves.

I cannot say but that now I began to faint in my resolutions; my heart failed me very much, and sorely I repented of my rashness. When I had been out, and met with such terrible things as these I have talked of, I say I repented my rashness in venturing to abide in town. I wished often that I had not taken upon me to stay, but had gone away with my brother and his family.

Terrified by those frightful objects, I would retire home sometimes and resolve to go out no more; and perhaps I would keep those resolutions for three or four days, which time I spent in the most serious thankfulness for my preservation and the preservation of my family, and the constant confession of my sins, giving myself up to God every day, and applying to Him with fasting, humiliation, and meditation. Such intervals as I had I employed in reading books and in writing down my memorandums of what occurred to me every day, and out of which afterwards I took most of this work, as it relates to my observations without doors. What I wrote of my private meditations I reserve for private use, and desire it may not be made public on any account whatever.

I also wrote other meditations upon divine subjects, such as occurred to me at that time and were profitable to myself, but not fit for any other view, and therefore I say no more of that.

I had a very good friend, a physician, whose name was Heath, whom I frequently visited during this dismal time, and to whose advice I was very much obliged for many things which he directed me to take, by way of preventing the infection when I went out, as he found I frequently did, and to hold in my mouth when I was in the streets. He also came very often to see me, and as he was a good Christian as well as a good physician, his agreeable conversation was a very great support to me in the worst of this terrible time.

It was now the beginning of August, and the plague grew very violent and terrible in the place where I lived, and Dr Heath coming to visit me, and finding that I ventured so often out in the streets, earnestly persuaded me to lock myself up and my family, and not to suffer any of us to go out of doors; to keep all our windows fast, shutters and curtains close, and never to open them; but first, to make a very strong smoke in the room where the window or door was to be opened, with rozen and pitch, brimstone or gunpowder and the like; and we did this for some time; but as I had not laid in a store of provision for such a retreat, it was impossible that we could keep within doors entirely. However, I attempted, though it was so very late, to do something towards it; and first, as I had convenience both for brewing and baking, I went and bought two sacks of meal, and for several weeks, having an oven, we baked all our own bread; also I bought malt, and brewed as much beer as all the casks I had would hold, and which seemed enough to serve my house for five or six weeks; also I laid in a quantity of salt butter and Cheshire cheese; but I had no flesh-meat, and the plague raged so violently among the butchers and slaughter-houses on the other side of our street, where they are known to dwell in great numbers, that it was not advisable so much as to go over the street among them.

And here I must observe again, that this necessity of going out of our houses to buy provisions was in a great measure the ruin of the whole city, for the people catched the distemper on these occasions one of another, and even the provisions themselves were often tainted; at least I have great reason to believe so; and therefore I cannot say with satisfaction what I know is repeated with great assurance, that the market-people and such as brought provisions to town were never infected. I am certain the butchers of Whitechappel, where the greatest part of the flesh-meat was killed, were dreadfully visited, and that at least to such a degree that few of their shops were kept open, and those that remained of them killed their meat at Mile End and that way, and brought it to market upon horses.

However, the poor people could not lay up provisions, and there was a necessity that they must go to market to buy, and others to send servants or their children; and as this was a necessity which renewed itself daily, it brought abundance of unsound people to the markets, and a great many that went thither sound brought death home with them.

It is true people used all possible precaution. When any one bought a joint of meat in the market they would not take it off the butcher's hand, but took it off the hooks themselves. On the other hand, the butcher would not touch the money, but have it put into a pot full of vinegar, which he kept for that purpose. The buyer carried always small money to make up any odd sum, that they might take no change. They carried bottles of scents and perfumes in their hands, and all the means that could be used were used, but then the poor could not do even these things, and they went at all hazards.

Innumerable dismal stories we heard every day on this very account. Sometimes a man or woman dropped down dead in the very markets, for many people that had the plague upon them knew nothing of it till the inward gangrene had affected their vitals, and they died in a few moments. This caused that many died frequently in that manner in the streets suddenly, without any warning; others perhaps had time to go to the next bulk or stall, or to any door-porch, and just sit down and die, as I have said before.

These objects were so frequent in the streets that when the plague came to be very raging on one side, there was scarce any passing by the streets but that several dead bodies would be lying here and there upon the ground. On the other hand, it is observable that though at first the people would stop as they went along and call to the neighbours to come out on such an occasion, yet afterward no notice was taken of them; but that if at any time we found a corpse lying, go across the way and not come near it; or, if in a narrow lane or passage, go back again and seek some other way to go on the business we were upon; and in those cases the corpse was always left till the officers had notice to come and take them away, or till night, when the bearers attending the dead-cart would take them up and carry them away. Nor did those undaunted creatures who performed these offices fail to search their pockets, and sometimes strip off their clothes if they were well dressed, as sometimes they were, and carry off what they could get.

But to return to the markets. The butchers took that care that if any person died in the market they had the officers always at band to take them up upon hand-barrows and carry them to the next churchyard; and this was so frequent that such were not entered in the weekly bill, 'Found dead in the streets or fields', as is the case now, but they went into the general articles of the great distemper.

But now the fury of the distemper increased to such a degree that even the markets were but very thinly furnished with provisions or frequented with buyers compared to what they were before; and the Lord Mayor caused the country people who brought provisions to be stopped in the streets leading into the town, and to sit down there with their goods, where they sold what they brought, and went immediately away; and this encouraged the country people greatly-to do so, for they sold their provisions at the very entrances into the town, and even in the fields, as particularly in the fields beyond Whitechappel, in Spittlefields; also in St George's Fields in Southwark, in Bunhill Fields, and in a great field called Wood's Close, near Islington. Thither the Lord Mayor, aldermen, and magistrates sent their officers and servants to buy for their families, themselves keeping within doors as much as possible, and the like did many other people; and after this method was taken the country people came with great cheerfulness, and brought provisions of all sorts, and very seldom got any harm, which, I suppose, added also to that report of their being miraculously preserved.

As for my little family, having thus, as I have said, laid in a store of bread, butter, cheese, and beer, I took my friend and physician's advice, and locked myself up, and my family, and resolved to suffer the hardship of living a few months without flesh-meat, rather than to purchase it at the hazard of our lives.

But though I confined my family, I could not prevail upon my unsatisfied curiosity to stay within entirely myself; and though I generally came frighted and terrified home, yet I could not restrain; only that indeed I did not do it so frequently as at first.

I had some little obligations, indeed, upon me to go to my brother's house, which was in Coleman Street parish and which he had left to my care, and I went at first every day, but afterwards only once or twice a week.

In these walks I had many dismal scenes before my eyes, as particularly of persons falling dead in the streets, terrible shrieks and screechings of women, who, in their agonies, would throw open their chamber windows and cry out in a dismal, surprising manner. It is impossible to describe the variety of postures in which the passions of the poor people would express themselves.

Passing through Tokenhouse Yard, in Lothbury, of a sudden a casement violently opened just over my head, and a woman gave three frightful screeches, and then cried, 'Oh! death, death, death!' in a most inimitable tone, and which struck me with horror and a chillness in my very blood. There was nobody to be seen in the whole street, neither did any other window open, for people had no curiosity now in any case, nor could anybody help one another, so I went on to pass into Bell Alley.

Just in Bell Alley, on the right hand of the passage, there was a more terrible cry than that, though it was not so directed out at the window; but the whole family was in a terrible fright, and I could hear women and children run screaming about the rooms like distracted, when a garret-window opened and somebody from a window on the other side the alley called and asked, 'What is the matter?' upon which, from the first window, it was answered, 'Oh Lord, my old master has hanged himself!' The other asked again, 'Is he quite dead?' and the first answered, 'Ay, ay, quite dead; quite dead and cold!' This person was a merchant and a deputy alderman, and very rich. I care not to mention the name, though I knew his name too, but that would be an hardship to the family, which is now flourishing again.

But this is but one; it is scarce credible what dreadful cases happened in particular families every day. People in the rage of the distemper, or in the torment of their swellings, which was indeed intolerable, running out of their own government, raving and distracted, and oftentimes laying violent hands upon themselves, throwing themselves out at their windows, shooting themselves &c.; mothers murdering their own children in their lunacy, some dying of mere grief as a passion, some of mere fright and surprise without any infection at all, others frighted into idiotism and foolish distractions, some into despair and lunacy, others into melancholy madness.

The pain of the swelling was in particular very violent, and to some intolerable; the physicians and surgeons may be said to have tortured many poor creatures even to death. The swellings in some grew hard, and they applied violent drawing-plaisters or poultices to break them, and if these did not do they cut and scarified them in a terrible manner. In some those swellings were made hard partly by the force of the distemper and partly by their being too violently drawn, and were so hard that no instrument could cut them, and then they burnt them with caustics, so that many died raving mad with the torment, and some in the very operation. In these distresses, some, for want of help to hold them down in their beds, or to look to them, laid hands upon themselves as above. Some broke out into the streets, perhaps naked, and would run directly down to the river if they were not stopped by the watchman or other officers, and plunge themselves into the water wherever they found it.

It often pierced my very soul to hear the groans and cries of those who were thus tormented, but of the two this was counted the most promising particular in the whole infection, for if these swellings could be brought to a head, and to break and run, or, as the surgeons call it, to digest, the patient generally recovered; whereas those who, like the gentlewoman's daughter, were struck with death at the beginning, and had the tokens come out upon them, often went about indifferent easy till a little before they died, and some till the moment they dropped down, as in apoplexies and epilepsies is often the case. Such would be taken suddenly very sick, and would run to a bench or bulk, or any convenient place that offered itself, or to their own houses if possible, as I mentioned before, and there sit down, grow faint, and die. This kind of dying was much the same as it was with those who die of common mortifications, who die swooning, and, as it were, go away in a dream. Such as died thus had very little notice of their being infected at all till the gangrene was spread through their whole body; nor could physicians themselves know certainly how it was with them till they opened their breasts or other parts of their body and saw the tokens.

We had at this time a great many frightful stories told us of nurses and watchmen who looked after the dying people; that is to say, hired nurses who attended infected people, using them barbarously, starving them, smothering them, or by other wicked means hastening their end, that is to say, murdering of them; and watchmen, being set to guard houses that were shut up when there has been but one person left, and perhaps that one lying sick, that they have broke in and murdered that body, and immediately thrown them out into the dead-cart! And so they have gone scarce cold to the grave.

I cannot say but that some such murders were committed, and I think two were sent to prison for it, but died before they could be tried; and I have heard that three others, at several times, were excused for murders of that kind; but I must say I believe nothing of its being so common a crime as some have since been pleased to say, nor did it seem to be so rational where the people were brought so low as not to be able to help themselves, for such seldom recovered, and there was no temptation to commit a murder, at least none equal to the fact, where they were sure persons would die in so short a time, and could not live.

That there were a great many robberies and wicked practices committed even in this dreadful time I do not deny. The power of avarice was so strong in some that they would run any hazard to steal and to plunder; and particularly in houses where all the families or inhabitants have been dead and carried out, they would break in at all hazards, and without regard to the danger of infection, take even the clothes off the dead bodies and the bed-clothes from others where they lay dead.

This, I suppose, must be the case of a family in Houndsditch, where a man and his daughter, the rest of the family being, as I suppose, carried away before by the dead-cart, were found stark naked, one in one chamber and one in another, lying dead on the floor, and the clothes of the beds, from whence 'tis supposed they were rolled off by thieves, stolen and carried quite away.

It is indeed to be observed that the women were in all this calamity the most rash, fearless, and desperate creatures, and as there were vast numbers that went about as nurses to tend those that were sick, they committed a great many petty thieveries in the houses where they were employed; and some of them were publicly whipped for it, when perhaps they ought rather to have been hanged for examples, for numbers of houses were robbed on these occasions, till at length the parish officers were sent to recommend nurses to the sick, and always took an account whom it was they sent, so as that they might call them to account if the house had been abused where they were placed.

But these robberies extended chiefly to wearing-clothes, linen, and what rings or money they could come at when the person died who was under their care, but not to a general plunder of the houses; and I could give you an account of one of these nurses, who, several years after, being on her deathbed, confessed with the utmost horror the robberies she had committed at the time of her being a nurse, and by which she had enriched herself to a great degree. But as for murders, I do not find that there was ever any proof of the facts in the manner as it has been reported, except as above.

They did tell me, indeed, of a nurse in one place that laid a wet cloth upon the face of a dying patient whom she tended, and so put an end to his life, who was just expiring before; and another that smothered a young woman she was looking to when she was in a fainting fit, and would have come to herself; some that killed them by giving them one thing, some another, and some starved them by giving them nothing at all. But these stories had two marks of suspicion that always attended them, which caused me always to slight them and to look on them as mere stories that people continually frighted one another with. First, that wherever it was that we heard it, they always placed the scene at the farther end of the town, opposite or most remote from where you were to hear it. If you heard it in Whitechappel, it had happened at St Giles's, or at Westminster, or Holborn, or that end of the town. If you heard of it at that end of the town, then it was done in Whitechappel, or the Minories, or about Cripplegate parish. If you heard of it in the city, why, then it happened in Southwark; and if you heard of it in Southwark, then it was done in the city, and the like.

In the next place, of what part soever you heard the story, the particulars were always the same, especially that of laying a wet double cloth on a dying man's face, and that of smothering a young gentlewoman; so that it was apparent, at least to my judgement, that there was more of tale than of truth in those things.

However, I cannot say but it had some effect upon the people, and particularly that, as I said before, they grew more cautious whom they took into their houses, and whom they trusted their lives with, and had them always recommended if they could; and where they could not find such, for they were not very plenty, they applied to the parish officers.

But here again the misery of that time lay upon the poor who, being infected, had neither food or physic, neither physician or apothecary to assist them, or nurse to attend them. Many of those died calling for help, and even for sustenance, out at their windows in a most miserable and deplorable manner; but it must be added that whenever the cases of such persons or families were represented to my Lord Mayor they always were relieved.

It is true, in some houses where the people were not very poor, yet where they had sent perhaps their wives and children away, and if they had any servants they had been dismissed; —I say it is true that to save the expenses, many such as these shut themselves in, and not having help, died alone.

A neighbour and acquaintance of mine, having some money owing to him from a shopkeeper in Whitecross Street or thereabouts, sent his apprentice, a youth about eighteen years of age, to endeavour to get the money. He came to the door, and finding it shut, knocked pretty hard; and, as he thought, heard somebody answer within, but was not sure, so he waited, and after some stay knocked again, and then a third time, when he heard somebody coming downstairs.

At length the man of the house came to the door; he had on his breeches or drawers, and a yellow flannel waistcoat, no stockings, a pair of slipped-shoes, a white cap on his head, and, as the young man said, 'death in his face'.

When he opened the door, says he, 'What do you disturb me thus for?' The boy, though a little surprised, replied, 'I come from such a one, and my master sent me for the money which he says you know of.' 'Very well, child,' returns the living ghost; 'call as you go by at Cripplegate Church, and bid them ring the bell'; and with these words shut the door again, and went up again, and died the same day; nay, perhaps the same hour. This the young man told me himself, and I have reason to believe it. This was while the plague was not come to a height. I think it was in June, towards the latter end of the month; it must be before the dead-carts came about, and while they used the ceremony of ringing the bell for the dead, which was over for certain, in that parish at least, before the month of July, for by the 25th of July there died 550 and upwards in a week, and then they could no more bury in form, rich or poor.

I have mentioned above that notwithstanding this dreadful calamity, yet the numbers of thieves were abroad upon all occasions, where they had found any prey, and that these were generally women. It was one morning about eleven O'clock, I had walked out to my brother's house in Coleman Street parish, as I often did, to see that all was safe.

My brother's house had a little court before it, and a brick wall and a gate in it, and within that several warehouses where his goods of several sorts lay. It happened that in one of these warehouses were several packs of women's high-crowned hats, which came out of the country and were, as I suppose, for exportation: whither, I know not.

I was surprised that when I came near my brother's door, which was in a place they called Swan Alley, I met three or four women with high-crowned hats on their heads; and, as I remembered afterwards, one, if not more, had some hats likewise in their hands; but as I did not see them come out at my brother's door, and not knowing that my brother had any such goods in his warehouse, I did not offer to say anything to them, but went across the way to shun meeting them, as was usual to do at that time, for fear of the plague. But when I came nearer to the gate I met another woman with more hats come out of the gate. 'What business, mistress,' said I, 'have you had there?' 'There are more people there,' said she; 'I have had no more business there than they.' I was hasty to get to the gate then, and said no more to her, by which means she got away. But just as I came to the gate, I saw two more coming across the yard to come out with hats also on their heads and under their arms, at which I threw the gate to behind me, which having a spring lock fastened itself; and turning to the women, 'Forsooth,' said I, 'what are you doing here?' and seized upon the hats, and took them from them. One of them, who, I confess, did not look like a thief—'Indeed,' says she, 'we are wrong, but we were told they were goods that had no owner. Be pleased to take them again; and look yonder, there are more such customers as we.' She cried and looked pitifully, so I took the hats from her and opened the gate, and bade them be gone, for I pitied the women indeed; but when I looked towards the warehouse, as she directed, there were six or seven more, all women, fitting themselves with hats as unconcerned and quiet as if they had been at a hatter's shop buying for their money.

I was surprised, not at the sight of so many thieves only, but at the circumstances I was in; being now to thrust myself in among so many people, who for some weeks had been so shy of myself that if I met anybody in the street I would cross the way from them.

They were equally surprised, though on another account. They all told me they were neighbours, that they had heard anyone might take them, that they were nobody's goods, and the like. I talked big to them at first, went back to the gate and took out the key, so that they were all my prisoners, threatened to lock them all into the warehouse, and go and fetch my Lord Mayor's officers for them.

They begged heartily, protested they found the gate open, and the warehouse door open; and that it had no doubt been broken open by some who expected to find goods of greater value: which indeed was reasonable to believe, because the lock was broke, and a padlock that hung to the door on the outside also loose, and an abundance of the hats carried away.

At length I considered that this was not a time to be cruel and rigorous; and besides that, it would necessarily oblige me to go much about, to have several people come to me, and I go to several whose circumstances of health I knew nothing of; and that even at this time the plague was so high as that there died 4000 a week; so that in showing my resentment, or even in seeking justice for my brother's goods, I might lose my own life; so I contented myself with taking the names and places where some of them lived, who were really inhabitants in the neighbourhood, and threatening that my brother should call them to an account for it when he returned to his habitation.

Then I talked a little upon another foot with them, and asked them how they could do such things as these in a time of such general calamity, and, as it were, in the face of God's most dreadful judgements, when the plague was at their very doors, and, it may be, in their very houses, and they did not know but that the dead-cart might stop at their doors in a few hours to carry them to their graves.

I could not perceive that my discourse made much impression upon them all that while, till it happened that there came two men of the neighbourhood, hearing of the disturbance, and knowing my brother, for they had been both dependents upon his family, and they came to my assistance. These being, as I said, neighbours, presently knew three of the women and told me who they were and where they lived; and it seems they had given me a true account of themselves before.

This brings these two men to a further remembrance. The name of one was John Hayward, who was at that time undersexton of the parish of St Stephen, Coleman Street. By undersexton was understood at that time gravedigger and bearer of the dead. This man carried, or assisted to carry, all the dead to their graves which were buried in that large parish, and who were carried in form; and after that form of burying was stopped, went with the dead-cart and the bell to fetch the dead bodies from the houses where they lay, and fetched many of them out of the chambers and houses; for the parish was, and is still, remarkable particularly, above all the parishes in London, for a great number of alleys and thoroughfares, very long, into which no carts could come, and where they were obliged to go and fetch the bodies a very long way; which alleys now remain to witness it, such as White's Alley, Cross Key Court, Swan Alley, Bell Alley, White Horse Alley, and many more. Here they went with a kind of hand-barrow and laid the dead bodies on it, and carried them out to the carts; which work he performed and never had the distemper at all, but lived about twenty years after it, and was sexton of the parish to the time of his death. His wife at the same time was a nurse to infected people, and tended many that died in the parish, being for her honesty recommended by the parish officers; yet she never was infected neither.

He never used any preservative against the infection, other than holding garlic and rue in his mouth, and smoking tobacco. This I also had from his own mouth. And his wife's remedy was washing her head in vinegar and sprinkling her head-clothes so with vinegar as to keep them always moist, and if the smell of any of those she waited on was more than ordinary offensive, she snuffed vinegar up her nose and sprinkled vinegar upon her head-clothes, and held a handkerchief wetted with vinegar to her mouth.

It must be confessed that though the plague was chiefly among the poor, yet were the poor the most venturous and fearless of it, and went about their employment with a sort of brutal courage; I must call it so, for it was founded neither on religion nor prudence; scarce did they use any caution, but ran into any business which they could get employment in, though it was the most hazardous. Such was that of tending the sick, watching houses shut up, carrying infected persons to the pest-house, and, which was still worse, carrying the dead away to their graves.

It was under this John Hayward's care, and within his bounds, that the story of the piper, with which people have made themselves so merry, happened, and he assured me that it was true. It is said that it was a blind piper; but, as John told me, the fellow was not blind, but an ignorant, weak, poor man, and usually walked his rounds about ten o'clock at night and went piping along from door to door, and the people usually took him in at public-houses where they knew him, and would give him drink and victuals, and sometimes farthings; and he in return would pipe and sing and talk simply, which diverted the people; and thus he lived. It was but a very bad time for this diversion while things were as I have told, yet the poor fellow went about as usual, but was almost starved; and when anybody asked how he did he would answer, the dead cart had not taken him yet, but that they had promised to call for him next week.

It happened one night that this poor fellow, whether somebody had given him too much drink or no—John Hayward said he had not drink in his house, but that they had given him a little more victuals than ordinary at a public-house in Coleman Street—and the poor fellow, having not usually had a bellyful for perhaps not a good while, was laid all along upon the top of a bulk or stall, and fast asleep, at a door in the street near London Wall, towards Cripplegate-, and that upon the same bulk or stall the people of some house, in the alley of which the house was a corner, hearing a bell which they always rang before the cart came, had laid a body really dead of the plague just by him, thinking, too, that this poor fellow had been a dead body, as the other was, and laid there by some of the neighbours.

Accordingly, when John Hayward with his bell and the cart came along, finding two dead bodies lie upon the stall, they took them up with the instrument they used and threw them into the cart, and, all this while the piper slept soundly.

From hence they passed along and took in other dead bodies, till, as honest John Hayward told me, they almost buried him alive in the cart; yet all this while he slept soundly. At length the cart came to the place where the bodies were to be thrown into the ground, which, as I do remember, was at Mount Mill; and as the cart usually stopped some time before they were ready to shoot out the melancholy load they had in it, as soon as the cart stopped the fellow awaked and struggled a little to get his head out from among the dead bodies, when, raising himself up in the cart, he called out, 'Hey! where am I?' This frighted the fellow that attended about the work; but after some pause John Hayward, recovering himself, said, 'Lord, bless us! There's somebody in the cart not quite dead!' So another called to him and said, 'Who are you?' The fellow answered, 'I am the poor piper. Where am I?' 'Where are you?' says Hayward. 'Why, you are in the dead-cart, and we are going to bury you.' 'But I an't dead though, am I?' says the piper, which made them laugh a little though, as John said, they were heartily frighted at first; so they helped the poor fellow down, and he went about his business.

I know the story goes he set up his pipes in the cart and frighted the bearers and others so that they ran away; but John Hayward did not tell the story so, nor say anything of his piping at all; but that he was a poor piper, and that he was carried away as above I am fully satisfied of the truth of.

It is to be noted here that the dead-carts in the city were not confined to particular parishes, but one cart went through several parishes, according as the number of dead presented; nor were they tied to carry the dead to their respective parishes, but many of the dead taken up in the city were carried to the burying-ground in the out-parts for want of room.

I have already mentioned the surprise that this judgement was at first among the people. I must be allowed to give some of my observations on the more serious and religious part. Surely never city, at least of this bulk and magnitude, was taken in a condition so perfectly unprepared for such a dreadful visitation, whether I am to speak of the civil preparations or religious. They were, indeed, as if they had had no warning, no expectation, no apprehensions, and consequently the least provision imaginable was made for it in a public way. For example, the Lord Mayor and sheriffs had made no provision as magistrates for the regulations which were to be observed. They had gone into no measures for relief of the poor. The citizens had no public magazines or storehouses for corn or meal for the subsistence of the poor, which if they had provided themselves, as in such cases is done abroad, many miserable families who were now reduced to the utmost distress would have been relieved, and that in a better manner than now could be done.

The stock of the city's money I can say but little to. The Chamber of London was said to be exceedingly rich, and it may be concluded that they were so, by the vast of money issued from thence in the rebuilding the public edifices after the fire of London, and in building new works, such as, for the first part, the Guildhall, Blackwell Hall, part of Leadenhall, half the Exchange, the Session House, the Compter, the prisons of Ludgate, Newgate, &c., several of the wharfs and stairs and landing-places on the river; all which were either burned down or damaged by the great fire of London, the next year after the plague; and of the second sort, the Monument, Fleet Ditch with its bridges, and the Hospital of Bethlem or Bedlam, &c. But possibly the managers of the city's credit at that time made more conscience of breaking in upon the orphan's money to show charity to the distressed citizens than the managers in the following years did to beautify the city and re-edify the buildings; though, in the first case, the losers would have thought their fortunes better bestowed, and the public faith of the city have been less subjected to scandal and reproach.

It must be acknowledged that the absent citizens, who, though they were fled for safety into the country, were yet greatly interested in the welfare of those whom they left behind, forgot not to contribute liberally to the relief of the poor, and large sums were also collected among trading towns in the remotest parts of England; and, as I have heard also, the nobility and the gentry in all parts of England took the deplorable condition of the city into their consideration, and sent up large sums of money in charity to the Lord Mayor and magistrates for the relief of the poor. The king also, as I was told, ordered a thousand pounds a week to be distributed in four parts: one quarter to the city and liberty of Westminster; one quarter or part among the inhabitants of the Southwark side of the water; one quarter to the liberty and parts within of the city, exclusive of the city within the walls; and one-fourth part to the suburbs in the county of Middlesex, and the east and north parts of the city. But this latter I only speak of as a report.

Certain it is, the greatest part of the poor or families who formerly lived by their labour, or by retail trade, lived now on charity; and had there not been prodigious sums of money given by charitable, well-minded Christians for the support of such, the city could never have subsisted. There were, no question, accounts kept of their charity, and of the just distribution of it by the magistrates. But as such multitudes of those very officers died through whose hands it was distributed, and also that, as I have been told, most of the accounts of those things were lost in the great fire which happened in the very next year, and which burnt even the chamberlain's office and many of their papers, so I could never come at the particular account, which I used great endeavours to have seen.

It may, however, be a direction in case of the approach of a like visitation, which God keep the city from;—I say, it may be of use to observe that by the care of the Lord Mayor and aldermen at that time in distributing weekly great sums of money for relief of the poor, a multitude of people who would otherwise have perished, were relieved, and their lives preserved. And here let me enter into a brief state of the case of the poor at that time, and what way apprehended from them, from whence may be judged hereafter what may be expected if the like distress should come upon the city.

At the beginning of the plague, when there was now no more hope but that the whole city would be visited; when, as I have said, all that had friends or estates in the country retired with their families; and when, indeed, one would have thought the very city itself was running out of the gates, and that there would be nobody left behind; you may be sure from that hour all trade, except such as related to immediate subsistence, was, as it were, at a full stop.

This is so lively a case, and contains in it so much of the real condition of the people, that I think I cannot be too particular in it, and therefore I descend to the several arrangements or classes of people who fell into immediate distress upon this occasion. For example:

1. All master-workmen in manufactures, especially such as belonged to ornament and the less necessary parts of the people's dress, clothes, and furniture for houses, such as riband-weavers and other weavers, gold and silver lace makers, and gold and silver wire drawers, sempstresses, milliners, shoemakers, hatmakers, and glovemakers; also upholsterers, joiners, cabinet-makers, looking-glass makers, and innumerable trades which depend upon such as these;—I say, the master-workmen in such stopped their work, dismissed their journeymen and workmen, and all their dependents.

2. As merchandising was at a full stop, for very few ships ventured to come up the river and none at all went out, so all the extraordinary officers of the customs, likewise the watermen, carmen, porters, and all the poor whose labour depended upon the merchants, were at once dismissed and put out of business.

3. All the tradesmen usually employed in building or repairing of houses were at a full stop, for the people were far from wanting to build houses when so many thousand houses were at once stripped of their inhabitants; so that this one article turned all the ordinary workmen of that kind out of business, such as bricklayers, masons, carpenters, joiners, plasterers, painters, glaziers, smiths, plumbers, and all the labourers depending on such.

4. As navigation was at a stop, our ships neither coming in or going out as before, so the seamen were all out of employment, and many of them in the last and lowest degree of distress; and with the seamen were all the several tradesmen and workmen belonging to and depending upon the building and fitting out of ships, such as ship-carpenters, caulkers, ropemakers, dry coopers, sailmakers, anchorsmiths, and other smiths; blockmakers, carvers, gunsmiths, ship-chandlers, ship-carvers, and the like. The masters of those perhaps might live upon their

substance, but the traders were universally at a stop, and consequently all their workmen discharged. Add to these that the river was in a manner without boats, and all or most part of the watermen, lightermen, boat-builders, and lighter-builders in like manner idle and laid by.

5. All families retrenched their living as much as possible, as well those that fled as those that stayed; so that an innumerable multitude of footmen, serving-men, shopkeepers, journeymen, merchants' bookkeepers, and such sort of people, and especially poor maid-servants, were turned off, and left friendless and helpless, without employment and without habitation, and this was really a dismal article.

I might be more particular as to this part, but it may suffice to mention in general, all trades being stopped, employment ceased: the labour, and by that the bread, of the poor were cut off; and at first indeed the cries of the poor were most lamentable to hear, though by the distribution of charity their misery that way was greatly abated. Many indeed fled into the counties, but thousands of them having stayed in London till nothing but desperation sent them away, death overtook them on the road, and they served for no better than the messengers of death; indeed, others carrying the infection along with them, spread it very unhappily into the remotest parts of the kingdom.

Many of these were the miserable objects of despair which I have mentioned before, and were removed by the destruction which followed. These might be said to perish not by the infection itself but by the consequence of it; indeed, namely, by hunger and distress and the want of all things: being without lodging, without money, without friends, without means to get their bread, or without anyone to give it them; for many of them were without what we call legal settlements, and so could not claim of the parishes, and all the support they had was by application to the magistrates for relief, which relief was (to give the magistrates their due) carefully and cheerfully administered as they found it necessary, and those that stayed behind never felt the want and distress of that kind which they felt who went away in the manner above noted.

Let any one who is acquainted with what multitudes of people get their daily bread in this city by their labour, whether artificers or mere workmen—I say, let any man consider what must be the miserable condition of this town if, on a sudden, they should be all turned out of employment, that labour should cease, and wages for work be no more.

This was the case with us at that time; and had not the sums of money contributed in charity by well-disposed people of every kind, as well abroad as at home, been prodigiously great, it had not been in the power of the Lord Mayor and sheriffs to have kept the public peace. Nor were they without apprehensions, as it was, that desperation should push the people upon tumults, and cause them to rifle the houses of rich men and plunder the markets of provisions; in which case the country people, who brought provisions very freely and boldly to town, would have been terrified from coming any more, and the town would have sunk under an unavoidable famine.

But the prudence of my Lord Mayor and the Court of Aldermen within the city, and of the justices of peace in the out-parts, was such, and they were supported with money from all parts so well, that the poor people were kept quiet, and their wants everywhere relieved, as far as was possible to be done.

Two things besides this contributed to prevent the mob doing any mischief. One was, that really the rich themselves had not laid up stores of provisions in their houses as indeed they ought to have done, and which if they had been wise enough to have done, and locked themselves entirely up, as some few did, they had perhaps escaped the disease better. But as it appeared they had not, so the mob had no notion of finding stores of provisions there if they had broken in as it is plain they were sometimes very near doing, and which: if they had, they had finished the ruin of the whole city, for there were no regular troops to have withstood them, nor could the trained bands have been brought together to defend the city, no men being to be found to bear arms.

But the vigilance of the Lord Mayor and such magistrates as could be had (for some, even of the aldermen, were dead, and some absent) prevented this; and they did it by the most kind and gentle methods they could think of, as particularly by relieving the most desperate with money, and putting others into business, and particularly that employment of watching houses that were infected and shut up. And as the number of these were very great (for it was said there was at one time ten thousand houses shut up, and every house had two watchmen to guard it, viz., one by night and the other by day), this gave opportunity to employ a very great number of poor men at a time.

The women and servants that were turned off from their places were likewise employed as nurses to tend the sick in all places, and this took off a very great number of them.

And, which though a melancholy article in itself, yet was a deliverance in its kind: namely, the plague, which raged in a dreadful manner from the middle of August to the middle of October, carried off in that time thirty or forty thousand of these very people which, had they been left, would certainly have been an insufferable burden by their poverty; that is to say, the whole city could not have supported the expense of them, or have provided food for them; and they would in time have been even driven to the necessity of plundering either the city itself or the country adjacent, to have subsisted themselves, which would first or last have put the whole nation, as well as the city, into the utmost terror and confusion.

It was observable, then, that this calamity of the people made them very humble; for now for about nine weeks together there died near a thousand a day, one day with another, even by the account of the weekly bills, which yet, I have reason to be assured, never gave a full account, by many thousands; the confusion being such, and the carts working in the dark when they carried the dead, that in some places no account at all was kept, but they worked on, the clerks and sextons not attending for weeks together, and not knowing what number they carried. This account is verified by the following bills of mortality:—

	Of all diseases:	Plague:
From August 8 to August 15	5319	3880
From August 15 to August 22	5568	4237
From August 22 to August 29	7496	6102
From August 29 to September 5	8252	6988
From September 5 to September 12	7690	6544
From September 12 to September 19	8297	7165
From September 19 to September 26	6460	5533
From September 26 to October 3	5720	4979
From October 3 to October 10	5068	4327
	59,870	49,705

So that the gross of the people were carried off in these two months; for, as the whole number which was brought in to die of the plague was but 68,590, here is 50,000 of them, within a trifle, in two months; I say 50,000, because, as there wants 295 in the number above, so there wants two days of two months in the account of time.

Now when I say that the parish officers did not give in a full account, or were not to be depended upon for their account, let any one but consider how men could be exact in such a time of dreadful distress, and when many of them were taken sick themselves and perhaps died in the very time when their accounts were to be given in; I mean the parish clerks, besides inferior officers; for though these poor men ventured at all hazards, yet they were far from being exempt from the common calamity, especially if it be true that the parish of Stepney had, within the year, 116 sextons, gravediggers, and their assistants; that is to say, bearers, bellmen, and drivers of carts for carrying off the dead bodies.

Indeed the work was not of a nature to allow them leisure to take an exact tale of the dead bodies, which were all huddled together in the dark into a pit; which pit or trench no man could come nigh but at the utmost peril. I observed often that in the parishes of Aldgate and Cripplegate, Whitechappel and Stepney, there were five, six, seven, and eight hundred in a week in the bills; whereas if we may believe the opinion of those that lived in the city all the time as well as I, there died sometimes 2000 a week in those parishes; and I saw it under the hand of one that made as strict an examination into that part as he could, that there really died an hundred thousand people of the plague in that one year whereas in the bills, the articles of the plague, it was but 68,590.

If I may be allowed to give my opinion, by what I saw with my eyes and heard from other people that were eye-witnesses, I do verily believe the same, viz., that there died at least 100,000 of the plague only, besides other distempers and besides those which died in the fields and highways and secret Places out of the compass of the communication, as it was called, and who were not put down in the bills though they really belonged to the body of the inhabitants. It was known to us all that abundance of poor despairing creatures who had the distemper upon them, and were grown stupid or melancholy by their misery, as many were, wandered away into the fields and Woods, and into secret uncouth places almost anywhere, to creep into a bush or hedge and die.

The inhabitants of the villages adjacent would, in pity, carry them food and set it at a distance, that they might fetch it, if they were able; and sometimes they were not able, and the next time they went they should find the poor wretches lie dead and the food untouched. The number of these miserable objects were many, and I know so many that perished thus, and so exactly where, that I believe I could go to the very place and dig their bones up still; for the country people would go and dig a hole at a distance from them, and then with long poles, and hooks at the end of them, drag the bodies into these pits, and then throw the earth in from as far as they could cast it, to cover them, taking notice how the wind blew, and so coming on that side which the seamen call to windward, that the scent of the bodies might blow from them; and thus great numbers went out of the world who were never known, or any account of them taken, as well within the bills of mortality as without.

This, indeed, I had in the main only from the relation of others, for I seldom walked into the fields, except towards Bethnal Green and Hackney, or as hereafter. But when I did walk, I always saw a great many poor wanderers at a distance; but I could know little of their cases, for whether it were in the street or in the fields, if we had seen anybody coming, it was a general method to walk away; yet I believe the account is exactly true.

As this puts me upon mentioning my walking the streets and fields, I cannot omit taking notice what a desolate place the city was at that time. The great street I lived in (which is known to be one of the broadest of all the streets of London, I mean of the suburbs as well as the liberties) all the side where the butchers lived, especially without the bars, was more like a green field than a paved street, and the people generally went in the middle with the horses and carts. It is true that the farthest end towards Whitechappel Church was not all paved, but even the part that was paved was full of grass also; but this need not seem strange, since the great streets within the city, such as Leadenhall Street, Bishopsgate Street, Cornhill, and even the Exchange itself, had grass growing in them in several places; neither cart or coach were seen in the streets from morning to evening, except some country carts to bring roots and beans, or peas, hay, and straw, to the market, and those but very few compared to what was usual. As for coaches, they were scarce used but to carry sick people to the pest-house, and to other hospitals, and some few to carry physicians to such places as they thought fit to venture to visit; for really coaches were dangerous things, and people did not care to venture into them, because they did not know who might have been carried in them last, and sick, infected people were, as I have said, ordinarily carried in them to the pest-houses, and sometimes people expired in them as they went along.

It is true, when the infection came to such a height as I have now mentioned, there were very few physicians which cared to stir abroad to sick houses, and very many of the most eminent of the faculty were dead, as well as the surgeons also; for now it was indeed a dismal time, and for about a month together, not taking any notice of the bills of mortality, I believe there did not die less than 1500 or 1700 a day, one day with another.

One of the worst days we had in the whole time, as I thought, was in the beginning of September, when, indeed, good people began to think that God was resolved to make a full end of the people in this miserable city. This was at that time when the plague was fully come into the eastern parishes. The parish of Aldgate, if I may give my opinion, buried above a thousand a week for two weeks, though the bills did not say so many;—but it surrounded me at so dismal a rate that there was not a house in twenty uninfected in the Minories, in Houndsditch, and in those parts of Aldgate parish about the Butcher Row and the alleys over against me. I say, in those places death reigned in every corner. Whitechappel parish was in the same condition, and though much less than the parish I lived in, yet buried near 600 a week by the bills, and in my opinion near twice as many. Whole families, and indeed whole streets of families, were swept away together; insomuch that it was frequent for neighbours to call to the bellman to go to such-and-such houses and fetch out the people, for that they were all dead.

And, indeed, the work of removing the dead bodies by carts was now grown so very odious and dangerous that it was complained of that the bearers did not take care to clear such houses where all the inhabitants were dead, but that sometimes the bodies lay several days unburied, till the neighbouring families were offended with the stench, and consequently infected; and this neglect of the officers was such that the churchwardens and constables were summoned to look after it, and even the justices of the Hamlets were obliged to venture their lives among them to quicken and encourage them, for innumerable of the bearers died of the distemper, infected by the bodies they were obliged to come so near. And had it not been that the number of poor people who wanted employment and wanted bread (as I have said before) was so great that necessity drove them to undertake anything and venture anything, they would never have found people to be employed. And then the bodies of the dead would have lain above ground, and have perished and rotted in a dreadful manner.

But the magistrates cannot be enough commended in this, that they kept such good order for the burying of the dead, that as fast as any of these they employed to carry off and bury the dead fell sick or died, as was many times the case, they immediately supplied the places with others, which, by reason of the great number of poor that was left out of business, as above, was not hard to do. This occasioned, that notwithstanding the infinite number of people which died and were sick, almost all together, yet they were always cleared away and carried off every night, so that it was never to be said of London that the living were not able to bury the dead.

As the desolation was greater during those terrible times, so the amazement of the people increased, and a thousand unaccountable things they would do in the violence of their fright, as others did the same in the agonies of their distemper, and this part was very affecting. Some went roaring and crying and wringing their hands along the street; some would go praying and lifting up their hands to heaven, calling upon God for mercy. I cannot say, indeed, whether this was not in their distraction, but, be it so, it was still an indication of a more serious mind, when they had the use of their senses, and was much better, even as it was, than the frightful yellings and cryings that every day, and especially in the evenings, were heard in some streets. I suppose the world has heard of the famous Solomon Eagle, an enthusiast. He, though not infected at all but in his head, went about denouncing of judgement upon the city in a frightful manner, sometimes quite naked, and with a pan of burning charcoal on his head. What he said, or pretended, indeed I could not learn.

I will not say whether that clergyman was distracted or not, or whether he did it in pure zeal for the poor people, who went every evening through the streets of Whitechappel, and, with his hands lifted up, repeated that part of the Liturgy of the Church continually, 'Spare us, good Lord; spare Thy people, whom Thou has redeemed with Thy most precious blood.' I say, I cannot speak positively of these things, because these were only the dismal objects which represented themselves to me as I looked through my chamber windows (for I seldom opened the casements), while I confined myself within doors during that most violent raging of the pestilence; when, indeed, as I have said, many began to think, and even to say, that there would none escape; and indeed I began to think so too, and therefore kept within doors for about a fortnight and never stirred out. But I could not hold it. Besides, there were some people who, notwithstanding the danger, did not omit publicly to attend the worship of God, even in the most dangerous times; and though it is true that a great many clergymen did shut up their churches, and fled, as other people did, for the safety of their lives, yet all did not do so. Some ventured to officiate and to keep up the assemblies of the people by constant prayers, and sometimes sermons or brief exhortations to repentance and reformation, and this as long as any would come to hear them. And Dissenters did the like also, and even in the very churches where the parish ministers were either dead or fled; nor was there any room for making difference at such a time as this was.

It was indeed a lamentable thing to hear the miserable lamentations of poor dying creatures calling out for ministers to comfort them and pray with them, to counsel them and to direct them, calling out to God for pardon and mercy, and confessing aloud their past sins. It would make the stoutest heart bleed to hear how many warnings were then given by dying penitents to others not to put off and delay their repentance to the day of distress; that such a time of calamity as this was no time for repentance, was no time to call upon God. I wish I could repeat the very sound of those groans and of those exclamations that I heard from some poor dying creatures when in the height of their agonies and distress, and that I could make him that reads this hear, as I imagine I now hear them, for the sound seems still to ring in my ears.

If I could but tell this part in such moving accents as should alarm the very soul of the reader, I should rejoice that I recorded those things, however short and imperfect.

It pleased God that I was still spared, and very hearty and sound in health, but very impatient of being pent up within doors without air, as I had been for fourteen days or thereabouts; and I could not restrain myself, but I would go to carry a letter for my brother to the post-house. Then it was indeed that I observed a profound silence in the streets. When I came to the post-house, as I went to put in my letter I saw a man stand in one corner of the yard and talking to another at a window, and a third had opened a door belonging to the office. In the middle of the yard lay a small leather purse with two keys hanging at it, with money in it, but nobody would meddle with it. I asked how long it had lain there; the man at the window said it had lain almost an hour, but that they had not meddled with it, because they did not know but the person who dropped it might come back to look for it. I had no such need of money, nor was the sum so big that I had any inclination to meddle with it, or to get the money at the hazard it might be attended with; so I seemed to go away, when the man who had opened the door said he would take it up, but so that if the right owner came for it he should be sure to have it. So he went in and fetched a pail of water and set it down hard by the purse, then went again and fetch some gunpowder, and cast a good deal of powder upon the purse, and then made a train from that which he had thrown loose upon the purse. The train reached about two yards. After this he goes in a third time and fetches out a pair of tongs red hot, and which he had prepared, I suppose, on purpose; and first setting fire to the train of powder, that singed the purse and also smoked the air sufficiently. But he was not content with that, but he then takes up the purse with the tongs, holding it so long till the tongs burnt through the purse, and then he shook the money out into the pail of water, so he carried it in. The money, as I remember, was about thirteen shilling and some smooth groats and brass farthings.

There might perhaps have been several poor people, as I have observed above, that would have been hardy enough to have ventured for the sake of the money; but you may easily see by what I have observed that the few people who were spared were very careful of themselves at that time when the distress was so exceeding great.

Much about the same time I walked out into the fields towards Bow; for I had a great mind to see how things were managed in the river and among the ships; and as I had some concern in shipping, I had a notion that it had been one of the best ways of securing one's self from the infection to have retired into a ship; and musing how to satisfy my curiosity in that point, I turned away over the fields from Bow to Bromley, and down to Blackwall to the stairs which are there for landing or taking water.

Here I saw a poor man walking on the bank, or sea-wall, as they call it, by himself. I walked a while also about, seeing the houses all shut up. At last I fell into some talk, at a distance, with this poor man; first I asked him how people did thereabouts. 'Alas, sir!' says he, 'almost desolate; all dead or sick. Here are very few families in this part, or in that village' (pointing at Poplar), 'where half of them are not dead already, and the rest sick.' Then he pointing to one house, 'There they are all dead', said he, 'and the house stands open; nobody dares go into it. A poor thief', says he, 'ventured in to steal something, but he paid dear for his theft, for he was carried to the churchyard too last night.' Then he pointed to several other houses. 'There', says he, 'they are all dead, the man and his wife, and five children. There', says he, 'they are shut up; you see a watchman at the door'; and so of other houses. 'Why,' says I, 'what do you here all alone?' 'Why,' says he, 'I am a poor, desolate man; it has pleased God I am not yet visited, though my family is, and one of my children dead.' 'How do you mean, then,' said I, 'that you are not visited?' 'Why,' says he, 'that's my house' (pointing to a very little, low-boarded house), 'and there my poor wife and two children live,' said he, 'if they may be said to live, for my wife and one of the children are visited, but I do not come at them.' And with that word I saw the tears run very plentifully down his face; and so they did down mine too, I assure you.

'But,' said I, 'why do you not come at them? How can you abandon your own flesh and blood?' 'Oh, sir,' says he, 'the Lord forbid! I do not abandon them; I work for them as much as I am able; and, blessed be the Lord, I keep them from want'; and with that I observed he lifted up his eyes to heaven, with a countenance that presently told me I had happened on a man that was no hypocrite, but a serious, religious, good man, and his ejaculation was an expression of thankfulness that, in such a condition as he was in, he should be able to say his family did not want. 'Well,' says I, 'honest man, that is a great mercy as things go now with the poor. But how do you live, then, and how are you kept from the dreadful calamity that is now upon us all?' 'Why, sir,' says he, 'I am a waterman, and there's my boat,' says he, 'and the boat serves me for a house. I work in it in the day, and I sleep in it in the night; and what I get I lay down upon that stone,' says he, showing me a broad stone on the other side of the street, a good way from his house; 'and then,' says he, 'I halloo, and call to them till I make them hear; and they come and fetch it.'

'Well, friend,' says I, 'but how can you get any money as a waterman? Does any body go by water these times?' 'Yes, sir,' says he, 'in the way I am employed there does. Do you see there,' says he, 'five ships lie at anchor' (pointing down the river a good way below the town), 'and do you see', says he, 'eight or ten ships lie at the chain there, and at anchor yonder?' (pointing above the town). 'All those ships have families on board, of their merchants and owners, and such-like, who have locked themselves up and live on board, close shut in, for fear of the infection; and I tend on them to fetch things for them, carry letters, and do what is absolutely necessary, that they may not be obliged to come on shore; and every night I fasten my boat on board one of the ship's boats, and there I sleep by myself, and, blessed be God, I am preserved hitherto.'

'Well,' said I, 'friend, but will they let you come on board after you have been on shore here, when this is such a terrible place, and so infected as it is?'

'Why, as to that,' said he, 'I very seldom go up the ship-side, but deliver what I bring to their boat, or lie by the side, and they hoist it on board. If I did, I think they are in no danger from me, for I never go into any house on shore, or touch anybody, no, not of my own family; but I fetch provisions for them.'

'Nay,' says I, 'but that may be worse, for you must have those provisions of somebody or other; and since all this part of the town is so infected, it is dangerous so much as to speak with anybody, for the village', said I, 'is, as it were, the beginning of London, though it be at some distance from it.'

'That is true,' added he; 'but you do not understand me right; I do not buy provisions for them here. I row up to Greenwich and buy fresh meat there, and sometimes I row down the river to Woolwich and buy there; then I go to single farm-houses on the Kentish side, where I am known, and buy fowls and eggs and butter, and bring to the ships, as they direct me, sometimes one, sometimes the other. I seldom come on shore here, and I came now only to call on my wife and hear how my family do, and give them a little money, which I received last night.'

'Poor man!' said I; 'and how much hast thou gotten for them?'

'I have gotten four shillings,' said he, 'which is a great sum, as things go now with poor men; but they have given me a bag of bread too, and a salt fish and some flesh; so all helps out.' 'Well,' said I, 'and have you given it them yet?'

'No,' said he; 'but I have called, and my wife has answered that she cannot come out yet, but in half-an-hour she hopes to come, and I am waiting for her. Poor woman!' says he, 'she is brought sadly down. She has a swelling, and it is broke, and I hope she will recover; but I fear the child will die, but it is the Lord—'

Here he stopped, and wept very much.

'Well, honest friend,' said I, 'thou hast a sure Comforter, if thou hast brought thyself to be resigned to the will of God; He is dealing with us all in judgement.'

'Oh, sir!' says he, 'it is infinite mercy if any of us are spared, and who am I to repine!'

'Sayest thou so?' said I, 'and how much less is my faith than thine?' And here my heart smote me, suggesting how much better this poor man's foundation was on which he stayed in the danger than mine; that he had nowhere to fly; that he had a family to bind him to attendance, which I had not; and mine was mere presumption, his a true dependence and a courage resting on God; and yet that he used all possible caution for his safety.

I turned a little way from the man while these thoughts engaged me, for, indeed, I could no more refrain from tears than he.

At length, after some further talk, the poor woman opened the door and called, 'Robert, Robert'. He answered, and bid her stay a few moments and he would come; so he ran down the common stairs to his boat and fetched up a sack, in which was the provisions he had brought from the ships; and when he returned he hallooed again. Then he went to the great stone which he showed me and emptied the sack, and laid all out, everything by themselves, and then retired; and his wife came with a little boy to fetch them away, and called and said such a captain had sent such a thing, and such a captain such a thing, and at the end adds, 'God has sent it all; give thanks to Him.' When the poor woman had taken up all, she was so weak she could not carry it at once in, though the weight was not much neither; so she left the biscuit, which was in a little bag, and left a little boy to watch it till she came again.

'Well, but', says I to him, 'did you leave her the four shillings too, which you said was your week's pay?'

'Yes, yes,' says he; 'you shall hear her own it.' So he calls again, 'Rachel, Rachel,' which it seems was her name, 'did you take up the money?' 'Yes,' said she. 'How much was it?' said he. 'Four shillings and a groat,' said she. 'Well, well,' says he, 'the Lord keep you all'; and so he turned to go away.

As I could not refrain contributing tears to this man's story, so neither could I refrain my charity for his assistance. So I called him, 'Hark thee, friend,' said I, 'come hither, for I believe thou art in health, that I may venture thee'; so I pulled out my hand, which was in my pocket before, 'Here,' says I, 'go and call thy Rachel once more, and give her a little more comfort from me. God will never forsake a family that trust in Him as thou dost.' So I gave him four other shillings, and bid him go lay them on the stone and call his wife.

I have not words to express the poor man's thankfulness, neither could he express it himself but by tears running down his face. He called his wife, and told her God had moved the heart of a stranger, upon hearing their condition, to give them all that money, and a great deal more such as that he said to her. The woman, too, made signs of the like thankfulness, as well to Heaven as to me, and joyfully picked it up; and I parted with no money all that year that I thought better bestowed.

I then asked the poor man if the distemper had not reached to Greenwich. He said it had not till about a fortnight before; but that then he feared it had, but that it was only at that end of the town which lay south towards Deptford Bridge; that he went only to a butcher's shop and a grocer's, where he generally bought such things as they sent him for, but was very careful.

I asked him then how it came to pass that those people who had so shut themselves up in the ships had not laid in sufficient stores of all things necessary. He said some of them had—but, on the other hand, some did not come on board till they were frighted into it and till it was too dangerous for them to go to the proper people to lay in quantities of things, and that he waited on two ships, which he showed me, that had laid in little or nothing but biscuit bread and ship beer, and that he had bought everything else almost for them. I asked him if there was any more ships that had separated themselves as those had done. He told me yes, all the way up from the point, right against Greenwich, to within the shore of Limehouse and Redriff, all the ships that could have room rid two and two in the middle of the stream, and that some of them had several families on board. I asked him if the distemper had not reached them. He said he believed it had not, except two or three ships whose people had not been so watchful to keep the seamen from going on shore as others had been, and he said it was a very fine sight to see how the ships lay up the Pool.

When he said he was going over to Greenwich as soon as the tide began to come in, I asked if he would let me go with him and bring me back, for that I had a great mind to see how the ships were ranged, as he had told me. He told me, if I would assure him on the word of a Christian and of an honest man that I had not the distemper, he would. I assured him that I had not; that it had pleased God to preserve me; that I lived in Whitechappel, but was too impatient of being so long within doors, and that I had ventured out so far for the refreshment of a little air, but that none in my house had so much as been touched with it.

Well, sir,' says he, 'as your charity has been moved to pity me and my poor family, sure you cannot have so little pity left as to put yourself into my boat if you were not sound in health which would be nothing less than killing me and ruining my whole family.' The poor man troubled me so much when he spoke of his family with such a sensible concern and in such an affectionate manner, that I could not satisfy myself at first to go at all. I told him I would lay aside my curiosity rather than make him uneasy, though I was sure, and very thankful for it, that I had no more distemper upon me than the freshest man in the world. Well, he would not have me put it off neither, but to let me see how confident he was that I was just to him, now importuned me to go; so when the tide came up to his boat I went in, and he carried me to Greenwich. While he bought the things which he had in his charge to buy, I walked up to the top of the hill under which the town stands, and on the east side of the town, to get a prospect of the river. But it was a surprising sight to see the number of ships which lay in rows, two and two, and some places two or three such lines in the breadth of the river, and this not only up quite to the town, between the houses which we call Ratcliff and Redriff, which they name the Pool, but even down the whole river as far as the head of Long Reach, which is as far as the hills give us leave to see it.

I cannot guess at the number of ships, but I think there must be several hundreds of sail; and I could not but applaud the contrivance: for ten thousand people and more who attended ship affairs were certainly sheltered here from the violence of the contagion, and lived very safe and very easy.

I returned to my own dwelling very well satisfied with my day's journey, and particularly with the poor man; also I rejoiced to see that such little sanctuaries were provided for so many families in a time of such desolation. I observed also that, as the violence of the plague had increased, so the ships which had families on board removed and went farther off, till, as I was told, some went quite away to sea, and put into such harbours and safe roads on the north coast as they could best come at.

But it was also true that all the people who thus left the land and lived on board the ships were not entirely safe from the infection, for many died and were thrown overboard into the river, some in coffins, and some, as I heard, without coffins, whose bodies were seen sometimes to drive up and down with the tide in the river.

But I believe I may venture to say that in those ships which were thus infected it either happened where the people had recourse to them too late, and did not fly to the ship till they had stayed too long on shore and had the distemper upon them (though perhaps they might not perceive it) and so the distemper did not come to them on board the ships, but they really carried it with them; or it was in these ships where the poor waterman said they had not had time to furnish themselves with provisions, but were obliged to send often on shore to buy what they had occasion for, or suffered boats to come to them from the shore. And so the distemper was brought insensibly among them.

And here I cannot but take notice that the strange temper of the people of London at that time contributed extremely to their own destruction. The plague began, as I have observed, at the other end of the town, namely, in Long Acre, Drury Lane, &c., and came on towards the city very gradually and slowly. It was felt at first in December, then again in February, then again in

April, and always but a very little at a time; then it stopped till May, and even the last week in May there was but seventeen, and all at that end of the town; and all this while, even so long as till there died above 3000 a week, yet had the people in Redriff, and in Wapping and Ratcliff, on both sides of the river, and almost all Southwark side, a mighty fancy that they should not be visited, or at least that it would not be so violent among them. Some people fancied the smell of the pitch and tar, and such other things as oil and rosin and brimstone, which is so much used by all trades relating to shipping, would preserve them. Others argued it, because it was in its extreamest violence in Westminster and the parish of St Giles and St Andrew, &c., and began to abate again before it came among them—which was true indeed, in part. For example—

From the 8th to the 15th August—
- - St Giles-in-the-Fields 242
- - Cripplegate 886
- - Stepney 197
- - St Margaret, Bermondsey 24
- - Rotherhithe 3
- - Total this week 4030

From the 15th to the 22nd August—
- - St Giles-in-the-Fields 175
- - Cripplegate 847
- - Stepney 273
- - St Margaret, Bermondsey 36
- - Rotherhithe 2
- - Total this week 5319

N.B.—That it was observed the numbers mentioned in Stepney parish at that time were generally all on that side where Stepney parish joined to Shoreditch, which we now call Spittlefields, where the parish of Stepney comes up to the very wall of Shoreditch Churchyard, and the plague at this time was abated at St Giles-in-the-Fields, and raged most violently in Cripplegate, Bishopsgate, and Shoreditch parishes; but there was not ten people a week that died of it in all that part of Stepney parish which takes in Limehouse, Ratcliff Highway, and which are now the parishes of Shadwell and Wapping, even to St Katherine's by the Tower, till after the whole month of August was expired. But they paid for it afterwards, as I shall observe by-and-by.

This, I say, made the people of Redriff and Wapping, Ratcliff and Limehouse, so secure, and flatter themselves so much with the plague's going off without reaching them, that they took no care either to fly into the country or shut themselves up. Nay, so far were they from stirring that they rather received their friends and relations from the city into their houses, and several from other places really took sanctuary in that part of the town as a Place of safety, and as a place which they thought God would pass over, and not visit as the rest was visited.

And this was the reason that when it came upon them they were more surprised, more unprovided, and more at a loss what to do than they were in other places; for when it came among them really and with violence, as it did indeed in September and October, there was then no stirring out into the country, nobody would suffer a stranger to come near them, no, nor near the towns where they dwelt; and, as I have been told, several that wandered into the country on Surrey side were found starved to death in the woods and commons, that country being more open and more woody than any other part so near London, especially about

Norwood and the parishes of Camberwell, Dullege, and Lusum, where, it seems, nobody durst relieve the poor distressed people for fear of the infection.

This notion having, as I said, prevailed with the people in that part of the town, was in part the occasion, as I said before, that they had recourse to ships for their retreat; and where they did this early and with prudence, furnishing themselves so with provisions that they had no need to go on shore for supplies or suffer boats to come on board to bring them,—I say, where they did so they had certainly the safest retreat of any people whatsoever; but the distress was such that people ran on board, in their fright, without bread to eat, and some into ships that had no men on board to remove them farther off, or to take the boat and go down the river to buy provisions where it might be done safely, and these often suffered and were infected on board as much as on shore.

As the richer sort got into ships, so the lower rank got into hoys, smacks, lighters, and fishing-boats; and many, especially watermen, lay in their boats; but those made sad work of it, especially the latter, for, going about for provision, and perhaps to get their subsistence, the infection got in among them and made a fearful havoc; many of the watermen died alone in their wherries as they rid at their roads, as well as above bridge as below, and were not found sometimes till they were not in condition for anybody to touch or come near them.

Indeed, the distress of the people at this seafaring end of the town was very deplorable, and deserved the greatest commiseration. But, alas! this was a time when every one's private safety lay so near them that they had no room to pity the distresses of others; for every one had death, as it were, at his door, and many even in their families, and knew not what to do or whither to fly.

This, I say, took away all compassion; self-preservation, indeed, appeared here to be the first law. For the children ran away from their parents as they languished in the utmost distress. And in some places, though not so frequent as the other, parents did the like to their children; nay, some dreadful examples there were, and particularly two in one week, of distressed mothers, raving and distracted, killing their own children; one whereof was not far off from where I dwelt, the poor lunatic creature not living herself long enough to be sensible of the sin of what she had done, much less to be punished for it.

It is not, indeed, to be wondered at: for the danger of immediate death to ourselves took away all bowels of love, all concern for one another. I speak in general, for there were many instances of immovable affection, pity, and duty in many, and some that came to my knowledge, that is to say, by hearsay; for I shall not take upon me to vouch the truth of the particulars.

To introduce one, let me first mention that one of the most deplorable cases in all the present calamity was that of women with child, who, when they came to the hour of their sorrows, and their pains come upon them, could neither have help of one kind or another; neither midwife or neighbouring women to come near them. Most of the midwives were dead, especially of such as served the poor; and many, if not all the midwives of note, were fled into the country; so that it was next to impossible for a poor woman that could not pay an immoderate price to get any midwife to come to her—and if they did, those they could get were generally unskilful and ignorant creatures; and the consequence of this was that a most unusual and incredible number of women were reduced to the utmost distress. Some were delivered and spoiled by the rashness and ignorance of those who pretended to lay them. Children without number were, I might say, murdered by the same but a more justifiable ignorance: pretending they would save the mother, whatever became of the child; and many times both mother and child were lost in the same manner; and especially where the mother had the distemper, there nobody would come near them and both sometimes perished. Sometimes the mother has died of the plague, and the infant, it may be, half born, or born but not parted from the mother. Some died in the very pains of their travail, and not delivered at all; and so many were the cases of this kind that it is hard to judge of them.

Something of it will appear in the unusual numbers which are put into the weekly bills (though I am far from allowing them to be able to give anything of a full account) under the articles of—

Child-bed.
    Abortive and Still-born.
    Christmas and Infants.

Take the weeks in which the plague was most violent, and compare them with the weeks before the distemper began, even in the same year. For example:—

	Child-bed:	Abortive:	Still-born:
From January 3 to January 10	7	1	13
From January 10 to January 17	8	6	11
From January 17 to January 24	9	5	15
From January 24 to January 31	3	2	9
From January 31 to February 7	3	3	8
From February 7 to February 14	6	2	11
From February 14 to February 21	5	2	13
From February 21 to February 28	2	2	10
From February 28 to March 7	5	1	10
	48	24	100
From August 1 to August 8	25	5	11
From August 8 to August 15	23	6	8
From August 15 to August 22	28	4	4
From August 22 to August 29	40	6	10
From August 29 to September 5	38	2	11
From September 5 to September 12	39	23	
From September 12 to September 19	42	5	17
From September 19 to September 26	42	6	10
From September 26 to October 3	14	4	9
	291	61	80

TO THE DISPARITY of these numbers it is to be considered and allowed for, that according to our usual opinion who were then upon the spot, there were not one-third of the people in the town during the months of August and September as were in the months of January and February. In a word, the usual number that used to die of these three articles, and, as I hear, did die of them the year before, was thus:—

1664.
    Child-bed... 189
    Abortive and still-born... 458

— 647

1665.
   Child-bed... 625
   Abortive and still-born.. 617
   — 1242

This inequality, I say, is exceedingly augmented when the numbers of people are considered. I pretend not to make any exact calculation of the numbers of people which were at this time in the city, but I shall make a probable conjecture at that part by-and-by. What I have said now is to explain the misery of those poor creatures above; so that it might well be said, as in the Scripture, Woe be to those who are with child, and to those which give suck in that day. For, indeed, it was a woe to them in particular.

I was not conversant in many particular families where these things happened, but the outcries of the miserable were heard afar off. As to those who were with child, we have seen some calculation made; 291 women dead in child-bed in nine weeks, out of one-third part of the number of whom there usually died in that time but eighty-four of the same disaster. Let the reader calculate the proportion.

There is no room to doubt but the misery of those that gave suck was in proportion as great. Our bills of mortality could give but little light in this, yet some it did. There were several more than usual starved at nurse, but this was nothing. The misery was where they were, first, starved for want of a nurse, the mother dying and all the family and the infants found dead by them, merely for want; and, if I may speak my opinion, I do believe that many hundreds of poor helpless infants perished in this manner. Secondly, not starved, but poisoned by the nurse. Nay, even where the mother has been nurse, and having received the infection, has poisoned, that is, infected the infant with her milk even before they knew they were infected themselves; nay, and the infant has died in such a case before the mother. I cannot but remember to leave this admonition upon record, if ever such another dreadful visitation should happen in this city, that all women that are with child or that give suck should be gone, if they have any possible means, out of the place, because their misery, if infected, will so much exceed all other people's.

I could tell here dismal stories of living infants being found sucking the breasts of their mothers, or nurses, after they have been dead of the plague. Of a mother in the parish where I lived, who, having a child that was not well, sent for an apothecary to view the child; and when he came, as the relation goes, was giving the child suck at her breast, and to all appearance was herself very well; but when the apothecary came close to her he saw the tokens upon that breast with which she was suckling the child. He was surprised enough, to be sure, but, not willing to fright the poor woman too much, he desired she would give the child into his hand; so he takes the child, and going to a cradle in the room, lays it in, and opening its cloths, found the tokens upon the child too, and both died before he could get home to send a preventive medicine to the father of the child, to whom he had told their condition. Whether the child infected the nurse-mother or the mother the child was not certain, but the last most likely. Likewise of a child brought home to the parents from a nurse that had died of the plague, yet the tender mother would not refuse to take in her child, and laid it in her bosom, by which she was infected; and died with the child in her arms dead also.

It would make the hardest heart move at the instances that were frequently found of tender mothers tending and watching with their dear children, and even dying before them, and sometimes taking the distemper from them and dying, when the child for whom the affectionate heart had been sacrificed has got over it and escaped.

The like of a tradesman in East Smithfield, whose wife was big with child of her first child, and fell in labour, having the plague upon her. He could neither get midwife to assist her or nurse to tend her, and two servants which he kept fled both from her. He ran from house to house like one distracted, but could get no help; the utmost he could get was, that a watchman, who attended at an infected house shut up, promised to send a nurse in the morning. The poor man, with his heart broke, went back, assisted his wife what he could, acted the part of the midwife, brought the child dead into the world, and his wife in about an hour died in his arms, where he held her dead body fast till the morning, when the watchman came and brought the nurse as he had promised; and coming up the stairs (for he had left the door open, or only latched), they found the man sitting with his dead wife in his arms, and so overwhelmed with grief that he died in a few hours after without any sign of the infection upon him, but merely sunk under the weight of his grief.

I have heard also of some who, on the death of their relations, have grown stupid with the insupportable sorrow; and of one, in particular, who was so absolutely overcome with the pressure upon his spirits that by degrees his head sank into his body, so between his shoulders that the crown of his head was very little seen above the bone of his shoulders; and by degrees losing both voice and sense, his face, looking forward, lay against his collarbone and could not be kept up any otherwise, unless held up by the hands of other people; and the poor man never came to himself again, but languished near a year in that condition, and died. Nor was he ever once seen to lift up his eyes or to look upon any particular object.

I cannot undertake to give any other than a summary of such passages as these, because it was not possible to come at the particulars, where sometimes the whole families where such things happened were carried off by the distemper. But there were innumerable cases of this kind which presented to the eye and the ear, even in passing along the streets, as I have hinted above. Nor is it easy to give any story of this or that family which there was not divers parallel stories to be met with of the same kind.

But as I am now talking of the time when the plague raged at the easternmost part of the town—how for a long time the people of those parts had flattered themselves that they should escape, and how they were surprised when it came upon them as it did; for, indeed, it came upon them like an armed man when it did come;—I say, this brings me back to the three poor men who wandered from Wapping, not knowing whither to go or what to do, and whom I mentioned before; one a biscuit-baker, one a sailmaker, and the other a joiner, all of Wapping, or there-abouts.

The sleepiness and security of that part, as I have observed, was such that they not only did not shift for themselves as others did, but they boasted of being safe, and of safety being with them; and many people fled out of the city, and out of the infected suburbs, to Wapping, Ratcliff, Limehouse, Poplar, and such Places, as to Places of security; and it is not at all unlikely that their doing this helped to bring the plague that way faster than it might otherwise have come. For though I am much for people flying away and emptying such a town as this upon the first appearance of a like visitation, and that all people who have any possible retreat should make use of it in time and be gone, yet I must say, when all that will fly are gone, those that are left and must stand it should stand stock-still where they are, and not shift from one end of the town or one part of the town to the other; for that is the bane and mischief of the whole, and they carry the plague from house to house in their very clothes.

Wherefore were we ordered to kill all the dogs and cats, but because as they were domestic animals, and are apt to run from house to house and from street to street, so they are capable of carrying the effluvia or infectious streams of bodies infected even in their furs and hair? And therefore it was that, in the beginning of the infection, an order was published by the Lord

Mayor, and by the magistrates, according to the advice of the physicians, that all the dogs and cats should be immediately killed, and an officer was appointed for the execution.

It is incredible, if their account is to be depended upon, what a prodigious number of those creatures were destroyed. I think they talked of forty thousand dogs, and five times as many cats; few houses being without a cat, some having several, sometimes five or six in a house. All possible endeavours were used also to destroy the mice and rats, especially the latter, by laying ratsbane and other poisons for them, and a prodigious multitude of them were also destroyed.

I often reflected upon the unprovided condition that the whole body of the people were in at the first coming of this calamity upon them, and how it was for want of timely entering into measures and managements, as well public as private, that all the confusions that followed were brought upon us, and that such a prodigious number of people sank in that disaster, which, if proper steps had been taken, might, Providence concurring, have been avoided, and which, if posterity think fit, they may take a caution and warning from. But I shall come to this part again.

I come back to my three men. Their story has a moral in every part of it, and their whole conduct, and that of some whom they joined with, is a pattern for all poor men to follow, or women either, if ever such a time comes again; and if there was no other end in recording it, I think this a very just one, whether my account be exactly according to fact or no.

Two of them are said to be brothers, the one an old soldier, but now a biscuit-maker; the other a lame sailor, but now a sailmaker; the third a joiner. Says John the biscuit-maker one day to Thomas his brother, the sailmaker, 'Brother Tom, what will become of us? The plague grows hot in the city, and increases this way. What shall we do?'

'Truly,' says Thomas, 'I am at a great loss what to do, for I find if it comes down into Wapping I shall be turned out of my lodging.' And thus they began to talk of it beforehand.

John. Turned out of your lodging, Tom! If you are, I don't know who will take you in; for people are so afraid of one another now, there's no getting a lodging anywhere.

Thomas. Why, the people where I lodge are good, civil people, and have kindness enough for me too; but they say I go abroad every day to my work, and it will be dangerous; and they talk of locking themselves up and letting nobody come near them.

John. Why, they are in the right, to be sure, if they resolve to venture staying in town.

Thomas. Nay, I might even resolve to stay within doors too, for, except a suit of sails that my master has in hand, and which I am just finishing, I am like to get no more work a great while. There's no trade stirs now. Workmen and servants are turned off everywhere, so that I might be glad to be locked up too; but I do not see they will be willing to consent to that, any more than to the other.

John. Why, what will you do then, brother? And what shall I do? for I am almost as bad as you. The people where I lodge are all gone into the country but a maid, and she is to go next week, and to shut the house quite up, so that I shall be turned adrift to the wide world before you, and I am resolved to go away too, if I knew but where to go.

Thomas. We were both distracted we did not go away at first; then we might have travelled anywhere. There's no stirring now; we shall be starved if we pretend to go out of town. They won't let us have victuals, no, not for our money, nor let us come into the towns, much less into their houses.

John. And that which is almost as bad, I have but little money to help myself with neither.

Thomas. As to that, we might make shift, I have a little, though not much; but I tell you there's no stirring on the road. I know a couple of poor honest men in our street have attempted to travel, and at Barnet, or Whetstone, or thereabouts, the people offered to fire at them if they pretended to go forward, so they are come back again quite discouraged.

John. I would have ventured their fire if I had been there. If I had been denied food for my money they should have seen me take it before their faces, and if I had tendered money for it they could not have taken any course with me by law.

Thomas. You talk your old soldier's language, as if you were in the Low Countries now, but this is a serious thing. The people have good reason to keep anybody off that they are not satisfied are sound, at such a time as this, and we must not plunder them.

John. No, brother, you mistake the case, and mistake me too. I would plunder nobody; but for any town upon the road to deny me leave to pass through the town in the open highway, and deny me provisions for my money, is to say the town has a right to starve me to death, which cannot be true.

Thomas. But they do not deny you liberty to go back again from whence you came, and therefore they do not starve you.

John. But the next town behind me will, by the same rule, deny me leave to go back, and so they do starve me between them. Besides, there is no law to prohibit my travelling wherever I will on the road.

Thomas. But there will be so much difficulty in disputing with them at every town on the road that it is not for poor men to do it or undertake it, at such a time as this is especially.

John. Why, brother, our condition at this rate is worse than anybody else's, for we can neither go away nor stay here. I am of the same mind with the lepers of Samaria: 'If we stay here we are sure to die', I mean especially as you and I are stated, without a dwelling-house of our own, and without lodging in anybody else's. There is no lying in the street at such a time as this; we had as good go into the dead-cart at once. Therefore I say, if we stay here we are sure to die, and if we go away we can but die; I am resolved to be gone.

Thomas. You will go away. Whither will you go, and what can you do? I would as willingly go away as you, if I knew whither. But we have no acquaintance, no friends. Here we were born, and here we must die.

John. Look you, Tom, the whole kingdom is my native country as well as this town. You may as well say I must not go out of my house if it is on fire as that I must not go out of the town I was born in when it is infected with the plague. I was born in England, and have a right to live in it if I can.

Thomas. But you know every vagrant person may by the laws of England be taken up, and passed back to their last legal settlement.

John. But how shall they make me vagrant? I desire only to travel on, upon my lawful occasions.

Thomas. What lawful occasions can we pretend to travel, or rather wander upon? They will not be put off with words.

John. Is not flying to save our lives a lawful occasion? And do they not all know that the fact is true? We cannot be said to dissemble.

Thomas. But suppose they let us pass, whither shall we go?

John. Anywhere, to save our lives; it is time enough to consider that when we are got out of this town. If I am once out of this dreadful place, I care not where I go.

Thomas. We shall be driven to great extremities. I know not what to think of it.

John. Well, Tom, consider of it a little.

This was about the beginning of July; and though the plague was come forward in the west and north parts of the town, yet all Wapping, as I have observed before, and Redriff, and Ratcliff, and Limehouse, and Poplar, in short, Deptford and Greenwich, all both sides of the river from the Hermitage, and from over against it, quite down to Blackwall, was entirely free; there had not one person died of the plague in all Stepney parish, and not one on the south side of Whitechappel Road, no, not in any parish; and yet the weekly bill was that very week risen up to 1006.

It was a fortnight after this before the two brothers met again, and then the case was a little altered, and the plague was exceedingly advanced and the number greatly increased; the bill was up at 2785, and prodigiously increasing, though still both sides of the river, as below, kept pretty well. But some began to die in Redriff, and about five or six in Ratcliff Highway, when the sailmaker came to his brother John express, and in some fright; for he was absolutely warned out of his lodging, and had only a week to provide himself. His brother John was in as bad a case, for he was quite out, and had only begged leave of his master, the biscuit-maker, to lodge in an outhouse belonging to his workhouse, where he only lay upon straw, with some biscuit-sacks, or bread-sacks, as they called them, laid upon it, and some of the same sacks to cover him.

Here they resolved (seeing all employment being at an end, and no work or wages to be had), they would make the best of their way to get out of the reach of the dreadful infection, and, being as good husbands as they could, would endeavour to live upon what they had as long as it would last, and then work for more if they could get work anywhere, of any kind, let it be what it would.

While they were considering to put this resolution in practice in the best manner they could, the third man, who was acquainted very well with the sailmaker, came to know of the design, and got leave to be one of the number; and thus they prepared to set out.

It happened that they had not an equal share of money; but as the sailmaker, who had the best stock, was, besides his being lame, the most unfit to expect to get anything by working in the country, so he was content that what money they had should all go into one public stock, on condition that whatever any one of them could gain more than another, it should without any grudging be all added to the public stock.

They resolved to load themselves with as little baggage as possible because they resolved at first to travel on foot, and to go a great way that they might, if possible, be effectually safe; and a great many consultations they had with themselves before they could agree about what way they should travel, which they were so far from adjusting that even to the morning they set out they were not resolved on it.

At last the seaman put in a hint that determined it. 'First,' says he, 'the weather is very hot, and therefore I am for travelling north, that we may not have the sun upon our faces and beating on our breasts, which will heat and suffocate us; and I have been told', says he, 'that it is not good to overheat our blood at a time when, for aught we know, the infection may be in the very air. In the next place,' says he, 'I am for going the way that may be contrary to the wind, as it may blow when we set out, that we may not have the wind blow the air of the city on our backs as we go.' These two cautions were approved of, if it could be brought so to hit that the wind might not be in the south when they set out to go north.

John the baker, who had been a soldier, then put in his opinion. 'First,' says he, 'we none of us expect to get any lodging on the road, and it will be a little too hard to lie just in the open air. Though it be warm weather, yet it may be wet and damp, and we have a double reason to take care of our healths at such a time as this; and therefore,' says he, 'you, brother Tom, that are a sailmaker, might easily make us a little tent, and I will undertake to set it up every night, and take it down, and a fig for all the inns in England; if we have a good tent over our heads we shall do well enough.'

The joiner opposed this, and told them, let them leave that to him; he would undertake to build them a house every night with his hatchet and mallet, though he had no other tools, which should be fully to their satisfaction, and as good as a tent.

The soldier and the joiner disputed that point some time, but at last the soldier carried it for a tent. The only objection against it was, that it must be carried with them, and that would increase their baggage too much, the weather being hot; but the sailmaker had a piece of good hap, fell in which made that easy, for his master whom he worked for, having a rope-walk as well as sailmaking trade, had a little, poor horse that he made no use of then; and being willing to assist the three honest men, he gave them the horse for the carrying their baggage; also for a small matter of three days' work that his man did for him before he went, he let him have an old top-gallant sail that was worn out, but was sufficient and more than enough to make a very good tent. The soldier showed how to shape it, and they soon by his direction made their tent, and fitted it with poles or staves for the purpose; and thus they were furnished for their journey, viz., three men, one tent, one horse, one gun—for the soldier would not go without arms, for now he said he was no more a biscuit-baker, but a trooper.

The joiner had a small bag of tools such as might be useful if he should get any work abroad, as well for their subsistence as his own. What money they had they brought all into one public stock, and thus they began their journey. It seems that in the morning when they set out the wind blew, as the sailor said, by his pocket-compass, at N.W. by W. So they directed, or rather resolved to direct, their course N.W.

But then a difficulty came in their way, that, as they set out from the hither end of Wapping, near the Hermitage, and that the plague was now very violent, especially on the north side of the city, as in Shoreditch and Cripplegate parish, they did not think it safe for them to go near those parts; so they went away east through Ratcliff Highway as far as Ratcliff Cross, and leaving Stepney Church still on their left hand, being afraid to come up from Ratcliff Cross to Mile End, because they must come just by the churchyard, and because the wind, that seemed to blow more from the west, blew directly from the side of the city where the plague was hottest. So, I say, leaving Stepney they fetched a long compass, and going to Poplar and Bromley, came into the great road just at Bow.

Here the watch placed upon Bow Bridge would have questioned them, but they, crossing the road into a narrow way that turns out of the hither end of the town of Bow to Old Ford, avoided any inquiry there, and travelled to Old Ford. The constables everywhere were upon their guard not so much, It seems, to stop people passing by as to stop them from taking up their abode in their towns, and withal because of a report that was newly raised at that time: and that, indeed, was not very improbable, viz., that the poor people in London, being distressed and starved for want of work, and by that means for want of bread, were up in arms and had raised a tumult, and that they would come out to all the towns round to plunder for bread. This, I say, was only a rumour, and it was very well it was no more. But it was not so far off from being a reality as it has been thought, for in a few weeks more the poor people became so desperate by the calamity they suffered that they were with great difficulty kept from going out into the fields and towns, and tearing all in pieces wherever they came; and, as I have observed before, nothing hindered them but that the plague raged so violently and fell in upon them so furiously that they rather went to the grave by thousands than into the fields in mobs by thousands; for, in the parts about the parishes of St Sepulcher, Clarkenwell, Cripplegate, Bishopsgate, and Shoreditch, which were the places where the mob began to threaten, the distemper came on so furiously that there died in those few parishes even then, before the plague was come to its height, no less than 5361 people in the first three weeks in August; when at the same time the parts about Wapping, Radcliff, and Rotherhithe were, as before described, hardly touched, or but very lightly; so that in a word though, as I said before, the good management of the Lord Mayor and justices did much to prevent the rage and desperation of the people from breaking out in rabbles and tumults, and in short from the poor plundering the rich,—I say, though they did much, the dead-carts did more: for as I have said that in five parishes only there died above 5000 in twenty days, so there might be probably three times that number sick all that time; for some recovered, and great numbers fell sick every day and died afterwards. Besides, I must still be allowed to say that if the bills of mortality said five thousand, I always believed it was near twice as many in reality, there being no room to believe that the account they gave was right, or that indeed they were among such confusions as I saw them in, in any condition to keep an exact account.

But to return to my travellers. Here they were only examined, and as they seemed rather coming from the country than from the city, they found the people the easier with them; that they talked to them, let them come into a public-house where the constable and his warders were, and gave them drink and some victuals which greatly refreshed and encouraged them; and here it came into their heads to say, when they should be inquired of afterwards, not that they came from London, but that they came out of Essex.

To forward this little fraud, they obtained so much favour of the constable at Old Ford as to give them a certificate of their passing from Essex through that village, and that they had not been at London; which, though false in the common acceptance of London in the county, yet was literally true, Wapping or Ratcliff being no part either of the city or liberty.

This certificate directed to the next constable that was at Homerton, one of the hamlets of the parish of Hackney, was so serviceable to them that it procured them, not a free passage there only, but a full certificate of health from a justice of the peace, who upon the constable's application granted it without much difficulty; and thus they passed through the long divided town of Hackney (for it lay then in several separated hamlets), and travelled on till they came into the great north road on the top of Stamford Hill.

By this time they began to be weary, and so in the back-road from Hackney, a little before it opened into the said great road, they resolved to set up their tent and encamp for the first night, which they did accordingly, with this addition, that finding a barn, or a building like a barn, and first searching as well as they could to be sure there was nobody in it, they set up their tent, with the head of it against the barn. This they did also because the wind blew that night very high, and they were but young at such a way of lodging, as well as at the managing their tent.

Here they went to sleep; but the joiner, a grave and sober man, and not pleased with their lying at this loose rate the first night, could not sleep, and resolved, after trying to sleep to no purpose, that he would get out, and, taking the gun in his hand, stand sentinel and guard his companions. So with the gun in his hand, he walked to and again before the barn, for that stood in the field near the road, but within the hedge. He had not been long upon the scout but he heard a noise of people coming on, as if it had been a great number, and they came on, as he thought, directly towards the barn. He did not presently awake his companions; but in a few minutes more, their noise growing louder and louder, the biscuit-baker called to him and asked him what was the matter, and quickly started out too. The other, being the lame sailmaker and most weary, lay still in the tent.

As they expected, so the people whom they had heard came on directly to the barn, when one of our travellers challenged, like soldiers upon the guard, with 'Who comes there?' The people did not answer immediately, but one of them speaking to another that was behind him, 'Alas! alas! we are all disappointed,' says he. 'Here are some people before us; the barn is taken up.'

They all stopped upon that, as under some surprise, and it seems there was about thirteen of them in all, and some women among them. They consulted together what they should do, and by their discourse our travellers soon found they were poor, distressed people too, like themselves, seeking shelter and safety; and besides, our travellers had no need to be afraid of their coming up to disturb them, for as soon as they heard the words, 'Who comes there?' these could hear the women say, as if frighted, 'Do not go near them. How do you know but they may have the plague?' And when one of the men said, 'Let us but speak to them', the women said, 'No, don't by any means. We have escaped thus far by the goodness of God; do not let us run into danger now, we beseech you.'

Our travellers found by this that they were a good, sober sort of people, and flying for their lives, as they were; and, as they were encouraged by it, so John said to the joiner, his comrade, 'Let us encourage them too as much as we can'; so he called to them, 'Hark ye, good people,' says the joiner, 'we find by your talk that you are flying from the same dreadful enemy as we are. Do not be afraid of us; we are only three poor men of us. If you are free from the distemper you shall not be hurt by us. We are not in the barn, but in a little tent here in the outside, and we will remove for you; we can set up our tent again immediately anywhere else'; and upon this a parley began between the joiner, whose name was Richard, and one of their men, who said his name was Ford.

Ford. And do you assure us that you are all sound men?

Richard. Nay, we are concerned to tell you of it, that you may not be uneasy or think yourselves in danger; but you see we do not desire you should put yourselves into any danger, and therefore I tell you that we have not made use of the barn, so we will remove from it, that you may be safe and we also.

Ford. That is very kind and charitable; but if we have reason to be satisfied that you are sound and free from the visitation, why should we make you remove now you are settled in your lodging, and, it may be, are laid down to rest? We will go into the barn, if you please, to rest ourselves a while, and we need not disturb you.

Richard. Well, but you are more than we are. I hope you will assure us that you are all of you sound too, for the danger is as great from you to us as from us to you.

Ford. Blessed be God that some do escape, though it is but few; what may be our portion still we know not, but hitherto we are preserved.

Richard. What part of the town do you come from? Was the plague come to the places where you lived?

Ford. Ay, ay, in a most frightful and terrible manner, or else we had not fled away as we do; but we believe there will be very few left alive behind us.

Richard. What part do you come from?

Ford. We are most of us of Cripplegate parish, only two or three of Clerkenwell parish, but on the hither side.

Richard. How then was it that you came away no sooner?

Ford. We have been away some time, and kept together as well as we could at the hither end of Islington, where we got leave to lie in an old uninhabited house, and had some bedding and conveniences of our own that we brought with us; but the plague is come up into Islington too, and a house next door to our poor dwelling was infected and shut up; and we are come away in a fright.

Richard. And what way are you going?

Ford. As our lot shall cast us; we know not whither, but God will guide those that look up to Him.

They parleyed no further at that time, but came all up to the barn, and with some difficulty got into it. There was nothing but hay in the barn, but it was almost full of that, and they accommodated themselves as well as they could, and went to rest; but our travellers observed that before they went to sleep an ancient man who it seems was father of one of the women, went to prayer with all the company, recommending themselves to the blessing and direction of Providence, before they went to sleep.

It was soon day at that time of the year, and as Richard the joiner had kept guard the first part of the night, so John the soldier relieved him, and he had the post in the morning, and they began to be acquainted with one another. It seems when they left Islington they intended to have gone north, away to Highgate, but were stopped at Holloway, and there they would not let them pass; so they crossed over the fields and hills to the eastward, and came out at the Boarded River, and so avoiding the towns, they left Hornsey on the left hand and Newington on the right hand, and came into the great road about Stamford Hill on that side, as the three travellers had done on the other side. And now they had thoughts of going over the river in the marshes, and make forwards to Epping Forest, where they hoped they should get leave to rest. It seems they were not poor, at least not so poor as to be in want; at least they had enough to subsist them moderately for two or three months, when, as they said, they were in hopes the cold weather would check the infection, or at least the violence of it would have spent itself, and would abate, if it were only for want of people left alive to be infected.

This was much the fate of our three travellers, only that they seemed to be the better furnished for travelling, and had it in their view to go farther off; for as to the first, they did not propose to go farther than one day's journey, that so they might have intelligence every two or three days how things were at London.

But here our travellers found themselves under an unexpected inconvenience: namely that of their horse, for by means of the horse to carry their baggage they were obliged to keep in the road, whereas the people of this other band went over the fields or roads, path or no path, way or no way, as they pleased; neither had they any occasion to pass through any town, or come near any town, other than to buy such things as they wanted for their necessary subsistence, and in that indeed they were put to much difficulty; of which in its place.

But our three travellers were obliged to keep the road, or else they must commit spoil, and do the country a great deal of damage in breaking down fences and gates to go over enclosed fields, which they were loth to do if they could help it.

Our three travellers, however, had a great mind to join themselves to this company and take their lot with them; and after some discourse they laid aside their first design which looked northward, and resolved to follow the other into Essex; so in the morning they took up their tent and loaded their horse, and away they travelled all together.

They had some difficulty in passing the ferry at the river-side, the ferryman being afraid of them; but after some parley at a distance, the ferryman was content to bring his boat to a place distant from the usual ferry, and leave it there for them to take it; so putting themselves over, he directed them to leave the boat, and he, having another boat, said he would fetch it again, which it seems, however, he did not do for above eight days.

Here, giving the ferryman money beforehand, they had a supply of victuals and drink, which he brought and left in the boat for them; but not without, as I said, having received the money beforehand. But now our travellers were at a great loss and difficulty how to get the horse over, the boat being small and not fit for it: and at last could not do it without unloading the baggage and making him swim over.

From the river they travelled towards the forest, but when they came to Walthamstow the people of that town denied to admit them, as was the case everywhere. The constables and their watchmen kept them off at a distance and parleyed with them. They gave the same account of themselves as before, but these gave no credit to what they said, giving it for a reason that two or three companies had already come that way and made the like pretences, but that they had given several people the distemper in the towns where they had passed; and had been afterwards so hardly used by the country (though with justice, too, as they had deserved) that about Brentwood, or that way, several of them perished in the fields—whether of the plague or of mere want and distress they could not tell.

This was a good reason indeed why the people of Walthamstow should be very cautious, and why they should resolve not to entertain anybody that they were not well satisfied of. But, as Richard the joiner and one of the other men who parleyed with them told them, it was no reason why they should block up the roads and refuse to let people pass through the town, and who asked nothing of them but to go through the street; that if their people were afraid of them, they might go into their houses and shut their doors; they would neither show them civility nor incivility, but go on about their business.

The constables and attendants, not to be persuaded by reason, continued obstinate, and would hearken to nothing; so the two men that talked with them went back to their fellows to consult what was to be done. It was very discouraging in the whole, and they knew not what to do for a good while; but at last John the soldier and biscuit-maker, considering a while, 'Come,' says he, 'leave the rest of the parley to me.' He had not appeared yet, so he sets the joiner, Richard, to work to cut some poles out of the trees and shape them as like guns as he could, and in a little time he had five or six fair muskets, which at a distance would not be known; and about the part where the lock of a gun is he caused them to wrap cloth and rags such as they had, as soldiers do in wet weather to preserve the locks of their pieces from rust; the rest was discoloured with clay or mud, such as they could get; and all this while the rest of them sat under the trees by his direction, in two or three bodies, where they made fires at a good distance from one another.

While this was doing he advanced himself and two or three with him, and set up their tent in the lane within sight of the barrier which the town's men had made, and set a sentinel just by it with the real gun, the only one they had, and who walked to and fro with the gun on his shoulder, so as that the people of the town might see them. Also, he tied the horse to a gate in the hedge just by, and got some dry sticks together and kindled a fire on the other side of the tent, so that the people of the town could see the fire and the smoke, but could not see what they were doing at it.

After the country people had looked upon them very earnestly a great while, and, by all that they could see, could not but suppose that they were a great many in company, they began to be uneasy, not for their going away, but for staying where they were; and above all, perceiving they had horses and arms, for they had seen one horse and one gun at the tent, and they had seen others of them walk about the field on the inside of the hedge by the side of the lane with their muskets, as they took them to be, shouldered; I say, upon such a sight as this, you may be assured they were alarmed and terribly frighted, and it seems they went to a justice of the peace to know what they should do. What the justice advised them to I know not, but towards the evening they called from the barrier, as above, to the sentinel at the tent.

'What do you want?' says John.[1]

'Why, what do you intend to do?' says the constable. 'To do,' says John; 'what would you have us to do?' Constable. Why don't you be gone? What do you stay there for?

John. Why do you stop us on the king's highway, and pretend to refuse us leave to go on our way?

Constable. We are not bound to tell you our reason, though we did let you know it was because of the plague.

John. We told you we were all sound and free from the plague, which we were not bound to have satisfied you of, and yet you pretend to stop us on the highway.

Constable. We have a right to stop it up, and our own safety obliges us to it. Besides, this is not the king's highway; 'tis a way upon sufferance. You see here is a gate, and if we do let people pass here, we make them pay toll.

John. We have a right to seek our own safety as well as you, and you may see we are flying for our lives: and 'tis very unchristian and unjust to stop us.

Constable. You may go back from whence you came; we do not hinder you from that.

John. No; it is a stronger enemy than you that keeps us from doing that, or else we should not have come hither.

Constable. Well, you may go any other way, then.

John. No, no; I suppose you see we are able to send you going, and all the people of your parish, and come through your town when we will; but since you have stopped us here, we are content. You see we have encamped here, and here we will live. We hope you will furnish us with victuals.

Constable. We furnish you! What mean you by that?

John. Why, you would not have us starve, would you? If you stop us here, you must keep us.

Constable. You will be ill kept at our maintenance.

John. If you stint us, we shall make ourselves the better allowance.

Constable. Why, you will not pretend to quarter upon us by force, will you?

John. We have offered no violence to you yet. Why do you seem to oblige us to it? I am an old soldier, and cannot starve, and if you think that we shall be obliged to go back for want of provisions, you are mistaken.

Constable. Since you threaten us, we shall take care to be strong enough for you. I have orders to raise the county upon you.

John. It is you that threaten, not we. And since you are for mischief, you cannot blame us if we do not give you time for it; we shall begin our march in a few minutes.[2]

Constable. What is it you demand of us?

John. At first we desired nothing of you but leave to go through the town; we should have offered no injury to any of you, neither would you have had any injury or loss by us. We are not thieves, but poor people in distress, and flying from the dreadful plague in London, which devours thousands every week. We wonder how you could be so unmerciful!

Constable. Self-preservation obliges us.

John. What! To shut up your compassion in a case of such distress as this?

Constable. Well, if you will pass over the fields on your left hand, and behind that part of the town, I will endeavour to have gates opened for you.

John. Our horsemen[3] cannot pass with our baggage that way; it does not lead into the road that we want to go, and why should you force us out of the road? Besides, you have kept us here all day without any provisions but such as we brought with us. I think you ought to send us some provisions for our relief.

Constable. If you will go another way we will send you some provisions.

John. That is the way to have all the towns in the county stop up the ways against us.

Constable. If they all furnish you with food, what will you be the worse? I see you have tents; you want no lodging.

John. Well, what quantity of provisions will you send us?

Constable. How many are you?

John. Nay, we do not ask enough for all our company; we are in three companies. If you will send us bread for twenty men and about six or seven women for three days, and show us the way over the field you speak of, we desire not to put your people into any fear for us; we will go out of our way to oblige you, though we are as free from infection as you are.[4]

Constable. And will you assure us that your other people shall offer us no new disturbance?

John. No, no you may depend on it.

Constable. You must oblige yourself, too, that none of your people shall come a step nearer than where the provisions we send you shall be set down.

John. I answer for it we will not.

Accordingly they sent to the place twenty loaves of bread and three or four large pieces of good beef, and opened some gates, through which they passed; but none of them had courage so much as to look out to see them go, and, as it was evening, if they had looked they could not have seen them as to know how few they were.

This was John the soldier's management. But this gave such an alarm to the county, that had they really been two or three hundred the whole county would have been raised upon them, and they would have been sent to prison, or perhaps knocked on the head.

They were soon made sensible of this, for two days afterwards they found several parties of horsemen and footmen also about, in pursuit of three companies of men, armed, as they said, with muskets, who were broke out from London and had the plague upon them, and that were not only spreading the distemper among the people, but plundering the country.

As they saw now the consequence of their case, they soon saw the danger they were in; so they resolved by the advice also of the old soldier to divide themselves again. John and his two comrades, with the horse, went away, as if towards Waltham; the other in two companies, but all a little asunder, and went towards Epping.

The first night they encamped all in the forest, and not far off of one another, but not setting up the tent, lest that should discover them. On the other hand, Richard went to work with his axe and his hatchet, and cutting down branches of trees, he built three tents or hovels, in which they all encamped with as much convenience as they could expect.

The provisions they had at Walthamstow served them very plentifully this night; and as for the next, they left it to Providence. They had fared so well with the old soldier's conduct that they now willingly made him their leader, and the first of his conduct appeared to be very good. He told them that they were now at a proper distance enough from London; that as they need not be immediately beholden to the country for relief, so they ought to be as careful the country did not infect them as that they did not infect the country; that what little money they had, they must be as frugal of as they could; that as he would not have them think of offering the country any violence, so they must endeavour to make the sense of their condition go as far with the country as it could. They all referred themselves to his direction, so they left their three houses standing, and the next day went away towards Epping. The captain also (for so they now called him), and his two fellow-travellers, laid aside their design of going to Waltham, and all went together.

When they came near Epping they halted, choosing out a proper place in the open forest, not very near the highway, but not far out of it on the north side, under a little cluster of low pollard-trees. Here they pitched their little camp—which consisted of three large tents or huts made of poles which their carpenter, and such as were his assistants, cut down and fixed in the ground in a circle, binding all the small ends together at the top and thickening the sides with boughs of trees and bushes, so that they were completely close and warm. They had, besides this, a little tent where the women lay by themselves, and a hut to put the horse in.

It happened that the next day, or next but one, was market-day at Epping, when Captain John and one of the other men went to market and bought some provisions; that is to say, bread, and some mutton and beef; and two of the women went separately, as if they had not belonged to the rest, and bought more. John took the horse to bring it home, and the sack which the carpenter carried his tools in, to put it in. The carpenter went to work and made them benches and stools to sit on, such as the wood he could get would afford, and a kind of table to dine on.

They were taken no notice of for two or three days, but after that abundance of people ran out of the town to look at them, and all the country was alarmed about them. The people at first seemed afraid to come near them; and, on the other hand, they desired the people to keep off, for there was a rumour that the plague was at Waltham, and that it had been in Epping two or three days; so John called out to them not to come to them, 'for,' says he, 'we are all whole and sound people here, and we would not have you bring the plague among us, nor pretend we brought it among you.'

After this the parish officers came up to them and parleyed with them at a distance, and desired to know who they were, and by what authority they pretended to fix their stand at that place. John answered very frankly, they were poor distressed people from London who, foreseeing the misery they should be reduced to if plague spread into the city, had fled out in time for their lives, and, having no acquaintance or relations to fly to, had first taken up at Islington; but, the plague being come into that town, were fled farther; and as they supposed that the people of Epping might have refused them coming into their town, they had pitched their tents thus in the open field and in the forest, being willing to bear all the hardships of such a disconsolate lodging rather than have any one think or be afraid that they should receive injury by them.

At first the Epping people talked roughly to them, and told them they must remove; that this was no place for them; and that they pretended to be sound and well, but that they might be infected with the plague for aught they knew, and might infect the whole country, and they could not suffer them there.

John argued very calmly with them a great while, and told them that London was the place by which they—that is, the townsmen of Epping and all the country round them—subsisted; to whom they sold the produce of their lands, and out of whom they made their rent of their farms; and to be so cruel to the inhabitants of London, or to any of those by whom they gained so much, was very hard, and they would be loth to have it remembered hereafter, and have it told how barbarous, how inhospitable, and how unkind they were to the people of London when they fled from the face of the most terrible enemy in the world; that it would be enough to make the name of an Epping man hateful through all the city, and to have the rabble stone them in the very streets whenever they came so much as to market; that they were not yet secure from being visited themselves, and that, as he heard, Waltham was already; that they would think it very hard that when any of them fled for fear before they were touched, they should be denied the liberty of lying so much as in the open fields.

The Epping men told them again, that they, indeed, said they were sound and free from the infection, but that they had no assurance of it; and that it was reported that there had been a great rabble of people at Walthamstow, who made such pretences of being sound as they did, but that they threatened to plunder the town and force their way, whether the parish officers would or no; that there were near two hundred of them, and had arms and tents like Low Country soldiers; that they extorted provisions from the town, by threatening them with living upon them at free quarter, showing their arms, and talking in the language of soldiers; and that several of them being gone away toward Rumford and Brentwood, the country had been infected by them, and the plague spread into both those large towns, so that the people durst not go to market there as usual; that it was very likely they were some of that party; and if so, they deserved to be sent to the county jail, and be secured till they had made satisfaction for the damage they had done, and for the terror and fright they had put the country into.

John answered that what other people had done was nothing to them; that they assured them they were all of one company; that they had never been more in number than they saw them at that time (which, by the way, was very true); that they came out in two separate companies, but joined by the way, their cases being the same; that they were ready to give what account of themselves anybody could desire of them, and to give in their names and places of abode, that so they might be called to an account for any disorder that they might be guilty of; that the townsmen might see they were content to live hardly, and only desired a little room to breathe in on the forest where it was wholesome; for where it was not they could not stay, and would decamp if they found it otherwise there.

'But,' said the townsmen, 'we have a great charge of poor upon our hands already, and we must take care not to increase it; we suppose you can give us no security against your being chargeable to our parish and to the inhabitants, any more than you can of being dangerous to us as to the infection.'

'Why, look you,' says John, 'as to being chargeable to you, we hope we shall not. If you will relieve us with provisions for our present necessity, we will be very thankful; as we all lived without charity when we were at home, so we will oblige ourselves fully to repay you, if God pleases to bring us back to our own families and houses in safety, and to restore health to the people of London.

'As to our dying here: we assure you, if any of us die, we that survive will bury them, and put you to no expense, except it should be that we should all die; and then, indeed, the last man not being able to bury himself, would put you to that single expense which I am persuaded', says John, 'he would leave enough behind him to pay you for the expense of.

'On the other hand,' says John, 'if you shut up all bowels of compassion, and not relieve us at all, we shall not extort anything by violence or steal from any one; but when what little we have is spent, if we perish for want, God's will be done.'

John wrought so upon the townsmen, by talking thus rationally and smoothly to them, that they went away; and though they did not give any consent to their staying there, yet they did not molest them; and the poor people continued there three or four days longer without any disturbance. In this time they had got some remote acquaintance with a victualling-house at the outskirts of the town, to whom they called at a distance to bring some little things that they wanted, and which they caused to be set down at a distance, and always paid for very honestly.

During this time the younger people of the town came frequently pretty near them, and would stand and look at them, and sometimes talk with them at some space between; and particularly it was observed that the first Sabbath-day the poor people kept retired, worshipped God together, and were heard to sing psalms.

These things, and a quiet, inoffensive behaviour, began to get them the good opinion of the country, and people began to pity them and speak very well of them; the consequence of which was, that upon the occasion of a very wet, rainy night, a certain gentleman who lived in the neighbourhood sent them a little cart with twelve trusses or bundles of straw, as well for them to lodge upon as to cover and thatch their huts and to keep them dry. The minister of a parish not far off, not knowing of the other, sent them also about two bushels of wheat and half a bushel of white peas.

They were very thankful, to be sure, for this relief, and particularly the straw was a—very great comfort to them; for though the ingenious carpenter had made frames for them to lie in like troughs, and filled them with leaves of trees, and such things as they could get, and had cut all their tent-cloth out to make coverlids, yet they lay damp and hard and unwholesome till this straw came, which was to them like feather-beds, and, as John said, more welcome than feather-beds would have been at another time.

This gentleman and the minister having thus begun, and given an example of charity to these wanderers, others quickly followed, and they received every day some benevolence or other from the people, but chiefly from the gentlemen who dwelt in the country round them. Some sent them chairs, stools, tables, and such household things as they gave notice they wanted; some sent them blankets, rugs, and coverlids, some earthenware, and some kitchen ware for ordering their food.

Encouraged by this good usage, their carpenter in a few days built them a large shed or house with rafters, and a roof in form, and an upper floor, in which they lodged warm: for the weather began to be damp and cold in the beginning of September. But this house, being well thatched, and the sides and roof made very thick, kept out the cold well enough. He made, also, an earthen wall at one end with a chimney in it, and another of the company, with a vast deal of trouble and pains, made a funnel to the chimney to carry out the smoke.

Here they lived comfortably, though coarsely, till the beginning of September, when they had the bad news to hear, whether true or not, that the plague, which was very hot at Waltham Abbey on one side and at Rumford and Brentwood on the other side, was also coming to Epping, to Woodford, and to most of the towns upon the Forest, and which, as they said, was brought down among them chiefly by the higlers, and such people as went to and from London with provisions.

If this was true, it was an evident contradiction to that report which was afterwards spread all over England, but which, as I have said, I cannot confirm of my own knowledge: namely, that the market-people carrying provisions to the city never got the infection or carried it back into the country; both which, I have been assured, has been false.

It might be that they were preserved even beyond expectation, though not to a miracle, that abundance went and came and were not touched; and that was much for the encouragement of the poor people of London, who had been completely miserable if the people that brought provisions to the markets had not been many times wonderfully preserved, or at least more preserved than could be reasonably expected.

But now these new inmates began to be disturbed more effectually, for the towns about them were really infected, and they began to be afraid to trust one another so much as to go abroad for such things as they wanted, and this pinched them very hard, for now they had little or nothing but what the charitable gentlemen of the country supplied them with. But, for their encouragement, it happened that other gentlemen in the country who had not sent them anything before, began to hear of them and supply them, and one sent them a large pig—that is to say, a porker—another two sheep, and another sent them a calf. In short, they had meat enough, and sometimes had cheese and milk, and all such things. They were chiefly put to it for bread, for when the gentlemen sent them corn they had nowhere to bake it or to grind it. This made them eat the first two bushel of wheat that was sent them in parched corn, as the Israelites of old did, without grinding or making bread of it.

At last they found means to carry their corn to a windmill near Woodford, where they had it ground, and afterwards the biscuit-maker made a hearth so hollow and dry that he could bake biscuit-cakes tolerably well; and thus they came into a condition to live without any assistance or supplies from the towns; and it was well they did, for the country was soon after fully infected, and about 120 were said to have died of the distemper in the villages near them, which was a terrible thing to them.

On this they called a new council, and now the towns had no need to be afraid they should settle near them; but, on the contrary, several families of the poorer sort of the inhabitants quitted their houses and built huts in the forest after the same manner as they had done. But it was observed that several of these poor people that had so removed had the sickness even in their huts or booths; the reason of which was plain, namely, not because they removed into the air, but, (1) because they did not remove time enough; that is to say, not till, by openly conversing with the other people their neighbours, they had the distemper upon them, or (as may be said) among them, and so carried it about them whither they went. Or (2) because they were not careful enough, after they were safely removed out of the towns, not to come in again and mingle with the diseased people.

But be it which of these it will, when our travellers began to perceive that the plague was not only in the towns, but even in the tents and huts on the forest near them, they began then not only to be afraid, but to think of decamping and removing; for had they stayed they would have been in manifest danger of their lives.

It is not to be wondered that they were greatly afflicted at being obliged to quit the place where they had been so kindly received, and where they had been treated with so much humanity and charity; but necessity and the hazard of life, which they came out so far to preserve, prevailed with them, and they saw no remedy. John, however, thought of a remedy for their present misfortune: namely, that he would first acquaint that gentleman who was their principal benefactor with the distress they were in, and to crave his assistance and advice.

The good, charitable gentleman encouraged them to quit the Place for fear they should be cut off from any retreat at all by the violence of the distemper; but whither they should go, that he found very hard to direct them to. At last John asked of him whether he, being a justice of the peace, would give them certificates of health to other justices whom they might come before; that so whatever might be their lot, they might not be repulsed now they had been also so long from London. This his worship immediately granted, and gave them proper letters of health, and from thence they were at liberty to travel whither they pleased.

Accordingly they had a full certificate of health, intimating that they had resided in a village in the county of Essex so long that, being examined and scrutinised sufficiently, and having been retired from all conversation for above forty days, without any appearance of sickness, they were therefore certainly concluded to be sound men, and might be safely entertained anywhere, having at last removed rather for fear of the plague which was come into such a town, rather than for having any signal of infection upon them, or upon any belonging to them.

With this certificate they removed, though with great reluctance; and John inclining not to go far from home, they moved towards the marshes on the side of Waltham. But here they found a man who, it seems, kept a weir or stop upon the river, made to raise the water for the barges which go up and down the river, and he terrified them with dismal stories of the sickness having been spread into all the towns on the river and near the river, on the side of Middlesex and Hertfordshire; that is to say, into Waltham, Waltham Cross, Enfield, and Ware, and all the towns on the road, that they were afraid to go that way; though it seems the man imposed upon them, for that the thing was not really true.

However, it terrified them, and they resolved to move across the forest towards Rumford and Brentwood; but they heard that there were numbers of people fled out of London that way, who lay up and down in the forest called Henalt Forest, reaching near Rumford, and who, having no subsistence or habitation, not only lived oddly and suffered great extremities in the woods and fields for want of relief, but were said to be made so desperate by those extremities as that they offered many violences to the county, robbed and plundered, and killed cattle, and the like; that others, building huts and hovels by the roadside, begged, and that with an importunity next door to demanding relief; so that the county was very uneasy, and had been obliged to take some of them up.

This in the first place intimated to them, that they would be sure to find the charity and kindness of the county, which they had found here where they were before, hardened and shut up against them; and that, on the other hand, they would be questioned wherever they came, and would be in danger of violence from others in like cases as themselves.

Upon all these considerations John, their captain, in all their names, went back to their good friend and benefactor, who had relieved them before, and laying their case truly before him, humbly asked his advice; and he as kindly advised them to take up their old quarters again, or if not, to remove but a little farther out of the road, and directed them to a proper place for them; and as they really wanted some house rather than huts to shelter them at that time of the year, it growing on towards Michaelmas, they found an old decayed house which had been formerly some cottage or little habitation but was so out of repair as scarce habitable; and by the consent of a farmer to whose farm it belonged, they got leave to make what use of it they could.

The ingenious joiner, and all the rest, by his directions went to work with it, and in a very few days made it capable to shelter them all in case of bad weather; and in which there was an old chimney and old oven, though both lying in ruins; yet they made them both fit for use, and, raising additions, sheds, and leantos on every side, they soon made the house capable to hold them all.

They chiefly wanted boards to make window-shutters, floors, doors, and several other things; but as the gentlemen above favoured them, and the country was by that means made easy with them, and above all, that they were known to be all sound and in good health, everybody helped them with what they could spare.

Here they encamped for good and all, and resolved to remove no more. They saw plainly how terribly alarmed that county was everywhere at anybody that came from London, and that they should have no admittance anywhere but with the utmost difficulty; at least no friendly reception and assistance as they had received here.

Now, although they received great assistance and encouragement from the country gentlemen and from the people round about them, yet they were put to great straits: for the weather grew cold and wet in October and November, and they had not been used to so much hardship; so that they got colds in their limbs, and distempers, but never had the infection; and thus about December they came home to the city again.

I give this story thus at large, principally to give an account what became of the great numbers of people which immediately appeared in the city as soon as the sickness abated; for, as I have said, great numbers of those that were able and had retreats in the country fled to those retreats. So, when it was increased to such a frightful extremity as I have related, the middling people who had not friends fled to all parts of the country where they could get shelter, as well those that had money to relieve themselves as those that had not. Those that had money always fled farthest, because they were able to subsist themselves; but those who were empty suffered, as I have said, great hardships, and were often driven by necessity to relieve their wants at the expense of the country. By that means the country was made very uneasy at them, and sometimes took them up; though even then they scarce knew what to do with them, and were always very backward to punish them, but often, too, they forced them from place to place till they were obliged to come back again to London.

I have, since my knowing this story of John and his brother, inquired and found that there were a great many of the poor disconsolate people, as above, fled into the country every way; and some of them got little sheds and barns and outhouses to live in, where they could obtain so much kindness of the country, and especially where they had any the least satisfactory account to give of themselves, and particularly that they did not come out of London too late. But others, and that in great numbers, built themselves little huts and retreats in the fields and woods, and lived like hermits in holes and caves, or any place they could find, and where, we may be sure, they suffered great extremities, such that many of them were obliged to come back again whatever the danger was; and so those little huts were often found empty, and the country people supposed the inhabitants lay dead in them of the plague, and would not go near them for fear—no, not in a great while; nor is it unlikely but that some of the unhappy wanderers might die so all alone, even sometimes for want of help, as particularly in one tent or hut was found a man dead, and on the gate of a field just by was cut with his knife in uneven letters the following words, by which it may be supposed the other man escaped, or that, one dying first, the other buried him as well as he could:—

> O mIsErY!
> We BoTH ShaLL DyE,
> WoE, WoE.

I have given an account already of what I found to have been the case down the river among the seafaring men; how the ships lay in the offing, as it's called, in rows or lines astern of one another, quite down from the Pool as far as I could see. I have been told that they lay in the same manner quite down the river as low as Gravesend, and some far beyond: even everywhere or in every place where they could ride with safety as to wind and weather; nor did I ever hear that the plague reached to any of the people on board those ships—except such as lay up in the Pool, or as high as Deptford Reach, although the people went frequently on shore to the country towns and villages and farmers' houses, to buy fresh provisions, fowls, pigs, calves, and the like for their supply.

Likewise I found that the watermen on the river above the bridge found means to convey themselves away up the river as far as they could go, and that they had, many of them, their whole families in their boats, covered with tilts and bales, as they call them, and furnished with straw within for their lodging, and that they lay thus all along by the shore in the marshes, some of them setting up little tents with their sails, and so lying under them on shore in the day, and going into their boats at night; and in this manner, as I have heard, the river-sides were lined with boats and people as long as they had anything to subsist on, or could get anything of the country; and indeed the country people, as well Gentlemen as others, on these and all other occasions, were very forward to relieve them—but they were by no means willing to receive them into their towns and houses, and for that we cannot blame them.

There was one unhappy citizen within my knowledge who had been visited in a dreadful manner, so that his wife and all his children were dead, and himself and two servants only left, with an elderly woman, a near relation, who had nursed those that were dead as well as she could. This disconsolate man goes to a village near the town, though not within the bills of mortality, and finding an empty house there, inquires out the owner, and took the house. After a few days he got a cart and loaded it with goods, and carries them down to the house; the people of the village opposed his driving the cart along; but with some arguings and some force, the men that drove the cart along got through the street up to the door of the house. There the constable resisted them again, and would not let them be brought in. The man caused the goods to be unloaden and laid at the door, and sent the cart away; upon which they carried the man before a justice of peace; that is to say, they commanded him to go, which he did. The justice ordered him to cause the cart to fetch away the goods again, which he refused to do; upon which the justice ordered the constable to pursue the carters and fetch them back, and make them reload the goods and carry them away, or to set them in the stocks till they came for further orders; and if they could not find them, nor the man would not consent to take them away, they should cause them to be drawn with hooks from the house-door and burned in the street. The poor distressed man upon this fetched the goods again, but with grievous cries and lamentations at the hardship of his case. But there was no remedy; self-preservation obliged the people to those severities which they would not otherwise have been concerned in. Whether this poor man lived or died I cannot tell, but it was reported that he had the plague upon him at that time; and perhaps the people might report that to justify their usage of him; but it was not unlikely that either he or his goods, or both, were dangerous, when his whole family had been dead of the distempers so little a while before.

I know that the inhabitants of the towns adjacent to London were much blamed for cruelty to the poor people that ran from the contagion in their distress, and many very severe things were done, as may be seen from what has been said; but I cannot but say also that, where there was room for charity and assistance to the people, without apparent danger to themselves, they were willing enough to help and relieve them. But as every town were indeed judges in their own case, so the poor people who ran abroad in their extremities were often ill-used and driven back again into the town; and this caused infinite exclamations and outcries against the country towns, and made the clamour very popular.

And yet, more or less, (with) all the caution, there was not a town of any note within ten (or, I believe, twenty) miles of the city but what was more or less infected and had some died among them. I have heard the accounts of several, such as they were reckoned up, as follows:—

In Enfield 32.....................In Uxbridge 117
" Hornsey 58 ...." Hertford 90
" Newington 17..................." Ware 160
" Tottenham 42.................. " Hodsdon 30
" Edmonton 19..................." Waltham Abbey 23
" Barnet and Hadly 19............" Epping 26
" St Albans 121..................." Deptford 623
" Watford 45......................" Greenwich 231
" Eltham and Lusum 85.........." Kingston 122
" Croydon 61......................" Stanes 82
" Brentwood 70..................." Chertsey 18
" Rumford 109..................." Windsor 103
" Barking Abbot 200
" Brentford 432 ....Cum aliis.

Another thing might render the country more strict with respect to the citizens, and especially with respect to the poor, and this was what I hinted at before: namely, that there was a seeming propensity or a wicked inclination in those that were infected to infect others.

There have been great debates among our physicians as to the reason of this. Some will have it to be in the nature of the disease, and that it impresses every one that is seized upon by it with a kind of a rage, and a hatred against their own kind—as if there was a malignity not only in the distemper to communicate itself, but in the very nature of man, prompting him with evil will or an evil eye, that, as they say in the case of a mad dog, who though the gentlest creature before of any of his kind, yet then will fly upon and bite any one that comes next him, and those as soon as any who had been most observed by him before.

Others placed it to the account of the corruption of human nature, who cannot bear to see itself more miserable than others of its own species, and has a kind of involuntary wish that all men were as unhappy or in as bad a condition as itself.

Others say it was only a kind of desperation, not knowing or regarding what they did, and consequently unconcerned at the danger or safety not only of anybody near them, but even of themselves also. And indeed, when men are once come to a condition to abandon themselves, and be unconcerned for the safety or at the danger of themselves, it cannot be so much wondered that they should be careless of the safety of other people.

But I choose to give this grave debate a quite different turn, and answer it or resolve it all by saying that I do not grant the fact. On the contrary, I say that the thing is not really so, but that it was a general complaint raised by the people inhabiting the outlying villages against the citizens to justify, or at least excuse, those hardships and severities so much talked of, and in which complaints both sides may be said to have injured one another; that is to say, the citizens pressing to be received and harboured in time of distress, and with the plague upon them, complain of the cruelty and injustice of the country people in being refused entrance and forced back again with their goods and families; and the inhabitants, finding themselves so imposed upon, and the citizens breaking in as it were upon them whether they would or no, complain that when they were infected they were not only regardless of others, but even willing to infect them; neither of which were really true—that is to say, in the colours they were described in.

It is true there is something to be said for the frequent alarms which were given to the country of the resolution of the people of London to come out by force, not only for relief, but to plunder and rob; that they ran about the streets with the distemper upon them without any control; and that no care was taken to shut up houses, and confine the sick people from infecting others; whereas, to do the Londoners justice, they never practised such things, except in such particular cases as I have mentioned above, and such like. On the other hand, everything was managed with so much care, and such excellent order was observed in the whole city and suburbs by the care of the Lord Mayor and aldermen and by the justices of the peace, church-wardens, &c., in the outparts, that London may be a pattern to all the cities in the world for the good government and the excellent order that was everywhere kept, even in the time of the most violent infection, and when the people were in the utmost consternation and distress. But of this I shall speak by itself.

One thing, it is to be observed, was owing principally to the prudence of the magistrates, and ought to be mentioned to their honour: viz., the moderation which they used in the great and difficult work of shutting up of houses. It is true, as I have mentioned, that the shutting up of houses was a great subject of discontent, and I may say indeed the only subject of discontent among the people at that time; for the confining the sound in the same house with the sick was counted very terrible, and the complaints of people so confined were very grievous. They were heard into the very streets, and they were sometimes such that called for resentment, though oftener for compassion. They had no way to converse with any of their friends but out at their windows, where they would make such piteous lamentations as often moved the hearts of those they talked with, and of others who, passing by, heard their story; and as those complaints oftentimes reproached the severity, and sometimes the insolence, of the watchmen placed at their doors, those watchmen would answer saucily enough, and perhaps be apt to affront the people who were in the street talking to the said families; for which, or for their ill-treatment of the families, I think seven or eight of them in several places were killed; I know not whether I should say murdered or not, because I cannot enter into the particular cases. It is true the watchmen were on their duty, and acting in the post where they were placed by a lawful authority; and killing any public legal officer in the execution of his office is always, in the language of the law, called murder. But as they were not authorised by the magistrates' instructions, or by the power they acted under, to be injurious or abusive either to the people who were under their observation or to any that concerned themselves for them; so when they did so, they might be said to act themselves, not their office; to act as private persons, not as persons employed; and consequently, if they brought mischief upon themselves by such an undue behaviour, that mischief was upon their own heads; and indeed they had so much the hearty curses of the people, whether they deserved it or not, that whatever befell them nobody pitied them, and everybody was apt to say they deserved it, whatever it was. Nor do I remember that anybody was ever punished, at least to any considerable degree, for whatever was done to the watchmen that guarded their houses.

What variety of stratagems were used to escape and get out of houses thus shut up, by which the watchmen were deceived or overpowered, and that the people got away, I have taken notice of already, and shall say no more to that. But I say the magistrates did moderate and ease families upon many occasions in this case, and particularly in that of taking away, or suffering to be removed, the sick persons out of such houses when they were willing to be removed either to a pest-house or other Places; and sometimes giving the well persons in the family so shut up, leave to remove upon information given that they were well, and that they would confine themselves in such houses where they went so long as should be required of them. The concern, also, of the magistrates for the supplying such poor families as were infected—I say, supplying them with necessaries, as well physic as food—was very great, and in which they did not content themselves with giving the necessary orders to the officers appointed, but the aldermen in person, and on horseback, frequently rode to such houses and caused the people to be asked at their windows whether they were duly attended or not; also, whether they wanted anything that was necessary, and if the officers had constantly carried their messages and fetched them such things as they wanted or not. And if they answered in the affirmative, all was well; but if they complained that they were ill supplied, and that the officer did not do his duty, or did not treat them civilly, they (the officers) were generally removed, and others placed in their stead.

It is true such complaint might be unjust, and if the officer had such arguments to use as would convince the magistrate that he was right, and that the people had injured him, he was continued and they reproved. But this part could not well bear a particular inquiry, for the parties could very ill be well heard and answered in the street from the windows, as was the case then. The magistrates, therefore, generally chose to favour the people and remove the man, as what seemed to be the least wrong and of the least ill consequence; seeing if the watchman was injured, yet they could easily make him amends by giving him another post of the like nature; but if the family was injured, there was no satisfaction could be made to them, the damage perhaps being irreparable, as it concerned their lives.

A great variety of these cases frequently happened between the watchmen and the poor people shut up, besides those I formerly mentioned about escaping. Sometimes the watchmen were absent, sometimes drunk, sometimes asleep when the people wanted them, and such never failed to be punished severely, as indeed they deserved.

But after all that was or could be done in these cases, the shutting up of houses, so as to confine those that were well with those that were sick, had very great inconveniences in it, and some that were very tragical, and which merited to have been considered if there had been room for it. But it was authorised by a law, it had the public good in view as the end chiefly aimed at, and all the private injuries that were done by the putting it in execution must be put to the account of the public benefit.

It is doubtful to this day whether, in the whole, it contributed anything to the stop of the infection; and indeed I cannot say it did, for nothing could run with greater fury and rage than the infection did when it was in its chief violence, though the houses infected were shut up as exactly and as effectually as it was possible. Certain it is that if all the infected persons were effectually shut in, no sound person could have been infected by them, because they could not have come near them. But the case was this (and I shall only touch it here): namely, that the infection was propagated insensibly, and by such persons as were not visibly infected, who neither knew whom they infected or who they were infected by.

A house in Whitechappel was shut up for the sake of one infected maid, who had only spots, not the tokens come out upon her, and recovered; yet these people obtained no liberty to stir, neither for air or exercise, forty days. Want of breath, fear, anger, vexation, and all the other gifts attending such an injurious treatment cast the mistress of the family into a fever, and visitors came into the house and said it was the plague, though the physicians declared it was not. However, the family were obliged to begin their quarantine anew on the report of the visitors or examiner, though their former quarantine wanted but a few days of being finished. This oppressed them so with anger and grief, and, as before, straitened them also so much as to room, and for want of breathing and free air, that most of the family fell sick, one of one distemper, one of another, chiefly scorbutic ailments; only one, a violent colic; till, after several prolongings of their confinement, some or other of those that came in with the visitors to inspect the persons that were ill, in hopes of releasing them, brought the distemper with them and infected the whole house; and all or most of them died, not of the plague as really upon them before, but of the plague that those people brought them, who should have been careful to have protected them from it. And this was a thing which frequently happened, and was indeed one of the worst consequences of shutting houses up.

I had about this time a little hardship put upon me, which I was at first greatly afflicted at, and very much disturbed about though, as it proved, it did not expose me to any disaster; and this was being appointed by the alderman of Portsoken Ward one of the examiners of the houses in the precinct where I lived. We had a large parish, and had no less than eighteen examiners, as the order called us; the people called us visitors. I endeavoured with all my might to be excused from such an employment, and used many arguments with the alderman's deputy to be excused; particularly I alleged that I was against shutting up houses at all, and that it would be very hard to oblige me to be an instrument in that which was against my judgement, and which I did verily believe would not answer the end it was intended for; but all the abatement I could get was only, that whereas the officer was appointed by my Lord Mayor to continue two months, I should be obliged to hold it but three weeks, on condition nevertheless that I could then get some other sufficient housekeeper to serve the rest of the time for me—which was, in short, but a very small favour, it being very difficult to get any man to accept of such an employment, that was fit to be entrusted with it.

It is true that shutting up of houses had one effect, which I am sensible was of moment, namely, it confined the distempered people, who would otherwise have been both very troublesome and very dangerous in their running about streets with the distemper upon them —which, when they were delirious, they would have done in a most frightful manner, and as indeed they began to do at first very much, till they were thus restrained; nay, so very open they were that the poor would go about and beg at people's doors, and say they had the plague upon them, and beg rags for their sores, or both, or anything that delirious nature happened to think of.

A poor, unhappy gentlewoman, a substantial citizen's wife, was (if the story be true) murdered by one of these creatures in Aldersgate Street, or that way. He was going along the street, raving mad to be sure, and singing; the people only said he was drunk, but he himself said he had the plague upon him, which it seems was true; and meeting this gentlewoman, he would kiss her. She was terribly frighted, as he was only a rude fellow, and she ran from him, but the street being very thin of people, there was nobody near enough to help her. When she saw he would overtake her, she turned and gave him a thrust so forcibly, he being but weak, and pushed him down backward. But very unhappily, she being so near, he caught hold of her and pulled her down also, and getting up first, mastered her and kissed her; and which was worst of all, when he had done, told her he had the plague, and why should not she have it as well as he? She was frighted enough before, being also young with child; but when she heard him say he had the plague, she screamed out and fell down into a swoon, or in a fit, which, though she recovered a little, yet killed her in a very few days; and I never heard whether she had the plague or no.

Another infected person came and knocked at the door of a citizen's house where they knew him very well; the servant let him in, and being told the master of the house was above, he ran up and came into the room to them as the whole family was at supper. They began to rise up, a little surprised, not knowing what the matter was; but he bid them sit still, he only came to take his leave of them. They asked him, 'Why, Mr—, where are you going?' 'Going,' says he; 'I have got the sickness, and shall die tomorrow night.' 'Tis easy to believe, though not to describe, the consternation they were all in. The women and the man's daughters, which were but little girls, were frighted almost to death and got up, one running out at one door and one at another, some downstairs and some upstairs, and getting together as well as they could, locked themselves into their chambers and screamed out at the window for help, as if they had been frighted out of their wits. The master, more composed than they, though both frighted and provoked, was going to lay hands on him and throw him downstairs, being in a passion; but then, considering a little the condition of the man and the danger of touching him, horror seized his mind, and he stood still like one astonished. The poor distempered man all this while, being as well diseased in his brain as in his body, stood still like one amazed. At length he turns round: 'Ay!' says he, with all the seeming calmness imaginable, 'is it so with you all? Are you all disturbed at me? Why, then I'll e'en go home and die there.' And so he goes immediately downstairs. The servant that had let him in goes down after him with a candle, but was afraid to go past him and open the door, so he stood on the stairs to see what he would do. The man went and opened the door, and went out and flung the door after him. It was some while before the family recovered the fright, but as no ill consequence attended, they have had occasion since to speak of it (You may be sure) with great satisfaction. Though the man was gone, it was some time—nay, as I heard, some days before they recovered themselves of the hurry they were in; nor did they go up and down the house with any assurance till they had burnt a great variety of fumes and perfumes in all the rooms, and made a great many smokes of pitch, of gunpowder, and of sulphur, all separately shifted, and washed their clothes, and the like. As to the poor man, whether he lived or died I don't remember.

It is most certain that, if by the shutting up of houses the sick had not been confined, multitudes who in the height of their fever were delirious and distracted would have been continually running up and down the streets; and even as it was a very great number did so, and offered all sorts of violence to those they met, even just as a mad dog runs on and bites at every one he meets; nor can I doubt but that, should one of those infected, diseased creatures have bitten any man or woman while the frenzy of the distemper was upon them, they, I mean the person so wounded, would as certainly have been incurably infected as one that was sick before, and had the tokens upon him.

I heard of one infected creature who, running out of his bed in his shirt in the anguish and agony of his swellings, of which he had three upon him, got his shoes on and went to put on his coat; but the nurse resisting, and snatching the coat from him, he threw her down, ran over her, ran downstairs and into the street, directly to the Thames in his shirt; the nurse running after him, and calling to the watch to stop him; but the watchman, frighted at the man, and afraid to touch him, let him go on; upon which he ran down to the Stillyard stairs, threw away his shirt, and plunged into the Thames, and, being a good swimmer, swam quite over the river; and the tide being coming in, as they call it (that is, running westward) he reached the land not till he came about the Falcon stairs, where landing, and finding no people there, it being in the night, he ran about the streets there, naked as he was, for a good while, when, it being by that time high water, he takes the river again, and swam back to the Stillyard, landed, ran up the streets again to his own house, knocking at the door, went up the stairs and into his bed again; and that this terrible experiment cured him of the plague, that is to say, that the violent motion of his arms and legs stretched the parts where the swellings he had upon him were, that is to say, under his arms and his groin, and caused them to ripen and break; and that the cold of the water abated the fever in his blood.

I have only to add that I do not relate this any more than some of the other, as a fact within my own knowledge, so as that I can vouch the truth of them, and especially that of the man being cured by the extravagant adventure, which I confess I do not think very possible; but it may serve to confirm the many desperate things which the distressed people falling into deliriums, and what we call light-headedness, were frequently run upon at that time, and how infinitely more such there would have been if such people had not been confined by the shutting up of houses; and this I take to be the best, if not the only good thing which was performed by that severe method.

On the other hand, the complaints and the murmurings were very bitter against the thing itself. It would pierce the hearts of all that came by to hear the piteous cries of those infected people, who, being thus out of their understandings by the violence of their pain or the heat of their blood, were either shut in or perhaps tied in their beds and chairs, to prevent their doing themselves hurt—and who would make a dreadful outcry at their being confined, and at their being not permitted to die at large, as they called it, and as they would have done before.

This running of distempered people about the streets was very dismal, and the magistrates did their utmost to prevent it; but as it was generally in the night and always sudden when such attempts were made, the officers could not be at hand to prevent it; and even when any got out in the day, the officers appointed did not care to meddle with them, because, as they were all grievously infected, to be sure, when they were come to that height, so they were more than ordinarily infectious, and it was one of the most dangerous things that could be to touch them. On the other hand, they generally ran on, not knowing what they did, till they dropped down stark dead, or till they had exhausted their spirits so as that they would fall and then die in perhaps half-an-hour or an hour; and, which was most piteous to hear, they were sure to come to themselves entirely in that half-hour or hour, and then to make most grievous and piercing cries and lamentations in the deep, afflicting sense of the condition they were in. This was much of it before the order for shutting up of houses was strictly put in execution, for at first the watchmen were not so vigorous and severe as they were afterward in the keeping the people in; that is to say, before they were (I mean some of them) severely punished for their neglect, failing in their duty, and letting people who were under their care slip away, or conniving at their going abroad, whether sick or well. But after they saw the officers appointed to examine into their conduct were resolved to have them do their duty or be punished for the omission, they were more exact, and the people were strictly restrained; which was a thing they took so ill and bore so impatiently that their discontents can hardly be described. But there was an absolute necessity for it, that must be confessed, unless some other measures had been timely entered upon, and it was too late for that.

Had not this particular (of the sick being restrained as above) been our case at that time, London would have been the most dreadful place that ever was in the world; there would, for aught I know, have as many people died in the streets as died in their houses; for when the distemper was at its height it generally made them raving and delirious, and when they were so they would never be persuaded to keep in their beds but by force; and many who were not tied threw themselves out of windows when they found they could not get leave to go out of their doors.

It was for want of people conversing one with another, in this time of calamity, that it was impossible any particular person could come at the knowledge of all the extraordinary cases that occurred in different families; and particularly I believe it was never known to this day how many people in their deliriums drowned themselves in the Thames, and in the river which runs from the marshes by Hackney, which we generally called Ware River, or Hackney River. As to those which were set down in the weekly bill, they were indeed few; nor could it be known of any of those whether they drowned themselves by accident or not. But I believe I might reckon up more who within the compass of my knowledge or observation really drowned themselves in that year, than are put down in the bill of all put together: for many of the bodies were never found who yet were known to be lost; and the like in other methods of self-destruction. There was also one man in or about Whitecross Street burned himself to death in his bed; some said it was done by himself, others that it was by the treachery of the nurse that attended him; but that he had the plague upon him was agreed by all.

It was a merciful disposition of Providence also, and which I have many times thought of at that time, that no fires, or no considerable ones at least, happened in the city during that year, which, if it had been otherwise, would have been very dreadful; and either the people must have let them alone unquenched, or have come together in great crowds and throngs, unconcerned at the danger of the infection, not concerned at the houses they went into, at the goods they handled, or at the persons or the people they came among. But so it was, that excepting that in Cripplegate parish, and two or three little eruptions of fires, which were presently extinguished, there was no disaster of that kind happened in the whole year. They told us a story of a house in a place called Swan Alley, passing from Goswell Street, near the end of Old Street, into St John Street, that a family was infected there in so terrible a manner that every one of the house died. The last person lay dead on the floor, and, as it is supposed, had lain herself all along to die just before the fire; the fire, it seems, had fallen from its place, being of wood, and had taken hold of the boards and the joists they lay on, and burnt as far as just to the body, but had not taken hold of the dead body (though she had little more than her shift on) and had gone out of itself, not burning the rest of the house, though it was a slight timber house. How true this might be I do not determine, but the city being to suffer severely the next year by fire, this year it felt very little of that calamity.

Indeed, considering the deliriums which the agony threw people into, and how I have mentioned in their madness, when they were alone, they did many desperate things, it was very strange there were no more disasters of that kind.

It has been frequently asked me, and I cannot say that I ever knew how to give a direct answer to it, how it came to pass that so many infected people appeared abroad in the streets at the same time that the houses which were infected were so vigilantly searched, and all of them shut up and guarded as they were.

I confess I know not what answer to give to this, unless it be this: that in so great and populous a city as this is it was impossible to discover every house that was infected as soon as it was so, or to shut up all the houses that were infected; so that people had the liberty of going about the streets, even where they Pleased, unless they were known to belong to such-and-such infected houses.

It is true that, as several physicians told my Lord Mayor, the fury of the contagion was such at some particular times, and people sickened so fast and died so soon, that it was impossible, and indeed to no purpose, to go about to inquire who was sick and who was well, or to shut them up with such exactness as the thing required, almost every house in a whole street being infected, and in many places every person in some of the houses; and that which was still worse, by the time that the houses were known to be infected, most of the persons infected would be stone dead, and the rest run away for fear of being shut up; so that it was to very small purpose to call them infected houses and shut them up, the infection having ravaged and taken its leave of the house before it was really known that the family was any way touched.

This might be sufficient to convince any reasonable person that as it was not in the power of the magistrates or of any human methods of policy, to prevent the spreading the infection, so that this way of shutting up of houses was perfectly insufficient for that end. Indeed it seemed to have no manner of public good in it, equal or proportionable to the grievous burden that it was to the particular families that were so shut up; and, as far as I was employed by the public in directing that severity, I frequently found occasion to see that it was incapable of answering the end. For example, as I was desired, as a visitor or examiner, to inquire into the particulars of several families which were infected, we scarce came to any house where the plague had visibly appeared in the family but that some of the family were fled and gone. The magistrates would resent this, and charge the examiners with being remiss in their examination or inspection. But by that means houses were long infected before it was known. Now, as I was in this dangerous office but half the appointed time, which was two months, it was long enough to inform myself that we were no way capable of coming at the knowledge of the true state of any family but by inquiring at the door or of the neighbours. As for going into every house to search, that was a part no authority would offer to impose on the inhabitants, or any citizen would undertake: for it would have been exposing us to certain infection and death, and to the ruin of our own families as well as of ourselves; nor would any citizen of probity, and that could be depended upon, have stayed in the town if they had been made liable to such a severity.

Seeing then that we could come at the certainty of things by no method but that of inquiry of the neighbours or of the family, and on that we could not justly depend, it was not possible but that the uncertainty of this matter would remain as above.

It is true masters of families were bound by the order to give notice to the examiner of the place wherein he lived, within two hours after he should discover it, of any person being sick in his house (that is to say, having signs of the infection)—but they found so many ways to evade this and excuse their negligence that they seldom gave that notice till they had taken measures to have every one escape out of the house who had a mind to escape, whether they were sick or sound; and while this was so, it is easy to see that the shutting up of houses was no way to be depended upon as a sufficient method for putting a stop to the infection because, as I have said elsewhere, many of those that so went out of those infected houses had the plague really upon them, though they might really think themselves sound. And some of these were the people that walked the streets till they fell down dead, not that they were suddenly struck with the distemper as with a bullet that killed with the stroke, but that they really had the infection in their blood long before; only, that as it preyed secretly on the vitals, it appeared not till it seized the heart with a mortal power, and the patient died in a moment, as with a sudden fainting or an apoplectic fit.

I know that some even of our physicians thought for a time that those people that so died in the streets were seized but that moment they fell, as if they had been touched by a stroke from heaven as men are killed by a flash of lightning—but they found reason to alter their opinion afterward; for upon examining the bodies of such after they were dead, they always either had tokens upon them or other evident proofs of the distemper having been longer upon them than they had otherwise expected.

This often was the reason that, as I have said, we that were examiners were not able to come at the knowledge of the infection being entered into a house till it was too late to shut it up, and sometimes not till the people that were left were all dead. In Petticoat Lane two houses together were infected, and several people sick; but the distemper was so well concealed, the examiner, who was my neighbour, got no knowledge of it till notice was sent him that the people were all dead, and that the carts should call there to fetch them away. The two heads of the families concerted their measures, and so ordered their matters as that when the examiner was in the neighbourhood they appeared generally at a time, and answered, that is, lied, for one another, or got some of the neighbourhood to say they were all in health—and perhaps knew no better —till, death making it impossible to keep it any longer as a secret, the dead-carts were called in the night to both the houses, and so it became public. But when the examiner ordered the constable to shut up the houses there was nobody left in them but three people, two in one house and one in the other, just dying, and a nurse in each house who acknowledged that they had buried five before, that the houses had been infected nine or ten days, and that for all the rest of the two families, which were many, they were gone, some sick, some well, or whether sick or well could not be known.

In like manner, at another house in the same lane, a man having his family infected but very unwilling to be shut up, when he could conceal it no longer, shut up himself; that is to say, he set the great red cross upon his door with the words, 'Lord have mercy upon us', and so deluded the examiner, who supposed it had been done by the constable by order of the other examiner, for there were two examiners to every district or precinct. By this means he had free egress and regress into his house again and out of it, as he pleased, notwithstanding it was infected, till at length his stratagem was found out; and then he, with the sound part of his servants and family, made off and escaped, so they were not shut up at all.

These things made it very hard, if not impossible, as I have said, to prevent the spreading of an infection by the shutting up of houses—unless the people would think the shutting of their houses no grievance, and be so willing to have it done as that they would give notice duly and faithfully to the magistrates of their being infected as soon as it was known by themselves; but as that cannot be expected from them, and the examiners cannot be supposed, as above, to go into their houses to visit and search, all the good of shutting up houses will be defeated, and few houses will be shut up in time, except those of the poor, who cannot conceal it, and of some people who will be discovered by the terror and consternation which the things put them into.

I got myself discharged of the dangerous office I was in as soon as I could get another admitted, whom I had obtained for a little money to accept of it; and so, instead of serving the two months, which was directed, I was not above three weeks in it; and a great while too, considering it was in the month of August, at which time the distemper began to rage with great violence at our end of the town.

In the execution of this office I could not refrain speaking my opinion among my neighbours as to this shutting up the people in their houses; in which we saw most evidently the severities that were used, though grievous in themselves, had also this particular objection against them: namely, that they did not answer the end, as I have said, but that the distempered people went day by day about the streets; and it was our united opinion that a method to have removed the sound from the sick, in case of a particular house being visited, would have been much more reasonable on many accounts, leaving nobody with the sick persons but such as should on such occasion request to stay and declare themselves content to be shut up with them.

Our scheme for removing those that were sound from those that were sick was only in such houses as were infected, and confining the sick was no confinement; those that could not stir would not complain while they were in their senses and while they had the power of judging.

Indeed, when they came to be delirious and light-headed, then they would cry out of the cruelty of being confined; but for the removal of those that were well, we thought it highly reasonable and just, for their own sakes, they should be removed from the sick, and that for other people's safety they should keep retired for a while, to see that they were sound, and might not infect others; and we thought twenty or thirty days enough for this.

Now, certainly, if houses had been provided on purpose for those that were sound to perform this demi-quarantine in, they would have much less reason to think themselves injured in such a restraint than in being confined with infected people in the houses where they lived.

It is here, however, to be observed that after the funerals became so many that people could not toll the bell, mourn or weep, or wear black for one another, as they did before; no, nor so much as make coffins for those that died; so after a while the fury of the infection appeared to be so increased that, in short, they shut up no houses at all. It seemed enough that all the remedies of that kind had been used till they were found fruitless, and that the plague spread itself with an irresistible fury; so that as the fire the succeeding year spread itself, and burned with such violence that the citizens, in despair, gave over their endeavours to extinguish it, so in the plague it came at last to such violence that the people sat still looking at one another, and seemed quite abandoned to despair; whole streets seemed to be desolated, and not to be shut up only, but to be emptied of their inhabitants; doors were left open, windows stood shattering with the wind in empty houses for want of people to shut them. In a word, people began to give up themselves to their fears and to think that all regulations and methods were in vain, and that there was nothing to be hoped for but an universal desolation; and it was even in the height of this general despair that it Pleased God to stay His hand, and to slacken the fury of the contagion in such a manner as was even surprising, like its beginning, and demonstrated it to be His own particular hand, and that above, if not without the agency of means, as I shall take notice of in its proper place.

But I must still speak of the plague as in its height, raging even to desolation, and the people under the most dreadful consternation, even, as I have said, to despair. It is hardly credible to what excess the passions of men carried them in this extremity of the distemper, and this part, I think, was as moving as the rest. What could affect a man in his full power of reflection, and what could make deeper impressions on the soul, than to see a man almost naked, and got out of his house, or perhaps out of his bed, into the street, come out of Harrow Alley, a populous conjunction or collection of alleys, courts, and passages in the Butcher Row in Whitechappel,—I say, what could be more affecting than to see this poor man come out into the open street, run dancing and singing and making a thousand antic gestures, with five or six women and children running after him, crying and calling upon him for the Lord's sake to come back, and entreating the help of others to bring him back, but all in vain, nobody daring to lay a hand upon him or to come near him?

This was a most grievous and afflicting thing to me, who saw it all from my own windows; for all this while the poor afflicted man was, as I observed it, even then in the utmost agony of pain, having (as they said) two swellings upon him which could not be brought to break or to suppurate; but, by laying strong caustics on them, the surgeons had, it seems, hopes to break them—which caustics were then upon him, burning his flesh as with a hot iron. I cannot say what became of this poor man, but I think he continued roving about in that manner till he fell down and died.

No wonder the aspect of the city itself was frightful. The usual concourse of people in the streets, and which used to be supplied from our end of the town, was abated. The Exchange was not kept shut, indeed, but it was no more frequented. The fires were lost; they had been almost extinguished for some days by a very smart and hasty rain. But that was not all; some of the physicians insisted that they were not only no benefit, but injurious to the health of people. This they made a loud clamour about, and complained to the Lord Mayor about it. On the other hand, others of the same faculty, and eminent too, opposed them, and gave their reasons why the fires were, and must be, useful to assuage the violence of the distemper. I cannot give a full account of their arguments on both sides; only this I remember, that they cavilled very much with one another. Some were for fires, but that they must be made of wood and not coal, and of particular sorts of wood too, such as fir in particular, or cedar, because of the strong effluvia of turpentine; others were for coal and not wood, because of the sulphur and bitumen; and others were for neither one or other. Upon the whole, the Lord Mayor ordered no more fires, and especially on this account, namely, that the plague was so fierce that they saw evidently it defied all means, and rather seemed to increase than decrease upon any application to check and abate it; and yet this amazement of the magistrates proceeded rather from want of being able to apply any means successfully than from any unwillingness either to expose themselves or undertake the care and weight of business; for, to do them justice, they neither spared their pains nor their persons. But nothing answered; the infection raged, and the people were now frighted and terrified to the last degree: so that, as I may say, they gave themselves up, and, as I mentioned above, abandoned themselves to their despair.

But let me observe here that, when I say the people abandoned themselves to despair, I do not mean to what men call a religious despair, or a despair of their eternal state, but I mean a despair of their being able to escape the infection or to outlive the plague which they saw was so raging and so irresistible in its force that indeed few people that were touched with it in its height, about August and September, escaped; and, which is very particular, contrary to its ordinary operation in June and July, and the beginning of August, when, as I have observed, many were infected, and continued so many days, and then went off after having had the poison in their blood a long time; but now, on the contrary, most of the people who were taken during the two last weeks in August and in the three first weeks in September, generally died in two or three days at furthest, and many the very same day they were taken; whether the dog-days, or, as our astrologers pretended to express themselves, the influence of the dog-star, had that malignant effect, or all those who had the seeds of infection before in them brought it up to a maturity at that time altogether, I know not; but this was the time when it was reported that above 3000 people died in one night; and they that would have us believe they more critically observed it pretend to say that they all died within the space of two hours, viz., between the hours of one and three in the morning.

As to the suddenness of people's dying at this time, more than before, there were innumerable instances of it, and I could name several in my neighbourhood. One family without the Bars, and not far from me, were all seemingly well on the Monday, being ten in family. That evening one maid and one apprentice were taken ill and died the next morning—when the other apprentice and two children were touched, whereof one died the same evening, and the other two on Wednesday. In a word, by Saturday at noon the master, mistress, four children, and four servants were all gone, and the house left entirely empty, except an ancient woman who came in to take charge of the goods for the master of the family's brother, who lived not far off, and who had not been sick.

Many houses were then left desolate, all the people being carried away dead, and especially in an alley farther on the same side beyond the Bars, going in at the sign of Moses and Aaron, there were several houses together which, they said, had not one person left alive in them; and some that died last in several of those houses were left a little too long before they were fetched out to be buried; the reason of which was not, as some have written very untruly, that the living were not sufficient to bury the dead, but that the mortality was so great in the yard or alley that there was nobody left to give notice to the buriers or sextons that there were any dead bodies there to be buried. It was said, how true I know not, that some of those bodies were so much corrupted and so rotten that it was with difficulty they were carried; and as the carts could not come any nearer than to the Alley Gate in the High Street, it was so much the more difficult to bring them along; but I am not certain how many bodies were then left. I am sure that ordinarily it was not so.

As I have mentioned how the people were brought into a condition to despair of life and abandon themselves, so this very thing had a strange effect among us for three or four weeks; that is, it made them bold and venturous: they were no more shy of one another, or restrained within doors, but went anywhere and everywhere, and began to converse. One would say to another, 'I do not ask you how you are, or say how I am; it is certain we shall all go; so 'tis no matter who is all sick or who is sound'; and so they ran desperately into any place or any company.

As it brought the people into public company, so it was surprising how it brought them to crowd into the churches. They inquired no more into whom they sat near to or far from, what offensive smells they met with, or what condition the people seemed to be in; but, looking upon themselves all as so many dead corpses, they came to the churches without the least caution, and crowded together as if their lives were of no consequence compared to the work which they came about there. Indeed, the zeal which they showed in coming, and the earnestness and affection they showed in their attention to what they heard, made it manifest what a value people would all put upon the worship of God if they thought every day they attended at the church that it would be their last.

Nor was it without other strange effects, for it took away, all manner of prejudice at or scruple about the person whom they found in the pulpit when they came to the churches. It cannot be doubted but that many of the ministers of the parish churches were cut off, among others, in so common and dreadful a calamity; and others had not courage enough to stand it, but removed into the country as they found means for escape. As then some parish churches were quite vacant and forsaken, the people made no scruple of desiring such Dissenters as had been a few years before deprived of their livings by virtue of the Act of Parliament called the Act of Uniformity to preach in the churches; nor did the church ministers in that case make any difficulty of accepting their assistance; so that many of those whom they called silenced ministers had their mouths opened on this occasion and preached publicly to the people.

Here we may observe and I hope it will not be amiss to take notice of it that a near view of death would soon reconcile men of good principles one to another, and that it is chiefly owing to our easy situation in life and our putting these things far from us that our breaches are fomented, ill blood continued, prejudices, breach of charity and of Christian union, so much kept and so far carried on among us as it is. Another plague year would reconcile all these differences; a close conversing with death, or with diseases that threaten death, would scum off the gall from our tempers, remove the animosities among us, and bring us to see with differing eyes than those which we looked on things with before. As the people who had been used to join with the Church were reconciled at this time with the admitting the Dissenters to preach to them, so the Dissenters, who with an uncommon prejudice had broken off from the communion of the Church of England, were now content to come to their parish churches and to conform to the worship which they did not approve of before; but as the terror of the infection abated, those things all returned again to their less desirable channel and to the course they were in before.

I mention this but historically. I have no mind to enter into arguments to move either or both sides to a more charitable compliance one with another. I do not see that it is probable such a discourse would be either suitable or successful; the breaches seem rather to widen, and tend to a widening further, than to closing, and who am I that I should think myself able to influence either one side or other? But this I may repeat again, that 'tis evident death will reconcile us all; on the other side the grave we shall be all brethren again. In heaven, whither I hope we may come from all parties and persuasions, we shall find neither prejudice or scruple; there we shall be of one principle and of one opinion. Why we cannot be content to go hand in hand to the Place where we shall join heart and hand without the least hesitation, and with the most complete harmony and affection—I say, why we cannot do so here I can say nothing to, neither shall I say anything more of it but that it remains to be lamented.

I could dwell a great while upon the calamities of this dreadful time, and go on to describe the objects that appeared among us every day, the dreadful extravagancies which the distraction of sick people drove them into; how the streets began now to be fuller of frightful objects, and families to be made even a terror to themselves. But after I have told you, as I have above, that one man, being tied in his bed, and finding no other way to deliver himself, set the bed on fire with his candle, which unhappily stood within his reach, and burnt himself in his bed; and how another, by the insufferable torment he bore, danced and sung naked in the streets, not knowing one ecstasy from another; I say, after I have mentioned these things, what can be added more? What can be said to represent the misery of these times more lively to the reader, or to give him a more perfect idea of a complicated distress?

I must acknowledge that this time was terrible, that I was sometimes at the end of all my resolutions, and that I had not the courage that I had at the beginning. As the extremity brought other people abroad, it drove me home, and except having made my voyage down to Blackwall and Greenwich, as I have related, which was an excursion, I kept afterwards very much within doors, as I had for about a fortnight before. I have said already that I repented several times that I had ventured to stay in town, and had not gone away with my brother and his family, but it was too late for that now; and after I had retreated and stayed within doors a good while before my impatience led me abroad, then they called me, as I have said, to an ugly and dangerous office which brought me out again; but as that was expired while the height of the distemper lasted, I retired again, and continued close ten or twelve days more, during which many dismal spectacles represented themselves in my view out of my own windows and in our own street—as that particularly from Harrow Alley, of the poor outrageous creature which danced and sung in his agony; and many others there were. Scarce a day or night passed over but some dismal thing or other happened at the end of that Harrow Alley, which was a place full of poor people, most of them belonging to the butchers or to employments depending upon the butchery.

Sometimes heaps and throngs of people would burst out of the alley, most of them women, making a dreadful clamour, mixed or compounded of screeches, cryings, and calling one another, that we could not conceive what to make of it. Almost all the dead part of the night the dead-cart stood at the end of that alley, for if it went in it could not well turn again, and could go in but a little way. There, I say, it stood to receive dead bodies, and as the churchyard was but a little way off, if it went away full it would soon be back again. It is impossible to describe the most horrible cries and noise the poor people would make at their bringing the dead bodies of their children and friends out of the cart, and by the number one would have thought there had been none left behind, or that there were people enough for a small city living in those places. Several times they cried 'Murder', sometimes 'Fire'; but it was easy to perceive it was all distraction, and the complaints of distressed and distempered people.

I believe it was everywhere thus as that time, for the plague raged for six or seven weeks beyond all that I have expressed, and came even to such a height that, in the extremity, they began to break into that excellent order of which I have spoken so much in behalf of the magistrates; namely, that no dead bodies were seen in the street or burials in the daytime: for there was a necessity in this extremity to bear with its being otherwise for a little while.

One thing I cannot omit here, and indeed I thought it was extraordinary, at least it seemed a remarkable hand of Divine justice: viz., that all the predictors, astrologers, fortune-tellers, and what they called cunning-men, conjurers, and the like: calculators of nativities and dreamers of dream, and such people, were gone and vanished; not one of them was to be found. I am verily persuaded that a great number of them fell in the heat of the calamity, having ventured to stay upon the prospect of getting great estates; and indeed their gain was but too great for a time, through the madness and folly of the people. But now they were silent; many of them went to their long home, not able to foretell their own fate or to calculate their own nativities. Some have been critical enough to say that every one of them died. I dare not affirm that; but this I must own, that I never heard of one of them that ever appeared after the calamity was over.

But to return to my particular observations during this dreadful part of the visitation. I am now come, as I have said, to the month of September, which was the most dreadful of its kind, I believe, that ever London saw; for, by all the accounts which I have seen of the preceding visitations which have been in London, nothing has been like it, the number in the weekly bill amounting to almost 40,000 from the 22nd of August to the 26th of September, being but five weeks. The particulars of the bills are as follows, viz.:—

From August the 22nd to the 29th..................7496
From August 29th to 5th September..................8252
From September the 5th to the 12th..................7690
From September the 12th to the 19th..................8297
38,195

This was a prodigious number of itself, but if I should add the reasons which I have to believe that this account was deficient, and how deficient it was, you would, with me, make no scruple to believe that there died above ten thousand a week for all those weeks, one week with another, and a proportion for several weeks both before and after. The confusion among the people, especially within the city, at that time, was inexpressible. The terror was so great at last that the courage of the people appointed to carry away the dead began to fail them; nay, several of them died, although they had the distemper before and were recovered, and some of them dropped down when they have been carrying the bodies even at the pit side, and just ready to throw them in; and this confusion was greater in the city because they had flattered themselves with hopes of escaping, and thought the bitterness of death was past. One cart, they told us, going up Shoreditch was forsaken of the drivers, or being left to one man to drive, he died in the street; and the horses going on overthrew the cart, and left the bodies, some thrown out here, some there, in a dismal manner. Another cart was, it seems, found in the great pit in Finsbury Fields, the driver being dead, or having been gone and abandoned it, and the horses running too near it, the cart fell in and drew the horses in also. It was suggested that the driver was thrown in with it and that the cart fell upon him, by reason his whip was seen to be in the pit among the bodies; but that, I suppose, could not be certain.

In our parish of Aldgate the dead-carts were several times, as I have heard, found standing at the churchyard gate full of dead bodies, but neither bellman or driver or any one else with it; neither in these or many other cases did they know what bodies they had in their cart, for sometimes they were let down with ropes out of balconies and out of windows, and sometimes the bearers brought them to the cart, sometimes other people; nor, as the men themselves said, did they trouble themselves to keep any account of the numbers.

The vigilance of the magistrates was now put to the utmost trial—and, it must be confessed, can never be enough acknowledged on this occasion also; whatever expense or trouble they were at, two things were never neglected in the city or suburbs either:—

(1) Provisions were always to be had in full plenty, and the price not much raised neither, hardly worth speaking.

(2) No dead bodies lay unburied or uncovered; and if one walked from one end of the city to another, no funeral or sign of it was to be seen in the daytime, except a little, as I have said above, in the three first weeks in September.

This last article perhaps will hardly be believed when some accounts which others have published since that shall be seen, wherein they say that the dead lay unburied, which I am assured was utterly false; at least, if it had been anywhere so, it must have been in houses where the living were gone from the dead (having found means, as I have observed, to escape) and where no notice was given to the officers. All which amounts to nothing at all in the case in hand; for this I am positive in, having myself been employed a little in the direction of that part in the parish in which I lived, and where as great a desolation was made in proportion to the number of inhabitants as was anywhere; I say, I am sure that there were no dead bodies remained unburied; that is to say, none that the proper officers knew of; none for want of people to carry them off, and buriers to put them into the ground and cover them; and this is sufficient to the argument; for what might lie in houses and holes, as in Moses and Aaron Alley, is nothing; for it is most certain they were buried as soon as they were found. As to the first article (namely, of provisions, the scarcity or dearness), though I have mentioned it before and shall speak of it again, yet I must observe here:—

(1) The price of bread in particular was not much raised; for in the beginning of the year, viz., in the first week in March, the penny wheaten loaf was ten ounces and a half; and in the height of the contagion it was to be had at nine ounces and a half, and never dearer, no, not all that season. And about the beginning of November it was sold ten ounces and a half again; the like of which, I believe, was never heard of in any city, under so dreadful a visitation, before.

(2) Neither was there (which I wondered much at) any want of bakers or ovens kept open to supply the people with the bread; but this was indeed alleged by some families, viz., that their maidservants, going to the bakehouses with their dough to be baked, which was then the custom, sometimes came home with the sickness (that is to say the plague) upon them.

In all this dreadful visitation there were, as I have said before, but two pest-houses made use of, viz., one in the fields beyond Old Street and one in Westminster; neither was there any compulsion used in carrying people thither. Indeed there was no need of compulsion in the case, for there were thousands of poor distressed people who, having no help or conveniences or supplies but of charity, would have been very glad to have been carried thither and been taken care of; which, indeed, was the only thing that I think was wanting in the whole public management of the city, seeing nobody was here allowed to be brought to the pest-house but where money was given, or security for money, either at their introducing or upon their being cured and sent out—for very many were sent out again whole; and very good physicians were appointed to those places, so that many people did very well there, of which I shall make mention again. The principal sort of people sent thither were, as I have said, servants who got the distemper by going on errands to fetch necessaries to the families where they lived, and who in that case, if they came home sick, were removed to preserve the rest of the house; and they were so well looked after there in all the time of the visitation that there was but 156 buried in all at the London pest-house, and 159 at that of Westminster.

By having more pest-houses I am far from meaning a forcing all people into such places. Had the shutting up of houses been omitted and the sick hurried out of their dwellings to pest-houses, as some proposed, it seems, at that time as well as since, it would certainly have been much worse than it was. The very removing the sick would have been a spreading of the infection, and rather because that removing could not effectually clear the house where the sick person was of the distemper; and the rest of the family, being then left at liberty, would certainly spread it among others.

The methods also in private families, which would have been universally used to have concealed the distemper and to have concealed the persons being sick, would have been such that the distemper would sometimes have seized a whole family before any visitors or examiners could have known of it. On the other hand, the prodigious numbers which would have been sick at a time would have exceeded all the capacity of public pest-houses to receive them, or of public officers to discover and remove them.

This was well considered in those days, and I have heard them talk of it often. The magistrates had enough to do to bring people to submit to having their houses shut up, and many ways they deceived the watchmen and got out, as I have observed. But that difficulty made it apparent that they would have found it impracticable to have gone the other way to work, for they could never have forced the sick people out of their beds and out of their dwellings. It must not have been my Lord Mayor's officers, but an army of officers, that must have attempted it; and the people, on the other hand, would have been enraged and desperate, and would have killed those that should have offered to have meddled with them or with their children and relations, whatever had befallen them for it; so that they would have made the people, who, as it was, were in the most terrible distraction imaginable, I say, they would have made them stark mad; whereas the magistrates found it proper on several accounts to treat them with lenity and compassion, and not with violence and terror, such as dragging the sick out of their houses or obliging them to remove themselves, would have been.

This leads me again to mention the time when the plague first began; that is to say, when it became certain that it would spread over the whole town, when, as I have said, the better sort of people first took the alarm and began to hurry themselves out of town. It was true, as I observed in its place, that the throng was so great, and the coaches, horses, waggons, and carts were so many, driving and dragging the people away, that it looked as if all the city was running away; and had any regulations been published that had been terrifying at that time, especially such as would pretend to dispose of the people otherwise than they would dispose of themselves, it would have put both the city and suburbs into the utmost confusion.

But the magistrates wisely caused the people to be encouraged, made very good bye-laws for the regulating the citizens, keeping good order in the streets, and making everything as eligible as possible to all sorts of people.

In the first place, the Lord Mayor and the sheriffs, the Court of Aldermen, and a certain number of the Common Council men, or their deputies, came to a resolution and published it, viz., that they would not quit the city themselves, but that they would be always at hand for the preserving good order in every place and for the doing justice on all occasions; as also for the distributing the public charity to the poor; and, in a word, for the doing the duty and discharging the trust reposed in them by the citizens to the utmost of their power.

In pursuance of these orders, the Lord Mayor, sheriffs, &c., held councils every day, more or less, for making such dispositions as they found needful for preserving the civil peace; and though they used the people with all possible gentleness and clemency, yet all manner of presumptuous rogues such as thieves, housebreakers, plunderers of the dead or of the sick, were duly punished, and several declarations were continually published by the Lord Mayor and Court of Aldermen against such.

Also all constables and churchwardens were enjoined to stay in the city upon severe penalties, or to depute such able and sufficient housekeepers as the deputy aldermen or Common Council men of the precinct should approve, and for whom they should give security; and also security in case of mortality that they would forthwith constitute other constables in their stead.

These things re-established the minds of the people very much, especially in the first of their fright, when they talked of making so universal a flight that the city would have been in danger of being entirely deserted of its inhabitants except the poor, and the country of being plundered and laid waste by the multitude. Nor were the magistrates deficient in performing their part as boldly as they promised it; for my Lord Mayor and the sheriffs were continually in the streets and at places of the greatest danger, and though they did not care for having too great a resort of people crowding about them, yet in emergent cases they never denied the people access to them, and heard with patience all their grievances and complaints. My Lord Mayor had a low gallery built on purpose in his hall, where he stood a little removed from the crowd when any complaint came to be heard, that he might appear with as much safety as possible.

Likewise the proper officers, called my Lord Mayor's officers, constantly attended in their turns, as they were in waiting; and if any of them were sick or infected, as some of them were, others were instantly employed to fill up and officiate in their places till it was known whether the other should live or die.

In like manner the sheriffs and aldermen did in their several stations and wards, where they were placed by office, and the sheriff's officers or sergeants were appointed to receive orders from the respective aldermen in their turn, so that justice was executed in all cases without interruption. In the next place, it was one of their particular cares to see the orders for the freedom of the markets observed, and in this part either the Lord Mayor or one or both of the sheriffs were every market-day on horseback to see their orders executed and to see that the country people had all possible encouragement and freedom in their coming to the markets and going back again, and that no nuisances or frightful objects should be seen in the streets to terrify them or make them unwilling to come. Also the bakers were taken under particular order, and the Master of the Bakers' Company was, with his court of assistants, directed to see the order of my Lord Mayor for their regulation put in execution, and the due assize of bread (which was weekly appointed by my Lord Mayor) observed; and all the bakers were obliged to keep their oven going constantly, on pain of losing the privileges of a freeman of the city of London.

By this means bread was always to be had in plenty, and as cheap as usual, as I said above; and provisions were never wanting in the markets, even to such a degree that I often wondered at it, and reproached myself with being so timorous and cautious in stirring abroad, when the country people came freely and boldly to market, as if there had been no manner of infection in the city, or danger of catching it.

It was indeed one admirable piece of conduct in the said magistrates that the streets were kept constantly clear and free from all manner of frightful objects, dead bodies, or any such things as were indecent or unpleasant—unless where anybody fell down suddenly or died in the streets, as I have said above; and these were generally covered with some cloth or blanket, or removed into the next churchyard till night. All the needful works that carried terror with them, that were both dismal and dangerous, were done in the night; if any diseased bodies were removed, or dead bodies buried, or infected clothes burnt, it was done in the night; and all the bodies which were thrown into the great pits in the several churchyards or burying-grounds, as has been observed, were so removed in the night, and everything was covered and closed before day. So that in the daytime there was not the least signal of the calamity to be seen or heard of, except what was to be observed from the emptiness of the streets, and sometimes from the passionate outcries and lamentations of the people, out at their windows, and from the numbers of houses and shops shut up.

Nor was the silence and emptiness of the streets so much in the city as in the out-parts, except just at one particular time when, as I have mentioned, the plague came east and spread over all the city. It was indeed a merciful disposition of God, that as the plague began at one end of the town first (as has been observed at large) so it proceeded progressively to other parts, and did not come on this way, or eastward, till it had spent its fury in the West part of the town; and so, as it came on one way, it abated another. For example, it began at St Giles's and the Westminster end of the town, and it was in its height in all that part by about the middle of July, viz., in St Giles-in-the-Fields, St Andrew's, Holborn, St Clement Danes, St Martin-in-the-Fields, and in Westminster. The latter end of July it decreased in those parishes; and coming east, it increased prodigiously in Cripplegate, St Sepulcher's, St James's, Clarkenwell, and St Bride's and Aldersgate. While it was in all these parishes, the city and all the parishes of the Southwark side of the water and all Stepney, Whitechappel, Aldgate, Wapping, and Ratcliff, were very little touched; so that people went about their business unconcerned, carried on their trades, kept open their shops, and conversed freely with one another in all the city, the east and north-east suburbs, and in Southwark, almost as if the plague had not been among us.

Even when the north and north-west suburbs were fully infected, viz., Cripplegate, Clarkenwell, Bishopsgate, and Shoreditch, yet still all the rest were tolerably well. For example from 25th July to 1st August the bill stood thus of all diseases:—

St Giles, Cripplegate 554
St Sepulchers 250
Clarkenwell 103
Bishopsgate 116
Shoreditch 110
Stepney parish 127
Aldgate 92
Whitechappel 104
All the ninety-seven parishes within the walls 228
All the parishes in Southwark 205
Total 1889

So that, in short, there died more that week in the two parishes of Cripplegate and St Sepulcher by forty-eight than in all the city, all the east suburbs, and all the Southwark parishes put together. This caused the reputation of the city's health to continue all over England—and especially in the counties and markets adjacent, from whence our supply of provisions chiefly came even much longer than that health itself continued; for when the people came into the streets from the country by Shoreditch and Bishopsgate, or by Old Street and Smithfield, they would see the out-streets empty and the houses and shops shut, and the few people that were stirring there walk in the middle of the streets. But when they came within the city, there things looked better, and the markets and shops were open, and the people walking about the streets as usual, though not quite so many; and this continued till the latter end of August and the beginning of September.

But then the case altered quite; the distemper abated in the west and north-west parishes, and the weight of the infection lay on the city and the eastern suburbs, and the Southwark side, and this in a frightful manner. Then, indeed, the city began to look dismal, shops to be shut, and the streets desolate. In the High Street, indeed, necessity made people stir abroad on many occasions; and there would be in the middle of the day a pretty many people, but in the mornings and evenings scarce any to be seen, even there, no, not in Cornhill and Cheapside.

These observations of mine were abundantly confirmed by the weekly bills of mortality for those weeks, an abstract of which, as they respect the parishes which. I have mentioned and as they make the calculations I speak of very evident, take as follows.

The weekly bill, which makes out this decrease of the burials in the west and north side of the city, stands thus—

From the 12th of September to the 19th—
- St Giles, Cripplegate 456
- St Giles-in-the-Fields 140
- Clarkenwell 77
- St Sepulcher 214
- St Leonard, Shoreditch 183
- Stepney parish 716
- Aldgate 623
- Whitechappel 532
- In the ninety-seven parishes within the walls 1493
- In the eight parishes on Southwark side 1636
- Total 6060

Here is a strange change of things indeed, and a sad change it was; and had it held for two months more than it did, very few people would have been left alive. But then such, I say, was the merciful disposition of God that, when it was thus, the west and north part which had been so dreadfully visited at first, grew, as you see, much better; and as the people disappeared here, they began to look abroad again there; and the next week or two altered it still more; that is, more to the encouragement of the other part of the town. For example:—

From the 19th of September to the 26th—
- St Giles, Cripplegate 277
- St Giles-in-the-Fields 119
- Clarkenwell 76
- St Sepulchers 193
- St Leonard, Shoreditch 146
- Stepney parish 616
- Aldgate 496
- Whitechappel 346
- In the ninety-seven parishes within the walls 1268
- In the eight parishes on Southwark side 1390
- Total 4927

From the 26th of September to the 3rd of October—
- St Giles, Cripplegate 196
- St Giles-in-the-Fields 95
- Clarkenwell 48

- St Sepulchers 137
- St Leonard, Shoreditch 128
- Stepney parish 674
- Aldgate 372
- Whitechappel 328
- In the ninety-seven parishes within the walls 1149
- In the eight parishes on Southwark side 1201
- Total 4382

And now the misery of the city and of the said east and south parts was complete indeed; for, as you see, the weight of the distemper lay upon those parts, that is to say, the city, the eight parishes over the river, with the parishes of Aldgate, Whitechappel, and Stepney; and this was the time that the bills came up to such a monstrous height as that I mentioned before, and that eight or nine, and, as I believe, ten or twelve thousand a week, died; for it is my settled opinion that they never could come at any just account of the numbers, for the reasons which I have given already.

Nay, one of the most eminent physicians, who has since published in Latin an account of those times, and of his observations says that in one week there died twelve thousand people, and that particularly there died four thousand in one night; though I do not remember that there ever was any such particular night so remarkably fatal as that such a number died in it. However, all this confirms what I have said above of the uncertainty of the bills of mortality, &c., of which I shall say more hereafter.

And here let me take leave to enter again, though it may seem a repetition of circumstances, into a description of the miserable condition of the city itself, and of those parts where I lived at this particular time. The city and those other parts, notwithstanding the great numbers of people that were gone into the country, was vastly full of people; and perhaps the fuller because people had for a long time a strong belief that the plague would not come into the city, nor into Southwark, no, nor into Wapping or Ratcliff at all; nay, such was the assurance of the people on that head that many removed from the suburbs on the west and north sides, into those eastern and south sides as for safety; and, as I verily believe, carried the plague amongst them there perhaps sooner than they would otherwise have had it.

Here also I ought to leave a further remark for the use of posterity, concerning the manner of people's infecting one another; namely, that it was not the sick people only from whom the plague was immediately received by others that were sound, but the well. To explain myself: by the sick people I mean those who were known to be sick, had taken their beds, had been under cure, or had swellings and tumours upon them, and the like; these everybody could beware of; they were either in their beds or in such condition as could not be concealed.

By the well I mean such as had received the contagion, and had it really upon them, and in their blood, yet did not show the consequences of it in their countenances: nay, even were not sensible of it themselves, as many were not for several days. These breathed death in every place, and upon everybody who came near them; nay, their very clothes retained the infection, their hands would infect the things they touched, especially if they were warm and sweaty, and they were generally apt to sweat too.

Now it was impossible to know these people, nor did they sometimes, as I have said, know themselves to be infected. These were the people that so often dropped down and fainted in the streets; for oftentimes they would go about the streets to the last, till on a sudden they would sweat, grow faint, sit down at a door and die. It is true, finding themselves thus, they would struggle hard to get home to their own doors, or at other times would be just able to go into their houses and die instantly; other times they would go about till they had the very tokens come out upon them, and yet not know it, and would die in an hour or two after they came home, but be well as long as they were abroad. These were the dangerous people; these were the people of whom the well people ought to have been afraid; but then, on the other side, it was impossible to know them.

And this is the reason why it is impossible in a visitation to prevent the spreading of the plague by the utmost human vigilance: viz., that it is impossible to know the infected people from the sound, or that the infected people should perfectly know themselves. I knew a man who conversed freely in London all the season of the plague in 1665, and kept about him an antidote or cordial on purpose to take when he thought himself in any danger, and he had such a rule to know or have warning of the danger by as indeed I never met with before or since. How far it may be depended on I know not. He had a wound in his leg, and whenever he came among any people that were not sound, and the infection began to affect him, he said he could know it by that signal, viz., that his wound in his leg would smart, and look pale and white; so as soon as ever he felt it smart it was time for him to withdraw, or to take care of himself, taking his drink, which he always carried about him for that purpose. Now it seems he found his wound would smart many times when he was in company with such who thought themselves to be sound, and who appeared so to one another; but he would presently rise up and say publicly, 'Friends, here is somebody in the room that has the plague', and so would immediately break up the company. This was indeed a faithful monitor to all people that the plague is not to be avoided by those that converse promiscuously in a town infected, and people have it when they know it not, and that they likewise give it to others when they know not that they have it themselves; and in this case shutting up the well or removing the sick will not do it, unless they can go back and shut up all those that the sick had conversed with, even before they knew themselves to be sick, and none knows how far to carry that back, or where to stop; for none knows when or where or how they may have received the infection, or from whom.

This I take to be the reason which makes so many people talk of the air being corrupted and infected, and that they need not be cautious of whom they converse with, for that the contagion was in the air. I have seen them in strange agitations and surprises on this account. 'I have never come near any infected body', says the disturbed person; 'I have conversed with none but sound, healthy people, and yet I have gotten the distemper!' 'I am sure I am struck from Heaven', says another, and he falls to the serious part. Again, the first goes on exclaiming, 'I have come near no infection or any infected person; I am sure it is the air. We draw in death when we breathe, and therefore 'tis the hand of God; there is no withstanding it.' And this at last made many people, being hardened to the danger, grow less concerned at it; and less cautious towards the latter end of the time, and when it was come to its height, than they were at first. Then, with a kind of a Turkish predestinarianism, they would say, if it pleased God to strike them, it was all one whether they went abroad or stayed at home; they could not escape it, and therefore they went boldly about, even into infected houses and infected company; visited sick people; and, in short, lay in the beds with their wives or relations when they were infected. And what was the consequence, but the same that is the consequence in Turkey, and in those countries where they do those things—namely, that they were infected too, and died by hundreds and thousands?

I would be far from lessening the awe of the judgements of God and the reverence to His providence which ought always to be on our minds on such occasions as these. Doubtless the visitation itself is a stroke from Heaven upon a city, or country, or nation where it falls; a messenger of His vengeance, and a loud call to that nation or country or city to humiliation and repentance, according to that of the prophet Jeremiah (xviii. 7, 8): 'At what instant I shall speak concerning a nation, and concerning a kingdom, to pluck up, and to pull down, and to destroy it; if that nation against whom I have pronounced turn from their evil, I will repent of the evil that I thought to do unto them.' Now to prompt due impressions of the awe of God on the minds of men on such occasions, and not to lessen them, it is that I have left those minutes upon record.

I say, therefore, I reflect upon no man for putting the reason of those things upon the immediate hand of God, and the appointment and direction of His providence; nay, on the contrary, there were many wonderful deliverances of persons from infection, and deliverances of persons when infected, which intimate singular and remarkable providence in the particular instances to which they refer; and I esteem my own deliverance to be one next to miraculous, and do record it with thankfulness.

But when I am speaking of the plague as a distemper arising from natural causes, we must consider it as it was really propagated by natural means; nor is it at all the less a judgement for its being under the conduct of human causes and effects; for, as the Divine Power has formed the whole scheme of nature and maintains nature in its course, so the same Power thinks fit to let His own actings with men, whether of mercy or judgement, to go on in the ordinary course of natural causes; and He is pleased to act by those natural causes as the ordinary means, excepting and reserving to Himself nevertheless a power to act in a supernatural way when He sees occasion. Now 'tis evident that in the case of an infection there is no apparent extraordinary occasion for supernatural operation, but the ordinary course of things appears sufficiently armed, and made capable of all the effects that Heaven usually directs by a contagion. Among these causes and effects, this of the secret conveyance of infection, imperceptible and unavoidable, is more than sufficient to execute the fierceness of Divine vengeance, without putting it upon supernaturals and miracle.

The acute penetrating nature of the disease itself was such, and the infection was received so imperceptibly, that the most exact caution could not secure us while in the place. But I must be allowed to believe—and I have so many examples fresh in my memory to convince me of it, that I think none can resist their evidence—I say, I must be allowed to believe that no one in this whole nation ever received the sickness or infection but who received it in the ordinary way of infection from somebody, or the clothes or touch or stench of somebody that was infected before.

The manner of its coming first to London proves this also, viz., by goods brought over from Holland, and brought thither from the Levant; the first breaking of it out in a house in Long Acre where those goods were carried and first opened; its spreading from that house to other houses by the visible unwary conversing with those who were sick; and the infecting the parish officers who were employed about the persons dead, and the like. These are known authorities for this great foundation point—that it went on and proceeded from person to person and from house to house, and no otherwise. In the first house that was infected there died four persons. A neighbour, hearing the mistress of the first house was sick, went to visit her, and went home and gave the distemper to her family, and died, and all her household. A minister, called to pray with the first sick person in the second house, was said to sicken immediately and die with several more in his house. Then the physicians began to consider, for they did not at first dream of a general contagion. But the physicians being sent to inspect the bodies, they assured the people that it was neither more or less than the plague, with all its terrifying particulars, and that it threatened an universal infection, so many people having already conversed with the sick or distempered, and having, as might be supposed, received infection from them, that it would be impossible to put a stop to it.

Here the opinion of the physicians agreed with my observation afterwards, namely, that the danger was spreading insensibly, for the sick could infect none but those that came within reach of the sick person; but that one man who may have really received the infection and knows it not, but goes abroad and about as a sound person, may give the plague to a thousand people, and they to greater numbers in proportion, and neither the person giving the infection or the persons receiving it know anything of it, and perhaps not feel the effects of it for several days after.

For example, many persons in the time of this visitation never perceived that they were infected till they found to their unspeakable surprise, the tokens come out upon them; after which they seldom lived six hours; for those spots they called the tokens were really gangrene spots, or mortified flesh in small knobs as broad as a little silver penny, and hard as a piece of callus or horn; so that, when the disease was come up to that length, there was nothing could follow but certain death; and yet, as I said, they knew nothing of their being infected, nor found themselves so much as out of order, till those mortal marks were upon them. But everybody must allow that they were infected in a high degree before, and must have been so some time, and consequently their breath, their sweat, their very clothes, were contagious for many days before. This occasioned a vast variety of cases which physicians would have much more opportunity to remember than I; but some came within the compass of my observation or hearing, of which I shall name a few.

A certain citizen who had lived safe and untouched till the month of September, when the weight of the distemper lay more in the city than it had done before, was mighty cheerful, and something too bold (as I think it was) in his talk of how secure he was, how cautious he had been, and how he had never come near any sick body. Says another citizen, a neighbour of his, to him one day, 'Do not be too confident, Mr—; it is hard to say who is sick and who is well, for we see men alive and well to outward appearance one hour, and dead the next.' 'That is true', says the first man, for he was not a man presumptuously secure, but had escaped a long while —and men, as I said above, especially in the city began to be over-easy upon that score. 'That is true,' says he; 'I do not think myself secure, but I hope I have not been in company with any person that there has been any danger in.' 'No?' says his neighbour. 'Was not you at the Bull Head Tavern in Gracechurch Street with Mr—the night before last?' 'Yes,' says the first, 'I was; but there was nobody there that we had any reason to think dangerous.' Upon which his neighbour said no more, being unwilling to surprise him; but this made him more inquisitive, and as his neighbour appeared backward, he was the more impatient, and in a kind of warmth says he aloud, 'Why, he is not dead, is he?' Upon which his neighbour still was silent, but cast up his eyes and said something to himself; at which the first citizen turned pale, and said no more but this, 'Then I am a dead man too', and went home immediately and sent for a neighbouring apothecary to give him something preventive, for he had not yet found himself ill; but the apothecary, opening his breast, fetched a sigh, and said no more but this, 'Look up to God'; and the man died in a few hours.

Now let any man judge from a case like this if it is possible for the regulations of magistrates, either by shutting up the sick or removing them, to stop an infection which spreads itself from man to man even while they are perfectly well and insensible of its approach, and may be so for many days.

It may be proper to ask here how long it may be supposed men might have the seeds of the contagion in them before it discovered itself in this fatal manner, and how long they might go about seemingly whole, and yet be contagious to all those that came near them. I believe the most experienced physicians cannot answer this question directly any more than I can; and something an ordinary observer may take notice of, which may pass their observations. The opinion of physicians abroad seems to be that it may lie dormant in the spirits or in the blood-vessels a very considerable time. Why else do they exact a quarantine of those who came into their harbours and ports from suspected places? Forty days is, one would think, too long for nature to struggle with such an enemy as this, and not conquer it or yield to it. But I could not think, by my own observation, that they can be infected so as to be contagious to others above fifteen or sixteen days at furthest; and on that score it was, that when a house was shut up in the city and any one had died of the plague, but nobody appeared to be ill in the family for sixteen or eighteen days after, they were not so strict but that they would connive at their going privately abroad; nor would people be much afraid of them afterward, but rather think they were fortified the better, having not been vulnerable when the enemy was in their own house; but we sometimes found it had lain much longer concealed.

Upon the foot of all these observations I must say that though Providence seemed to direct my conduct to be otherwise, yet it is my opinion, and I must leave it as a prescription, viz., that the best physic against the plague is to run away from it. I know people encourage themselves by saying God is able to keep us in the midst of danger, and able to overtake us when we think ourselves out of danger; and this kept thousands in the town whose carcases went into the great pits by cartloads, and who, if they had fled from the danger, had, I believe, been safe from the disaster; at least 'tis probable they had been safe.

And were this very fundamental only duly considered by the people on any future occasion of this or the like nature, I am persuaded it would put them upon quite different measures for managing the people from those that they took in 1665, or than any that have been taken abroad that I have heard of. In a word, they would consider of separating the people into smaller bodies, and removing them in time farther from one another—and not let such a contagion as this, which is indeed chiefly dangerous to collected bodies of people, find a million of people in a body together, as was very near the case before, and would certainly be the case if it should ever appear again.

The plague, like a great fire, if a few houses only are contiguous where it happens, can only burn a few houses; or if it begins in a single, or, as we call it, a lone house, can only burn that lone house where it begins. But if it begins in a close-built town or city and gets a head, there its fury increases: it rages over the whole place, and consumes all it can reach.

I could propose many schemes on the foot of which the government of this city, if ever they should be under the apprehensions of such another enemy (God forbid they should), might ease themselves of the greatest part of the dangerous people that belong to them; I mean such as the begging, starving, labouring poor, and among them chiefly those who, in case of a siege, are called the useless mouths; who being then prudently and to their own advantage disposed of, and the wealthy inhabitants disposing of themselves and of their servants and children, the city and its adjacent parts would be so effectually evacuated that there would not be above a tenth part of its people left together for the disease to take hold upon. But suppose them to be a fifth part, and that two hundred and fifty thousand people were left: and if it did seize upon them, they would, by their living so much at large, be much better prepared to defend themselves against the infection, and be less liable to the effects of it than if the same number of people lived close together in one smaller city such as Dublin or Amsterdam or the like.

It is true hundreds, yea, thousands of families fled away at this last plague, but then of them, many fled too late, and not only died in their flight, but carried the distemper with them into the countries where they went and infected those whom they went among for safety; which confounded the thing, and made that be a propagation of the distemper which was the best means to prevent it; and this too is an evidence of it, and brings me back to what I only hinted at before, but must speak more fully to here, namely, that men went about apparently well many days after they had the taint of the disease in their vitals, and after their spirits were so seized as that they could never escape it, and that all the while they did so they were dangerous to others; I say, this proves that so it was; for such people infected the very towns they went through, as well as the families they went among; and it was by that means that almost all the great towns in England had the distemper among them, more or less, and always they would tell you such a Londoner or such a Londoner brought it down.

It must not be omitted that when I speak of those people who were really thus dangerous, I suppose them to be utterly ignorant of their own conditions; for if they really knew their circumstances to be such as indeed they were, they must have been a kind of wilful murtherers if they would have gone abroad among healthy people—and it would have verified indeed the suggestion which I mentioned above, and which I thought seemed untrue: viz., that the infected people were utterly careless as to giving the infection to others, and rather forward to do it than not; and I believe it was partly from this very thing that they raised that suggestion, which I hope was not really true in fact.

I confess no particular case is sufficient to prove a general, but I could name several people within the knowledge of some of their neighbours and families yet living who showed the contrary to an extreme. One man, a master of a family in my neighbourhood, having had the distemper, he thought he had it given him by a poor workman whom he employed, and whom he went to his house to see, or went for some work that he wanted to have finished; and he had some apprehensions even while he was at the poor workman's door, but did not discover it fully; but the next day it discovered itself, and he was taken very in, upon which he immediately caused himself to be carried into an outbuilding which he had in his yard, and where there was a chamber over a workhouse (the man being a brazier). Here he lay, and here he died, and would be tended by none of his neighbours, but by a nurse from abroad; and would not suffer his wife, nor children, nor servants to come up into the room, lest they should be infected—but sent them his blessing and prayers for them by the nurse, who spoke it to them at a distance, and all this for fear of giving them the distemper; and without which he knew, as they were kept up, they could not have it.

And here I must observe also that the plague, as I suppose all distempers do, operated in a different manner on differing constitutions; some were immediately overwhelmed with it, and it came to violent fevers, vomitings, insufferable headaches, pains in the back, and so up to ravings and ragings with those pains; others with swellings and tumours in the neck or groin, or armpits, which till they could be broke put them into insufferable agonies and torment; while others, as I have observed, were silently infected, the fever preying upon their spirits insensibly, and they seeing little of it till they fell into swooning, and faintings, and death without pain. I am not physician enough to enter into the particular reasons and manner of these differing effects of one and the same distemper, and of its differing operation in several bodies; nor is it my business here to record the observations which I really made, because the doctors themselves have done that part much more effectually than I can do, and because my opinion may in some things differ from theirs. I am only relating what I know, or have heard, or believe of the particular cases, and what fell within the compass of my view, and the different nature of the infection as it appeared in the particular cases which I have related; but this may be added too: that though the former sort of those cases, namely, those openly visited, were the worst for themselves as to pain—I mean those that had such fevers, vomitings, headaches, pains, and swellings, because they died in such a dreadful manner—yet the latter had the worst state of the disease; for in the former they frequently recovered, especially if the swellings broke; but the latter was inevitable death; no cure, no help, could be possible, nothing could follow but death. And it was worse also to others, because, as above, it secretly and unperceived by others or by themselves, communicated death to those they conversed with, the penetrating poison insinuating itself into their blood in a manner which it is impossible to describe, or indeed conceive.

This infecting and being infected without so much as its being known to either person is evident from two sorts of cases which frequently happened at that time; and there is hardly anybody living who was in London during the infection but must have known several of the cases of both sorts.

(1) Fathers and mothers have gone about as if they had been well, and have believed themselves to be so, till they have insensibly infected and been the destruction of their whole families, which they would have been far from doing if they had the least apprehensions of their being unsound and dangerous themselves. A family, whose story I have heard, was thus infected by the father; and the distemper began to appear upon some of them even before he found it upon himself. But searching more narrowly, it appeared he had been affected some time; and as soon as he found that his family had been poisoned by himself he went distracted, and would have laid violent hands upon himself, but was kept from that by those who looked to him, and in a few days died.

(2) The other particular is, that many people having been well to the best of their own judgement, or by the best observation which they could make of themselves for several days, and only finding a decay of appetite, or a light sickness upon their stomachs; nay, some whose appetite has been strong, and even craving, and only a light pain in their heads, have sent for physicians to know what ailed them, and have been found, to their great surprise, at the brink of death: the tokens upon them, or the plague grown up to an incurable height.

It was very sad to reflect how such a person as this last mentioned above had been a walking destroyer perhaps for a week or a fortnight before that; how he had ruined those that he would have hazarded his life to save, and had been breathing death upon them, even perhaps in his tender kissing and embracings of his own children. Yet thus certainly it was, and often has been, and I could give many particular cases where it has been so. If then the blow is thus insensibly striking—if the arrow flies thus unseen, and cannot be discovered—to what purpose are all the schemes for shutting up or removing the sick people? Those schemes cannot take place but upon those that appear to be sick, or to be infected; whereas there are among them at the same time thousands of people who seem to be well, but are all that while carrying death with them into all companies which they come into.

This frequently puzzled our physicians, and especially the apothecaries and surgeons, who knew not how to discover the sick from the sound; they all allowed that it was really so, that many people had the plague in their very blood, and preying upon their spirits, and were in themselves but walking putrefied carcases whose breath was infectious and their sweat poison, and yet were as well to look on as other people, and even knew it not themselves; I say, they all allowed that it was really true in fact, but they knew not how to propose a discovery.

My friend Dr Heath was of opinion that it might be known by the smell of their breath; but then, as he said, who durst smell to that breath for his information? since, to know it, he must draw the stench of the plague up into his own brain, in order to distinguish the smell! I have heard it was the opinion of others that it might be distinguished by the party's breathing upon a piece of glass, where, the breath condensing, there might living creatures be seen by a microscope, of strange, monstrous, and frightful shapes, such as dragons, snakes, serpents, and devils, horrible to behold. But this I very much question the truth of, and we had no microscopes at that time, as I remember, to make the experiment with.

It was the opinion also of another learned man, that the breath of such a person would poison and instantly kill a bird; not only a small bird, but even a cock or hen, and that, if it did not immediately kill the latter, it would cause them to be roupy, as they call it; particularly that if they had laid any eggs at any time, they would be all rotten. But those are opinions which I never found supported by any experiments, or heard of others that had seen it; so I leave them as I find them; only with this remark, namely, that I think the probabilities are very strong for them.

Some have proposed that such persons should breathe hard upon warm water, and that they would leave an unusual scum upon it, or upon several other things, especially such as are of a glutinous substance and are apt to receive a scum and support it.

But from the whole I found that the nature of this contagion was such that it was impossible to discover it at all, or to prevent its spreading from one to another by any human skill.

Here was indeed one difficulty which I could never thoroughly get over to this time, and which there is but one way of answering that I know of, and it is this, viz., the first person that died of the plague was on December 20, or thereabouts, 1664, and in or about long Acre; whence the first person had the infection was generally said to be from a parcel of silks imported from Holland, and first opened in that house.

But after this we heard no more of any person dying of the plague, or of the distemper being in that place, till the 9th of February, which was about seven weeks after, and then one more was buried out of the same house. Then it was hushed, and we were perfectly easy as to the public for a great while; for there were no more entered in the weekly bill to be dead of the plague till the 22nd of April, when there was two more buried, not out of the same house, but out of the same street; and, as near as I can remember, it was out of the next house to the first. This was nine weeks asunder, and after this we had no more till a fortnight, and then it broke out in several streets and spread every way. Now the question seems to lie thus: Where lay the seeds of the infection all this while? How came it to stop so long, and not stop any longer? Either the distemper did not come immediately by contagion from body to body, or, if it did, then a body may be capable to continue infected without the disease discovering itself many days, nay, weeks together; even not a quarantine of days only, but soixantine; not only forty days, but sixty days or longer.

It is true there was, as I observed at first, and is well known to many yet living, a very cold winter and a long frost which continued three months; and this, the doctors say, might check the infection; but then the learned must allow me to say that if, according to their notion, the disease was (as I may say) only frozen up, it would like a frozen river have returned to its usual force and current when it thawed—whereas the principal recess of this infection, which was from February to April, was after the frost was broken and the weather mild and warm.

But there is another way of solving all this difficulty, which I think my own remembrance of the thing will supply; and that is, the fact is not granted—namely, that there died none in those long intervals, viz., from the 20th of December to the 9th of February, and from thence to the 22nd of April. The weekly bills are the only evidence on the other side, and those bills were not of credit enough, at least with me, to support an hypothesis or determine a question of such importance as this; for it was our received opinion at that time, and I believe upon very good grounds, that the fraud lay in the parish officers, searchers, and persons appointed to give account of the dead, and what diseases they died of; and as people were very loth at first to have the neighbours believe their houses were infected, so they gave money to procure, or otherwise procured, the dead persons to be returned as dying of other distempers; and this I know was practised afterwards in many places, I believe I might say in all places where the distemper came, as will be seen by the vast increase of the numbers placed in the weekly bills under other articles of diseases during the time of the infection. For example, in the months of July and August, when the plague was coming on to its highest pitch, it was very ordinary to have from a thousand to twelve hundred, nay, to almost fifteen hundred a week of other distempers. Not that the numbers of those distempers were really increased to such a degree, but the great number of families and houses where really the infection was, obtained the favour to have their dead be returned of other distempers, to prevent the shutting up their houses. For example:—

Dead of other diseases beside the plague —
    From the 18th July to the 25th..........942
    From the 25th July to the 1st August..........1004
    From the 1st August to the 8th..........1213
    From the 8th August to the 15th..........1439
    From the 15th August to the 22nd..........1331
    From the 22nd August to the 29th..........1394
    From the 29th August to the 5th September..........1264
    From the 5th September to the 12th..........1056
    From the 12th September to the 19th..........1132
    From the 19th September to the 26th..........927

Now it was not doubted but the greatest part of these, or a great part of them, were dead of the plague, but the officers were prevailed with to return them as above, and the numbers of some particular articles of distempers discovered is as follows:—

Aug1-8..Aug8-15..Aug15-22..Aug22-29..Aug29-Sep5..Sep5-12..Sep12-19..Sep19-26

Fever							
314	*353*	*348*	*383*	*364*	*332*	*309*	*268*

Spotted Fever
...174.....190...........166........165.........157...........97.........101.........65

Surfeit
....85.......87...........74.........99.........68...........45.........49..........36

Teeth
....90.....113...........111........133.........138...........128.......121........112
—
...663.....743..........699........780.........727...........602.......580........481

There were several other articles which bore a proportion to these, and which, it is easy to perceive, were increased on the same account, as aged, consumptions, vomitings, imposthumes, gripes, and the like, many of which were not doubted to be infected people; but as it was of the utmost consequence to families not to be known to be infected, if it was possible to avoid it, so they took all the measures they could to have it not believed, and if any died in their houses, to get them returned to the examiners, and by the searchers, as having died of other distempers.

This, I say, will account for the long interval which, as I have said, was between the dying of the first persons that were returned in the bill to be dead of the plague and the time when the distemper spread openly and could not be concealed.

Besides, the weekly bills themselves at that time evidently discover the truth; for, while there was no mention of the plague, and no increase after it had been mentioned, yet it was apparent that there was an increase of those distempers which bordered nearest upon it; for example, there were eight, twelve, seventeen of the spotted fever in a week, when there were none, or but very few, of the plague; whereas before, one, three, or four were the ordinary weekly numbers of that distemper. Likewise, as I observed before, the burials increased weekly in that particular parish and the parishes adjacent more than in any other parish, although there were none set down of the plague; all which tells us, that the infection was handed on, and the succession of the distemper really preserved, though it seemed to us at that time to be ceased, and to come again in a manner surprising.

It might be, also, that the infection might remain in other parts of the same parcel of goods which at first it came in, and which might not be perhaps opened, or at least not fully, or in the clothes of the first infected person; for I cannot think that anybody could be seized with the contagion in a fatal and mortal degree for nine weeks together, and support his state of health so well as even not to discover it to themselves; yet if it were so, the argument is the stronger in favour of what I am saying: namely, that the infection is retained in bodies apparently well, and conveyed from them to those they converse with, while it is known to neither the one nor the other.

Great were the confusions at that time upon this very account, and when people began to be convinced that the infection was received in this surprising manner from persons apparently well, they began to be exceeding shy and jealous of every one that came near them. Once, on a public day, whether a Sabbath-day or not I do not remember, in Aldgate Church, in a pew full of people, on a sudden one fancied she smelt an ill smell. Immediately she fancies the plague was in the pew, whispers her notion or suspicion to the next, then rises and goes out of the pew. It immediately took with the next, and so to them all; and every one of them, and of the two or three adjoining pews, got up and went out of the church, nobody knowing what it was offended them, or from whom.

This immediately filled everybody's mouths with one preparation or other, such as the old woman directed, and some perhaps as physicians directed, in order to prevent infection by the breath of others; insomuch that if we came to go into a church when it was anything full of people, there would be such a mixture of smells at the entrance that it was much more strong, though perhaps not so wholesome, than if you were going into an apothecary's or druggist's shop. In a word, the whole church was like a smelling-bottle; in one corner it was all perfumes; in another, aromatics, balsamics, and variety of drugs and herbs; in another, salts and spirits, as every one was furnished for their own preservation. Yet I observed that after people were possessed, as I have said, with the belief, or rather assurance, of the infection being thus carried on by persons apparently in health, the churches and meeting-houses were much thinner of people than at other times before that they used to be. For this is to be said of the people of London, that during the whole time of the pestilence the churches or meetings were never wholly shut up, nor did the people decline coming out to the public worship of God, except only in some parishes when the violence of the distemper was more particularly in that parish at that time, and even then no longer than it continued to be so.

Indeed nothing was more strange than to see with what courage the people went to the public service of God, even at that time when they were afraid to stir out of their own houses upon any other occasion; this, I mean, before the time of desperation, which I have mentioned already. This was a proof of the exceeding populousness of the city at the time of the infection, notwithstanding the great numbers that were gone into the country at the first alarm, and that fled out into the forests and woods when they were further terrified with the extraordinary increase of it. For when we came to see the crowds and throngs of people which appeared on the Sabbath-days at the churches, and especially in those parts of the town where the plague was abated, or where it was not yet come to its height, it was amazing. But of this I shall speak again presently. I return in the meantime to the article of infecting one another at first, before people came to right notions of the infection, and of infecting one another. People were only shy of those that were really sick, a man with a cap upon his head, or with clothes round his neck, which was the case of those that had swellings there. Such was indeed frightful; but when we saw a gentleman dressed, with his band on and his gloves in his hand, his hat upon his head, and his hair combed, of such we had not the least apprehensions, and people conversed a great while freely, especially with their neighbours and such as they knew. But when the physicians assured us that the danger was as well from the sound (that is, the seemingly sound) as the sick, and that those people who thought themselves entirely free were oftentimes the most fatal, and that it came to be generally understood that people were sensible of it, and of the reason of it; then, I say, they began to be jealous of everybody, and a vast number of people locked themselves up, so as not to come abroad into any company at all, nor suffer any that had been abroad in promiscuous company to come into their houses, or near them—at least not so near them as to be within the reach of their breath or of any smell from them; and when they were obliged to converse at a distance with strangers, they would always have preservatives in their mouths and about their clothes to repel and keep off the infection.

It must be acknowledged that when people began to use these cautions they were less exposed to danger, and the infection did not break into such houses so furiously as it did into others before; and thousands of families were preserved (speaking with due reserve to the direction of Divine Providence) by that means.

But it was impossible to beat anything into the heads of the poor. They went on with the usual impetuosity of their tempers, full of outcries and lamentations when taken, but madly careless of themselves, foolhardy and obstinate, while they were well. Where they could get employment they pushed into any kind of business, the most dangerous and the most liable to infection; and if they were spoken to, their answer would be, 'I must trust to God for that; if I am taken, then I am provided for, and there is an end of me', and the like. Or thus, 'Why, what must I do? I can't starve. I had as good have the plague as perish for want. I have no work; what could I do? I must do this or beg.' Suppose it was burying the dead, or attending the sick, or watching infected houses, which were all terrible hazards; but their tale was generally the same. It is true, necessity was a very justifiable, warrantable plea, and nothing could be better; but their way of talk was much the same where the necessities were not the same. This adventurous conduct of the poor was that which brought the plague among them in a most furious manner; and this, joined to the distress of their circumstances when taken, was the reason why they died so by heaps; for I cannot say I could observe one jot of better husbandry among them, I mean the labouring poor, while they were all well and getting money than there was before, but as lavish, as extravagant, and as thoughtless for tomorrow as ever; so that when they came to be taken sick they were immediately in the utmost distress, as well for want as for sickness, as well for lack of food as lack of health.

This misery of the poor I had many occasions to be an eyewitness of, and sometimes also of the charitable assistance that some pious people daily gave to such, sending them relief and supplies both of food, physic, and other help, as they found they wanted; and indeed it is a debt of justice due to the temper of the people of that day to take notice here, that not only great sums, very great sums of money were charitably sent to the Lord Mayor and aldermen for the assistance and support of the poor distempered people, but abundance of private people daily distributed large sums of money for their relief, and sent people about to inquire into the condition of particular distressed and visited families, and relieved them; nay, some pious ladies were so transported with zeal in so good a work, and so confident in the protection of Providence in discharge of the great duty of charity, that they went about in person distributing alms to the poor, and even visiting poor families, though sick and infected, in their very houses, appointing nurses to attend those that wanted attending, and ordering apothecaries and surgeons, the first to supply them with drugs or plasters, and such things as they wanted; and the last to lance and dress the swellings and tumours, where such were wanting; giving their blessing to the poor in substantial relief to them, as well as hearty prayers for them.

I will not undertake to say, as some do, that none of those charitable people were suffered to fall under the calamity itself; but this I may say, that I never knew any one of them that miscarried, which I mention for the encouragement of others in case of the like distress; and doubtless, if they that give to the poor lend to the Lord, and He will repay them, those that hazard their lives to give to the poor, and to comfort and assist the poor in such a misery as this, may hope to be protected in the work.

Nor was this charity so extraordinary eminent only in a few, but (for I cannot lightly quit this point) the charity of the rich, as well in the city and suburbs as from the country, was so great that, in a word, a prodigious number of people who must otherwise inevitably have perished for want as well as sickness were supported and subsisted by it; and though I could never, nor I believe any one else, come to a full knowledge of what was so contributed, yet I do believe that, as I heard one say that was a critical observer of that part, there was not only many thousand pounds contributed, but many hundred thousand pounds, to the relief of the poor of this distressed, afflicted city; nay, one man affirmed to me that he could reckon up above one hundred thousand pounds a week, which was distributed by the churchwardens at the several parish vestries by the Lord Mayor and aldermen in the several wards and precincts, and by the particular direction of the court and of the justices respectively in the parts where they resided, over and above the private charity distributed by pious bands in the manner I speak of; and this continued for many weeks together.

I confess this is a very great sum; but if it be true that there was distributed in the parish of Cripplegate only, 17,800 in one week to the relief of the poor, as I heard reported, and which I really believe was true, the other may not be improbable.

It was doubtless to be reckoned among the many signal good providences which attended this great city, and of which there were many other worth recording,—I say, this was a very remarkable one, that it pleased God thus to move the hearts of the people in all parts of the kingdom so cheerfully to contribute to the relief and support of the poor at London, the good consequences of which were felt many ways, and particularly in preserving the lives and recovering the health of so many thousands, and keeping so many thousands of families from perishing and starving.

And now I am talking of the merciful disposition of Providence in this time of calamity, I cannot but mention again, though I have spoken several times of it already on other accounts, I mean that of the progression of the distemper; how it began at one end of the town, and proceeded gradually and slowly from one part to another, and like a dark cloud that passes over our heads, which, as it thickens and overcasts the air at one end, clears up at the other end; so, while the plague went on raging from west to east, as it went forwards east, it abated in the west, by which means those parts of the town which were not seized, or who were left, and where it had spent its fury, were (as it were) spared to help and assist the other; whereas, had the distemper spread itself over the whole city and suburbs, at once, raging in all places alike, as it has done since in some places abroad, the whole body of the people must have been overwhelmed, and there would have died twenty thousand a day, as they say there did at Naples; nor would the people have been able to have helped or assisted one another.

For it must be observed that where the plague was in its full force, there indeed the people were very miserable, and the consternation was inexpressible. But a little before it reached even to that place, or presently after it was gone, they were quite another sort of people; and I cannot but acknowledge that there was too much of that common temper of mankind to be found among us all at that time, namely, to forget the deliverance when the danger is past. But I shall come to speak of that part again.

It must not be forgot here to take some notice of the state of trade during the time of this common calamity, and this with respect to foreign trade, as also to our home trade.

As to foreign trade, there needs little to be said. The trading nations of Europe were all afraid of us; no port of France, or Holland, or Spain, or Italy would admit our ships or correspond with us; indeed we stood on ill terms with the Dutch, and were in a furious war with them, but though in a bad condition to fight abroad, who had such dreadful enemies to struggle with at home.

Our merchants were accordingly at a full stop; their ships could go nowhere—that is to say, to no place abroad; their manufactures and merchandise—that is to say, of our growth—would not be touched abroad. They were as much afraid of our goods as they were of our people; and indeed they had reason: for our woollen manufactures are as retentive of infection as human bodies, and if packed up by persons infected, would receive the infection and be as dangerous to touch as a man would be that was infected; and therefore, when any English vessel arrived in foreign countries, if they did take the goods on shore, they always caused the bales to be opened and aired in places appointed for that purpose. But from London they would not suffer them to come into port, much less to unlade their goods, upon any terms whatever, and this strictness was especially used with them in Spain and Italy. In Turkey and the islands of the Arches indeed, as they are called, as well those belonging to the Turks as to the Venetians, they were not so very rigid. In the first there was no obstruction at all; and four ships which were then in the river loading for Italy—that is, for Leghorn and Naples—being denied product, as they call it, went on to Turkey, and were freely admitted to unlade their cargo without any difficulty; only that when they arrived there, some of their cargo was not fit for sale in that country; and other parts of it being consigned to merchants at Leghorn, the captains of the ships had no right nor any orders to dispose of the goods; so that great inconveniences followed to the merchants. But this was nothing but what the necessity of affairs required, and the merchants at Leghorn and Naples having notice given them, sent again from thence to take care of the effects which were particularly consigned to those ports, and to bring back in other ships such as were improper for the markets at Smyrna and Scanderoon.

The inconveniences in Spain and Portugal were still greater, for they would by no means suffer our ships, especially those from London, to come into any of their ports, much less to unlade. There was a report that one of our ships having by stealth delivered her cargo, among which was some bales of English cloth, cotton, kerseys, and such-like goods, the Spaniards caused all the goods to be burned, and punished the men with death who were concerned in carrying them on shore. This, I believe, was in part true, though I do not affirm it; but it is not at all unlikely, seeing the danger was really very great, the infection being so violent in London.

I heard likewise that the plague was carried into those countries by some of our ships, and particularly to the port of Faro in the kingdom of Algarve, belonging to the King of Portugal, and that several persons died of it there; but it was not confirmed.

On the other hand, though the Spaniards and Portuguese were so shy of us, it is most certain that the plague (as has been said) keeping at first much at that end of the town next Westminster, the merchandising part of the town (such as the city and the water-side) was perfectly sound till at least the beginning of July, and the ships in the river till the beginning of August; for to the 1st of July there had died but seven within the whole city, and but sixty within the liberties, but one in all the parishes of Stepney, Aldgate, and Whitechappel, and but two in the eight parishes of Southwark. But it was the same thing abroad, for the bad news was gone over the whole world that the city of London was infected with the plague, and there was no inquiring there how the infection proceeded, or at which part of the town it was begun or was reached to.

Besides, after it began to spread it increased so fast, and the bills grew so high all on a sudden, that it was to no purpose to lessen the report of it, or endeavour to make the people abroad think it better than it was; the account which the weekly bills gave in was sufficient; and that there died two thousand to three or four thousand a week was sufficient to alarm the whole trading part of the world; and the following time, being so dreadful also in the very city itself, put the whole world, I say, upon their guard against it.

You may be sure, also, that the report of these things lost nothing in the carriage. The plague was itself very terrible, and the distress of the people very great, as you may observe of what I have said. But the rumour was infinitely greater, and it must not be wondered that our friends abroad (as my brother's correspondents in particular were told there, namely, in Portugal and Italy, where he chiefly traded) [said] that in London there died twenty thousand in a week; that the dead bodies lay unburied by heaps; that the living were not sufficient to bury the dead or the sound to look after the sick; that all the kingdom was infected likewise, so that it was an universal malady such as was never heard of in those parts of the world; and they could hardly believe us when we gave them an account how things really were, and how there was not above one-tenth part of the people dead; that there was 500,000, left that lived all the time in the town; that now the people began to walk the streets again, and those who were fled to return, there was no miss of the usual throng of people in the streets, except as every family might miss their relations and neighbours, and the like. I say they could not believe these things; and if inquiry were now to be made in Naples, or in other cities on the coast of Italy, they would tell you that there was a dreadful infection in London so many years ago, in which, as above, there died twenty thousand in a week, &c., just as we have had it reported in London that there was a plague in the city of Naples in the year 1656, in which there died 20,000 people in a day, of which I have had very good satisfaction that it was utterly false.

But these extravagant reports were very prejudicial to our trade, as well as unjust and injurious in themselves, for it was a long time after the plague was quite over before our trade could recover itself in those parts of the world; and the Flemings and Dutch (but especially the last) made very great advantages of it, having all the market to themselves, and even buying our manufactures in several parts of England where the plague was not, and carrying them to Holland and Flanders, and from thence transporting them to Spain and to Italy as if they had been of their own making.

But they were detected sometimes and punished: that is to say, their goods confiscated and ships also; for if it was true that our manufactures as well as our people were infected, and that it was dangerous to touch or to open and receive the smell of them, then those people ran the hazard by that clandestine trade not only of carrying the contagion into their own country, but also of infecting the nations to whom they traded with those goods; which, considering how many lives might be lost in consequence of such an action, must be a trade that no men of conscience could suffer themselves to be concerned in.

I do not take upon me to say that any harm was done, I mean of that kind, by those people. But I doubt I need not make any such proviso in the case of our own country; for either by our people of London, or by the commerce which made their conversing with all sorts of people in every country and of every considerable town necessary, I say, by this means the plague was first or last spread all over the kingdom, as well in London as in all the cities and great towns, especially in the trading manufacturing towns and seaports; so that, first or last, all the considerable places in England were visited more or less, and the kingdom of Ireland in some places, but not so universally. How it fared with the people in Scotland I had no opportunity to inquire.

It is to be observed that while the plague continued so violent in London, the outports, as they are called, enjoyed a very great trade, especially to the adjacent countries and to our own plantations. For example, the towns of Colchester, Yarmouth, and Hull, on that side of England, exported to Holland and Hamburg the manufactures of the adjacent countries for several months after the trade with London was, as it were, entirely shut up; likewise the cities of Bristol and Exeter, with the port of Plymouth, had the like advantage to Spain, to the Canaries, to Guinea, and to the West Indies, and particularly to Ireland; but as the plague spread itself every way after it had been in London to such a degree as it was in August and September, so all or most of those cities and towns were infected first or last; and then trade was, as it were, under a general embargo or at a full stop—as I shall observe further when I speak of our home trade.

One thing, however, must be observed: that as to ships coming in from abroad (as many, you may be sure, did) some who were out in all parts of the world a considerable while before, and some who when they went out knew nothing of an infection, or at least of one so terrible— these came up the river boldly, and delivered their cargoes as they were obliged to do, except just in the two months of August and September, when the weight of the infection lying, as I may say, all below Bridge, nobody durst appear in business for a while. But as this continued but for a few weeks, the homeward-bound ships, especially such whose cargoes were not liable to spoil, came to an anchor for a time short of the Pool,[5] or fresh-water part of the river, even as low as the river Medway, where several of them ran in; and others lay at the Nore, and in the Hope below Gravesend. So that by the latter end of October there was a very great fleet of homeward-bound ships to come up, such as the like had not been known for many years.

Two particular trades were carried on by water-carriage all the while of the infection, and that with little or no interruption, very much to the advantage and comfort of the poor distressed people of the city: and those were the coasting trade for corn and the Newcastle trade for coals.

The first of these was particularly carried on by small vessels from the port of Hull and other places on the Humber, by which great quantities of corn were brought in from Yorkshire and Lincolnshire. The other part of this corn-trade was from Lynn, in Norfolk, from Wells and Burnham, and from Yarmouth, all in the same county; and the third branch was from the river Medway, and from Milton, Feversham, Margate, and Sandwich, and all the other little places and ports round the coast of Kent and Essex.

There was also a very good trade from the coast of Suffolk with corn, butter, and cheese; these vessels kept a constant course of trade, and without interruption came up to that market known still by the name of Bear Key, where they supplied the city plentifully with corn when land-carriage began to fail, and when the people began to be sick of coming from many places in the country.

This also was much of it owing to the prudence and conduct of the Lord Mayor, who took such care to keep the masters and seamen from danger when they came up, causing their corn to be bought off at any time they wanted a market (which, however, was very seldom), and causing the corn-factors immediately to unlade and deliver the vessels loaden with corn, that they had very little occasion to come out of their ships or vessels, the money being always carried on board to them and put into a pail of vinegar before it was carried.

The second trade was that of coals from Newcastle-upon-Tyne, without which the city would have been greatly distressed; for not in the streets only, but in private houses and families, great quantities of coals were then burnt, even all the summer long and when the weather was hottest, which was done by the advice of the physicians. Some indeed opposed it, and insisted that to keep the houses and rooms hot was a means to propagate the temper, which was a fermentation and heat already in the blood; that it was known to spread and increase in hot weather and abate in cold; and therefore they alleged that all contagious distempers are the worse for heat, because the contagion was nourished and gained strength in hot weather, and was, as it were, propagated in heat.

Others said they granted that heat in the climate might propagate infection—as sultry, hot weather fills the air with vermin and nourishes innumerable numbers and kinds of venomous creatures which breed in our food, in the plants, and even in our bodies, by the very stench of which infection may be propagated; also that heat in the air, or heat of weather, as we ordinarily call it, makes bodies relax and faint, exhausts the spirits, opens the pores, and makes us more apt to receive infection, or any evil influence, be it from noxious pestilential vapours or any other thing in the air; but that the heat of fire, and especially of coal fires kept in our houses, or near us, had a quite different operation; the heat being not of the same kind, but quick and fierce, tending not to nourish but to consume and dissipate all those noxious fumes which the other kind of heat rather exhaled and stagnated than separated and burnt up. Besides, it was alleged that the sulphurous and nitrous particles that are often found to be in the coal, with that bituminous substance which burns, are all assisting to clear and purge the air, and render it wholesome and safe to breathe in after the noxious particles, as above, are dispersed and burnt up.

The latter opinion prevailed at that time, and, as I must confess, I think with good reason; and the experience of the citizens confirmed it, many houses which had constant fires kept in the rooms having never been infected at all; and I must join my experience to it, for I found the keeping good fires kept our rooms sweet and wholesome, and I do verily believe made our whole family so, more than would otherwise have been.

But I return to the coals as a trade. It was with no little difficulty that this trade was kept open, and particularly because, as we were in an open war with the Dutch at that time, the Dutch capers at first took a great many of our collier-ships, which made the rest cautious, and made them to stay to come in fleets together. But after some time the capers were either afraid to take them, or their masters, the States, were afraid they should, and forbade them, lest the plague should be among them, which made them fare the better.

For the security of those northern traders, the coal-ships were ordered by my Lord Mayor not to come up into the Pool above a certain number at a time, and ordered lighters and other vessels such as the woodmongers (that is, the wharf-keepers or coal-sellers) furnished, to go down and take out the coals as low as Deptford and Greenwich, and some farther down.

Others delivered great quantities of coals in particular places where the ships could come to the shore, as at Greenwich, Blackwall, and other places, in vast heaps, as if to be kept for sale; but were then fetched away after the ships which brought them were gone, so that the seamen had no communication with the river-men, nor so much as came near one another.

Yet all this caution could not effectually prevent the distemper getting among the colliery: that is to say among the ships, by which a great many seamen died of it; and that which was still worse was, that they carried it down to Ipswich and Yarmouth, to Newcastle-upon-Tyne, and other places on the coast—where, especially at Newcastle and at Sunderland, it carried off a great number of people.

The making so many fires, as above, did indeed consume an unusual quantity of coals; and that upon one or two stops of the ships coming up, whether by contrary weather or by the interruption of enemies I do not remember, but the price of coals was exceeding dear, even as high as 4 l. a chalder; but it soon abated when the ships came in, and as afterwards they had a freer passage, the price was very reasonable all the rest of that year.

The public fires which were made on these occasions, as I have calculated it, must necessarily have cost the city about 200 chalders of coals a week, if they had continued, which was indeed a very great quantity; but as it was thought necessary, nothing was spared. However, as some of the physicians cried them down, they were not kept alight above four or five days. The fires were ordered thus:—

One at the Custom House, one at Billingsgate, one at Queenhith, and one at the Three Cranes; one in Blackfriars, and one at the gate of Bridewell; one at the corner of Leadenhal Street and Gracechurch; one at the north and one at the south gate of the Royal Exchange; one at Guild Hall, and one at Blackwell Hall gate; one at the Lord Mayor's door in St Helen's, one at the west entrance into St Paul's, and one at the entrance into Bow Church. I do not remember whether there was any at the city gates, but one at the Bridge-foot there was, just by St Magnus Church.

I know some have quarrelled since that at the experiment, and said that there died the more people because of those fires; but I am persuaded those that say so offer no evidence to prove it, neither can I believe it on any account whatever.

It remains to give some account of the state of trade at home in England during this dreadful time, and particularly as it relates to the manufactures and the trade in the city. At the first breaking out of the infection there was, as it is easy to suppose, a very great fright among the people, and consequently a general stop of trade, except in provisions and necessaries of life; and even in those things, as there was a vast number of people fled and a very great number always sick, besides the number which died, so there could not be above two-thirds, if above one-half, of the consumption of provisions in the city as used to be.

It pleased God to send a very plentiful year of corn and fruit, but not of hay or grass—by which means bread was cheap, by reason of the plenty of corn. Flesh was cheap, by reason of the scarcity of grass; but butter and cheese were dear for the same reason, and hay in the market just beyond Whitechappel Bars was sold at 4 pound per load. But that affected not the poor. There was a most excessive plenty of all sorts of fruit, such as apples, pears, plums, cherries, grapes, and they were the cheaper because of the want of people; but this made the poor eat them to excess, and this brought them into fluxes, griping of the guts, surfeits, and the like, which often precipitated them into the plague.

But to come to matters of trade. First, foreign exportation being stopped or at least very much interrupted and rendered difficult, a general stop of all those manufactures followed of course which were usually brought for exportation; and though sometimes merchants abroad were importunate for goods, yet little was sent, the passages being so generally stopped that the English ships would not be admitted, as is said already, into their port.

This put a stop to the manufactures that were for exportation in most parts of England, except in some out-ports; and even that was soon stopped, for they all had the plague in their turn. But though this was felt all over England, yet, what was still worse, all intercourse of trade for home consumption of manufactures, especially those which usually circulated through the Londoner's hands, was stopped at once, the trade of the city being stopped.

All kinds of handicrafts in the city, &c., tradesmen and mechanics, were, as I have said before, out of employ; and this occasioned the putting-off and dismissing an innumerable number of journeymen and workmen of all sorts, seeing nothing was done relating to such trades but what might be said to be absolutely necessary.

This caused the multitude of single people in London to be unprovided for, as also families whose living depended upon the labour of the heads of those families; I say, this reduced them to extreme misery; and I must confess it is for the honour of the city of London, and will be for many ages, as long as this is to be spoken of, that they were able to supply with charitable provision the wants of so many thousands of those as afterwards fell sick and were distressed: so that it may be safely averred that nobody perished for want, at least that the magistrates had any notice given them of.

This stagnation of our manufacturing trade in the country would have put the people there to much greater difficulties, but that the master-workmen, clothiers and others, to the uttermost of their stocks and strength, kept on making their goods to keep the poor at work, believing that soon as the sickness should abate they would have a quick demand in proportion to the decay of their trade at that time. But as none but those masters that were rich could do thus, and that many were poor and not able, the manufacturing trade in England suffered greatly, and the poor were pinched all over England by the calamity of the city of London only.

It is true that the next year made them full amends by another terrible calamity upon the city; so that the city by one calamity impoverished and weakened the country, and by another calamity, even terrible too of its kind, enriched the country and made them again amends; for an infinite quantity of household Stuff, wearing apparel, and other things, besides whole warehouses filled with merchandise and manufactures such as come from all parts of England, were consumed in the fire of London the next year after this terrible visitation. It is incredible what a trade this made all over the whole kingdom, to make good the want and to supply that loss; so that, in short, all the manufacturing hands in the nation were set on work, and were little enough for several years to supply the market and answer the demands. All foreign markets also were empty of our goods by the stop which had been occasioned by the plague, and before an open trade was allowed again; and the prodigious demand at home falling in, joined to make a quick vent for all sort of goods; so that there never was known such a trade all over England for the time as was in the first seven years after the plague, and after the fire of London.

It remains now that I should say something of the merciful part of this terrible judgement. The last week in September, the plague being come to its crisis, its fury began to assuage. I remember my friend Dr Heath, coming to see me the week before, told me he was sure that the violence of it would assuage in a few days; but when I saw the weekly bill of that week, which was the highest of the whole year, being 8297 of all diseases, I upbraided him with it, and asked him what he had made his judgement from. His answer, however, was not so much to seek as I thought it would have been. 'Look you,' says he, 'by the number which are at this time sick and infected, there should have been twenty thousand dead the last week instead of eight thousand, if the inveterate mortal contagion had been as it was two weeks ago; for then it ordinarily killed in two or three days, now not under eight or ten; and then not above one in five recovered, whereas I have observed that now not above two in five miscarry. And, observe it from me, the next bill will decrease, and you will see many more people recover than used to do; for though a vast multitude are now everywhere infected, and as many every day fall sick, yet there will not so many die as there did, for the malignity of the distemper is abated';—adding that he began now to hope, nay, more than hope, that the infection had passed its crisis and was going off; and accordingly so it was, for the next week being, as I said, the last in September, the bill decreased almost two thousand.

It is true the plague was still at a frightful height, and the next bill was no less than 6460, and the next to that, 5720; but still my friend's observation was just, and it did appear the people did recover faster and more in number than they used to do; and indeed, if it had not been so, what had been the condition of the city of London? For, according to my friend, there were not fewer than 60,000 people at that time infected, whereof, as above, 20,477 died, and near 40,000 recovered; whereas, had it been as it was before, 50,000 of that number would very probably have died, if not more, and 50,000 more would have sickened; for, in a word, the whole mass of people began to sicken, and it looked as if none would escape.

But this remark of my friend's appeared more evident in a few weeks more, for the decrease went on, and another week in October it decreased 1843, so that the number dead of the plague was but 2665; and the next week it decreased 1413 more, and yet it was seen plainly that there was abundance of people sick, nay, abundance more than ordinary, and abundance fell sick every day but (as above) the malignity of the disease abated.

Such is the precipitant disposition of our people (whether it is so or not all over the world, that's none of my particular business to inquire), but I saw it apparently here, that as upon the first fright of the infection they shunned one another, and fled from one another's houses and from the city with an unaccountable and, as I thought, unnecessary fright, so now, upon this notion spreading, viz., that the distemper was not so catching as formerly, and that if it was catched it was not so mortal, and seeing abundance of people who really fell sick recover again daily, they took to such a precipitant courage, and grew so entirely regardless of themselves and of the infection, that they made no more of the plague than of an ordinary fever, nor indeed so much. They not only went boldly into company with those who had tumours and carbuncles upon them that were running, and consequently contagious, but ate and drank with them, nay, into their houses to visit them, and even, as I was told, into their very chambers where they lay sick.

This I could not see rational. My friend Dr Heath allowed, and it was plain to experience, that the distemper was as catching as ever, and as many fell sick, but only he alleged that so many of those that fell sick did not die; but I think that while many did die, and that at best the distemper itself was very terrible, the sores and swellings very tormenting, and the danger of death not left out of the circumstances of sickness, though not so frequent as before; all those things, together with the exceeding tediousness of the cure, the loathsomeness of the disease, and many other articles, were enough to deter any man living from a dangerous mixture with the sick people, and make them as anxious almost to avoid the infections as before.

Nay, there was another thing which made the mere catching of the distemper frightful, and that was the terrible burning of the caustics which the surgeons laid on the swellings to bring them to break and to run, without which the danger of death was very great, even to the last. Also, the insufferable torment of the swellings, which, though it might not make people raving and distracted, as they were before, and as I have given several instances of already, yet they put the patient to inexpressible torment; and those that fell into it, though they did escape with life, yet they made bitter complaints of those that had told them there was no danger, and sadly repented their rashness and folly in venturing to run into the reach of it.

Nor did this unwary conduct of the people end here, for a great many that thus cast off their cautions suffered more deeply still, and though many escaped, yet many died; and at least it had this public mischief attending it, that it made the decrease of burials slower than it would otherwise have been. For as this notion ran like lightning through the city, and people's heads were possessed with it, even as soon as the first great decrease in the bills appeared, we found that the two next bills did not decrease in proportion; the reason I take to be the people's running so rashly into danger, giving up all their former cautions and care, and all the shyness which they used to practise, depending that the sickness would not reach them—or that if it did, they should not die.

The physicians opposed this thoughtless humour of the people with all their might, and gave out printed directions, spreading them all over the city and suburbs, advising the people to continue reserved, and to use still the utmost caution in their ordinary conduct, notwithstanding the decrease of the distemper, terrifying them with the danger of bringing a relapse upon the whole city, and telling them how such a relapse might be more fatal and dangerous than the whole visitation that had been already; with many arguments and reasons to explain and prove that part to them, and which are too long to repeat here.

But it was all to no purpose; the audacious creatures were so possessed with the first joy and so surprised with the satisfaction of seeing a vast decrease in the weekly bills, that they were impenetrable by any new terrors, and would not be persuaded but that the bitterness of death was past; and it was to no more purpose to talk to them than to an east wind; but they opened shops, went about streets, did business, and conversed with anybody that came in their way to converse with, whether with business or without, neither inquiring of their health or so much as being apprehensive of any danger from them, though they knew them not to be sound.

This imprudent, rash conduct cost a great many their lives who had with great care and caution shut themselves up and kept retired, as it were, from all mankind, and had by that means, under God's providence, been preserved through all the heat of that infection.

This rash and foolish conduct, I say, of the people went so far that the ministers took notice to them of it at last, and laid before them both the folly and danger of it; and this checked it a little, so that they grew more cautious. But it had another effect, which they could not check; for as the first rumour had spread not over the city only, but into the country, it had the like effect: and the people were so tired with being so long from London, and so eager to come back, that they flocked to town without fear or forecast, and began to show themselves in the streets as if all the danger was over. It was indeed surprising to see it, for though there died still from 1000 to 1800 a week, yet the people flocked to town as if all had been well.

The consequence of this was, that the bills increased again 400 the very first week in November; and if I might believe the physicians, there was above 3000 fell sick that week, most of them new-comers, too.

One John Cock, a barber in St Martin's-le-Grand, was an eminent example of this; I mean of the hasty return of the people when the plague was abated. This John Cock had left the town with his whole family, and locked up his house, and was gone in the country, as many others did; and finding the plague so decreased in November that there died but 905 per week of all diseases, he ventured home again. He had in his family ten persons; that is to say, himself and wife, five children, two apprentices, and a maid-servant. He had not returned to his house above a week, and began to open his shop and carry on his trade, but the distemper broke out in his family, and within about five days they all died, except one; that is to say, himself, his wife, all his five children, and his two apprentices; and only the maid remained alive.

But the mercy of God was greater to the rest than we had reason to expect; for the malignity (as I have said) of the distemper was spent, the contagion was exhausted, and also the winter weather came on apace, and the air was clear and cold, with sharp frosts; and this increasing still, most of those that had fallen sick recovered, and the health of the city began to return. There were indeed some returns of the distemper even in the month of December, and the bills increased near a hundred; but it went off again, and so in a short while things began to return to their own channel. And wonderful it was to see how populous the city was again all on a sudden, so that a stranger could not miss the numbers that were lost. Neither was there any miss of the inhabitants as to their dwellings—few or no empty houses were to be seen, or if there were some, there was no want of tenants for them.

I wish I could say that as the city had a new face, so the manners of the people had a new appearance. I doubt not but there were many that retained a sincere sense of their deliverance, and were that heartily thankful to that Sovereign Hand that had protected them in so dangerous a time; it would be very uncharitable to judge otherwise in a city so populous, and where the people were so devout as they were here in the time of the visitation itself; but except what of this was to be found in particular families and faces, it must be acknowledged that the general practice of the people was just as it was before, and very little difference was to be seen.

Some, indeed, said things were worse; that the morals of the people declined from this very time; that the people, hardened by the danger they had been in, like seamen after a storm is over, were more wicked and more stupid, more bold and hardened, in their vices and immoralities than they were before; but I will not carry it so far neither. It would take up a history of no small length to give a particular of all the gradations by which the course of things in this city came to be restored again, and to run in their own channel as they did before.

Some parts of England were now infected as violently as London had been; the cities of Norwich, Peterborough, Lincoln, Colchester, and other places were now visited; and the magistrates of London began to set rules for our conduct as to corresponding with those cities. It is true we could not pretend to forbid their people coming to London, because it was impossible to know them asunder; so, after many consultations, the Lord Mayor and Court of Aldermen were obliged to drop it. All they could do was to warn and caution the people not to entertain in their houses or converse with any people who they knew came from such infected places.

But they might as well have talked to the air, for the people of London thought themselves so plague-free now that they were past all admonitions; they seemed to depend upon it that the air was restored, and that the air was like a man that had had the smallpox, not capable of being infected again. This revived that notion that the infection was all in the air, that there was no such thing as contagion from the sick people to the sound; and so strongly did this whimsy prevail among people that they ran all together promiscuously, sick and well. Not the Mahometans, who, prepossessed with the principle of predestination, value nothing of contagion, let it be in what it will, could be more obstinate than the people of London; they that were perfectly sound, and came out of the wholesome air, as we call it, into the city, made nothing of going into the same houses and chambers, nay, even into the same beds, with those that had the distemper upon them, and were not recovered.

Some, indeed, paid for their audacious boldness with the price of their lives; an infinite number fell sick, and the physicians had more work than ever, only with this difference, that more of their patients recovered; that is to say, they generally recovered, but certainly there were more people infected and fell sick now, when there did not die above a thousand or twelve hundred in a week, than there was when there died five or six thousand a week, so entirely negligent were the people at that time in the great and dangerous case of health and infection, and so ill were they able to take or accept of the advice of those who cautioned them for their good.

The people being thus returned, as it were, in general, it was very strange to find that in their inquiring after their friends, some whole families were so entirely swept away that there was no remembrance of them left, neither was anybody to be found to possess or show any title to that little they had left; for in such cases what was to be found was generally embezzled and purloined, some gone one way, some another.

It was said such abandoned effects came to the king, as the universal heir; upon which we are told, and I suppose it was in part true, that the king granted all such, as deodands, to the Lord Mayor and Court of Aldermen of London, to be applied to the use of the poor, of whom there were very many. For it is to be observed, that though the occasions of relief and the objects of distress were very many more in the time of the violence of the plague than now after all was over, yet the distress of the poor was more now a great deal than it was then, because all the sluices of general charity were now shut. People supposed the main occasion to be over, and so stopped their hands; whereas particular objects were still very moving, and the distress of those that were poor was very great indeed.

Though the health of the city was now very much restored, yet foreign trade did not begin to stir, neither would foreigners admit our ships into their ports for a great while. As for the Dutch, the misunderstandings between our court and them had broken out into a war the year before, so that our trade that way was wholly interrupted; but Spain and Portugal, Italy and Barbary, as also Hamburg and all the ports in the Baltic, these were all shy of us a great while, and would not restore trade with us for many months.

The distemper sweeping away such multitudes, as I have observed, many if not all the out-parishes were obliged to make new burying-grounds, besides that I have mentioned in Bunhill Fields, some of which were continued, and remain in use to this day. But others were left off, and (which I confess I mention with some reflection) being converted into other uses or built upon afterwards, the dead bodies were disturbed, abused, dug up again, some even before the flesh of them was perished from the bones, and removed like dung or rubbish to other places. Some of those which came within the reach of my observation are as follow:

(1) A piece of ground beyond Goswell Street, near Mount Mill, being some of the remains of the old lines or fortifications of the city, where abundance were buried promiscuously from the parishes of Aldersgate, Clerkenwell, and even out of the city. This ground, as I take it, was since made a physic garden, and after that has been built upon.

(2) A piece of ground just over the Black Ditch, as it was then called, at the end of Holloway Lane, in Shoreditch parish. It has been since made a yard for keeping hogs, and for other ordinary uses, but is quite out of use as a burying-ground.

(3) The upper end of Hand Alley, in Bishopsgate Street, which was then a green field, and was taken in particularly for Bishopsgate parish, though many of the carts out of the city brought their dead thither also, particularly out of the parish of St All-hallows on the Wall. This place I cannot mention without much regret. It was, as I remember, about two or three years after the plague was ceased that Sir Robert Clayton came to be possessed of the ground. It was reported, how true I know not, that it fell to the king for want of heirs, all those who had any right to it being carried off by the pestilence, and that Sir Robert Clayton obtained a grant of it from King Charles II. But however he came by it, certain it is the ground was let out to build on, or built upon, by his order. The first house built upon it was a large fair house, still standing, which faces the street or way now called Hand Alley which, though called an alley, is as wide as a street. The houses in the same row with that house northward are built on the very same ground where the poor people were buried, and the bodies, on opening the ground for the foundations, were dug up, some of them remaining so plain to be seen that the women's skulls were distinguished by their long hair, and of others the flesh was not quite perished; so that the people began to exclaim loudly against it, and some suggested that it might endanger a return of the contagion; after which the bones and bodies, as fast as they came at them, were carried to another part of the same ground and thrown all together into a deep pit, dug on purpose, which now is to be known in that it is not built on, but is a passage to another house at the upper end of Rose Alley, just against the door of a meeting-house which has been built there many years since; and the ground is palisadoed off from the rest of the passage, in a little square; there lie the bones and remains of near two thousand bodies, carried by the dead carts to their grave in that one year.

(4) Besides this, there was a piece of ground in Moorfields; by the going into the street which is now called Old Bethlem, which was enlarged much, though not wholly taken in on the same occasion.

[N.B.—The author of this journal lies buried in that very ground, being at his own desire, his sister having been buried there a few years before.]

(5) Stepney parish, extending itself from the east part of London to the north, even to the very edge of Shoreditch Churchyard, had a piece of ground taken in to bury their dead close to the said churchyard, and which for that very reason was left open, and is since, I suppose, taken into the same churchyard. And they had also two other burying-places in Spittlefields, one where since a chapel or tabernacle has been built for ease to this great parish, and another in Petticoat Lane.

There were no less than five other grounds made use of for the parish of Stepney at that time: one where now stands the parish church of St Paul, Shadwell, and the other where now stands the parish church of St John's at Wapping, both which had not the names of parishes at that time, but were belonging to Stepney parish.

I could name many more, but these coming within my particular knowledge, the circumstance, I thought, made it of use to record them. From the whole, it may be observed that they were obliged in this time of distress to take in new burying-grounds in most of the out-parishes for laying the prodigious numbers of people which died in so short a space of time; but why care was not taken to keep those places separate from ordinary uses, that so the bodies might rest undisturbed, that I cannot answer for, and must confess I think it was wrong. Who were to blame I know not.

I should have mentioned that the Quakers had at that time also a burying-ground set apart to their use, and which they still make use of; and they had also a particular dead-cart to fetch their dead from their houses; and the famous Solomon Eagle, who, as I mentioned before, had predicted the plague as a judgement, and ran naked through the streets, telling the people that it was come upon them to punish them for their sins, had his own wife died the very next day of the plague, and was carried, one of the first in the Quakers' dead-cart, to their new burying-ground.

I might have thronged this account with many more remarkable things which occurred in the time of the infection, and particularly what passed between the Lord Mayor and the Court, which was then at Oxford, and what directions were from time to time received from the Government for their conduct on this critical occasion. But really the Court concerned themselves so little, and that little they did was of so small import, that I do not see it of much moment to mention any part of it here: except that of appointing a monthly fast in the city and the sending the royal charity to the relief of the poor, both which I have mentioned before.

Great was the reproach thrown on those physicians who left their patients during the sickness, and now they came to town again nobody cared to employ them. They were called deserters, and frequently bills were set up upon their doors and written, 'Here is a doctor to be let', so that several of those physicians were fain for a while to sit still and look about them, or at least remove their dwellings, and set up in new places and among new acquaintance. The like was the case with the clergy, whom the people were indeed very abusive to, writing verses and scandalous reflections upon them, setting upon the church-door, 'Here is a pulpit to be let', or sometimes, 'to be sold', which was worse.

It was not the least of our misfortunes that with our infection, when it ceased, there did not cease the spirit of strife and contention, slander and reproach, which was really the great troubler of the nation's peace before. It was said to be the remains of the old animosities, which had so lately involved us all in blood and disorder. But as the late Act of Indemnity had laid asleep the quarrel itself, so the Government had recommended family and personal peace upon all occasions to the whole nation.

But it could not be obtained; and particularly after the ceasing of the plague in London, when any one that had seen the condition which the people had been in, and how they caressed one another at that time, promised to have more charity for the future, and to raise no more reproaches; I say, any one that had seen them then would have thought they would have come together with another spirit at last. But, I say, it could not be obtained. The quarrel remained; the Church and the Presbyterians were incompatible. As soon as the plague was removed, the Dissenting ousted ministers who had supplied the pulpits which were deserted by the incumbents retired; they could expect no other but that they should immediately fall upon them and harass them with their penal laws, accept their preaching while they were sick, and persecute them as soon as they were recovered again; this even we that were of the Church thought was very hard, and could by no means approve of it.

But it was the Government, and we could say nothing to hinder it; we could only say it was not our doing, and we could not answer for it.

On the other hand, the Dissenters reproaching those ministers of the Church with going away and deserting their charge, abandoning the people in their danger, and when they had most need of comfort, and the like: this we could by no means approve, for all men have not the same faith and the same courage, and the Scripture commands us to judge the most favourably and according to charity.

A plague is a formidable enemy, and is armed with terrors that every man is not sufficiently fortified to resist or prepared to stand the shock against. It is very certain that a great many of the clergy who were in circumstances to do it withdrew and fled for the safety of their lives; but 'tis true also that a great many of them stayed, and many of them fell in the calamity and in the discharge of their duty.

It is true some of the Dissenting turned-out ministers stayed, and their courage is to be commended and highly valued—but these were not abundance; it cannot be said that they all stayed, and that none retired into the country, any more than it can be said of the Church clergy that they all went away. Neither did all those that went away go without substituting curates and others in their places, to do the offices needful and to visit the sick, as far as it was practicable; so that, upon the whole, an allowance of charity might have been made on both sides, and we should have considered that such a time as this of 1665 is not to be paralleled in history, and that it is not the stoutest courage that will always support men in such cases. I had not said this, but had rather chosen to record the courage and religious zeal of those of both sides, who did hazard themselves for the service of the poor people in their distress, without remembering that any failed in their duty on either side. But the want of temper among us has made the contrary to this necessary: some that stayed not only boasting too much of themselves, but reviling those that fled, branding them with cowardice, deserting their flocks, and acting the part of the hireling, and the like. I recommend it to the charity of all good people to look back and reflect duly upon the terrors of the time, and whoever does so will see that it is not an ordinary strength that could support it. It was not like appearing in the head of an army or charging a body of horse in the field, but it was charging Death itself on his pale horse; to stay was indeed to die, and it could be esteemed nothing less, especially as things appeared at the latter end of August and the beginning of September, and as there was reason to expect them at that time; for no man expected, and I dare say believed, that the distemper would take so sudden a turn as it did, and fall immediately two thousand in a week, when there was such a prodigious number of people sick at that time as it was known there was; and then it was that many shifted away that had stayed most of the time before.

Besides, if God gave strength to some more than to others, was it to boast of their ability to abide the stroke, and upbraid those that had not the same gift and support, or ought not they rather to have been humble and thankful if they were rendered more useful than their brethren?

I think it ought to be recorded to the honour of such men, as well clergy as physicians, surgeons, apothecaries, magistrates, and officers of every kind, as also all useful people who ventured their lives in discharge of their duty, as most certainly all such as stayed did to the last degree; and several of all these kinds did not only venture but lose their lives on that sad occasion.

I was once making a list of all such, I mean of all those professions and employments who thus died, as I call it, in the way of their duty; but it was impossible for a private man to come at a certainty in the particulars. I only remember that there died sixteen clergymen, two aldermen, five physicians, thirteen surgeons, within the city and liberties before the beginning of September. But this being, as I said before, the great crisis and extremity of the infection, it can be no complete list. As to inferior people, I think there died six-and-forty constables and head-boroughs in the two parishes of Stepney and Whitechappel; but I could not carry my list on, for when the violent rage of the distemper in September came upon us, it drove us out of all measures. Men did then no more die by tale and by number. They might put out a weekly bill, and call them seven or eight thousand, or what they pleased; 'tis certain they died by heaps, and were buried by heaps, that is to say, without account. And if I might believe some people, who were more abroad and more conversant with those things than I though I was public enough for one that had no more business to do than I had,—I say, if I may believe them, there was not many less buried those first three weeks in September than 20,000 per week. However, the others aver the truth of it; yet I rather choose to keep to the public account; seven and eight thousand per week is enough to make good all that I have said of the terror of those times;— and it is much to the satisfaction of me that write, as well as those that read, to be able to say that everything is set down with moderation, and rather within compass than beyond it.

Upon all these accounts, I say, I could wish, when we were recovered, our conduct had been more distinguished for charity and kindness in remembrance of the past calamity, and not so much a valuing ourselves upon our boldness in staying, as if all men were cowards that fly from the hand of God, or that those who stay do not sometimes owe their courage to their ignorance, and despising the hand of their Maker—which is a criminal kind of desperation, and not a true courage.

I cannot but leave it upon record that the civil officers, such as constables, head-boroughs, Lord Mayor's and sheriffs'-men, as also parish officers, whose business it was to take charge of the poor, did their duties in general with as much courage as any, and perhaps with more, because their work was attended with more hazards, and lay more among the poor, who were more subject to be infected, and in the most pitiful plight when they were taken with the infection. But then it must be added, too, that a great number of them died; indeed it was scarce possible it should be otherwise.

I have not said one word here about the physic or preparations that we ordinarily made use of on this terrible occasion—I mean we that went frequently abroad and up down street, as I did; much of this was talked of in the books and bills of our quack doctors, of whom I have said enough already. It may, however, be added, that the College of Physicians were daily publishing several preparations, which they had considered of in the process of their practice, and which, being to be had in print, I avoid repeating them for that reason.

One thing I could not help observing: what befell one of the quacks, who published that he had a most excellent preservative against the plague, which whoever kept about them should never be infected or liable to infection. This man, who, we may reasonably suppose, did not go abroad without some of this excellent preservative in his pocket, yet was taken by the distemper, and carried off in two or three days.

I am not of the number of the physic-haters or physic-despisers; on the contrary, I have often mentioned the regard I had to the dictates of my particular friend Dr Heath; but yet I must acknowledge I made use of little or nothing—except, as I have observed, to keep a preparation of strong scent to have ready, in case I met with anything of offensive smells or went too near any burying-place or dead body.

Neither did I do what I know some did: keep the spirits always high and hot with cordials and wine and such things; and which, as I observed, one learned physician used himself so much to as that he could not leave them off when the infection was quite gone, and so became a sot for all his life after.

I remember my friend the doctor used to say that there was a certain set of drugs and preparations which were all certainly good and useful in the case of an infection; out of which, or with which, physicians might make an infinite variety of medicines, as the ringers of bells make several hundred different rounds of music by the changing and order or sound but in six bells, and that all these preparations shall be really very good: 'Therefore,' said he, 'I do not wonder that so vast a throng of medicines is offered in the present calamity, and almost every physician prescribes or prepares a different thing, as his judgement or experience guides him; but', says my friend, 'let all the prescriptions of all the physicians in London be examined, and it will be found that they are all compounded of the same things, with such variations only as the particular fancy of the doctor leads him to; so that', says he, 'every man, judging a little of his own constitution and manner of his living, and circumstances of his being infected, may direct his own medicines out of the ordinary drugs and preparations. Only that', says he, 'some recommend one thing as most sovereign, and some another. Some', says he, 'think that pill. ruff., which is called itself the anti-pestilential pill is the best preparation that can be made; others think that Venice treacle is sufficient of itself to resist the contagion; and I', says he, 'think as both these think, viz., that the last is good to take beforehand to prevent it, and the first, if touched, to expel it.' According to this opinion, I several times took Venice treacle, and a sound sweat upon it, and thought myself as well fortified against the infection as any one could be fortified by the power of physic.

As for quackery and mountebanks, of which the town was so full, I listened to none of them, and have observed often since, with some wonder, that for two years after the plague I scarcely saw or heard of one of them about town. Some fancied they were all swept away in the infection to a man, and were for calling it a particular mark of God's vengeance upon them for leading the poor people into the pit of destruction, merely for the lucre of a little money they got by them; but I cannot go that length neither. That abundance of them died is certain—many of them came within the reach of my own knowledge—but that all of them were swept off I much question. I believe rather they fled into the country and tried their practices upon the people there, who were in apprehension of the infection before it came among them.

This, however, is certain, not a man of them appeared for a great while in or about London. There were, indeed, several doctors who published bills recommending their several physical preparations for cleansing the body, as they call it, after the plague, and needful, as they said, for such people to take who had been visited and had been cured; whereas I must own I believe that it was the opinion of the most eminent physicians at that time that the plague was itself a sufficient purge, and that those who escaped the infection needed no physic to cleanse their bodies of any other things; the running sores, the tumours, &c., which were broke and kept open by the directions of the physicians, having sufficiently cleansed them; and that all other distempers, and causes of distempers, were effectually carried off that way; and as the physicians gave this as their opinions wherever they came, the quacks got little business.

There were, indeed, several little hurries which happened after the decrease of the plague, and which, whether they were contrived to fright and disorder the people, as some imagined, I cannot say, but sometimes we were told the plague would return by such a time; and the famous Solomon Eagle, the naked Quaker I have mentioned, prophesied evil tidings every day; and several others telling us that London had not been sufficiently scourged, and that sorer and severer strokes were yet behind. Had they stopped there, or had they descended to particulars, and told us that the city should the next year be destroyed by fire, then, indeed, when we had seen it come to pass, we should not have been to blame to have paid more than a common respect to their prophetic spirits; at least we should have wondered at them, and have been more serious in our inquiries after the meaning of it, and whence they had the foreknowledge. But as they generally told us of a relapse into the plague, we have had no concern since that about them; yet by those frequent clamours, we were all kept with some kind of apprehensions constantly upon us; and if any died suddenly, or if the spotted fevers at any time increased, we were presently alarmed; much more if the number of the plague increased, for to the end of the year there were always between 200 and 300 of the plague. On any of these occasions, I say, we were alarmed anew.

Those who remember the city of London before the fire must remember that there was then no such place as we now call Newgate Market, but that in the middle of the street which is now called Blowbladder Street, and which had its name from the butchers, who used to kill and dress their sheep there (and who, it seems, had a custom to blow up their meat with pipes to make it look thicker and fatter than it was, and were punished there for it by the Lord Mayor); I say, from the end of the street towards Newgate there stood two long rows of shambles for the selling meat.

It was in those shambles that two persons falling down dead, as they were buying meat, gave rise to a rumour that the meat was all infected; which, though it might affright the people, and spoiled the market for two or three days, yet it appeared plainly afterwards that there was nothing of truth in the suggestion. But nobody can account for the possession of fear when it takes hold of the mind.

However, it Pleased God, by the continuing of the winter weather, so to restore the health of the city that by February following we reckoned the distemper quite ceased, and then we were not so easily frighted again.

There was still a question among the learned, and at first perplexed the people a little: and that was in what manner to purge the house and goods where the plague had been, and how to render them habitable again, which had been left empty during the time of the plague. Abundance of perfumes and preparations were prescribed by physicians, some of one kind and some of another, in which the people who listened to them put themselves to a great, and indeed, in my opinion, to an unnecessary expense; and the poorer people, who only set open their windows night and day, burned brimstone, pitch, and gunpowder, and such things in their rooms, did as well as the best; nay, the eager people who, as I said above, came home in haste and at all hazards, found little or no inconvenience in their houses, nor in the goods, and did little or nothing to them.

However, in general, prudent, cautious people did enter into some measures for airing and sweetening their houses, and burned perfumes, incense, benjamin, rozin, and sulphur in their rooms close shut up, and then let the air carry it all out with a blast of gunpowder; others caused large fires to be made all day and all night for several days and nights; by the same token that two or three were pleased to set their houses on fire, and so effectually sweetened them by burning them down to the ground; as particularly one at Ratcliff, one in Holbourn, and one at Westminster; besides two or three that were set on fire, but the fire was happily got out again before it went far enough to burn down the houses; and one citizen's servant, I think it was in Thames Street, carried so much gunpowder into his master's house, for clearing it of the infection, and managed it so foolishly, that he blew up part of the roof of the house. But the time was not fully come that the city was to be purged by fire, nor was it far off; for within nine months more I saw it all lying in ashes; when, as some of our quacking philosophers pretend, the seeds of the plague were entirely destroyed, and not before; a notion too ridiculous to speak of here: since, had the seeds of the plague remained in the houses, not to be destroyed but by fire, how has it been that they have not since broken out, seeing all those buildings in the suburbs and liberties, all in the great parishes of Stepney, Whitechappel, Aldgate, Bishopsgate, Shoreditch, Cripplegate, and St Giles, where the fire never came, and where the plague raged with the greatest violence, remain still in the same condition they were in before?

But to leave these things just as I found them, it was certain that those people who were more than ordinarily cautious of their health, did take particular directions for what they called seasoning of their houses, and abundance of costly things were consumed on that account which I cannot but say not only seasoned those houses, as they desired, but filled the air with very grateful and wholesome smells which others had the share of the benefit of as well as those who were at the expenses of them.

And yet after all, though the poor came to town very precipitantly, as I have said, yet I must say the rich made no such haste. The men of business, indeed, came up, but many of them did not bring their families to town till the spring came on, and that they saw reason to depend upon it that the plague would not return.

The Court, indeed, came up soon after Christmas, but the nobility and gentry, except such as depended upon and had employment under the administration, did not come so soon.

I should have taken notice here that, notwithstanding the violence of the plague in London and in other places, yet it was very observable that it was never on board the fleet; and yet for some time there was a strange press in the river, and even in the streets, for seamen to man the fleet. But it was in the beginning of the year, when the plague was scarce begun, and not at all come down to that part of the city where they usually press for seamen; and though a war with the Dutch was not at all grateful to the people at that time, and the seamen went with a kind of reluctancy into the service, and many complained of being dragged into it by force, yet it proved in the event a happy violence to several of them, who had probably perished in the general calamity, and who, after the summer service was over, though they had cause to lament the desolation of their families—who, when they came back, were many of them in their graves —yet they had room to be thankful that they were carried out of the reach of it, though so much against their wills. We indeed had a hot war with the Dutch that year, and one very great engagement at sea in which the Dutch were worsted, but we lost a great many men and some ships. But, as I observed, the plague was not in the fleet, and when they came to lay up the ships in the river the violent part of it began to abate.

I would be glad if I could close the account of this melancholy year with some particular examples historically; I mean of the thankfulness to God, our preserver, for our being delivered from this dreadful calamity. Certainly the circumstance of the deliverance, as well as the terrible enemy we were delivered from, called upon the whole nation for it. The circumstances of the deliverance were indeed very remarkable, as I have in part mentioned already, and particularly the dreadful condition which we were all in when we were to the surprise of the whole town made joyful with the hope of a stop of the infection.

Nothing but the immediate finger of God, nothing but omnipotent power, could have done it. The contagion despised all medicine; death raged in every corner; and had it gone on as it did then, a few weeks more would have cleared the town of all, and everything that had a soul. Men everywhere began to despair; every heart failed them for fear; people were made desperate through the anguish of their souls, and the terrors of death sat in the very faces and countenances of the people.

In that very moment when we might very well say, 'Vain was the help of man',—I say, in that very moment it pleased God, with a most agreeable surprise, to cause the fury of it to abate, even of itself; and the malignity declining, as I have said, though infinite numbers were sick, yet fewer died, and the very first weeks' bill decreased 1843; a vast number indeed!

It is impossible to express the change that appeared in the very countenances of the people that Thursday morning when the weekly bill came out. It might have been perceived in their countenances that a secret surprise and smile of joy sat on everybody's face. They shook one another by the hands in the streets, who would hardly go on the same side of the way with one another before. Where the streets were not too broad they would open their windows and call from one house to another, and ask how they did, and if they had heard the good news that the plague was abated. Some would return, when they said good news, and ask, 'What good news?' and when they answered that the plague was abated and the bills decreased almost two thousand, they would cry out, 'God be praised!' and would weep aloud for joy, telling them they had heard nothing of it; and such was the joy of the people that it was, as it were, life to them from the grave. I could almost set down as many extravagant things done in the excess of their joy as of their grief; but that would be to lessen the value of it.

I must confess myself to have been very much dejected just before this happened; for the prodigious number that were taken sick the week or two before, besides those that died, was such, and the lamentations were so great everywhere, that a man must have seemed to have acted even against his reason if he had so much as expected to escape; and as there was hardly a house but mine in all my neighbourhood but was infected, so had it gone on it would not have been long that there would have been any more neighbours to be infected. Indeed it is hardly credible what dreadful havoc the last three weeks had made, for if I might believe the person whose calculations I always found very well grounded, there were not less than 30,000 people dead and near 100.000 fallen sick in the three weeks I speak of; for the number that sickened was surprising, indeed it was astonishing, and those whose courage upheld them all the time before, sank under it now.

In the middle of their distress, when the condition of the city of London was so truly calamitous, just then it pleased God—as it were by His immediate hand to disarm this enemy; the poison was taken out of the sting. It was wonderful; even the physicians themselves were surprised at it. Wherever they visited they found their patients better; either they had sweated kindly, or the tumours were broke, or the carbuncles went down and the inflammations round them changed colour, or the fever was gone, or the violent headache was assuaged, or some good symptom was in the case; so that in a few days everybody was recovering, whole families that were infected and down, that had ministers praying with them, and expected death every hour, were revived and healed, and none died at all out of them.

Nor was this by any new medicine found out, or new method of cure discovered, or by any experience in the operation which the physicians or surgeons attained to; but it was evidently from the secret invisible hand of Him that had at first sent this disease as a judgement upon us; and let the atheistic part of mankind call my saying what they please, it is no enthusiasm; it was acknowledged at that time by all mankind. The disease was enervated and its malignity spent; and let it proceed from whencesoever it will, let the philosophers search for reasons in nature to account for it by, and labour as much as they will to lessen the debt they owe to their Maker, those physicians who had the least share of religion in them were obliged to acknowledge that it was all supernatural, that it was extraordinary, and that no account could be given of it.

If I should say that this is a visible summons to us all to thankfulness, especially we that were under the terror of its increase, perhaps it may be thought by some, after the sense of the thing was over, an officious canting of religious things, preaching a sermon instead of writing a history, making myself a teacher instead of giving my observations of things; and this restrains me very much from going on here as I might otherwise do. But if ten lepers were healed, and but one returned to give thanks, I desire to be as that one, and to be thankful for myself.

Nor will I deny but there were abundance of people who, to all appearance, were very thankful at that time; for their mouths were stopped, even the mouths of those whose hearts were not extraordinary long affected with it. But the impression was so strong at that time that it could not be resisted; no, not by the worst of the people.

It was a common thing to meet people in the street that were strangers, and that we knew nothing at all of, expressing their surprise. Going one day through Aldgate, and a pretty many people being passing and repassing, there comes a man out of the end of the Minories, and looking a little up the street and down, he throws his hands abroad, 'Lord, what an alteration is here! Why, last week I came along here, and hardly anybody was to be seen.' Another man—I heard him—adds to his words, ''Tis all wonderful; 'tis all a dream.' 'Blessed be God,' says a third man, and let us give thanks to Him, for 'tis all His own doing, human help and human skill was at an end.' These were all strangers to one another. But such salutations as these were frequent in the street every day; and in spite of a loose behaviour, the very common people went along the streets giving God thanks for their deliverance.

It was now, as I said before, the people had cast off all apprehensions, and that too fast; indeed we were no more afraid now to pass by a man with a white cap upon his head, or with a cloth wrapt round his neck, or with his leg limping, occasioned by the sores in his groin, all which were frightful to the last degree, but the week before. But now the street was full of them, and these poor recovering creatures, give them their due, appeared very sensible of their unexpected deliverance; and I should wrong them very much if I should not acknowledge that I believe many of them were really thankful. But I must own that, for the generality of the people, it might too justly be said of them as was said of the children of Israel after their being delivered from the host of Pharaoh, when they passed the Red Sea, and looked back and saw the Egyptians overwhelmed in the water: viz., that they sang His praise, but they soon forgot His works.

I can go no farther here. I should be counted censorious, and perhaps unjust, if I should enter into the unpleasing work of reflecting, whatever cause there was for it, upon the unthankfulness and return of all manner of wickedness among us, which I was so much an eye-witness of myself. I shall conclude the account of this calamitous year therefore with a coarse but sincere stanza of my own, which I placed at the end of my ordinary memorandums the same year they were written:—

> *A dreadful plague in London was*
> *In the year sixty-five,*
> *Which swept an hundred thousand souls*
> *Away; yet I alive!*

> — H. F.

1. It seems John was in the tent, but hearing them call, he steps out, and taking the gun upon his shoulder, talked to them as if he had been the sentinel placed there upon the guard by some officer that was his superior. [Footnote in the original.]
2. This frighted the constable and the people that were with him, that they immediately changed their note.
3. They had but one horse among them. [Footnotes in the original.]
4. Here he called to one of his men, and bade him order Captain Richard and his people to march the lower way on the side of the marches, and meet them in the forest; which was all a sham, for they had no Captain Richard, or any such company. [Footnote in the original.]
5. That part of the river where the ships lie up when they come home is called the Pool, and takes in all the river on both sides of the water, from the Tower to Cuckold's Point and Limehouse. [Footnote in the original.]

THE LAST MAN

MARY SHELLEY

❧ I ❧

INTRODUCTION

I visited Naples in the year 1818. On the 8th of December of that year, my companion and I crossed the Bay, to visit the antiquities which are scattered on the shores of Baiae. The translucent and shining waters of the calm sea covered fragments of old Roman villas, which were interlaced by sea-weed, and received diamond tints from the chequering of the sun-beams; the blue and pellucid element was such as Galatea might have skimmed in her car of mother of pearl; or Cleopatra, more fitly than the Nile, have chosen as the path of her magic ship. Though it was winter, the atmosphere seemed more appropriate to early spring; and its genial warmth contributed to inspire those sensations of placid delight, which are the portion of every traveler, as he lingers, loath to quit the tranquil bays and radiant promontories of Baiae.

We visited the so called Elysian Fields and Avernus: and wandered through various ruined temples, baths, and classic spots; at length we entered the gloomy cavern of the Cumaean Sibyl. Our Lazzeroni bore flaring torches, which shone red, and almost dusky, in the murky subterranean passages, whose darkness thirstily surrounding them, seemed eager to imbibe more and more of the element of light. We passed by a natural archway, leading to a second gallery, and enquired, if we could not enter there also. The guides pointed to the reflection of their torches on the water that paved it, leaving us to form our own conclusion; but adding it was a pity, for it led to the Sibyl's Cave. Our curiosity and enthusiasm were excited by this circumstance, and we insisted upon attempting the passage. As is usually the case in the prosecution of such enterprises, the difficulties decreased on examination. We found, on each side of the humid pathway, "dry land for the sole of the foot."

At length we arrived at a large, desert, dark cavern, which the Lazzeroni assured us was the Sibyl's Cave. We were sufficiently disappointed—Yet we examined it with care, as if its blank, rocky walls could still bear trace of celestial visitant. On one side was a small opening. Whither does this lead? we asked: can we enter here?—"Questo poi, no,"—said the wild looking savage, who held the torch; "you can advance but a short distance, and nobody visits it."

"Nevertheless, I will try it," said my companion; "it may lead to the real cavern. Shall I go alone, or will you accompany me?"

I signified my readiness to proceed, but our guides protested against such a measure. With great volubility, in their native Neapolitan dialect, with which we were not very familiar, they told us that there were spectres, that the roof would fall in, that it was too narrow to admit us, that there was a deep hole within, filled with water, and we might be drowned. My friend shortened the harangue, by taking the man's torch from him; and we proceeded alone.

The passage, which at first scarcely admitted us, quickly grew narrower and lower; we were almost bent double; yet still we persisted in making our way through it. At length we entered a wider space, and the low roof heightened; but, as we congratulated ourselves on this change, our torch was extinguished by a current of air, and we were left in utter darkness. The guides bring with them materials for renewing the light, but we had none—our only resource was to return as we came. We groped round the widened space to find the entrance, and after a time fancied that we had succeeded. This proved however to be a second passage, which evidently ascended. It terminated like the former; though something approaching to a ray, we could not tell whence, shed a very doubtful twilight in the space. By degrees, our eyes grew somewhat accustomed to this dimness, and we perceived that there was no direct passage leading us further; but that it was possible to climb one side of the cavern to a low arch at top, which promised a more easy path, from whence we now discovered that this light proceeded. With considerable difficulty we scrambled up, and came to another passage with still more of illumination, and this led to another ascent like the former.

After a succession of these, which our resolution alone permitted us to surmount, we arrived at a wide cavern with an arched dome-like roof. An aperture in the midst let in the light of heaven; but this was overgrown with brambles and underwood, which acted as a veil, obscuring the day, and giving a solemn religious hue to the apartment. It was spacious, and nearly circular, with a raised seat of stone, about the size of a Grecian couch, at one end. The only sign that life had been here, was the perfect snow-white skeleton of a goat, which had probably not perceived the opening as it grazed on the hill above, and had fallen headlong. Ages perhaps had elapsed since this catastrophe; and the ruin it had made above, had been repaired by the growth of vegetation during many hundred summers.

The rest of the furniture of the cavern consisted of piles of leaves, fragments of bark, and a white filmy substance, resembling the inner part of the green hood which shelters the grain of the unripe Indian corn. We were fatigued by our struggles to attain this point, and seated ourselves on the rocky couch, while the sounds of tinkling sheep-bells, and shout of shepherd-boy, reached us from above.

At length my friend, who had taken up some of the leaves strewed about, exclaimed, "This is the Sibyl's cave; these are Sibylline leaves." On examination, we found that all the leaves, bark, and other substances, were traced with written characters. What appeared to us more astonishing, was that these writings were expressed in various languages: some unknown to my companion, ancient Chaldee, and Egyptian hieroglyphics, old as the Pyramids. Stranger still, some were in modern dialects, English and Italian. We could make out little by the dim light, but they seemed to contain prophecies, detailed relations of events but lately passed; names, now well known, but of modern date; and often exclamations of exultation or woe, of victory or defeat, were traced on their thin scant pages. This was certainly the Sibyl's Cave; not indeed exactly as Virgil describes it, but the whole of this land had been so convulsed by earthquake and volcano, that the change was not wonderful, though the traces of ruin were effaced by time; and we probably owed the preservation of these leaves, to the accident which had closed the mouth of the cavern, and the swift-growing vegetation which had rendered its sole opening impervious to the storm. We made a hasty selection of such of the leaves, whose writing one at least of us could understand; and then, laden with our treasure, we bade adieu to the dim hypaethric cavern, and after much difficulty succeeded in rejoining our guides.

During our stay at Naples, we often returned to this cave, sometimes alone, skimming the sun-lit sea, and each time added to our store. Since that period, whenever the world's circumstance has not imperiously called me away, or the temper of my mind impeded such study, I have been employed in deciphering these sacred remains. Their meaning, wondrous and eloquent, has often repaid my toil, soothing me in sorrow, and exciting my imagination to daring flights, through the immensity of nature and the mind of man. For a while my labours were not solitary; but that time is gone; and, with the selected and matchless companion of my toils, their dearest reward is also lost to me—

> Di mie tenere frondi altro lavoro
> Credea mostrarte; e qual fero pianeta
> Ne' nvidio insieme, o mio nobil tesoro?

I present the public with my latest discoveries in the slight Sibylline pages. Scattered and unconnected as they were, I have been obliged to add links, and model the work into a consistent form. But the main substance rests on the truths contained in these poetic rhapsodies, and the divine intuition which the Cumaean damsel obtained from heaven.

I have often wondered at the subject of her verses, and at the English dress of the Latin poet. Sometimes I have thought, that, obscure and chaotic as they are, they owe their present form to me, their decipherer. As if we should give to another artist, the painted fragments which form the mosaic copy of Raphael's Transfiguration in St. Peter's; he would put them together in a form, whose mode would be fashioned by his own peculiar mind and talent. Doubtless the leaves of the Cumaean Sibyl have suffered distortion and diminution of interest and excellence in my hands. My only excuse for thus transforming them, is that they were unintelligible in their pristine condition.

My labours have cheered long hours of solitude, and taken me out of a world, which has averted its once benignant face from me, to one glowing with imagination and power. Will my readers ask how I could find solace from the narration of misery and woeful change? This is one of the mysteries of our nature, which holds full sway over me, and from whose influence I cannot escape. I confess, that I have not been unmoved by the development of the tale; and that I have been depressed, nay, agonized, at some parts of the recital, which I have faithfully transcribed from my materials. Yet such is human nature, that the excitement of mind was dear to me, and that the imagination, painter of tempest and earthquake, or, worse, the stormy and ruin-fraught passions of man, softened my real sorrows and endless regrets, by clothing these fictitious ones in that ideality, which takes the mortal sting from pain.

I hardly know whether this apology is necessary. For the merits of my adaptation and translation must decide how far I have well bestowed my time and imperfect powers, in giving form and substance to the frail and attenuated Leaves of the Sibyl.

I AM the native of a sea-surrounded nook, a cloud-enshadowed land, which, when the surface of the globe, with its shoreless ocean and trackless continents, presents itself to my mind, appears only as an inconsiderable speck in the immense whole; and yet, when balanced in the scale of mental power, far outweighed countries of larger extent and more numerous population. So true it is, that man's mind alone was the creator of all that was good or great to man, and that Nature herself was only his first minister. England, seated far north in the turbid sea, now visits my dreams in the semblance of a vast and well-manned ship, which mastered the winds and rode proudly over the waves. In my boyish days she was the universe to me. When I stood on my native hills, and saw plain and mountain stretch out to the utmost limits of my vision, speckled by the dwellings of my countrymen, and subdued to fertility by their labours, the earth's very centre was fixed for me in that spot, and the rest of her orb was as a fable, to have forgotten which would have cost neither my imagination nor understanding an effort.

My fortunes have been, from the beginning, an exemplification of the power that mutability may possess over the varied tenor of man's life. With regard to myself, this came almost by inheritance. My father was one of those men on whom nature had bestowed to prodigality the envied gifts of wit and imagination, and then left his bark of life to be impelled by these winds, without adding reason as the rudder, or judgment as the pilot for the voyage. His extraction was obscure; but circumstances brought him early into public notice, and his small paternal property was soon dissipated in the splendid scene of fashion and luxury in which he was an actor. During the short years of thoughtless youth, he was adored by the high-bred triflers of the day, nor least by the youthful sovereign, who escaped from the intrigues of party, and the arduous duties of kingly business, to find never-failing amusement and exhilaration of spirit in his society. My father's impulses, never under his own controul, perpetually led him into difficulties from which his ingenuity alone could extricate him; and the accumulating pile of debts of honour and of trade, which would have bent to earth any other, was supported by him with a light spirit and tameless hilarity; while his company was so necessary at the tables and assemblies of the rich, that his derelictions were considered venial, and he himself received with intoxicating flattery.

This kind of popularity, like every other, is evanescent: and the difficulties of every kind with which he had to contend, increased in a frightful ratio compared with his small means of extricating himself. At such times the king, in his enthusiasm for him, would come to his relief, and then kindly take his friend to task; my father gave the best promises for amendment, but his social disposition, his craving for the usual diet of admiration, and more than all, the fiend of gambling, which fully possessed him, made his good resolutions transient, his promises vain. With the quick sensibility peculiar to his temperament, he perceived his power in the brilliant circle to be on the wane. The king married; and the haughty princess of Austria, who became, as queen of England, the head of fashion, looked with harsh eyes on his defects, and with contempt on the affection her royal husband entertained for him. My father felt that his fall was near; but so far from profiting by this last calm before the storm to save himself, he sought to forget anticipated evil by making still greater sacrifices to the deity of pleasure, deceitful and cruel arbiter of his destiny.

The king, who was a man of excellent dispositions, but easily led, had now become a willing disciple of his imperious consort. He was induced to look with extreme disapprobation, and at last with distaste, on my father's imprudence and follies. It is true that his presence dissipated these clouds; his warm-hearted frankness, brilliant sallies, and confiding demeanour were irresistible: it was only when at a distance, while still renewed tales of his errors were poured into his royal friend's ear, that he lost his influence. The queen's dextrous management was employed to prolong these absences, and gather together accusations. At length the king was brought to see in him a source of perpetual disquiet, knowing that he should pay for the short-lived pleasure of his society by tedious homilies, and more painful narrations of excesses, the truth of which he could not disprove. The result was, that he would make one more attempt to reclaim him, and in case of ill success, cast him off forever.

Such a scene must have been one of deepest interest and high-wrought passion. A powerful king, conspicuous for a goodness which had heretofore made him meek, and now lofty in his admonitions, with alternate entreaty and reproof, besought his friend to attend to his real interests, resolutely to avoid those fascinations which in fact were fast deserting him, and to spend his great powers on a worthy field, in which he, his sovereign, would be his prop, his stay, and his pioneer. My father felt this kindness; for a moment ambitious dreams floated before him; and he thought that it would be well to exchange his present pursuits for nobler duties. With sincerity and fervour he gave the required promise: as a pledge of continued favour, he received from his royal master a sum of money to defray pressing debts, and enable him to enter under good auspices his new career. That very night, while yet full of gratitude and good resolves, this whole sum, and its amount doubled, was lost at the gaming-table. In his desire to repair his first losses, my father risked double stakes, and thus incurred a debt of honour he was wholly unable to pay. Ashamed to apply again to the king, he turned his back upon London, its false delights and clinging miseries; and, with poverty for his sole companion, buried himself in solitude among the hills and lakes of Cumberland. His wit, his bon mots, the record of his personal attractions, fascinating manners, and social talents, were long remembered and repeated from mouth to mouth. Ask where now was this favourite of fashion, this companion of the noble, this excelling beam, which gilt with alien splendour the assemblies of the courtly and the gay—you heard that he was under a cloud, a lost man; not one thought it belonged to him to repay pleasure by real services, or that his long reign of brilliant wit deserved a pension on retiring. The king lamented his absence; he loved to repeat his sayings, relate the adventures they had had together, and exalt his talents—but here ended his reminiscence.

Meanwhile my father, forgotten, could not forget. He repined for the loss of what was more necessary to him than air or food—the excitements of pleasure, the admiration of the noble, the luxurious and polished living of the great. A nervous fever was the consequence; during which he was nursed by the daughter of a poor cottager, under whose roof he lodged. She was lovely, gentle, and, above all, kind to him; nor can it afford astonishment, that the late idol of high-bred beauty should, even in a fallen state, appear a being of an elevated and wondrous nature to the lowly cottage-girl. The attachment between them led to the ill-fated marriage, of which I was the offspring. Notwithstanding the tenderness and sweetness of my mother, her husband still deplored his degraded state. Unaccustomed to industry, he knew not in what way to contribute to the support of his increasing family. Sometimes he thought of applying to the king; pride and shame for a while withheld him; and, before his necessities became so imperious as to compel him to some kind of exertion, he died. For one brief interval before this catastrophe, he looked forward to the future, and contemplated with anguish the desolate situation in which his wife and children would be left. His last effort was a letter to the king, full of touching eloquence, and of occasional flashes of that brilliant spirit which was an integral part of him. He bequeathed his widow and orphans to the friendship of his royal master, and felt satisfied that, by this means, their prosperity was better assured in his death than in his life. This letter was enclosed to the care of a nobleman, who, he did not doubt, would perform the last and inexpensive office of placing it in the king's own hand.

He died in debt, and his little property was seized immediately by his creditors. My mother, pennyless and burthened with two children, waited week after week, and month after month, in sickening expectation of a reply, which never came. She had no experience beyond her father's cottage; and the mansion of the lord of the manor was the chiefest type of grandeur she could conceive. During my father's life, she had been made familiar with the name of royalty and the courtly circle; but such things, ill according with her personal experience, appeared, after the loss of him who gave substance and reality to them, vague and fantastical. If, under any circumstances, she could have acquired sufficient courage to address the noble persons mentioned by her husband, the ill success of his own application caused her to banish the idea. She saw therefore no escape from dire penury: perpetual care, joined to sorrow for the loss of the wondrous being, whom she continued to contemplate with ardent admiration, hard labour, and naturally delicate health, at length released her from the sad continuity of want and misery.

The condition of her orphan children was peculiarly desolate. Her own father had been an emigrant from another part of the country, and had died long since: they had no one relation to take them by the hand; they were outcasts, paupers, unfriended beings, to whom the most scanty pittance was a matter of favour, and who were treated merely as children of peasants, yet poorer than the poorest, who, dying, had left them, a thankless bequest, to the close-handed charity of the land.

I, the elder of the two, was five years old when my mother died. A remembrance of the discourses of my parents, and the communications which my mother endeavoured to impress upon me concerning my father's friends, in slight hope that I might one day derive benefit from the knowledge, floated like an indistinct dream through my brain. I conceived that I was different and superior to my protectors and companions, but I knew not how or wherefore. The sense of injury, associated with the name of king and noble, clung to me; but I could draw no conclusions from such feelings, to serve as a guide to action. My first real knowledge of myself was as an unprotected orphan among the valleys and fells of Cumberland. I was in the service of a farmer; and with crook in hand, my dog at my side, I shepherded a numerous flock on the near uplands. I cannot say much in praise of such a life; and its pains far exceeded its pleasures. There was freedom in it, a companionship with nature, and a reckless loneliness; but these, romantic as they were, did not accord with the love of action and desire of human sympathy, characteristic of youth. Neither the care of my flock, nor the change of seasons, were sufficient to tame my eager spirit; my out-door life and unemployed time were the temptations that led me early into lawless habits. I associated with others friendless like myself; I formed them into a band, I was their chief and captain. All shepherd-boys alike, while our flocks were spread over the pastures, we schemed and executed many a mischievous prank, which drew on us the anger and revenge of the rustics. I was the leader and protector of my comrades, and as I became distinguished among them, their misdeeds were usually visited upon me. But while I endured punishment and pain in their defence with the spirit of an hero, I claimed as my reward their praise and obedience.

In such a school my disposition became rugged, but firm. The appetite for admiration and small capacity for self-controul which I inherited from my father, nursed by adversity, made me daring and reckless. I was rough as the elements, and unlearned as the animals I tended. I often compared myself to them, and finding that my chief superiority consisted in power, I soon persuaded myself that it was in power only that I was inferior to the chiefest potentates of the earth. Thus untaught in refined philosophy, and pursued by a restless feeling of degradation from my true station in society, I wandered among the hills of civilized England as uncouth a savage as the wolf-bred founder of old Rome. I owned but one law, it was that of the strongest, and my greatest deed of virtue was never to submit.

Yet let me a little retract from this sentence I have passed on myself. My mother, when dying, had, in addition to her other half-forgotten and misapplied lessons, committed, with solemn exhortation, her other child to my fraternal guardianship; and this one duty I performed to the best of my ability, with all the zeal and affection of which my nature was capable. My sister was three years younger than myself; I had nursed her as an infant, and when the difference of our sexes, by giving us various occupations, in a great measure divided us, yet she continued to be the object of my careful love. Orphans, in the fullest sense of the term, we were poorest among the poor, and despised among the unhonoured. If my daring and courage obtained for me a kind of respectful aversion, her youth and sex, since they did not excite tenderness, by proving her to be weak, were the causes of numberless mortifications to her; and her own disposition was not so constituted as to diminish the evil effects of her lowly station.

She was a singular being, and, like me, inherited much of the peculiar disposition of our father. Her countenance was all expression; her eyes were not dark, but impenetrably deep; you seemed to discover space after space in their intellectual glance, and to feel that the soul which was their soul, comprehended an universe of thought in its ken. She was pale and fair, and her golden hair clustered on her temples, contrasting its rich hue with the living marble beneath. Her coarse peasant-dress, little consonant apparently with the refinement of feeling which her face expressed, yet in a strange manner accorded with it. She was like one of Guido's saints, with heaven in her heart and in her look, so that when you saw her you only thought of that within, and costume and even feature were secondary to the mind that beamed in her countenance.

Yet though lovely and full of noble feeling, my poor Perdita (for this was the fanciful name my sister had received from her dying parent), was not altogether saintly in her disposition.

Her manners were cold and repulsive. If she had been nurtured by those who had regarded her with affection, she might have been different; but unloved and neglected, she repaid want of kindness with distrust and silence. She was submissive to those who held authority over her, but a perpetual cloud dwelt on her brow; she looked as if she expected enmity from every one who approached her, and her actions were instigated by the same feeling. All the time she could command she spent in solitude. She would ramble to the most unfrequented places, and scale dangerous heights, that in those unvisited spots she might wrap herself in loneliness. Often she passed whole hours walking up and down the paths of the woods; she wove garlands of flowers and ivy, or watched the flickering of the shadows and glancing of the leaves; sometimes she sat beside a stream, and as her thoughts paused, threw flowers or pebbles into the waters, watching how those swam and these sank; or she would set afloat boats formed of bark of trees or leaves, with a feather for a sail, and intensely watch the navigation of her craft among the rapids and shallows of the brook. Meanwhile her active fancy wove a thousand combinations; she dreamt "of moving accidents by flood and field"—she lost herself delightedly in these self-created wanderings, and returned with unwilling spirit to the dull detail of common life. Poverty was the cloud that veiled her excellencies, and all that was good in her seemed about to perish from want of the genial dew of affection. She had not even the same advantage as I in the recollection of her parents; she clung to me, her brother, as her only friend, but her alliance with me completed the distaste that her protectors felt for her; and every error was magnified by them into crimes. If she had been bred in that sphere of life to which by inheritance the delicate framework of her mind and person was adapted, she would have been the object almost of adoration, for her virtues were as eminent as her defects. All the genius that ennobled the blood of her father illustrated hers; a generous tide flowed in her veins; artifice, envy, or meanness, were at the antipodes of her nature; her countenance, when enlightened by amiable feeling, might have belonged to a queen of nations; her eyes were bright; her look fearless.

Although by our situation and dispositions we were almost equally cut off from the usual forms of social intercourse, we formed a strong contrast to each other. I always required the stimulants of companionship and applause. Perdita was all-sufficient to herself. Notwithstanding my lawless habits, my disposition was sociable, hers recluse. My life was spent among tangible realities, hers was a dream. I might be said even to love my enemies, since by exciting me they in a sort bestowed happiness upon me; Perdita almost disliked her friends, for they interfered with her visionary moods. All my feelings, even of exultation and triumph, were changed to bitterness, if unparticipated; Perdita, even in joy, fled to loneliness, and could go on from day to day, neither expressing her emotions, nor seeking a fellow-feeling in another mind. Nay, she could love and dwell with tenderness on the look and voice of her friend, while her demeanour expressed the coldest reserve. A sensation with her became a sentiment, and she never spoke until she had mingled her perceptions of outward objects with others which were the native growth of her own mind. She was like a fruitful soil that imbibed the airs and dews of heaven, and gave them forth again to light in loveliest forms of fruits and flowers; but then she was often dark and rugged as that soil, raked up, and new sown with unseen seed.

She dwelt in a cottage whose trim grass-plat sloped down to the waters of the lake of Ulswater; a beech wood stretched up the hill behind, and a purling brook gently falling from the acclivity ran through poplar-shaded banks into the lake. I lived with a farmer whose house was built higher up among the hills: a dark crag rose behind it, and, exposed to the north, the snow lay in its crevices the summer through. Before dawn I led my flock to the sheep-walks, and guarded them through the day. It was a life of toil; for rain and cold were more frequent than sunshine; but it was my pride to contemn the elements. My trusty dog watched the sheep as I slipped away to the rendezvous of my comrades, and thence to the accomplishment of our schemes. At noon we met again, and we threw away in contempt our peasant fare, as we built our fire-place and kindled the cheering blaze destined to cook the game stolen from the neighbouring preserves. Then came the tale of hair-breadth escapes, combats with dogs, ambush and flight, as gypsy-like we encompassed our pot. The search after a stray lamb, or the devices by which we elude or endeavoured to elude punishment, filled up the hours of afternoon; in the evening my flock went to its fold, and I to my sister.

It was seldom indeed that we escaped, to use an old-fashioned phrase, scot free. Our dainty fare was often exchanged for blows and imprisonment. Once, when thirteen years of age, I was sent for a month to the county jail. I came out, my morals unimproved, my hatred to my oppressors increased tenfold. Bread and water did not tame my blood, nor solitary confinement inspire me with gentle thoughts. I was angry, impatient, miserable; my only happy hours were those during which I devised schemes of revenge; these were perfected in my forced solitude, so that during the whole of the following season, and I was freed early in September, I never failed to provide excellent and plenteous fare for myself and my comrades. This was a glorious winter. The sharp frost and heavy snows tamed the animals, and kept the country gentlemen by their firesides; we got more game than we could eat, and my faithful dog grew sleek upon our refuse.

Thus years passed on; and years only added fresh love of freedom, and contempt for all that was not as wild and rude as myself. At the age of sixteen I had shot up in appearance to man's estate; I was tall and athletic; I was practised to feats of strength, and inured to the inclemency of the elements. My skin was embrowned by the sun; my step was firm with conscious power. I feared no man, and loved none. In after life I looked back with wonder to what I then was; how utterly worthless I should have become if I had pursued my lawless career. My life was like that of an animal, and my mind was in danger of degenerating into that which informs brute nature. Until now, my savage habits had done me no radical mischief; my physical powers had grown up and flourished under their influence, and my mind, undergoing the same discipline, was imbued with all the hardy virtues. But now my boasted independence was daily instigating me to acts of tyranny, and freedom was becoming licentiousness. I stood on the brink of manhood; passions, strong as the trees of a forest, had already taken root within me, and were about to shadow with their noxious overgrowth, my path of life.

I panted for enterprises beyond my childish exploits, and formed distempered dreams of future action. I avoided my ancient comrades, and I soon lost them. They arrived at the age when they were sent to fulfil their destined situations in life; while I, an outcast, with none to lead or drive me forward, paused. The old began to point at me as an example, the young to wonder at me as a being distinct from themselves; I hated them, and began, last and worst degradation, to hate myself. I clung to my ferocious habits, yet half despised them; I continued my war against civilization, and yet entertained a wish to belong to it.

I revolved again and again all that I remembered my mother to have told me of my father's former life; I contemplated the few relics I possessed belonging to him, which spoke of greater refinement than could be found among the mountain cottages; but nothing in all this served as a guide to lead me to another and pleasanter way of life. My father had been connected with nobles, but all I knew of such connection was subsequent neglect. The name of the king,—he to whom my dying father had addressed his latest prayers, and who had barbarously slighted them, was associated only with the ideas of unkindness, injustice, and consequent resentment. I was born for something greater than I was—and greater I would become; but greatness, at least to my distorted perceptions, was no necessary associate of goodness, and my wild thoughts were unchecked by moral considerations when they rioted in dreams of distinction. Thus I stood upon a pinnacle, a sea of evil rolled at my feet; I was about to precipitate myself into it, and rush like a torrent over all obstructions to the object of my wishes— when a stranger influence came over the current of my fortunes, and changed their boisterous course to what was in comparison like the gentle meanderings of a meadow-encircling streamlet.

2

I LIVED FAR from the busy haunts of men, and the rumour of wars or political changes came worn to a mere sound, to our mountain abodes. England had been the scene of momentous struggles, during my early boyhood. In the year 2073, the last of its kings, the ancient friend of my father, had abdicated in compliance with the gentle force of the remonstrances of his subjects, and a republic was instituted. Large estates were secured to the dethroned monarch and his family; he received the title of Earl of Windsor, and Windsor Castle, an ancient royalty, with its wide demesnes were a part of his allotted wealth. He died soon after, leaving two children, a son and a daughter.

The ex-queen, a princess of the house of Austria, had long impelled her husband to withstand the necessity of the times. She was haughty and fearless; she cherished a love of power, and a bitter contempt for him who had despoiled himself of a kingdom. For her children's sake alone she consented to remain, shorn of regality, a member of the English republic. When she became a widow, she turned all her thoughts to the educating her son Adrian, second Earl of Windsor, so as to accomplish her ambitious ends; and with his mother's milk he imbibed, and was intended to grow up in the steady purpose of re-acquiring his lost crown. Adrian was now fifteen years of age. He was addicted to study, and imbued beyond his years with learning and talent: report said that he had already begun to thwart his mother's views, and to entertain republican principles. However this might be, the haughty Countess entrusted none with the secrets of her family-tuition. Adrian was bred up in solitude, and kept apart from the natural companions of his age and rank. Some unknown circumstance now induced his mother to send him from under her immediate tutelage; and we heard that he was about to visit Cumberland. A thousand tales were rife, explanatory of the Countess of Windsor's conduct; none true probably; but each day it became more certain that we should have the noble scion of the late regal house of England among us.

There was a large estate with a mansion attached to it, belonging to this family, at Ulswater. A large park was one of its appendages, laid out with great taste, and plentifully stocked with game. I had often made depredations on these preserves; and the neglected state of the property facilitated my incursions. When it was decided that the young Earl of Windsor should visit Cumberland, workmen arrived to put the house and grounds in order for his reception. The apartments were restored to their pristine splendour, and the park, all disrepairs restored, was guarded with unusual care.

I was beyond measure disturbed by this intelligence. It roused all my dormant recollections, my suspended sentiments of injury, and gave rise to the new one of revenge. I could no longer attend to my occupations; all my plans and devices were forgotten; I seemed about to begin life anew, and that under no good auspices. The tug of war, I thought, was now to begin. He would come triumphantly to the district to which my parent had fled broken-hearted; he would find the ill-fated offspring, bequeathed with such vain confidence to his royal father, miserable paupers. That he should know of our existence, and treat us, near at hand, with the same contumely which his father had practised in distance and absence, appeared to me the certain consequence of all that had gone before. Thus then I should meet this titled stripling—the son of my father's friend. He would be hedged in by servants; nobles, and the sons of nobles, were his companions; all England rang with his name; and his coming, like a thunderstorm, was heard from far: while I, unlettered and unfashioned, should, if I came in contact with him, in the judgment of his courtly followers, bear evidence in my very person to the propriety of that ingratitude which had made me the degraded being I appeared.

With my mind fully occupied by these ideas, I might be said as if fascinated, to haunt the destined abode of the young Earl. I watched the progress of the improvements, and stood by the unlading waggons, as various articles of luxury, brought from London, were taken forth and conveyed into the mansion. It was part of the Ex-Queen's plan, to surround her son with princely magnificence. I beheld rich carpets and silken hangings, ornaments of gold, richly embossed metals, emblazoned furniture, and all the appendages of high rank arranged, so that nothing but what was regal in splendour should reach the eye of one of royal descent. I looked on these; I turned my gaze to my own mean dress.—Whence sprung this difference? Whence but from ingratitude, from falsehood, from a dereliction on the part of the prince's father, of all noble sympathy and generous feeling. Doubtless, he also, whose blood received a mingling tide from his proud mother—he, the acknowledged focus of the kingdom's wealth and nobility, had been taught to repeat my father's name with disdain, and to scoff at my just claims to protection. I strove to think that all this grandeur was but more glaring infamy, and that, by planting his gold-enwoven flag beside my tarnished and tattered banner, he proclaimed not his superiority, but his debasement. Yet I envied him. His stud of beautiful horses, his arms of costly workmanship, the praise that attended him, the adoration, ready servitor, high place and high esteem,—I considered them as forcibly wrenched from me, and envied them all with novel and tormenting bitterness.

To crown my vexation of spirit, Perdita, the visionary Perdita, seemed to awake to real life with transport, when she told me that the Earl of Windsor was about to arrive.

"And this pleases you?" I observed, moodily.

"Indeed it does, Lionel," she replied; "I quite long to see him; he is the descendant of our kings, the first noble of the land: every one admires and loves him, and they say that his rank is his least merit; he is generous, brave, and affable."

"You have learnt a pretty lesson, Perdita," said I, "and repeat it so literally, that you forget the while the proofs we have of the Earl's virtues; his generosity to us is manifest in our plenty, his bravery in the protection he affords us, his affability in the notice he takes of us. His rank his least merit, do you say? Why, all his virtues are derived from his station only; because he is rich, he is called generous; because he is powerful, brave; because he is well served, he is affable. Let them call him so, let all England believe him to be thus—we know him—he is our enemy—our penurious, dastardly, arrogant enemy; if he were gifted with one particle of the virtues you call his, he would do justly by us, if it were only to shew, that if he must strike, it should not be a fallen foe. His father injured my father—his father, unassailable on his throne, dared despise him who only stooped beneath himself, when he deigned to associate with the royal ingrate. We, descendants from the one and the other, must be enemies also. He shall find that I can feel my injuries; he shall learn to dread my revenge!"

A few days after he arrived. Every inhabitant of the most miserable cottage, went to swell the stream of population that poured forth to meet him: even Perdita, in spite of my late philippic, crept near the highway, to behold this idol of all hearts. I, driven half mad, as I met party after party of the country people, in their holiday best, descending the hills, escaped to their cloud-veiled summits, and looking on the sterile rocks about me, exclaimed—"They do not cry, long live the Earl!" Nor, when night came, accompanied by drizzling rain and cold, would I return home; for I knew that each cottage rang with the praises of Adrian; as I felt my limbs grow numb and chill, my pain served as food for my insane aversion; nay, I almost triumphed in it, since it seemed to afford me reason and excuse for my hatred of my unheeding adversary. All was attributed to him, for I confounded so entirely the idea of father and son, that I forgot that the latter might be wholly unconscious of his parent's neglect of us; and as I struck my aching head with my hand, I cried: "He shall hear of this! I will be revenged! I will not suffer like a spaniel! He shall know, beggar and friendless as I am, that I will not tamely submit to injury!" Each day, each hour added to these exaggerated wrongs. His praises were so many adder's stings infixed in my vulnerable breast. If I saw him at a distance, riding a beautiful horse, my blood boiled with rage; the air seemed poisoned by his presence, and my very native English was changed to a vile jargon, since every phrase I heard was coupled with his name and honour. I panted to relieve this painful heart-burning by some misdeed that should rouse him to a sense of my antipathy. It was the height of his offending, that he should occasion in me such intolerable sensations, and not deign himself to afford any demonstration that he was aware that I even lived to feel them.

It soon became known that Adrian took great delight in his park and preserves. He never sported, but spent hours in watching the tribes of lovely and almost tame animals with which it was stocked, and ordered that greater care should be taken of them than ever. Here was an opening for my plans of offence, and I made use of it with all the brute impetuosity I derived from my active mode of life. I proposed the enterprise of poaching on his demesne to my few remaining comrades, who were the most determined and lawless of the crew; but they all shrunk from the peril; so I was left to achieve my revenge myself. At first my exploits were unperceived; I increased in daring; footsteps on the dewy grass, torn boughs, and marks of slaughter, at length betrayed me to the game-keepers. They kept better watch; I was taken, and sent to prison. I entered its gloomy walls in a fit of triumphant extasy: "He feels me now," I cried, "and shall, again and again!"—I passed but one day in confinement; in the evening I was liberated, as I was told, by the order of the Earl himself. This news precipitated me from my self-raised pinnacle of honour. He despises me, I thought; but he shall learn that I despise him, and hold in equal contempt his punishments and his clemency. On the second night after my release, I was again taken by the gamekeepers—again imprisoned, and again released; and again, such was my pertinacity, did the fourth night find me in the forbidden park. The gamekeepers were more enraged than their lord by my obstinacy. They had received orders that if I were again taken, I should be brought to the Earl; and his lenity made them expect a conclusion which they considered ill befitting my crime. One of them, who had been from the first the leader among those who had seized me, resolved to satisfy his own resentment, before he made me over to the higher powers.

The late setting of the moon, and the extreme caution I was obliged to use in this my third expedition, consumed so much time, that something like a qualm of fear came over me when I perceived dark night yield to twilight. I crept along by the fern, on my hands and knees, seeking the shadowy coverts of the underwood, while the birds awoke with unwelcome song above, and the fresh morning wind, playing among the boughs, made me suspect a footfall at each turn. My heart beat quick as I approached the palings; my hand was on one of them, a leap would take me to the other side, when two keepers sprang from an ambush upon me: one knocked me down, and proceeded to inflict a severe horse-whipping. I started up—a knife was in my grasp; I made a plunge at his raised right arm, and inflicted a deep, wide wound in his hand. The rage and yells of the wounded man, the howling execrations of his comrade, which I answered with equal bitterness and fury, echoed through the dell; morning broke more and more, ill accordant in its celestial beauty with our brute and noisy contest. I and my enemy were still struggling, when the wounded man exclaimed, "The Earl!" I sprang out of the herculean hold of the keeper, panting from my exertions; I cast furious glances on my persecutors, and placing myself with my back to a tree, resolved to defend myself to the last. My garments were torn, and they, as well as my hands, were stained with the blood of the man I had wounded; one hand grasped the dead birds—my hard-earned prey, the other held the knife; my hair was matted; my face besmeared with the same guilty signs that bore witness against me on the dripping instrument I clenched; my whole appearance was haggard and squalid. Tall and muscular as I was in form, I must have looked like, what indeed I was, the merest ruffian that ever trod the earth.

The name of the Earl startled me, and caused all the indignant blood that warmed my heart to rush into my cheeks; I had never seen him before; I figured to myself a haughty, assuming youth, who would take me to task, if he deigned to speak to me, with all the arrogance of superiority. My reply was ready; a reproach I deemed calculated to sting his very heart. He came up the while; and his appearance blew aside, with gentle western breath, my cloudy wrath: a tall, slim, fair boy, with a physiognomy expressive of the excess of sensibility and refinement stood before me; the morning sunbeams tinged with gold his silken hair, and spread light and glory over his beaming countenance. "How is this?" he cried. The men eagerly began their defence; he put them aside, saying, "Two of you at once on a mere lad— for shame!" He came up to me: "Verney," he cried, "Lionel Verney, do we meet thus for the first time? We were born to be friends to each other; and though ill fortune has divided us, will you not acknowledge the hereditary bond of friendship which I trust will hereafter unite us?"

As he spoke, his earnest eyes, fixed on me, seemed to read my very soul: my heart, my savage revengeful heart, felt the influence of sweet benignity sink upon it; while his thrilling voice, like sweetest melody, awoke a mute echo within me, stirring to its depths the life-blood in my frame. I desired to reply, to acknowledge his goodness, accept his proffered friendship; but words, fitting words, were not afforded to the rough mountaineer; I would have held out my hand, but its guilty stain restrained me. Adrian took pity on my faltering mien: "Come with me," he said, "I have much to say to you; come home with me—you know who I am?"

"Yes," I exclaimed, "I do believe that I now know you, and that you will pardon my mistakes—my crime."

Adrian smiled gently; and after giving his orders to the gamekeepers, he came up to me; putting his arm in mine, we walked together to the mansion.

It was not his rank—after all that I have said, surely it will not be suspected that it was Adrian's rank, that, from the first, subdued my heart of hearts, and laid my entire spirit prostrate before him. Nor was it I alone who felt thus intimately his perfections. His sensibility and courtesy fascinated every one. His vivacity, intelligence, and active spirit of benevolence, completed the conquest. Even at this early age, he was deep read and imbued with the spirit of high philosophy. This spirit gave a tone of irresistible persuasion to his intercourse with others, so that he seemed like an inspired musician, who struck, with unerring skill, the "lyre of mind," and produced thence divine harmony. In person, he hardly appeared of this world; his slight frame was overinformed by the soul that dwelt within; he was all mind; "Man but a rush against" his breast, and it would have conquered his strength; but the might of his smile would have tamed an hungry lion, or caused a legion of armed men to lay their weapons at his feet.

I spent the day with him. At first he did not recur to the past, or indeed to any personal occurrences. He wished probably to inspire me with confidence, and give me time to gather together my scattered thoughts. He talked of general subjects, and gave me ideas I had never before conceived. We sat in his library, and he spoke of the old Greek sages, and of the power which they had acquired over the minds of men, through the force of love and wisdom only. The room was decorated with the busts of many of them, and he described their characters to me. As he spoke, I felt subject to him; and all my boasted pride and strength were subdued by the honeyed accents of this blue-eyed boy. The trim and paled demesne of civilization, which I had before regarded from my wild jungle as inaccessible, had its wicket opened by him; I stepped within, and felt, as I entered, that I trod my native soil.

As evening came on, he reverted to the past. "I have a tale to relate," he said, "and much explanation to give concerning the past; perhaps you can assist me to curtail it. Do you remember your father? I had never the happiness of seeing him, but his name is one of my earliest recollections: he stands written in my mind's tablets as the type of all that was gallant, amiable, and fascinating in man. His wit was not more conspicuous than the overflowing goodness of his heart, which he poured in such full measure on his friends, as to leave, alas! small remnant for himself."

Encouraged by this encomium, I proceeded, in answer to his inquiries, to relate what I remembered of my parent; and he gave an account of those circumstances which had brought about a neglect of my father's testamentary letter. When, in after times, Adrian's father, then king of England, felt his situation become more perilous, his line of conduct more embarrassed, again and again he wished for his early friend, who might stand a mound against the impetuous anger of his queen, a mediator between him and the parliament. From the time that he had quitted London, on the fatal night of his defeat at the gaming-table, the king had received no tidings concerning him; and when, after the lapse of years, he exerted himself to discover him, every trace was lost. With fonder regret than ever, he clung to his memory; and gave it in charge to his son, if ever he should meet this valued friend, in his name to bestow every succour, and to assure him that, to the last, his attachment survived separation and silence.

A short time before Adrian's visit to Cumberland, the heir of the nobleman to whom my father had confided his last appeal to his royal master, put this letter, its seal unbroken, into the young Earl's hands. It had been found cast aside with a mass of papers of old date, and accident alone brought it to light. Adrian read it with deep interest; and found there that living spirit of genius and wit he had so often heard commemorated. He discovered the name of the spot whither my father had retreated, and where he died; he learnt the existence of his orphan children; and during the short interval between his arrival at Ulswater and our meeting in the park, he had been occupied in making inquiries concerning us, and arranging a variety of plans for our benefit, preliminary to his introducing himself to our notice.

The mode in which he spoke of my father was gratifying to my vanity; the veil which he delicately cast over his benevolence, in alleging a duteous fulfilment of the king's latest will, was soothing to my pride. Other feelings, less ambiguous, were called into play by his conciliating manner and the generous warmth of his expressions, respect rarely before experienced, admiration, and love—he had touched my rocky heart with his magic power, and the stream of affection gushed forth, imperishable and pure. In the evening we parted; he pressed my hand: "We shall meet again; come to me to-morrow." I clasped that kind hand; I tried to answer; a fervent "God bless you!" was all my ignorance could frame of speech, and I darted away, oppressed by my new emotions.

I could not rest. I sought the hills; a west wind swept them, and the stars glittered above. I ran on, careless of outward objects, but trying to master the struggling spirit within me by means of bodily fatigue. "This," I thought, "is power! Not to be strong of limb, hard of heart, ferocious, and daring; but kind compassionate and soft."—Stopping short, I clasped my hands, and with the fervour of a new proselyte, cried, "Doubt me not, Adrian, I also will become wise and good!" and then quite overcome, I wept aloud.

As this gust of passion passed from me, I felt more composed. I lay on the ground, and giving the reins to my thoughts, repassed in my mind my former life; and began, fold by fold, to unwind the many errors of my heart, and to discover how brutish, savage, and worthless I had hitherto been. I could not however at that time feel remorse, for methought I was born anew; my soul threw off the burthen of past sin, to commence a new career in innocence and love. Nothing harsh or rough remained to jar with the soft feelings which the transactions of the day had inspired; I was as a child lisping its devotions after its mother, and my plastic soul was remoulded by a master hand, which I neither desired nor was able to resist.

This was the first commencement of my friendship with Adrian, and I must commemorate this day as the most fortunate of my life. I now began to be human. I was admitted within that sacred boundary which divides the intellectual and moral nature of man from that which characterizes animals. My best feelings were called into play to give fitting responses to the generosity, wisdom, and amenity of my new friend. He, with a noble goodness all his own, took infinite delight in bestowing to prodigality the treasures of his mind and fortune on the long-neglected son of his father's friend, the offspring of that gifted being whose excellencies and talents he had heard commemorated from infancy.

After his abdication the late king had retreated from the sphere of politics, yet his domestic circle afforded him small content. The ex-queen had none of the virtues of domestic life, and those of courage and daring which she possessed were rendered null by the secession of her husband: she despised him, and did not care to conceal her sentiments. The king had, in compliance with her exactions, cast off his old friends, but he had acquired no new ones under her guidance. In this dearth of sympathy, he had recourse to his almost infant son; and the early development of talent and sensibility rendered Adrian no unfitting depository of his father's confidence. He was never weary of listening to the latter's often repeated accounts of old times, in which my father had played a distinguished part; his keen remarks were repeated to the boy, and remembered by him; his wit, his fascinations, his very faults were hallowed by the regret of affection; his loss was sincerely deplored. Even the queen's dislike of the favourite was ineffectual to deprive him of his son's admiration: it was bitter, sarcastic, contemptuous—but as she bestowed her heavy censure alike on his virtues as his errors, on his devoted friendship and his ill-bestowed loves, on his disinterestedness and his prodigality, on his pre-possessing grace of manner, and the facility with which he yielded to temptation, her double shot proved too heavy, and fell short of the mark. Nor did her angry dislike prevent Adrian from imaging my father, as he had said, the type of all that was gallant, amiable, and fascinating in man. It was not strange therefore, that when he heard of the existence of the offspring of this celebrated person, he should have formed the plan of bestowing on them all the advantages his rank made him rich to afford. When he found me a vagabond shepherd of the hills, a poacher, an unlettered savage, still his kindness did not fail. In addition to the opinion he entertained that his father was to a degree culpable of neglect towards us, and that he was bound to every possible reparation, he was pleased to say that under all my ruggedness there glimmered forth an elevation of spirit, which could be distinguished from mere animal courage, and that I inherited a similarity of countenance to my father, which gave proof that all his virtues and talents had not died with him. Whatever those might be which descended to me, my noble young friend resolved should not be lost for want of culture.

Acting upon this plan in our subsequent intercourse, he led me to wish to participate in that cultivation which graced his own intellect. My active mind, when once it seized upon this new idea, fastened on it with extreme avidity. At first it was the great object of my ambition to rival the merits of my father, and render myself worthy of the friendship of Adrian. But curiosity soon awoke, and an earnest love of knowledge, which caused me to pass days and nights in reading and study. I was already well acquainted with what I may term the panorama of nature, the change of seasons, and the various appearances of heaven and earth. But I was at once startled and enchanted by my sudden extension of vision, when the curtain, which had been drawn before the intellectual world, was withdrawn, and I saw the universe, not only as it presented itself to my outward senses, but as it had appeared to the wisest among men. Poetry and its creations, philosophy and its researches and classifications, alike awoke the sleeping ideas in my mind, and gave me new ones.

I felt as the sailor, who from the topmast first discovered the shore of America; and like him I hastened to tell my companions of my discoveries in unknown regions. But I was unable to excite in any breast the same craving appetite for knowledge that existed in mine. Even Perdita was unable to understand me. I had lived in what is generally called the world of reality, and it was awakening to a new country to find that there was a deeper meaning in all I saw, besides that which my eyes conveyed to me. The visionary Perdita beheld in all this only a new gloss upon an old reading, and her own was sufficiently inexhaustible to content her. She listened to me as she had done to the narration of my adventures, and sometimes took an interest in this species of information; but she did not, as I did, look on it as an integral part of her being, which having obtained, I could no more put off than the universal sense of touch.

We both agreed in loving Adrian: although she not having yet escaped from childhood could not appreciate as I did the extent of his merits, or feel the same sympathy in his pursuits and opinions. I was for ever with him. There was a sensibility and sweetness in his disposition, that gave a tender and unearthly tone to our converse. Then he was gay as a lark carolling from its skiey tower, soaring in thought as an eagle, innocent as the mild-eyed dove. He could dispel the seriousness of Perdita, and take the sting from the torturing activity of my nature. I looked back to my restless desires and painful struggles with my fellow beings as to a troubled dream, and felt myself as much changed as if I had transmigrated into another form, whose fresh sensorium and mechanism of nerves had altered the reflection of the apparent universe in the mirror of mind. But it was not so; I was the same in strength, in earnest craving for sympathy, in my yearning for active exertion. My manly virtues did not desert me, for the witch Urania spared the locks of Sampson, while he reposed at her feet; but all was softened and humanized. Nor did Adrian instruct me only in the cold truths of history and philosophy. At the same time that he taught me by their means to subdue my own reckless and uncultured spirit, he opened to my view the living page of his own heart, and gave me to feel and understand its wondrous character.

The ex-queen of England had, even during infancy, endeavoured to implant daring and ambitious designs in the mind of her son. She saw that he was endowed with genius and surpassing talent; these she cultivated for the sake of afterwards using them for the furtherance of her own views. She encouraged his craving for knowledge and his impetuous courage; she even tolerated his tameless love of freedom, under the hope that this would, as is too often the case, lead to a passion for command. She endeavoured to bring him up in a sense of resentment towards, and a desire to revenge himself upon, those who had been instrumental in bringing about his father's abdication. In this she did not succeed. The accounts furnished him, however distorted, of a great and wise nation asserting its right to govern itself, excited his admiration: in early days he became a republican from principle. Still his mother did not despair. To the love of rule and haughty pride of birth she added determined ambition, patience, and self-control. She devoted herself to the study of her son's disposition. By the application of praise, censure, and exhortation, she tried to seek and strike the fitting chords; and though the melody that followed her touch seemed discord to her, she built her hopes on his talents, and felt sure that she would at last win him. The kind of banishment he now experienced arose from other causes.

The ex-queen had also a daughter, now twelve years of age; his fairy sister, Adrian was wont to call her; a lovely, animated, little thing, all sensibility and truth. With these, her children, the noble widow constantly resided at Windsor; and admitted no visitors, except her own partisans, travellers from her native Germany, and a few of the foreign ministers. Among these, and highly distinguished by her, was Prince Zaimi, ambassador to England from the free States of Greece; and his daughter, the young Princess Evadne, passed much of her time at Windsor Castle. In company with this sprightly and clever Greek girl, the Countess would relax from her usual state. Her views with regard to her own children, placed all her words and actions relative to them under restraint: but Evadne was a plaything she could in no way fear; nor were her talents and vivacity slight alleviations to the monotony of the Countess's life.

Evadne was eighteen years of age. Although they spent much time together at Windsor, the extreme youth of Adrian prevented any suspicion as to the nature of their intercourse. But he was ardent and tender of heart beyond the common nature of man, and had already learnt to love, while the beauteous Greek smiled benignantly on the boy. It was strange to me, who, though older than Adrian, had never loved, to witness the whole heart's sacrifice of my friend. There was neither jealousy, inquietude, or mistrust in his sentiment; it was devotion and faith. His life was swallowed up in the existence of his beloved; and his heart beat only in unison with the pulsations that vivified hers. This was the secret law of his life—he loved and was beloved. The universe was to him a dwelling, to inhabit with his chosen one; and not either a scheme of society or an enchainment of events, that could impart to him either happiness or misery. What, though life and the system of social intercourse were a wilderness, a tiger-haunted jungle! Through the midst of its errors, in the depths of its savage recesses, there was a disentangled and flowery pathway, through which they might journey in safety and delight. Their track would be like the passage of the Red Sea, which they might traverse with unwet feet, though a wall of destruction were impending on either side.

Alas! why must I record the hapless delusion of this matchless specimen of humanity? What is there in our nature that is for ever urging us on towards pain and misery? We are not formed for enjoyment; and, however we may be attuned to the reception of pleasureable emotion, disappointment is the never-failing pilot of our life's bark, and ruthlessly carries us on to the shoals. Who was better framed than this highly-gifted youth to love and be beloved, and to reap unalienable joy from an unblamed passion? If his heart had slept but a few years longer, he might have been saved; but it awoke in its infancy; it had power, but no knowledge; and it was ruined, even as a too early-blowing bud is nipt by the killing frost.

I did not accuse Evadne of hypocrisy or a wish to deceive her lover; but the first letter that I saw of hers convinced me that she did not love him; it was written with elegance, and, foreigner as she was, with great command of language. The hand-writing itself was exquisitely beautiful; there was something in her very paper and its folds, which even I, who did not love, and was withal unskilled in such matters, could discern as being tasteful. There was much kindness, gratitude, and sweetness in her expression, but no love. Evadne was two years older than Adrian; and who, at eighteen, ever loved one so much their junior? I compared her placid epistles with the burning ones of Adrian. His soul seemed to distil itself into the words he wrote; and they breathed on the paper, bearing with them a portion of the life of love, which was his life. The very writing used to exhaust him; and he would weep over them, merely from the excess of emotion they awakened in his heart.

Adrian's soul was painted in his countenance, and concealment or deceit were at the antipodes to the dreadless frankness of his nature. Evadne made it her earnest request that the tale of their loves should not be revealed to his mother; and after for a while contesting the point, he yielded it to her. A vain concession; his demeanour quickly betrayed his secret to the quick eyes of the ex-queen. With the same wary prudence that characterized her whole conduct, she concealed her discovery, but hastened to remove her son from the sphere of the attractive Greek. He was sent to Cumberland; but the plan of correspondence between the lovers, arranged by Evadne, was effectually hidden from her. Thus the absence of Adrian, concerted for the purpose of separating, united them in firmer bonds than ever. To me he discoursed ceaselessly of his beloved Ionian. Her country, its ancient annals, its late memorable struggles, were all made to partake in her glory and excellence. He submitted to be away from her, because she commanded this submission; but for her influence, he would have declared his attachment before all England, and resisted, with unshaken constancy, his mother's opposition. Evadne's feminine prudence perceived how useless any assertion of his resolves would be, till added years gave weight to his power. Perhaps there was besides a lurking dislike to bind herself in the face of the world to one whom she did not love—not love, at least, with that passionate enthusiasm which her heart told her she might one day feel towards another. He obeyed her injunctions, and passed a year in exile in Cumberland.

❧ 3 ❧

Happy, thrice happy, were the months, and weeks, and hours of that year. Friendship, hand in hand with admiration, tenderness and respect, built a bower of delight in my heart, late rough as an untrod wild in America, as the homeless wind or herbless sea. Insatiate thirst for knowledge, and boundless affection for Adrian, combined to keep both my heart and understanding occupied, and I was consequently happy. What happiness is so true and unclouded, as the overflowing and talkative delight of young people. In our boat, upon my native lake, beside the streams and the pale bordering poplars—in valley and over hill, my crook thrown aside, a nobler flock to tend than silly sheep, even a flock of new-born ideas, I read or listened to Adrian; and his discourse, whether it concerned his love or his theories for the improvement of man, alike entranced me. Sometimes my lawless mood would return, my love of peril, my resistance to authority; but this was in his absence; under the mild sway of his dear eyes, I was obedient and good as a boy of five years old, who does his mother's bidding.

After a residence of about a year at Ulswater, Adrian visited London, and came back full of plans for our benefit. You must begin life, he said: you are seventeen, and longer delay would render the necessary apprenticeship more and more irksome. He foresaw that his own life would be one of struggle, and I must partake his labours with him. The better to fit me for this task, we must now separate. He found my name a good passport to preferment, and he had procured for me the situation of private secretary to the Ambassador at Vienna, where I should enter on my career under the best auspices. In two years, I should return to my country, with a name well known and a reputation already founded.

And Perdita?—Perdita was to become the pupil, friend and younger sister of Evadne. With his usual thoughtfulness, he had provided for her independence in this situation. How refuse the offers of this generous friend?—I did not wish to refuse them; but in my heart of hearts, I made a vow to devote life, knowledge, and power, all of which, in as much as they were of any value, he had bestowed on me—all, all my capacities and hopes, to him alone I would devote.

Thus I promised myself, as I journeyed towards my destination with roused and ardent expectation: expectation of the fulfilment of all that in boyhood we promise ourselves of power and enjoyment in maturity. Methought the time was now arrived, when, childish occupations laid aside, I should enter into life. Even in the Elysian fields, Virgil describes the souls of the happy as eager to drink of the wave which was to restore them to this mortal coil. The young are seldom in Elysium, for their desires, outstripping possibility, leave them as poor as a moneyless debtor. We are told by the wisest philosophers of the dangers of the world, the deceits of men, and the treason of our own hearts: but not the less fearlessly does each put off his frail bark from the port, spread the sail, and strain his oar, to attain the multitudinous streams of the sea of life. How few in youth's prime, moor their vessels on the "golden sands," and collect the painted shells that strew them. But all at close of day, with riven planks and rent canvas make for shore, and are either wrecked ere they reach it, or find some wave-beaten haven, some desart strand, whereon to cast themselves and die unmourned.

A truce to philosophy!—Life is before me, and I rush into possession. Hope, glory, love, and blameless ambition are my guides, and my soul knows no dread. What has been, though sweet, is gone; the present is good only because it is about to change, and the to come is all my own. Do I fear, that my heart palpitates? high aspirations cause the flow of my blood; my eyes seem to penetrate the cloudy midnight of time, and to discern within the depths of its darkness, the fruition of all my soul desires.

Now pause!—During my journey I might dream, and with buoyant wings reach the summit of life's high edifice. Now that I am arrived at its base, my pinions are furled, the mighty stairs are before me, and step by step I must ascend the wondrous fane—

Speak!—What door is opened?

Behold me in a new capacity. A diplomatist: one among the pleasure-seeking society of a gay city; a youth of promise; favourite of the Ambassador. All was strange and admirable to the shepherd of Cumberland. With breathless amaze I entered on the gay scene, whose actors were

—the lilies glorious as Solomon, Who toil not, neither do they spin.

Soon, too soon, I entered the giddy whirl; forgetting my studious hours, and the companionship of Adrian. Passionate desire of sympathy, and ardent pursuit for a wished-for object still characterized me. The sight of beauty entranced me, and attractive manners in man or woman won my entire confidence. I called it rapture, when a smile made my heart beat; and I felt the life's blood tingle in my frame, when I approached the idol which for awhile I worshipped. The mere flow of animal spirits was Paradise, and at night's close I only desired a renewal of the intoxicating delusion. The dazzling light of ornamented rooms; lovely forms arrayed in splendid dresses; the motions of a dance, the voluptuous tones of exquisite music, cradled my senses in one delightful dream.

And is not this in its kind happiness? I appeal to moralists and sages. I ask if in the calm of their measured reveries, if in the deep meditations which fill their hours, they feel the extasy of a youthful tyro in the school of pleasure? Can the calm beams of their heaven-seeking eyes equal the flashes of mingling passion which blind his, or does the influence of cold philosophy steep their soul in a joy equal to his, engaged

In this dear work of youthful revelry.

But in truth, neither the lonely meditations of the hermit, nor the tumultuous raptures of the reveller, are capable of satisfying man's heart. From the one we gather unquiet speculation, from the other satiety. The mind flags beneath the weight of thought, and droops in the heartless intercourse of those whose sole aim is amusement. There is no fruition in their vacant kindness, and sharp rocks lurk beneath the smiling ripples of these shallow waters.

Thus I felt, when disappointment, weariness, and solitude drove me back upon my heart, to gather thence the joy of which it had become barren. My flagging spirits asked for something to speak to the affections; and not finding it, I drooped. Thus, notwithstanding the thoughtless delight that waited on its commencement, the impression I have of my life at Vienna is melancholy. Goethe has said, that in youth we cannot be happy unless we love. I did not love; but I was devoured by a restless wish to be something to others. I became the victim of ingratitude and cold coquetry—then I desponded, and imagined that my discontent gave me a right to hate the world. I receded to solitude; I had recourse to my books, and my desire again to enjoy the society of Adrian became a burning thirst.

Emulation, that in its excess almost assumed the venomous properties of envy, gave a sting to these feelings. At this period the name and exploits of one of my countrymen filled the world with admiration. Relations of what he had done, conjectures concerning his future actions, were the never-failing topics of the hour. I was not angry on my own account, but I felt as if the praises which this idol received were leaves torn from laurels destined for Adrian. But I must enter into some account of this darling of fame—this favourite of the wonder-loving world.

Lord Raymond was the sole remnant of a noble but impoverished family. From early youth he had considered his pedigree with complacency, and bitterly lamented his want of wealth. His first wish was aggrandisement; and the means that led towards this end were secondary considerations. Haughty, yet trembling to every demonstration of respect; ambitious, but too proud to shew his ambition; willing to achieve honour, yet a votary of pleasure,— he entered upon life. He was met on the threshold by some insult, real or imaginary; some repulse, where he least expected it; some disappointment, hard for his pride to bear. He writhed beneath an injury he was unable to revenge; and he quitted England with a vow not to return, till the good time should arrive, when she might feel the power of him she now despised.

He became an adventurer in the Greek wars. His reckless courage and comprehensive genius brought him into notice. He became the darling hero of this rising people. His foreign birth, and he refused to throw off his allegiance to his native country, alone prevented him from filling the first offices in the state. But, though others might rank higher in title and ceremony, Lord Raymond held a station above and beyond all this. He led the Greek armies to victory; their triumphs were all his own. When he appeared, whole towns poured forth their population to meet him; new songs were adapted to their national airs, whose themes were his glory, valour, and munificence. A truce was concluded between the Greeks and Turks. At the same time, Lord Raymond, by some unlooked-for chance, became the possessor of an immense fortune in England, whither he returned, crowned with glory, to receive the mead of honour and distinction before denied to his pretensions. His proud heart rebelled against this change. In what was the despised Raymond not the same? If the acquisition of power in the shape of wealth caused this alteration, that power should they feel as an iron yoke. Power therefore was the aim of all his endeavours; aggrandizement the mark at which he forever shot. In open ambition or close intrigue, his end was the same—to attain the first station in his own country.

This account filled me with curiosity. The events that in succession followed his return to England, gave me keener feelings. Among his other advantages, Lord Raymond was supremely handsome; every one admired him; of women he was the idol. He was courteous, honey-tongued—an adept in fascinating arts. What could not this man achieve in the busy English world? Change succeeded to change; the entire history did not reach me; for Adrian had ceased to write, and Perdita was a laconic correspondent. The rumour went that Adrian had become— how write the fatal word—mad: that Lord Raymond was the favourite of the ex-queen, her daughter's destined husband. Nay, more, that this aspiring noble revived the claim of the house of Windsor to the crown, and that, on the event of Adrian's incurable disorder and his marriage with the sister, the brow of the ambitious Raymond might be encircled with the magic ring of regality.

Such a tale filled the trumpet of many voiced fame; such a tale rendered my longer stay at Vienna, away from the friend of my youth, intolerable. Now I must fulfil my vow; now range myself at his side, and be his ally and support till death. Farewell to courtly pleasure; to politic intrigue; to the maze of passion and folly! All hail, England! Native England, receive thy child! thou art the scene of all my hopes, the mighty theatre on which is acted the only drama that can, heart and soul, bear me along with it in its development. A voice most irresistible, a power omnipotent, drew me thither. After an absence of two years I landed on its shores, not daring to make any inquiries, fearful of every remark. My first visit would be to my sister, who inhabited a little cottage, a part of Adrian's gift, on the borders of Windsor Forest. From her I should learn the truth concerning our protector; I should hear why she had withdrawn from the protection of the Princess Evadne, and be instructed as to the influence which this overtopping and towering Raymond exercised over the fortunes of my friend.

I had never before been in the neighbourhood of Windsor; the fertility and beauty of the country around now struck me with admiration, which increased as I approached the antique wood. The ruins of majestic oaks which had grown, flourished, and decayed during the progress of centuries, marked where the limits of the forest once reached, while the shattered palings and neglected underwood shewed that this part was deserted for the younger plantations, which owed their birth to the beginning of the nineteenth century, and now stood in the pride of maturity. Perdita's humble dwelling was situated on the skirts of the most ancient portion; before it was stretched Bishopgate Heath, which towards the east appeared interminable, and was bounded to the west by Chapel Wood and the grove of Virginia Water. Behind, the cottage was shadowed by the venerable fathers of the forest, under which the deer came to graze, and which for the most part hollow and decayed, formed fantastic groups that contrasted with the regular beauty of the younger trees. These, the offspring of a later period, stood erect and seemed ready to advance fearlessly into coming time; while those out worn stragglers, blasted and broke, clung to each other, their weak boughs sighing as the wind buffetted them—a weather-beaten crew.

A light railing surrounded the garden of the cottage, which, low-roofed, seemed to submit to the majesty of nature, and cower amidst the venerable remains of forgotten time. Flowers, the children of the spring, adorned her garden and casements; in the midst of lowliness there was an air of elegance which spoke the graceful taste of the inmate. With a beating heart I entered the enclosure; as I stood at the entrance, I heard her voice, melodious as it had ever been, which before I saw her assured me of her welfare.

A moment more and Perdita appeared; she stood before me in the fresh bloom of youthful womanhood, different from and yet the same as the mountain girl I had left. Her eyes could not be deeper than they were in childhood, nor her countenance more expressive; but the expression was changed and improved; intelligence sat on her brow; when she smiled her face was embellished by the softest sensibility, and her low, modulated voice seemed tuned by love. Her person was formed in the most feminine proportions; she was not tall, but her mountain life had given freedom to her motions, so that her light step scarce made her foot-fall heard as she tript across the hall to meet me. When we had parted, I had clasped her to my bosom with unrestrained warmth; we met again, and new feelings were awakened; when each beheld the other, childhood passed, as full grown actors on this changeful scene. The pause was but for a moment; the flood of association and natural feeling which had been checked, again rushed in full tide upon our hearts, and with tenderest emotion we were swiftly locked in each other's embrace.

This burst of passionate feeling over, with calmed thoughts we sat together, talking of the past and present. I alluded to the coldness of her letters; but the few minutes we had spent together sufficiently explained the origin of this. New feelings had arisen within her, which she was unable to express in writing to one whom she had only known in childhood; but we saw each other again, and our intimacy was renewed as if nothing had intervened to check it. I detailed the incidents of my sojourn abroad, and then questioned her as to the changes that had taken place at home, the causes of Adrian's absence, and her secluded life.

The tears that suffused my sister's eyes when I mentioned our friend, and her heightened colour seemed to vouch for the truth of the reports that had reached me. But their import was too terrible for me to give instant credit to my suspicion. Was there indeed anarchy in the sublime universe of Adrian's thoughts, did madness scatter the well-appointed legions, and was he no longer the lord of his own soul? Beloved friend, this ill world was no clime for your gentle spirit; you delivered up its governance to false humanity, which stript it of its leaves ere winter-time, and laid bare its quivering life to the evil ministration of roughest winds. Have those gentle eyes, those "channels of the soul" lost their meaning, or do they only in their glare disclose the horrible tale of its aberrations? Does that voice no longer "discourse excellent music?" Horrible, most horrible! I veil my eyes in terror of the change, and gushing tears bear witness to my sympathy for this unimaginable ruin.

In obedience to my request Perdita detailed the melancholy circumstances that led to this event.

The frank and unsuspicious mind of Adrian, gifted as it was by every natural grace, endowed with transcendant powers of intellect, unblemished by the shadow of defect (unless his dreadless independence of thought was to be construed into one), was devoted, even as a victim to sacrifice, to his love for Evadne. He entrusted to her keeping the treasures of his soul, his aspirations after excellence, and his plans for the improvement of mankind. As manhood dawned upon him, his schemes and theories, far from being changed by personal and prudential motives, acquired new strength from the powers he felt arise within him; and his love for Evadne became deep-rooted, as he each day became more certain that the path he pursued was full of difficulty, and that he must seek his reward, not in the applause or gratitude of his fellow creatures, hardly in the success of his plans, but in the approbation of his own heart, and in her love and sympathy, which was to lighten every toil and recompence every sacrifice.

In solitude, and through many wanderings afar from the haunts of men, he matured his views for the reform of the English government, and the improvement of the people. It would have been well if he had concealed his sentiments, until he had come into possession of the power which would secure their practical development. But he was impatient of the years that must intervene, he was frank of heart and fearless. He gave not only a brief denial to his mother's schemes, but published his intention of using his influence to diminish the power of the aristocracy, to effect a greater equalization of wealth and privilege, and to introduce a perfect system of republican government into England. At first his mother treated his theories as the wild ravings of inexperience. But they were so systematically arranged, and his arguments so well supported, that though still in appearance incredulous, she began to fear him. She tried to reason with him, and finding him inflexible, learned to hate him.

Strange to say, this feeling was infectious. His enthusiasm for good which did not exist; his contempt for the sacredness of authority; his ardour and imprudence were all at the antipodes of the usual routine of life; the worldly feared him; the young and inexperienced did not understand the lofty severity of his moral views, and disliked him as a being different from themselves. Evadne entered but coldly into his systems. She thought he did well to assert his own will, but she wished that will to have been more intelligible to the multitude. She had none of the spirit of a martyr, and did not incline to share the shame and defeat of a fallen patriot.

She was aware of the purity of his motives, the generosity of his disposition, his true and ardent attachment to her; and she entertained a great affection for him. He repaid this spirit of kindness with the fondest gratitude, and made her the treasure-house of all his hopes.

At this time Lord Raymond returned from Greece. No two persons could be more opposite than Adrian and he. With all the incongruities of his character, Raymond was emphatically a man of the world. His passions were violent; as these often obtained the mastery over him, he could not always square his conduct to the obvious line of self-interest, but self-gratification at least was the paramount object with him. He looked on the structure of society as but a part of the machinery which supported the web on which his life was traced. The earth was spread out as an highway for him; the heavens built up as a canopy for him.

Adrian felt that he made a part of a great whole. He owned affinity not only with mankind, but all nature was akin to him; the mountains and sky were his friends; the winds of heaven and the offspring of earth his playmates; while he the focus only of this mighty mirror, felt his life mingle with the universe of existence. His soul was sympathy, and dedicated to the worship of beauty and excellence. Adrian and Raymond now came into contact, and a spirit of aversion rose between them. Adrian despised the narrow views of the politician, and Raymond held in supreme contempt the benevolent visions of the philanthropist.

With the coming of Raymond was formed the storm that laid waste at one fell blow the gardens of delight and sheltered paths which Adrian fancied that he had secured to himself, as a refuge from defeat and contumely. Raymond, the deliverer of Greece, the graceful soldier, who bore in his mien a tinge of all that, peculiar to her native clime, Evadne cherished as most dear— Raymond was loved by Evadne. Overpowered by her new sensations, she did not pause to examine them, or to regulate her conduct by any sentiments except the tyrannical one which suddenly usurped the empire of her heart. She yielded to its influence, and the too natural consequence in a mind unattuned to soft emotions was, that the attentions of Adrian became distasteful to her. She grew capricious; her gentle conduct towards him was exchanged for asperity and repulsive coldness. When she perceived the wild or pathetic appeal of his expressive countenance, she would relent, and for a while resume her ancient kindness. But these fluctuations shook to its depths the soul of the sensitive youth; he no longer deemed the world subject to him, because he possessed Evadne's love; he felt in every nerve that the dire storms of the mental universe were about to attack his fragile being, which quivered at the expectation of its advent.

Perdita, who then resided with Evadne, saw the torture that Adrian endured. She loved him as a kind elder brother; a relation to guide, protect, and instruct her, without the too frequent tyranny of parental authority. She adored his virtues, and with mixed contempt and indignation she saw Evadne pile drear sorrow on his head, for the sake of one who hardly marked her. In his solitary despair Adrian would often seek my sister, and in covered terms express his misery, while fortitude and agony divided the throne of his mind. Soon, alas! was one to conquer. Anger made no part of his emotion. With whom should he be angry? Not with Raymond, who was unconscious of the misery he occasioned; not with Evadne, for her his soul wept tears of blood—poor, mistaken girl, slave not tyrant was she, and amidst his own anguish he grieved for her future destiny. Once a writing of his fell into Perdita's hands; it was blotted with tears—well might any blot it with the like—

"Life"—it began thus—"is not the thing romance writers describe it; going through the measures of a dance, and after various evolutions arriving at a conclusion, when the dancers may sit down and repose. While there is life there is action and change. We go on, each thought linked to the one which was its parent, each act to a previous act. No joy or sorrow dies barren of progeny, which forever generated and generating, weaves the chain that make our life:

Un dia llama a otro dia y ass i llama, y encadena llanto a llanto, y pena a pena.

Truly disappointment is the guardian deity of human life; she sits at the threshold of unborn time, and marshals the events as they come forth. Once my heart sat lightly in my bosom; all the beauty of the world was doubly beautiful, irradiated by the sun-light shed from my own soul. O wherefore are love and ruin forever joined in this our mortal dream? So that when we make our hearts a lair for that gently seeming beast, its companion enters with it, and pitilessly lays waste what might have been an home and a shelter."

By degrees his health was shaken by his misery, and then his intellect yielded to the same tyranny. His manners grew wild; he was sometimes ferocious, sometimes absorbed in speechless melancholy. Suddenly Evadne quitted London for Paris; he followed, and overtook her when the vessel was about to sail; none knew what passed between them, but Perdita had never seen him since; he lived in seclusion, no one knew where, attended by such persons as his mother selected for that purpose.

✲ 4 ✲

THE NEXT DAY Lord Raymond called at Perdita's cottage, on his way to Windsor Castle. My sister's heightened colour and sparkling eyes half revealed her secret to me. He was perfectly self-possessed; he accosted us both with courtesy, seemed immediately to enter into our feelings, and to make one with us. I scanned his physiognomy, which varied as he spoke, yet was beautiful in every change. The usual expression of his eyes was soft, though at times he could make them even glare with ferocity; his complexion was colourless; and every trait spoke predominate self-will; his smile was pleasing, though disdain too often curled his lips—lips which to female eyes were the very throne of beauty and love. His voice, usually gentle, often startled you by a sharp discordant note, which shewed that his usual low tone was rather the work of study than nature. Thus full of contradictions, unbending yet haughty, gentle yet fierce, tender and again neglectful, he by some strange art found easy entrance to the admiration and affection of women; now caressing and now tyrannizing over them according to his mood, but in every change a despot.

At the present time Raymond evidently wished to appear amiable. Wit, hilarity, and deep observation were mingled in his talk, rendering every sentence that he uttered as a flash of light. He soon conquered my latent distaste; I endeavoured to watch him and Perdita, and to keep in mind everything I had heard to his disadvantage. But all appeared so ingenuous, and all was so fascinating, that I forgot everything except the pleasure his society afforded me. Under the idea of initiating me in the scene of English politics and society, of which I was soon to become a part, he narrated a number of anecdotes, and sketched many characters; his discourse, rich and varied, flowed on, pervading all my senses with pleasure. But for one thing he would have been completely triumphant. He alluded to Adrian, and spoke of him with that disparagement that the worldly wise always attach to enthusiasm. He perceived the cloud gathering, and tried to dissipate it; but the strength of my feelings would not permit me to pass thus lightly over this sacred subject; so I said emphatically, "Permit me to remark, that I am devotedly attached to the Earl of Windsor; he is my best friend and benefactor. I reverence his goodness, I accord with his opinions, and bitterly lament his present, and I trust temporary, illness. That illness, from its peculiarity, makes it painful to me beyond words to hear him mentioned, unless in terms of respect and affection."

Raymond replied; but there was nothing conciliatory in his reply. I saw that in his heart he despised those dedicated to any but worldly idols. "Every man," he said, "dreams about something, love, honour, and pleasure; you dream of friendship, and devote yourself to a maniac; well, if that be your vocation, doubtless you are in the right to follow it."—

Some reflection seemed to sting him, and the spasm of pain that for a moment convulsed his countenance, checked my indignation. "Happy are dreamers," he continued, "so that they be not awakened! Would I could dream! but 'broad and garish day' is the element in which I live; the dazzling glare of reality inverts the scene for me. Even the ghost of friendship has departed, and love"——He broke off; nor could I guess whether the disdain that curled his lip was directed against the passion, or against himself for being its slave.

This account may be taken as a sample of my intercourse with Lord Raymond. I became intimate with him, and each day afforded me occasion to admire more and more his powerful and versatile talents, that together with his eloquence, which was graceful and witty, and his wealth now immense, caused him to be feared, loved, and hated beyond any other man in England.

My descent, which claimed interest, if not respect, my former connection with Adrian, the favour of the ambassador, whose secretary I had been, and now my intimacy with Lord Raymond, gave me easy access to the fashionable and political circles of England. To my inexperience we at first appeared on the eve of a civil war; each party was violent, acrimonious, and unyielding. Parliament was divided by three factions, aristocrats, democrats, and royalists. After Adrian's declared predeliction to the republican form of government, the latter party had nearly died away, chiefless, guideless; but, when Lord Raymond came forward as its leader, it revived with redoubled force. Some were royalists from prejudice and ancient affection, and there were many moderately inclined who feared alike the capricious tyranny of the popular party, and the unbending despotism of the aristocrats. More than a third of the members ranged themselves under Raymond, and their number was perpetually increasing. The aristocrats built their hopes on their preponderant wealth and influence; the reformers on the force of the nation itself; the debates were violent, more violent the discourses held by each knot of politicians as they assembled to arrange their measures. Opprobrious epithets were bandied about, resistance even to the death threatened; meetings of the populace disturbed the quiet order of the country; except in war, how could all this end? Even as the destructive flames were ready to break forth, I saw them shrink back; allayed by the absence of the military, by the aversion entertained by everyone to any violence, save that of speech, and by the cordial politeness and even friendship of the hostile leaders when they met in private society. I was from a thousand motives induced to attend minutely to the course of events, and watch each turn with intense anxiety.

I could not but perceive that Perdita loved Raymond; methought also that he regarded the fair daughter of Verney with admiration and tenderness. Yet I knew that he was urging forward his marriage with the presumptive heiress of the Earldom of Windsor, with keen expectation of the advantages that would thence accrue to him. All the ex-queen's friends were his friends; no week passed that he did not hold consultations with her at Windsor.

I had never seen the sister of Adrian. I had heard that she was lovely, amiable, and fascinating. Wherefore should I see her? There are times when we have an indefinable sentiment of impending change for better or for worse, to arise from an event; and, be it for better or for worse, we fear the change, and shun the event. For this reason I avoided this high-born damsel.

To me she was everything and nothing; her very name mentioned by another made me start and tremble; the endless discussion concerning her union with Lord Raymond was real agony to me. Methought that, Adrian withdrawn from active life, and this beauteous Idris, a victim probably to her mother's ambitious schemes, I ought to come forward to protect her from undue influence, guard her from unhappiness, and secure to her freedom of choice, the right of every human being. Yet how was I to do this? She herself would disdain my interference. Since then I must be an object of indifference or contempt to her, better, far better avoid her, nor expose myself before her and the scornful world to the chance of playing the mad game of a fond, foolish Icarus. One day, several months after my return to England, I quitted London to visit my sister. Her society was my chief solace and delight; and my spirits always rose at the expectation of seeing her. Her conversation was full of pointed remark and discernment; in her pleasant alcove, redolent with sweetest flowers, adorned by magnificent casts, antique vases, and copies of the finest pictures of Raphael, Correggio, and Claude, painted by herself, I fancied myself in a fairy retreat untainted by and inaccessible to the noisy contentions of politicians and the frivolous pursuits of fashion. On this occasion, my sister was not alone; nor could I fail to recognise her companion: it was Idris, the till now unseen object of my mad idolatry.

In what fitting terms of wonder and delight, in what choice expression and soft flow of language, can I usher in the loveliest, wisest, best? How in poor assemblage of words convey the halo of glory that surrounded her, the thousand graces that waited unwearied on her. The first thing that struck you on beholding that charming countenance was its perfect goodness and frankness; candour sat upon her brow, simplicity in her eyes, heavenly benignity in her smile. Her tall slim figure bent gracefully as a poplar to the breezy west, and her gait, goddess-like, was as that of a winged angel new alit from heaven's high floor; the pearly fairness of her complexion was stained by a pure suffusion; her voice resembled the low, subdued tenor of a flute. It is easiest perhaps to describe by contrast. I have detailed the perfections of my sister; and yet she was utterly unlike Idris. Perdita, even where she loved, was reserved and timid; Idris was frank and confiding. The one recoiled to solitude, that she might there entrench herself from disappointment and injury; the other walked forth in open day, believing that none would harm her. Wordsworth has compared a beloved female to two fair objects in nature; but his lines always appeared to me rather a contrast than a similitude:

> A violet by a mossy stone
> Half hidden from the eye,
> Fair as a star when only one
> Is shining in the sky.

Such a violet was sweet Perdita, trembling to entrust herself to the very air, cowering from observation, yet betrayed by her excellences; and repaying with a thousand graces the labour of those who sought her in her lonely bye-path. Idris was as the star, set in single splendour in the dim anadem of balmy evening; ready to enlighten and delight the subject world, shielded herself from every taint by her unimagined distance from all that was not like herself akin to heaven.

I found this vision of beauty in Perdita's alcove, in earnest conversation with its inmate. When my sister saw me, she rose, and taking my hand, said, "He is here, even at our wish; this is Lionel, my brother." Idris arose also, and bent on me her eyes of celestial blue, and with grace peculiar said—"You hardly need an introduction; we have a picture, highly valued by my father, which declares at once your name. Verney, you will acknowledge this tie, and as my brother's friend, I feel that I may trust you."

Then, with lids humid with a tear and trembling voice, she continued— "Dear friends, do not think it strange that now, visiting you for the first time, I ask your assistance, and confide my wishes and fears to you. To you alone do I dare speak; I have heard you commended by impartial spectators; you are my brother's friends, therefore you must be mine. What can I say? if you refuse to aid me, I am lost indeed!" She cast up her eyes, while wonder held her auditors mute; then, as if carried away by her feelings, she cried—"My brother! beloved, ill-fated Adrian! how speak of your misfortunes? Doubtless you have both heard the current tale; perhaps believe the slander; but he is not mad! Were an angel from the foot of God's throne to assert it, never, never would I believe it. He is wronged, betrayed, imprisoned—save him! Verney, you must do this; seek him out in whatever part of the island he is immured; find him, rescue him from his persecutors, restore him to himself, to me—on the wide earth I have none to love but only him!"

Her earnest appeal, so sweetly and passionately expressed, filled me with wonder and sympathy; and, when she added, with thrilling voice and look, "Do you consent to undertake this enterprise?" I vowed, with energy and truth, to devote myself in life and death to the restoration and welfare of Adrian. We then conversed on the plan I should pursue, and discussed the probable means of discovering his residence. While we were in earnest discourse, Lord Raymond entered unannounced: I saw Perdita tremble and grow deadly pale, and the cheeks of Idris glow with purest blushes. He must have been astonished at our conclave, disturbed by it I should have thought; but nothing of this appeared; he saluted my companions, and addressed me with a cordial greeting. Idris appeared suspended for a moment, and then with extreme sweetness, she said, "Lord Raymond, I confide in your goodness and honour."

Smiling haughtily, he bent his head, and replied, with emphasis, "Do you indeed confide, Lady Idris?"

She endeavoured to read his thought, and then answered with dignity, "As you please. It is certainly best not to compromise oneself by any concealment."

"Pardon me," he replied, "if I have offended. Whether you trust me or not, rely on my doing my utmost to further your wishes, whatever they may be."

Idris smiled her thanks, and rose to take leave. Lord Raymond requested permission to accompany her to Windsor Castle, to which she consented, and they quitted the cottage together. My sister and I were left—truly like two fools, who fancied that they had obtained a golden treasure, till daylight shewed it to be lead—two silly, luckless flies, who had played in sunbeams and were caught in a spider's web. I leaned against the casement, and watched those two glorious creatures, till they disappeared in the forest-glades; and then I turned. Perdita had not moved; her eyes fixed on the ground, her cheeks pale, her very lips white, motionless and rigid, every feature stamped by woe, she sat. Half frightened, I would have taken her hand; but she shudderingly withdrew it, and strove to collect herself. I entreated her to speak to me: "Not now," she replied, "nor do you speak to me, my dear Lionel; you can say nothing, for you know nothing. I will see you to-morrow; in the meantime, adieu!" She rose, and walked from the room; but pausing at the door, and leaning against it, as if her over-busy thoughts had taken from her the power of supporting herself, she said, "Lord Raymond will probably return. Will you tell him that he must excuse me to-day, for I am not well. I will see him to-morrow if he wishes it, and you also. You had better return to London with him; you can there make the enquiries agreed upon, concerning the Earl of Windsor and visit me again to-morrow, before you proceed on your journey—till then, farewell!"

She spoke falteringly, and concluded with a heavy sigh. I gave my assent to her request; and she left me. I felt as if, from the order of the systematic world, I had plunged into chaos, obscure, contrary, unintelligible. That Raymond should marry Idris was more than ever intolerable; yet my passion, though a giant from its birth, was too strange, wild, and impracticable, for me to feel at once the misery I perceived in Perdita. How should I act? She had not confided in me; I could not demand an explanation from Raymond without the hazard of betraying what was perhaps her most treasured secret. I would obtain the truth from her the following day—in the meantime—But, while I was occupied by multiplying reflections, Lord Raymond returned. He asked for my sister; and I delivered her message. After musing on it for a moment, he asked me if I were about to return to London, and if I would accompany him: I consented. He was full of thought, and remained silent during a considerable part of our ride; at length he said, "I must apologize to you for my abstraction; the truth is, Ryland's motion comes on to-night, and I am considering my reply."

Ryland was the leader of the popular party, a hard-headed man, and in his way eloquent; he had obtained leave to bring in a bill making it treason to endeavour to change the present state of the English government and the standing laws of the republic. This attack was directed against Raymond and his machinations for the restoration of the monarchy.

Raymond asked me if I would accompany him to the House that evening. I remembered my pursuit for intelligence concerning Adrian; and, knowing that my time would be fully occupied, I excused myself. "Nay," said my companion, "I can free you from your present impediment. You are going to make enquiries concerning the Earl of Windsor. I can answer them at once, he is at the Duke of Athol's seat at Dunkeld. On the first approach of his disorder, he travelled about from one place to another; until, arriving at that romantic seclusion he refused to quit it, and we made arrangements with the Duke for his continuing there."

I was hurt by the careless tone with which he conveyed this information, and replied coldly: "I am obliged to you for your intelligence, and will avail myself of it."

"You shall, Verney," said he, "and if you continue of the same mind, I will facilitate your views. But first witness, I beseech you, the result of this night's contest, and the triumph I am about to achieve, if I may so call it, while I fear that victory is to me defeat. What can I do? My dearest hopes appear to be near their fulfilment. The ex-queen gives me Idris; Adrian is totally unfitted to succeed to the earldom, and that earldom in my hands becomes a kingdom. By the reigning God it is true; the paltry earldom of Windsor shall no longer content him, who will inherit the rights which must forever appertain to the person who possesses it. The Countess can never forget that she has been a queen, and she disdains to leave a diminished inheritance to her children; her power and my wit will rebuild the throne, and this brow will be clasped by a kingly diadem.—I can do this—I can marry Idris."——

He stopped abruptly, his countenance darkened, and its expression changed again and again under the influence of internal passion. I asked, "Does Lady Idris love you?"

"What a question," replied he laughing. "She will of course, as I shall her, when we are married."

"You begin late," said I, ironically, "marriage is usually considered the grave, and not the cradle of love. So you are about to love her, but do not already?"

"Do not catechise me, Lionel; I will do my duty by her, be assured. Love! I must steel my heart against that; expel it from its tower of strength, barricade it out: the fountain of love must cease to play, its waters be dried up, and all passionate thoughts attendant on it die—that is to say, the love which would rule me, not that which I rule. Idris is a gentle, pretty, sweet little girl; it is impossible not to have an affection for her, and I have a very sincere one; only do not speak of love —love, the tyrant and the tyrant-queller; love, until now my conqueror, now my slave; the hungry fire, the untameable beast, the fanged snake—no—no—I will have nothing to do with that love. Tell me, Lionel, do you consent that I should marry this young lady?"

He bent his keen eyes upon me, and my uncontrollable heart swelled in my bosom. I replied in a calm voice—but how far from calm was the thought imaged by my still words—"Never! I can never consent that Lady Idris should be united to one who does not love her."

"Because you love her yourself."

"Your Lordship might have spared that taunt; I do not, dare not love her."

"At least," he continued haughtily, "she does not love you. I would not marry a reigning sovereign, were I not sure that her heart was free. But, O, Lionel! a kingdom is a word of might, and gently sounding are the terms that compose the style of royalty. Were not the mightiest men of the olden times kings? Alexander was a king; Solomon, the wisest of men, was a king; Napoleon was a king; Caesar died in his attempt to become one, and Cromwell, the puritan and king-killer, aspired to regality. The father of Adrian yielded up the already broken sceptre of England; but I will rear the fallen plant, join its dismembered frame, and exalt it above all the flowers of the field.

"You need not wonder that I freely discover Adrian's abode. Do not suppose that I am wicked or foolish enough to found my purposed sovereignty on a fraud, and one so easily discovered as the truth or falsehood of the Earl's insanity. I am just come from him. Before I decided on my marriage with Idris, I resolved to see him myself again, and to judge of the probability of his recovery.—He is irrecoverably mad."

I gasped for breath—

"I will not detail to you," continued Raymond, "the melancholy particulars. You shall see him, and judge for yourself; although I fear this visit, useless to him, will be insufferably painful to you. It has weighed on my spirits ever since. Excellent and gentle as he is even in the downfall of his reason, I do not worship him as you do, but I would give all my hopes of a crown and my right hand to boot, to see him restored to himself."

His voice expressed the deepest compassion: "Thou most unaccountable being," I cried, "whither will thy actions tend, in all this maze of purpose in which thou seemest lost?"

"Whither indeed? To a crown, a golden be-gemmed crown, I hope; and yet I dare not trust and though I dream of a crown and wake for one, ever and anon a busy devil whispers to me, that it is but a fool's cap that I seek, and that were I wise, I should trample on it, and take in its stead, that which is worth all the crowns of the east and presidentships of the west."

"And what is that?"

"If I do make it my choice, then you shall know; at present I dare not speak, even think of it."

Again he was silent, and after a pause turned to me laughingly. When scorn did not inspire his mirth, when it was genuine gaiety that painted his features with a joyous expression, his beauty became super-eminent, divine. "Verney," said he, "my first act when I become King of England, will be to unite with the Greeks, take Constantinople, and subdue all Asia. I intend to be a warrior, a conqueror; Napoleon's name shall vail to mine; and enthusiasts, instead of visiting his rocky grave, and exalting the merits of the fallen, shall adore my majesty, and magnify my illustrious achievements."

I listened to Raymond with intense interest. Could I be other than all ear, to one who seemed to govern the whole earth in his grasping imagination, and who only quailed when he attempted to rule himself. Then on his word and will depended my own happiness—the fate of all dear to me. I endeavoured to divine the concealed meaning of his words. Perdita's name was not mentioned; yet I could not doubt that love for her caused the vacillation of purpose that he exhibited. And who was so worthy of love as my noble-minded sister? Who deserved the hand of this self-exalted king more than she whose glance belonged to a queen of nations? who loved him, as he did her; notwithstanding that disappointment quelled her passion, and ambition held strong combat with his.

We went together to the House in the evening. Raymond, while he knew that his plans and prospects were to be discussed and decided during the expected debate, was gay and careless. An hum, like that of ten thousand hives of swarming bees, stunned us as we entered the coffee-room. Knots of politicians were assembled with anxious brows and loud or deep voices. The aristocratical party, the richest and most influential men in England, appeared less agitated than the others, for the question was to be discussed without their interference. Near the fire was Ryland and his supporters. Ryland was a man of obscure birth and of immense wealth, inherited from his father, who had been a manufacturer. He had witnessed, when a young man, the abdication of the king, and the amalgamation of the two houses of Lords and Commons; he had sympathized with these popular encroachments, and it had been the business of his life to consolidate and increase them. Since then, the influence of the landed proprietors had augmented; and at first Ryland was not sorry to observe the machinations of Lord Raymond, which drew off many of his opponent's partisans. But the thing was now going too far. The poorer nobility hailed the return of sovereignty, as an event which would restore them to their power and rights, now lost. The half extinct spirit of royalty roused itself in the minds of men; and they, willing slaves, self-constituted subjects, were ready to bend their necks to the yoke. Some erect and manly spirits still remained, pillars of state; but the word republic had grown stale to the vulgar ear; and many—the event would prove whether it was a majority— pined for the tinsel and show of royalty. Ryland was roused to resistance; he asserted that his sufferance alone had permitted the increase of this party; but the time for indulgence was passed, and with one motion of his arm he would sweep away the cobwebs that blinded his countrymen.

When Raymond entered the coffee-room, his presence was hailed by his friends almost with a shout. They gathered round him, counted their numbers, and detailed the reasons why they were now to receive an addition of such and such members, who had not yet declared themselves. Some trifling business of the House having been gone through, the leaders took their seats in the chamber; the clamour of voices continued, till Ryland arose to speak, and then the slightest whispered observation was audible. All eyes were fixed upon him as he stood— ponderous of frame, sonorous of voice, and with a manner which, though not graceful, was impressive. I turned from his marked, iron countenance to Raymond, whose face, veiled by a smile, would not betray his care; yet his lips quivered somewhat, and his hand clasped the bench on which he sat, with a convulsive strength that made the muscles start again.

Ryland began by praising the present state of the British empire. He recalled past years to their memory; the miserable contentions which in the time of our fathers arose almost to civil war, the abdication of the late king, and the foundation of the republic. He described this republic; shewed how it gave privilege to each individual in the state, to rise to consequence, and even to temporary sovereignty. He compared the royal and republican spirit; shewed how the one tended to enslave the minds of men; while all the institutions of the other served to raise even the meanest among us to something great and good. He shewed how England had become powerful, and its inhabitants valiant and wise, by means of the freedom they enjoyed. As he spoke, every heart swelled with pride, and every cheek glowed with delight to remember, that each one there was English, and that each supported and contributed to the happy state of things now commemorated. Ryland's fervour increased—his eyes lighted up— his voice assumed the tone of passion. There was one man, he continued, who wished to alter all this, and bring us back to our days of impotence and contention:—one man, who would dare arrogate the honour which was due to all who claimed England as their birthplace, and set his name and style above the name and style of his country. I saw at this juncture that Raymond changed colour; his eyes were withdrawn from the orator, and cast on the ground; the listeners turned from one to the other; but in the meantime the speaker's voice filled their ears—the thunder of his denunciations influenced their senses. The very boldness of his language gave him weight; each knew that he spoke truth—a truth known, but not acknowledged. He tore from reality the mask with which she had been clothed; and the purposes of Raymond, which before had crept around, ensnaring by stealth, now stood a hunted stag—even at bay—as all perceived who watched the irrepressible changes of his countenance. Ryland ended by moving, that any attempt to re-erect the kingly power should be declared treason, and he a traitor who should endeavour to change the present form of government. Cheers and loud acclamations followed the close of his speech.

After his motion had been seconded, Lord Raymond rose,—his countenance bland, his voice softly melodious, his manner soothing, his grace and sweetness came like the mild breathing of a flute, after the loud, organ-like voice of his adversary. He rose, he said, to speak in favour of the honourable member's motion, with one slight amendment subjoined. He was ready to go back to old times, and commemorate the contests of our fathers, and the monarch's abdication. Nobly and greatly, he said, had the illustrious and last sovereign of England sacrificed himself to the apparent good of his country, and divested himself of a power which could only be maintained by the blood of his subjects—these subjects named so no more, these, his friends and equals, had in gratitude conferred certain favours and distinctions on him and his family forever. An ample estate was allotted to them, and they took the first rank among the peers of Great Britain. Yet it might be conjectured that they had not forgotten their ancient heritage; and it was hard that his heir should suffer alike with any other pretender, if he attempted to regain what by ancient right and inheritance belonged to him. He did not say that he should favour such an attempt; but he did say that such an attempt would be venial; and, if the aspirant did not go so far as to declare war, and erect a standard in the kingdom, his fault ought to be regarded with an indulgent eye. In his amendment he proposed, that an exception should be made in the bill in favour of any person who claimed the sovereign power in right of the earls of Windsor. Nor did Raymond make an end without drawing in vivid and glowing colours, the splendour of a kingdom, in opposition to the commercial spirit of republicanism. He asserted, that each individual under the English monarchy, was then as now, capable of attaining high rank and power—with one only exception, that of the function of chief magistrate; higher and nobler rank, than a bartering, timorous commonwealth could afford. And for this one exception, to what did it amount? The nature of riches and influence forcibly confined the list of candidates to a few of the wealthiest; and it was much to be feared, that the ill-humour and contention generated by this triennial struggle, would counterbalance its advantages in impartial eyes. I can ill record the flow of language and graceful turns of expression, the wit and easy raillery that gave vigour and influence to his speech. His manner, timid at first, became firm—his changeful face was lit up to superhuman brilliancy; his voice, various as music, was like that enchanting.

It were useless to record the debate that followed this harangue. Party speeches were delivered, which clothed the question in cant, and veiled its simple meaning in a woven wind of words. The motion was lost; Ryland withdrew in rage and despair; and Raymond, gay and exulting, retired to dream of his future kingdom.

Is THERE SUCH a feeling as love at first sight? And if there be, in what does its nature differ from love founded in long observation and slow growth? Perhaps its effects are not so permanent; but they are, while they last, as violent and intense. We walk the pathless mazes of society, vacant of joy, till we hold this clue, leading us through that labyrinth to paradise. Our nature dim, like to an unlighted torch, sleeps in formless blank till the fire attain it; this life of life, this light to moon, and glory to the sun. What does it matter, whether the fire be struck from flint and steel, nourished with care into a flame, slowly communicated to the dark wick, or whether swiftly the radiant power of light and warmth passes from a kindred power, and shines at once the beacon and the hope. In the deepest fountain of my heart the pulses were stirred; around, above, beneath, the clinging Memory as a cloak enwrapt me. In no one moment of coming time did I feel as I had done in time gone by. The spirit of Idris hovered in the air I breathed; her eyes were ever and for ever bent on mine; her remembered smile blinded my faint gaze, and caused me to walk as one, not in eclipse, not in darkness and vacancy—but in a new and brilliant light, too novel, too dazzling for my human senses. On every leaf, on every small division of the universe, (as on the hyacinth ai is engraved) was imprinted the talisman of my existence—SHE LIVES! SHE IS! —I had not time yet to analyze my feeling, to take myself to task, and leash in the tameless passion; all was one idea, one feeling, one knowledge —it was my life!

But the die was cast—Raymond would marry Idris. The merry marriage bells rung in my ears; I heard the nation's gratulation which followed the union; the ambitious noble uprose with swift eagle-flight, from the lowly ground to regal supremacy—and to the love of Idris. Yet, not so! She did not love him; she had called me her friend; she had smiled on me; to me she had entrusted her heart's dearest hope, the welfare of Adrian. This reflection thawed my congealing blood, and again the tide of life and love flowed impetuously onward, again to ebb as my busy thoughts changed.

The debate had ended at three in the morning. My soul was in tumults; I traversed the streets with eager rapidity. Truly, I was mad that night— love—which I have named a giant from its birth, wrestled with despair! My heart, the field of combat, was wounded by the iron heel of the one, watered by the gushing tears of the other. Day, hateful to me, dawned; I retreated to my lodgings—I threw myself on a couch—I slept—was it sleep?—for thought was still alive—love and despair struggled still, and I writhed with unendurable pain.

I awoke half stupefied; I felt a heavy oppression on me, but knew not wherefore; I entered, as it were, the council-chamber of my brain, and questioned the various ministers of thought therein assembled; too soon I remembered all; too soon my limbs quivered beneath the tormenting power; soon, too soon, I knew myself a slave!

Suddenly, unannounced, Lord Raymond entered my apartment. He came in gaily, singing the Tyrolese song of liberty; noticed me with a gracious nod, and threw himself on a sopha opposite the copy of a bust of the Apollo Belvidere. After one or two trivial remarks, to which I sullenly replied, he suddenly cried, looking at the bust, "I am called like that victor! Not a bad idea; the head will serve for my new coinage, and be an omen to all dutiful subjects of my future success."

He said this in his most gay, yet benevolent manner, and smiled, not disdainfully, but in playful mockery of himself. Then his countenance suddenly darkened, and in that shrill tone peculiar to himself, he cried, "I fought a good battle last night; higher conquest the plains of Greece never saw me achieve. Now I am the first man in the state, burthen of every ballad, and object of old women's mumbled devotions. What are your meditations? You, who fancy that you can read the human soul, as your native lake reads each crevice and folding of its surrounding hills—say what you think of me; king-expectant, angel or devil, which?"

This ironical tone was discord to my bursting, over-boiling-heart; I was nettled by his insolence, and replied with bitterness; "There is a spirit, neither angel or devil, damned to limbo merely." I saw his cheeks become pale, and his lips whiten and quiver; his anger served but to enkindle mine, and I answered with a determined look his eyes which glared on me; suddenly they were withdrawn, cast down, a tear, I thought, wetted the dark lashes; I was softened, and with involuntary emotion added, "Not that you are such, my dear lord."

I paused, even awed by the agitation he evinced; "Yes," he said at length, rising and biting his lip, as he strove to curb his passion; "Such am I! You do not know me, Verney; neither you, nor our audience of last night, nor does universal England know aught of me. I stand here, it would seem, an elected king; this hand is about to grasp a sceptre; these brows feel in each nerve the coming diadem. I appear to have strength, power, victory; standing as a dome-supporting column stands; and I am—a reed! I have ambition, and that attains its aim; my nightly dreams are realized, my waking hopes fulfilled; a kingdom awaits my acceptance, my enemies are overthrown. But here," and he struck his heart with violence, "here is the rebel, here the stumbling-block; this over-ruling heart, which I may drain of its living blood; but, while one fluttering pulsation remains, I am its slave."

He spoke with a broken voice, then bowed his head, and, hiding his face in his hands, wept. I was still smarting from my own disappointment; yet this scene oppressed me even to terror, nor could I interrupt his access of passion. It subsided at length; and, throwing himself on the couch, he remained silent and motionless, except that his changeful features shewed a strong internal conflict. At last he rose, and said in his usual tone of voice, "The time grows on us, Verney, I must away. Let me not forget my chiefest errand here. Will you accompany me to Windsor to-morrow? You will not be dishonoured by my society, and as this is probably the last service, or disservice you can do me, will you grant my request?"

He held out his hand with almost a bashful air. Swiftly I thought—Yes, I will witness the last scene of the drama. Beside which, his mien conquered me, and an affectionate sentiment towards him, again filled my heart—I bade him command me. "Aye, that I will," said he gaily, "that's my cue now; be with me to-morrow morning by seven; be secret and faithful; and you shall be groom of the stole ere long."

So saying, he hastened away, vaulted on his horse, and with a gesture as if he gave me his hand to kiss, bade me another laughing adieu. Left to myself, I strove with painful intensity to divine the motive of his request and foresee the events of the coming day. The hours passed on unperceived; my head ached with thought, the nerves seemed teeming with the over full fraught—I clasped my burning brow, as if my fevered hand could medicine its pain. I was punctual to the appointed hour on the following day, and found Lord Raymond waiting for me. We got into his carriage, and proceeded towards Windsor. I had tutored myself, and was resolved by no outward sign to disclose my internal agitation.

"What a mistake Ryland made," said Raymond, "when he thought to overpower me the other night. He spoke well, very well; such an harangue would have succeeded better addressed to me singly, than to the fools and knaves assembled yonder. Had I been alone, I should have listened to him with a wish to hear reason, but when he endeavoured to vanquish me in my own territory, with my own weapons, he put me on my mettle, and the event was such as all might have expected."

I smiled incredulously, and replied: "I am of Ryland's way of thinking, and will, if you please, repeat all his arguments; we shall see how far you will be induced by them, to change the royal for the patriotic style."

"The repetition would be useless," said Raymond, "since I well remember them, and have many others, self-suggested, which speak with unanswerable persuasion."

He did not explain himself, nor did I make any remark on his reply. Our silence endured for some miles, till the country with open fields, or shady woods and parks, presented pleasant objects to our view. After some observations on the scenery and seats, Raymond said: "Philosophers have called man a microcosm of nature, and find a reflection in the internal mind for all this machinery visibly at work around us. This theory has often been a source of amusement to me; and many an idle hour have I spent, exercising my ingenuity in finding resemblances. Does not Lord Bacon say that, 'the falling from a discord to a concord, which maketh great sweetness in music, hath an agreement with the affections, which are re-integrated to the better after some dislikes?' What a sea is the tide of passion, whose fountains are in our own nature! Our virtues are the quick-sands, which shew themselves at calm and low water; but let the waves arise and the winds buffet them, and the poor devil whose hope was in their durability, finds them sink from under him. The fashions of the world, its exigencies, educations and pursuits, are winds to drive our wills, like clouds all one way; but let a thunderstorm arise in the shape of love, hate, or ambition, and the rack goes backward, stemming the opposing air in triumph."

"Yet," replied I, "nature always presents to our eyes the appearance of a patient: while there is an active principle in man which is capable of ruling fortune, and at least of tacking against the gale, till it in some mode conquers it."

"There is more of what is specious than true in your distinction," said my companion. "Did we form ourselves, choosing our dispositions, and our powers? I find myself, for one, as a stringed instrument with chords and stops—but I have no power to turn the pegs, or pitch my thoughts to a higher or lower key."

"Other men," I observed, "may be better musicians."

"I talk not of others, but myself," replied Raymond, "and I am as fair an example to go by as another. I cannot set my heart to a particular tune, or run voluntary changes on my will. We are born; we choose neither our parents, nor our station; we are educated by others, or by the world's circumstance, and this cultivation, mingling with our innate disposition, is the soil in which our desires, passions, and motives grow."

"There is much truth in what you say," said I, "and yet no man ever acts upon this theory.

Who, when he makes a choice, says, Thus I choose, because I am necessitated? Does he not on the contrary feel a freedom of will within him, which, though you may call it fallacious, still actuates him as he decides?"

"Exactly so," replied Raymond, "another link of the breakless chain. Were I now to commit an act which would annihilate my hopes, and pluck the regal garment from my mortal limbs, to clothe them in ordinary weeds, would this, think you, be an act of free-will on my part?"

As we talked thus, I perceived that we were not going the ordinary road to Windsor, but through Englefield Green, towards Bishopgate Heath. I began to divine that Idris was not the object of our journey, but that I was brought to witness the scene that was to decide the fate of Raymond—and of Perdita. Raymond had evidently vacillated during his journey, and irresolution was marked in every gesture as we entered Perdita's cottage. I watched him curiously, determined that, if this hesitation should continue, I would assist Perdita to overcome herself, and teach her to disdain the wavering love of him, who balanced between the possession of a crown, and of her, whose excellence and affection transcended the worth of a kingdom.

We found her in her flower-adorned alcove; she was reading the newspaper report of the debate in parliament, that apparently doomed her to hopelessness. That heart-sinking feeling was painted in her sunk eyes and spiritless attitude; a cloud was on her beauty, and frequent sighs were tokens of her distress. This sight had an instantaneous effect on Raymond; his eyes beamed with tenderness, and remorse clothed his manners with earnestness and truth. He sat beside her; and, taking the paper from her hand, said, "Not a word more shall my sweet Perdita read of this contention of madmen and fools. I must not permit you to be acquainted with the extent of my delusion, lest you despise me; although, believe me, a wish to appear before you, not vanquished, but as a conqueror, inspired me during my wordy war."

Perdita looked at him like one amazed; her expressive countenance shone for a moment with tenderness; to see him only was happiness. But a bitter thought swiftly shadowed her joy; she bent her eyes on the ground, endeavouring to master the passion of tears that threatened to overwhelm her. Raymond continued, "I will not act a part with you, dear girl, or appear other than what I am, weak and unworthy, more fit to excite your disdain than your love. Yet you do love me; I feel and know that you do, and thence I draw my most cherished hopes. If pride guided you, or even reason, you might well reject me. Do so; if your high heart, incapable of my infirmity of purpose, refuses to bend to the lowness of mine. Turn from me, if you will,—if you can. If your whole soul does not urge you to forgive me—if your entire heart does not open wide its door to admit me to its very centre, forsake me, never speak to me again. I, though sinning against you almost beyond remission, I also am proud; there must be no reserve in your pardon—no drawback to the gift of your affection."

Perdita looked down, confused, yet pleased. My presence embarrassed her; so that she dared not turn to meet her lover's eye, or trust her voice to assure him of her affection; while a blush mantled her cheek, and her disconsolate air was exchanged for one expressive of deep-felt joy. Raymond encircled her waist with his arm, and continued, "I do not deny that I have balanced between you and the highest hope that mortal men can entertain; but I do so no longer. Take me—mould me to your will, possess my heart and soul to all eternity. If you refuse to contribute to my happiness, I quit England to-night, and will never set foot in it again.

"Lionel, you hear: witness for me: persuade your sister to forgive the injury I have done her; persuade her to be mine."

"There needs no persuasion," said the blushing Perdita, "except your own dear promises, and my ready heart, which whispers to me that they are true."

That same evening we all three walked together in the forest, and, with the garrulity which happiness inspires, they detailed to me the history of their loves. It was pleasant to see the haughty Raymond and reserved Perdita changed through happy love into prattling, playful children, both losing their characteristic dignity in the fulness of mutual contentment. A night or two ago Lord Raymond, with a brow of care, and a heart oppressed with thought, bent all his energies to silence or persuade the legislators of England that a sceptre was not too weighty for his hand, while visions of dominion, war, and triumph floated before him; now, frolicsome as a lively boy sporting under his mother's approving eye, the hopes of his ambition were complete, when he pressed the small fair hand of Perdita to his lips; while she, radiant with delight, looked on the still pool, not truly admiring herself, but drinking in with rapture the reflection there made of the form of herself and her lover, shewn for the first time in dear conjunction.

I rambled away from them. If the rapture of assured sympathy was theirs, I enjoyed that of restored hope. I looked on the regal towers of Windsor. High is the wall and strong the barrier that separate me from my Star of Beauty. But not impassible. She will not be his. A few more years dwell in thy native garden, sweet flower, till I by toil and time acquire a right to gather thee. Despair not, nor bid me despair! What must I do now? First I must seek Adrian, and restore him to her. Patience, gentleness, and untired affection, shall recall him, if it be true, as Raymond says, that he is mad; energy and courage shall rescue him, if he be unjustly imprisoned.

After the lovers again joined me, we supped together in the alcove. Truly it was a fairy's supper; for though the air was perfumed by the scent of fruits and wine, we none of us either ate or drank—even the beauty of the night was unobserved; their extasy could not be increased by outward objects, and I was wrapt in reverie. At about midnight Raymond and I took leave of my sister, to return to town. He was all gaiety; scraps of songs fell from his lips; every thought of his mind—every object about us, gleamed under the sunshine of his mirth. He accused me of melancholy, of ill-humour and envy.

"Not so," said I, "though I confess that my thoughts are not occupied as pleasantly as yours are. You promised to facilitate my visit to Adrian; I conjure you to perform your promise. I cannot linger here; I long to soothe —perhaps to cure the malady of my first and best friend. I shall immediately depart for Dunkeld."

"Thou bird of night," replied Raymond, "what an eclipse do you throw across my bright thoughts, forcing me to call to mind that melancholy ruin, which stands in mental desolation, more irreparable than a fragment of a carved column in a weed-grown field. You dream that you can restore him? Daedalus never wound so inextricable an error round Minotaur, as madness has woven about his imprisoned reason. Nor you, nor any other Theseus, can thread the labyrinth, to which perhaps some unkind Ariadne has the clue."

"You allude to Evadne Zaimi: but she is not in England."

"And were she," said Raymond, "I would not advise her seeing him. Better to decay in absolute delirium, than to be the victim of the methodical unreason of ill-bestowed love. The long duration of his malady has probably erased from his mind all vestige of her; and it were well that it should never again be imprinted. You will find him at Dunkeld; gentle and tractable he wanders up the hills, and through the wood, or sits listening beside the waterfall. You may see him—his hair stuck with wild flowers —his eyes full of untraceable meaning—his voice broken—his person wasted to a shadow. He plucks flowers and weeds, and weaves chaplets of them, or sails yellow leaves and bits of bark on the stream, rejoicing in their safety, or weeping at their wreck. The very memory half unmans me. By Heaven! the first tears I have shed since boyhood rushed scalding into my eyes when I saw him."

It needed not this last account to spur me on to visit him. I only doubted whether or not I should endeavour to see Idris again, before I departed. This doubt was decided on the following day. Early in the morning Raymond came to me; intelligence had arrived that Adrian was dangerously ill, and it appeared impossible that his failing strength should surmount the disorder. "To-morrow," said Raymond, "his mother and sister set out for Scotland to see him once again."

"And I go to-day," I cried; "this very hour I will engage a sailing balloon; I shall be there in forty-eight hours at furthest, perhaps in less, if the wind is fair. Farewell, Raymond; be happy in having chosen the better part in life. This turn of fortune revives me. I feared madness, not sickness—I have a presentiment that Adrian will not die; perhaps this illness is a crisis, and he may recover."

Everything favoured my journey. The balloon rose about half a mile from the earth, and with a favourable wind it hurried through the air, its feathered vans cleaving the unopposing atmosphere. Notwithstanding the melancholy object of my journey, my spirits were exhilarated by reviving hope, by the swift motion of the airy pinnace, and the balmy visitation of the sunny air. The pilot hardly moved the plumed steerage, and the slender mechanism of the wings, wide unfurled, gave forth a murmuring noise, soothing to the sense. Plain and hill, stream and corn-field, were discernible below, while we unimpeded sped on swift and secure, as a wild swan in his spring-tide flight. The machine obeyed the slightest motion of the helm; and, the wind blowing steadily, there was no let or obstacle to our course. Such was the power of man over the elements; a power long sought, and lately won; yet foretold in by-gone time by the prince of poets, whose verses I quoted much to the astonishment of my pilot, when I told him how many hundred years ago they had been written:—

> Oh! human wit, thou can'st invent much ill,
> Thou searchest strange arts: who would think by skill,
> An heavy man like a light bird should stray,
> And through the empty heavens find a way?

I alighted at Perth; and, though much fatigued by a constant exposure to the air for many hours, I would not rest, but merely altering my mode of conveyance, I went by land instead of air, to Dunkeld. The sun was rising as I entered the opening of the hills. After the revolution of ages Birnam hill was again covered with a young forest, while more aged pines, planted at the very commencement of the nineteenth century by the then Duke of Athol, gave solemnity and beauty to the scene. The rising sun first tinged the pine tops; and my mind, rendered through my mountain education deeply susceptible of the graces of nature, and now on the eve of again beholding my beloved and perhaps dying friend, was strangely influenced by the sight of those distant beams: surely they were ominous, and as such I regarded them, good omens for Adrian, on whose life my happiness depended.

Poor fellow! he lay stretched on a bed of sickness, his cheeks glowing with the hues of fever, his eyes half closed, his breath irregular and difficult. Yet it was less painful to see him thus, than to find him fulfilling the animal functions uninterruptedly, his mind sick the while. I established myself at his bedside; I never quitted it day or night. Bitter task was it, to behold his spirit waver between death and life: to see his warm cheek, and know that the very fire which burned too fiercely there, was consuming the vital fuel; to hear his moaning voice, which might never again articulate words of love and wisdom; to witness the ineffectual motions of his limbs, soon to be wrapt in their mortal shroud. Such for three days and nights appeared the consummation which fate had decreed for my labours, and I became haggard and spectre-like, through anxiety and watching. At length his eyes unclosed faintly, yet with a look of returning life; he became pale and weak; but the rigidity of his features was softened by approaching convalescence. He knew me. What a brimful cup of joyful agony it was, when his face first gleamed with the glance of recognition—when he pressed my hand, now more fevered than his own, and when he pronounced my name! No trace of his past insanity remained, to dash my joy with sorrow.

This same evening his mother and sister arrived. The Countess of Windsor was by nature full of energetic feeling; but she had very seldom in her life permitted the concentrated emotions of her heart to shew themselves on her features. The studied immovability of her countenance; her slow, equable manner, and soft but unmelodious voice, were a mask, hiding her fiery passions, and the impatience of her disposition. She did not in the least resemble either of her children; her black and sparkling eye, lit up by pride, was totally unlike the blue lustre, and frank, benignant expression of either Adrian or Idris. There was something grand and majestic in her motions, but nothing persuasive, nothing amiable. Tall, thin, and strait, her face still handsome, her raven hair hardly tinged with grey, her forehead arched and beautiful, had not the eye-brows been somewhat scattered—it was impossible not to be struck by her, almost to fear her. Idris appeared to be the only being who could resist her mother, notwithstanding the extreme mildness of her character. But there was a fearlessness and frankness about her, which said that she would not encroach on another's liberty, but held her own sacred and unassailable.

The Countess cast no look of kindness on my worn-out frame, though afterwards she thanked me coldly for my attentions. Not so Idris; her first glance was for her brother; she took his hand, she kissed his eye-lids, and hung over him with looks of compassion and love. Her eyes glistened with tears when she thanked me, and the grace of her expressions was enhanced, not diminished, by the fervour, which caused her almost to falter as she spoke. Her mother, all eyes and ears, soon interrupted us; and I saw, that she wished to dismiss me quietly, as one whose services, now that his relatives had arrived, were of no use to her son. I was harassed and ill, resolved not to give up my post, yet doubting in what way I should assert it; when Adrian called me, and clasping my hand, bade me not leave him. His mother, apparently inattentive, at once understood what was meant, and seeing the hold we had upon her, yielded the point to us.

The days that followed were full of pain to me; so that I sometimes regretted that I had not yielded at once to the haughty lady, who watched all my motions, and turned my beloved task of nursing my friend to a work of pain and irritation. Never did any woman appear so entirely made of mind, as the Countess of Windsor. Her passions had subdued her appetites, even her natural wants; she slept little, and hardly ate at all; her body was evidently considered by her as a mere machine, whose health was necessary for the accomplishment of her schemes, but whose senses formed no part of her enjoyment. There is something fearful in one who can thus conquer the animal part of our nature, if the victory be not the effect of consummate virtue; nor was it without a mixture of this feeling, that I beheld the figure of the Countess awake when others slept, fasting when I, abstemious naturally, and rendered so by the fever that preyed on me, was forced to recruit myself with food. She resolved to prevent or diminish my opportunities of acquiring influence over her children, and circumvented my plans by a hard, quiet, stubborn resolution, that seemed not to belong to flesh and blood. War was at last tacitly acknowledged between us. We had many pitched battles, during which no word was spoken, hardly a look was interchanged, but in which each resolved not to submit to the other. The Countess had the advantage of position; so I was vanquished, though I would not yield.

I became sick at heart. My countenance was painted with the hues of ill health and vexation. Adrian and Idris saw this; they attributed it to my long watching and anxiety; they urged me to rest, and take care of myself, while I most truly assured them, that my best medicine was their good wishes; those, and the assured convalescence of my friend, now daily more apparent. The faint rose again blushed on his cheek; his brow and lips lost the ashy paleness of threatened dissolution; such was the dear reward of my unremitting attention—and bounteous heaven added overflowing recompence, when it gave me also the thanks and smiles of Idris.

After the lapse of a few weeks, we left Dunkeld. Idris and her mother returned immediately to Windsor, while Adrian and I followed by slow journies and frequent stoppages, occasioned by his continued weakness. As we traversed the various counties of fertile England, all wore an exhilarating appearance to my companion, who had been so long secluded by disease from the enjoyments of weather and scenery. We passed through busy towns and cultivated plains. The husbandmen were getting in their plenteous harvests, and the women and children, occupied by light rustic toils, formed groupes of happy, healthful persons, the very sight of whom carried cheerfulness to the heart. One evening, quitting our inn, we strolled down a shady lane, then up a grassy slope, till we came to an eminence, that commanded an extensive view of hill and dale, meandering rivers, dark woods, and shining villages. The sun was setting; and the clouds, straying, like new-shorn sheep, through the vast fields of sky, received the golden colour of his parting beams; the distant uplands shone out, and the busy hum of evening came, harmonized by distance, on our ear. Adrian, who felt all the fresh spirit infused by returning health, clasped his hands in delight, and exclaimed with transport:

"O happy earth, and happy inhabitants of earth! A stately palace has God built for you, O man! and worthy are you of your dwelling! Behold the verdant carpet spread at our feet, and the azure canopy above; the fields of earth which generate and nurture all things, and the track of heaven, which contains and clasps all things. Now, at this evening hour, at the period of repose and refection, methinks all hearts breathe one hymn of love and thanksgiving, and we, like priests of old on the mountain-tops, give a voice to their sentiment.

"Assuredly a most benignant power built up the majestic fabric we inhabit, and framed the laws by which it endures. If mere existence, and not happiness, had been the final end of our being, what need of the profuse luxuries which we enjoy? Why should our dwelling place be so lovely, and why should the instincts of nature minister pleasurable sensations? The very sustaining of our animal machine is made delightful; and our sustenance, the fruits of the field, is painted with transcendant hues, endued with grateful odours, and palatable to our taste. Why should this be, if HE were not good? We need houses to protect us from the seasons, and behold the materials with which we are provided; the growth of trees with their adornment of leaves; while rocks of stone piled above the plains variegate the prospect with their pleasant irregularity.

"Nor are outward objects alone the receptacles of the Spirit of Good. Look into the mind of man, where wisdom reigns enthroned; where imagination, the painter, sits, with his pencil dipt in hues lovelier than those of sunset, adorning familiar life with glowing tints. What a noble boon, worthy the giver, is the imagination! it takes from reality its leaden hue: it envelopes all thought and sensation in a radiant veil, and with an hand of beauty beckons us from the sterile seas of life, to her gardens, and bowers, and glades of bliss. And is not love a gift of the divinity? Love, and her child, Hope, which can bestow wealth on poverty, strength on the weak, and happiness on the sorrowing.

"My lot has not been fortunate. I have consorted long with grief, entered the gloomy labyrinth of madness, and emerged, but half alive. Yet I thank God that I have lived! I thank God, that I have beheld his throne, the heavens, and earth, his footstool. I am glad that I have seen the changes of his day; to behold the sun, fountain of light, and the gentle pilgrim moon; to have seen the fire bearing flowers of the sky, and the flowery stars of earth; to have witnessed the sowing and the harvest. I am glad that I have loved, and have experienced sympathetic joy and sorrow with my fellow-creatures. I am glad now to feel the current of thought flow through my mind, as the blood through the articulations of my frame; mere existence is pleasure; and I thank God that I live!

"And all ye happy nurslings of mother-earth, do ye not echo my words? Ye who are linked by the affectionate ties of nature, companions, friends, lovers! fathers, who toil with joy for their offspring; women, who while gazing on the living forms of their children, forget the pains of maternity; children, who neither toil nor spin, but love and are loved!

"Oh, that death and sickness were banished from our earthly home! that hatred, tyranny, and fear could no longer make their lair in the human heart! that each man might find a brother in his fellow, and a nest of repose amid the wide plains of his inheritance! that the source of tears were dry, and that lips might no longer form expressions of sorrow. Sleeping thus under the beneficent eye of heaven, can evil visit thee, O Earth, or grief cradle to their graves thy luckless children? Whisper it not, let the demons hear and rejoice! The choice is with us; let us will it, and our habitation becomes a paradise. For the will of man is omnipotent, blunting the arrows of death, soothing the bed of disease, and wiping away the tears of agony. And what is each human being worth, if he do not put forth his strength to aid his fellow-creatures? My soul is a fading spark, my nature frail as a spent wave; but I dedicate all of intellect and strength that remains to me, to that one work, and take upon me the task, as far as I am able, of bestowing blessings on my fellow-men!"

His voice trembled, his eyes were cast up, his hands clasped, and his fragile person was bent, as it were, with excess of emotion. The spirit of life seemed to linger in his form, as a dying flame on an altar flickers on the embers of an accepted sacrifice.

❧ 6 ❧

WHEN WE ARRIVED AT WINDSOR, I found that Raymond and Perdita had departed for the continent. I took possession of my sister's cottage, and blessed myself that I lived within view of Windsor Castle. It was a curious fact, that at this period, when by the marriage of Perdita I was allied to one of the richest individuals in England, and was bound by the most intimate friendship to its chiefest noble, I experienced the greatest excess of poverty that I had ever known. My knowledge of the worldly principles of Lord Raymond, would have ever prevented me from applying to him, however deep my distress might have been. It was in vain that I repeated to myself with regard to Adrian, that his purse was open to me; that one in soul, as we were, our fortunes ought also to be common. I could never, while with him, think of his bounty as a remedy to my poverty; and I even put aside hastily his offers of supplies, assuring him of a falsehood, that I needed them not. How could I say to this generous being, "Maintain me in idleness. You who have dedicated your powers of mind and fortune to the benefit of your species, shall you so misdirect your exertions, as to support in uselessness the strong, healthy, and capable?"

And yet I dared not request him to use his influence that I might obtain an honourable provision for myself—for then I should have been obliged to leave Windsor. I hovered forever around the walls of its Castle, beneath its enshadowing thickets; my sole companions were my books and my loving thoughts. I studied the wisdom of the ancients, and gazed on the happy walls that sheltered the beloved of my soul. My mind was nevertheless idle. I pored over the poetry of old times; I studied the metaphysics of Plato and Berkeley. I read the histories of Greece and Rome, and of England's former periods, and I watched the movements of the lady of my heart. At night I could see her shadow on the walls of her apartment; by day I viewed her in her flower-garden, or riding in the park with her usual companions. Methought the charm would be broken if I were seen, but I heard the music of her voice and was happy. I gave to each heroine of whom I read, her beauty and matchless excellences—such was Antigone, when she guided the blind Oedipus to the grove of the Eumenides, and discharged the funeral rites of Polynices; such was Miranda in the unvisited cave of Prospero; such Haidee, on the sands of the Ionian island. I was mad with excess of passionate devotion; but pride, tameless as fire, invested my nature, and prevented me from betraying myself by word or look.

In the mean time, while I thus pampered myself with rich mental repasts, a peasant would have disdained my scanty fare, which I sometimes robbed from the squirrels of the forest. I was, I own, often tempted to recur to the lawless feats of my boy-hood, and knock down the almost tame pheasants that perched upon the trees, and bent their bright eyes on me. But they were the property of Adrian, the nurslings of Idris; and so, although my imagination rendered sensual by privation, made me think that they would better become the spit in my kitchen, than the green leaves of the forest,

> Nathelesse,
> *I checked my haughty will, and did not eat;*

but supped upon sentiment, and dreamt vainly of "such morsels sweet," as I might not waking attain.

But, at this period, the whole scheme of my existence was about to change. The orphan and neglected son of Verney, was on the eve of being linked to the mechanism of society by a golden chain, and to enter into all the duties and affections of life. Miracles were to be wrought in my favour, the machine of social life pushed with vast effort backward. Attend, O reader! while I narrate this tale of wonders!

One day as Adrian and Idris were riding through the forest, with their mother and accustomed companions, Idris, drawing her brother aside from the rest of the cavalcade, suddenly asked him, "What had become of his friend, Lionel Verney?"

"Even from this spot," replied Adrian, pointing to my sister's cottage, "you can see his dwelling."

"Indeed!" said Idris, "and why, if he be so near, does he not come to see us, and make one of our society?"

"I often visit him," replied Adrian; "but you may easily guess the motives, which prevent him from coming where his presence may annoy any one among us."

"I do guess them," said Idris, "and such as they are, I would not venture to combat them. Tell me, however, in what way he passes his time; what he is doing and thinking in his cottage retreat?"

"Nay, my sweet sister," replied Adrian, "you ask me more than I can well answer; but if you feel interest in him, why not visit him? He will feel highly honoured, and thus you may repay a part of the obligation I owe him, and compensate for the injuries fortune has done him."

"I will most readily accompany you to his abode," said the lady, "not that I wish that either of us should unburthen ourselves of our debt, which, being no less than your life, must remain unpayable ever. But let us go; to-morrow we will arrange to ride out together, and proceeding towards that part of the forest, call upon him."

The next evening therefore, though the autumnal change had brought on cold and rain, Adrian and Idris entered my cottage. They found me Curius-like, feasting on sorry fruits for supper; but they brought gifts richer than the golden bribes of the Sabines, nor could I refuse the invaluable store of friendship and delight which they bestowed. Surely the glorious twins of Latona were not more welcome, when, in the infancy of the world, they were brought forth to beautify and enlighten this "sterile promontory," than were this angelic pair to my lowly dwelling and grateful heart. We sat like one family round my hearth. Our talk was on subjects, unconnected with the emotions that evidently occupied each; but we each divined the other's thought, and as our voices spoke of indifferent matters, our eyes, in mute language, told a thousand things no tongue could have uttered.

They left me in an hour's time. They left me happy—how unspeakably happy. It did not require the measured sounds of human language to syllable the story of my extasy. Idris had visited me; Idris I should again and again see—my imagination did not wander beyond the completeness of this knowledge. I trod air; no doubt, no fear, no hope even, disturbed me; I clasped with my soul the fulness of contentment, satisfied, undesiring, beatified.

For many days Adrian and Idris continued to visit me thus. In this dear intercourse, love, in the guise of enthusiastic friendship, infused more and more of his omnipotent spirit. Idris felt it. Yes, divinity of the world, I read your characters in her looks and gesture; I heard your melodious voice echoed by her—you prepared for us a soft and flowery path, all gentle thoughts adorned it—your name, O Love, was not spoken, but you stood the Genius of the Hour, veiled, and time, but no mortal hand, might raise the curtain. Organs of articulate sound did not proclaim the union of our hearts; for untoward circumstance allowed no opportunity for the expression that hovered on our lips. Oh my pen! haste thou to write what was, before the thought of what is, arrests the hand that guides thee. If I lift up my eyes and see the desart earth, and feel that those dear eyes have spent their mortal lustre, and that those beauteous lips are silent, their "crimson leaves" faded, forever I am mute!

But you live, my Idris, even now you move before me! There was a glade, O reader! a grassy opening in the wood; the retiring trees left its velvet expanse as a temple for love; the silver Thames bounded it on one side, and a willow bending down dipt in the water its Naiad hair, dishevelled by the wind's viewless hand. The oaks around were the home of a tribe of nightingales—there am I now; Idris, in youth's dear prime, is by my side —remember, I am just twenty-two, and seventeen summers have scarcely passed over the beloved of my heart. The river swollen by autumnal rains, deluged the low lands, and Adrian in his favourite boat is employed in the dangerous pastime of plucking the topmost bough from a submerged oak. Are you weary of life, O Adrian, that you thus play with danger?—

He has obtained his prize, and he pilots his boat through the flood; our eyes were fixed on him fearfully, but the stream carried him away from us; he was forced to land far lower down, and to make a considerable circuit before he could join us. "He is safe!" said Idris, as he leapt on shore, and waved the bough over his head in token of success; "we will wait for him here."

We were alone together; the sun had set; the song of the nightingales began; the evening star shone distinct in the flood of light, which was yet unfaded in the west. The blue eyes of my angelic girl were fixed on this sweet emblem of herself: "How the light palpitates," she said, "which is that star's life. Its vacillating effulgence seems to say that its state, even like ours upon earth, is wavering and inconstant; it fears, methinks, and it loves."

"Gaze not on the star, dear, generous friend," I cried, "read not love in its trembling rays; look not upon distant worlds; speak not of the mere imagination of a sentiment. I have long been silent; long even to sickness have I desired to speak to you, and submit my soul, my life, my entire being to you. Look not on the star, dear love, or do, and let that eternal spark plead for me; let it be my witness and my advocate, silent as it shines—love is to me as light to the star; even so long as that is uneclipsed by annihilation, so long shall I love you."

Veiled forever to the world's callous eye must be the transport of that moment. Still do I feel her graceful form press against my full-fraught heart—still does sight, and pulse, and breath sicken and fail, at the remembrance of that first kiss. Slowly and silently we went to meet Adrian, whom we heard approaching.

I entreated Adrian to return to me after he had conducted his sister home. And that same evening, walking among the moon-lit forest paths, I poured forth my whole heart, its transport and its hope, to my friend. For a moment he looked disturbed—"I might have foreseen this," he said, "what strife will now ensue! Pardon me, Lionel, nor wonder that the expectation of contest with my mother should jar me, when else I should delightedly confess that my best hopes are fulfilled, in confiding my sister to your protection. If you do not already know it, you will soon learn the deep hate my mother bears to the name Verney. I will converse with Idris; then all that a friend can do, I will do; to her it must belong to play the lover's part, if she be capable of it."

While the brother and sister were still hesitating in what manner they could best attempt to bring their mother over to their party, she, suspecting our meetings, taxed her children with them; taxed her fair daughter with deceit, and an unbecoming attachment for one whose only merit was being the son of the profligate favourite of her imprudent father; and who was doubtless as worthless as he from whom he boasted his descent. The eyes of Idris flashed at this accusation; she replied, "I do not deny that I love Verney; prove to me that he is worthless; and I will never see him more."

"Dear Madam," said Adrian, "let me entreat you to see him, to cultivate his friendship. You will wonder then, as I do, at the extent of his accomplishments, and the brilliancy of his talents." (Pardon me, gentle reader, this is not futile vanity;—not futile, since to know that Adrian felt thus, brings joy even now to my lone heart).

"Mad and foolish boy!" exclaimed the angry lady, "you have chosen with dreams and theories to overthrow my schemes for your own aggrandizement; but you shall not do the same by those I have formed for your sister. I but too well understand the fascination you both labour under; since I had the same struggle with your father, to make him cast off the parent of this youth, who hid his evil propensities with the smoothness and subtlety of a viper. In those days how often did I hear of his attractions, his wide spread conquests, his wit, his refined manners. It is well when flies only are caught by such spiders' webs; but is it for the high-born and powerful to bow their necks to the flimsy yoke of these unmeaning pretensions? Were your sister indeed the insignificant person she deserves to be, I would willingly leave her to the fate, the wretched fate, of the wife of a man, whose very person, resembling as it does his wretched father, ought to remind you of the folly and vice it typifies—but remember, Lady Idris, it is not alone the once royal blood of England that colours your veins, you are a Princess of Austria, and every life-drop is akin to emperors and kings. Are you then a fit mate for an uneducated shepherd-boy, whose only inheritance is his father's tarnished name?"

"I can make but one defence," replied Idris, "the same offered by my brother; see Lionel, converse with my shepherd-boy"——The Countess interrupted her indignantly—"Yours!"—she cried: and then, smoothing her impassioned features to a disdainful smile, she continued—"We will talk of this another time. All I now ask, all your mother, Idris, requests is, that you will not see this upstart during the interval of one month."

"I dare not comply," said Idris, "it would pain him too much. I have no right to play with his feelings, to accept his proffered love, and then sting him with neglect."

"This is going too far," her mother answered, with quivering lips, and eyes again instinct by anger.

"Nay, Madam," said Adrian, "unless my sister consent never to see him again, it is surely an useless torment to separate them for a month."

"Certainly," replied the ex-queen, with bitter scorn, "his love, and her love, and both their childish flutterings, are to be put in fit comparison with my years of hope and anxiety, with the duties of the offspring of kings, with the high and dignified conduct which one of her descent ought to pursue. But it is unworthy of me to argue and complain. Perhaps you will have the goodness to promise me not to marry during that interval?"

This was asked only half ironically; and Idris wondered why her mother should extort from her a solemn vow not to do, what she had never dreamed of doing—but the promise was required and given.

All went on cheerfully now; we met as usual, and talked without dread of our future plans. The Countess was so gentle, and even beyond her wont, amiable with her children, that they began to entertain hopes of her ultimate consent. She was too unlike them, too utterly alien to their tastes, for them to find delight in her society, or in the prospect of its continuance, but it gave them pleasure to see her conciliating and kind. Once even, Adrian ventured to propose her receiving me. She refused with a smile, reminding him that for the present his sister had promised to be patient.

One day, after the lapse of nearly a month, Adrian received a letter from a friend in London, requesting his immediate presence for the furtherance of some important object. Guileless himself, Adrian feared no deceit. I rode with him as far as Staines: he was in high spirits; and, since I could not see Idris during his absence, he promised a speedy return. His gaiety, which was extreme, had the strange effect of awakening in me contrary feelings; a presentiment of evil hung over me; I loitered on my return; I counted the hours that must elapse before I saw Idris again. Wherefore should this be? What evil might not happen in the mean time? Might not her mother take advantage of Adrian's absence to urge her beyond her sufferance, perhaps to entrap her? I resolved, let what would befall, to see and converse with her the following day. This determination soothed me. To-morrow, loveliest and best, hope and joy of my life, to-morrow I will see thee—Fool, to dream of a moment's delay!

I went to rest. At past midnight I was awaked by a violent knocking. It was now deep winter; it had snowed, and was still snowing; the wind whistled in the leafless trees, despoiling them of the white flakes as they fell; its drear moaning, and the continued knocking, mingled wildly with my dreams— at length I was wide awake; hastily dressing myself, I hurried to discover the cause of this disturbance, and to open my door to the unexpected visitor. Pale as the snow that showered about her, with clasped hands, Idris stood before me. "Save me!" she exclaimed, and would have sunk to the ground had I not supported her. In a moment however she revived, and, with energy, almost with violence, entreated me to saddle horses, to take her away, away to London—to her brother—at least to save her. I had no horses—she wrung her hands. "What can I do?" she cried, "I am lost—we are both for ever lost! But come—come with me, Lionel; here I must not stay,—we can get a chaise at the nearest post-house; yet perhaps we have time! come, O come with me to save and protect me!"

When I heard her piteous demands, while with disordered dress, dishevelled hair, and aghast looks, she wrung her hands—the idea shot across me is she also mad?—"Sweet one," and I folded her to my heart, "better repose than wander further;—rest—my beloved, I will make a fire—you are chill."

"Rest!" she cried, "repose! you rave, Lionel! If you delay we are lost; come, I pray you, unless you would cast me off forever."

That Idris, the princely born, nursling of wealth and luxury, should have come through the tempestuous winter-night from her regal abode, and standing at my lowly door, conjure me to fly with her through darkness and storm—was surely a dream—again her plaintive tones, the sight of her loveliness assured me that it was no vision. Looking timidly around, as if she feared to be overheard, she whispered: "I have discovered—to-morrow —that is, to-day—already the to-morrow is come—before dawn, foreigners, Austrians, my mother's hirelings, are to carry me off to Germany, to prison, to marriage—to anything, except you and my brother —take me away, or soon they will be here!"

I was frightened by her vehemence, and imagined some mistake in her incoherent tale; but I no longer hesitated to obey her. She had come by herself from the Castle, three long miles, at midnight, through the heavy snow; we must reach Englefield Green, a mile and a half further, before we could obtain a chaise. She told me, that she had kept up her strength and courage till her arrival at my cottage, and then both failed. Now she could hardly walk. Supporting her as I did, still she lagged: and at the distance of half a mile, after many stoppages, shivering fits, and half faintings, she slipt from my supporting arm on the snow, and with a torrent of tears averred that she must be taken, for that she could not proceed. I lifted her up in my arms; her light form rested on my breast.—I felt no burthen, except the internal one of contrary and contending emotions. Brimming delight now invested me. Again her chill limbs touched me as a torpedo; and I shuddered in sympathy with her pain and fright. Her head lay on my shoulder, her breath waved my hair, her heart beat near mine, transport made me tremble, blinded me, annihilated me—till a suppressed groan, bursting from her lips, the chattering of her teeth, which she strove vainly to subdue, and all the signs of suffering she evinced, recalled me to the necessity of speed and succour. At last I said to her, "There is Englefield Green; there the inn. But, if you are seen thus strangely circumstanced, dear Idris, even now your enemies may learn your flight too soon: were it not better that I hired the chaise alone? I will put you in safety meanwhile, and return to you immediately."

She answered that I was right, and might do with her as I pleased. I observed the door of a small out-house a-jar. I pushed it open; and, with some hay strewed about, I formed a couch for her, placing her exhausted frame on it, and covering her with my cloak. I feared to leave her, she looked so wan and faint—but in a moment she re-acquired animation, and, with that, fear; and again she implored me not to delay. To call up the people of the inn, and obtain a conveyance and horses, even though I harnessed them myself, was the work of many minutes; minutes, each freighted with the weight of ages. I caused the chaise to advance a little, waited till the people of the inn had retired, and then made the post-boy draw up the carriage to the spot where Idris, impatient, and now somewhat recovered, stood waiting for me. I lifted her into the chaise; I assured her that with our four horses we should arrive in London before five o'clock, the hour when she would be sought and missed. I besought her to calm herself; a kindly shower of tears relieved her, and by degrees she related her tale of fear and peril.

That same night after Adrian's departure, her mother had warmly expostulated with her on the subject of her attachment to me. Every motive, every threat, every angry taunt was urged in vain. She seemed to consider that through me she had lost Raymond; I was the evil influence of her life; I was even accused of increasing and confirming the mad and base apostacy of Adrian from all views of advancement and grandeur; and now this miserable mountaineer was to steal her daughter. Never, Idris related, did the angry lady deign to recur to gentleness and persuasion; if she had, the task of resistance would have been exquisitely painful. As it was, the sweet girl's generous nature was roused to defend, and ally herself with, my despised cause. Her mother ended with a look of contempt and covert triumph, which for a moment awakened the suspicions of Idris. When they parted for the night, the Countess said, "To-morrow I trust your tone will be changed: be composed; I have agitated you; go to rest; and I will send you a medicine I always take when unduly restless—it will give you a quiet night."

By the time that she had with uneasy thoughts laid her fair cheek upon her pillow, her mother's servant brought a draught; a suspicion again crossed her at this novel proceeding, sufficiently alarming to determine her not to take the potion; but dislike of contention, and a wish to discover whether there was any just foundation for her conjectures, made her, she said, almost instinctively, and in contradiction to her usual frankness, pretend to swallow the medicine. Then, agitated as she had been by her mother's violence, and now by unaccustomed fears, she lay unable to sleep, starting at every sound. Soon her door opened softly, and on her springing up, she heard a whisper, "Not asleep yet," and the door again closed. With a beating heart she expected another visit, and when after an interval her chamber was again invaded, having first assured herself that the intruders were her mother and an attendant, she composed herself to feigned sleep. A step approached her bed, she dared not move, she strove to calm her palpitations, which became more violent, when she heard her mother say mutteringly, "Pretty simpleton, little do you think that your game is already at an end forever."

For a moment the poor girl fancied that her mother believed that she had drank poison: she was on the point of springing up; when the Countess, already at a distance from the bed, spoke in a low voice to her companion, and again Idris listened: "Hasten," said she, "there is no time to lose— it is long past eleven; they will be here at five; take merely the clothes necessary for her journey, and her jewel-casket." The servant obeyed; few words were spoken on either side; but those were caught at with avidity by the intended victim. She heard the name of her own maid mentioned;—"No, no," replied her mother, "she does not go with us; Lady Idris must forget England, and all belonging to it." And again she heard, "She will not wake till late to-morrow, and we shall then be at sea."——"All is ready," at length the woman announced. The Countess again came to her daughter's bedside: "In Austria at least," she said, "you will obey. In Austria, where obedience can be enforced, and no choice left but between an honourable prison and a fitting marriage."

Both then withdrew; though, as she went, the Countess said, "Softly; all sleep; though all have not been prepared for sleep, like her. I would not have any one suspect, or she might be roused to resistance, and perhaps escape. Come with me to my room; we will remain there till the hour agreed upon." They went. Idris, panic-struck, but animated and strengthened even by her excessive fear, dressed herself hurriedly, and going down a flight of back-stairs, avoiding the vicinity of her mother's apartment, she contrived to escape from the castle by a low window, and came through snow, wind, and obscurity to my cottage; nor lost her courage, until she arrived, and, depositing her fate in my hands, gave herself up to the desperation and weariness that overwhelmed her.

I comforted her as well as I might. Joy and exultation, were mine, to possess, and to save her. Yet not to excite fresh agitation in her, "per non turbar quel bel viso sereno," I curbed my delight. I strove to quiet the eager dancing of my heart; I turned from her my eyes, beaming with too much tenderness, and proudly, to dark night, and the inclement atmosphere, murmured the expressions of my transport. We reached London, methought, all too soon; and yet I could not regret our speedy arrival, when I witnessed the extasy with which my beloved girl found herself in her brother's arms, safe from every evil, under his unblamed protection.

Adrian wrote a brief note to his mother, informing her that Idris was under his care and guardianship. Several days elapsed, and at last an answer came, dated from Cologne. "It was useless," the haughty and disappointed lady wrote, "for the Earl of Windsor and his sister to address again the injured parent, whose only expectation of tranquility must be derived from oblivion of their existence. Her desires had been blasted, her schemes overthrown. She did not complain; in her brother's court she would find, not compensation for their disobedience (filial unkindness admitted of none), but such a state of things and mode of life, as might best reconcile her to her fate. Under such circumstances, she positively declined any communication with them."

Such were the strange and incredible events, that finally brought about my union with the sister of my best friend, with my adored Idris. With simplicity and courage she set aside the prejudices and opposition which were obstacles to my happiness, nor scrupled to give her hand, where she had given her heart. To be worthy of her, to raise myself to her height through the exertion of talents and virtue, to repay her love with devoted, unwearied tenderness, were the only thanks I could offer for the matchless gift.

7

AND NOW LET THE READER, passing over some short period of time, be introduced to our happy circle. Adrian, Idris and I, were established in Windsor Castle; Lord Raymond and my sister, inhabited a house which the former had built on the borders of the Great Park, near Perdita's cottage, as was still named the low-roofed abode, where we two, poor even in hope, had each received the assurance of our felicity. We had our separate occupations and our common amusements. Sometimes we passed whole days under the leafy covert of the forest with our books and music. This occurred during those rare days in this country, when the sun mounts his etherial throne in unclouded majesty, and the windless atmosphere is as a bath of pellucid and grateful water, wrapping the senses in tranquility. When the clouds veiled the sky, and the wind scattered them there and here, rending their woof, and strewing its fragments through the aerial plains—then we rode out, and sought new spots of beauty and repose. When the frequent rains shut us within doors, evening recreation followed morning study, ushered in by music and song. Idris had a natural musical talent; and her voice, which had been carefully cultivated, was full and sweet. Raymond and I made a part of the concert, and Adrian and Perdita were devout listeners. Then we were as gay as summer insects, playful as children; we ever met one another with smiles, and read content and joy in each other's countenances. Our prime festivals were held in Perdita's cottage; nor were we ever weary of talking of the past or dreaming of the future. Jealousy and disquiet were unknown among us; nor did a fear or hope of change ever disturb our tranquility. Others said, We might be happy—we said—We are.

When any separation took place between us, it generally so happened, that Idris and Perdita would ramble away together, and we remained to discuss the affairs of nations, and the philosophy of life. The very difference of our dispositions gave zest to these conversations. Adrian had the superiority in learning and eloquence; but Raymond possessed a quick penetration, and a practical knowledge of life, which usually displayed itself in opposition to Adrian, and thus kept up the ball of discussion. At other times we made excursions of many days' duration, and crossed the country to visit any spot noted for beauty or historical association. Sometimes we went up to London, and entered into the amusements of the busy throng; sometimes our retreat was invaded by visitors from among them. This change made us only the more sensible to the delights of the intimate intercourse of our own circle, the tranquility of our divine forest, and our happy evenings in the halls of our beloved Castle.

The disposition of Idris was peculiarly frank, soft, and affectionate. Her temper was unalterably sweet; and although firm and resolute on any point that touched her heart, she was yielding to those she loved. The nature of Perdita was less perfect; but tenderness and happiness improved her temper, and softened her natural reserve. Her understanding was clear and comprehensive, her imagination vivid; she was sincere, generous, and reasonable. Adrian, the matchless brother of my soul, the sensitive and excellent Adrian, loving all, and beloved by all, yet seemed destined not to find the half of himself, which was to complete his happiness. He often left us, and wandered by himself in the woods, or sailed in his little skiff, his books his only companions. He was often the gayest of our party, at the same time that he was the only one visited by fits of despondency; his slender frame seemed overcharged with the weight of life, and his soul appeared rather to inhabit his body than unite with it. I was hardly more devoted to my Idris than to her brother, and she loved him as her teacher, her friend, the benefactor who had secured to her the fulfilment of her dearest wishes. Raymond, the ambitious, restless Raymond, reposed midway on the great high-road of life, and was content to give up all his schemes of sovereignty and fame, to make one of us, the flowers of the field. His kingdom was the heart of Perdita, his subjects her thoughts; by her he was loved, respected as a superior being, obeyed, waited on. No office, no devotion, no watching was irksome to her, as it regarded him. She would sit apart from us and watch him; she would weep for joy to think that he was hers. She erected a temple for him in the depth of her being, and each faculty was a priestess vowed to his service. Sometimes she might be wayward and capricious; but her repentance was bitter, her return entire, and even this inequality of temper suited him who was not formed by nature to float idly down the stream of life.

During the first year of their marriage, Perdita presented Raymond with a lovely girl. It was curious to trace in this miniature model the very traits of its father. The same half-disdainful lips and smile of triumph, the same intelligent eyes, the same brow and chestnut hair; her very hands and taper fingers resembled his. How very dear she was to Perdita! In progress of time, I also became a father, and our little darlings, our playthings and delights, called forth a thousand new and delicious feelings.

Years passed thus,—even years. Each month brought forth its successor, each year one like to that gone by; truly, our lives were a living comment on that beautiful sentiment of Plutarch, that "our souls have a natural inclination to love, being born as much to love, as to feel, to reason, to understand and remember." We talked of change and active pursuits, but still remained at Windsor, incapable of violating the charm that attached us to our secluded life.

> *Pareamo aver qui tutto il ben raccolto*
> *Che fra mortali in piu parte si rimembra.*

Now also that our children gave us occupation, we found excuses for our idleness, in the idea of bringing them up to a more splendid career. At length our tranquility was disturbed, and the course of events, which for five years had flowed on in hushing tranquility, was broken by breakers and obstacles, that woke us from our pleasant dream.

A new Lord Protector of England was to be chosen; and, at Raymond's request, we removed to London, to witness, and even take a part in the election. If Raymond had been united to Idris, this post had been his stepping-stone to higher dignity; and his desire for power and fame had been crowned with fullest measure. He had exchanged a sceptre for a lute, a kingdom for Perdita.

Did he think of this as we journeyed up to town? I watched him, but could make but little of him. He was particularly gay, playing with his child, and turning to sport every word that was uttered. Perhaps he did this because he saw a cloud upon Perdita's brow. She tried to rouse herself, but her eyes every now and then filled with tears, and she looked wistfully on Raymond and her girl, as if fearful that some evil would betide them. And so she felt. A presentiment of ill hung over her. She leaned from the window looking on the forest, and the turrets of the Castle, and as these became hid by intervening objects, she passionately exclaimed—"Scenes of happiness! scenes sacred to devoted love, when shall I see you again! and when I see ye, shall I be still the beloved and joyous Perdita, or shall I, heart-broken and lost, wander among your groves, the ghost of what I am!"

"Why, silly one," cried Raymond, "what is your little head pondering upon, that of a sudden you have become so sublimely dismal? Cheer up, or I shall make you over to Idris, and call Adrian into the carriage, who, I see by his gesture, sympathizes with my good spirits."

Adrian was on horseback; he rode up to the carriage, and his gaiety, in addition to that of Raymond, dispelled my sister's melancholy. We entered London in the evening, and went to our several abodes near Hyde Park.

The following morning Lord Raymond visited me early. "I come to you," he said, "only half assured that you will assist me in my project, but resolved to go through with it, whether you concur with me or not. Promise me secrecy however; for if you will not contribute to my success, at least you must not baffle me."

"Well, I promise. And now——"

"And now, my dear fellow, for what are we come to London? To be present at the election of a Protector, and to give our yea or nay for his shuffling Grace of——? or for that noisy Ryland? Do you believe, Verney, that I brought you to town for that? No, we will have a Protector of our own. We will set up a candidate, and ensure his success. We will nominate Adrian, and do our best to bestow on him the power to which he is entitled by his birth, and which he merits through his virtues.

"Do not answer; I know all your objections, and will reply to them in order. First, Whether he will or will not consent to become a great man? Leave the task of persuasion on that point to me; I do not ask you to assist me there. Secondly, Whether he ought to exchange his employment of plucking blackberries, and nursing wounded partridges in the forest, for the command of a nation? My dear Lionel, we are married men, and find employment sufficient in amusing our wives, and dancing our children. But Adrian is alone, wifeless, childless, unoccupied. I have long observed him. He pines for want of some interest in life. His heart, exhausted by his early sufferings, reposes like a new-healed limb, and shrinks from all excitement. But his understanding, his charity, his virtues, want a field for exercise and display; and we will procure it for him. Besides, is it not a shame, that the genius of Adrian should fade from the earth like a flower in an untrod mountain-path, fruitless? Do you think Nature composed his surpassing machine for no purpose? Believe me, he was destined to be the author of infinite good to his native England. Has she not bestowed on him every gift in prodigality?— birth, wealth, talent, goodness? Does not every one love and admire him? and does he not delight singly in such efforts as manifest his love to all? Come, I see that you are already persuaded, and will second me when I propose him to-night in parliament."

"You have got up all your arguments in excellent order," I replied; "and, if Adrian consent, they are unanswerable. One only condition I would make, —that you do nothing without his concurrence."

"I believe you are in the right," said Raymond; "although I had thought at first to arrange the affair differently. Be it so. I will go instantly to Adrian; and, if he inclines to consent, you will not destroy my labour by persuading him to return, and turn squirrel again in Windsor Forest. Idris, you will not act the traitor towards me?"

"Trust me," replied she, "I will preserve a strict neutrality."

"For my part," said I, "I am too well convinced of the worth of our friend, and the rich harvest of benefits that all England would reap from his Protectorship, to deprive my countrymen of such a blessing, if he consent to bestow it on them."

In the evening Adrian visited us.—"Do you cabal also against me," said he, laughing; "and will you make common cause with Raymond, in dragging a poor visionary from the clouds to surround him with the fire-works and blasts of earthly grandeur, instead of heavenly rays and airs? I thought you knew me better."

"I do know you better," I replied "than to think that you would be happy in such a situation; but the good you would do to others may be an inducement, since the time is probably arrived when you can put your theories into practice, and you may bring about such reformation and change, as will conduce to that perfect system of government which you delight to portray."

"You speak of an almost-forgotten dream," said Adrian, his countenance slightly clouding as he spoke; "the visions of my boyhood have long since faded in the light of reality; I know now that I am not a man fitted to govern nations; sufficient for me, if I keep in wholesome rule the little kingdom of my own mortality.

"But do not you see, Lionel, the drift of our noble friend; a drift, perhaps, unknown to himself, but apparent to me. Lord Raymond was never born to be a drone in the hive, and to find content in our pastoral life. He thinks, that he ought to be satisfied; he imagines, that his present situation precludes the possibility of aggrandisement; he does not therefore, even in his own heart, plan change for himself. But do you not see, that, under the idea of exalting me, he is chalking out a new path for himself; a path of action from which he has long wandered?

"Let us assist him. He, the noble, the warlike, the great in every quality that can adorn the mind and person of man; he is fitted to be the Protector of England. If I—that is, if we propose him, he will assuredly be elected, and will find, in the functions of that high office, scope for the towering powers of his mind. Even Perdita will rejoice. Perdita, in whom ambition was a covered fire until she married Raymond, which event was for a time the fulfilment of her hopes; Perdita will rejoice in the glory and advancement of her lord—and, coyly and prettily, not be discontented with her share. In the mean time, we, the wise of the land, will return to our Castle, and, Cincinnatus-like, take to our usual labours, until our friend shall require our presence and assistance here."

The more Adrian reasoned upon this scheme, the more feasible it appeared. His own determination never to enter into public life was insurmountable, and the delicacy of his health was a sufficient argument against it. The next step was to induce Raymond to confess his secret wishes for dignity and fame. He entered while we were speaking. The way in which Adrian had received his project for setting him up as a candidate for the Protectorship, and his replies, had already awakened in his mind, the view of the subject which we were now discussing. His countenance and manner betrayed irresolution and anxiety; but the anxiety arose from a fear that we should not prosecute, or not succeed in our idea; and his irresolution, from a doubt whether we should risk a defeat. A few words from us decided him, and hope and joy sparkled in his eyes; the idea of embarking in a career, so congenial to his early habits and cherished wishes, made him as before energetic and bold. We discussed his chances, the merits of the other candidates, and the dispositions of the voters.

After all we miscalculated. Raymond had lost much of his popularity, and was deserted by his peculiar partisans. Absence from the busy stage had caused him to be forgotten by the people; his former parliamentary supporters were principally composed of royalists, who had been willing to make an idol of him when he appeared as the heir of the Earldom of Windsor; but who were indifferent to him, when he came forward with no other attributes and distinctions than they conceived to be common to many among themselves. Still he had many friends, admirers of his transcendent talents; his presence in the house, his eloquence, address and imposing beauty, were calculated to produce an electric effect. Adrian also, notwithstanding his recluse habits and theories, so adverse to the spirit of party, had many friends, and they were easily induced to vote for a candidate of his selection.

The Duke of——, and Mr. Ryland, Lord Raymond's old antagonist, were the other candidates. The Duke was supported by all the aristocrats of the republic, who considered him their proper representative. Ryland was the popular candidate; when Lord Raymond was first added to the list, his chance of success appeared small. We retired from the debate which had followed on his nomination: we, his nominators, mortified; he dispirited to excess. Perdita reproached us bitterly. Her expectations had been strongly excited; she had urged nothing against our project, on the contrary, she was evidently pleased by it; but its evident ill success changed the current of her ideas. She felt, that, once awakened, Raymond would never return unrepining to Windsor. His habits were unhinged; his restless mind roused from its sleep, ambition must now be his companion through life; and if he did not succeed in his present attempt, she foresaw that unhappiness and cureless discontent would follow. Perhaps her own disappointment added a sting to her thoughts and words; she did not spare us, and our own reflections added to our disquietude.

It was necessary to follow up our nomination, and to persuade Raymond to present himself to the electors on the following evening. For a long time he was obstinate. He would embark in a balloon; he would sail for a distant quarter of the world, where his name and humiliation were unknown. But this was useless; his attempt was registered; his purpose published to the world; his shame could never be erased from the memories of men. It was as well to fail at last after a struggle, as to fly now at the beginning of his enterprise.

From the moment that he adopted this idea, he was changed. His depression and anxiety fled; he became all life and activity. The smile of triumph shone on his countenance; determined to pursue his object to the uttermost, his manner and expression seem ominous of the accomplishment of his wishes. Not so Perdita. She was frightened by his gaiety, for she dreaded a greater revulsion at the end. If his appearance even inspired us with hope, it only rendered the state of her mind more painful. She feared to lose sight of him; yet she dreaded to remark any change in the temper of his mind. She listened eagerly to him, yet tantalized herself by giving to his words a meaning foreign to their true interpretation, and adverse to her hopes. She dared not be present at the contest; yet she remained at home a prey to double solicitude. She wept over her little girl; she looked, she spoke, as if she dreaded the occurrence of some frightful calamity. She was half mad from the effects of uncontrollable agitation.

Lord Raymond presented himself to the house with fearless confidence and insinuating address. After the Duke of——and Mr. Ryland had finished their speeches, he commenced. Assuredly he had not conned his lesson; and at first he hesitated, pausing in his ideas, and in the choice of his expressions. By degrees he warmed; his words flowed with ease, his language was full of vigour, and his voice of persuasion. He reverted to his past life, his successes in Greece, his favour at home. Why should he lose this, now that added years, prudence, and the pledge which his marriage gave to his country, ought to increase, rather than diminish his claims to confidence? He spoke of the state of England; the necessary measures to be taken to ensure its security, and confirm its prosperity. He drew a glowing picture of its present situation. As he spoke, every sound was hushed, every thought suspended by intense attention.

His graceful elocution enchained the senses of his hearers. In some degree also he was fitted to reconcile all parties. His birth pleased the aristocracy; his being the candidate recommended by Adrian, a man intimately allied to the popular party, caused a number, who had no great reliance either on the Duke or Mr. Ryland, to range on his side.

The contest was keen and doubtful. Neither Adrian nor myself would have been so anxious, if our own success had depended on our exertions; but we had egged our friend on to the enterprise, and it became us to ensure his triumph. Idris, who entertained the highest opinion of his abilities, was warmly interested in the event: and my poor sister, who dared not hope, and to whom fear was misery, was plunged into a fever of disquietude.

Day after day passed while we discussed our projects for the evening, and each night was occupied by debates which offered no conclusion. At last the crisis came: the night when parliament, which had so long delayed its choice, must decide: as the hour of twelve passed, and the new day began, it was by virtue of the constitution dissolved, its power extinct.

We assembled at Raymond's house, we and our partisans. At half past five o'clock we proceeded to the House. Idris endeavoured to calm Perdita; but the poor girl's agitation deprived her of all power of self-command. She walked up and down the room,—gazed wildly when any one entered, fancying that they might be the announcers of her doom. I must do justice to my sweet sister: it was not for herself that she was thus agonized. She alone knew the weight which Raymond attached to his success. Even to us he assumed gaiety and hope, and assumed them so well, that we did not divine the secret workings of his mind. Sometimes a nervous trembling, a sharp dissonance of voice, and momentary fits of absence revealed to Perdita the violence he did himself; but we, intent on our plans, observed only his ready laugh, his joke intruded on all occasions, the flow of his spirits which seemed incapable of ebb. Besides, Perdita was with him in his retirement; she saw the moodiness that succeeded to this forced hilarity; she marked his disturbed sleep, his painful irritability—once she had seen his tears—hers had scarce ceased to flow, since she had beheld the big drops which disappointed pride had caused to gather in his eye, but which pride was unable to dispel. What wonder then, that her feelings were wrought to this pitch! I thus accounted to myself for her agitation; but this was not all, and the sequel revealed another excuse.

One moment we seized before our departure, to take leave of our beloved girls. I had small hope of success, and entreated Idris to watch over my sister. As I approached the latter, she seized my hand, and drew me into another apartment; she threw herself into my arms, and wept and sobbed bitterly and long. I tried to soothe her; I bade her hope; I asked what tremendous consequences would ensue even on our failure. "My brother," she cried, "protector of my childhood, dear, most dear Lionel, my fate hangs by a thread. I have you all about me now—you, the companion of my infancy; Adrian, as dear to me as if bound by the ties of blood; Idris, the sister of my heart, and her lovely offspring. This, O this may be the last time that you will surround me thus!"

Abruptly she stopped, and then cried: "What have I said?—foolish false girl that I am!" She looked wildly on me, and then suddenly calming herself, apologized for what she called her unmeaning words, saying that she must indeed be insane, for, while Raymond lived, she must be happy; and then, though she still wept, she suffered me tranquilly to depart. Raymond only took her hand when he went, and looked on her expressively; she answered by a look of intelligence and assent.

Poor girl! what she then suffered! I could never entirely forgive Raymond for the trials he imposed on her, occasioned as they were by a selfish feeling on his part. He had schemed, if he failed in his present attempt, without taking leave of any of us, to embark for Greece, and never again to revisit England. Perdita acceded to his wishes; for his contentment was the chief object of her life, the crown of her enjoyment; but to leave us all, her companions, the beloved partners of her happiest years, and in the interim to conceal this frightful determination, was a task that almost conquered her strength of mind. She had been employed in arranging for their departure; she had promised Raymond during this decisive evening, to take advantage of our absence, to go one stage of the journey, and he, after his defeat was ascertained, would slip away from us, and join her.

Although, when I was informed of this scheme, I was bitterly offended by the small attention which Raymond paid to my sister's feelings, I was led by reflection to consider, that he acted under the force of such strong excitement, as to take from him the consciousness, and, consequently, the guilt of a fault. If he had permitted us to witness his agitation, he would have been more under the guidance of reason; but his struggles for the shew of composure, acted with such violence on his nerves, as to destroy his power of self-command. I am convinced that, at the worst, he would have returned from the seashore to take leave of us, and to make us the partners of his council. But the task imposed on Perdita was not the less painful. He had extorted from her a vow of secrecy; and her part of the drama, since it was to be performed alone, was the most agonizing that could be devised. But to return to my narrative.

The debates had hitherto been long and loud; they had often been protracted merely for the sake of delay. But now each seemed fearful lest the fatal moment should pass, while the choice was yet undecided. Unwonted silence reigned in the house, the members spoke in whispers, and the ordinary business was transacted with celerity and quietness. During the first stage of the election, the Duke of——had been thrown out; the question therefore lay between Lord Raymond and Mr. Ryland. The latter had felt secure of victory, until the appearance of Raymond; and, since his name had been inserted as a candidate, he had canvassed with eagerness. He had appeared each evening, impatience and anger marked in his looks, scowling on us from the opposite side of St. Stephen's, as if his mere frown would cast eclipse on our hopes.

Every thing in the English constitution had been regulated for the better preservation of peace. On the last day, two candidates only were allowed to remain; and to obviate, if possible, the last struggle between these, a bribe was offered to him who should voluntarily resign his pretensions; a place of great emolument and honour was given him, and his success facilitated at a future election. Strange to say however, no instance had yet occurred, where either candidate had had recourse to this expedient; in consequence the law had become obsolete, nor had been referred to by any of us in our discussions. To our extreme surprise, when it was moved that we should resolve ourselves into a committee for the election of the Lord Protector, the member who had nominated Ryland, rose and informed us that this candidate had resigned his pretensions. His information was at first received with silence; a confused murmur succeeded; and, when the chairman declared Lord Raymond duly chosen, it amounted to a shout of applause and victory. It seemed as if, far from any dread of defeat even if Mr. Ryland had not resigned, every voice would have been united in favour of our candidate. In fact, now that the idea of contest was dismissed, all hearts returned to their former respect and admiration of our accomplished friend. Each felt, that England had never seen a Protector so capable of fulfilling the arduous duties of that high office. One voice made of many voices, resounded through the chamber; it syllabled the name of Raymond.

He entered. I was on one of the highest seats, and saw him walk up the passage to the table of the speaker. The native modesty of his disposition conquered the joy of his triumph. He looked round timidly; a mist seemed before his eyes. Adrian, who was beside me, hastened to him, and jumping down the benches, was at his side in a moment. His appearance re-animated our friend; and, when he came to speak and act, his hesitation vanished, and he shone out supreme in majesty and victory. The former Protector tendered him the oaths, and presented him with the insignia of office, performing the ceremonies of installation. The house then dissolved. The chief members of the state crowded round the new magistrate, and conducted him to the palace of government. Adrian suddenly vanished; and, by the time that Raymond's supporters were reduced to our intimate friends merely, returned leading Idris to congratulate her friend on his success.

But where was Perdita? In securing solicitously an unobserved retreat in case of failure, Raymond had forgotten to arrange the mode by which she was to hear of his success; and she had been too much agitated to revert to this circumstance. When Idris entered, so far had Raymond forgotten himself, that he asked for my sister; one word, which told of her mysterious disappearance, recalled him. Adrian it is true had already gone to seek the fugitive, imagining that her tameless anxiety had led her to the purlieus of the House, and that some sinister event detained her. But Raymond, without explaining himself, suddenly quitted us, and in another moment we heard him gallop down the street, in spite of the wind and rain that scattered tempest over the earth. We did not know how far he had to go, and soon separated, supposing that in a short time he would return to the palace with Perdita, and that they would not be sorry to find themselves alone.

Perdita had arrived with her child at Dartford, weeping and inconsolable. She directed everything to be prepared for the continuance of their journey, and placing her lovely sleeping charge on a bed, passed several hours in acute suffering. Sometimes she observed the war of elements, thinking that they also declared against her, and listened to the pattering of the rain in gloomy despair. Sometimes she hung over her child, tracing her resemblance to the father, and fearful lest in after life she should display the same passions and uncontrollable impulses, that rendered him unhappy. Again, with a gush of pride and delight, she marked in the features of her little girl, the same smile of beauty that often irradiated Raymond's countenance. The sight of it soothed her. She thought of the treasure she possessed in the affections of her lord; of his accomplishments, surpassing those of his contemporaries, his genius, his devotion to her.— Soon she thought, that all she possessed in the world, except him, might well be spared, nay, given with delight, a propitiatory offering, to secure the supreme good she retained in him. Soon she imagined, that fate demanded this sacrifice from her, as a mark she was devoted to Raymond, and that it must be made with cheerfulness. She figured to herself their life in the Greek isle he had selected for their retreat; her task of soothing him; her cares for the beauteous Clara, her rides in his company, her dedication of herself to his consolation. The picture then presented itself to her in such glowing colours, that she feared the reverse, and a life of magnificence and power in London; where Raymond would no longer be hers only, nor she the sole source of happiness to him. So far as she merely was concerned, she began to hope for defeat; and it was only on his account that her feelings vacillated, as she heard him gallop into the court-yard of the inn. That he should come to her alone, wetted by the storm, careless of every thing except speed, what else could it mean, than that, vanquished and solitary, they were to take their way from native England, the scene of shame, and hide themselves in the myrtle groves of the Grecian isles?

In a moment she was in his arms. The knowledge of his success had become so much a part of himself, that he forgot that it was necessary to impart it to his companion. She only felt in his embrace a dear assurance that while he possessed her, he would not despair. "This is kind," she cried; "this is noble, my own beloved! O fear not disgrace or lowly fortune, while you have your Perdita; fear not sorrow, while our child lives and smiles. Let us go even where you will; the love that accompanies us will prevent our regrets."

Locked in his embrace, she spoke thus, and cast back her head, seeking an assent to her words in his eyes—they were sparkling with ineffable delight. "Why, my little Lady Protectress," said he, playfully, "what is this you say? And what pretty scheme have you woven of exile and obscurity, while a brighter web, a gold-enwoven tissue, is that which, in truth, you ought to contemplate?"

He kissed her brow—but the wayward girl, half sorry at his triumph, agitated by swift change of thought, hid her face in his bosom and wept. He comforted her; he instilled into her his own hopes and desires; and soon her countenance beamed with sympathy. How very happy were they that night! How full even to bursting was their sense of joy!

8

HAVING SEEN our friend properly installed in his new office, we turned our eyes towards Windsor. The nearness of this place to London was such, as to take away the idea of painful separation, when we quitted Raymond and Perdita. We took leave of them in the Protectoral Palace. It was pretty enough to see my sister enter as it were into the spirit of the drama, and endeavour to fill her station with becoming dignity. Her internal pride and humility of manner were now more than ever at war. Her timidity was not artificial, but arose from that fear of not being properly appreciated, that slight estimation of the neglect of the world, which also characterized Raymond. But then Perdita thought more constantly of others than he; and part of her bashfulness arose from a wish to take from those around her a sense of inferiority; a feeling which never crossed her mind. From the circumstances of her birth and education, Idris would have been better fitted for the formulae of ceremony; but the very ease which accompanied such actions with her, arising from habit, rendered them tedious; while, with every drawback, Perdita evidently enjoyed her situation. She was too full of new ideas to feel much pain when we departed; she took an affectionate leave of us, and promised to visit us soon; but she did not regret the circumstances that caused our separation. The spirits of Raymond were unbounded; he did not know what to do with his new got power; his head was full of plans; he had as yet decided on none— but he promised himself, his friends, and the world, that the aera of his Protectorship should be signalized by some act of surpassing glory. Thus, we talked of them, and moralized, as with diminished numbers we returned to Windsor Castle. We felt extreme delight at our escape from political turmoil, and sought our solitude with redoubled zest. We did not want for occupation; but my eager disposition was now turned to the field of intellectual exertion only; and hard study I found to be an excellent medicine to allay a fever of spirit with which in indolence, I should doubtless have been assailed. Perdita had permitted us to take Clara back with us to Windsor; and she and my two lovely infants were perpetual sources of interest and amusement.

The only circumstance that disturbed our peace, was the health of Adrian. It evidently declined, without any symptom which could lead us to suspect his disease, unless indeed his brightened eyes, animated look, and flustering cheeks, made us dread consumption; but he was without pain or fear. He betook himself to books with ardour, and reposed from study in the society he best loved, that of his sister and myself. Sometimes he went up to London to visit Raymond, and watch the progress of events. Clara often accompanied him in these excursions; partly that she might see her parents, partly because Adrian delighted in the prattle, and intelligent looks of this lovely child.

Meanwhile all went on well in London. The new elections were finished; parliament met, and Raymond was occupied in a thousand beneficial schemes. Canals, aqueducts, bridges, stately buildings, and various edifices for public utility, were entered upon; he was continually surrounded by projectors and projects, which were to render England one scene of fertility and magnificence; the state of poverty was to be abolished; men were to be transported from place to place almost with the same facility as the Princes Houssain, Ali, and Ahmed, in the Arabian Nights. The physical state of man would soon not yield to the beatitude of angels; disease was to be banished; labour lightened of its heaviest burden. Nor did this seem extravagant. The arts of life, and the discoveries of science had augmented in a ratio which left all calculation behind; food sprung up, so to say, spontaneously—machines existed to supply with facility every want of the population. An evil direction still survived; and men were not happy, not because they could not, but because they would not rouse themselves to vanquish self-raised obstacles. Raymond was to inspire them with his beneficial will, and the mechanism of society, once systematised according to faultless rules, would never again swerve into disorder. For these hopes he abandoned his long-cherished ambition of being enregistered in the annals of nations as a successful warrior; laying aside his sword, peace and its enduring glories became his aim— the title he coveted was that of the benefactor of his country.

Among other works of art in which he was engaged, he had projected the erection of a national gallery for statues and pictures. He possessed many himself, which he designed to present to the Republic; and, as the edifice was to be the great ornament of his Protectorship, he was very fastidious in his choice of the plan on which it would be built. Hundreds were brought to him and rejected. He sent even to Italy and Greece for drawings; but, as the design was to be characterized by originality as well as by perfect beauty, his endeavours were for a time without avail. At length a drawing came, with an address where communications might be sent, and no artist's name affixed. The design was new and elegant, but faulty; so faulty, that although drawn with the hand and eye of taste, it was evidently the work of one who was not an architect. Raymond contemplated it with delight; the more he gazed, the more pleased he was; and yet the errors multiplied under inspection. He wrote to the address given, desiring to see the draughtsman, that such alterations might be made, as should be suggested in a consultation between him and the original conceiver.

A Greek came. A middle-aged man, with some intelligence of manner, but with so common-place a physiognomy, that Raymond could scarcely believe that he was the designer. He acknowledged that he was not an architect; but the idea of the building had struck him, though he had sent it without the smallest hope of its being accepted. He was a man of few words. Raymond questioned him; but his reserved answers soon made him turn from the man to the drawing. He pointed out the errors, and the alterations that he wished to be made; he offered the Greek a pencil that he might correct the sketch on the spot; this was refused by his visitor, who said that he perfectly understood, and would work at it at home. At length Raymond suffered him to depart.

The next day he returned. The design had been re-drawn; but many defects still remained, and several of the instructions given had been misunderstood. "Come," said Raymond, "I yielded to you yesterday, now comply with my request—take the pencil."

The Greek took it, but he handled it in no artist-like way; at length he said: "I must confess to you, my Lord, that I did not make this drawing. It is impossible for you to see the real designer; your instructions must pass through me. Condescend therefore to have patience with my ignorance, and to explain your wishes to me; in time I am certain that you will be satisfied."

Raymond questioned vainly; the mysterious Greek would say no more. Would an architect be permitted to see the artist? This also was refused. Raymond repeated his instructions, and the visitor retired. Our friend resolved however not to be foiled in his wish. He suspected, that unaccustomed poverty was the cause of the mystery, and that the artist was unwilling to be seen in the garb and abode of want. Raymond was only the more excited by this consideration to discover him; impelled by the interest he took in obscure talent, he therefore ordered a person skilled in such matters, to follow the Greek the next time he came, and observe the house in which he should enter. His emissary obeyed, and brought the desired intelligence. He had traced the man to one of the most penurious streets in the metropolis. Raymond did not wonder, that, thus situated, the artist had shrunk from notice, but he did not for this alter his resolve.

On the same evening, he went alone to the house named to him. Poverty, dirt, and squalid misery characterized its appearance. Alas! thought Raymond, I have much to do before England becomes a Paradise. He knocked; the door was opened by a string from above—the broken, wretched staircase was immediately before him, but no person appeared; he knocked again, vainly—and then, impatient of further delay, he ascended the dark, creaking stairs. His main wish, more particularly now that he witnessed the abject dwelling of the artist, was to relieve one, possessed of talent, but depressed by want. He pictured to himself a youth, whose eyes sparkled with genius, whose person was attenuated by famine. He half feared to displease him; but he trusted that his generous kindness would be administered so delicately, as not to excite repulse. What human heart is shut to kindness? and though poverty, in its excess, might render the sufferer unapt to submit to the supposed degradation of a benefit, the zeal of the benefactor must at last relax him into thankfulness. These thoughts encouraged Raymond, as he stood at the door of the highest room of the house. After trying vainly to enter the other apartments, he perceived just within the threshold of this one, a pair of small Turkish slippers; the door was ajar, but all was silent within. It was probable that the inmate was absent, but secure that he had found the right person, our adventurous Protector was tempted to enter, to leave a purse on the table, and silently depart. In pursuance of this idea, he pushed open the door gently—but the room was inhabited.

Raymond had never visited the dwellings of want, and the scene that now presented itself struck him to the heart. The floor was sunk in many places; the walls ragged and bare—the ceiling weather-stained—a tattered bed stood in the corner; there were but two chairs in the room, and a rough broken table, on which was a light in a tin candlestick;—yet in the midst of such drear and heart sickening poverty, there was an air of order and cleanliness that surprised him. The thought was fleeting; for his attention was instantly drawn towards the inhabitant of this wretched abode. It was a female. She sat at the table; one small hand shaded her eyes from the candle; the other held a pencil; her looks were fixed on a drawing before her, which Raymond recognized as the design presented to him. Her whole appearance awakened his deepest interest. Her dark hair was braided and twined in thick knots like the head-dress of a Grecian statue; her garb was mean, but her attitude might have been selected as a model of grace. Raymond had a confused remembrance that he had seen such a form before; he walked across the room; she did not raise her eyes, merely asking in Romaic, who is there? "A friend," replied Raymond in the same dialect. She looked up wondering, and he saw that it was Evadne Zaimi. Evadne, once the idol of Adrian's affections; and who, for the sake of her present visitor, had disdained the noble youth, and then, neglected by him she loved, with crushed hopes and a stinging sense of misery, had returned to her native Greece. What revolution of fortune could have brought her to England, and housed her thus?

Raymond recognized her; and his manner changed from polite beneficence to the warmest protestations of kindness and sympathy. The sight of her, in her present situation, passed like an arrow into his soul. He sat by her, he took her hand, and said a thousand things which breathed the deepest spirit of compassion and affection. Evadne did not answer; her large dark eyes were cast down, at length a tear glimmered on the lashes. "Thus," she cried, "kindness can do, what no want, no misery ever effected; I weep." She shed indeed many tears; her head sunk unconsciously on the shoulder of Raymond; he held her hand: he kissed her sunken tear-stained cheek. He told her, that her sufferings were now over: no one possessed the art of consoling like Raymond; he did not reason or declaim, but his look shone with sympathy; he brought pleasant images before the sufferer; his caresses excited no distrust, for they arose purely from the feeling which leads a mother to kiss her wounded child; a desire to demonstrate in every possible way the truth of his feelings, and the keenness of his wish to pour balm into the lacerated mind of the unfortunate. As Evadne regained her composure, his manner became even gay; he sported with the idea of her poverty. Something told him that it was not its real evils that lay heavily at her heart, but the debasement and disgrace attendant on it; as he talked, he divested it of these; sometimes speaking of her fortitude with energetic praise; then, alluding to her past state, he called her his Princess in disguise. He made her warm offers of service; she was too much occupied by more engrossing thoughts, either to accept or reject them; at length he left her, making a promise to repeat his visit the next day. He returned home, full of mingled feelings, of pain excited by Evadne's wretchedness, and pleasure at the prospect of relieving it. Some motive for which he did not account, even to himself, prevented him from relating his adventure to Perdita.

The next day he threw such disguise over his person as a cloak afforded, and revisited Evadne. As he went, he bought a basket of costly fruits, such as were natives of her own country, and throwing over these various beautiful flowers, bore it himself to the miserable garret of his friend. "Behold," cried he, as he entered, "what bird's food I have brought for my sparrow on the house-top."

Evadne now related the tale of her misfortunes. Her father, though of high rank, had in the end dissipated his fortune, and even destroyed his reputation and influence through a course of dissolute indulgence. His health was impaired beyond hope of cure; and it became his earnest wish, before he died, to preserve his daughter from the poverty which would be the portion of her orphan state. He therefore accepted for her, and persuaded her to accede to, a proposal of marriage, from a wealthy Greek merchant settled at Constantinople. She quitted her native Greece; her father died; by degrees she was cut off from all the companions and ties of her youth.

The war, which about a year before the present time had broken out between Greece and Turkey, brought about many reverses of fortune. Her husband became bankrupt, and then in a tumult and threatened massacre on the part of the Turks, they were obliged to fly at midnight, and reached in an open boat an English vessel under sail, which brought them immediately to this island. The few jewels they had saved, supported them awhile. The whole strength of Evadne's mind was exerted to support the failing spirits of her husband. Loss of property, hopelessness as to his future prospects, the inoccupation to which poverty condemned him, combined to reduce him to a state bordering on insanity. Five months after their arrival in England, he committed suicide.

"You will ask me," continued Evadne, "what I have done since; why I have not applied for succour to the rich Greeks resident here; why I have not returned to my native country? My answer to these questions must needs appear to you unsatisfactory, yet they have sufficed to lead me on, day after day, enduring every wretchedness, rather than by such means to seek relief. Shall the daughter of the noble, though prodigal Zaimi, appear a beggar before her compeers or inferiors—superiors she had none. Shall I bow my head before them, and with servile gesture sell my nobility for life? Had I a child, or any tie to bind me to existence, I might descend to this—but, as it is—the world has been to me a harsh step-mother; fain would I leave the abode she seems to grudge, and in the grave forget my pride, my struggles, my despair. The time will soon come; grief and famine have already sapped the foundations of my being; a very short time, and I shall have passed away; unstained by the crime of self-destruction, unstung by the memory of degradation, my spirit will throw aside the miserable coil, and find such recompense as fortitude and resignation may deserve. This may seem madness to you, yet you also have pride and resolution; do not then wonder that my pride is tameless, my resolution unalterable."

Having thus finished her tale, and given such an account as she deemed fit, of the motives of her abstaining from all endeavour to obtain aid from her countrymen, Evadne paused; yet she seemed to have more to say, to which she was unable to give words. In the meantime Raymond was eloquent. His desire of restoring his lovely friend to her rank in society, and to her lost prosperity, animated him, and he poured forth with energy, all his wishes and intentions on that subject. But he was checked; Evadne exacted a promise, that he should conceal from all her friends her existence in England. "The relatives of the Earl of Windsor," said she haughtily, "doubtless think that I injured him; perhaps the Earl himself would be the first to acquit me, but probably I do not deserve acquittal. I acted then, as I ever must, from impulse. This abode of penury may at least prove the disinterestedness of my conduct. No matter: I do not wish to plead my cause before any of them, not even before your Lordship, had you not first discovered me. The tenor of my actions will prove that I had rather die, than be a mark for scorn—behold the proud Evadne in her tatters! look on the beggar-princess! There is aspic venom in the thought—promise me that my secret shall not be violated by you."

Raymond promised; but then a new discussion ensued. Evadne required another engagement on his part, that he would not without her concurrence enter into any project for her benefit, nor himself offer relief. "Do not degrade me in my own eyes," she said; "poverty has long been my nurse; hard-visaged she is, but honest. If dishonour, or what I conceive to be dishonour, come near me, I am lost." Raymond adduced many arguments and fervent persuasions to overcome her feeling, but she remained unconvinced; and, agitated by the discussion, she wildly and passionately made a solemn vow, to fly and hide herself where he never could discover her, where famine would soon bring death to conclude her woes, if he persisted in his to her disgracing offers. She could support herself, she said. And then she shewed him how, by executing various designs and paintings, she earned a pittance for her support. Raymond yielded for the present. He felt assured, after he had for a while humoured her self-will, that in the end friendship and reason would gain the day.

But the feelings that actuated Evadne were rooted in the depths of her being, and were such in their growth as he had no means of understanding. Evadne loved Raymond. He was the hero of her imagination, the image carved by love in the unchanged texture of her heart. Seven years ago, in her youthful prime, she had become attached to him; he had served her country against the Turks; he had in her own land acquired that military glory peculiarly dear to the Greeks, since they were still obliged inch by inch to fight for their security. Yet when he returned thence, and first appeared in public life in England, her love did not purchase his, which then vacillated between Perdita and a crown. While he was yet undecided, she had quitted England; the news of his marriage reached her, and her hopes, poorly nurtured blossoms, withered and fell. The glory of life was gone for her; the roseate halo of love, which had imbued every object with its own colour, faded;—she was content to take life as it was, and to make the best of leaden-coloured reality. She married; and, carrying her restless energy of character with her into new scenes, she turned her thoughts to ambition, and aimed at the title and power of Princess of Wallachia; while her patriotic feelings were soothed by the idea of the good she might do her country, when her husband should be chief of this principality. She lived to find ambition, as unreal a delusion as love. Her intrigues with Russia for the furtherance of her object, excited the jealousy of the Porte, and the animosity of the Greek government. She was considered a traitor by both, the ruin of her husband followed; they avoided death by a timely flight, and she fell from the height of her desires to penury in England. Much of this tale she concealed from Raymond; nor did she confess, that repulse and denial, as to a criminal convicted of the worst of crimes, that of bringing the scythe of foreign despotism to cut away the new springing liberties of her country, would have followed her application to any among the Greeks.

She knew that she was the cause of her husband's utter ruin; and she strung herself to bear the consequences. The reproaches which agony extorted; or worse, cureless, uncomplaining depression, when his mind was sunk in a torpor, not the less painful because it was silent and moveless. She reproached herself with the crime of his death; guilt and its punishments appeared to surround her; in vain she endeavoured to allay remorse by the memory of her real integrity; the rest of the world, and she among them, judged of her actions, by their consequences. She prayed for her husband's soul; she conjured the Supreme to place on her head the crime of his self-destruction—she vowed to live to expiate his fault.

In the midst of such wretchedness as must soon have destroyed her, one thought only was matter of consolation. She lived in the same country, breathed the same air as Raymond. His name as Protector was the burthen of every tongue; his achievements, projects, and magnificence, the argument of every story. Nothing is so precious to a woman's heart as the glory and excellence of him she loves; thus in every horror Evadne revelled in his fame and prosperity. While her husband lived, this feeling was regarded by her as a crime, repressed, repented of. When he died, the tide of love resumed its ancient flow, it deluged her soul with its tumultuous waves, and she gave herself up a prey to its uncontrollable power.

But never, O, never, should he see her in her degraded state. Never should he behold her fallen, as she deemed, from her pride of beauty, the poverty-stricken inhabitant of a garret, with a name which had become a reproach, and a weight of guilt on her soul. But though impenetrably veiled from him, his public office permitted her to become acquainted with all his actions, his daily course of life, even his conversation. She allowed herself one luxury, she saw the newspapers every day, and feasted on the praise and actions of the Protector. Not that this indulgence was devoid of accompanying grief. Perdita's name was forever joined with his; their conjugal felicity was celebrated even by the authentic testimony of facts. They were continually together, nor could the unfortunate Evadne read the monosyllable that designated his name, without, at the same time, being presented with the image of her who was the faithful companion of all his labours and pleasures. They, their Excellencies, met her eyes in each line, mingling an evil potion that poisoned her very blood.

It was in the newspaper that she saw the advertisement for the design for a national gallery. Combining with taste her remembrance of the edifices which she had seen in the east, and by an effort of genius enduing them with unity of design, she executed the plan which had been sent to the Protector. She triumphed in the idea of bestowing, unknown and forgotten as she was, a benefit upon him she loved; and with enthusiastic pride looked forward to the accomplishment of a work of hers, which, immortalized in stone, would go down to posterity stamped with the name of Raymond. She awaited with eagerness the return of her messenger from the palace; she listened insatiate to his account of each word, each look of the Protector; she felt bliss in this communication with her beloved, although he knew not to whom he addressed his instructions. The drawing itself became ineffably dear to her. He had seen it, and praised it; it was again retouched by her, each stroke of her pencil was as a chord of thrilling music, and bore to her the idea of a temple raised to celebrate the deepest and most unutterable emotions of her soul. These contemplations engaged her, when the voice of Raymond first struck her ear, a voice, once heard, never to be forgotten; she mastered her gush of feelings, and welcomed him with quiet gentleness.

Pride and tenderness now struggled, and at length made a compromise together. She would see Raymond, since destiny had led him to her, and her constancy and devotion must merit his friendship. But her rights with regard to him, and her cherished independence, should not be injured by the idea of interest, or the intervention of the complicated feelings attendant on pecuniary obligation, and the relative situations of the benefactor, and benefited. Her mind was of uncommon strength; she could subdue her sensible wants to her mental wishes, and suffer cold, hunger and misery, rather than concede to fortune a contested point. Alas! that in human nature such a pitch of mental discipline, and disdainful negligence of nature itself, should not have been allied to the extreme of moral excellence! But the resolution that permitted her to resist the pains of privation, sprung from the too great energy of her passions; and the concentrated self-will of which this was a sign, was destined to destroy even the very idol, to preserve whose respect she submitted to this detail of wretchedness.

Their intercourse continued. By degrees Evadne related to her friend the whole of her story, the stain her name had received in Greece, the weight of sin which had accrued to her from the death of her husband. When Raymond offered to clear her reputation, and demonstrate to the world her real patriotism, she declared that it was only through her present sufferings that she hoped for any relief to the stings of conscience; that, in her state of mind, diseased as he might think it, the necessity of occupation was salutary medicine; she ended by extorting a promise that for the space of one month he would refrain from the discussion of her interests, engaging after that time to yield in part to his wishes. She could not disguise to herself that any change would separate her from him; now she saw him each day. His connection with Adrian and Perdita was never mentioned; he was to her a meteor, a companionless star, which at its appointed hour rose in her hemisphere, whose appearance brought felicity, and which, although it set, was never eclipsed. He came each day to her abode of penury, and his presence transformed it to a temple redolent with sweets, radiant with heaven's own light; he partook of her delirium. "They built a wall between them and the world"—Without, a thousand harpies raved, remorse and misery, expecting the destined moment for their invasion. Within, was the peace as of innocence, reckless blindless, deluding joy, hope, whose still anchor rested on placid but unconstant water.

Thus, while Raymond had been wrapt in visions of power and fame, while he looked forward to entire dominion over the elements and the mind of man, the territory of his own heart escaped his notice; and from that unthought of source arose the mighty torrent that overwhelmed his will, and carried to the oblivious sea, fame, hope, and happiness.

❧ 9 ❧

I N THE MEAN time what did Perdita?

During the first months of his Protectorate, Raymond and she had been inseparable; each project was discussed with her, each plan approved by her. I never beheld any one so perfectly happy as my sweet sister. Her expressive eyes were two stars whose beams were love; hope and light-heartedness sat on her cloudless brow. She fed even to tears of joy on the praise and glory of her Lord; her whole existence was one sacrifice to him, and if in the humility of her heart she felt self-complacency, it arose from the reflection that she had won the distinguished hero of the age, and had for years preserved him, even after time had taken from love its usual nourishment. Her own feeling was as entire as at its birth. Five years had failed to destroy the dazzling unreality of passion. Most men ruthlessly destroy the sacred veil, with which the female heart is wont to adorn the idol of its affections. Not so Raymond; he was an enchanter, whose reign was forever undiminished; a king whose power never was suspended: follow him through the details of common life, still the same charm of grace and majesty adorned him; nor could he be despoiled of the innate deification with which nature had invested him. Perdita grew in beauty and excellence under his eye; I no longer recognised my reserved abstracted sister in the fascinating and open-hearted wife of Raymond. The genius that enlightened her countenance, was now united to an expression of benevolence, which gave divine perfection to her beauty.

Happiness is in its highest degree the sister of goodness. Suffering and amiability may exist together, and writers have loved to depict their conjunction; there is a human and touching harmony in the picture. But perfect happiness is an attribute of angels; and those who possess it, appear angelic. Fear has been said to be the parent of religion: even of that religion is it the generator, which leads its votaries to sacrifice human victims at its altars; but the religion which springs from happiness is a lovelier growth; the religion which makes the heart breathe forth fervent thanksgiving, and causes us to pour out the overflowings of the soul before the author of our being; that which is the parent of the imagination and the nurse of poetry; that which bestows benevolent intelligence on the visible mechanism of the world, and makes earth a temple with heaven for its cope. Such happiness, goodness, and religion inhabited the mind of Perdita.

During the five years we had spent together, a knot of happy human beings at Windsor Castle, her blissful lot had been the frequent theme of my sister's conversation. From early habit, and natural affection, she selected me in preference to Adrian or Idris, to be the partner in her overflowings of delight; perhaps, though apparently much unlike, some secret point of resemblance, the offspring of consanguinity, induced this preference. Often at sunset, I have walked with her, in the sober, enshadowed forest paths, and listened with joyful sympathy. Security gave dignity to her passion; the certainty of a full return, left her with no wish unfulfilled. The birth of her daughter, embryo copy of her Raymond, filled up the measure of her content, and produced a sacred and indissoluble tie between them. Sometimes she felt proud that he had preferred her to the hopes of a crown. Sometimes she remembered that she had suffered keen anguish, when he hesitated in his choice. But this memory of past discontent only served to enhance her present joy. What had been hardly won, was now, entirely possessed, doubly dear. She would look at him at a distance with the same rapture, (O, far more exuberant rapture!) that one might feel, who after the perils of a tempest, should find himself in the desired port; she would hasten towards him, to feel more certain in his arms, the reality of her bliss. This warmth of affection, added to the depth of her understanding, and the brilliancy of her imagination, made her beyond words dear to Raymond.

If a feeling of dissatisfaction ever crossed her, it arose from the idea that he was not perfectly happy. Desire of renown, and presumptuous ambition, had characterized his youth. The one he had acquired in Greece; the other he had sacrificed to love. His intellect found sufficient field for exercise in his domestic circle, whose members, all adorned by refinement and literature, were many of them, like himself, distinguished by genius. Yet active life was the genuine soil for his virtues; and he sometimes suffered tedium from the monotonous succession of events in our retirement. Pride made him recoil from complaint; and gratitude and affection to Perdita, generally acted as an opiate to all desire, save that of meriting her love. We all observed the visitation of these feelings, and none regretted them so much as Perdita. Her life consecrated to him, was a slight sacrifice to reward his choice, but was not that sufficient—Did he need any gratification that she was unable to bestow? This was the only cloud in the azure of her happiness.

His passage to power had been full of pain to both. He however attained his wish; he filled the situation for which nature seemed to have moulded him. His activity was fed in wholesome measure, without either exhaustion or satiety; his taste and genius found worthy expression in each of the modes human beings have invented to encage and manifest the spirit of beauty; the goodness of his heart made him never weary of conducing to the well-being of his fellow-creatures; his magnificent spirit, and aspirations for the respect and love of mankind, now received fruition; true, his exaltation was temporary; perhaps it were better that it should be so. Habit would not dull his sense of the enjoyment of power; nor struggles, disappointment and defeat await the end of that which would expire at its maturity. He determined to extract and condense all of glory, power, and achievement, which might have resulted from a long reign, into the three years of his Protectorate.

Raymond was eminently social. All that he now enjoyed would have been devoid of pleasure to him, had it been unparticipated. But in Perdita he possessed all that his heart could desire. Her love gave birth to sympathy; her intelligence made her understand him at a word; her powers of intellect enabled her to assist and guide him. He felt her worth. During the early years of their union, the inequality of her temper, and yet unsubdued self-will which tarnished her character, had been a slight drawback to the fulness of his sentiment. Now that unchanged serenity, and gentle compliance were added to her other qualifications, his respect equalled his love. Years added to the strictness of their union. They did not now guess at, and totter on the pathway, divining the mode to please, hoping, yet fearing the continuance of bliss. Five years gave a sober certainty to their emotions, though it did not rob them of their etherial nature. It had given them a child; but it had not detracted from the personal attractions of my sister. Timidity, which in her had almost amounted to awkwardness, was exchanged for a graceful decision of manner; frankness, instead of reserve, characterized her physiognomy; and her voice was attuned to thrilling softness. She was now three and twenty, in the pride of womanhood, fulfilling the precious duties of wife and mother, possessed of all her heart had ever coveted. Raymond was ten years older; to his previous beauty, noble mien, and commanding aspect, he now added gentlest benevolence, winning tenderness, graceful and unwearied attention to the wishes of another.

The first secret that had existed between them was the visits of Raymond to Evadne. He had been struck by the fortitude and beauty of the ill-fated Greek; and, when her constant tenderness towards him unfolded itself, he asked with astonishment, by what act of his he had merited this passionate and unrequited love. She was for a while the sole object of his reveries; and Perdita became aware that his thoughts and time were bestowed on a subject unparticipated by her. My sister was by nature destitute of the common feelings of anxious, petulant jealousy. The treasure which she possessed in the affections of Raymond, was more necessary to her being, than the life-blood that animated her veins—more truly than Othello she might say,

> To be once in doubt,
> Is—once to be resolved.

On the present occasion she did not suspect any alienation of affection; but she conjectured that some circumstance connected with his high place, had occasioned this mystery. She was startled and pained. She began to count the long days, and months, and years which must elapse, before he would be restored to a private station, and unreservedly to her. She was not content that, even for a time, he should practice concealment with her. She often repined; but her trust in the singleness of his affection was undisturbed; and, when they were together, unchecked by fear, she opened her heart to the fullest delight.

Time went on. Raymond, stopping mid-way in his wild career, paused suddenly to think of consequences. Two results presented themselves in the view he took of the future. That his intercourse with Evadne should continue a secret to, or that finally it should be discovered by Perdita. The destitute condition, and highly wrought feelings of his friend prevented him from adverting to the possibility of exiling himself from her. In the first event he had bidden an eternal farewell to open-hearted converse, and entire sympathy with the companion of his life. The veil must be thicker than that invented by Turkish jealousy; the wall higher than the unscaleable tower of Vathek, which should conceal from her the workings of his heart, and hide from her view the secret of his actions. This idea was intolerably painful to him. Frankness and social feelings were the essence of Raymond's nature; without them his qualities became common-place; without these to spread glory over his intercourse with Perdita, his vaunted exchange of a throne for her love, was as weak and empty as the rainbow hues which vanish when the sun is down. But there was no remedy. Genius, devotion, and courage; the adornments of his mind, and the energies of his soul, all exerted to their uttermost stretch, could not roll back one hair's breadth the wheel of time's chariot; that which had been was written with the adamantine pen of reality, on the everlasting volume of the past; nor could agony and tears suffice to wash out one iota from the act fulfilled.

But this was the best side of the question. What, if circumstance should lead Perdita to suspect, and suspecting to be resolved? The fibres of his frame became relaxed, and cold dew stood on his forehead, at this idea. Many men may scoff at his dread; but he read the future; and the peace of Perdita was too dear to him, her speechless agony too certain, and too fearful, not to unman him. His course was speedily decided upon. If the worst befell; if she learnt the truth, he would neither stand her reproaches, or the anguish of her altered looks. He would forsake her, England, his friends, the scenes of his youth, the hopes of coming time, he would seek another country, and in other scenes begin life again. Having resolved on this, he became calmer. He endeavoured to guide with prudence the steeds of destiny through the devious road which he had chosen, and bent all his efforts the better to conceal what he could not alter.

The perfect confidence that subsisted between Perdita and him, rendered every communication common between them. They opened each other's letters, even as, until now, the inmost fold of the heart of each was disclosed to the other. A letter came unawares, Perdita read it. Had it contained confirmation, she must have been annihilated. As it was, trembling, cold, and pale, she sought Raymond. He was alone, examining some petitions lately presented. She entered silently, sat on a sofa opposite to him, and gazed on him with a look of such despair, that wildest shrieks and dire moans would have been tame exhibitions of misery, compared to the living incarnation of the thing itself exhibited by her.

At first he did not take his eyes from the papers; when he raised them, he was struck by the wretchedness manifest on her altered cheek; for a moment he forgot his own acts and fears, and asked with consternation—"Dearest girl, what is the matter; what has happened?"

"Nothing," she replied at first; "and yet not so," she continued, hurrying on in her speech; "you have secrets, Raymond; where have you been lately, whom have you seen, what do you conceal from me?—why am I banished from your confidence? Yet this is not it—I do not intend to entrap you with questions—one will suffice—am I completely a wretch?"

With trembling hand she gave him the paper, and sat white and motionless looking at him while he read it. He recognised the hand-writing of Evadne, and the colour mounted in his cheeks. With lightning-speed he conceived the contents of the letter; all was now cast on one die; falsehood and artifice were trifles in comparison with the impending ruin. He would either entirely dispel Perdita's suspicions, or quit her forever. "My dear girl," he said, "I have been to blame; but you must pardon me. I was in the wrong to commence a system of concealment; but I did it for the sake of sparing you pain; and each day has rendered it more difficult for me to alter my plan. Besides, I was instigated by delicacy towards the unhappy writer of these few lines."

Perdita gasped: "Well," she cried, "well, go on!"

"That is all—this paper tells all. I am placed in the most difficult circumstances. I have done my best, though perhaps I have done wrong. My love for you is inviolate."

Perdita shook her head doubtingly: "It cannot be," she cried, "I know that it is not. You would deceive me, but I will not be deceived. I have lost you, myself, my life!"

"Do you not believe me?" said Raymond haughtily.

"To believe you," she exclaimed, "I would give up all, and expire with joy, so that in death I could feel that you were true—but that cannot be!"

"Perdita," continued Raymond, "you do not see the precipice on which you stand. You may believe that I did not enter on my present line of conduct without reluctance and pain. I knew that it was possible that your suspicions might be excited; but I trusted that my simple word would cause them to disappear. I built my hope on your confidence. Do you think that I will be questioned, and my replies disdainfully set aside? Do you think that I will be suspected, perhaps watched, cross-questioned, and disbelieved? I am not yet fallen so low; my honour is not yet so tarnished. You have loved me; I adored you. But all human sentiments come to an end. Let our affection expire—but let it not be exchanged for distrust and recrimination. Heretofore we have been friends—lovers—let us not become enemies, mutual spies. I cannot live the object of suspicion—you cannot believe me—let us part!"

"Exactly so," cried Perdita, "I knew that it would come to this! Are we not already parted? Does not a stream, boundless as ocean, deep as vacuum, yawn between us?"

Raymond rose, his voice was broken, his features convulsed, his manner calm as the earthquake-cradling atmosphere, he replied: "I am rejoiced that you take my decision so philosophically. Doubtless you will play the part of the injured wife to admiration. Sometimes you may be stung with the feeling that you have wronged me, but the condolence of your relatives, the pity of the world, the complacency which the consciousness of your own immaculate innocence will bestow, will be excellent balm;—me you will never see more!"

Raymond moved towards the door. He forgot that each word he spoke was false. He personated his assumption of innocence even to self-deception. Have not actors wept, as they portrayed imagined passion? A more intense feeling of the reality of fiction possessed Raymond. He spoke with pride; he felt injured. Perdita looked up; she saw his angry glance; his hand was on the lock of the door. She started up, she threw herself on his neck, she gasped and sobbed; he took her hand, and leading her to the sofa, sat down near her. Her head fell on his shoulder, she trembled, alternate changes of fire and ice ran through her limbs: observing her emotion he spoke with softened accents:

"The blow is given. I will not part from you in anger;—I owe you too much. I owe you six years of unalloyed happiness. But they are passed. I will not live the mark of suspicion, the object of jealousy. I love you too well. In an eternal separation only can either of us hope for dignity and propriety of action. We shall not then be degraded from our true characters. Faith and devotion have hitherto been the essence of our intercourse;—these lost, let us not cling to the seedless husk of life, the unkernelled shell. You have your child, your brother, Idris, Adrian"—

"And you," cried Perdita, "the writer of that letter."

Uncontrollable indignation flashed from the eyes of Raymond. He knew that this accusation at least was false. "Entertain this belief," he cried, "hug it to your heart—make it a pillow to your head, an opiate for your eyes —I am content. But, by the God that made me, hell is not more false than the word you have spoken!"

Perdita was struck by the impassioned seriousness of his asseverations. She replied with earnestness, "I do not refuse to believe you, Raymond; on the contrary I promise to put implicit faith in your simple word. Only assure me that your love and faith towards me have never been violated; and suspicion, and doubt, and jealousy will at once be dispersed. We shall continue as we have ever done, one heart, one hope, one life."

"I have already assured you of my fidelity," said Raymond with disdainful coldness, "triple assertions will avail nothing where one is despised. I will say no more; for I can add nothing to what I have already said, to what you before contemptuously set aside. This contention is unworthy of both of us; and I confess that I am weary of replying to charges at once unfounded and unkind."

Perdita tried to read his countenance, which he angrily averted. There was so much of truth and nature in his resentment, that her doubts were dispelled. Her countenance, which for years had not expressed a feeling unallied to affection, became again radiant and satisfied. She found it however no easy task to soften and reconcile Raymond. At first he refused to stay to hear her.

But she would not be put off; secure of his unaltered love, she was willing to undertake any labour, use any entreaty, to dispel his anger. She obtained an hearing, he sat in haughty silence, but he listened. She first assured him of her boundless confidence; of this he must be conscious, since but for that she would not seek to detain him. She enumerated their years of happiness; she brought before him past scenes of intimacy and happiness; she pictured their future life, she mentioned their child—tears unbidden now filled her eyes. She tried to disperse them, but they refused to be checked—her utterance was choaked. She had not wept before. Raymond could not resist these signs of distress: he felt perhaps somewhat ashamed of the part he acted of the injured man, he who was in truth the injurer. And then he devoutly loved Perdita; the bend of her head, her glossy ringlets, the turn of her form were to him subjects of deep tenderness and admiration; as she spoke, her melodious tones entered his soul; he soon softened towards her, comforting and caressing her, and endeavouring to cheat himself into the belief that he had never wronged her.

Raymond staggered forth from this scene, as a man might do, who had been just put to the torture, and looked forward to when it would be again inflicted. He had sinned against his own honour, by affirming, swearing to, a direct falsehood; true this he had palmed on a woman, and it might therefore be deemed less base—by others—not by him;—for whom had he deceived?— his own trusting, devoted, affectionate Perdita, whose generous belief galled him doubly, when he remembered the parade of innocence with which it had been exacted. The mind of Raymond was not so rough cast, nor had been so rudely handled, in the circumstance of life, as to make him proof to these considerations—on the contrary, he was all nerve; his spirit was as a pure fire, which fades and shrinks from every contagion of foul atmosphere: but now the contagion had become incorporated with its essence, and the change was the more painful. Truth and falsehood, love and hate lost their eternal boundaries, heaven rushed in to mingle with hell; while his sensitive mind, turned to a field for such battle, was stung to madness. He heartily despised himself, he was angry with Perdita, and the idea of Evadne was attended by all that was hideous and cruel. His passions, always his masters, acquired fresh strength, from the long sleep in which love had cradled them, the clinging weight of destiny bent him down; he was goaded, tortured, fiercely impatient of that worst of miseries, the sense of remorse. This troubled state yielded by degrees, to sullen animosity, and depression of spirits. His dependants, even his equals, if in his present post he had any, were startled to find anger, derision, and bitterness in one, before distinguished for suavity and benevolence of manner. He transacted public business with distaste, and hastened from it to the solitude which was at once his bane and relief. He mounted a fiery horse, that which had borne him forward to victory in Greece; he fatigued himself with deadening exercise, losing the pangs of a troubled mind in animal sensation.

He slowly recovered himself; yet, at last, as one might from the effects of poison, he lifted his head from above the vapours of fever and passion into the still atmosphere of calm reflection. He meditated on what was best to be done. He was first struck by the space of time that had elapsed, since madness, rather than any reasonable impulse, had regulated his actions. A month had gone by, and during that time he had not seen Evadne. Her power, which was linked to few of the enduring emotions of his heart, had greatly decayed. He was no longer her slave—no longer her lover: he would never see her more, and by the completeness of his return, deserve the confidence of Perdita.

Yet, as he thus determined, fancy conjured up the miserable abode of the Greek girl. An abode, which from noble and lofty principle, she had refused to exchange for one of greater luxury. He thought of the splendour of her situation and appearance when he first knew her; he thought of her life at Constantinople, attended by every circumstance of oriental magnificence;

of her present penury, her daily task of industry, her lorn state, her faded, famine-struck cheek. Compassion swelled his breast; he would see her once again; he would devise some plan for restoring her to society, and the enjoyment of her rank; their separation would then follow, as a matter of course.

Again he thought, how during this long month, he had avoided Perdita, flying from her as from the stings of his own conscience. But he was awake now; all this should be remedied; and future devotion erase the memory of this only blot on the serenity of their life. He became cheerful, as he thought of this, and soberly and resolutely marked out the line of conduct he would adopt. He remembered that he had promised Perdita to be present this very evening (the 19th of October, anniversary of his election as Protector) at a festival given in his honour. Good augury should this festival be of the happiness of future years. First, he would look in on Evadne; he would not stay; but he owed her some account, some compensation for his long and unannounced absence; and then to Perdita, to the forgotten world, to the duties of society, the splendour of rank, the enjoyment of power.

After the scene sketched in the preceding pages, Perdita had contemplated an entire change in the manners and conduct of Raymond. She expected freedom of communication, and a return to those habits of affectionate intercourse which had formed the delight of her life. But Raymond did not join her in any of her avocations. He transacted the business of the day apart from her; he went out, she knew not whither. The pain inflicted by this disappointment was tormenting and keen. She looked on it as a deceitful dream, and tried to throw off the consciousness of it; but like the shirt of Nessus, it clung to her very flesh, and ate with sharp agony into her vital principle. She possessed that (though such an assertion may appear a paradox) which belongs to few, a capacity of happiness. Her delicate organization and creative imagination rendered her peculiarly susceptible of pleasurable emotion. The overflowing warmth of her heart, by making love a plant of deep root and stately growth, had attuned her whole soul to the reception of happiness, when she found in Raymond all that could adorn love and satisfy her imagination. But if the sentiment on which the fabric of her existence was founded, became common place through participation, the endless succession of attentions and graceful action snapt by transfer, his universe of love wrested from her, happiness must depart, and then be exchanged for its opposite. The same peculiarities of character rendered her sorrows agonies; her fancy magnified them, her sensibility made her forever open to their renewed impression; love envenomed the heart-piercing sting. There was neither submission, patience, nor self-abandonment in her grief; she fought with it, struggled beneath it, and rendered every pang more sharp by resistance. Again and again the idea recurred, that he loved another. She did him justice; she believed that he felt a tender affection for her; but give a paltry prize to him who in some life-pending lottery has calculated on the possession of tens of thousands, and it will disappoint him more than a blank. The affection and amity of a Raymond might be inestimable; but, beyond that affection, embosomed deeper than friendship, was the indivisible treasure of love. Take the sum in its completeness, and no arithmetic can calculate its price; take from it the smallest portion, give it but the name of parts, separate it into degrees and sections, and like the magician's coin, the valueless gold of the mine, is turned to vilest substance. There is a meaning in the eye of love; a cadence in its voice, an irradiation in its smile, the talisman of whose enchantments one only can possess; its spirit is elemental, its essence single, its divinity an unit. The very heart and soul of Raymond and Perdita had mingled, even as two mountain brooks that join in their descent, and murmuring and sparkling flow over shining pebbles, beside starry flowers; but let one desert its primal course, or be dammed up by choaking obstruction, and the other shrinks in its altered banks. Perdita was sensible of the failing of the tide that fed her life. Unable to support the slow withering of her hopes, she suddenly formed a plan, resolving to terminate at once the period of misery, and to bring to an happy conclusion the late disastrous events.

The anniversary was at hand of the exaltation of Raymond to the office of Protector; and it was customary to celebrate this day by a splendid festival. A variety of feelings urged Perdita to shed double magnificence over the scene; yet, as she arrayed herself for the evening gala, she wondered herself at the pains she took, to render sumptuous the celebration of an event which appeared to her the beginning of her sufferings. Woe befall the day, she thought, woe, tears, and mourning betide the hour, that gave Raymond another hope than love, another wish than my devotion; and thrice joyful the moment when he shall be restored to me! God knows, I put my trust in his vows, and believe his asserted faith—but for that, I would not seek what I am now resolved to attain. Shall two years more be thus passed, each day adding to our alienation, each act being another stone piled on the barrier which separates us? No, my Raymond, my only beloved, sole possession of Perdita! This night, this splendid assembly, these sumptuous apartments, and this adornment of your tearful girl, are all united to celebrate your abdication. Once for me, you relinquished the prospect of a crown. That was in days of early love, when I could only hold out the hope, not the assurance of happiness. Now you have the experience of all that I can give, the heart's devotion, taintless love, and unhesitating subjection to you. You must choose between these and your protectorate. This, proud noble, is your last night! Perdita has bestowed on it all of magnificent and dazzling that your heart best loves—but, from these gorgeous rooms, from this princely attendance, from power and elevation, you must return with to-morrow's sun to our rural abode; for I would not buy an immortality of joy, by the endurance of one more week sister to the last.

Brooding over this plan, resolved when the hour should come, to propose, and insist upon its accomplishment, secure of his consent, the heart of Perdita was lightened, or rather exalted. Her cheek was flushed by the expectation of struggle; her eyes sparkled with the hope of triumph. Having cast her fate upon a die, and feeling secure of winning, she, whom I have named as bearing the stamp of queen of nations on her noble brow, now rose superior to humanity, and seemed in calm power, to arrest with her finger, the wheel of destiny. She had never before looked so supremely lovely.

We, the Arcadian shepherds of the tale, had intended to be present at this festivity, but Perdita wrote to entreat us not to come, or to absent ourselves from Windsor; for she (though she did not reveal her scheme to us) resolved the next morning to return with Raymond to our dear circle, there to renew a course of life in which she had found entire felicity. Late in the evening she entered the apartments appropriated to the festival. Raymond had quitted the palace the night before; he had promised to grace the assembly, but he had not yet returned. Still she felt sure that he would come at last; and the wider the breach might appear at this crisis, the more secure she was of closing it for ever.

It was as I said, the nineteenth of October; the autumn was far advanced and dreary. The wind howled; the half bare trees were despoiled of the remainder of their summer ornament; the state of the air which induced the decay of vegetation, was hostile to cheerfulness or hope. Raymond had been exalted by the determination he had made; but with the declining day his spirits declined. First he was to visit Evadne, and then to hasten to the palace of the Protectorate. As he walked through the wretched streets in the neighbourhood of the luckless Greek's abode, his heart smote him for the whole course of his conduct towards her. First, his having entered into any engagement that should permit her to remain in such a state of degradation; and then, after a short wild dream, having left her to drear solitude, anxious conjecture, and bitter, still—disappointed expectation. What had she done the while, how supported his absence and neglect? Light grew dim in these close streets, and when the well-known door was opened, the staircase was shrouded in perfect night. He groped his way up, he entered the garret, he found Evadne stretched speechless, almost lifeless on her wretched bed. He called for the people of the house, but could learn nothing from them, except that they knew nothing. Her story was plain to him, plain and distinct as the remorse and horror that darted their fangs into him. When she found herself forsaken by him, she lost the heart to pursue her usual avocations; pride forbade every application to him; famine was welcomed as the kind porter to the gates of death, within whose opening folds she should now, without sin, quickly repose. No creature came near her, as her strength failed.

If she died, where could there be found on record a murderer, whose cruel act might compare with his? What fiend more wanton in his mischief, what damned soul more worthy of perdition! But he was not reserved for this agony of self-reproach. He sent for medical assistance; the hours passed, spun by suspense into ages; the darkness of the long autumnal night yielded to day, before her life was secure. He had her then removed to a more commodious dwelling, and hovered about her, again and again to assure himself that she was safe.

In the midst of his greatest suspense and fear as to the event, he remembered the festival given in his honour, by Perdita; in his honour then, when misery and death were affixing indelible disgrace to his name, honour to him whose crimes deserved a scaffold; this was the worst mockery. Still Perdita would expect him; he wrote a few incoherent words on a scrap of paper, testifying that he was well, and bade the woman of the house take it to the palace, and deliver it into the hands of the wife of the Lord Protector. The woman, who did not know him, contemptuously asked, how he thought she should gain admittance, particularly on a festal night, to that lady's presence? Raymond gave her his ring to ensure the respect of the menials. Thus, while Perdita was entertaining her guests, and anxiously awaiting the arrival of her lord, his ring was brought her; and she was told that a poor woman had a note to deliver to her from its wearer.

The vanity of the old gossip was raised by her commission, which, after all, she did not understand, since she had no suspicion, even now that Evadne's visitor was Lord Raymond. Perdita dreaded a fall from his horse, or some similar accident—till the woman's answers woke other fears. From a feeling of cunning blindly exercised, the officious, if not malignant messenger, did not speak of Evadne's illness; but she garrulously gave an account of Raymond's frequent visits, adding to her narration such circumstances, as, while they convinced Perdita of its truth, exaggerated the unkindness and perfidy of Raymond. Worst of all, his absence now from the festival, his message wholly unaccounted for, except by the disgraceful hints of the woman, appeared the deadliest insult. Again she looked at the ring, it was a small ruby, almost heart-shaped, which she had herself given him. She looked at the hand-writing, which she could not mistake, and repeated to herself the words—"Do not, I charge you, I entreat you, permit your guests to wonder at my absence:" the while the old crone going on with her talk, filled her ear with a strange medley of truth and falsehood. At length Perdita dismissed her.

The poor girl returned to the assembly, where her presence had not been missed. She glided into a recess somewhat obscured, and leaning against an ornamental column there placed, tried to recover herself. Her faculties were palsied. She gazed on some flowers that stood near in a carved vase: that morning she had arranged them, they were rare and lovely plants; even now all aghast as she was, she observed their brilliant colours and starry shapes.—"Divine infoliations of the spirit of beauty," she exclaimed, "Ye droop not, neither do ye mourn; the despair that clasps my heart, has not spread contagion over you!—Why am I not a partner of your insensibility, a sharer in your calm!"

She paused. "To my task," she continued mentally, "my guests must not perceive the reality, either as it regards him or me. I obey; they shall not, though I die the moment they are gone. They shall behold the antipodes of what is real—for I will appear to live—while I am—dead." It required all her self-command, to suppress the gush of tears self-pity caused at this idea. After many struggles, she succeeded, and turned to join the company.

All her efforts were now directed to the dissembling her internal conflict. She had to play the part of a courteous hostess; to attend to all; to shine the focus of enjoyment and grace. She had to do this, while in deep woe she sighed for loneliness, and would gladly have exchanged her crowded rooms for dark forest depths, or a drear, night-enshadowed heath. But she became gay. She could not keep in the medium, nor be, as was usual with her, placidly content. Every one remarked her exhilaration of spirits; as all actions appear graceful in the eye of rank, her guests surrounded her applaudingly, although there was a sharpness in her laugh, and an abruptness in her sallies, which might have betrayed her secret to an attentive observer. She went on, feeling that, if she had paused for a moment, the checked waters of misery would have deluged her soul, that her wrecked hopes would raise their wailing voices, and that those who now echoed her mirth, and provoked her repartees, would have shrunk in fear from her convulsive despair. Her only consolation during the violence which she did herself, was to watch the motions of an illuminated clock, and internally count the moments which must elapse before she could be alone.

At length the rooms began to thin. Mocking her own desires, she rallied her guests on their early departure. One by one they left her—at length she pressed the hand of her last visitor. "How cold and damp your hand is," said her friend; "you are over fatigued, pray hasten to rest." Perdita smiled faintly—her guest left her; the carriage rolling down the street assured the final departure. Then, as if pursued by an enemy, as if wings had been at her feet, she flew to her own apartment, she dismissed her attendants, she locked the doors, she threw herself wildly on the floor, she bit her lips even to blood to suppress her shrieks, and lay long a prey to the vulture of despair, striving not to think, while multitudinous ideas made a home of her heart; and ideas, horrid as furies, cruel as vipers, and poured in with such swift succession, that they seemed to jostle and wound each other, while they worked her up to madness.

At length she rose, more composed, not less miserable. She stood before a large mirror—she gazed on her reflected image; her light and graceful dress, the jewels that studded her hair, and encircled her beauteous arms and neck, her small feet shod in satin, her profuse and glossy tresses, all were to her clouded brow and woe-begone countenance like a gorgeous frame to a dark tempest-pourtraying picture. "Vase am I," she thought, "vase brimful of despair's direst essence. Farewell, Perdita! farewell, poor girl! never again will you see yourself thus; luxury and wealth are no longer yours; in the excess of your poverty you may envy the homeless beggar; most truly am I without a home! I live on a barren desert, which, wide and interminable, brings forth neither fruit or flower; in the midst is a solitary rock, to which thou, Perdita, art chained, and thou seest the dreary level stretch far away."

She threw open her window, which looked on the palace-garden. Light and darkness were struggling together, and the orient was streaked by roseate and golden rays. One star only trembled in the depth of the kindling atmosphere. The morning air blowing freshly over the dewy plants, rushed into the heated room. "All things go on," thought Perdita, "all things proceed, decay, and perish! When noontide has passed, and the weary day has driven her team to their western stalls, the fires of heaven rise from the East, moving in their accustomed path, they ascend and descend the skiey hill. When their course is fulfilled, the dial begins to cast westward an uncertain shadow; the eye-lids of day are opened, and birds and flowers, the startled vegetation, and fresh breeze awaken; the sun at length appears, and in majestic procession climbs the capitol of heaven. All proceeds, changes and dies, except the sense of misery in my bursting heart.

"Ay, all proceeds and changes: what wonder then, that love has journied on to its setting, and that the lord of my life has changed? We call the supernal lights fixed, yet they wander about yonder plain, and if I look again where I looked an hour ago, the face of the eternal heavens is altered. The silly moon and inconstant planets vary nightly their erratic dance; the sun itself, sovereign of the sky, ever and anon deserts his throne, and leaves his dominion to night and winter. Nature grows old, and shakes in her decaying limbs,—creation has become bankrupt! What wonder then, that eclipse and death have led to destruction the light of thy life, O Perdita!"

❧ 10 ❧

THUS SAD AND disarranged were the thoughts of my poor sister, when she became assured of the infidelity of Raymond. All her virtues and all her defects tended to make the blow incurable. Her affection for me, her brother, for Adrian and Idris, was subject as it were to the reigning passion of her heart; even her maternal tenderness borrowed half its force from the delight she had in tracing Raymond's features and expression in the infant's countenance. She had been reserved and even stern in childhood; but love had softened the asperities of her character, and her union with Raymond had caused her talents and affections to unfold themselves; the one betrayed, and the other lost, she in some degree returned to her ancient disposition. The concentrated pride of her nature, forgotten during her blissful dream, awoke, and with its adder's sting pierced her heart; her humility of spirit augmented the power of the venom; she had been exalted in her own estimation, while distinguished by his love: of what worth was she, now that he thrust her from this preferment? She had been proud of having won and preserved him—but another had won him from her, and her exultation was as cold as a water quenched ember.

We, in our retirement, remained long in ignorance of her misfortune. Soon after the festival she had sent for her child, and then she seemed to have forgotten us. Adrian observed a change during a visit that he afterward paid them; but he could not tell its extent, or divine the cause. They still appeared in public together, and lived under the same roof. Raymond was as usual courteous, though there was, on occasions, an unbidden haughtiness, or painful abruptness in his manners, which startled his gentle friend; his brow was not clouded but disdain sat on his lips, and his voice was harsh. Perdita was all kindness and attention to her lord; but she was silent, and beyond words sad. She had grown thin and pale; and her eyes often filled with tears. Sometimes she looked at Raymond, as if to say—That it should be so! At others her countenance expressed—I will still do all I can to make you happy. But Adrian read with uncertain aim the charactery of her face, and might mistake.—Clara was always with her, and she seemed most at ease, when, in an obscure corner, she could sit holding her child's hand, silent and lonely. Still Adrian was unable to guess the truth; he entreated them to visit us at Windsor, and they promised to come during the following month.

It was May before they arrived: the season had decked the forest trees with leaves, and its paths with a thousand flowers. We had notice of their intention the day before; and, early in the morning, Perdita arrived with her daughter. Raymond would follow soon, she said; he had been detained by business. According to Adrian's account, I had expected to find her sad; but, on the contrary, she appeared in the highest spirits: true, she had grown thin, her eyes were somewhat hollow, and her cheeks sunk, though tinged by a bright glow. She was delighted to see us; caressed our children, praised their growth and improvement; Clara also was pleased to meet again her young friend Alfred; all kinds of childish games were entered into, in which Perdita joined. She communicated her gaiety to us, and as we amused ourselves on the Castle Terrace, it appeared that a happier, less care-worn party could not have been assembled. "This is better, Mamma," said Clara, "than being in that dismal London, where you often cry, and never laugh as you do now."—"Silence, little foolish thing," replied her mother, "and remember any one that mentions London is sent to Coventry for an hour."

Soon after, Raymond arrived. He did not join as usual in the playful spirit of the rest; but, entering into conversation with Adrian and myself, by degrees we seceded from our companions, and Idris and Perdita only remained with the children. Raymond talked of his new buildings; of his plan for an establishment for the better education of the poor; as usual Adrian and he entered into argument, and the time slipped away unperceived.

We assembled again towards evening, and Perdita insisted on our having recourse to music. She wanted, she said, to give us a specimen of her new accomplishment; for since she had been in London, she had applied herself to music, and sang, without much power, but with a great deal of sweetness. We were not permitted by her to select any but light-hearted melodies; and all the Operas of Mozart were called into service, that we might choose the most exhilarating of his airs. Among the other transcendant attributes of Mozart's music, it possesses more than any other that of appearing to come from the heart; you enter into the passions expressed by him, and are transported with grief, joy, anger, or confusion, as he, our soul's master, chooses to inspire. For some time, the spirit of hilarity was kept up; but, at length, Perdita receded from the piano, for Raymond had joined in the trio of "Taci ingiusto core," in Don Giovanni, whose arch entreaty was softened by him into tenderness, and thrilled her heart with memories of the changed past; it was the same voice, the same tone, the self-same sounds and words, which often before she had received, as the homage of love to her—no longer was it that; and this concord of sound with its dissonance of expression penetrated her with regret and despair. Soon after Idris, who was at the harp, turned to that passionate and sorrowful air in Figaro, "Porgi, amor, qualche risforo," in which the deserted Countess laments the change of the faithless Almaviva. The soul of tender sorrow is breathed forth in this strain; and the sweet voice of Idris, sustained by the mournful chords of her instrument, added to the expression of the words. During the pathetic appeal with which it concludes, a stifled sob attracted our attention to Perdita, the cessation of the music recalled her to herself, she hastened out of the hall—I followed her. At first, she seemed to wish to shun me; and then, yielding to my earnest questioning, she threw herself on my neck, and wept aloud:—"Once more," she cried, "once more on your friendly breast, my beloved brother, can the lost Perdita pour forth her sorrows. I had imposed a law of silence on myself; and for months I have kept it. I do wrong in weeping now, and greater wrong in giving words to my grief. I will not speak! Be it enough for you to know that I am miserable—be it enough for you to know, that the painted veil of life is rent, that I sit for ever shrouded in darkness and gloom, that grief is my sister, everlasting lamentation my mate!"

I endeavoured to console her; I did not question her! but I caressed her, assured her of my deepest affection and my intense interest in the changes of her fortune:—"Dear words," she cried, "expressions of love come upon my ear, like the remembered sounds of forgotten music, that had been dear to me. They are vain, I know; how very vain in their attempt to soothe or comfort me. Dearest Lionel, you cannot guess what I have suffered during these long months. I have read of mourners in ancient days, who clothed themselves in sackcloth, scattered dust upon their heads, ate their bread mingled with ashes, and took up their abode on the bleak mountain tops, reproaching heaven and earth aloud with their misfortunes. Why this is the very luxury of sorrow! thus one might go on from day to day contriving new extravagances, revelling in the paraphernalia of woe, wedded to all the appurtenances of despair. Alas! I must forever conceal the wretchedness that consumes me. I must weave a veil of dazzling falsehood to hide my grief from vulgar eyes, smoothe my brow, and paint my lips in deceitful smiles— even in solitude I dare not think how lost I am, lest I become insane and rave."

The tears and agitation of my poor sister had rendered her unfit to return to the circle we had left—so I persuaded her to let me drive her through the park; and, during the ride, I induced her to confide the tale of her unhappiness to me, fancying that talking of it would lighten the burthen, and certain that, if there were a remedy, it should be found and secured to her.

Several weeks had elapsed since the festival of the anniversary, and she had been unable to calm her mind, or to subdue her thoughts to any regular train. Sometimes she reproached herself for taking too bitterly to heart, that which many would esteem an imaginary evil; but this was no subject for reason; and, ignorant as she was of the motives and true conduct of Raymond, things assumed for her even a worse appearance, than the reality warranted. He was seldom at the palace; never, but when he was assured that his public duties would prevent his remaining alone with Perdita. They seldom addressed each other, shunning explanation, each fearing any communication the other might make. Suddenly, however, the manners of Raymond changed; he appeared to desire to find opportunities of bringing about a return to kindness and intimacy with my sister. The tide of love towards her appeared to flow again; he could never forget, how once he had been devoted to her, making her the shrine and storehouse wherein to place every thought and every sentiment. Shame seemed to hold him back; yet he evidently wished to establish a renewal of confidence and affection. From the moment Perdita had sufficiently recovered herself to form any plan of action, she had laid one down, which now she prepared to follow. She received these tokens of returning love with gentleness; she did not shun his company; but she endeavoured to place a barrier in the way of familiar intercourse or painful discussion, which mingled pride and shame prevented Raymond from surmounting. He began at last to shew signs of angry impatience, and Perdita became aware that the system she had adopted could not continue; she must explain herself to him; she could not summon courage to speak—she wrote thus:—

"Read this letter with patience, I entreat you. It will contain no reproaches. Reproach is indeed an idle word: for what should I reproach you?

"Allow me in some degree to explain my feeling; without that, we shall both grope in the dark, mistaking one another; erring from the path which may conduct, one of us at least, to a more eligible mode of life than that led by either during the last few weeks.

"I loved you—I love you—neither anger nor pride dictates these lines; but a feeling beyond, deeper, and more unalterable than either. My affections are wounded; it is impossible to heal them:—cease then the vain endeavour, if indeed that way your endeavours tend. Forgiveness! Return! Idle words are these! I forgive the pain I endure; but the trodden path cannot be retraced.

"Common affection might have been satisfied with common usages. I believed that you read my heart, and knew its devotion, its unalienable fidelity towards you. I never loved any but you. You came the embodied image of my fondest dreams. The praise of men, power and high aspirations attended your career. Love for you invested the world for me in enchanted light; it was no longer the earth I trod—the earth, common mother, yielding only trite and stale repetition of objects and circumstances old and worn out. I lived in a temple glorified by intensest sense of devotion and rapture; I walked, a consecrated being, contemplating only your power, your excellence;

> For O, you stood beside me, like my youth,
> Transformed for me the real to a dream,
> Cloathing the palpable and familiar
> With golden exhalations of the dawn.

'The bloom has vanished from my life'—there is no morning to this all investing night; no rising to the set-sun of love. In those days the rest of the world was nothing to me: all other men —I never considered nor felt what they were; nor did I look on you as one of them. Separated from them; exalted in my heart; sole possessor of my affections; single object of my hopes, the best half of myself.

"Ah, Raymond, were we not happy? Did the sun shine on any, who could enjoy its light with purer and more intense bliss? It was not—it is not a common infidelity at which I repine. It is the disunion of an whole which may not have parts; it is the carelessness with which you have shaken off the mantle of election with which to me you were invested, and have become one among the many. Dream not to alter this. Is not love a divinity, because it is immortal? Did not I appear sanctified, even to myself, because this love had for its temple my heart? I have gazed on you as you slept, melted even to tears, as the idea filled my mind, that all I possessed lay cradled in those idolized, but mortal lineaments before me. Yet, even then, I have checked thick-coming fears with one thought; I would not fear death, for the emotions that linked us must be immortal.

"And now I do not fear death. I should be well pleased to close my eyes, never more to open them again. And yet I fear it; even as I fear all things; for in any state of being linked by the chain of memory with this, happiness would not return—even in Paradise, I must feel that your love was less enduring than the mortal beatings of my fragile heart, every pulse of which knells audibly,

> The funeral note
> Of love, deep buried, without resurrection.
> No—no—me miserable; for love extinct there is no resurrection!

"Yet I love you. Yet, and for ever, would I contribute all I possess to your welfare. On account of a tattling world; for the sake of my—of our child, I would remain by you, Raymond, share your fortunes, partake your counsel. Shall it be thus? We are no longer lovers; nor can I call myself a friend to any; since, lost as I am, I have no thought to spare from my own wretched, engrossing self. But it will please me to see you each day! to listen to the public voice praising you; to keep up your paternal love for our girl; to hear your voice; to know that I am near you, though you are no longer mine.

"If you wish to break the chains that bind us, say the word, and it shall be done—I will take all the blame on myself, of harshness or unkindness, in the world's eye.

"Yet, as I have said, I should be best pleased, at least for the present, to live under the same roof with you. When the fever of my young life is spent; when placid age shall tame the vulture that devours me, friendship may come, love and hope being dead. May this be true? Can my soul, inextricably linked to this perishable frame, become lethargic and cold, even as this sensitive mechanism shall lose its youthful elasticity? Then, with lack-lustre eyes, grey hairs, and wrinkled brow, though now the words sound hollow and meaningless, then, tottering on the grave's extreme edge, I may be—your affectionate and true friend,

"PERDITA."

Raymond's answer was brief. What indeed could he reply to her complaints, to her griefs which she jealously paled round, keeping out all thought of remedy. "Notwithstanding your bitter letter," he wrote, "for bitter I must call it, you are the chief person in my estimation, and it is your happiness that I would principally consult. Do that which seems best to you: and if you can receive gratification from one mode of life in preference to another, do not let me be any obstacle. I foresee that the plan which you mark out in your letter will not endure long; but you are mistress of yourself, and it is my sincere wish to contribute as far as you will permit me to your happiness."

"Raymond has prophesied well," said Perdita, "alas, that it should be so! our present mode of life cannot continue long, yet I will not be the first to propose alteration. He beholds in me one whom he has injured even unto death; and I derive no hope from his kindness; no change can possibly be brought about even by his best intentions. As well might Cleopatra have worn as an ornament the vinegar which contained her dissolved pearl, as I be content with the love that Raymond can now offer me."

I own that I did not see her misfortune with the same eyes as Perdita. At all events methought that the wound could be healed; and, if they remained together, it would be so. I endeavoured therefore to sooth and soften her mind; and it was not until after many endeavours that I gave up the task as impracticable. Perdita listened to me impatiently, and answered with some asperity:—"Do you think that any of your arguments are new to me? or that my own burning wishes and intense anguish have not suggested them all a thousand times, with far more eagerness and subtlety than you can put into them? Lionel, you cannot understand what woman's love is. In days of happiness I have often repeated to myself, with a grateful heart and exulting spirit, all that Raymond sacrificed for me. I was a poor, uneducated, unbefriended, mountain girl, raised from nothingness by him. All that I possessed of the luxuries of life came from him. He gave me an illustrious name and noble station; the world's respect reflected from his own glory: all this joined to his own undying love, inspired me with sensations towards him, akin to those with which we regard the Giver of life. I gave him love only. I devoted myself to him: imperfect creature that I was, I took myself to task, that I might become worthy of him. I watched over my hasty temper, subdued my burning impatience of character, schooled my self-engrossing thoughts, educating myself to the best perfection I might attain, that the fruit of my exertions might be his happiness. I took no merit to myself for this. He deserved it all—all labour, all devotion, all sacrifice; I would have toiled up a scaleless Alp, to pluck a flower that would please him. I was ready to quit you all, my beloved and gifted companions, and to live only with him, for him. I could not do otherwise, even if I had wished; for if we are said to have two souls, he was my better soul, to which the other was a perpetual slave. One only return did he owe me, even fidelity. I earned that; I deserved it. Because I was mountain bred, unallied to the noble and wealthy, shall he think to repay me by an empty name and station? Let him take them back; without his love they are nothing to me. Their only merit in my eyes was that they were his."

Thus passionately Perdita ran on. When I adverted to the question of their entire separation, she replied: "Be it so! One day the period will arrive; I know it, and feel it. But in this I am a coward. This imperfect companionship, and our masquerade of union, are strangely dear to me. It is painful, I allow, destructive, impracticable. It keeps up a perpetual fever in my veins; it frets my immedicable wound; it is instinct with poison. Yet I must cling to it; perhaps it will kill me soon, and thus perform a thankful office."

In the mean time, Raymond had remained with Adrian and Idris. He was naturally frank; the continued absence of Perdita and myself became remarkable; and Raymond soon found relief from the constraint of months, by an unreserved confidence with his two friends. He related to them the situation in which he had found Evadne. At first, from delicacy to Adrian he concealed her name; but it was divulged in the course of his narrative, and her former lover heard with the most acute agitation the history of her sufferings. Idris had shared Perdita's ill opinion of the Greek; but Raymond's account softened and interested her. Evadne's constancy, fortitude, even her ill-fated and ill-regulated love, were matter of admiration and pity; especially when, from the detail of the events of the nineteenth of October, it was apparent that she preferred suffering and death to any in her eyes degrading application for the pity and assistance of her lover. Her subsequent conduct did not diminish this interest. At first, relieved from famine and the grave, watched over by Raymond with the tenderest assiduity, with that feeling of repose peculiar to convalescence, Evadne gave herself up to rapturous gratitude and love. But reflection returned with health. She questioned him with regard to the motives which had occasioned his critical absence. She framed her enquiries with Greek subtlety; she formed her conclusions with the decision and firmness peculiar to her disposition. She could not divine, that the breach which she had occasioned between Raymond and Perdita was already irreparable: but she knew, that under the present system it would be widened each day, and that its result must be to destroy her lover's happiness, and to implant the fangs of remorse in his heart. From the moment that she perceived the right line of conduct, she resolved to adopt it, and to part from Raymond for ever. Conflicting passions, long-cherished love, and self-inflicted disappointment, made her regard death alone as sufficient refuge for her woe. But the same feelings and opinions which had before restrained her, acted with redoubled force; for she knew that the reflection that he had occasioned her death, would pursue Raymond through life, poisoning every enjoyment, clouding every prospect. Besides, though the violence of her anguish made life hateful, it had not yet produced that monotonous, lethargic sense of changeless misery which for the most part produces suicide. Her energy of character induced her still to combat with the ills of life; even those attendant on hopeless love presented themselves, rather in the shape of an adversary to be overcome, than of a victor to whom she must submit. Besides, she had memories of past tenderness to cherish, smiles, words, and even tears, to con over, which, though remembered in desertion and sorrow, were to be preferred to the forgetfulness of the grave. It was impossible to guess at the whole of her plan. Her letter to Raymond gave no clue for discovery; it assured him, that she was in no danger of wanting the means of life; she promised in it to preserve herself, and some future day perhaps to present herself to him in a station not unworthy of her. She then bade him, with the eloquence of despair and of unalterable love, a last farewell.

All these circumstances were now related to Adrian and Idris. Raymond then lamented the cureless evil of his situation with Perdita. He declared, notwithstanding her harshness, he even called it coldness, that he loved her. He had been ready once with the humility of a penitent, and the duty of a vassal, to surrender himself to her; giving up his very soul to her tutelage, to become her pupil, her slave, her bondsman. She had rejected these advances; and the time for such exuberant submission, which must be founded on love and nourished by it, was now passed. Still all his wishes and endeavours were directed towards her peace, and his chief discomfort arose from the perception that he exerted himself in vain. If she were to continue inflexible in the line of conduct she now pursued, they must part. The combinations and occurrences of this senseless mode of intercourse were maddening to him. Yet he would not propose the separation. He was haunted by the fear of causing the death of one or other of the beings implicated in these events; and he could not persuade himself to undertake to direct the course of events, lest, ignorant of the land he traversed, he should lead those attached to the car into irremediable ruin.

After a discussion on this subject, which lasted for several hours, he took leave of his friends, and returned to town, unwilling to meet Perdita before us, conscious, as we all must be, of the thoughts uppermost in the minds of both. Perdita prepared to follow him with her child. Idris endeavoured to persuade her to remain. My poor sister looked at the counsellor with affright. She knew that Raymond had conversed with her; had he instigated this request?—was this to be the prelude to their eternal separation?—I have said, that the defects of her character awoke and acquired vigour from her unnatural position. She regarded with suspicion the invitation of Idris; she embraced me, as if she were about to be deprived of my affection also: calling me her more than brother, her only friend, her last hope, she pathetically conjured me not to cease to love her; and with increased anxiety she departed for London, the scene and cause of all her misery.

The scenes that followed, convinced her that she had not yet fathomed the obscure gulph into which she had plunged. Her unhappiness assumed every day a new shape; every day some unexpected event seemed to close, while in fact it led onward, the train of calamities which now befell her.

The selected passion of the soul of Raymond was ambition. Readiness of talent, a capacity of entering into, and leading the dispositions of men; earnest desire of distinction were the awakeners and nurses of his ambition. But other ingredients mingled with these, and prevented him from becoming the calculating, determined character, which alone forms a successful hero. He was obstinate, but not firm; benevolent in his first movements; harsh and reckless when provoked. Above all, he was remorseless and unyielding in the pursuit of any object of desire, however lawless. Love of pleasure, and the softer sensibilities of our nature, made a prominent part of his character, conquering the conqueror; holding him in at the moment of acquisition; sweeping away ambition's web; making him forget the toil of weeks, for the sake of one moment's indulgence of the new and actual object of his wishes. Obeying these impulses, he had become the husband of Perdita: egged on by them, he found himself the lover of Evadne. He had now lost both. He had neither the ennobling self-gratulation, which constancy inspires, to console him, nor the voluptuous sense of abandonment to a forbidden, but intoxicating passion. His heart was exhausted by the recent events; his enjoyment of life was destroyed by the resentment of Perdita, and the flight of Evadne; and the inflexibility of the former, set the last seal upon the annihilation of his hopes. As long as their disunion remained a secret, he cherished an expectation of re-awakening past tenderness in her bosom; now that we were all made acquainted with these occurrences, and that Perdita, by declaring her resolves to others, in a manner pledged herself to their accomplishment, he gave up the idea of re-union as futile, and sought only, since he was unable to influence her to change, to reconcile himself to the present state of things. He made a vow against love and its train of struggles, disappointment and remorse, and sought in mere sensual enjoyment, a remedy for the injurious inroads of passion.

Debasement of character is the certain follower of such pursuits. Yet this consequence would not have been immediately remarkable, if Raymond had continued to apply himself to the execution of his plans for the public benefit, and the fulfilling his duties as Protector. But, extreme in all things, given up to immediate impressions, he entered with ardour into this new pursuit of pleasure, and followed up the incongruous intimacies occasioned by it without reflection or foresight. The council-chamber was deserted; the crowds which attended on him as agents to his various projects were neglected. Festivity, and even libertinism, became the order of the day.

Perdita beheld with affright the increasing disorder. For a moment she thought that she could stem the torrent, and that Raymond could be induced to hear reason from her.—Vain hope! The moment of her influence was passed. He listened with haughtiness, replied disdainfully; and, if in truth, she succeeded in awakening his conscience, the sole effect was that he sought an opiate for the pang in oblivious riot. With the energy natural to her, Perdita then endeavoured to supply his place. Their still apparent union permitted her to do much; but no woman could, in the end, present a remedy to the increasing negligence of the Protector; who, as if seized with a paroxysm of insanity, trampled on all ceremony, all order, all duty, and gave himself up to license.

Reports of these strange proceedings reached us, and we were undecided what method to adopt to restore our friend to himself and his country, when Perdita suddenly appeared among us. She detailed the progress of the mournful change, and entreated Adrian and myself to go up to London, and endeavour to remedy the increasing evil:—"Tell him," she cried, "tell Lord Raymond, that my presence shall no longer annoy him. That he need not plunge into this destructive dissipation for the sake of disgusting me, and causing me to fly. This purpose is now accomplished; he will never see me more. But let me, it is my last entreaty, let me in the praises of his countrymen and the prosperity of England, find the choice of my youth justified."

During our ride up to town, Adrian and I discussed and argued upon Raymond's conduct, and his falling off from the hopes of permanent excellence on his part, which he had before given us cause to entertain. My friend and I had both been educated in one school, or rather I was his pupil in the opinion, that steady adherence to principle was the only road to honour; a ceaseless observance of the laws of general utility, the only conscientious aim of human ambition. But though we both entertained these ideas, we differed in their application. Resentment added also a sting to my censure; and I reprobated Raymond's conduct in severe terms. Adrian was more benign, more considerate. He admitted that the principles that I laid down were the best; but he denied that they were the only ones. Quoting the text, there are many mansions in my father's house, he insisted that the modes of becoming good or great, varied as much as the dispositions of men, of whom it might be said, as of the leaves of the forest, there were no two alike.

We arrived in London at about eleven at night. We conjectured, notwithstanding what we had heard, that we should find Raymond in St. Stephen's: thither we sped. The chamber was full—but there was no Protector; and there was an austere discontent manifest on the countenances of the leaders, and a whispering and busy tattle among the underlings, not less ominous. We hastened to the palace of the Protectorate. We found Raymond in his dining room with six others: the bottle was being pushed about merrily, and had made considerable inroads on the understanding of one or two. He who sat near Raymond was telling a story, which convulsed the rest with laughter.

Raymond sat among them, though while he entered into the spirit of the hour, his natural dignity never forsook him. He was gay, playful, fascinating—but never did he overstep the modesty of nature, or the respect due to himself, in his wildest sallies. Yet I own, that considering the task which Raymond had taken on himself as Protector of England, and the cares to which it became him to attend, I was exceedingly provoked to observe the worthless fellows on whom his time was wasted, and the jovial if not drunken spirit which seemed on the point of robbing him of his better self. I stood watching the scene, while Adrian flitted like a shadow in among them, and, by a word and look of sobriety, endeavoured to restore order in the assembly. Raymond expressed himself delighted to see him, declaring that he should make one in the festivity of the night.

This action of Adrian provoked me. I was indignant that he should sit at the same table with the companions of Raymond—men of abandoned characters, or rather without any, the refuse of high-bred luxury, the disgrace of their country. "Let me entreat Adrian," I cried, "not to comply: rather join with me in endeavouring to withdraw Lord Raymond from this scene, and restore him to other society."

"My good fellow," said Raymond, "this is neither the time nor place for the delivery of a moral lecture: take my word for it that my amusements and society are not so bad as you imagine. We are neither hypocrites or fools —for the rest, 'Dost thou think because thou art virtuous, there shall be no more cakes and ale?'"

I turned angrily away: "Verney," said Adrian, "you are very cynical: sit down; or if you will not, perhaps, as you are not a frequent visitor, Lord Raymond will humour you, and accompany us, as we had previously agreed upon, to parliament."

Raymond looked keenly at him; he could read benignity only in his gentle lineaments; he turned to me, observing with scorn my moody and stern demeanour. "Come," said Adrian, "I have promised for you, enable me to keep my engagement. Come with us."—Raymond made an uneasy movement, and laconically replied—"I won't!"

The party in the mean time had broken up. They looked at the pictures, strolled into the other apartments, talked of billiards, and one by one vanished. Raymond strode angrily up and down the room. I stood ready to receive and reply to his reproaches. Adrian leaned against the wall. "This is infinitely ridiculous," he cried, "if you were school-boys, you could not conduct yourselves more unreasonably."

"You do not understand," said Raymond. "This is only part of a system:—a scheme of tyranny to which I will never submit. Because I am Protector of England, am I to be the only slave in its empire? My privacy invaded, my actions censured, my friends insulted? But I will get rid of the whole together.—Be you witnesses," and he took the star, insignia of office, from his breast, and threw it on the table. "I renounce my office, I abdicate my power—assume it who will!"—

"Let him assume it," exclaimed Adrian, "who can pronounce himself, or whom the world will pronounce to be your superior. There does not exist the man in England with adequate presumption. Know yourself, Raymond, and your indignation will cease; your complacency return. A few months ago, whenever we prayed for the prosperity of our country, or our own, we at the same time prayed for the life and welfare of the Protector, as indissolubly linked to it. Your hours were devoted to our benefit, your ambition was to obtain our commendation. You decorated our towns with edifices, you bestowed on us useful establishments, you gifted the soil with abundant fertility. The powerful and unjust cowered at the steps of your judgment-seat, and the poor and oppressed arose like morn-awakened flowers under the sunshine of your protection.

"Can you wonder that we are all aghast and mourn, when this appears changed? But, come, this splenetic fit is already passed; resume your functions; your partisans will hail you; your enemies be silenced; our love, honour, and duty will again be manifested towards you. Master yourself, Raymond, and the world is subject to you."

"All this would be very good sense, if addressed to another," replied Raymond, moodily, "con the lesson yourself, and you, the first peer of the land, may become its sovereign. You the good, the wise, the just, may rule all hearts. But I perceive, too soon for my own happiness, too late for England's good, that I undertook a task to which I am unequal. I cannot rule myself. My passions are my masters; my smallest impulse my tyrant. Do you think that I renounced the

Protectorate (and I have renounced it) in a fit of spleen? By the God that lives, I swear never to take up that bauble again; never again to burthen myself with the weight of care and misery, of which that is the visible sign.

"Once I desired to be a king. It was in the hey-day of youth, in the pride of boyish folly. I knew myself when I renounced it. I renounced it to gain —no matter what—for that also I have lost. For many months I have submitted to this mock majesty—this solemn jest. I am its dupe no longer. I will be free.

"I have lost that which adorned and dignified my life; that which linked me to other men. Again I am a solitary man; and I will become again, as in my early years, a wanderer, a soldier of fortune. My friends, for Verney, I feel that you are my friend, do not endeavour to shake my resolve. Perdita, wedded to an imagination, careless of what is behind the veil, whose charactery is in truth faulty and vile, Perdita has renounced me. With her it was pretty enough to play a sovereign's part; and, as in the recesses of your beloved forest we acted masques, and imagined ourselves Arcadian shepherds, to please the fancy of the moment—so was I content, more for Perdita's sake than my own, to take on me the character of one of the great ones of the earth; to lead her behind the scenes of grandeur, to vary her life with a short act of magnificence and power. This was to be the colour; love and confidence the substance of our existence. But we must live, and not act our lives; pursuing the shadow, I lost the reality—now I renounce both.

"Adrian, I am about to return to Greece, to become again a soldier, perhaps a conqueror. Will you accompany me? You will behold new scenes; see a new people; witness the mighty struggle there going forward between civilization and barbarism; behold, and perhaps direct the efforts of a young and vigorous population, for liberty and order. Come with me. I have expected you. I waited for this moment; all is prepared;—will you accompany me?"

"I will," replied Adrian. "Immediately?"

"To-morrow if you will."

"Reflect!" I cried.

"Wherefore?" asked Raymond—"My dear fellow, I have done nothing else than reflect on this step the live-long summer; and be assured that Adrian has condensed an age of reflection into this little moment. Do not talk of reflection; from this moment I abjure it; this is my only happy moment during a long interval of time. I must go, Lionel—the Gods will it; and I must. Do not endeavour to deprive me of my companion, the out-cast's friend.

"One word more concerning unkind, unjust Perdita. For a time, I thought that, by watching a complying moment, fostering the still warm ashes, I might relume in her the flame of love. It is more cold within her, than a fire left by gypsies in winter-time, the spent embers crowned by a pyramid of snow. Then, in endeavouring to do violence to my own disposition, I made all worse than before. Still I think, that time, and even absence, may restore her to me. Remember, that I love her still, that my dearest hope is that she will again be mine. I know, though she does not, how false the veil is which she has spread over the reality—do not endeavour to rend this deceptive covering, but by degrees withdraw it. Present her with a mirror, in which she may know herself; and, when she is an adept in that necessary but difficult science, she will wonder at her present mistake, and hasten to restore to me, what is by right mine, her forgiveness, her kind thoughts, her love."

ꙮ I I ꙮ

AFTER THESE EVENTS, it was long before we were able to attain any degree of composure. A moral tempest had wrecked our richly freighted vessel, and we, remnants of the diminished crew, were aghast at the losses and changes which we had undergone. Idris passionately loved her brother, and could ill brook an absence whose duration was uncertain; his society was dear and necessary to me—I had followed up my chosen literary occupations with delight under his tutorship and assistance; his mild philosophy, unerring reason, and enthusiastic friendship were the best ingredient, the exalted spirit of our circle; even the children bitterly regretted the loss of their kind playfellow. Deeper grief oppressed Perdita. In spite of resentment, by day and night she figured to herself the toils and dangers of the wanderers. Raymond absent, struggling with difficulties, lost to the power and rank of the Protectorate, exposed to the perils of war, became an object of anxious interest; not that she felt any inclination to recall him, if recall must imply a return to their former union. Such return she felt to be impossible; and while she believed it to be thus, and with anguish regretted that so it should be, she continued angry and impatient with him, who occasioned her misery. These perplexities and regrets caused her to bathe her pillow with nightly tears, and to reduce her in person and in mind to the shadow of what she had been. She sought solitude, and avoided us when in gaiety and unrestrained affection we met in a family circle. Lonely musings, interminable wanderings, and solemn music were her only pastimes. She neglected even her child; shutting her heart against all tenderness, she grew reserved towards me, her first and fast friend.

I could not see her thus lost, without exerting myself to remedy the evil —remediless I knew, if I could not in the end bring her to reconcile herself to Raymond. Before he went I used every argument, every persuasion to induce her to stop his journey. She answered the one with a gush of tears—telling me that to be persuaded—life and the goods of life were a cheap exchange. It was not will that she wanted, but the capacity; again and again she declared, it were as easy to enchain the sea, to put reins on the wind's viewless courses, as for her to take truth for falsehood, deceit for honesty, heartless communion for sincere, confiding love. She answered my reasonings more briefly, declaring with disdain, that the reason was hers; and, until I could persuade her that the past could be unacted, that maturity could go back to the cradle, and that all that was could become as though it had never been, it was useless to assure her that no real change had taken place in her fate. And thus with stern pride she suffered him to go, though her very heart-strings cracked at the fulfilling of the act, which rent from her all that made life valuable.

To change the scene for her, and even for ourselves, all unhinged by the cloud that had come over us, I persuaded my two remaining companions that it were better that we should absent ourselves for a time from Windsor. We visited the north of England, my native Ulswater, and lingered in scenes dear from a thousand associations. We lengthened our tour into Scotland, that we might see Loch Katrine and Loch Lomond; thence we crossed to Ireland, and passed several weeks in the neighbourhood of Killarney. The change of scene operated to a great degree as I expected; after a year's absence, Perdita returned in gentler and more docile mood to Windsor. The first sight of this place for a time unhinged her. Here every spot was distinct with associations now grown bitter. The forest glades, the ferny dells, and lawny uplands, the cultivated and cheerful country spread around the silver pathway of ancient Thames, all earth, air, and wave, took up one choral voice, inspired by memory, instinct with plaintive regret.

But my essay towards bringing her to a saner view of her own situation, did not end here. Perdita was still to a great degree uneducated. When first she left her peasant life, and resided with the elegant and cultivated Evadne, the only accomplishment she brought to any perfection was that of painting, for which she had a taste almost amounting to genius. This had occupied her in her lonely cottage, when she quitted her Greek friend's protection. Her pallet and easel were now thrown aside; did she try to paint, thronging recollections made her hand tremble, her eyes fill with tears. With this occupation she gave up almost every other; and her mind preyed upon itself almost to madness.

For my own part, since Adrian had first withdrawn me from my selvatic wilderness to his own paradise of order and beauty, I had been wedded to literature. I felt convinced that however it might have been in former times, in the present stage of the world, no man's faculties could be developed, no man's moral principle be enlarged and liberal, without an extensive acquaintance with books. To me they stood in the place of an active career, of ambition, and those palpable excitements necessary to the multitude. The collation of philosophical opinions, the study of historical facts, the acquirement of languages, were at once my recreation, and the serious aim of my life. I turned author myself. My productions however were sufficiently unpretending; they were confined to the biography of favourite historical characters, especially those whom I believed to have been traduced, or about whom clung obscurity and doubt.

As my authorship increased, I acquired new sympathies and pleasures. I found another and a valuable link to enchain me to my fellow-creatures; my point of sight was extended, and the inclinations and capacities of all human beings became deeply interesting to me. Kings have been called the fathers of their people. Suddenly I became as it were the father of all mankind. Posterity became my heirs. My thoughts were gems to enrich the treasure house of man's intellectual possessions; each sentiment was a precious gift I bestowed on them. Let not these aspirations be attributed to vanity. They were not expressed in words, nor even reduced to form in my own mind; but they filled my soul, exalting my thoughts, raising a glow of enthusiasm, and led me out of the obscure path in which I before walked, into the bright noon-enlightened highway of mankind, making me, citizen of the world, a candidate for immortal honors, an eager aspirant to the praise and sympathy of my fellow men.

No one certainly ever enjoyed the pleasures of composition more intensely than I. If I left the woods, the solemn music of the waving branches, and the majestic temple of nature, I sought the vast halls of the Castle, and looked over wide, fertile England, spread beneath our

regal mount, and listened the while to inspiring strains of music. At such times solemn
harmonies or spirit-stirring airs gave wings to my lagging thoughts, permitting them,
methought, to penetrate the last veil of nature and her God, and to display the highest beauty
in visible expression to the understandings of men. As the music went on, my ideas seemed to
quit their mortal dwelling house; they shook their pinions and began a flight, sailing on the
placid current of thought, filling the creation with new glory, and rousing sublime imagery that
else had slept voiceless. Then I would hasten to my desk, weave the new-found web of mind in
firm texture and brilliant colours, leaving the fashioning of the material to a calmer moment.

But this account, which might as properly belong to a former period of my life as to the
present moment, leads me far afield. It was the pleasure I took in literature, the discipline of
mind I found arise from it, that made me eager to lead Perdita to the same pursuits. I began
with light hand and gentle allurement; first exciting her curiosity, and then satisfying it in such
a way as might occasion her, at the same time that she half forgot her sorrows in occupation, to
find in the hours that succeeded a reaction of benevolence and toleration.

Intellectual activity, though not directed towards books, had always been my sister's
characteristic. It had been displayed early in life, leading her out to solitary musing among her
native mountains, causing her to form innumerous combinations from common objects, giving
strength to her perceptions, and swiftness to their arrangement. Love had come, as the rod of
the master-prophet, to swallow up every minor propensity. Love had doubled all her
excellencies, and placed a diadem on her genius. Was she to cease to love? Take the colours and
odour from the rose, change the sweet nutriment of mother's milk to gall and poison; as easily
might you wean Perdita from love. She grieved for the loss of Raymond with an anguish, that
exiled all smile from her lips, and trenched sad lines on her brow of beauty. But each day
seemed to change the nature of her suffering, and every succeeding hour forced her to alter (if
so I may style it) the fashion of her soul's mourning garb. For a time music was able to satisfy
the cravings of her mental hunger, and her melancholy thoughts renewed themselves in each
change of key, and varied with every alteration in the strain. My schooling first impelled her
towards books; and, if music had been the food of sorrow, the productions of the wise became
its medicine. The acquisition of unknown languages was too tedious an occupation, for one
who referred every expression to the universe within, and read not, as many do, for the mere
sake of filling up time; but who was still questioning herself and her author, moulding every
idea in a thousand ways, ardently desirous for the discovery of truth in every sentence. She
sought to improve her understanding; mechanically her heart and dispositions became soft and
gentle under this benign discipline. After awhile she discovered, that amidst all her newly
acquired knowledge, her own character, which formerly she fancied that she thoroughly
understood, became the first in rank among the terrae incognitae, the pathless wilds of a
country that had no chart. Erringly and strangely she began the task of self-examination with
self-condemnation. And then again she became aware of her own excellencies, and began to
balance with juster scales the shades of good and evil. I, who longed beyond words, to restore
her to the happiness it was still in her power to enjoy, watched with anxiety the result of these
internal proceedings.

But man is a strange animal. We cannot calculate on his forces like that of an engine; and,
though an impulse draw with a forty-horse power at what appears willing to yield to one, yet
in contempt of calculation the movement is not effected. Neither grief, philosophy, nor love
could make Perdita think with mildness of the dereliction of Raymond. She now took pleasure
in my society; towards Idris she felt and displayed a full and affectionate sense of her worth—
she restored to her child in abundant measure her tenderness and care. But I could discover,
amidst all her repinings, deep resentment towards Raymond, and an unfading sense of injury,

that plucked from me my hope, when I appeared nearest to its fulfilment. Among other painful restrictions, she has occasioned it to become a law among us, never to mention Raymond's name before her. She refused to read any communications from Greece, desiring me only to mention when any arrived, and whether the wanderers were well. It was curious that even little Clara observed this law towards her mother. This lovely child was nearly eight years of age. Formerly she had been a light-hearted infant, fanciful, but gay and childish. After the departure of her father, thought became impressed on her young brow. Children, unadepts in language, seldom find words to express their thoughts, nor could we tell in what manner the late events had impressed themselves on her mind. But certainly she had made deep observations while she noted in silence the changes that passed around her. She never mentioned her father to Perdita, she appeared half afraid when she spoke of him to me, and though I tried to draw her out on the subject, and to dispel the gloom that hung about her ideas concerning him, I could not succeed. Yet each foreign post-day she watched for the arrival of letters—knew the post mark, and watched me as I read. I found her often poring over the article of Greek intelligence in the newspaper.

There is no more painful sight than that of untimely care in children, and it was particularly observable in one whose disposition had heretofore been mirthful. Yet there was so much sweetness and docility about Clara, that your admiration was excited; and if the moods of mind are calculated to paint the cheek with beauty, and endow motions with grace, surely her contemplations must have been celestial; since every lineament was moulded into loveliness, and her motions were more harmonious than the elegant boundings of the fawns of her native forest. I sometimes expostulated with Perdita on the subject of her reserve; but she rejected my counsels, while her daughter's sensibility excited in her a tenderness still more passionate.

After the lapse of more than a year, Adrian returned from Greece.

When our exiles had first arrived, a truce was in existence between the Turks and Greeks; a truce that was as sleep to the mortal frame, signal of renewed activity on waking. With the numerous soldiers of Asia, with all of warlike stores, ships, and military engines, that wealth and power could command, the Turks at once resolved to crush an enemy, which creeping on by degrees, had from their stronghold in the Morea, acquired Thrace and Macedonia, and had led their armies even to the gates of Constantinople, while their extensive commercial relations gave every European nation an interest in their success. Greece prepared for a vigorous resistance; it rose to a man; and the women, sacrificing their costly ornaments, accoutred their sons for the war, and bade them conquer or die with the spirit of the Spartan mother. The talents and courage of Raymond were highly esteemed among the Greeks. Born at Athens, that city claimed him for her own, and by giving him the command of her peculiar division in the army, the commander-in-chief only possessed superior power. He was numbered among her citizens, his name was added to the list of Grecian heroes. His judgment, activity, and consummate bravery, justified their choice. The Earl of Windsor became a volunteer under his friend.

"It is well," said Adrian, "to prate of war in these pleasant shades, and with much ill-spent oil make a show of joy, because many thousand of our fellow-creatures leave with pain this sweet air and natal earth. I shall not be suspected of being averse to the Greek cause; I know and feel its necessity; it is beyond every other a good cause. I have defended it with my sword, and was willing that my spirit should be breathed out in its defence; freedom is of more worth than life, and the Greeks do well to defend their privilege unto death. But let us not deceive ourselves. The Turks are men; each fibre, each limb is as feeling as our own, and every spasm, be it mental or bodily, is as truly felt in a Turk's heart or brain, as in a Greek's. The last action at which I was present was the taking of ——. The Turks resisted to the last, the garrison perished on the ramparts, and we entered by assault. Every breathing creature within the walls was massacred. Think you, amidst the shrieks of violated innocence and helpless infancy, I did not feel in every nerve the cry of a fellow being? They were men and women, the sufferers, before they were Mahometans, and when they rise turbanless from the grave, in what except their good or evil actions will they be the better or worse than we? Two soldiers contended for a girl, whose rich dress and extreme beauty excited the brutal appetites of these wretches, who, perhaps good men among their families, were changed by the fury of the moment into incarnated evils. An old man, with a silver beard, decrepid and bald, he might be her grandfather, interposed to save her; the battle axe of one of them clove his skull. I rushed to her defence, but rage made them blind and deaf; they did not distinguish my Christian garb or heed my words—words were blunt weapons then, for while war cried "havoc," and murder gave fit echo, how could I—

> *Turn back the tide of ills, relieving wrong*
> *With mild accost of soothing eloquence?*

One of the fellows, enraged at my interference, struck me with his bayonet in the side, and I fell senseless.

"This wound will probably shorten my life, having shattered a frame, weak of itself. But I am content to die. I have learnt in Greece that one man, more or less, is of small import, while human bodies remain to fill up the thinned ranks of the soldiery; and that the identity of an individual may be overlooked, so that the muster roll contain its full numbers. All this has a different effect upon Raymond. He is able to contemplate the ideal of war, while I am sensible only to its realities. He is a soldier, a general. He can influence the blood-thirsty war-dogs, while I resist their propensities vainly. The cause is simple. Burke has said that, 'in all bodies those who would lead, must also, in a considerable degree, follow.' —I cannot follow; for I do not sympathize in their dreams of massacre and glory—to follow and to lead in such a career, is the natural bent of Raymond's mind. He is always successful, and bids fair, at the same time that he acquires high name and station for himself, to secure liberty, probably extended empire, to the Greeks."

Perdita's mind was not softened by this account. He, she thought, can be great and happy without me. Would that I also had a career! Would that I could freight some untried bark with all my hopes, energies, and desires, and launch it forth into the ocean of life—bound for some attainable point, with ambition or pleasure at the helm! But adverse winds detain me on shore; like Ulysses, I sit at the water's edge and weep. But my nerveless hands can neither fell the trees, nor smooth the planks. Under the influence of these melancholy thoughts, she became more than ever in love with sorrow. Yet Adrian's presence did some good; he at once broke through the law of silence observed concerning Raymond. At first she started from the unaccustomed sound; soon she got used to it and to love it, and she listened with avidity to the account of his achievements. Clara got rid also of her restraint; Adrian and she had been old playfellows; and now, as they walked or rode together, he yielded to her earnest entreaty, and repeated, for the hundredth time, some tale of her father's bravery, munificence, or justice.

Each vessel in the mean time brought exhilarating tidings from Greece. The presence of a friend in its armies and councils made us enter into the details with enthusiasm; and a short letter now and then from Raymond told us how he was engrossed by the interests of his adopted country. The Greeks were strongly attached to their commercial pursuits, and would have been satisfied with their present acquisitions, had not the Turks roused them by invasion. The patriots were victorious; a spirit of conquest was instilled; and already they looked on

Constantinople as their own. Raymond rose perpetually in their estimation; but one man held a superior command to him in their armies. He was conspicuous for his conduct and choice of position in a battle fought in the plains of Thrace, on the banks of the Hebrus, which was to decide the fate of Islam. The Mahometans were defeated, and driven entirely from the country west of this river. The battle was sanguinary, the loss of the Turks apparently irreparable; the Greeks, in losing one man, forgot the nameless crowd strewed upon the bloody field, and they ceased to value themselves on a victory, which cost them— Raymond.

At the battle of Makri he had led the charge of cavalry, and pursued the fugitives even to the banks of the Hebrus. His favourite horse was found grazing by the margin of the tranquil river. It became a question whether he had fallen among the unrecognized; but no broken ornament or stained trapping betrayed his fate. It was suspected that the Turks, finding themselves possessed of so illustrious a captive, resolved to satisfy their cruelty rather than their avarice, and fearful of the interference of England, had come to the determination of concealing for ever the cold-blooded murder of the soldier they most hated and feared in the squadrons of their enemy.

Raymond was not forgotten in England. His abdication of the Protectorate had caused an unexampled sensation; and, when his magnificent and manly system was contrasted with the narrow views of succeeding politicians, the period of his elevation was referred to with sorrow. The perpetual recurrence of his name, joined to most honourable testimonials, in the Greek gazettes, kept up the interest he had excited. He seemed the favourite child of fortune, and his untimely loss eclipsed the world, and shewed forth the remnant of mankind with diminished lustre. They clung with eagerness to the hope held out that he might yet be alive. Their minister at Constantinople was urged to make the necessary perquisitions, and should his existence be ascertained, to demand his release. It was to be hoped that their efforts would succeed, and that though now a prisoner, the sport of cruelty and the mark of hate, he would be rescued from danger and restored to the happiness, power, and honour which he deserved.

The effect of this intelligence upon my sister was striking. She never for a moment credited the story of his death; she resolved instantly to go to Greece. Reasoning and persuasion were thrown away upon her; she would endure no hindrance, no delay. It may be advanced for a truth, that, if argument or entreaty can turn any one from a desperate purpose, whose motive and end depends on the strength of the affections only, then it is right so to turn them, since their docility shews, that neither the motive nor the end were of sufficient force to bear them through the obstacles attendant on their undertaking. If, on the contrary, they are proof against expostulation, this very steadiness is an omen of success; and it becomes the duty of those who love them, to assist in smoothing the obstructions in their path. Such sentiments actuated our little circle. Finding Perdita immoveable, we consulted as to the best means of furthering her purpose. She could not go alone to a country where she had no friends, where she might arrive only to hear the dreadful news, which must overwhelm her with grief and remorse. Adrian, whose health had always been weak, now suffered considerable aggravation of suffering from the effects of his wound. Idris could not endure to leave him in this state; nor was it right either to quit or take with us a young family for a journey of this description. I resolved at length to accompany Perdita. The separation from my Idris was painful—but necessity reconciled us to it in some degree: necessity and the hope of saving Raymond, and restoring him again to happiness and Perdita. No delay was to ensue. Two days after we came to our determination, we set out for Portsmouth, and embarked. The season was May, the weather stormless; we were promised a prosperous voyage. Cherishing the most fervent hopes, embarked on the waste ocean, we saw with delight the receding shore of Britain, and on the wings of desire outspeeded our well filled sails towards the South. The light curling waves bore us onward,

and old ocean smiled at the freight of love and hope committed to his charge; it stroked gently
its tempestuous plains, and the path was smoothed for us. Day and night the wind right aft,
gave steady impulse to our keel—nor did rough gale, or treacherous sand, or destructive rock
interpose an obstacle between my sister and the land which was to restore her to her first
beloved,

Her dear heart's confessor—a heart within that heart.

❧ II ❧

DURING THIS VOYAGE, when on calm evenings we conversed on deck, watching the glancing of the waves and the changeful appearances of the sky, I discovered the total revolution that the disasters of Raymond had wrought in the mind of my sister. Were they the same waters of love, which, lately cold and cutting as ice, repelling as that, now loosened from their frozen chains, flowed through the regions of her soul in gushing and grateful exuberance? She did not believe that he was dead, but she knew that he was in danger, and the hope of assisting in his liberation, and the idea of soothing by tenderness the ills that he might have undergone, elevated and harmonized the late jarring element of her being. I was not so sanguine as she as to the result of our voyage. She was not sanguine, but secure; and the expectation of seeing the lover she had banished, the husband, friend, heart's companion from whom she had long been alienated, wrapt her senses in delight, her mind in placidity. It was beginning life again; it was leaving barren sands for an abode of fertile beauty; it was a harbour after a tempest, an opiate after sleepless nights, a happy waking from a terrible dream.

Little Clara accompanied us; the poor child did not well understand what was going forward. She heard that we were bound for Greece, that she would see her father, and now, for the first time, she prattled of him to her mother.

On landing at Athens we found difficulties increase upon us: nor could the storied earth or balmy atmosphere inspire us with enthusiasm or pleasure, while the fate of Raymond was in jeopardy. No man had ever excited so strong an interest in the public mind; this was apparent even among the phlegmatic English, from whom he had long been absent. The Athenians had expected their hero to return in triumph; the women had taught their children to lisp his name joined to thanksgiving; his manly beauty, his courage, his devotion to their cause, made him appear in their eyes almost as one of the ancient deities of the soil descended from their native Olympus to defend them. When they spoke of his probable death and certain captivity, tears streamed from their eyes; even as the women of Syria sorrowed for Adonis, did the wives and mothers of Greece lament our English Raymond—Athens was a city of mourning.

All these shews of despair struck Perdita with affright. With that sanguine but confused expectation, which desire engendered while she was at a distance from reality, she had formed an image in her mind of instantaneous change, when she should set her foot on Grecian shores. She fancied that Raymond would already be free, and that her tender attentions would come to entirely obliterate even the memory of his mischance. But his fate was still uncertain; she began to fear the worst, and to feel that her soul's hope was cast on a chance that might prove a blank. The wife and lovely child of Lord Raymond became objects of intense interest in Athens. The gates of their abode were besieged, audible prayers were breathed for his restoration; all these circumstances added to the dismay and fears of Perdita.

My exertions were unremitted: after a time I left Athens, and joined the army stationed at Kishan in Thrace. Bribery, threats, and intrigue, soon discovered the secret that Raymond was alive, a prisoner, suffering the most rigorous confinement and wanton cruelties. We put in movement every impulse of policy and money to redeem him from their hands.

The impatience of my sister's disposition now returned on her, awakened by repentance, sharpened by remorse. The very beauty of the Grecian climate, during the season of spring, added torture to her sensations. The unexampled loveliness of the flower-clad earth—the genial sunshine and grateful shade—the melody of the birds—the majesty of the woods— the splendour of the marble ruins—the clear effulgence of the stars by night—the combination of all that was exciting and voluptuous in this transcending land, by inspiring a quicker spirit of life and an added sensitiveness to every articulation of her frame, only gave edge to the poignancy of her grief. Each long hour was counted, and "He suffers" was the burthen of all her thoughts. She abstained from food; she lay on the bare earth, and, by such mimickry of his enforced torments, endeavoured to hold communion with his distant pain. I remembered in one of her harshest moments a quotation of mine had roused her to anger and disdain. "Perdita," I had said, "some day you will discover that you have done wrong in again casting Raymond on the thorns of life. When disappointment has sullied his beauty, when a soldier's hardships have bent his manly form, and loneliness made even triumph bitter to him, then you will repent; and regret for the irreparable change

"will move In hearts all rocky now, the late remorse of love."[1]

The stinging "remorse of love" now pierced her heart. She accused herself of his journey to Greece—his dangers—his imprisonment. She pictured to herself the anguish of his solitude; she remembered with what eager delight he had in former days made her the partner of his joyful hopes— with what grateful affection he received her sympathy in his cares. She called to mind how often he had declared that solitude was to him the greatest of all evils, and how death itself was to him more full of fear and pain when he pictured to himself a lonely grave. "My best girl," he had said, "relieves me from these phantasies. United to her, cherished in her dear heart, never again shall I know the misery of finding myself alone. Even if I die before you, my Perdita, treasure up my ashes till yours may mingle with mine. It is a foolish sentiment for one who is not a materialist, yet, methinks, even in that dark cell, I may feel that my inanimate dust mingles with yours, and thus have a companion in decay." In her resentful mood, these expressions had been remembered with acrimony and disdain; they visited her in her softened hour, taking sleep from her eyes, all hope of rest from her uneasy mind.

Two months passed thus, when at last we obtained a promise of Raymond's release. Confinement and hardship had undermined his health; the Turks feared an accomplishment of the threats of the English government, if he died under their hands; they looked upon his recovery as impossible; they delivered him up as a dying man, willingly making over to us the rites of burial.

He came by sea from Constantinople to Athens. The wind, favourable to him, blew so strongly in shore, that we were unable, as we had at first intended, to meet him on his watery road. The watchtower of Athens was besieged by inquirers, each sail eagerly looked out for; till on the first of May the gallant frigate bore in sight, freighted with treasure more invaluable than the wealth which, piloted from Mexico, the vexed Pacific swallowed, or that was conveyed over its tranquil bosom to enrich the crown of Spain. At early dawn the vessel was discovered bearing in shore; it was conjectured that it would cast anchor about five miles from land. The news spread through Athens, and the whole city poured out at the gate of the Piraeus, down the roads, through the vineyards, the olive woods and plantations of fig-trees, towards the harbour. The noisy joy of the populace, the gaudy colours of their dress, the tumult of carriages and horses, the march of soldiers intermixed, the waving of banners and sound of martial music added to the high excitement of the scene; while round us reposed in solemn majesty the relics of antient time. To our right the Acropolis rose high, spectatress of a thousand changes, of ancient glory, Turkish slavery, and the restoration of dear-bought liberty; tombs and cenotaphs were strewed thick around, adorned by ever renewing vegetation; the mighty dead hovered over their monuments, and beheld in our enthusiasm and congregated numbers a renewal of the scenes in which they had been the actors. Perdita and Clara rode in a close carriage; I attended them on horseback. At length we arrived at the harbour; it was agitated by the outward swell of the sea; the beach, as far could be discerned, was covered by a moving multitude, which, urged by those behind toward the sea, again rushed back as the heavy waves with sullen roar burst close to them. I applied my glass, and could discern that the frigate had already cast anchor, fearful of the danger of approaching nearer to a lee shore: a boat was lowered; with a pang I saw that Raymond was unable to descend the vessel's side; he was let down in a chair, and lay wrapt in cloaks at the bottom of the boat.

I dismounted, and called to some sailors who were rowing about the harbour to pull up, and take me into their skiff; Perdita at the same moment alighted from her carriage—she seized my arm—"Take me with you," she cried; she was trembling and pale; Clara clung to her—"You must not," I said, "the sea is rough—he will soon be here—do you not see his boat?" The little bark to which I had beckoned had now pulled up; before I could stop her, Perdita, assisted by the sailors was in it—Clara followed her mother—a loud shout echoed from the crowd as we pulled out of the inner harbour; while my sister at the prow, had caught hold of one of the men who was using a glass, asking a thousand questions, careless of the spray that broke over her, deaf, sightless to all, except the little speck that, just visible on the top of the waves, evidently neared. We approached with all the speed six rowers could give; the orderly and picturesque dress of the soldiers on the beach, the sounds of exulting music, the stirring breeze and waving flags, the unchecked exclamations of the eager crowd, whose dark looks and foreign garb were purely eastern; the sight of temple-crowned rock, the white marble of the buildings glittering in the sun, and standing in bright relief against the dark ridge of lofty mountains beyond; the near roar of the sea, the splash of oars, and dash of spray, all steeped my soul in a delirium, unfelt, unimagined in the common course of common life. Trembling, I was unable to continue to look through the glass with which I had watched the motion of the crew, when the frigate's boat had first been launched. We rapidly drew near, so that at length the number and forms of those within could be discerned; its dark sides grew big, and the splash of its oars became audible: I could distinguish the languid form of my friend, as he half raised himself at our approach.

Perdita's questions had ceased; she leaned on my arm, panting with emotions too acute for tears—our men pulled alongside the other boat. As a last effort, my sister mustered her strength, her firmness; she stepped from one boat to the other, and then with a shriek she sprang towards Raymond, knelt at his side, and glueing her lips to the hand she seized, her face shrouded by her long hair, gave herself up to tears.

Raymond had somewhat raised himself at our approach, but it was with difficulty that he exerted himself even thus much. With sunken cheek and hollow eyes, pale and gaunt, how could I recognize the beloved of Perdita? I continued awe-struck and mute—he looked smilingly on the poor girl; the smile was his. A day of sun-shine falling on a dark valley, displays its before hidden characteristics; and now this smile, the same with which he first spoke love to Perdita, with which he had welcomed the protectorate, playing on his altered countenance, made me in my heart's core feel that this was Raymond.

He stretched out to me his other hand; I discerned the trace of manacles on his bared wrist. I heard my sister's sobs, and thought, happy are women who can weep, and in a passionate caress disburthen the oppression of their feelings; shame and habitual restraint hold back a man. I would have given worlds to have acted as in days of boyhood, have strained him to my breast, pressed his hand to my lips, and wept over him; my swelling heart choked me; the natural current would not be checked; the big rebellious tears gathered in my eyes; I turned aside, and they dropped in the sea—they came fast and faster;—yet I could hardly be ashamed, for I saw that the rough sailors were not unmoved, and Raymond's eyes alone were dry from among our crew. He lay in that blessed calm which convalescence always induces, enjoying in secure tranquility his liberty and re-union with her whom he adored. Perdita at length subdued her burst of passion, and rose, —she looked round for Clara; the child frightened, not recognizing her father, and neglected by us, had crept to the other end of the boat; she came at her mother's call. Perdita presented her to Raymond; her first words were: "Beloved, embrace our child!"

"Come hither, sweet one," said her father, "do you not know me?" she knew his voice, and cast herself in his arms with half bashful but uncontrollable emotion.

Perceiving the weakness of Raymond, I was afraid of ill consequences from the pressure of the crowd on his landing. But they were awed as I had been, at the change of his appearance. The music died away, the shouts abruptly ended; the soldiers had cleared a space in which a carriage was drawn up. He was placed in it; Perdita and Clara entered with him, and his escort closed round it; a hollow murmur, akin to the roaring of the near waves, went through the multitude; they fell back as the carriage advanced, and fearful of injuring him they had come to welcome, by loud testimonies of joy, they satisfied themselves with bending in a low salaam as the carriage passed; it went slowly along the road of the Piraeus; passed by antique temple and heroic tomb, beneath the craggy rock of the citadel. The sound of the waves was left behind; that of the multitude continued at intervals, supressed and hoarse; and though, in the city, the houses, churches, and public buildings were decorated with tapestry and banners—though the soldiery lined the streets, and the inhabitants in thousands were assembled to give him hail, the same solemn silence prevailed, the soldiery presented arms, the banners vailed, many a white hand waved a streamer, and vainly sought to discern the hero in the vehicle, which, closed and encompassed by the city guards, drew him to the palace allotted for his abode.

Raymond was weak and exhausted, yet the interest he perceived to be excited on his account, filled him with proud pleasure. He was nearly killed with kindness. It is true, the populace retained themselves; but there arose a perpetual hum and bustle from the throng round the palace, which added to the noise of fireworks, the frequent explosion of arms, the tramp to and fro of horsemen and carriages, to which effervescence he was the focus, retarded his recovery. So we retired awhile to Eleusis, and here rest and tender care added each day to the strength of our invalid. The zealous attention of Perdita claimed the first rank in the causes which induced his rapid recovery; but the second was surely the delight he felt in the affection and good will of the Greeks. We are said to love much those whom we greatly benefit. Raymond had fought and conquered for the Athenians; he had suffered, on their account, peril, imprisonment, and hardship; their gratitude affected him deeply, and he inly vowed to unite his fate for ever to that of a people so enthusiastically devoted to him.

Social feeling and sympathy constituted a marked feature in my disposition. In early youth, the living drama acted around me, drew me heart and soul into its vortex. I was now conscious of a change. I loved, I hoped, I enjoyed; but there was something besides this. I was inquisitive as to the internal principles of action of those around me: anxious to read their thoughts justly, and for ever occupied in divining their inmost mind. All events, at the same time that they deeply interested me, arranged themselves in pictures before me. I gave the right place to every personage in the groupe, the just balance to every sentiment. This undercurrent of thought, often soothed me amidst distress, and even agony. It gave ideality to that, from which, taken in naked truth, the soul would have revolted: it bestowed pictorial colours on misery and disease, and not unfrequently relieved me from despair in deplorable changes. This faculty, or instinct, was now rouzed. I watched the re-awakened devotion of my sister; Clara's timid, but concentrated admiration of her father, and Raymond's appetite for renown, and sensitiveness to the demonstrations of affection of the Athenians. Attentively perusing this animated volume, I was the less surprised at the tale I read on the new-turned page.

The Turkish army were at this time besieging Rodosto; and the Greeks, hastening their preparations, and sending each day reinforcements, were on the eve of forcing the enemy to battle. Each people looked on the coming struggle as that which would be to a great degree decisive; as, in case of victory, the next step would be the siege of Constantinople by the Greeks. Raymond, being somewhat recovered, prepared to re-assume his command in the army.

Perdita did not oppose herself to his determination. She only stipulated to be permitted to accompany him. She had set down no rule of conduct for herself; but for her life she could not have opposed his slightest wish, or do other than acquiesce cheerfully in all his projects. One word, in truth, had alarmed her more than battles or sieges, during which she trusted Raymond's high command would exempt him from danger. That word, as yet it was not more to her, was PLAGUE. This enemy to the human race had begun early in June to raise its serpent-head on the shores of the Nile; parts of Asia, not usually subject to this evil, were infected. It was in Constantinople; but as each year that city experienced a like visitation, small attention was paid to those accounts which declared more people to have died there already, than usually made up the accustomed prey of the whole of the hotter months. However it might be, neither plague nor war could prevent Perdita from following her lord, or induce her to utter one objection to the plans which he proposed. To be near him, to be loved by him, to feel him again her own, was the limit of her desires. The object of her life was to do him pleasure: it had been so before, but with a difference. In past times, without thought or foresight she had made him happy, being so herself, and in any question of choice, consulted her own wishes, as being one with his. Now she sedulously put herself out of the question, sacrificing even her anxiety for his health and welfare to her resolve not to oppose any of his desires. Love of the Greek people, appetite for glory, and hatred of the barbarian government under which he had suffered even to the approach of death, stimulated him. He wished to repay the kindness of the Athenians, to keep alive the splendid associations connected with his name, and to eradicate from Europe a power which, while every other nation advanced in civilization, stood still, a monument of antique barbarism. Having effected the reunion of Raymond and Perdita, I was eager to return to England; but his earnest request, added to awakening curiosity, and an indefinable anxiety to behold the catastrophe, now apparently at hand, in the long drawn history of Grecian and Turkish warfare, induced me to consent to prolong until the autumn, the period of my residence in Greece.

As soon as the health of Raymond was sufficiently re-established, he prepared to join the

Grecian camp, hear Kishan, a town of some importance, situated to the east of the Hebrus; in which Perdita and Clara were to remain until the event of the expected battle. We quitted Athens on the 2nd of June. Raymond had recovered from the gaunt and pallid looks of fever. If I no longer saw the fresh glow of youth on his matured countenance, if care had besieged his brow, "And dug deep trenches in his beauty's field," if his hair, slightly mingled with grey, and his look, considerate even in its eagerness, gave signs of added years and past sufferings, yet there was something irresistibly affecting in the sight of one, lately snatched from the grave, renewing his career, untamed by sickness or disaster. The Athenians saw in him, not as heretofore, the heroic boy or desperate man, who was ready to die for them; but the prudent commander, who for their sakes was careful of his life, and could make his own warrior-propensities second to the scheme of conduct policy might point out.

All Athens accompanied us for several miles. When he had landed a month ago, the noisy populace had been hushed by sorrow and fear; but this was a festival day to all. The air resounded with their shouts; their picturesque costume, and the gay colours of which it was composed, flaunted in the sunshine; their eager gestures and rapid utterance accorded with their wild appearance. Raymond was the theme of every tongue, the hope of each wife, mother or betrothed bride, whose husband, child, or lover, making a part of the Greek army, were to be conducted to victory by him.

Notwithstanding the hazardous object of our journey, it was full of romantic interest, as we passed through the vallies, and over the hills, of this divine country. Raymond was inspirited by the intense sensations of recovered health; he felt that in being general of the Athenians, he filled a post worthy of his ambition; and, in his hope of the conquest of Constantinople, he counted on an event which would be as a landmark in the waste of ages, an exploit unequalled in the annals of man; when a city of grand historic association, the beauty of whose site was the wonder of the world, which for many hundred years had been the strong hold of the Moslems, should be rescued from slavery and barbarism, and restored to a people illustrious for genius, civilization, and a spirit of liberty. Perdita rested on his restored society, on his love, his hopes and fame, even as a Sybarite on a luxurious couch; every thought was transport, each emotion bathed as it were in a congenial and balmy element.

We arrived at Kishan on the 7th of July. The weather during our journey had been serene. Each day, before dawn, we left our night's encampment, and watched the shadows as they retreated from hill and valley, and the golden splendour of the sun's approach. The accompanying soldiers received, with national vivacity, enthusiastic pleasure from the sight of beautiful nature. The uprising of the star of day was hailed by triumphant strains, while the birds, heard by snatches, filled up the intervals of the music. At noon, we pitched our tents in some shady valley, or embowering wood among the mountains, while a stream prattling over pebbles induced grateful sleep. Our evening march, more calm, was yet more delightful than the morning restlessness of spirit. If the band played, involuntarily they chose airs of moderated passion; the farewell of love, or lament at absence, was followed and closed by some solemn hymn, which harmonized with the tranquil loveliness of evening, and elevated the soul to grand and religious thought. Often all sounds were suspended, that we might listen to the nightingale, while the fire-flies danced in bright measure, and the soft cooing of the aziolo spoke of fair weather to the travellers. Did we pass a valley? Soft shades encompassed us, and rocks tinged with beauteous hues. If we traversed a mountain, Greece, a living map, was spread beneath, her renowned pinnacles cleaving the ether; her rivers threading in silver line the fertile land. Afraid almost to breathe, we English travellers surveyed with extasy this splendid landscape, so different from the sober hues and melancholy graces of our native scenery. When we quitted Macedonia, the fertile but low plains of Thrace afforded fewer beauties; yet our journey continued to be interesting. An advanced guard gave information of our approach, and the country people were quickly in motion to do honour to Lord Raymond. The villages were decorated by triumphal arches of greenery by day, and lamps by night; tapestry waved from the windows, the ground was strewed with flowers, and the name of Raymond, joined to that of Greece, was echoed in the Evive of the peasant crowd.

When we arrived at Kishan, we learnt, that on hearing of the advance of Lord Raymond and his detachment, the Turkish army had retreated from Rodosto; but meeting with a reinforcement, they had re-trod their steps. In the meantime, Argyropylo, the Greek commander-in-chief, had advanced, so as to be between the Turks and Rodosto; a battle, it was said, was inevitable. Perdita and her child were to remain at Kishan. Raymond asked me, if I would not continue with them. "Now by the fells of Cumberland," I cried, "by all of the vagabond and poacher that appertains to me, I will stand at your side, draw my sword in the Greek cause, and be hailed as a victor along with you!"

All the plain, from Kishan to Rodosto, a distance of sixteen leagues, was alive with troops, or with the camp-followers, all in motion at the approach of a battle. The small garrisons were drawn from the various towns and fortresses, and went to swell the main army. We met baggage waggons, and many females of high and low rank returning to Fairy or Kishan, there to wait the issue of the expected day. When we arrived at Rodosto, we found that the field had been taken, and the scheme of the battle arranged. The sound of firing, early on the following morning, informed us that advanced posts of the armies were engaged. Regiment after regiment advanced, their colours flying and bands playing. They planted the cannon on the tumuli, sole elevations in this level country, and formed themselves into column and hollow square; while the pioneers threw up small mounds for their protection.

These then were the preparations for a battle, nay, the battle itself; far different from any thing the imagination had pictured. We read of centre and wing in Greek and Roman history; we fancy a spot, plain as a table, and soldiers small as chessmen; and drawn forth, so that the most ignorant of the game can discover science and order in the disposition of the forces. When I came to the reality, and saw regiments file off to the left far out of sight, fields intervening between the battalions, but a few troops sufficiently near me to observe their motions, I gave up all idea of understanding, even of seeing a battle, but attaching myself to Raymond attended with intense interest to his actions. He shewed himself collected, gallant and imperial; his commands were prompt, his intuition of the events of the day to me miraculous. In the mean time the cannon roared; the music lifted up its enlivening voice at intervals; and we on the highest of the mounds I mentioned, too far off to observe the fallen sheaves which death gathered into his storehouse, beheld the regiments, now lost in smoke, now banners and staves peering above the cloud, while shout and clamour drowned every sound.

Early in the day, Argyropylo was wounded dangerously, and Raymond assumed the command of the whole army. He made few remarks, till, on observing through his glass the sequel of an order he had given, his face, clouded for awhile with doubt, became radiant. "The day is ours," he cried, "the Turks fly from the bayonet." And then swiftly he dispatched his aides-de-camp to command the horse to fall on the routed enemy. The defeat became total; the cannon ceased to roar; the infantry rallied, and horse pursued the flying Turks along the dreary plain; the staff of Raymond was dispersed in various directions, to make observations, and bear commands. Even I was dispatched to a distant part of the field.

The ground on which the battle was fought, was a level plain—so level, that from the tumuli you saw the waving line of mountains on the wide-stretched horizon; yet the intervening space was unvaried by the least irregularity, save such undulations as resembled the waves of the sea. The whole of this part of Thrace had been so long a scene of contest, that it had remained uncultivated, and presented a dreary, barren appearance. The order I had received, was to make an observation of the direction which a detachment of the enemy might have taken, from a northern tumulus; the whole Turkish army, followed by the Greek, had poured eastward; none but the dead remained in the direction of my side. From the top of the mound, I looked far round—all was silent and deserted.

The last beams of the nearly sunken sun shot up from behind the far summit of Mount Athos; the sea of Marmora still glittered beneath its rays, while the Asiatic coast beyond was half hid in a haze of low cloud. Many a casque, and bayonet, and sword, fallen from unnerved arms, reflected the departing ray; they lay scattered far and near. From the east, a band of ravens, old inhabitants of the Turkish cemeteries, came sailing along towards their harvest; the sun disappeared. This hour, melancholy yet sweet, has always seemed to me the time when we are most naturally led to commune with higher powers; our mortal sternness departs, and gentle complacency invests the soul. But now, in the midst of the dying and the dead, how could a thought of heaven or a sensation of tranquility possess one of the murderers? During the busy day, my mind had yielded itself a willing slave to the state of things presented to it by its fellow-beings; historical association, hatred of the foe, and military enthusiasm had held dominion over me. Now, I looked on the evening star, as softly and calmly it hung pendulous in the orange hues of sunset. I turned to the corse-strewn earth; and felt ashamed of my species. So perhaps were the placid skies; for they quickly veiled themselves in mist, and in this change assisted the swift disappearance of twilight usual in the south; heavy masses of cloud floated up from the south east, and red and turbid lightning shot from their dark edges; the rushing wind disturbed the garments of the dead, and was chilled as it passed over their icy forms. Darkness gathered round; the objects about me became indistinct, I descended from my station, and with difficulty guided my horse, so as to avoid the slain.

Suddenly I heard a piercing shriek; a form seemed to rise from the earth; it flew swiftly towards me, sinking to the ground again as it drew near. All this passed so suddenly, that I with difficulty reined in my horse, so that it should not trample on the prostrate being. The dress of this person was that of a soldier, but the bared neck and arms, and the continued shrieks discovered a female thus disguised. I dismounted to her aid, while she, with heavy groans, and her hand placed on her side, resisted my attempt to lead her on. In the hurry of the moment I forgot that I was in Greece, and in my native accents endeavoured to soothe the sufferer. With wild and terrific exclamations did the lost, dying Evadne (for it was she) recognize the language of her lover; pain and fever from her wound had deranged her intellects, while her piteous cries and feeble efforts to escape, penetrated me with compassion. In wild delirium she called upon the name of Raymond; she exclaimed that I was keeping him from her, while the Turks with fearful instruments of torture were about to take his life. Then again she sadly lamented her hard fate; that a woman, with a woman's heart and sensibility, should be driven by hopeless love and vacant hopes to take up the trade of arms, and suffer beyond the endurance of man privation, labour, and pain—the while her dry, hot hand pressed mine, and her brow and lips burned with consuming fire.

As her strength grew less, I lifted her from the ground; her emaciated form hung over my arm, her sunken cheek rested on my breast; in a sepulchral voice she murmured:—"This is the end of love!—Yet not the end!"— and frenzy lent her strength as she cast her arm up to heaven: "there is the end! there we meet again. Many living deaths have I borne for thee, O Raymond, and now I expire, thy victim!—By my death I purchase thee— lo! the instruments of war, fire, the plague are my servitors. I dared, I conquered them all, till now! I have sold myself to death, with the sole condition that thou shouldst follow me—Fire, and war, and plague, unite for thy destruction—O my Raymond, there is no safety for thee!"

With an heavy heart I listened to the changes of her delirium; I made her a bed of cloaks; her violence decreased and a clammy dew stood on her brow as the paleness of death succeeded to the crimson of fever, I placed her on the cloaks. She continued to rave of her speedy meeting with her beloved in the grave, of his death nigh at hand; sometimes she solemnly declared that he was summoned; sometimes she bewailed his hard destiny. Her voice grew feebler, her speech interrupted; a few convulsive movements, and her muscles relaxed, the limbs fell, no more to be sustained, one deep sigh, and life was gone.

I bore her from the near neighbourhood of the dead; wrapt in cloaks, I placed her beneath a tree. Once more I looked on her altered face; the last time I saw her she was eighteen; beautiful as poet's vision, splendid as a Sultana of the East—Twelve years had past; twelve years of change, sorrow and hardship; her brilliant complexion had become worn and dark, her limbs had lost the roundness of youth and womanhood; her eyes had sunk deep,

> Crushed and o'erworn,
> The hours had drained her blood, and filled her brow
> With lines and wrinkles.[2]

With shuddering horror I veiled this monument of human passion and human misery; I heaped over her all of flags and heavy accoutrements I could find, to guard her from birds and beasts of prey, until I could bestow on her a fitting grave. Sadly and slowly I stemmed my course from among the heaps of slain, and, guided by the twinkling lights of the town, at length reached Rodosto.

---

1. Lord Byron's Fourth Canto of Childe Harolde.
2. Shakspeare's Sonnets.

❧ 2 ❧

ON MY ARRIVAL, I found that an order had already gone forth for the army to proceed immediately towards Constantinople; and the troops which had suffered least in the battle were already on their way. The town was full of tumult. The wound, and consequent inability of Argyropylo, caused Raymond to be the first in command. He rode through the town, visiting the wounded, and giving such orders as were necessary for the siege he meditated. Early in the morning the whole army was in motion. In the hurry I could hardly find an opportunity to bestow the last offices on Evadne. Attended only by my servant, I dug a deep grave for her at the foot of the tree, and without disturbing her warrior shroud, I placed her in it, heaping stones upon the grave. The dazzling sun and glare of daylight, deprived the scene of solemnity; from Evadne's low tomb, I joined Raymond and his staff, now on their way to the Golden City.

Constantinople was invested, trenches dug, and advances made. The whole Greek fleet blockaded it by sea; on land from the river Kyat Kbanah, near the Sweet Waters, to the Tower of Marmora, on the shores of the Propontis, along the whole line of the ancient walls, the trenches of the siege were drawn. We already possessed Pera; the Golden Horn itself, the city, bastioned by the sea, and the ivy-mantled walls of the Greek emperors was all of Europe that the Mahometans could call theirs. Our army looked on her as certain prey. They counted the garrison; it was impossible that it should be relieved; each sally was a victory; for, even when the Turks were triumphant, the loss of men they sustained was an irreparable injury. I rode one morning with Raymond to the lofty mound, not far from the Top Kapou, (Cannon-gate), on which Mahmoud planted his standard, and first saw the city. Still the same lofty domes and minarets towered above the verdurous walls, where Constantine had died, and the Turk had entered the city. The plain around was interspersed with cemeteries, Turk, Greek, and Armenian, with their growth of cypress trees; and other woods of more cheerful aspect, diversified the scene. Among them the Greek army was encamped, and their squadrons moved to and fro—now in regular march, now in swift career.

Raymond's eyes were fixed on the city. "I have counted the hours of her life," said he; "one month, and she falls. Remain with me till then; wait till you see the cross on St. Sophia; and then return to your peaceful glades."

"You then," I asked, "still remain in Greece?"

"Assuredly," replied Raymond. "Yet Lionel, when I say this, believe me I look back with regret to our tranquil life at Windsor. I am but half a soldier; I love the renown, but not the trade of war. Before the battle of Rodosto I was full of hope and spirit; to conquer there, and afterwards to take Constantinople, was the hope, the bourne, the fulfilment of my ambition. This enthusiasm is now spent, I know not why; I seem to myself to be entering a darksome gulph; the ardent spirit of the army is irksome to me, the rapture of triumph null."

He paused, and was lost in thought. His serious mien recalled, by some association, the half-forgotten Evadne to my mind, and I seized this opportunity to make enquiries from him concerning her strange lot. I asked him, if he had ever seen among the troops any one resembling her; if since he had returned to Greece he had heard of her?

He started at her name,—he looked uneasily on me. "Even so," he cried, "I knew you would speak of her. Long, long I had forgotten her. Since our encampment here, she daily, hourly visits my thoughts. When I am addressed, her name is the sound I expect: in every communication, I imagine that she will form a part. At length you have broken the spell; tell me what you know of her."

I related my meeting with her; the story of her death was told and re-told. With painful earnestness he questioned me concerning her prophecies with regard to him. I treated them as the ravings of a maniac. "No, no," he said, "do not deceive yourself,—me you cannot. She has said nothing but what I knew before—though this is confirmation. Fire, the sword, and plague! They may all be found in yonder city; on my head alone may they fall!"

From this day Raymond's melancholy increased. He secluded himself as much as the duties of his station permitted. When in company, sadness would in spite of every effort steal over his features, and he sat absent and mute among the busy crowd that thronged about him. Perdita rejoined him, and before her he forced himself to appear cheerful, for she, even as a mirror, changed as he changed, and if he were silent and anxious, she solicitously inquired concerning, and endeavoured to remove the cause of his seriousness. She resided at the palace of Sweet Waters, a summer seraglio of the Sultan; the beauty of the surrounding scenery, undefiled by war, and the freshness of the river, made this spot doubly delightful. Raymond felt no relief, received no pleasure from any show of heaven or earth. He often left Perdita, to wander in the grounds alone; or in a light shallop he floated idly on the pure waters, musing deeply. Sometimes I joined him; at such times his countenance was invariably solemn, his air dejected. He seemed relieved on seeing me, and would talk with some degree of interest on the affairs of the day. There was evidently something behind all this; yet, when he appeared about to speak of that which was nearest his heart, he would abruptly turn away, and with a sigh endeavour to deliver the painful idea to the winds.

It had often occurred, that, when, as I said, Raymond quitted Perdita's drawing-room, Clara came up to me, and gently drawing me aside, said, "Papa is gone; shall we go to him? I dare say he will be glad to see you." And, as accident permitted, I complied with or refused her request. One evening a numerous assembly of Greek chieftains were gathered together in the palace. The intriguing Palli, the accomplished Karazza, the warlike Ypsilanti, were among the principal. They talked of the events of the day; the skirmish at noon; the diminished numbers of the Infidels; their defeat and flight: they contemplated, after a short interval of time, the capture of the Golden City. They endeavoured to picture forth what would then happen, and spoke in lofty terms of the prosperity of Greece, when Constantinople should become its capital. The conversation then reverted to Asiatic intelligence, and the ravages the plague made in its chief cities; conjectures were hazarded as to the progress that disease might have made in the besieged city.

Raymond had joined in the former part of the discussion. In lively terms he demonstrated the extremities to which Constantinople was reduced; the wasted and haggard, though ferocious appearance of the troops; famine and pestilence was at work for them, he observed, and the infidels would soon be obliged to take refuge in their only hope—submission. Suddenly in the midst of his harangue he broke off, as if stung by some painful thought; he rose uneasily, and I perceived him at length quit the hall, and through the long corridor seek the open air. He did not return; and soon Clara crept round to me, making the accustomed invitation. I consented to her request, and taking her little hand, followed Raymond. We found him just about to embark in his boat, and he readily agreed to receive us as companions. After the heats of the day, the cooling land-breeze ruffled the river, and filled our little sail. The city looked dark to the south, while numerous lights along the near shores, and the beautiful aspect of the banks reposing in placid night, the waters keenly reflecting the heavenly lights, gave to this beauteous river a dower of loveliness that might have characterized a retreat in Paradise. Our single boatman attended to the sail; Raymond steered; Clara sat at his feet, clasping his knees with her arms, and laying her head on them. Raymond began the conversation somewhat abruptly.

"This, my friend, is probably the last time we shall have an opportunity of conversing freely; my plans are now in full operation, and my time will become more and more occupied. Besides, I wish at once to tell you my wishes and expectations, and then never again to revert to so painful a subject. First, I must thank you, Lionel, for having remained here at my request. Vanity first prompted me to ask you: vanity, I call it; yet even in this I see the hand of fate— your presence will soon be necessary; you will become the last resource of Perdita, her protector and consoler. You will take her back to Windsor."—

"Not without you," I said. "You do not mean to separate again?"

"Do not deceive yourself," replied Raymond, "the separation at hand is one over which I have no control; most near at hand is it; the days are already counted. May I trust you? For many days I have longed to disclose the mysterious presentiments that weigh on me, although I fear that you will ridicule them. Yet do not, my gentle friend; for, all childish and unwise as they are, they have become a part of me, and I dare not expect to shake them off.

"Yet how can I expect you to sympathize with me? You are of this world; I am not. You hold forth your hand; it is even as a part of yourself; and you do not yet divide the feeling of identity from the mortal form that shapes forth Lionel. How then can you understand me? Earth is to me a tomb, the firmament a vault, shrouding mere corruption. Time is no more, for I have stepped within the threshold of eternity; each man I meet appears a corse, which will soon be deserted of its animating spark, on the eve of decay and corruption.

> Cada piedra un piramide levanta, y cada flor costruye un monumento, cada edificio es un sepulcro altivo, cada soldado un esqueleto vivo."[1]

His accent was mournful,—he sighed deeply. "A few months ago," he continued, "I was thought to be dying; but life was strong within me. My affections were human; hope and love were the day-stars of my life. Now— they dream that the brows of the conqueror of the infidel faith are about to be encircled by triumphant laurel; they talk of honourable reward, of title, power, and wealth—all I ask of Greece is a grave. Let them raise a mound above my lifeless body, which may stand even when the dome of St. Sophia has fallen.

"Wherefore do I feel thus? At Rodosto I was full of hope; but when first I saw Constantinople, that feeling, with every other joyful one, departed. The last words of Evadne were the seal upon the warrant of my death. Yet I do not pretend to account for my mood by any particular event. All I can say is, that it is so. The plague I am told is in Constantinople, perhaps I have imbibed its effluvia—perhaps disease is the real cause of my prognostications. It matters little why or wherefore I am affected, no power can avert the stroke, and the shadow of Fate's uplifted hand already darkens me.

"To you, Lionel, I entrust your sister and her child. Never mention to her the fatal name of Evadne. She would doubly sorrow over the strange link that enchains me to her, making my spirit obey her dying voice, following her, as it is about to do, to the unknown country."

I listened to him with wonder; but that his sad demeanour and solemn utterance assured me of the truth and intensity of his feelings, I should with light derision have attempted to dissipate his fears. Whatever I was about to reply, was interrupted by the powerful emotions of Clara. Raymond had spoken, thoughtless of her presence, and she, poor child, heard with terror and faith the prophecy of his death. Her father was moved by her violent grief; he took her in his arms and soothed her, but his very soothings were solemn and fearful. "Weep not, sweet child," said he, "the coming death of one you have hardly known. I may die, but in death I can never forget or desert my own Clara. In after sorrow or joy, believe that you father's spirit is near, to save or sympathize with you. Be proud of me, and cherish your infant remembrance of me. Thus, sweetest, I shall not appear to die. One thing you must promise,—not to speak to any one but your uncle, of the conversation you have just overheard. When I am gone, you will console your mother, and tell her that death was only bitter because it divided me from her; that my last thoughts will be spent on her. But while I live, promise not to betray me; promise, my child."

With faltering accents Clara promised, while she still clung to her father in a transport of sorrow. Soon we returned to shore, and I endeavoured to obviate the impression made on the child's mind, by treating Raymond's fears lightly. We heard no more of them; for, as he had said, the siege, now drawing to a conclusion, became paramount in interest, engaging all his time and attention.

The empire of the Mahometans in Europe was at its close. The Greek fleet blockading every port of Stamboul, prevented the arrival of succour from Asia; all egress on the side towards land had become impracticable, except to such desperate sallies, as reduced the numbers of the enemy without making any impression on our lines. The garrison was now so much diminished, that it was evident that the city could easily have been carried by storm; but both humanity and policy dictated a slower mode of proceeding. We could hardly doubt that, if pursued to the utmost, its palaces, its temples and store of wealth would be destroyed in the fury of contending triumph and defeat. Already the defenceless citizens had suffered through the barbarity of the Janisaries; and, in time of storm, tumult and massacre, beauty, infancy and decrepitude, would have alike been sacrificed to the brutal ferocity of the soldiers. Famine and blockade were certain means of conquest; and on these we founded our hopes of victory.

Each day the soldiers of the garrison assaulted our advanced posts, and impeded the accomplishment of our works. Fire-boats were launched from the various ports, while our troops sometimes recoiled from the devoted courage of men who did not seek to live, but to sell their lives dearly. These contests were aggravated by the season: they took place during summer, when the southern Asiatic wind came laden with intolerable heat, when the streams were dried up in their shallow beds, and the vast basin of the sea appeared to glow under the unmitigated rays of the solsticial sun. Nor did night refresh the earth. Dew was denied; herbage and flowers there were none; the very trees drooped; and summer assumed the blighted appearance of winter, as it went forth in silence and flame to abridge the means of sustenance to man. In vain did the eye strive to find the wreck of some northern cloud in the stainless empyrean, which might bring hope of change and moisture to the oppressive and windless atmosphere. All was serene, burning, annihilating. We the besiegers were in the comparison little affected by these evils. The woods around afforded us shade,—the river secured to us a constant supply of water; nay, detachments were employed in furnishing the army with ice, which had been laid up on Haemus, and Athos, and the mountains of Macedonia, while cooling fruits and wholesome food renovated the strength of the labourers, and made us bear with less impatience the weight of the unrefreshing air. But in the city things wore a different face. The sun's rays were refracted from the pavement and buildings—the stoppage of the public fountains—the bad quality of the food, and scarcity even of that, produced a state of suffering, which was aggravated by the scourge of disease; while the garrison arrogated every superfluity to themselves, adding by waste and riot to the necessary evils of the time. Still they would not capitulate.

Suddenly the system of warfare was changed. We experienced no more assaults; and by night and day we continued our labours unimpeded. Stranger still, when the troops advanced near the city, the walls were vacant, and no cannon was pointed against the intruders. When these circumstances were reported to Raymond, he caused minute observations to be made as to what was doing within the walls, and when his scouts returned, reporting only the continued silence and desolation of the city, he commanded the army to be drawn out before the gates. No one appeared on the walls; the very portals, though locked and barred, seemed unguarded; above, the many domes and glittering crescents pierced heaven; while the old walls, survivors of ages, with ivy-crowned tower and weed-tangled buttress, stood as rocks in an uninhabited waste. From within the city neither shout nor cry, nor aught except the casual howling of a dog, broke the noon-day stillness. Even our soldiers were awed to silence; the music paused; the clang of arms was hushed. Each man asked his fellow in whispers, the meaning of this sudden peace; while Raymond from an height endeavoured, by means of glasses, to discover and observe the stratagem of the enemy. No form could be discerned on the terraces of the houses; in the higher parts of the town no moving shadow bespoke the presence of any living being: the very trees waved not, and mocked the stability of architecture with like immovability.

The tramp of horses, distinctly heard in the silence, was at length discerned. It was a troop sent by Karazza, the Admiral; they bore dispatches to the Lord General. The contents of these papers were important. The night before, the watch, on board one of the smaller vessels anchored near the seraglio wall, was roused by a slight splashing as of muffled oars; the alarm was given: twelve small boats, each containing three Janizaries, were descried endeavouring to make their way through the fleet to the opposite shore of Scutari. When they found themselves discovered they discharged their muskets, and some came to the front to cover the others, whose crews, exerting all their strength, endeavoured to escape with their light barks from among the dark hulls that environed them. They were in the end all sunk, and, with the exception of two or three prisoners, the crews drowned. Little could be got from the survivors; but their cautious answers caused it to be surmised that several expeditions had preceded this last, and that several Turks of rank and importance had been conveyed to Asia. The men disdainfully repelled the idea of having deserted the defence of their city; and one, the youngest among them, in answer to the taunt of a sailor, exclaimed, "Take it, Christian dogs! take the palaces, the gardens, the mosques, the abode of our fathers—take plague with them; pestilence is the enemy we fly; if she be your friend, hug her to your bosoms. The curse of Allah is on Stamboul, share ye her fate."

Such was the account sent by Karazza to Raymond: but a tale full of monstrous exaggerations, though founded on this, was spread by the accompanying troop among our soldiers. A murmur arose, the city was the prey of pestilence; already had a mighty power subjugated the inhabitants; Death had become lord of Constantinople.

I have heard a picture described, wherein all the inhabitants of earth were drawn out in fear to stand the encounter of Death. The feeble and decrepid fled; the warriors retreated, though they threatened even in flight. Wolves and lions, and various monsters of the desert roared against him; while the grim Unreality hovered shaking his spectral dart, a solitary but invincible assailant. Even so was it with the army of Greece. I am convinced, that had the myriad troops of Asia come from over the Propontis, and stood defenders of the Golden City, each and every Greek would have marched against the overwhelming numbers, and have devoted himself with patriotic fury for his country. But here no hedge of bayonets opposed itself, no death-dealing artillery, no formidable array of brave soldiers—the unguarded walls afforded easy entrance—the vacant palaces luxurious dwellings; but above the dome of St. Sophia the superstitious Greek saw Pestilence, and shrunk in trepidation from her influence.

Raymond was actuated by far other feelings. He descended the hill with a face beaming with triumph, and pointing with his sword to the gates, commanded his troops to—down with those barricades—the only obstacles now to completest victory. The soldiers answered his cheerful words with aghast and awe-struck looks; instinctively they drew back, and Raymond rode in the front of the lines:—"By my sword I swear," he cried, "that no ambush or stratagem endangers you. The enemy is already vanquished; the pleasant places, the noble dwellings and spoil of the city are already yours; force the gate; enter and possess the seats of your ancestors, your own inheritance!"

An universal shudder and fearful whispering passed through the lines; not a soldier moved. "Cowards!" exclaimed their general, exasperated, "give me an hatchet! I alone will enter! I will plant your standard; and when you see it wave from yon highest minaret, you may gain courage, and rally round it!"

One of the officers now came forward: "General," he said, "we neither fear the courage, nor arms, the open attack, nor secret ambush of the Moslems. We are ready to expose our breasts, exposed ten thousand times before, to the balls and scymetars of the infidels, and to fall gloriously for Greece. But we will not die in heaps, like dogs poisoned in summer-time, by the pestilential air of that city—we dare not go against the Plague!"

A multitude of men are feeble and inert, without a voice, a leader; give them that, and they regain the strength belonging to their numbers. Shouts from a thousand voices now rent the air —the cry of applause became universal. Raymond saw the danger; he was willing to save his troops from the crime of disobedience; for he knew, that contention once begun between the commander and his army, each act and word added to the weakness of the former, and bestowed power on the latter. He gave orders for the retreat to be sounded, and the regiments repaired in good order to the camp.

I hastened to carry the intelligence of these strange proceedings to Perdita; and we were soon joined by Raymond. He looked gloomy and perturbed. My sister was struck by my narrative: "How beyond the imagination of man," she exclaimed, "are the decrees of heaven, wondrous and inexplicable!"

"Foolish girl," cried Raymond angrily, "are you like my valiant soldiers, panic-struck? What is there inexplicable, pray, tell me, in so very natural an occurrence? Does not the plague rage each year in Stamboul? What wonder, that this year, when as we are told, its virulence is unexampled in Asia, that it should have occasioned double havoc in that city? What wonder then, in time of siege, want, extreme heat, and drought, that it should make unaccustomed ravages? Less wonder far is it, that the garrison, despairing of being able to hold out longer, should take advantage of the negligence of our fleet to escape at once from siege and capture. It is not pestilence —by the God that lives! it is not either plague or impending danger that makes us, like birds in harvest-time, terrified by a scarecrow, abstain from the ready prey—it is base superstition—And thus the aim of the valiant is made the shuttlecock of fools; the worthy ambition of the high-souled, the plaything of these tamed hares! But yet Stamboul shall be ours! By my past labours, by torture and imprisonment suffered for them, by my victories, by my sword, I swear—by my hopes of fame, by my former deserts now awaiting their reward, I deeply vow, with these hands to plant the cross on yonder mosque!"

"Dearest Raymond!" interrupted Perdita, in a supplicating accent.

He had been walking to and fro in the marble hall of the seraglio; his very lips were pale with rage, while, quivering, they shaped his angry words— his eyes shot fire—his gestures seemed restrained by their very vehemence. "Perdita," he continued, impatiently, "I know what you would say; I know that you love me, that you are good and gentle; but this is no woman's work—nor can a female heart guess at the hurricane which tears me!"

He seemed half afraid of his own violence, and suddenly quitted the hall: a look from Perdita shewed me her distress, and I followed him. He was pacing the garden: his passions were in a state of inconceivable turbulence. "Am I for ever," he cried, "to be the sport of fortune! Must man, the heaven-climber, be for ever the victim of the crawling reptiles of his species! Were I as you, Lionel, looking forward to many years of life, to a succession of love-enlightened days, to refined enjoyments and fresh-springing hopes, I might yield, and breaking my General's staff, seek repose in the glades of Windsor. But I am about to die!—nay, interrupt me not—soon I shall die. From the many-peopled earth, from the sympathies of man, from the loved resorts of my youth, from the kindness of my friends, from the affection of my only beloved Perdita, I am about to be removed. Such is the will of fate! Such the decree of the High Ruler from whom there is no appeal: to whom I submit. But to lose all—to lose with life and love, glory also! It shall not be!

"I, and in a few brief years, all you,—this panic-struck army, and all the population of fair Greece, will no longer be. But other generations will arise, and ever and for ever will continue, to be made happier by our present acts, to be glorified by our valour. The prayer of my youth was to be one among those who render the pages of earth's history splendid; who exalt the race of man, and make this little globe a dwelling of the mighty. Alas, for Raymond! the prayer of his youth is wasted—the hopes of his manhood are null!

"From my dungeon in yonder city I cried, soon I will be thy lord! When Evadne pronounced my death, I thought that the title of Victor of Constantinople would be written on my tomb, and I subdued all mortal fear. I stand before its vanquished walls, and dare not call myself a conqueror. So shall it not be! Did not Alexander leap from the walls of the city of the Oxydracae, to shew his coward troops the way to victory, encountering alone the swords of its defenders? Even so will I brave the plague—and though no man follow, I will plant the Grecian standard on the height of St. Sophia."

Reason came unavailing to such high-wrought feelings. In vain I shewed him, that when winter came, the cold would dissipate the pestilential air, and restore courage to the Greeks. "Talk not of other season than this!" he cried. "I have lived my last winter, and the date of this year, 2092, will be carved upon my tomb. Already do I see," he continued, looking up mournfully, "the bourne and precipitate edge of my existence, over which I plunge into the gloomy mystery of the life to come. I am prepared, so that I leave behind a trail of light so radiant, that my worst enemies cannot cloud it. I owe this to Greece, to you, to my surviving Perdita, and to myself, the victim of ambition."

We were interrupted by an attendant, who announced, that the staff of Raymond was assembled in the council-chamber. He requested me in the meantime to ride through the camp, and to observe and report to him the dispositions of the soldiers; he then left me. I had been excited to the utmost by the proceedings of the day, and now more than ever by the passionate language of Raymond. Alas! for human reason! He accused the Greeks of superstition: what name did he give to the faith he lent to the predictions of Evadne? I passed from the palace of Sweet Waters to the plain on which the encampment lay, and found its inhabitants in commotion. The arrival of several with fresh stories of marvels, from the fleet; the exaggerations bestowed on what was already known; tales of old prophecies, of fearful histories of whole regions which had been laid waste during the present year by pestilence, alarmed and occupied the troops. Discipline was lost; the army disbanded itself. Each individual, before a part of a great whole moving only in unison with others, now became resolved into the unit nature had made him, and thought of himself only. They stole off at first by ones and twos, then in larger companies, until, unimpeded by the officers, whole battalions sought the road that led to Macedonia.

About midnight I returned to the palace and sought Raymond; he was alone, and apparently composed; such composure, at least, was his as is inspired by a resolve to adhere to a certain line of conduct. He heard my account of the self-dissolution of the army with calmness, and then said, "You know, Verney, my fixed determination not to quit this place, until in the light of day Stamboul is confessedly ours. If the men I have about me shrink from following me, others, more courageous, are to be found. Go you before break of day, bear these dispatches to Karazza, add to them your own entreaties that he send me his marines and naval force; if I can get but one regiment to second me, the rest would follow of course. Let him send me this regiment. I shall expect your return by to-morrow noon."

Methought this was but a poor expedient; but I assured him of my obedience and zeal. I quitted him to take a few hours rest. With the breaking of morning I was accoutred for my ride. I lingered awhile, desirous of taking leave of Perdita, and from my window observed the approach of the sun. The golden splendour arose, and weary nature awoke to suffer yet another day of heat and thirsty decay. No flowers lifted up their dew-laden cups to meet the dawn; the dry grass had withered on the plains; the burning fields of air were vacant of birds; the cicale alone, children of the sun, began their shrill and deafening song among the cypresses and olives. I saw Raymond's coal-black charger brought to the palace gate; a small company of officers arrived soon after; care and fear was painted on each cheek, and in each eye, unrefreshed by sleep. I found Raymond and Perdita together. He was watching the rising sun, while with one arm he encircled his beloved's waist; she looked on him, the sun of her life, with earnest gaze of mingled anxiety and tenderness. Raymond started angrily when he saw me. "Here still?" he cried. "Is this your promised zeal?"

"Pardon me," I said, "but even as you speak, I am gone."

"Nay, pardon me," he replied; "I have no right to command or reproach; but my life hangs on your departure and speedy return. Farewell!"

His voice had recovered its bland tone, but a dark cloud still hung on his features. I would have delayed; I wished to recommend watchfulness to Perdita, but his presence restrained me. I had no pretence for my hesitation; and on his repeating his farewell, I clasped his outstretched hand; it was cold and clammy. "Take care of yourself, my dear Lord," I said.

"Nay," said Perdita, "that task shall be mine. Return speedily, Lionel." With an air of absence he was playing with her auburn locks, while she leaned on him; twice I turned back, only to look again on this matchless pair. At last, with slow and heavy steps, I had paced out of the hall, and sprung upon my horse. At that moment Clara flew towards me; clasping my knee she cried, "Make haste back, uncle! Dear uncle, I have such fearful dreams; I dare not tell my mother. Do not be long away!" I assured her of my impatience to return, and then, with a small escort rode along the plain towards the tower of Marmora.

I fulfilled my commission; I saw Karazza. He was somewhat surprised; he would see, he said, what could be done; but it required time; and Raymond had ordered me to return by noon. It was impossible to effect any thing in so short a time. I must stay till the next day; or come back, after having reported the present state of things to the general. My choice was easily made. A restlessness, a fear of what was about to betide, a doubt as to Raymond's purposes, urged me to return without delay to his quarters. Quitting the Seven Towers, I rode eastward towards the Sweet Waters. I took a circuitous path, principally for the sake of going to the top of the mount before mentioned, which commanded a view of the city. I had my glass with me. The city basked under the noon-day sun, and the venerable walls formed its picturesque boundary. Immediately before me was the Top Kapou, the gate near which Mahomet had made the breach by which he entered the city. Trees gigantic and aged grew near; before the gate I discerned a crowd of moving human figures—with intense curiosity I lifted my glass to my eye. I saw Lord Raymond on his charger; a small company of officers had gathered about him; and behind was a promiscuous concourse of soldiers and subalterns, their discipline lost, their arms thrown aside; no music sounded, no banners streamed. The only flag among them was one which Raymond carried; he pointed with it to the gate of the city. The circle round him fell back. With angry gestures he leapt from his horse, and seizing a hatchet that hung from his saddle-bow, went with the apparent intention of battering down the opposing gate. A few men came to aid him; their numbers increased; under their united blows the obstacle was vanquished, gate, portcullis, and fence were demolished; and the wide sun-lit way, leading to the heart of the city, now lay open before them. The men shrank back; they seemed afraid of what they had already done, and stood as if they expected some Mighty Phantom to stalk in offended majesty from the opening. Raymond sprung lightly on his horse, grasped the standard, and with words which I could not hear (but his gestures, being their fit accompaniment, were marked by passionate energy,) he seemed to adjure their assistance and companionship; even as he spoke, the crowd receded from him. Indignation now transported him; his words I guessed were fraught with disdain—then turning from his coward followers, he addressed himself to enter the city alone. His very horse seemed to back from the fatal entrance; his dog, his faithful dog, lay moaning and supplicating in his path—in a moment more, he had plunged the rowels into the sides of the stung animal, who bounded forward, and he, the gateway passed, was galloping up the broad and desart street.

Until this moment my soul had been in my eyes only. I had gazed with wonder, mixed with fear and enthusiasm. The latter feeling now predominated. I forgot the distance between us: "I will go with thee, Raymond!" I cried; but, my eye removed from the glass, I could scarce discern the pigmy forms of the crowd, which about a mile from me surrounded the gate; the form of Raymond was lost. Stung with impatience, I urged my horse with force of spur and loosened reins down the acclivity, that, before danger could arrive, I might be at the side of my noble, godlike friend. A number of buildings and trees intervened, when I had reached the plain, hiding the city from my view. But at that moment a crash was heard. Thunderlike it reverberated through the sky, while the air was darkened. A moment more and the old walls again met my sight, while over them hovered a murky cloud; fragments of buildings whirled above, half seen in smoke, while flames burst out beneath, and continued explosions filled the air with terrific thunders. Flying from the mass of falling ruin which leapt over the high walls, and shook the ivy towers, a crowd of soldiers made for the road by which I came; I was surrounded, hemmed in by them, unable to get forward. My impatience rose to its utmost; I stretched out my hands to the men; I conjured them to turn back and save their General, the conqueror of Stamboul, the liberator of Greece; tears, aye tears, in warm flow gushed from my eyes—I would not believe in his destruction; yet every mass that darkened the air seemed to bear with it a portion of the martyred Raymond. Horrible sights were shaped to me in the turbid cloud that hovered over the city; and my only relief was derived from the struggles I made to approach the gate. Yet when I effected my purpose, all I could discern within the precincts of the massive walls was a city of fire: the open way through which Raymond had ridden was enveloped in smoke and flame. After an interval the explosions ceased, but the flames still shot up from various quarters; the dome of St. Sophia had disappeared. Strange to say (the result perhaps of the concussion of air occasioned by the blowing up of the city) huge, white thunder clouds lifted themselves up from the southern horizon, and gathered over-head; they were the first blots on the blue expanse that I had seen for months, and amidst this havoc and despair they inspired pleasure. The vault above became obscured, lightning flashed from the heavy masses, followed instantaneously by crashing thunder; then the big rain fell. The flames of the city bent beneath it; and the smoke and dust arising from the ruins was dissipated.

I no sooner perceived an abatement of the flames than, hurried on by an irresistible impulse, I endeavoured to penetrate the town. I could only do this on foot, as the mass of ruin was impracticable for a horse. I had never entered the city before, and its ways were unknown to me. The streets were blocked up, the ruins smoking; I climbed up one heap, only to view others in succession; and nothing told me where the centre of the town might be, or towards what point Raymond might have directed his course. The rain ceased; the clouds sunk behind the horizon; it was now evening, and the sun descended swiftly the western sky. I scrambled on, until I came to a street, whose wooden houses, half-burnt, had been cooled by the rain, and were fortunately uninjured by the gunpowder. Up this I hurried—until now I had not seen a vestige of man. Yet none of the defaced human forms which I distinguished, could be Raymond; so I turned my eyes away, while my heart sickened within me. I came to an open space—a mountain of ruin in the midst, announced that some large mosque had occupied the space—and here, scattered about, I saw various articles of luxury and wealth, singed, destroyed—but shewing what they had been in their ruin—jewels, strings of pearls, embroidered robes, rich furs, glittering tapestries, and oriental ornaments, seemed to have been collected here in a pile destined for destruction; but the rain had stopped the havoc midway.

Hours passed, while in this scene of ruin I sought for Raymond. Insurmountable heaps sometimes opposed themselves; the still burning fires scorched me. The sun set; the atmosphere grew dim—and the evening star no longer shone companionless. The glare of flames attested the progress of destruction, while, during mingled light and obscurity, the piles around me took gigantic proportions and weird shapes. For a moment I could yield to the creative power of the imagination, and for a moment was soothed by the sublime fictions it presented to me. The beatings of my human heart drew me back to blank reality. Where, in this wilderness of death, art thou, O Raymond—ornament of England, deliverer of Greece, "hero of unwritten story," where in this burning chaos are thy dear relics strewed? I called aloud for him—through the darkness of night, over the scorching ruins of fallen Constantinople, his name was heard; no voice replied—echo even was mute.

I was overcome by weariness; the solitude depressed my spirits. The sultry air impregnated with dust, the heat and smoke of burning palaces, palsied my limbs. Hunger suddenly came acutely upon me. The excitement which had hitherto sustained me was lost; as a building, whose props are loosened, and whose foundations rock, totters and falls, so when enthusiasm and hope deserted me, did my strength fail. I sat on the sole remaining step of an edifice, which even in its downfall, was huge and magnificent; a few broken walls, not dislodged by gunpowder, stood in fantastic groupes, and a flame glimmered at intervals on the summit of the pile. For a time hunger and sleep contended, till the constellations reeled before my eyes and then were lost. I strove to rise, but my heavy lids closed, my limbs over-wearied, claimed repose—I rested my head on the stone, I yielded to the grateful sensation of utter forgetfulness; and in that scene of desolation, on that night of despair—I slept.

---

1. Calderon de la Barca.

THE STARS still shone brightly when I awoke, and Taurus high in the southern heaven shewed that it was midnight. I awoke from disturbed dreams. Methought I had been invited to Timon's last feast; I came with keen appetite, the covers were removed, the hot water sent up its unsatisfying steams, while I fled before the anger of the host, who assumed the form of Raymond; while to my diseased fancy, the vessels hurled by him after me, were surcharged with fetid vapour, and my friend's shape, altered by a thousand distortions, expanded into a gigantic phantom, bearing on its brow the sign of pestilence. The growing shadow rose and rose, filling, and then seeming to endeavour to burst beyond, the adamantine vault that bent over, sustaining and enclosing the world. The night-mare became torture; with a strong effort I threw off sleep, and recalled reason to her wonted functions. My first thought was Perdita; to her I must return; her I must support, drawing such food from despair as might best sustain her wounded heart; recalling her from the wild excesses of grief, by the austere laws of duty, and the soft tenderness of regret.

The position of the stars was my only guide. I turned from the awful ruin of the Golden City, and, after great exertion, succeeded in extricating myself from its enclosure. I met a company of soldiers outside the walls; I borrowed a horse from one of them, and hastened to my sister. The appearance of the plain was changed during this short interval; the encampment was broken up; the relics of the disbanded army met in small companies here and there; each face was clouded; every gesture spoke astonishment and dismay.

With an heavy heart I entered the palace, and stood fearful to advance, to speak, to look. In the midst of the hall was Perdita; she sat on the marble pavement, her head fallen on her bosom, her hair dishevelled, her fingers twined busily one within the other; she was pale as marble, and every feature was contracted by agony. She perceived me, and looked up enquiringly; her half glance of hope was misery; the words died before I could articulate them; I felt a ghastly smile wrinkle my lips. She understood my gesture; again her head fell; again her fingers worked restlessly. At last I recovered speech, but my voice terrified her; the hapless girl had understood my look, and for worlds she would not that the tale of her heavy misery should have been shaped out and confirmed by hard, irrevocable words. Nay, she seemed to wish to distract my thoughts from the subject: she rose from the floor: "Hush!" she said, whisperingly; "after much weeping, Clara sleeps; we must not disturb her." She seated herself then on the same ottoman where I had left her in the morning resting on the beating heart of her Raymond; I dared not approach her, but sat at a distant corner, watching her starting and nervous gestures. At length, in an abrupt manner she asked, "Where is he?"

"O, fear not," she continued, "fear not that I should entertain hope! Yet tell me, have you found him? To have him once more in my arms, to see him, however changed, is all I desire. Though Constantinople be heaped above him as a tomb, yet I must find him—then cover us with the city's weight, with a mountain piled above—I care not, so that one grave hold Raymond and his Perdita." Then weeping, she clung to me: "Take me to him," she cried, "unkind Lionel, why do you keep me here? Of myself I cannot find him —but you know where he lies—lead me thither."

At first these agonizing plaints filled me with intolerable compassion. But soon I endeavoured to extract patience for her from the ideas she suggested. I related my adventures of the night, my endeavours to find our lost one, and my disappointment. Turning her thoughts this way, I gave them an object which rescued them from insanity. With apparent calmness she discussed with me the probable spot where he might be found, and planned the means we should use for that purpose. Then hearing of my fatigue and abstinence, she herself brought me food. I seized the favourable moment, and endeavoured to awaken in her something beyond the killing torpor of grief. As I spoke, my subject carried me away; deep admiration; grief, the offspring of truest affection, the overflowing of a heart bursting with sympathy for all that had been great and sublime in the career of my friend, inspired me as I poured forth the praises of Raymond.

"Alas, for us," I cried, "who have lost this latest honour of the world! Beloved Raymond! He is gone to the nations of the dead; he has become one of those, who render the dark abode of the obscure grave illustrious by dwelling there. He has journied on the road that leads to it, and joined the mighty of soul who went before him. When the world was in its infancy death must have been terrible, and man left his friends and kindred to dwell, a solitary stranger, in an unknown country. But now, he who dies finds many companions gone before to prepare for his reception. The great of past ages people it, the exalted hero of our own days is counted among its inhabitants, while life becomes doubly 'the desart and the solitude.'

"What a noble creature was Raymond, the first among the men of our time. By the grandeur of his conceptions, the graceful daring of his actions, by his wit and beauty, he won and ruled the minds of all. Of one only fault he might have been accused; but his death has cancelled that. I have heard him called inconstant of purpose—when he deserted, for the sake of love, the hope of sovereignty, and when he abdicated the protectorship of England, men blamed his infirmity of purpose. Now his death has crowned his life, and to the end of time it will be remembered, that he devoted himself, a willing victim, to the glory of Greece. Such was his choice: he expected to die. He foresaw that he should leave this cheerful earth, the lightsome sky, and thy love, Perdita; yet he neither hesitated or turned back, going right onward to his mark of fame. While the earth lasts, his actions will be recorded with praise. Grecian maidens will in devotion strew flowers on his tomb, and make the air around it resonant with patriotic hymns, in which his name will find high record."

I saw the features of Perdita soften; the sternness of grief yielded to tenderness—I continued:—"Thus to honour him, is the sacred duty of his survivors. To make his name even as an holy spot of ground, enclosing it from all hostile attacks by our praise, shedding on it the blossoms of love and regret, guarding it from decay, and bequeathing it untainted to posterity. Such is the duty of his friends. A dearer one belongs to you, Perdita, mother of his child. Do you remember in her infancy, with what transport you beheld Clara, recognizing in her the united being of yourself and Raymond; joying to view in this living temple a manifestation of your eternal loves. Even such is she still. You say that you have lost Raymond. O, no!—yet he lives with you and in you there. From him she sprung, flesh of his flesh, bone of his bone—and not, as heretofore, are you content to trace in her downy cheek and delicate limbs, an affinity to Raymond, but in her enthusiastic affections, in the sweet qualities of her mind, you may still find him living, the good, the great, the beloved. Be it your care to foster this similarity—be it your care to render her worthy of him, so that, when she glory in her origin, she take not shame for what she is."

I could perceive that, when I recalled my sister's thoughts to her duties in life, she did not listen with the same patience as before. She appeared to suspect a plan of consolation on my part, from which she, cherishing her new-born grief, revolted. "You talk of the future," she said, "while the present is all to me. Let me find the earthly dwelling of my beloved; let us rescue that from common dust, so that in times to come men may point to the sacred tomb, and name it his—then to other thoughts, and a new course of life, or what else fate, in her cruel tyranny, may have marked out for me."

After a short repose I prepared to leave her, that I might endeavour to accomplish her wish. In the mean time we were joined by Clara, whose pallid cheek and scared look shewed the deep impression grief had made on her young mind. She seemed to be full of something to which she could not give words; but, seizing an opportunity afforded by Perdita's absence, she preferred to me an earnest prayer, that I would take her within view of the gate at which her father had entered Constantinople. She promised to commit no extravagance, to be docile, and immediately to return. I could not refuse; for Clara was not an ordinary child; her sensibility and intelligence seemed already to have endowed her with the rights of womanhood. With her therefore, before me on my horse, attended only by the servant who was to re-conduct her, we rode to the Top Kapou. We found a party of soldiers gathered round it. They were listening. "They are human cries," said one: "More like the howling of a dog," replied another; and again they bent to catch the sound of regular distant moans, which issued from the precincts of the ruined city. "That, Clara," I said, "is the gate, that the street which yestermorn your father rode up." Whatever Clara's intention had been in asking to be brought hither, it was balked by the presence of the soldiers. With earnest gaze she looked on the labyrinth of smoking piles which had been a city, and then expressed her readiness to return home. At this moment a melancholy howl struck on our ears; it was repeated; "Hark!" cried Clara, "he is there; that is Florio, my father's dog." It seemed to me impossible that she could recognise the sound, but she persisted in her assertion till she gained credit with the crowd about. At least it would be a benevolent action to rescue the sufferer, whether human or brute, from the desolation of the town; so, sending Clara back to her home, I again entered Constantinople. Encouraged by the impunity attendant on my former visit, several soldiers who had made a part of Raymond's body guard, who had loved him, and sincerely mourned his loss, accompanied me.

It is impossible to conjecture the strange enchainment of events which restored the lifeless form of my friend to our hands. In that part of the town where the fire had most raged the night before, and which now lay quenched, black and cold, the dying dog of Raymond crouched beside the mutilated form of its lord. At such a time sorrow has no voice; affliction, tamed by it is very vehemence, is mute. The poor animal recognised me, licked my hand, crept close to its lord, and died. He had been evidently thrown from his horse by some falling ruin, which had crushed his head, and defaced his whole person. I bent over the body, and took in my hand the edge of his cloak, less altered in appearance than the human frame it clothed. I pressed it to my lips, while the rough soldiers gathered around, mourning over this worthiest prey of death, as if regret and endless lamentation could re-illumine the extinguished spark, or call to its shattered prison-house of flesh the liberated spirit. Yesterday those limbs were worth an universe; they then enshrined a transcendant power, whose intents, words, and actions were worthy to be recorded in letters of gold; now the superstition of affection alone could give value to the shattered mechanism, which, incapable and clod-like, no more resembled Raymond, than the fallen rain is like the former mansion of cloud in which it climbed the highest skies, and gilded by the sun, attracted all eyes, and satiated the sense by its excess of beauty.

Such as he had now become, such as was his terrene vesture, defaced and spoiled, we wrapt it in our cloaks, and lifting the burthen in our arms, bore it from this city of the dead. The question arose as to where we should deposit him. In our road to the palace, we passed through the Greek cemetery; here on a tablet of black marble I caused him to be laid; the cypresses waved high above, their death-like gloom accorded with his state of nothingness. We cut branches of the funereal trees and placed them over him, and on these again his sword. I left a guard to protect this treasure of dust; and ordered perpetual torches to be burned around.

When I returned to Perdita, I found that she had already been informed of the success of my undertaking. He, her beloved, the sole and eternal object of her passionate tenderness, was restored her. Such was the maniac language of her enthusiasm. What though those limbs moved not, and those lips could no more frame modulated accents of wisdom and love! What though like a weed flung from the fruitless sea, he lay the prey of corruption— still that was the form she had caressed, those the lips that meeting hers, had drank the spirit of love from the commingling breath; that was the earthly mechanism of dissoluble clay she had called her own. True, she looked forward to another life; true, the burning spirit of love seemed to her unextinguishable throughout eternity. Yet at this time, with human fondness, she clung to all that her human senses permitted her to see and feel to be a part of Raymond.

Pale as marble, clear and beaming as that, she heard my tale, and enquired concerning the spot where he had been deposited. Her features had lost the distortion of grief; her eyes were brightened, her very person seemed dilated; while the excessive whiteness and even transparency of her skin, and something hollow in her voice, bore witness that not tranquility, but excess of excitement, occasioned the treacherous calm that settled on her countenance. I asked her where he should be buried. She replied, "At Athens; even at the Athens which he loved. Without the town, on the acclivity of Hymettus, there is a rocky recess which he pointed out to me as the spot where he would wish to repose."

My own desire certainly was that he should not be removed from the spot where he now lay. But her wish was of course to be complied with; and I entreated her to prepare without delay for our departure.

Behold now the melancholy train cross the flats of Thrace, and wind through the defiles, and over the mountains of Macedonia, coast the clear waves of the Peneus, cross the Larissean plain, pass the straits of Thermopylae, and ascending in succession Oeta and Parnassus, descend to the fertile plain of Athens. Women bear with resignation these long drawn ills, but to a man's impatient spirit, the slow motion of our cavalcade, the melancholy repose we took at noon, the perpetual presence of the pall, gorgeous though it was, that wrapt the rifled casket which had contained Raymond, the monotonous recurrence of day and night, unvaried by hope or change, all the circumstances of our march were intolerable. Perdita, shut up in herself, spoke little. Her carriage was closed; and, when we rested, she sat leaning her pale cheek on her white cold hand, with eyes fixed on the ground, indulging thoughts which refused communication or sympathy.

We descended from Parnassus, emerging from its many folds, and passed through Livadia on our road to Attica. Perdita would not enter Athens; but reposing at Marathon on the night of our arrival, conducted me on the following day, to the spot selected by her as the treasure house of Raymond's dear remains. It was in a recess near the head of the ravine to the south of Hymettus. The chasm, deep, black, and hoary, swept from the summit to the base; in the fissures of the rock myrtle underwood grew and wild thyme, the food of many nations of bees; enormous crags protruded into the cleft, some beetling over, others rising perpendicularly from it. At the foot of this sublime chasm, a fertile laughing valley reached from sea to sea, and beyond was spread the blue Aegean, sprinkled with islands, the light waves glancing beneath the sun. Close to the spot on which we stood, was a solitary rock, high and conical, which, divided on every side from the mountain, seemed a nature-hewn pyramid; with little labour this block was reduced to a perfect shape; the narrow cell was scooped out beneath in which Raymond was placed, and a short inscription, carved in the living stone, recorded the name of its tenant, the cause and aera of his death.

Every thing was accomplished with speed under my directions. I agreed to leave the finishing and guardianship of the tomb to the head of the religious establishment at Athens, and by the end of October prepared for my return to England. I mentioned this to Perdita. It was painful to appear to drag her from the last scene that spoke of her lost one; but to linger here was vain, and my very soul was sick with its yearning to rejoin my Idris and her babes. In reply, my sister requested me to accompany her the following evening to the tomb of Raymond. Some days had passed since I had visited the spot. The path to it had been enlarged, and steps hewn in the rock led us less circuitously than before, to the spot itself; the platform on which the pyramid stood was enlarged, and looking towards the south, in a recess overshadowed by the straggling branches of a wild fig-tree, I saw foundations dug, and props and rafters fixed, evidently the commencement of a cottage; standing on its unfinished threshold, the tomb was at our right-hand, the whole ravine, and plain, and azure sea immediately before us; the dark rocks received a glow from the descending sun, which glanced along the cultivated valley, and dyed in purple and orange the placid waves; we sat on a rocky elevation, and I gazed with rapture on the beauteous panorama of living and changeful colours, which varied and enhanced the graces of earth and ocean.

"Did I not do right," said Perdita, "in having my loved one conveyed hither? Hereafter this will be the cynosure of Greece. In such a spot death loses half its terrors, and even the inanimate dust appears to partake of the spirit of beauty which hallows this region. Lionel, he sleeps there; that is the grave of Raymond, he whom in my youth I first loved; whom my heart accompanied in days of separation and anger; to whom I am now joined for ever. Never—mark me—never will I leave this spot. Methinks his spirit remains here as well as that dust, which, uncommunicable though it be, is more precious in its nothingness than aught else widowed earth clasps to her sorrowing bosom. The myrtle bushes, the thyme, the little cyclamen, which peep from the fissures of the rock, all the produce of the place, bear affinity to him; the light that invests the hills participates in his essence, and sky and mountains, sea and valley, are imbued by the presence of his spirit. I will live and die here!

"Go you to England, Lionel; return to sweet Idris and dearest Adrian; return, and let my orphan girl be as a child of your own in your house. Look on me as dead; and truly if death be a mere change of state, I am dead. This is another world, from that which late I inhabited, from that which is now your home. Here I hold communion only with the has been, and to come. Go you to England, and leave me where alone I can consent to drag out the miserable days which I must still live."

A shower of tears terminated her sad harangue. I had expected some extravagant proposition, and remained silent awhile, collecting my thoughts that I might the better combat her fanciful scheme. "You cherish dreary thoughts, my dear Perdita," I said, "nor do I wonder that for a time your better reason should be influenced by passionate grief and a disturbed imagination. Even I am in love with this last home of Raymond's; nevertheless we must quit it."

"I expected this," cried Perdita; "I supposed that you would treat me as a mad, foolish girl. But do not deceive yourself; this cottage is built by my order; and here I shall remain, until the hour arrives when I may share his happier dwelling."

"My dearest girl!"

"And what is there so strange in my design? I might have deceived you; I might have talked of remaining here only a few months; in your anxiety to reach Windsor you would have left me, and without reproach or contention, I might have pursued my plan. But I disdained the artifice; or rather in my wretchedness it was my only consolation to pour out my heart to you, my brother, my only friend. You will not dispute with me? You know how wilful your poor, misery-stricken sister is. Take my girl with you; wean her from sights and thoughts of sorrow; let infantine hilarity revisit her heart, and animate her eyes; so could it never be, were she near me; it is far better for all of you that you should never see me again. For myself, I will not voluntarily seek death, that is, I will not, while I can command myself; and I can here. But drag me from this country; and my power of self control vanishes, nor can I answer for the violence my agony of grief may lead me to commit."

"You clothe your meaning, Perdita," I replied, "in powerful words, yet that meaning is selfish and unworthy of you. You have often agreed with me that there is but one solution to the intricate riddle of life; to improve ourselves, and contribute to the happiness of others: and now, in the very prime of life, you desert your principles, and shut yourself up in useless solitude. Will you think of Raymond less at Windsor, the scene of your early happiness? Will you commune less with his departed spirit, while you watch over and cultivate the rare excellence of his child? You have been sadly visited; nor do I wonder that a feeling akin to insanity should drive you to bitter and unreasonable imaginings. But a home of love awaits you in your native England. My tenderness and affection must soothe you; the society of Raymond's friends will be of more solace than these dreary speculations. We will all make it our first care, our dearest task, to contribute to your happiness."

Perdita shook her head; "If it could be so," she replied, "I were much in the wrong to disdain your offers. But it is not a matter of choice; I can live here only. I am a part of this scene; each and all its properties are a part of me. This is no sudden fancy; I live by it. The knowledge that I am here, rises with me in the morning, and enables me to endure the light; it is mingled with my food, which else were poison; it walks, it sleeps with me, for ever it accompanies me. Here I may even cease to repine, and may add my tardy consent to the decree which has taken him from me. He would rather have died such a death, which will be recorded in history to endless time, than have lived to old age unknown, unhonoured. Nor can I desire better, than, having been the chosen and beloved of his heart, here, in youth's prime, before added years can tarnish the best feelings of my nature, to watch his tomb, and speedily rejoin him in his blessed repose.

"So much, my dearest Lionel, I have said, wishing to persuade you that I do right. If you are unconvinced, I can add nothing further by way of argument, and I can only declare my fixed resolve. I stay here; force only can remove me. Be it so; drag me away—I return; confine me, imprison me, still I escape, and come here. Or would my brother rather devote the heart-broken Perdita to the straw and chains of a maniac, than suffer her to rest in peace beneath the shadow of His society, in this my own selected and beloved recess?"—

All this appeared to me, I own, methodized madness. I imagined, that it was my imperative duty to take her from scenes that thus forcibly reminded her of her loss. Nor did I doubt, that in the tranquility of our family circle at Windsor, she would recover some degree of composure, and in the end, of happiness. My affection for Clara also led me to oppose these fond dreams of cherished grief; her sensibility had already been too much excited; her infant heedlessness too soon exchanged for deep and anxious thought. The strange and romantic scheme of her mother, might confirm and perpetuate the painful view of life, which had intruded itself thus early on her contemplation.

On returning home, the captain of the steam packet with whom I had agreed to sail, came to tell me, that accidental circumstances hastened his departure, and that, if I went with him, I must come on board at five on the following morning. I hastily gave my consent to this arrangement, and as hastily formed a plan through which Perdita should be forced to become my companion. I believe that most people in my situation would have acted in the same manner. Yet this consideration does not, or rather did not in after time, diminish the reproaches of my conscience. At the moment, I felt convinced that I was acting for the best, and that all I did was right and even necessary.

I sat with Perdita and soothed her, by my seeming assent to her wild scheme. She received my concurrence with pleasure, and a thousand times over thanked her deceiving, deceitful brother. As night came on, her spirits, enlivened by my unexpected concession, regained an almost forgotten vivacity. I pretended to be alarmed by the feverish glow in her cheek; I entreated her to take a composing draught; I poured out the medicine, which she took docilely from me. I watched her as she drank it. Falsehood and artifice are in themselves so hateful, that, though I still thought I did right, a feeling of shame and guilt came painfully upon me. I left her, and soon heard that she slept soundly under the influence of the opiate I had administered. She was carried thus unconscious on board; the anchor weighed, and the wind being favourable, we stood far out to sea; with all the canvas spread, and the power of the engine to assist, we scudded swiftly and steadily through the chafed element.

It was late in the day before Perdita awoke, and a longer time elapsed before recovering from the torpor occasioned by the laudanum, she perceived her change of situation. She started wildly from her couch, and flew to the cabin window. The blue and troubled sea sped past the vessel, and was spread shoreless around: the sky was covered by a rack, which in its swift motion shewed how speedily she was borne away. The creaking of the masts, the clang of the wheels, the tramp above, all persuaded her that she was already far from the shores of Greece. —"Where are we?" she cried, "where are we going?"—

The attendant whom I had stationed to watch her, replied, "to England."—

"And my brother?"—

"Is on deck, Madam."

"Unkind! unkind!" exclaimed the poor victim, as with a deep sigh she looked on the waste of waters. Then without further remark, she threw herself on her couch, and closing her eyes remained motionless; so that but for the deep sighs that burst from her, it would have seemed that she slept.

As soon as I heard that she had spoken, I sent Clara to her, that the sight of the lovely innocent might inspire gentle and affectionate thoughts. But neither the presence of her child, nor a subsequent visit from me, could rouse my sister. She looked on Clara with a countenance of woful meaning, but she did not speak. When I appeared, she turned away, and in reply to my enquiries, only said, "You know not what you have done!"—I trusted that this sullenness betokened merely the struggle between disappointment and natural affection, and that in a few days she would be reconciled to her fate.

When night came on, she begged that Clara might sleep in a separate cabin. Her servant, however, remained with her. About midnight she spoke to the latter, saying that she had had a bad dream, and bade her go to her daughter, and bring word whether she rested quietly. The woman obeyed.

The breeze, that had flagged since sunset, now rose again. I was on deck, enjoying our swift progress. The quiet was disturbed only by the rush of waters as they divided before the steady keel, the murmur of the moveless and full sails, the wind whistling in the shrouds, and the regular motion of the engine. The sea was gently agitated, now shewing a white crest, and now resuming an uniform hue; the clouds had disappeared; and dark ether clipt the broad ocean, in which the constellations vainly sought their accustomed mirror. Our rate could not have been less than eight knots.

Suddenly I heard a splash in the sea. The sailors on watch rushed to the side of the vessel, with the cry—some one gone overboard. "It is not from deck," said the man at the helm, "something has been thrown from the aft cabin." A call for the boat to be lowered was echoed from the deck. I rushed into my sister's cabin; it was empty.

With sails abaft, the engine stopt, the vessel remained unwillingly stationary, until, after an hour's search, my poor Perdita was brought on board. But no care could re-animate her, no medicine cause her dear eyes to open, and the blood to flow again from her pulseless heart. One clenched hand contained a slip of paper, on which was written, "To Athens." To ensure her removal thither, and prevent the irrecoverable loss of her body in the wide sea, she had had the precaution to fasten a long shawl round her waist, and again to the staunchions of the cabin window. She had drifted somewhat under the keel of the vessel, and her being out of sight occasioned the delay in finding her. And thus the ill-starred girl died a victim to my senseless rashness. Thus, in early day, she left us for the company of the dead, and preferred to share the rocky grave of Raymond, before the animated scene this cheerful earth afforded, and the society of loving friends. Thus in her twenty-ninth year she died; having enjoyed some few years of the happiness of paradise, and sustaining a reverse to which her impatient spirit and affectionate disposition were unable to submit. As I marked the placid expression that had settled on her countenance in death, I felt, in spite of the pangs of remorse, in spite of heart-rending regret, that it was better to die so, than to drag on long, miserable years of repining and inconsolable grief. Stress of weather drove us up the Adriatic Gulph; and, our vessel being hardly fitted to weather a storm, we took refuge in the port of Ancona. Here I met Georgio Palli, the vice-admiral of the Greek fleet, a former friend and warm partizan of Raymond. I committed the remains of my lost Perdita to his care, for the purpose of having them transported to Hymettus, and placed in the cell her Raymond already occupied beneath the pyramid. This was all accomplished even as I wished. She reposed beside her beloved, and the tomb above was inscribed with the united names of Raymond and Perdita.

I then came to a resolution of pursuing our journey to England overland. My own heart was racked by regrets and remorse. The apprehension, that Raymond had departed for ever, that his name, blended eternally with the past, must be erased from every anticipation of the future, had come slowly upon me. I had always admired his talents; his noble aspirations; his grand conceptions of the glory and majesty of his ambition: his utter want of mean passions; his fortitude and daring. In Greece I had learnt to love him; his very waywardness, and self-abandonment to the impulses of superstition, attached me to him doubly; it might be weakness, but it was the antipodes of all that was grovelling and selfish. To these pangs were added the loss of Perdita, lost through my own accursed self-will and conceit. This dear one, my sole relation; whose progress I had marked from tender childhood through the varied path of life, and seen her throughout conspicuous for integrity, devotion, and true affection; for all that constitutes the peculiar graces of the female character, and beheld her at last the victim of too much loving, too constant an attachment to the perishable and lost, she, in her pride of beauty and life, had thrown aside the pleasant perception of the apparent world for the unreality of the grave, and had left poor Clara quite an orphan. I concealed from this beloved child that her mother's death was voluntary, and tried every means to awaken cheerfulness in her sorrow-stricken spirit.

One of my first acts for the recovery even of my own composure, was to bid farewell to the sea. Its hateful splash renewed again and again to my sense the death of my sister; its roar was a dirge; in every dark hull that was tossed on its inconstant bosom, I imaged a bier, that would convey to death all who trusted to its treacherous smiles. Farewell to the sea! Come, my Clara, sit beside me in this aerial bark; quickly and gently it cleaves the azure serene, and with soft undulation glides upon the current of the air; or, if storm shake its fragile mechanism, the green earth is below; we can descend, and take shelter on the stable continent. Here aloft, the companions of the swift-winged birds, we skim through the unresisting element, fleetly and fearlessly. The light boat heaves not, nor is opposed by death-bearing waves; the ether opens before the prow, and the shadow of the globe that upholds it, shelters us from the noon-day sun. Beneath are the plains of Italy, or the vast undulations of the wave-like Apennines: fertility reposes in their many folds, and woods crown the summits. The free and happy peasant, unshackled by the Austrian, bears the double harvest to the garner; and the refined citizens rear without dread the long blighted tree of knowledge in this garden of the world. We were lifted above the Alpine peaks, and from their deep and brawling ravines entered the plain of fair France, and after an airy journey of six days, we landed at Dieppe, furled the feathered wings, and closed the silken globe of our little pinnace. A heavy rain made this mode of travelling now incommodious; so we embarked in a steam-packet, and after a short passage landed at Portsmouth.

A strange story was rife here. A few days before, a tempest-struck vessel had appeared off the town: the hull was parched-looking and cracked, the sails rent, and bent in a careless, unseamanlike manner, the shrouds tangled and broken. She drifted towards the harbour, and was stranded on the sands at the entrance. In the morning the custom-house officers, together with a crowd of idlers, visited her. One only of the crew appeared to have arrived with her. He had got to shore, and had walked a few paces towards the town, and then, vanquished by malady and approaching death, had fallen on the inhospitable beach. He was found stiff, his hands clenched, and pressed against his breast. His skin, nearly black, his matted hair and bristly beard, were signs of a long protracted misery. It was whispered that he had died of the plague. No one ventured on board the vessel, and strange sights were averred to be seen at night, walking the deck, and hanging on the masts and shrouds. She soon went to pieces; I was shewn where she had been, and saw her disjoined timbers tossed on the waves. The body of the man who had landed, had been buried deep in the sands; and none could tell more, than that the vessel was American built, and that several months before the Fortunatas had sailed from Philadelphia, of which no tidings were afterwards received.

$\mathscr{H}$ 4 $\mathscr{H}$

I RETURNED to my family estate in the autumn of the year 2092. My heart had long been with them; and I felt sick with the hope and delight of seeing them again. The district which contained them appeared the abode of every kindly spirit. Happiness, love and peace, walked the forest paths, and tempered the atmosphere. After all the agitation and sorrow I had endured in Greece, I sought Windsor, as the storm-driven bird does the nest in which it may fold its wings in tranquility.

How unwise had the wanderers been, who had deserted its shelter, entangled themselves in the web of society, and entered on what men of the world call "life,"—that labyrinth of evil, that scheme of mutual torture. To live, according to this sense of the word, we must not only observe and learn, we must also feel; we must not be mere spectators of action, we must act; we must not describe, but be subjects of description. Deep sorrow must have been the inmate of our bosoms; fraud must have lain in wait for us; the artful must have deceived us; sickening doubt and false hope must have chequered our days; hilarity and joy, that lap the soul in ecstasy, must at times have possessed us. Who that knows what "life" is, would pine for this feverish species of existence? I have lived. I have spent days and nights of festivity; I have joined in ambitious hopes, and exulted in victory: now,—shut the door on the world, and build high the wall that is to separate me from the troubled scene enacted within its precincts. Let us live for each other and for happiness; let us seek peace in our dear home, near the inland murmur of streams, and the gracious waving of trees, the beauteous vesture of earth, and sublime pageantry of the skies. Let us leave "life," that we may live.

Idris was well content with this resolve of mine. Her native sprightliness needed no undue excitement, and her placid heart reposed contented on my love, the well-being of her children, and the beauty of surrounding nature. Her pride and blameless ambition was to create smiles in all around her, and to shed repose on the fragile existence of her brother. In spite of her tender nursing, the health of Adrian perceptibly declined. Walking, riding, the common occupations of life, overcame him: he felt no pain, but seemed to tremble for ever on the verge of annihilation. Yet, as he had lived on for months nearly in the same state, he did not inspire us with any immediate fear; and, though he talked of death as an event most familiar to his thoughts, he did not cease to exert himself to render others happy, or to cultivate his own astonishing powers of mind. Winter passed away; and spring, led by the months, awakened life in all nature. The forest was dressed in green; the young calves frisked on the new-sprung grass; the wind-winged shadows of light clouds sped over the green cornfields; the hermit cuckoo repeated his monotonous all-hail to the season; the nightingale, bird of love and minion of the evening star, filled the woods with song; while Venus lingered in the warm sunset, and the young green of the trees lay in gentle relief along the clear horizon.

Delight awoke in every heart, delight and exultation; for there was peace through all the world; the temple of Universal Janus was shut, and man died not that year by the hand of man.

"Let this last but twelve months," said Adrian; "and earth will become a Paradise. The energies of man were before directed to the destruction of his species: they now aim at its liberation and preservation. Man cannot repose, and his restless aspirations will now bring forth good instead of evil. The favoured countries of the south will throw off the iron yoke of servitude; poverty will quit us, and with that, sickness. What may not the forces, never before united, of liberty and peace achieve in this dwelling of man?"

"Dreaming, for ever dreaming, Windsor!" said Ryland, the old adversary of Raymond, and candidate for the Protectorate at the ensuing election. "Be assured that earth is not, nor ever can be heaven, while the seeds of hell are natives of her soil. When the seasons have become equal, when the air breeds no disorders, when its surface is no longer liable to blights and droughts, then sickness will cease; when men's passions are dead, poverty will depart. When love is no longer akin to hate, then brotherhood will exist: we are very far from that state at present."

"Not so far as you may suppose," observed a little old astronomer, by name Merrival, "the poles precede slowly, but securely; in an hundred thousand years—"

"We shall all be underground," said Ryland.

"The pole of the earth will coincide with the pole of the ecliptic," continued the astronomer, "an universal spring will be produced, and earth become a paradise."

"And we shall of course enjoy the benefit of the change," said Ryland, contemptuously.

"We have strange news here," I observed. I had the newspaper in my hand, and, as usual, had turned to the intelligence from Greece. "It seems that the total destruction of Constantinople, and the supposition that winter had purified the air of the fallen city, gave the Greeks courage to visit its site, and begin to rebuild it. But they tell us that the curse of God is on the place, for every one who has ventured within the walls has been tainted by the plague; that this disease has spread in Thrace and Macedonia; and now, fearing the virulence of infection during the coming heats, a cordon has been drawn on the frontiers of Thessaly, and a strict quarantine exacted." This intelligence brought us back from the prospect of paradise, held out after the lapse of an hundred thousand years, to the pain and misery at present existent upon earth. We talked of the ravages made last year by pestilence in every quarter of the world; and of the dreadful consequences of a second visitation. We discussed the best means of preventing infection, and of preserving health and activity in a large city thus afflicted— London, for instance. Merrival did not join in this conversation; drawing near Idris, he proceeded to assure her that the joyful prospect of an earthly paradise after an hundred thousand years, was clouded to him by the knowledge that in a certain period of time after, an earthly hell or purgatory, would occur, when the ecliptic and equator would be at right angles.[1] Our party at length broke up; "We are all dreaming this morning," said Ryland, "it is as wise to discuss the probability of a visitation of the plague in our well-governed metropolis, as to calculate the centuries which must escape before we can grow pine-apples here in the open air."

But, though it seemed absurd to calculate upon the arrival of the plague in London, I could not reflect without extreme pain on the desolation this evil would cause in Greece. The English for the most part talked of Thrace and Macedonia, as they would of a lunar territory, which, unknown to them, presented no distinct idea or interest to the minds. I had trod the soil. The faces of many of the inhabitants were familiar to me; in the towns, plains, hills, and defiles of these countries, I had enjoyed unspeakable delight, as I journied through them the year before. Some romantic village, some cottage, or elegant abode there situated, inhabited by the lovely and the good, rose before my mental sight, and the question haunted me, is the plague there also?—That same invincible monster, which hovered over and devoured Constantinople—that fiend more cruel than tempest, less tame than fire, is, alas, unchained in that beautiful country —these reflections would not allow me to rest.

The political state of England became agitated as the time drew near when the new Protector was to be elected. This event excited the more interest, since it was the current report, that if the popular candidate (Ryland) should be chosen, the question of the abolition of hereditary rank, and other feudal relics, would come under the consideration of parliament. Not a word had been spoken during the present session on any of these topics. Every thing would depend upon the choice of a Protector, and the elections of the ensuing year. Yet this very silence was awful, shewing the deep weight attributed to the question; the fear of either party to hazard an ill-timed attack, and the expectation of a furious contention when it should begin.

But although St. Stephen's did not echo with the voice which filled each heart, the newspapers teemed with nothing else; and in private companies the conversation however remotely begun, soon verged towards this central point, while voices were lowered and chairs drawn closer. The nobles did not hesitate to express their fear; the other party endeavoured to treat the matter lightly. "Shame on the country," said Ryland, "to lay so much stress upon words and frippery; it is a question of nothing; of the new painting of carriage-pannels and the embroidery of footmen's coats."

Yet could England indeed doff her lordly trappings, and be content with the democratic style of America? Were the pride of ancestry, the patrician spirit, the gentle courtesies and refined pursuits, splendid attributes of rank, to be erased among us? We were told that this would not be the case; that we were by nature a poetical people, a nation easily duped by words, ready to array clouds in splendour, and bestow honour on the dust. This spirit we could never lose; and it was to diffuse this concentrated spirit of birth, that the new law was to be brought forward. We were assured that, when the name and title of Englishman was the sole patent of nobility, we should all be noble; that when no man born under English sway, felt another his superior in rank, courtesy and refinement would become the birth-right of all our countrymen. Let not England be so far disgraced, as to have it imagined that it can be without nobles, nature's true nobility, who bear their patent in their mien, who are from their cradle elevated above the rest of their species, because they are better than the rest. Among a race of independent, and generous, and well educated men, in a country where the imagination is empress of men's minds, there needs be no fear that we should want a perpetual succession of the high-born and lordly. That party, however, could hardly yet be considered a minority in the kingdom, who extolled the ornament of the column, "the Corinthian capital of polished society;" they appealed to prejudices without number, to old attachments and young hopes; to the expectation of thousands who might one day become peers; they set up as a scarecrow, the spectre of all that was sordid, mechanic and base in the commercial republics.

The plague had come to Athens. Hundreds of English residents returned to their own country. Raymond's beloved Athenians, the free, the noble people of the divinest town in

Greece, fell like ripe corn before the merciless sickle of the adversary. Its pleasant places were deserted; its temples and palaces were converted into tombs; its energies, bent before towards the highest objects of human ambition, were now forced to converge to one point, the guarding against the innumerous arrows of the plague.

At any other time this disaster would have excited extreme compassion among us; but it was now passed over, while each mind was engaged by the coming controversy. It was not so with me; and the question of rank and right dwindled to insignificance in my eyes, when I pictured the scene of suffering Athens. I heard of the death of only sons; of wives and husbands most devoted; of the rending of ties twisted with the heart's fibres, of friend losing friend, and young mothers mourning for their first born; and these moving incidents were grouped and painted in my mind by the knowledge of the persons, by my esteem and affection for the sufferers. It was the admirers, friends, fellow soldiers of Raymond, families that had welcomed Perdita to Greece, and lamented with her the loss of her lord, that were swept away, and went to dwell with them in the undistinguishing tomb.

The plague at Athens had been preceded and caused by the contagion from the East; and the scene of havoc and death continued to be acted there, on a scale of fearful magnitude. A hope that the visitation of the present year would prove the last, kept up the spirits of the merchants connected with these countries; but the inhabitants were driven to despair, or to a resignation which, arising from fanaticism, assumed the same dark hue. America had also received the taint; and, were it yellow fever or plague, the epidemic was gifted with a virulence before unfelt. The devastation was not confined to the towns, but spread throughout the country; the hunter died in the woods, the peasant in the corn-fields, and the fisher on his native waters.

A strange story was brought to us from the East, to which little credit would have been given, had not the fact been attested by a multitude of witnesses, in various parts of the world. On the twenty-first of June, it was said that an hour before noon, a black sun arose: an orb, the size of that luminary, but dark, defined, whose beams were shadows, ascended from the west; in about an hour it had reached the meridian, and eclipsed the bright parent of day. Night fell upon every country, night, sudden, rayless, entire. The stars came out, shedding their ineffectual glimmerings on the light-widowed earth. But soon the dim orb passed from over the sun, and lingered down the eastern heaven. As it descended, its dusky rays crossed the brilliant ones of the sun, and deadened or distorted them. The shadows of things assumed strange and ghastly shapes. The wild animals in the woods took fright at the unknown shapes figured on the ground. They fled they knew not whither; and the citizens were filled with greater dread, at the convulsion which "shook lions into civil streets;"—birds, strong-winged eagles, suddenly blinded, fell in the market-places, while owls and bats shewed themselves welcoming the early night. Gradually the object of fear sank beneath the horizon, and to the last shot up shadowy beams into the otherwise radiant air. Such was the tale sent us from Asia, from the eastern extremity of Europe, and from Africa as far west as the Golden Coast. Whether this story were true or not, the effects were certain. Through Asia, from the banks of the Nile to the shores of the Caspian, from the Hellespont even to the sea of Oman, a sudden panic was driven. The men filled the mosques; the women, veiled, hastened to the tombs, and carried offerings to the dead, thus to preserve the living. The plague was forgotten, in this new fear which the black sun had spread; and, though the dead multiplied, and the streets of Ispahan, of Pekin, and of Delhi were strewed with pestilence-struck corpses, men passed on, gazing on the ominous sky, regardless of the death beneath their feet. The christians sought their churches,—christian maidens, even at the feast of roses, clad in white, with shining veils, sought, in long procession, the places consecrated to their religion, filling the air with their hymns; while, ever and anon, from the lips of some poor mourner in the crowd, a voice of wailing burst, and the rest looked up, fancying they could discern the sweeping wings of angels, who passed over the earth, lamenting the disasters about to fall on man.

In the sunny clime of Persia, in the crowded cities of China, amidst the aromatic groves of Cashmere, and along the southern shores of the Mediterranean, such scenes had place. Even in Greece the tale of the sun of darkness increased the fears and despair of the dying multitude. We, in our cloudy isle, were far removed from danger, and the only circumstance that brought these disasters at all home to us, was the daily arrival of vessels from the east, crowded with emigrants, mostly English; for the Moslems, though the fear of death was spread keenly among them, still clung together; that, if they were to die (and if they were, death would as readily meet them on the homeless sea, or in far England, as in Persia,)— if they were to die, their bones might rest in earth made sacred by the relics of true believers. Mecca had never before been so crowded with pilgrims; yet the Arabs neglected to pillage the caravans, but, humble and weaponless, they joined the procession, praying Mahomet to avert plague from their tents and deserts.

I cannot describe the rapturous delight with which I turned from political brawls at home, and the physical evils of distant countries, to my own dear home, to the selected abode of goodness and love; to peace, and the interchange of every sacred sympathy. Had I never quitted Windsor, these emotions would not have been so intense; but I had in Greece been the prey of fear and deplorable change; in Greece, after a period of anxiety and sorrow, I had seen depart two, whose very names were the symbol of greatness and virtue. But such miseries could never intrude upon the domestic circle left to me, while, secluded in our beloved forest, we passed our lives in tranquility. Some small change indeed the progress of years brought here; and time, as it is wont, stamped the traces of mortality on our pleasures and expectations. Idris, the most affectionate wife, sister and friend, was a tender and loving mother. The feeling was not with her as with many, a pastime; it was a passion. We had had three children; one, the second in age, died while I was in Greece. This had dashed the triumphant and rapturous emotions of maternity with grief and fear. Before this event, the little beings, sprung from herself, the young heirs of her transient life, seemed to have a sure lease of existence; now she dreaded that the pitiless destroyer might snatch her remaining darlings, as it had snatched their brother. The least illness caused throes of terror; she was miserable if she were at all absent from them; her treasure of happiness she had garnered in their fragile being, and kept forever on the watch, lest the insidious thief should as before steal these valued gems. She had fortunately small cause for fear. Alfred, now nine years old, was an upright, manly little fellow, with radiant brow, soft eyes, and gentle, though independent disposition. Our youngest was yet in infancy; but his downy cheek was sprinkled with the roses of health, and his unwearied vivacity filled our halls with innocent laughter.

Clara had passed the age which, from its mute ignorance, was the source of the fears of Idris. Clara was dear to her, to all. There was so much intelligence combined with innocence, sensibility with forbearance, and seriousness with perfect good-humour, a beauty so transcendant, united to such endearing simplicity, that she hung like a pearl in the shrine of our possessions, a treasure of wonder and excellence.

At the beginning of winter our Alfred, now nine years of age, first went to school at Eton. This appeared to him the primary step towards manhood, and he was proportionably pleased. Community of study and amusement developed the best parts of his character, his steady perseverance, generosity, and well-governed firmness. What deep and sacred emotions are excited in a father's bosom, when he first becomes convinced that his love for his child is not a mere instinct, but worthily bestowed, and that others, less akin, participate his approbation! It was supreme happiness to Idris and myself, to find that the frankness which Alfred's open brow indicated, the intelligence of his eyes, the tempered sensibility of his tones, were not delusions, but indications of talents and virtues, which would "grow with his growth, and strengthen with his strength." At this period, the termination of an animal's love for its offspring,—the true affection of the human parent commences. We no longer look on this dearest part of ourselves, as a tender plant which we must cherish, or a plaything for an idle hour. We build now on his intellectual faculties, we establish our hopes on his moral propensities. His weakness still imparts anxiety to this feeling, his ignorance prevents entire intimacy; but we begin to respect the future man, and to endeavour to secure his esteem, even as if he were our equal. What can a parent have more at heart than the good opinion of his child? In all our transactions with him our honour must be inviolate, the integrity of our relations untainted: fate and circumstance may, when he arrives at maturity, separate us for ever—but, as his aegis in danger, his consolation in hardship, let the ardent youth for ever bear with him through the rough path of life, love and honour for his parents.

We had lived so long in the vicinity of Eton, that its population of young folks was well known to us. Many of them had been Alfred's playmates, before they became his school-fellows. We now watched this youthful congregation with redoubled interest. We marked the difference of character among the boys, and endeavoured to read the future man in the stripling. There is nothing more lovely, to which the heart more yearns than a free-spirited boy, gentle, brave, and generous. Several of the Etonians had these characteristics; all were distinguished by a sense of honour, and spirit of enterprise; in some, as they verged towards manhood, this degenerated into presumption; but the younger ones, lads a little older than our own, were conspicuous for their gallant and sweet dispositions.

Here were the future governors of England; the men, who, when our ardour was cold, and our projects completed or destroyed for ever, when, our drama acted, we doffed the garb of the hour, and assumed the uniform of age, or of more equalizing death; here were the beings who were to carry on the vast machine of society; here were the lovers, husbands, fathers; here the landlord, the politician, the soldier; some fancied that they were even now ready to appear on the stage, eager to make one among the dramatis personae of active life. It was not long since I was like one of these beardless aspirants; when my boy shall have obtained the place I now hold, I shall have tottered into a grey-headed, wrinkled old man. Strange system! riddle of the Sphynx, most awe-striking! that thus man remains, while we the individuals pass away. Such is, to borrow the words of an eloquent and philosophic writer, "the mode of existence decreed to a permanent body composed of transitory parts; wherein, by the disposition of a stupendous wisdom, moulding together the great mysterious incorporation of the human race, the whole, at one time, is never old, or middle-aged, or young, but, in a condition of unchangeable constancy, moves on through the varied tenour of perpetual decay, fall, renovation, and progression."[2]

Willingly do I give place to thee, dear Alfred! advance, offspring of tender love, child of our hopes; advance a soldier on the road to which I have been the pioneer! I will make way for thee. I have already put off the carelessness of childhood, the unlined brow, and springy gait of early years, that they may adorn thee. Advance; and I will despoil myself still further for thy advantage. Time shall rob me of the graces of maturity, shall take the fire from my eyes, and agility from my limbs, shall steal the better part of life, eager expectation and passionate love, and shower them in double portion on thy dear head. Advance! avail thyself of the gift, thou and thy comrades; and in the drama you are about to act, do not disgrace those who taught you to enter on the stage, and to pronounce becomingly the parts assigned to you! May your progress be uninterrupted and secure; born during the spring-tide of the hopes of man, may you lead up the summer to which no winter may succeed!

---

1. See an ingenious Essay, entitled, "The Mythological Astronomy of the Ancients Demonstrated," by Mackey, a shoemaker, of Norwich printed in 1822.
2. Burke's Reflections on the French Revolution.

SOME DISORDER HAD SURELY CREPT into the course of the elements, destroying their benignant influence. The wind, prince of air, raged through his kingdom, lashing the sea into fury, and subduing the rebel earth into some sort of obedience.

> The God sends down his angry plagues from high,
> Famine and pestilence in heaps they die.
> Again in vengeance of his wrath he falls
> On their great hosts, and breaks their tottering walls;
> Arrests their navies on the ocean's plain,
> And whelms their strength with mountains of the main.[1]

Their deadly power shook the flourishing countries of the south, and during winter, even, we, in our northern retreat, began to quake under their ill effects.

That fable is unjust, which gives the superiority to the sun over the wind. Who has not seen the lightsome earth, the balmy atmosphere, and basking nature become dark, cold and ungenial, when the sleeping wind has awoke in the east? Or, when the dun clouds thickly veil the sky, while exhaustless stores of rain are poured down, until, the dank earth refusing to imbibe the superabundant moisture, it lies in pools on the surface; when the torch of day seems like a meteor, to be quenched; who has not seen the cloud-stirring north arise, the streaked blue appear, and soon an opening made in the vapours in the eye of the wind, through which the bright azure shines? The clouds become thin; an arch is formed for ever rising upwards, till, the universal cope being unveiled, the sun pours forth its rays, re-animated and fed by the breeze.

Then mighty art thou, O wind, to be throned above all other vicegerents of nature's power; whether thou comest destroying from the east, or pregnant with elementary life from the west; thee the clouds obey; the sun is subservient to thee; the shoreless ocean is thy slave! Thou sweepest over the earth, and oaks, the growth of centuries, submit to thy viewless axe; the snow-drift is scattered on the pinnacles of the Alps, the avalanche thunders down their vallies.

Thou holdest the keys of the frost, and canst first chain and then set free the streams; under thy gentle governance the buds and leaves are born, they flourish nursed by thee.

Why dost thou howl thus, O wind? By day and by night for four long months thy roarings have not ceased—the shores of the sea are strewn with wrecks, its keel-welcoming surface has become impassable, the earth has shed her beauty in obedience to thy command; the frail balloon dares no longer sail on the agitated air; thy ministers, the clouds, deluge the land with rain; rivers forsake their banks; the wild torrent tears up the mountain path; plain and wood, and verdant dell are despoiled of their loveliness; our very cities are wasted by thee. Alas, what will become of us? It seems as if the giant waves of ocean, and vast arms of the sea, were about to wrench the deep-rooted island from its centre; and cast it, a ruin and a wreck, upon the fields of the Atlantic.

What are we, the inhabitants of this globe, least among the many that people infinite space? Our minds embrace infinity; the visible mechanism of our being is subject to merest accident. Day by day we are forced to believe this. He whom a scratch has disorganized, he who disappears from apparent life under the influence of the hostile agency at work around us, had the same powers as I—I also am subject to the same laws. In the face of all this we call ourselves lords of the creation, wielders of the elements, masters of life and death, and we allege in excuse of this arrogance, that though the individual is destroyed, man continues for ever.

Thus, losing our identity, that of which we are chiefly conscious, we glory in the continuity of our species, and learn to regard death without terror. But when any whole nation becomes the victim of the destructive powers of exterior agents, then indeed man shrinks into insignificance, he feels his tenure of life insecure, his inheritance on earth cut off.

I remember, after having witnessed the destructive effects of a fire, I could not even behold a small one in a stove, without a sensation of fear. The mounting flames had curled round the building, as it fell, and was destroyed. They insinuated themselves into the substances about them, and the impediments to their progress yielded at their touch. Could we take integral parts of this power, and not be subject to its operation? Could we domesticate a cub of this wild beast, and not fear its growth and maturity?

Thus we began to feel, with regard to many-visaged death let loose on the chosen districts of our fair habitation, and above all, with regard to the plague. We feared the coming summer. Nations, bordering on the already infected countries, began to enter upon serious plans for the better keeping out of the enemy. We, a commercial people, were obliged to bring such schemes under consideration; and the question of contagion became matter of earnest disquisition.

That the plague was not what is commonly called contagious, like the scarlet fever, or extinct small-pox, was proved. It was called an epidemic. But the grand question was still unsettled of how this epidemic was generated and increased. If infection depended upon the air, the air was subject to infection. As for instance, a typhus fever has been brought by ships to one sea-port town; yet the very people who brought it there, were incapable of communicating it in a town more fortunately situated. But how are we to judge of airs, and pronounce—in such a city plague will die unproductive; in such another, nature has provided for it a plentiful harvest? In the same way, individuals may escape ninety-nine times, and receive the death-blow at the hundredth; because bodies are sometimes in a state to reject the infection of malady, and at others, thirsty to imbibe it. These reflections made our legislators pause, before they could decide on the laws to be put in force. The evil was so wide-spreading, so violent and immedicable, that no care, no prevention could be judged superfluous, which even added a chance to our escape.

These were questions of prudence; there was no immediate necessity for an earnest caution. England was still secure. France, Germany, Italy and Spain, were interposed, walls yet without a breach, between us and the plague. Our vessels truly were the sport of winds and waves, even as Gulliver was the toy of the Brobdignagians; but we on our stable abode could not be hurt in life or limb by these eruptions of nature. We could not fear—we did not. Yet a feeling of awe, a breathless sentiment of wonder, a painful sense of the degradation of humanity, was introduced into every heart. Nature, our mother, and our friend, had turned on us a brow of menace. She shewed us plainly, that, though she permitted us to assign her laws and subdue her apparent powers, yet, if she put forth but a finger, we must quake. She could take our globe, fringed with mountains, girded by the atmosphere, containing the condition of our being, and all that man's mind could invent or his force achieve; she could take the ball in her hand, and cast it into space, where life would be drunk up, and man and all his efforts for ever annihilated.

These speculations were rife among us; yet not the less we proceeded in our daily occupations, and our plans, whose accomplishment demanded the lapse of many years. No voice was heard telling us to hold! When foreign distresses came to be felt by us through the channels of commerce, we set ourselves to apply remedies. Subscriptions were made for the emigrants, and merchants bankrupt by the failure of trade. The English spirit awoke to its full activity, and, as it had ever done, set itself to resist the evil, and to stand in the breach which diseased nature had suffered chaos and death to make in the bounds and banks which had hitherto kept them out.

At the commencement of summer, we began to feel, that the mischief which had taken place in distant countries was greater than we had at first suspected. Quito was destroyed by an earthquake. Mexico laid waste by the united effects of storm, pestilence and famine. Crowds of emigrants inundated the west of Europe; and our island had become the refuge of thousands. In the mean time Ryland had been chosen Protector. He had sought this office with eagerness, under the idea of turning his whole forces to the suppression of the privileged orders of our community. His measures were thwarted, and his schemes interrupted by this new state of things. Many of the foreigners were utterly destitute; and their increasing numbers at length forbade a recourse to the usual modes of relief. Trade was stopped by the failure of the interchange of cargoes usual between us, and America, India, Egypt and Greece. A sudden break was made in the routine of our lives. In vain our Protector and his partisans sought to conceal this truth; in vain, day after day, he appointed a period for the discussion of the new laws concerning hereditary rank and privilege; in vain he endeavoured to represent the evil as partial and temporary. These disasters came home to so many bosoms, and, through the various channels of commerce, were carried so entirely into every class and division of the community, that of necessity they became the first question in the state, the chief subjects to which we must turn our attention.

Can it be true, each asked the other with wonder and dismay, that whole countries are laid waste, whole nations annihilated, by these disorders in nature? The vast cities of America, the fertile plains of Hindostan, the crowded abodes of the Chinese, are menaced with utter ruin. Where late the busy multitudes assembled for pleasure or profit, now only the sound of wailing and misery is heard. The air is empoisoned, and each human being inhales death, even while in youth and health, their hopes are in the flower. We called to mind the plague of 1348, when it was calculated that a third of mankind had been destroyed. As yet western Europe was uninfected; would it always be so?

O, yes, it would—Countrymen, fear not! In the still uncultivated wilds of America, what wonder that among its other giant destroyers, Plague should be numbered! It is of old a native of the East, sister of the tornado, the earthquake, and the simoon. Child of the sun, and nursling of the tropics, it would expire in these climes. It drinks the dark blood of the inhabitant of the south, but it never feasts on the pale-faced Celt. If perchance some stricken Asiatic come among us, plague dies with him, uncommunicated and innoxious. Let us weep for our brethren, though we can never experience their reverse. Let us lament over and assist the children of the garden of the earth. Late we envied their abodes, their spicy groves, fertile plains, and abundant loveliness. But in this mortal life extremes are always matched; the thorn grows with the rose, the poison tree and the cinnamon mingle their boughs. Persia, with its cloth of gold, marble halls, and infinite wealth, is now a tomb. The tent of the Arab is fallen in the sands, and his horse spurns the ground unbridled and unsaddled. The voice of lamentation fills the valley of Cashmere; its dells and woods, its cool fountains, and gardens of roses, are polluted by the dead; in Circassia and Georgia the spirit of beauty weeps over the ruin of its favourite temple— the form of woman.

Our own distresses, though they were occasioned by the fictitious reciprocity of commerce, increased in due proportion. Bankers, merchants, and manufacturers, whose trade depended on exports and interchange of wealth, became bankrupt. Such things, when they happen singly, affect only the immediate parties; but the prosperity of the nation was now shaken by frequent and extensive losses. Families, bred in opulence and luxury, were reduced to beggary. The very state of peace in which we gloried was injurious; there were no means of employing the idle, or of sending any overplus of population out of the country. Even the source of colonies was dried up, for in New Holland, Van Diemen's Land, and the Cape of Good Hope, plague raged. O, for some medicinal vial to purge unwholesome nature, and bring back the earth to its accustomed health!

Ryland was a man of strong intellects and quick and sound decision in the usual course of things, but he stood aghast at the multitude of evils that gathered round us. Must he tax the landed interest to assist our commercial population? To do this, he must gain the favour of the chief land-holders, the nobility of the country; and these were his vowed enemies—he must conciliate them by abandoning his favourite scheme of equalization; he must confirm them in their manorial rights; he must sell his cherished plans for the permanent good of his country, for temporary relief. He must aim no more at the dear object of his ambition; throwing his arms aside, he must for present ends give up the ultimate object of his endeavours. He came to Windsor to consult with us. Every day added to his difficulties; the arrival of fresh vessels with emigrants, the total cessation of commerce, the starving multitude that thronged around the palace of the Protectorate, were circumstances not to be tampered with. The blow was struck; the aristocracy obtained all they wished, and they subscribed to a twelvemonths' bill, which levied twenty per cent on all the rent-rolls of the country. Calm was now restored to the metropolis, and to the populous cities, before driven to desperation; and we returned to the consideration of distant calamities, wondering if the future would bring any alleviation to their excess. It was August; so there could be small hope of relief during the heats. On the contrary, the disease gained virulence, while starvation did its accustomed work. Thousands died unlamented; for beside the yet warm corpse the mourner was stretched, made mute by death.

On the eighteenth of this month news arrived in London that the plague was in France and Italy. These tidings were at first whispered about town; but no one dared express aloud the soul-quailing intelligence. When any one met a friend in the street, he only cried as he hurried on, "You know!"— while the other, with an ejaculation of fear and horror, would answer,— "What will become of us?" At length it was mentioned in the newspapers. The paragraph was inserted in an obscure part: "We regret to state that there can be no longer a doubt of the plague having been introduced at Leghorn, Genoa, and Marseilles." No word of comment followed; each reader made his own fearful one. We were as a man who hears that his house is burning, and yet hurries through the streets, borne along by a lurking hope of a mistake, till he turns the corner, and sees his sheltering roof enveloped in a flame. Before it had been a rumour; but now in words uneraseable, in definite and undeniable print, the knowledge went forth. Its obscurity of situation rendered it the more conspicuous: the diminutive letters grew gigantic to the bewildered eye of fear: they seemed graven with a pen of iron, impressed by fire, woven in the clouds, stamped on the very front of the universe.

The English, whether travellers or residents, came pouring in one great revulsive stream, back on their own country; and with them crowds of Italians and Spaniards. Our little island was filled even to bursting. At first an unusual quantity of specie made its appearance with the emigrants; but these people had no means of receiving back into their hands what they spent among us. With the advance of summer, and the increase of the distemper, rents were unpaid, and their remittances failed them. It was impossible to see these crowds of wretched, perishing creatures, late nurslings of luxury, and not stretch out a hand to save them. As at the conclusion of the eighteenth century, the English unlocked their hospitable store, for the relief of those driven from their homes by political revolution; so now they were not backward in affording aid to the victims of a more wide-spreading calamity. We had many foreign friends whom we eagerly sought out, and relieved from dreadful penury. Our Castle became an asylum for the unhappy. A little population occupied its halls. The revenue of its possessor, which had always found a mode of expenditure congenial to his generous nature, was now attended to more parsimoniously, that it might embrace a wider portion of utility. It was not however money, except partially, but the necessaries of life, that became scarce. It was difficult to find an immediate remedy. The usual one of imports was entirely cut off. In this emergency, to feed the very people to whom we had given refuge, we were obliged to yield to the plough and the mattock our pleasure-grounds and parks. Live stock diminished sensibly in the country, from the effects of the great demand in the market. Even the poor deer, our antlered proteges, were obliged to fall for the sake of worthier pensioners. The labour necessary to bring the lands to this sort of culture, employed and fed the offcasts of the diminished manufactories.

Adrian did not rest only with the exertions he could make with regard to his own possessions. He addressed himself to the wealthy of the land; he made proposals in parliament little adapted to please the rich; but his earnest pleadings and benevolent eloquence were irresistible. To give up their pleasure-grounds to the agriculturist, to diminish sensibly the number of horses kept for the purposes of luxury throughout the country, were means obvious, but unpleasing. Yet, to the honour of the English be it recorded, that, although natural disinclination made them delay awhile, yet when the misery of their fellow-creatures became glaring, an enthusiastic generosity inspired their decrees. The most luxurious were often the first to part with their indulgencies. As is common in communities, a fashion was set. The high-born ladies of the country would have deemed themselves disgraced if they had now enjoyed, what they before called a necessary, the ease of a carriage. Chairs, as in olden time, and Indian palanquins were introduced for the infirm; but else it was nothing singular to see females of rank going on foot to places of fashionable resort. It was more common, for all who possessed landed property to secede to their estates, attended by whole troops of the indigent, to cut down their woods to erect temporary dwellings, and to portion out their parks, parterres and flower-gardens, to necessitous families. Many of these, of high rank in their own countries, now, with hoe in hand, turned up the soil. It was found necessary at last to check the spirit of sacrifice, and to remind those whose generosity proceeded to lavish waste, that, until the present state of things became permanent, of which there was no likelihood, it was wrong to carry change so far as to make a reaction difficult. Experience demonstrated that in a year or two pestilence would cease; it were well that in the mean time we should not have destroyed our fine breeds of horses, or have utterly changed the face of the ornamented portion of the country.

It may be imagined that things were in a bad state indeed, before this spirit of benevolence could have struck such deep roots. The infection had now spread in the southern provinces of France. But that country had so many resources in the way of agriculture, that the rush of population from one part of it to another, and its increase through foreign emigration, was less felt than with us. The panic struck appeared of more injury, than disease and its natural concomitants.

Winter was hailed, a general and never-failing physician. The embrowning woods, and swollen rivers, the evening mists, and morning frosts, were welcomed with gratitude. The effects of purifying cold were immediately felt; and the lists of mortality abroad were curtailed each week. Many of our visitors left us: those whose homes were far in the south, fled delightedly from our northern winter, and sought their native land, secure of plenty even after their fearful visitation. We breathed again. What the coming summer would bring, we knew not; but the present months were our own, and our hopes of a cessation of pestilence were high.

---

1. Elton's translation of Hesiod's Works.

❦ 6 ❦

I HAVE LINGERED THUS LONG on the extreme bank, the wasting shoal that stretched into the stream of life, dallying with the shadow of death. Thus long, I have cradled my heart in retrospection of past happiness, when hope was. Why not for ever thus? I am not immortal; and the thread of my history might be spun out to the limits of my existence. But the same sentiment that first led me to pourtray scenes replete with tender recollections, now bids me hurry on. The same yearning of this warm, panting heart, that has made me in written words record my vagabond youth, my serene manhood, and the passions of my soul, makes me now recoil from further delay. I must complete my work.

Here then I stand, as I said, beside the fleet waters of the flowing years, and now away! Spread the sail, and strain with oar, hurrying by dark impending crags, adown steep rapids, even to the sea of desolation I have reached. Yet one moment, one brief interval before I put from shore— once, once again let me fancy myself as I was in 2094 in my abode at Windsor, let me close my eyes, and imagine that the immeasurable boughs of its oaks still shadow me, its castle walls anear. Let fancy pourtray the joyous scene of the twentieth of June, such as even now my aching heart recalls it.

Circumstances had called me to London; here I heard talk that symptoms of the plague had occurred in hospitals of that city. I returned to Windsor; my brow was clouded, my heart heavy; I entered the Little Park, as was my custom, at the Frogmore gate, on my way to the Castle. A great part of these grounds had been given to cultivation, and strips of potatoe-land and corn were scattered here and there. The rooks cawed loudly in the trees above; mixed with their hoarse cries I heard a lively strain of music. It was Alfred's birthday. The young people, the Etonians, and children of the neighbouring gentry, held a mock fair, to which all the country people were invited. The park was speckled by tents, whose flaunting colours and gaudy flags, waving in the sunshine, added to the gaiety of the scene. On a platform erected beneath the terrace, a number of the younger part of the assembly were dancing. I leaned against a tree to observe them. The band played the wild eastern air of Weber introduced in Abon Hassan; its volatile notes gave wings to the feet of the dancers, while the lookers-on unconsciously beat time. At first the tripping measure lifted my spirit with it, and for a moment my eyes gladly followed the mazes of the dance. The revulsion of thought passed like keen steel to my heart. Ye are all going to die, I thought; already your tomb is built up around you. Awhile, because you are gifted with agility and strength, you fancy that you live: but frail is the "bower of flesh" that encaskets life; dissoluble the silver cord than binds you to it. The joyous soul, charioted from pleasure to pleasure by the graceful mechanism of well-formed limbs, will suddenly feel the axle-tree give way, and spring and wheel dissolve in dust. Not one of you, O! fated crowd, can escape—not one! not my own ones! not my Idris and her babes! Horror and misery! Already the gay dance vanished, the green sward was strewn with corpses, the blue air above became fetid with deathly exhalations. Shriek, ye clarions! ye loud trumpets, howl! Pile dirge on dirge; rouse the funereal chords; let the air ring with dire wailing; let wild discord rush on the wings of the wind! Already I hear it, while guardian angels, attendant on humanity, their task achieved, hasten away, and their departure is announced by melancholy strains; faces all unseemly with weeping, forced open my lids; faster and faster many groups of these woe-begone countenances thronged around, exhibiting every variety of wretchedness—well known faces mingled with the distorted creations of fancy. Ashy pale, Raymond and Perdita sat apart, looking on with sad smiles. Adrian's countenance flitted across, tainted by death—Idris, with eyes languidly closed and livid lips, was about to slide into the wide grave. The confusion grew —their looks of sorrow changed to mockery; they nodded their heads in time to the music, whose clang became maddening.

I felt that this was insanity—I sprang forward to throw it off; I rushed into the midst of the crowd. Idris saw me: with light step she advanced; as I folded her in my arms, feeling, as I did, that I thus enclosed what was to me a world, yet frail as the waterdrop which the noon-day sun will drink from the water lily's cup; tears filled my eyes, unwont to be thus moistened. The joyful welcome of my boys, the soft gratulation of Clara, the pressure of Adrian's hand, contributed to unman me. I felt that they were near, that they were safe, yet methought this was all deceit;—the earth reeled, the firm-enrooted trees moved—dizziness came over me—I sank to the ground.

My beloved friends were alarmed—nay, they expressed their alarm so anxiously, that I dared not pronounce the word plague, that hovered on my lips, lest they should construe my perturbed looks into a symptom, and see infection in my languor. I had scarcely recovered, and with feigned hilarity had brought back smiles into my little circle, when we saw Ryland approach.

Ryland had something the appearance of a farmer; of a man whose muscles and full grown stature had been developed under the influence of vigorous exercise and exposure to the elements. This was to a great degree the case: for, though a large landed proprietor, yet, being a projector, and of an ardent and industrious disposition, he had on his own estate given himself up to agricultural labours. When he went as ambassador to the Northern States of America, he, for some time, planned his entire migration; and went so far as to make several journies far westward on that immense continent, for the purpose of choosing the site of his new abode. Ambition turned his thoughts from these designs—ambition, which labouring through various lets and hindrances, had now led him to the summit of his hopes, in making him Lord Protector of England.

His countenance was rough but intelligent—his ample brow and quick grey eyes seemed to look out, over his own plans, and the opposition of his enemies. His voice was stentorian: his hand stretched out in debate, seemed by its gigantic and muscular form, to warn his hearers that words were not his only weapons. Few people had discovered some cowardice and much infirmity of purpose under this imposing exterior. No man could crush a "butterfly on the wheel" with better effect; no man better cover a speedy retreat from a powerful adversary. This had been the secret of his secession at the time of Lord Raymond's election. In the unsteady glance of his eye, in his extreme desire to learn the opinions of all, in the feebleness of his handwriting, these qualities might be obscurely traced, but they were not generally known. He was now our Lord Protector. He had canvassed eagerly for this post. His protectorate was to be distinguished by every kind of innovation on the aristocracy. This his selected task was exchanged for the far different one of encountering the ruin caused by the convulsions of physical nature. He was incapable of meeting these evils by any comprehensive system; he had resorted to expedient after expedient, and could never be induced to put a remedy in force, till it came too late to be of use.

Certainly the Ryland that advanced towards us now, bore small resemblance to the powerful, ironical, seemingly fearless canvasser for the first rank among Englishmen. Our native oak, as his partisans called him, was visited truly by a nipping winter. He scarcely appeared half his usual height; his joints were unknit, his limbs would not support him; his face was contracted, his eye wandering; debility of purpose and dastard fear were expressed in every gesture.

In answer to our eager questions, one word alone fell, as it were involuntarily, from his convulsed lips: The Plague.—"Where?"—"Every where—we must fly—all fly—but whither? No man can tell—there is no refuge on earth, it comes on us like a thousand packs of wolves—we must all fly—where shall you go? Where can any of us go?"

These words were syllabled trembling by the iron man. Adrian replied, "Whither indeed would you fly? We must all remain; and do our best to help our suffering fellow-creatures."

"Help!" said Ryland, "there is no help!—great God, who talks of help!

All the world has the plague!"

"Then to avoid it, we must quit the world," observed Adrian, with a gentle smile.

Ryland groaned; cold drops stood on his brow. It was useless to oppose his paroxysm of terror: but we soothed and encouraged him, so that after an interval he was better able to explain to us the ground of his alarm. It had come sufficiently home to him. One of his servants, while waiting on him, had suddenly fallen down dead. The physician declared that he died of the plague. We endeavoured to calm him—but our own hearts were not calm. I saw the eye of Idris wander from me to her children, with an anxious appeal to my judgment. Adrian was absorbed in meditation. For myself, I own that Ryland's words rang in my ears; all the world was infected;—in what uncontaminated seclusion could I save my beloved treasures, until the shadow of death had passed from over the earth? We sunk into silence: a silence that drank in the doleful accounts and prognostications of our guest. We had receded from the crowd; and ascending the steps of the terrace, sought the Castle. Our change of cheer struck those nearest to us; and, by means of Ryland's servants, the report soon spread that he had fled from the plague in London. The sprightly parties broke up—they assembled in whispering groups. The spirit of gaiety was eclipsed; the music ceased; the young people left their occupations and gathered together. The lightness of heart which had dressed them in masquerade habits, had decorated their tents, and assembled them in fantastic groups, appeared a sin against, and a provocative to, the awful destiny that had laid its palsying hand upon hope and life. The merriment of the hour was an unholy mockery of the sorrows of man. The foreigners whom we had among us, who had fled from the plague in their own country, now saw their last asylum invaded; and, fear making them garrulous, they described to eager listeners the miseries they had beheld in cities visited by the calamity, and gave fearful accounts of the insidious and irremediable nature of the disease.

We had entered the Castle. Idris stood at a window that over-looked the park; her maternal eyes sought her own children among the young crowd. An Italian lad had got an audience about him, and with animated gestures was describing some scene of horror. Alfred stood immoveable before him, his whole attention absorbed. Little Evelyn had endeavoured to draw Clara away to play with him; but the Italian's tale arrested her, she crept near, her lustrous eyes fixed on the speaker. Either watching the crowd in the park, or occupied by painful reflection, we were all silent; Ryland stood by himself in an embrasure of the window; Adrian paced the hall, revolving some new and overpowering idea—suddenly he stopped and said: "I have long expected this; could we in reason expect that this island should be exempt from the universal visitation? The evil is come home to us, and we must not shrink from our fate. What are your plans, my Lord Protector, for the benefit of our country?"

"For heaven's love! Windsor," cried Ryland, "do not mock me with that title. Death and disease level all men. I neither pretend to protect nor govern an hospital—such will England quickly become."

"Do you then intend, now in time of peril, to recede from your duties?"

"Duties! speak rationally, my Lord!—when I am a plague-spotted corpse, where will my duties be? Every man for himself! the devil take the protectorship, say I, if it expose me to danger!"

"Faint-hearted man!" cried Adrian indignantly—"Your countrymen put their trust in you, and you betray them!"

"I betray them!" said Ryland, "the plague betrays me. Faint-hearted! It is well, shut up in your castle, out of danger, to boast yourself out of fear. Take the Protectorship who will; before God I renounce it!"

"And before God," replied his opponent, fervently, "do I receive it! No one will canvass for this honour now—none envy my danger or labours. Deposit your powers in my hands. Long have I fought with death, and much" (he stretched out his thin hand) "much have I suffered in the struggle. It is not by flying, but by facing the enemy, that we can conquer. If my last combat is now about to be fought, and I am to be worsted—so let it be!"

"But come, Ryland, recollect yourself! Men have hitherto thought you magnanimous and wise, will you cast aside these titles? Consider the panic your departure will occasion. Return to London. I will go with you. Encourage the people by your presence. I will incur all the danger. Shame! shame! if the first magistrate of England be foremost to renounce his duties."

Meanwhile among our guests in the park, all thoughts of festivity had faded. As summer-flies are scattered by rain, so did this congregation, late noisy and happy, in sadness and melancholy murmurs break up, dwindling away apace. With the set sun and the deepening twilight the park became nearly empty. Adrian and Ryland were still in earnest discussion. We had prepared a banquet for our guests in the lower hall of the castle; and thither Idris and I repaired to receive and entertain the few that remained. There is nothing more melancholy than a merry-meeting thus turned to sorrow: the gala dresses—the decorations, gay as they might otherwise be, receive a solemn and funereal appearance. If such change be painful from lighter causes, it weighed with intolerable heaviness from the knowledge that the earth's desolator had at last, even as an arch-fiend, lightly over-leaped the boundaries our precautions raised, and at once enthroned himself in the full and beating heart of our country. Idris sat at the top of the half-empty hall. Pale and tearful, she almost forgot her duties as hostess; her eyes were fixed on her children. Alfred's serious air shewed that he still revolved the tragic story related by the Italian boy. Evelyn was the only mirthful creature present: he sat on Clara's lap; and, making matter of glee from his own fancies, laughed aloud. The vaulted roof echoed again his infant tone. The poor mother who had brooded long over, and suppressed the expression of her anguish, now burst into tears, and folding her babe in her arms, hurried from the hall. Clara and Alfred followed. While the rest of the company, in confused murmur, which grew louder and louder, gave voice to their many fears.

The younger part gathered round me to ask my advice; and those who had friends in London were anxious beyond the rest, to ascertain the present extent of disease in the metropolis. I encouraged them with such thoughts of cheer as presented themselves. I told them exceedingly few deaths had yet been occasioned by pestilence, and gave them hopes, as we were the last visited, so the calamity might have lost its most venomous power before it had reached us. The cleanliness, habits of order, and the manner in which our cities were built, were all in our favour. As it was an epidemic, its chief force was derived from pernicious qualities in the air, and it would probably do little harm where this was naturally salubrious. At first, I had spoken only to those nearest me; but the whole assembly gathered about me, and I found that I was listened to by all. "My friends," I said, "our risk is common; our precautions and exertions shall be common also. If manly courage and resistance can save us, we will be saved. We will fight the enemy to the last. Plague shall not find us a ready prey; we will dispute every inch of ground; and, by methodical and inflexible laws, pile invincible barriers to the progress of our foe. Perhaps in no part of the world has she met with so systematic and determined an opposition. Perhaps no country is naturally so well protected against our invader; nor has nature anywhere been so well assisted by the hand of man. We will not despair. We are neither cowards nor fatalists; but, believing that God has placed the means for our preservation in our own hands, we will use those means to our utmost. Remember that cleanliness, sobriety, and even good-humour and benevolence, are our best medicines."

There was little I could add to this general exhortation; for the plague, though in London, was not among us. I dismissed the guests therefore; and they went thoughtful, more than sad, to await the events in store for them.

I now sought Adrian, anxious to hear the result of his discussion with Ryland. He had in part prevailed; the Lord Protector consented to return to London for a few weeks; during which time things should be so arranged, as to occasion less consternation at his departure. Adrian and Idris were together. The sadness with which the former had first heard that the plague was in London had vanished; the energy of his purpose informed his body with strength, the solemn joy of enthusiasm and self-devotion illuminated his countenance; and the weakness of his physical nature seemed to pass from him, as the cloud of humanity did, in the ancient fable, from the divine lover of Semele. He was endeavouring to encourage his sister, and to bring her to look on his intent in a less tragic light than she was prepared to do; and with passionate eloquence he unfolded his designs to her.

"Let me, at the first word," he said, "relieve your mind from all fear on my account. I will not task myself beyond my powers, nor will I needlessly seek danger. I feel that I know what ought to be done, and as my presence is necessary for the accomplishment of my plans, I will take especial care to preserve my life.

"I am now going to undertake an office fitted for me. I cannot intrigue, or work a tortuous path through the labyrinth of men's vices and passions; but I can bring patience, and sympathy, and such aid as art affords, to the bed of disease; I can raise from earth the miserable orphan, and awaken to new hopes the shut heart of the mourner. I can enchain the plague in limits, and set a term to the misery it would occasion; courage, forbearance, and watchfulness, are the forces I bring towards this great work.

"O, I shall be something now! From my birth I have aspired like the eagle —but, unlike the eagle, my wings have failed, and my vision has been blinded. Disappointment and sickness have hitherto held dominion over me; twin born with me, my would, was for ever enchained by the shall not, of these my tyrants. A shepherd-boy that tends a silly flock on the mountains, was more in the scale of society than I. Congratulate me then that I have found fitting scope for my powers. I have often thought of offering my services to the pestilence-stricken towns of France and Italy; but fear of paining you, and expectation of this catastrophe, withheld me. To England and to Englishmen I dedicate myself. If I can save one of her mighty spirits from the deadly shaft; if I can ward disease from one of her smiling cottages, I shall not have lived in vain."

Strange ambition this! Yet such was Adrian. He appeared given up to contemplation, averse to excitement, a lowly student, a man of visions— but afford him worthy theme, and—

> *Like to the lark at break of day arising,*
> *From sullen earth, sings hymns at heaven's gate.*[1]

so did he spring up from listlessness and unproductive thought, to the highest pitch of virtuous action.

With him went enthusiasm, the high-wrought resolve, the eye that without blenching could look at death. With us remained sorrow, anxiety, and unendurable expectation of evil. The man, says Lord Bacon, who hath wife and children, has given hostages to fortune. Vain was all philosophical reasoning—vain all fortitude—vain, vain, a reliance on probable good. I might heap high the scale with logic, courage, and resignation—but let one fear for Idris and our children enter the opposite one, and, over-weighed, it kicked the beam.

The plague was in London! Fools that we were not long ago to have foreseen this. We wept over the ruin of the boundless continents of the east, and the desolation of the western world; while we fancied that the little channel between our island and the rest of the earth was to preserve us alive among the dead. It were no mighty leap methinks from Calais to Dover. The eye easily discerns the sister land; they were united once; and the little path that runs between looks in a map but as a trodden footway through high grass. Yet this small interval was to save us: the sea was to rise a wall of adamant—without, disease and misery—within, a shelter from evil, a nook of the garden of paradise—a particle of celestial soil, which no evil could invade— truly we were wise in our generation, to imagine all these things!

But we are awake now. The plague is in London; the air of England is tainted, and her sons and daughters strew the unwholesome earth. And now, the sea, late our defence, seems our prison bound; hemmed in by its gulphs, we shall die like the famished inhabitants of a besieged town. Other nations have a fellowship in death; but we, shut out from all neighbourhood, must bury our own dead, and little England become a wide, wide tomb.

This feeling of universal misery assumed concentration and shape, when I looked on my wife and children; and the thought of danger to them possessed my whole being with fear. How could I save them? I revolved a thousand and a thousand plans. They should not die— first I would be gathered to nothingness, ere infection should come anear these idols of my soul. I would walk barefoot through the world, to find an uninfected spot; I would build my home on some wave-tossed plank, drifted about on the barren, shoreless ocean. I would betake me with them to some wild beast's den, where a tyger's cubs, which I would slay, had been reared in health. I would seek the mountain eagle's eirie, and live years suspended in some inaccessible recess of a sea-bounding cliff—no labour too great, no scheme too wild, if it promised life to them. O! ye heart-strings of mine, could ye be torn asunder, and my soul not spend itself in tears of blood for sorrow!

Idris, after the first shock, regained a portion of fortitude. She studiously shut out all prospect of the future, and cradled her heart in present blessings. She never for a moment lost sight of her children. But while they in health sported about her, she could cherish contentment and hope. A strange and wild restlessness came over me—the more intolerable, because I was forced to conceal it. My fears for Adrian were ceaseless; August had come; and the symptoms of plague increased rapidly in London. It was deserted by all who possessed the power of removing; and he, the brother of my soul, was exposed to the perils from which all but slaves enchained by circumstance fled. He remained to combat the fiend—his side unguarded, his toils unshared—infection might even reach him, and he die unattended and alone. By day and night these thoughts pursued me. I resolved to visit London, to see him; to quiet these agonizing throes by the sweet medicine of hope, or the opiate of despair.

It was not until I arrived at Brentford, that I perceived much change in the face of the country. The better sort of houses were shut up; the busy trade of the town palsied; there was an air of anxiety among the few passengers I met, and they looked wonderingly at my carriage —the first they had seen pass towards London, since pestilence sat on its high places, and possessed its busy streets. I met several funerals; they were slenderly attended by mourners, and were regarded by the spectators as omens of direst import. Some gazed on these processions with wild eagerness— others fled timidly—some wept aloud.

Adrian's chief endeavour, after the immediate succour of the sick, had been to disguise the symptoms and progress of the plague from the inhabitants of London. He knew that fear and melancholy forebodings were powerful assistants to disease; that desponding and brooding care rendered the physical nature of man peculiarly susceptible of infection. No unseemly sights were therefore discernible: the shops were in general open, the concourse of passengers in some degree kept up. But although the appearance of an infected town was avoided, to me, who had not beheld it since the commencement of the visitation, London appeared sufficiently changed. There were no carriages, and grass had sprung high in the streets; the houses had a desolate look; most of the shutters were closed; and there was a ghast and frightened stare in the persons I met, very different from the usual business-like demeanour of the Londoners. My solitary carriage attracted notice, as it rattled along towards the Protectoral Palace—and the fashionable streets leading to it wore a still more dreary and deserted appearance. I found Adrian's anti-chamber crowded—it was his hour for giving audience. I was unwilling to disturb his labours, and waited, watching the ingress and egress of the petitioners. They consisted of people of the middling and lower classes of society, whose means of subsistence failed with the cessation of trade, and of the busy spirit of money-making in all its branches, peculiar to our country. There was an air of anxiety, sometimes of terror in the new-comers, strongly contrasted with the resigned and even satisfied mien of those who had had audience. I could read the influence of my friend in their quickened motions and cheerful faces. Two o'clock struck, after which none were admitted; those who had been disappointed went sullenly or sorrowfully away, while I entered the audience-chamber.

I was struck by the improvement that appeared in the health of Adrian. He was no longer bent to the ground, like an over-nursed flower of spring, that, shooting up beyond its strength, is weighed down even by its own coronal of blossoms. His eyes were bright, his countenance composed, an air of concentrated energy was diffused over his whole person, much unlike its former languor. He sat at a table with several secretaries, who were arranging petitions, or registering the notes made during that day's audience. Two or three petitioners were still in attendance. I admired his justice and patience. Those who possessed a power of living out of London, he advised immediately to quit it, affording them the means of so doing. Others, whose trade was beneficial to the city, or who possessed no other refuge, he provided with advice for better avoiding the epidemic; relieving overloaded families, supplying the gaps made in others by death. Order, comfort, and even health, rose under his influence, as from the touch of a magician's wand.

"I am glad you are come," he said to me, when we were at last alone; "I can only spare a few minutes, and must tell you much in that time. The plague is now in progress—it is useless closing one's eyes to the fact—the deaths increase each week. What will come I cannot guess. As yet, thank God, I am equal to the government of the town; and I look only to the present. Ryland, whom I have so long detained, has stipulated that I shall suffer him to depart before the end of this month. The deputy appointed by parliament is dead; another therefore must be named; I have advanced my claim, and I believe that I shall have no competitor. To-night the question is to be decided, as there is a call of the house for the purpose. You must nominate me, Lionel; Ryland, for shame, cannot shew himself; but you, my friend, will do me this service?

How lovely is devotion! Here was a youth, royally sprung, bred in luxury, by nature averse to the usual struggles of a public life, and now, in time of danger, at a period when to live was the utmost scope of the ambitious, he, the beloved and heroic Adrian, made, in sweet simplicity, an offer to sacrifice himself for the public good. The very idea was generous and noble,—but, beyond this, his unpretending manner, his entire want of the assumption of a virtue, rendered his act ten times more touching. I would have withstood his request; but I had seen the good he diffused; I felt that his resolves were not to be shaken, so, with an heavy heart, I consented to do as he asked. He grasped my hand affectionately:—"Thank you," he said, "you have relieved me from a painful dilemma, and are, as you ever were, the best of my friends. Farewell—I must now leave you for a few hours. Go you and converse with Ryland. Although he deserts his post in London, he may be of the greatest service in the north of England, by receiving and assisting travellers, and contributing to supply the metropolis with food. Awaken him, I entreat you, to some sense of duty."

Adrian left me, as I afterwards learnt, upon his daily task of visiting the hospitals, and inspecting the crowded parts of London. I found Ryland much altered, even from what he had been when he visited Windsor. Perpetual fear had jaundiced his complexion, and shrivelled his whole person. I told him of the business of the evening, and a smile relaxed the contracted muscles. He desired to go; each day he expected to be infected by pestilence, each day he was unable to resist the gentle violence of Adrian's detention. The moment Adrian should be legally elected his deputy, he would escape to safety. Under this impression he listened to all I said; and, elevated almost to joy by the near prospect of his departure, he entered into a discussion concerning the plans he should adopt in his own county, forgetting, for the moment, his cherished resolution of shutting himself up from all communication in the mansion and grounds of his estate.

In the evening, Adrian and I proceeded to Westminster. As we went he reminded me of what I was to say and do, yet, strange to say, I entered the chamber without having once reflected on my purpose. Adrian remained in the coffee-room, while I, in compliance with his desire, took my seat in St. Stephen's. There reigned unusual silence in the chamber. I had not visited it since Raymond's protectorate; a period conspicuous for a numerous attendance of members, for the eloquence of the speakers, and the warmth of the debate. The benches were very empty, those by custom occupied by the hereditary members were vacant; the city members were there—the members for the commercial towns, few landed proprietors, and not many of those who entered parliament for the sake of a career. The first subject that occupied the attention of the house was an address from the Lord Protector, praying them to appoint a deputy during a necessary absence on his part.

A silence prevailed, till one of the members coming to me, whispered that the Earl of Windsor had sent him word that I was to move his election, in the absence of the person who had been first chosen for this office. Now for the first time I saw the full extent of my task, and I was overwhelmed by what I had brought on myself. Ryland had deserted his post through fear of the plague: from the same fear Adrian had no competitor. And I, the nearest kinsman of the Earl of Windsor, was to propose his election. I was to thrust this selected and matchless friend into the post of danger— impossible! the die was cast—I would offer myself as candidate.

The few members who were present, had come more for the sake of terminating the business by securing a legal attendance, than under the idea of a debate. I had risen mechanically—my knees trembled; irresolution hung on my voice, as I uttered a few words on the necessity of choosing a person adequate to the dangerous task in hand. But, when the idea of presenting myself in the room of my friend intruded, the load of doubt and pain was taken from off me. My words flowed spontaneously—my utterance was firm and quick. I adverted to what Adrian had already done—I promised the same vigilance in furthering all his views. I drew a touching picture of his vacillating health; I boasted of my own strength. I prayed them to save even from himself this scion of the noblest family in England. My alliance with him was the pledge of my sincerity, my union with his sister, my children, his presumptive heirs, were the hostages of my truth.

This unexpected turn in the debate was quickly communicated to Adrian. He hurried in, and witnessed the termination of my impassioned harangue. I did not see him: my soul was in my words,—my eyes could not perceive that which was; while a vision of Adrian's form, tainted by pestilence, and sinking in death, floated before them. He seized my hand, as I concluded— "Unkind!" he cried, "you have betrayed me!" then, springing forwards, with the air of one who had a right to command, he claimed the place of deputy as his own. He had bought it, he said, with danger, and paid for it with toil. His ambition rested there; and, after an interval devoted to the interests of his country, was I to step in, and reap the profit? Let them remember what London had been when he arrived: the panic that prevailed brought famine, while every moral and legal tie was loosened. He had restored order—this had been a work which required perseverance, patience, and energy; and he had neither slept nor waked but for the good of his country.—Would they dare wrong him thus? Would they wrest his hard-earned reward from him, to bestow it on one, who, never having mingled in public life, would come a tyro to the craft, in which he was an adept. He demanded the place of deputy as his right. Ryland had shewn that he preferred him. Never before had he, who was born even to the inheritance of the throne of England, never had he asked favour or honour from those now his equals, but who might have been his subjects. Would they refuse him? Could they thrust back from the path of distinction and laudable ambition, the heir of their ancient kings, and heap another disappointment on a fallen house.

No one had ever before heard Adrian allude to the rights of his ancestors. None had ever before suspected, that power, or the suffrage of the many, could in any manner become dear to him. He had begun his speech with vehemence; he ended with unassuming gentleness, making his appeal with the same humility, as if he had asked to be the first in wealth, honour, and power among Englishmen, and not, as was the truth, to be the foremost in the ranks of loathsome toils and inevitable death. A murmur of approbation rose after his speech. "Oh, do not listen to him," I cried, "he speaks false—false to himself,"—I was interrupted: and, silence being restored, we were ordered, as was the custom, to retire during the decision of the house. I fancied that they hesitated, and that there was some hope for me—I was mistaken—hardly had we quitted the chamber, before Adrian was recalled, and installed in his office of Lord Deputy to the Protector.

We returned together to the palace. "Why, Lionel," said Adrian, "what did you intend? you could not hope to conquer, and yet you gave me the pain of a triumph over my dearest friend."

"This is mockery," I replied, "you devote yourself,—you, the adored brother of Idris, the being, of all the world contains, dearest to our hearts—you devote yourself to an early death. I would have prevented this; my death would be a small evil—or rather I should not die; while you cannot hope to escape."

"As to the likelihood of escaping," said Adrian, "ten years hence the cold stars may shine on the graves of all of us; but as to my peculiar liability to infection, I could easily prove, both logically and physically, that in the midst of contagion I have a better chance of life than you.

"This is my post: I was born for this—to rule England in anarchy, to save her in danger—to devote myself for her. The blood of my forefathers cries aloud in my veins, and bids me be first among my countrymen. Or, if this mode of speech offend you, let me say, that my mother, the proud queen, instilled early into me a love of distinction, and all that, if the weakness of my physical nature and my peculiar opinions had not prevented such a design, might have made me long since struggle for the lost inheritance of my race. But now my mother, or, if you will, my mother's lessons, awaken within me. I cannot lead on to battle; I cannot, through intrigue and faithlessness rear again the throne upon the wreck of English public spirit. But I can be the first to support and guard my country, now that terrific disasters and ruin have laid strong hands upon her.

"That country and my beloved sister are all I have. I will protect the first—the latter I commit to your charge. If I survive, and she be lost, I were far better dead. Preserve her—for her own sake I know that you will—if you require any other spur, think that, in preserving her, you preserve me. Her faultless nature, one sum of perfections, is wrapt up in her affections—if they were hurt, she would droop like an unwatered floweret, and the slightest injury they receive is a nipping frost to her. Already she fears for us. She fears for the children she adores, and for you, the father of these, her lover, husband, protector; and you must be near her to support and encourage her. Return to Windsor then, my brother; for such you are by every tie —fill the double place my absence imposes on you, and let me, in all my sufferings here, turn my eyes towards that dear seclusion, and say—There is peace."

---

1. Shakespeare's Sonnets.

7

I DID PROCEED TO WINDSOR, but not with the intention of remaining there. I went but to obtain the consent of Idris, and then to return and take my station beside my unequalled friend; to share his labours, and save him, if so it must be, at the expence of my life. Yet I dreaded to witness the anguish which my resolve might excite in Idris. I had vowed to my own heart never to shadow her countenance even with transient grief, and should I prove recreant at the hour of greatest need? I had begun my journey with anxious haste; now I desired to draw it out through the course of days and months. I longed to avoid the necessity of action; I strove to escape from thought—vainly—futurity, like a dark image in a phantasmagoria, came nearer and more near, till it clasped the whole earth in its shadow.

A slight circumstance induced me to alter my usual route, and to return home by Egham and Bishopgate. I alighted at Perdita's ancient abode, her cottage; and, sending forward the carriage, determined to walk across the park to the castle. This spot, dedicated to sweetest recollections, the deserted house and neglected garden were well adapted to nurse my melancholy. In our happiest days, Perdita had adorned her cottage with every aid art might bring, to that which nature had selected to favour. In the same spirit of exaggeration she had, on the event of her separation from Raymond, caused it to be entirely neglected. It was now in ruin: the deer had climbed the broken palings, and reposed among the flowers; grass grew on the threshold, and the swinging lattice creaking to the wind, gave signal of utter desertion. The sky was blue above, and the air impregnated with fragrance by the rare flowers that grew among the weeds. The trees moved overhead, awakening nature's favourite melody—but the melancholy appearance of the choaked paths, and weed-grown flower-beds, dimmed even this gay summer scene. The time when in proud and happy security we assembled at this cottage, was gone—soon the present hours would join those past, and shadows of future ones rose dark and menacing from the womb of time, their cradle and their bier. For the first time in my life I envied the sleep of the dead, and thought with pleasure of one's bed under the sod, where grief and fear have no power. I passed through the gap of the broken paling—I felt, while I disdained, the choaking tears—I rushed into the depths of the forest. O death and change, rulers of our life, where are ye, that I may grapple with you! What was there in our tranquility, that excited your envy—in our happiness, that ye should destroy it? We were happy, loving, and beloved; the horn of Amalthea contained no blessing unshowered upon us, but, alas!

la fortuna deidad barbara importuna, oy cadaver y ayer flor, no permanece jamas![1]

As I wandered on thus ruminating, a number of country people passed me. They seemed full of careful thought, and a few words of their conversation that reached me, induced me to approach and make further enquiries. A party of people flying from London, as was frequent in those days, had come up the Thames in a boat. No one at Windsor would afford them shelter; so, going a little further up, they remained all night in a deserted hut near Bolter's lock. They pursued their way the following morning, leaving one of their company behind them, sick of the plague. This circumstance once spread abroad, none dared approach within half a mile of the infected neighbourhood, and the deserted wretch was left to fight with disease and death in solitude, as he best might. I was urged by compassion to hasten to the hut, for the purpose of ascertaining his situation, and administering to his wants.

As I advanced I met knots of country-people talking earnestly of this event: distant as they were from the apprehended contagion, fear was impressed on every countenance. I passed by a group of these terrorists, in a lane in the direct road to the hut. One of them stopped me, and, conjecturing that I was ignorant of the circumstance, told me not to go on, for that an infected person lay but at a short distance.

"I know it," I replied, "and I am going to see in what condition the poor fellow is."

A murmur of surprise and horror ran through the assembly. I continued:—

"This poor wretch is deserted, dying, succourless; in these unhappy times,
God knows how soon any or all of us may be in like want. I am going to do,
as I would be done by."

"But you will never be able to return to the Castle—Lady Idris—his children—" in confused speech were the words that struck my ear.

"Do you not know, my friends," I said, "that the Earl himself, now Lord Protector, visits daily, not only those probably infected by this disease, but the hospitals and pest houses, going near, and even touching the sick? yet he was never in better health. You labour under an entire mistake as to the nature of the plague; but do not fear, I do not ask any of you to accompany me, nor to believe me, until I return safe and sound from my patient."

So I left them, and hurried on. I soon arrived at the hut: the door was ajar. I entered, and one glance assured me that its former inhabitant was no more—he lay on a heap of straw, cold and stiff; while a pernicious effluvia filled the room, and various stains and marks served to shew the virulence of the disorder.

I had never before beheld one killed by pestilence. While every mind was full of dismay at its effects, a craving for excitement had led us to peruse De Foe's account, and the masterly delineations of the author of Arthur Mervyn. The pictures drawn in these books were so vivid, that we seemed to have experienced the results depicted by them. But cold were the sensations excited by words, burning though they were, and describing the death and misery of thousands, compared to what I felt in looking on the corpse of this unhappy stranger. This indeed was the plague. I raised his rigid limbs, I marked the distortion of his face, and the stony eyes lost to perception. As I was thus occupied, chill horror congealed my blood, making my flesh quiver and my hair to stand on end. Half insanely I spoke to the dead. So the plague killed you, I muttered. How came this? Was the coming painful? You look as if the enemy had tortured, before he murdered you. And now I leapt up precipitately, and escaped from the hut, before nature could revoke her laws, and inorganic words be breathed in answer from the lips of the departed.

On returning through the lane, I saw at a distance the same assemblage of persons which I had left. They hurried away, as soon as they saw me; my agitated mien added to their fear of coming near one who had entered within the verge of contagion.

At a distance from facts one draws conclusions which appear infallible, which yet when put to the test of reality, vanish like unreal dreams. I had ridiculed the fears of my countrymen, when they related to others; now that they came home to myself, I paused. The Rubicon, I felt, was passed; and it behoved me well to reflect what I should do on this hither side of disease and danger. According to the vulgar superstition, my dress, my person, the air I breathed, bore in it mortal danger to myself and others. Should I return to the Castle, to my wife and children, with this taint upon me? Not surely if I were infected; but I felt certain that I was not—a few hours would determine the question—I would spend these in the forest, in reflection on what was to come, and what my future actions were to be. In the feeling communicated to me by the sight of one struck by the plague, I forgot the events that had excited me so strongly in London; new and more painful prospects, by degrees were cleared of the mist which had hitherto veiled them. The question was no longer whether I should share Adrian's toils and danger; but in what manner I could, in Windsor and the neighbourhood, imitate the prudence and zeal which, under his government, produced order and plenty in London, and how, now pestilence had spread more widely, I could secure the health of my own family.

I spread the whole earth out as a map before me. On no one spot of its surface could I put my finger and say, here is safety. In the south, the disease, virulent and immedicable, had nearly annihilated the race of man; storm and inundation, poisonous winds and blights, filled up the measure of suffering. In the north it was worse—the lesser population gradually declined, and famine and plague kept watch on the survivors, who, helpless and feeble, were ready to fall an easy prey into their hands.

I contracted my view to England. The overgrown metropolis, the great heart of mighty Britain, was pulseless. Commerce had ceased. All resort for ambition or pleasure was cut off— the streets were grass-grown—the houses empty—the few, that from necessity remained, seemed already branded with the taint of inevitable pestilence. In the larger manufacturing towns the same tragedy was acted on a smaller, yet more disastrous scale. There was no Adrian to superintend and direct, while whole flocks of the poor were struck and killed. Yet we were not all to die. No truly, though thinned, the race of man would continue, and the great plague would, in after years, become matter of history and wonder. Doubtless this visitation was for extent unexampled—more need that we should work hard to dispute its progress; ere this men have gone out in sport, and slain their thousands and tens of thousands; but now man had become a creature of price; the life of one of them was of more worth than the so called treasures of kings. Look at his thought-endued countenance, his graceful limbs, his majestic brow, his wondrous mechanism—the type and model of this best work of God is not to be cast aside as a broken vessel—he shall be preserved, and his children and his children's children carry down the name and form of man to latest time.

Above all I must guard those entrusted by nature and fate to my especial care. And surely, if among all my fellow-creatures I were to select those who might stand forth examples of the greatness and goodness of man, I could choose no other than those allied to me by the most sacred ties. Some from among the family of man must survive, and these should be among the survivors; that should be my task—to accomplish it my own life were a small sacrifice. There then in that castle—in Windsor Castle, birth-place of Idris and my babes, should be the haven and retreat for the wrecked bark of human society. Its forest should be our world—its garden afford us food; within its walls I would establish the shaken throne of health. I was an outcast and a vagabond, when Adrian gently threw over me the silver net of love and civilization, and linked me inextricably to human charities and human excellence. I was one, who, though an aspirant after good, and an ardent lover of wisdom, was yet unenrolled in any list of worth, when Idris, the princely born, who was herself the personification of all that was divine in woman, she who walked the earth like a poet's dream, as a carved goddess endued with sense, or pictured saint stepping from the canvas—she, the most worthy, chose me, and gave me herself—a priceless gift.

During several hours I continued thus to meditate, till hunger and fatigue brought me back to the passing hour, then marked by long shadows cast from the descending sun. I had wandered towards Bracknel, far to the west of Windsor. The feeling of perfect health which I enjoyed, assured me that I was free from contagion. I remembered that Idris had been kept in ignorance of my proceedings. She might have heard of my return from London, and my visit to Bolter's Lock, which, connected with my continued absence, might tend greatly to alarm her. I returned to Windsor by the Long Walk, and passing through the town towards the Castle, I found it in a state of agitation and disturbance.

"It is too late to be ambitious," says Sir Thomas Browne. "We cannot hope to live so long in our names as some have done in their persons; one face of Janus holds no proportion to the other." Upon this text many fanatics arose, who prophesied that the end of time was come. The spirit of superstition had birth, from the wreck of our hopes, and antics wild and dangerous were played on the great theatre, while the remaining particle of futurity dwindled into a point in the eyes of the prognosticators. Weak-spirited women died of fear as they listened to their denunciations; men of robust form and seeming strength fell into idiotcy and madness, racked by the dread of coming eternity. A man of this kind was now pouring forth his eloquent despair among the inhabitants of Windsor. The scene of the morning, and my visit to the dead, which had been spread abroad, had alarmed the country-people, so they had become fit instruments to be played upon by a maniac.

The poor wretch had lost his young wife and lovely infant by the plague. He was a mechanic; and, rendered unable to attend to the occupation which supplied his necessities, famine was added to his other miseries. He left the chamber which contained his wife and child —wife and child no more, but "dead earth upon the earth"—wild with hunger, watching and grief, his diseased fancy made him believe himself sent by heaven to preach the end of time to the world. He entered the churches, and foretold to the congregations their speedy removal to the vaults below. He appeared like the forgotten spirit of the time in the theatres, and bade the spectators go home and die. He had been seized and confined; he had escaped and wandered from London among the neighbouring towns, and, with frantic gestures and thrilling words, he unveiled to each their hidden fears, and gave voice to the soundless thought they dared not syllable. He stood under the arcade of the town-hall of Windsor, and from this elevation harangued a trembling crowd.

"Hear, O ye inhabitants of the earth," he cried, "hear thou, all seeing, but most pitiless Heaven! hear thou too, O tempest-tossed heart, which breathes out these words, yet faints beneath their meaning! Death is among us! The earth is beautiful and flower-bedecked, but she is our grave! The clouds of heaven weep for us—the pageantry of the stars is but our funeral torchlight. Grey headed men, ye hoped for yet a few years in your long-known abode—but the lease is up, you must remove—children, ye will never reach maturity, even now the small grave is dug for ye— mothers, clasp them in your arms, one death embraces you!"

Shuddering, he stretched out his hands, his eyes cast up, seemed bursting from their sockets, while he appeared to follow shapes, to us invisible, in the yielding air—"There they are," he cried, "the dead! They rise in their shrouds, and pass in silent procession towards the far land of their doom—their bloodless lips move not—their shadowy limbs are void of motion, while still they glide onwards. We come," he exclaimed, springing forwards, "for what should we wait? Haste, my friends, apparel yourselves in the court-dress of death. Pestilence will usher you to his presence. Why thus long? they, the good, the wise, and the beloved, are gone before. Mothers, kiss you last—husbands, protectors no more, lead on the partners of your death! Come, O come! while the dear ones are yet in sight, for soon they will pass away, and we never never shall join them more."

From such ravings as these, he would suddenly become collected, and with unexaggerated but terrific words, paint the horrors of the time; describe with minute detail, the effects of the plague on the human frame, and tell heart-breaking tales of the snapping of dear affinities—the gasping horror of despair over the death-bed of the last beloved—so that groans and even shrieks burst from the crowd. One man in particular stood in front, his eyes fixt on the prophet, his mouth open, his limbs rigid, while his face changed to various colours, yellow, blue, and green, through intense fear. The maniac caught his glance, and turned his eye on him— one has heard of the gaze of the rattle-snake, which allures the trembling victim till he falls within his jaws. The maniac became composed; his person rose higher; authority beamed from his countenance. He looked on the peasant, who began to tremble, while he still gazed; his knees knocked together; his teeth chattered. He at last fell down in convulsions. "That man has the plague," said the maniac calmly. A shriek burst from the lips of the poor wretch; and then sudden motionlessness came over him; it was manifest to all that he was dead.

Cries of horror filled the place—every one endeavoured to effect his escape—in a few minutes the market place was cleared—the corpse lay on the ground; and the maniac, subdued and exhausted, sat beside it, leaning his gaunt cheek upon his thin hand. Soon some people, deputed by the magistrates, came to remove the body; the unfortunate being saw a jailor in each—he fled precipitately, while I passed onwards to the Castle.

Death, cruel and relentless, had entered these beloved walls. An old servant, who had nursed Idris in infancy, and who lived with us more on the footing of a revered relative than a domestic, had gone a few days before to visit a daughter, married, and settled in the neighbourhood of London. On the night of her return she sickened of the plague. From the haughty and unbending nature of the Countess of Windsor, Idris had few tender filial associations with her. This good woman had stood in the place of a mother, and her very deficiencies of education and knowledge, by rendering her humble and defenceless, endeared her to us—she was the especial favourite of the children. I found my poor girl, there is no exaggeration in the expression, wild with grief and dread. She hung over the patient in agony, which was not mitigated when her thoughts wandered towards her babes, for whom she feared infection. My arrival was like the newly discovered lamp of a lighthouse to sailors, who are weathering some dangerous point. She deposited her appalling doubts in my hands; she relied on my judgment, and was comforted by my participation in her sorrow. Soon our poor nurse expired; and the anguish of suspense was changed to deep regret, which though at first more painful, yet yielded with greater readiness to my consolations. Sleep, the sovereign balm, at length steeped her tearful eyes in forgetfulness.

She slept; and quiet prevailed in the Castle, whose inhabitants were hushed to repose. I was awake, and during the long hours of dead night, my busy thoughts worked in my brain, like ten thousand mill-wheels, rapid, acute, untameable. All slept—all England slept; and from my window, commanding a wide prospect of the star-illumined country, I saw the land stretched out in placid rest. I was awake, alive, while the brother of death possessed my race. What, if the more potent of these fraternal deities should obtain dominion over it? The silence of midnight, to speak truly, though apparently a paradox, rung in my ears. The solitude became intolerable —I placed my hand on the beating heart of Idris, I bent my head to catch the sound of her breath, to assure myself that she still existed—for a moment I doubted whether I should not awake her; so effeminate an horror ran through my frame.—Great God! would it one day be thus? One day all extinct, save myself, should I walk the earth alone? Were these warning voices, whose inarticulate and oracular sense forced belief upon me?

> Yet I would not call them
> Voices of warning, that announce to us
> Only the inevitable. As the sun,
> Ere it is risen, sometimes paints its image
> In the atmosphere—so often do the spirits
> Of great events stride on before the events,
> And in to-day already walks to-morrow.[2]

---

1. Calderon de la Barca.
2. Coleridge's Translation of Schiller's Wallenstein.

8

AFTER A LONG INTERVAL, I am again impelled by the restless spirit within me to continue my narration; but I must alter the mode which I have hitherto adopted. The details contained in the foregoing pages, apparently trivial, yet each slightest one weighing like lead in the depressed scale of human afflictions; this tedious dwelling on the sorrows of others, while my own were only in apprehension; this slowly laying bare of my soul's wounds: this journal of death; this long drawn and tortuous path, leading to the ocean of countless tears, awakens me again to keen grief. I had used this history as an opiate; while it described my beloved friends, fresh with life and glowing with hope, active assistants on the scene, I was soothed; there will be a more melancholy pleasure in painting the end of all. But the intermediate steps, the climbing the wall, raised up between what was and is, while I still looked back nor saw the concealed desert beyond, is a labour past my strength. Time and experience have placed me on an height from which I can comprehend the past as a whole; and in this way I must describe it, bringing forward the leading incidents, and disposing light and shade so as to form a picture in whose very darkness there will be harmony.

It would be needless to narrate those disastrous occurrences, for which a parallel might be found in any slighter visitation of our gigantic calamity. Does the reader wish to hear of the pest-houses, where death is the comforter—of the mournful passage of the death-cart—of the insensibility of the worthless, and the anguish of the loving heart—of harrowing shrieks and silence dire—of the variety of disease, desertion, famine, despair, and death? There are many books which can feed the appetite craving for these things; let them turn to the accounts of Boccaccio, De Foe, and Browne. The vast annihilation that has swallowed all things—the voiceless solitude of the once busy earth—the lonely state of singleness which hems me in, has deprived even such details of their stinging reality, and mellowing the lurid tints of past anguish with poetic hues, I am able to escape from the mosaic of circumstance, by perceiving and reflecting back the grouping and combined colouring of the past.

I had returned from London possessed by the idea, with the intimate feeling that it was my first duty to secure, as well as I was able, the well-being of my family, and then to return and take my post beside Adrian. The events that immediately followed on my arrival at Windsor changed this view of things. The plague was not in London alone, it was every where—it came on us, as Ryland had said, like a thousand packs of wolves, howling through the winter night, gaunt and fierce. When once disease was introduced into the rural districts, its effects appeared more horrible, more exigent, and more difficult to cure, than in towns. There was a companionship in suffering there, and, the neighbours keeping constant watch on each other, and inspired by the active benevolence of Adrian, succour was afforded, and the path of destruction smoothed. But in the country, among the scattered farm-houses, in lone cottages, in fields, and barns, tragedies were acted harrowing to the soul, unseen, unheard, unnoticed. Medical aid was less easily procured, food was more difficult to obtain, and human beings, unwithheld by shame, for they were unbeheld of their fellows, ventured on deeds of greater wickedness, or gave way more readily to their abject fears.

Deeds of heroism also occurred, whose very mention swells the heart and brings tears into the eyes. Such is human nature, that beauty and deformity are often closely linked. In reading history we are chiefly struck by the generosity and self-devotion that follow close on the heels of crime, veiling with supernal flowers the stain of blood. Such acts were not wanting to adorn the grim train that waited on the progress of the plague.

The inhabitants of Berkshire and Bucks had been long aware that the plague was in London, in Liverpool, Bristol, Manchester, York, in short, in all the more populous towns of England. They were not however the less astonished and dismayed when it appeared among themselves. They were impatient and angry in the midst of terror. They would do something to throw off the clinging evil, and, while in action, they fancied that a remedy was applied. The inhabitants of the smaller towns left their houses, pitched tents in the fields, wandering separate from each other careless of hunger or the sky's inclemency, while they imagined that they avoided the death-dealing disease. The farmers and cottagers, on the contrary, struck with the fear of solitude, and madly desirous of medical assistance, flocked into the towns.

But winter was coming, and with winter, hope. In August, the plague had appeared in the country of England, and during September it made its ravages. Towards the end of October it dwindled away, and was in some degree replaced by a typhus, of hardly less virulence. The autumn was warm and rainy: the infirm and sickly died off—happier they: many young people flushed with health and prosperity, made pale by wasting malady, became the inhabitants of the grave. The crop had failed, the bad corn, and want of foreign wines, added vigour to disease. Before Christmas half England was under water. The storms of the last winter were renewed; but the diminished shipping of this year caused us to feel less the tempests of the sea. The flood and storms did more harm to continental Europe than to us—giving, as it were, the last blow to the calamities which destroyed it. In Italy the rivers were unwatched by the diminished peasantry; and, like wild beasts from their lair when the hunters and dogs are afar, did Tiber, Arno, and Po, rush upon and destroy the fertility of the plains. Whole villages were carried away. Rome, and Florence, and Pisa were overflowed, and their marble palaces, late mirrored in tranquil streams, had their foundations shaken by their winter-gifted power. In Germany and Russia the injury was still more momentous.

But frost would come at last, and with it a renewal of our lease of earth. Frost would blunt the arrows of pestilence, and enchain the furious elements; and the land would in spring throw off her garment of snow, released from her menace of destruction. It was not until February that the desired signs of winter appeared. For three days the snow fell, ice stopped the current of the rivers, and the birds flew out from crackling branches of the frost-whitened trees. On the fourth morning all vanished. A south-west wind brought up rain—the sun came out, and mocking the usual laws of nature, seemed even at this early season to burn with solsticial force. It was no consolation, that with the first winds of March the lanes were filled with violets, the fruit trees covered with blossoms, that the corn sprung up, and the leaves came out, forced by the unseasonable heat. We feared the balmy air—we feared the cloudless sky, the flower-covered earth, and delightful woods, for we looked on the fabric of the universe no longer as our dwelling, but our tomb, and the fragrant land smelled to the apprehension of fear like a wide church-yard.

> Pisando la tierra dura de continuo el hombre esta y cada passo que da es sobre su sepultura.[1]

Yet notwithstanding these disadvantages winter was breathing time; and we exerted ourselves to make the best of it. Plague might not revive with the summer; but if it did, it should find us prepared. It is a part of man's nature to adapt itself through habit even to pain and sorrow. Pestilence had become a part of our future, our existence; it was to be guarded against, like the flooding of rivers, the encroachments of ocean, or the inclemency of the sky. After long suffering and bitter experience, some panacea might be discovered; as it was, all that received infection died— all however were not infected; and it became our part to fix deep the foundations, and raise high the barrier between contagion and the sane; to introduce such order as would conduce to the well-being of the survivors, and as would preserve hope and some portion of happiness to those who were spectators of the still renewed tragedy. Adrian had introduced systematic modes of proceeding in the metropolis, which, while they were unable to stop the progress of death, yet prevented other evils, vice and folly, from rendering the awful fate of the hour still more tremendous. I wished to imitate his example, but men are used to

> —move all together, if they move at all,[2]

and I could find no means of leading the inhabitants of scattered towns and villages, who forgot my words as soon as they heard them not, and veered with every baffling wind, that might arise from an apparent change of circumstance.

I adopted another plan. Those writers who have imagined a reign of peace and happiness on earth, have generally described a rural country, where each small township was directed by the elders and wise men. This was the key of my design. Each village, however small, usually contains a leader, one among themselves whom they venerate, whose advice they seek in difficulty, and whose good opinion they chiefly value. I was immediately drawn to make this observation by occurrences that presented themselves to my personal experience.

In the village of Little Marlow an old woman ruled the community. She had lived for some years in an alms-house, and on fine Sundays her threshold was constantly beset by a crowd, seeking her advice and listening to her admonitions. She had been a soldier's wife, and had seen the world; infirmity, induced by fevers caught in unwholesome quarters, had come on her before its time, and she seldom moved from her little cot. The plague entered the village; and, while fright and grief deprived the inhabitants of the little wisdom they possessed, old Martha stepped forward and said— "Before now I have been in a town where there was the plague."—"And you escaped?"—"No, but I recovered."—After this Martha was seated more firmly than ever on the regal seat, elevated by reverence and love. She entered the cottages of the sick; she relieved their wants with her own hand; she betrayed no fear, and inspired all who saw her with some portion of her own native courage. She attended the markets—she insisted upon being supplied with food for those who were too poor to purchase it. She shewed them how the well-being of each included the prosperity of all. She would not permit the gardens to be neglected, nor the very flowers in the cottage lattices to droop from want of care. Hope, she said, was better than a doctor's prescription, and every thing that could sustain and enliven the spirits, of more worth than drugs and mixtures.

It was the sight of Little Marlow, and my conversations with Martha, that led me to the plan I formed. I had before visited the manor houses and gentlemen's seats, and often found the inhabitants actuated by the purest benevolence, ready to lend their utmost aid for the welfare of their tenants. But this was not enough. The intimate sympathy generated by similar hopes and fears, similar experience and pursuits, was wanting here. The poor perceived that the rich possessed other means of preservation than those which could be partaken of by themselves, seclusion, and, as far as circumstances permitted, freedom from care. They could not place reliance on them, but turned with tenfold dependence to the succour and advice of their equals. I resolved therefore to go from village to village, seeking out the rustic archon of the place, and by systematizing their exertions, and enlightening their views, increase both their power and their use among their fellow-cottagers. Many changes also now occurred in these spontaneous regal elections: depositions and abdications were frequent, while, in the place of the old and prudent, the ardent youth would step forward, eager for action, regardless of danger. Often too, the voice to which all listened was suddenly silenced, the helping hand cold, the sympathetic eye closed, and the villagers feared still more the death that had selected a choice victim, shivering in dust the heart that had beat for them, reducing to incommunicable annihilation the mind for ever occupied with projects for their welfare.

Whoever labours for man must often find ingratitude, watered by vice and folly, spring from the grain which he has sown. Death, which had in our younger days walked the earth like "a thief that comes in the night," now, rising from his subterranean vault, girt with power, with dark banner floating, came a conqueror. Many saw, seated above his vice-regal throne, a supreme Providence, who directed his shafts, and guided his progress, and they bowed their heads in resignation, or at least in obedience. Others perceived only a passing casualty; they endeavoured to exchange terror for heedlessness, and plunged into licentiousness, to avoid the agonizing throes of worst apprehension. Thus, while the wise, the good, and the prudent were occupied by the labours of benevolence, the truce of winter produced other effects among the young, the thoughtless, and the vicious. During the colder months there was a general rush to London in search of amusement—the ties of public opinion were loosened; many were rich, heretofore poor—many had lost father and mother, the guardians of their morals, their mentors and restraints. It would have been useless to have opposed these impulses by barriers, which would only have driven those actuated by them to more pernicious indulgencies. The theatres were open and thronged; dance and midnight festival were frequented—in many of these decorum was violated, and the evils, which hitherto adhered to an advanced state of civilization, were doubled. The student left his books, the artist his study: the occupations of life were gone, but the amusements remained; enjoyment might be protracted to the verge of the grave. All factitious colouring disappeared —death rose like night, and, protected by its murky shadows the blush of modesty, the reserve of pride, the decorum of prudery were frequently thrown aside as useless veils. This was not universal. Among better natures, anguish and dread, the fear of eternal separation, and the awful wonder produced by unprecedented calamity, drew closer the ties of kindred and friendship. Philosophers opposed their principles, as barriers to the inundation of profligacy or despair, and the only ramparts to protect the invaded territory of human life; the religious, hoping now for their reward, clung fast to their creeds, as the rafts and planks which over the tempest-vexed sea of suffering, would bear them in safety to the harbour of the Unknown Continent. The loving heart, obliged to contract its view, bestowed its overflow of affection in triple portion on the few that remained. Yet, even among these, the present, as an unalienable possession, became all of time to which they dared commit the precious freight of their hopes.

The experience of immemorial time had taught us formerly to count our enjoyments by years, and extend our prospect of life through a lengthened period of progression and decay; the long road threaded a vast labyrinth, and the Valley of the Shadow of Death, in which it terminated, was hid by intervening objects. But an earthquake had changed the scene—under our very feet the earth yawned—deep and precipitous the gulph below opened to receive us, while the hours charioted us towards the chasm. But it was winter now, and months must elapse before we are hurled from our security. We became ephemera, to whom the interval between the rising and setting sun was as a long drawn year of common time. We should never see our children ripen into maturity, nor behold their downy cheeks roughen, their blithe hearts subdued by passion or care; but we had them now—they lived, and we lived—what more could we desire? With such schooling did my poor Idris try to hush thronging fears, and in some measure succeeded. It was not as in summer-time, when each hour might bring the dreaded fate—until summer, we felt sure; and this certainty, short lived as it must be, yet for awhile satisfied her maternal tenderness. I know not how to express or communicate the sense of concentrated, intense, though evanescent transport, that imparadized us in the present hour. Our joys were dearer because we saw their end; they were keener because we felt, to its fullest extent, their value; they were purer because their essence was sympathy— as a meteor is brighter than a star, did the felicity of this winter contain in itself the extracted delights of a long, long life.

How lovely is spring! As we looked from Windsor Terrace on the sixteen fertile counties spread beneath, speckled by happy cottages and wealthier towns, all looked as in former years, heart-cheering and fair. The land was ploughed, the slender blades of wheat broke through the dark soil, the fruit trees were covered with buds, the husbandman was abroad in the fields, the milk-maid tripped home with well-filled pails, the swallows and martins struck the sunny pools with their long, pointed wings, the new dropped lambs reposed on the young grass, the tender growth of leaves—

> Lifts its sweet head into the air, and feeds
> A silent space with ever sprouting green.[3]

Man himself seemed to regenerate, and feel the frost of winter yield to an elastic and warm renewal of life—reason told us that care and sorrow would grow with the opening year—but how to believe the ominous voice breathed up with pestiferous vapours from fear's dim cavern, while nature, laughing and scattering from her green lap flowers, and fruits, and sparkling waters, invited us to join the gay masque of young life she led upon the scene?

Where was the plague? "Here—every where!" one voice of horror and dismay exclaimed, when in the pleasant days of a sunny May the Destroyer of man brooded again over the earth, forcing the spirit to leave its organic chrysalis, and to enter upon an untried life. With one mighty sweep of its potent weapon, all caution, all care, all prudence were levelled low: death sat at the tables of the great, stretched itself on the cottager's pallet, seized the dastard who fled, quelled the brave man who resisted: despondency entered every heart, sorrow dimmed every eye.

Sights of woe now became familiar to me, and were I to tell all of anguish and pain that I witnessed, of the despairing moans of age, and the more terrible smiles of infancy in the bosom of horror, my reader, his limbs quivering and his hair on end, would wonder how I did not, seized with sudden frenzy, dash myself from some precipice, and so close my eyes for ever on the sad end of the world. But the powers of love, poetry, and creative fancy will dwell even beside the sick of the plague, with the squalid, and with the dying. A feeling of devotion, of duty, of a high and steady purpose, elevated me; a strange joy filled my heart. In the midst of saddest grief I seemed to tread air, while the spirit of good shed round me an ambrosial atmosphere, which blunted the sting of sympathy, and purified the air of sighs. If my wearied soul flagged in its career, I thought of my loved home, of the casket that contained my treasures, of the kiss of love and the filial caress, while my eyes were moistened by purest dew, and my heart was at once softened and refreshed by thrilling tenderness.

Maternal affection had not rendered Idris selfish; at the beginning of our calamity she had, with thoughtless enthusiasm, devoted herself to the care of the sick and helpless. I checked her; and she submitted to my rule. I told her how the fear of her danger palsied my exertions, how the knowledge of her safety strung my nerves to endurance. I shewed her the dangers which her children incurred during her absence; and she at length agreed not to go beyond the inclosure of the forest. Indeed, within the walls of the Castle we had a colony of the unhappy, deserted by their relatives, and in themselves helpless, sufficient to occupy her time and attention, while ceaseless anxiety for my welfare and the health of her children, however she strove to curb or conceal it, absorbed all her thoughts, and undermined the vital principle. After watching over and providing for their safety, her second care was to hide from me her anguish and tears. Each night I returned to the Castle, and found there repose and love awaiting me. Often I waited beside the bed of death till midnight, and through the obscurity of rainy, cloudy nights rode many miles, sustained by one circumstance only, the safety and sheltered repose of those I loved. If some scene of tremendous agony shook my frame and fevered my brow, I would lay my head on the lap of Idris, and the tumultuous pulses subsided into a temperate flow —her smile could raise me from hopelessness, her embrace bathe my sorrowing heart in calm peace. Summer advanced, and, crowned with the sun's potent rays, plague shot her unerring shafts over the earth. The nations beneath their influence bowed their heads, and died. The corn that sprung up in plenty, lay in autumn rotting on the ground, while the melancholy wretch who had gone out to gather bread for his children, lay stiff and plague-struck in the furrow. The green woods waved their boughs majestically, while the dying were spread beneath their shade, answering the solemn melody with inharmonious cries. The painted birds flitted through the shades; the careless deer reposed unhurt upon the fern—the oxen and the horses strayed from their unguarded stables, and grazed among the wheat, for death fell on man alone.

With summer and mortality grew our fears. My poor love and I looked at each other, and our babes.—"We will save them, Idris," I said, "I will save them. Years hence we shall recount to them our fears, then passed away with their occasion. Though they only should remain on the earth, still they shall live, nor shall their cheeks become pale nor their sweet voices languish." Our eldest in some degree understood the scenes passing around, and at times, he with serious looks questioned me concerning the reason of so vast a desolation. But he was only ten years old; and the hilarity of youth soon chased unreasonable care from his brow. Evelyn, a laughing cherub, a gamesome infant, without idea of pain or sorrow, would, shaking back his light curls from his eyes, make the halls re-echo with his merriment, and in a thousand artless ways attract our attention to his play. Clara, our lovely gentle Clara, was our stay, our solace, our delight. She made it her task to attend the sick, comfort the sorrowing, assist the aged, and partake the sports and awaken the gaiety of the young. She flitted through the rooms, like a good spirit, dispatched from the celestial kingdom, to illumine our dark hour with alien splendour. Gratitude and praise marked where her footsteps had been. Yet, when she stood in unassuming simplicity before us, playing with our children, or with girlish assiduity performing little kind offices for Idris, one wondered in what fair lineament of her pure loveliness, in what soft tone of her thrilling voice, so much of heroism, sagacity and active goodness resided.

The summer passed tediously, for we trusted that winter would at least check the disease. That it would vanish altogether was an hope too dear— too heartfelt, to be expressed. When such a thought was heedlessly uttered, the hearers, with a gush of tears and passionate sobs, bore witness how deep their fears were, how small their hopes. For my own part, my exertions for the public good permitted me to observe more closely than most others, the virulence and extensive ravages of our sightless enemy. A short month has destroyed a village, and where in May the first person sickened, in June the paths were deformed by unburied corpses—the houses tenantless, no smoke arising from the chimneys; and the housewife's clock marked only the hour when death had been triumphant. From such scenes I have sometimes saved a deserted infant—sometimes led a young and grieving mother from the lifeless image of her first born, or drawn the sturdy labourer from childish weeping over his extinct family.

July is gone. August must pass, and by the middle of September we may hope. Each day was eagerly counted; and the inhabitants of towns, desirous to leap this dangerous interval, plunged into dissipation, and strove, by riot, and what they wished to imagine to be pleasure, to banish thought and opiate despair. None but Adrian could have tamed the motley population of London, which, like a troop of unbitted steeds rushing to their pastures, had thrown aside all minor fears, through the operation of the fear paramount. Even Adrian was obliged in part to yield, that he might be able, if not to guide, at least to set bounds to the license of the times. The theatres were kept open; every place of public resort was frequented; though he endeavoured so to modify them, as might best quiet the agitation of the spectators, and at the same time prevent a reaction of misery when the excitement was over. Tragedies deep and dire were the chief favourites. Comedy brought with it too great a contrast to the inner despair: when such were attempted, it was not unfrequent for a comedian, in the midst of the laughter occasioned by his disporportioned buffoonery, to find a word or thought in his part that jarred with his own sense of wretchedness, and burst from mimic merriment into sobs and tears, while the spectators, seized with irresistible sympathy, wept, and the pantomimic revelry was changed to a real exhibition of tragic passion.

It was not in my nature to derive consolation from such scenes; from theatres, whose buffoon laughter and discordant mirth awakened distempered sympathy, or where fictitious tears and wailings mocked the heart-felt grief within; from festival or crowded meeting, where hilarity sprung from the worst feelings of our nature, or such enthralment of the better ones, as impressed it with garish and false varnish; from assemblies of mourners in the guise of revellers. Once however I witnessed a scene of singular interest at one of the theatres, where nature overpowered art, as an overflowing cataract will tear away the puny manufacture of a mock cascade, which had before been fed by a small portion of its waters.

I had come to London to see Adrian. He was not at the palace; and, though the attendants did not know whither he had gone, they did not expect him till late at night. It was between six and seven o'clock, a fine summer afternoon, and I spent my leisure hours in a ramble through the empty streets of London; now turning to avoid an approaching funeral, now urged by curiosity to observe the state of a particular spot; my wanderings were instinct with pain, for silence and desertion characterized every place I visited, and the few beings I met were so pale and woe-begone, so marked with care and depressed by fear, that weary of encountering only signs of misery, I began to retread my steps towards home.

I was now in Holborn, and passed by a public house filled with uproarious companions, whose songs, laughter, and shouts were more sorrowful than the pale looks and silence of the mourner. Such an one was near, hovering round this house. The sorry plight of her dress displayed her poverty, she was ghastly pale, and continued approaching, first the window and then the door of the house, as if fearful, yet longing to enter. A sudden burst of song and merriment seemed to sting her to the heart; she murmured, "Can he have the heart?" and then mustering her courage, she stepped within the threshold. The landlady met her in the passage; the poor creature asked, "Is my husband here? Can I see George?"

"See him," cried the woman, "yes, if you go to him; last night he was taken with the plague, and we sent him to the hospital."

The unfortunate inquirer staggered against a wall, a faint cry escaped her

—"O! were you cruel enough," she exclaimed, "to send him there?"

The landlady meanwhile hurried away; but a more compassionate bar-maid gave her a detailed account, the sum of which was, that her husband had been taken ill, after a night of riot, and sent by his boon companions with all expedition to St. Bartholomew's Hospital. I had watched this scene, for there was a gentleness about the poor woman that interested me; she now tottered away from the door, walking as well as she could down Holborn Hill; but her strength soon failed her; she leaned against a wall, and her head sunk on her bosom, while her pallid cheek became still more white. I went up to her and offered my services. She hardly looked up—"You can do me no good," she replied; "I must go to the hospital; if I do not die before I get there."

There were still a few hackney-coaches accustomed to stand about the streets, more truly from habit than for use. I put her in one of these, and entered with her that I might secure her entrance into the hospital. Our way was short, and she said little; except interrupted ejaculations of reproach that he had left her, exclamations on the unkindness of some of his friends, and hope that she would find him alive. There was a simple, natural earnestness about her that interested me in her fate, especially when she assured me that her husband was the best of men,—had been so, till want of business during these unhappy times had thrown him into bad company. "He could not bear to come home," she said, "only to see our children die. A man cannot have the patience a mother has, with her own flesh and blood."

We were set down at St. Bartholomew's, and entered the wretched precincts of the house of disease. The poor creature clung closer to me, as she saw with what heartless haste they bore the dead from the wards, and took them into a room, whose half-opened door displayed a number of corpses, horrible to behold by one unaccustomed to such scenes. We were directed to the ward where her husband had been first taken, and still was, the nurse said, if alive. My companion looked eagerly from one bed to the other, till at the end of the ward she espied, on a wretched bed, a squalid, haggard creature, writhing under the torture of disease. She rushed towards him, she embraced him, blessing God for his preservation.

The enthusiasm that inspired her with this strange joy, blinded her to the horrors about her; but they were intolerably agonizing to me. The ward was filled with an effluvia that caused my heart to heave with painful qualms. The dead were carried out, and the sick brought in, with like indifference; some were screaming with pain, others laughing from the influence of more terrible delirium; some were attended by weeping, despairing relations, others called aloud with thrilling tenderness or reproach on the friends who had deserted them, while the nurses went from bed to bed, incarnate images of despair, neglect, and death. I gave gold to my luckless companion; I recommended her to the care of the attendants; I then hastened away; while the tormentor, the imagination, busied itself in picturing my own loved ones, stretched on such beds, attended thus. The country afforded no such mass of horrors; solitary wretches died in the open fields; and I have found a survivor in a vacant village, contending at once with famine and disease; but the assembly of pestilence, the banqueting hall of death, was spread only in London.

I rambled on, oppressed, distracted by painful emotions—suddenly I found myself before Drury Lane Theatre. The play was Macbeth—the first actor of the age was there to exert his powers to drug with irreflection the auditors; such a medicine I yearned for, so I entered. The theatre was tolerably well filled. Shakspeare, whose popularity was established by the approval of four centuries, had not lost his influence even at this dread period; but was still "Ut magus," the wizard to rule our hearts and govern our imaginations. I came in during the interval between the third and fourth act. I looked round on the audience; the females were mostly of the lower classes, but the men were of all ranks, come hither to forget awhile the protracted scenes of wretchedness, which awaited them at their miserable homes. The curtain drew up, and the stage presented the scene of the witches' cave. The wildness and supernatural machinery of Macbeth, was a pledge that it could contain little directly connected with our present circumstances. Great pains had been taken in the scenery to give the semblance of reality to the impossible. The extreme darkness of the stage, whose only light was received from the fire under the cauldron, joined to a kind of mist that floated about it, rendered the unearthly shapes of the witches obscure and shadowy. It was not three decrepid old hags that bent over their pot throwing in the grim ingredients of the magic charm, but forms frightful, unreal, and fanciful. The entrance of Hecate, and the wild music that followed, took us out of this world. The cavern shape the stage assumed, the beetling rocks, the glare of the fire, the misty shades that crossed the scene at times, the music in harmony with all witch-like fancies, permitted the imagination to revel, without fear of contradiction, or reproof from reason or the heart. The entrance of Macbeth did not destroy the illusion, for he was actuated by the same feelings that inspired us, and while the work of magic proceeded we sympathized in his wonder and his daring, and gave ourselves up with our whole souls to the influence of scenic delusion. I felt the beneficial result of such excitement, in a renewal of those pleasing flights of fancy to which I had long been a stranger. The effect of this scene of incantation communicated a portion of its power to that which followed. We forgot that Malcolm and Macduff were mere human beings, acted upon by such simple passions as warmed our own breasts. By slow degrees however we were drawn to the real interest of the scene. A shudder like the swift passing of an electric shock ran through the house, when Rosse exclaimed, in answer to "Stands Scotland where it did?"

> *Alas, poor country;*
> *Almost afraid to know itself! It cannot*
> *Be called our mother, but our grave: where nothing,*
> *But who knows nothing, is once seen to smile;*
> *Where sighs, and groans, and shrieks that rent the air,*
> *Are made, not marked; where violent sorrow seems*
> *A modern extasy: the dead man's knell*
> *Is there scarce asked, for who; and good men's lives*
> *Expire before the flowers in their caps,*
> *Dying, or ere they sicken.*

Each word struck the sense, as our life's passing bell; we feared to look at each other, but bent our gaze on the stage, as if our eyes could fall innocuous on that alone. The person who played the part of Rosse, suddenly became aware of the dangerous ground he trod. He was an inferior actor, but truth now made him excellent; as he went on to announce to Macduff the slaughter of his family, he was afraid to speak, trembling from apprehension of a burst of grief from the audience, not from his fellow-mime. Each word was drawn out with difficulty; real anguish painted his features; his eyes were now lifted in sudden horror, now fixed in dread upon the ground. This shew of terror increased ours, we gasped with him, each neck was stretched out, each face changed with the actor's changes— at length while Macduff, who, attending to his part, was unobservant of the high wrought sympathy of the house, cried with well acted passion:

All my pretty ones?
Did you say all?—O hell kite! All?
What! all my pretty chickens, and their dam,
At one fell swoop!

A pang of tameless grief wrenched every heart, a burst of despair was echoed from every lip.—I had entered into the universal feeling—I had been absorbed by the terrors of Rosse—I re-echoed the cry of Macduff, and then rushed out as from an hell of torture, to find calm in the free air and silent street.

Free the air was not, or the street silent. Oh, how I longed then for the dear soothings of maternal Nature, as my wounded heart was still further stung by the roar of heartless merriment from the public-house, by the sight of the drunkard reeling home, having lost the memory of what he would find there in oblivious debauch, and by the more appalling salutations of those melancholy beings to whom the name of home was a mockery. I ran on at my utmost speed until I found myself I knew not how, close to Westminster Abbey, and was attracted by the deep and swelling tone of the organ. I entered with soothing awe the lighted chancel, and listened to the solemn religious chaunt, which spoke peace and hope to the unhappy. The notes, freighted with man's dearest prayers, re-echoed through the dim aisles, and the bleeding of the soul's wounds was staunched by heavenly balm. In spite of the misery I deprecated, and could not understand; in spite of the cold hearths of wide London, and the corpse-strewn fields of my native land; in spite of all the variety of agonizing emotions I had that evening experienced, I thought that in reply to our melodious adjurations, the Creator looked down in compassion and promise of relief; the awful peal of the heaven-winged music seemed fitting voice wherewith to commune with the Supreme; calm was produced by its sound, and by the sight of many other human creatures offering up prayers and submission with me. A sentiment approaching happiness followed the total resignation of one's being to the guardianship of the world's ruler. Alas! with the failing of this solemn strain, the elevated spirit sank again to earth. Suddenly one of the choristers died—he was lifted from his desk, the vaults below were hastily opened—he was consigned with a few muttered prayers to the darksome cavern, abode of thousands who had gone before—now wide yawning to receive even all who fulfilled the funeral rites. In vain I would then have turned from this scene, to darkened aisle or lofty dome, echoing with melodious praise. In the open air alone I found relief; among nature's beauteous works, her God reassumed his attribute of benevolence, and again I could trust that he who built up the mountains, planted the forests, and poured out the rivers, would erect another state for lost humanity, where we might awaken again to our affections, our happiness, and our faith.

Fortunately for me those circumstances were of rare occurrence that obliged me to visit London, and my duties were confined to the rural district which our lofty castle overlooked; and here labour stood in the place of pastime, to occupy such of the country people as were sufficiently exempt from sorrow or disease. My endeavours were directed towards urging them to their usual attention to their crops, and to the acting as if pestilence did not exist. The mower's scythe was at times heard; yet the joyless haymakers after they had listlessly turned the grass, forgot to cart it; the shepherd, when he had sheared his sheep, would let the wool lie to be scattered by the winds, deeming it useless to provide clothing for another winter. At times however the spirit of life was awakened by these employments; the sun, the refreshing breeze, the sweet smell of the hay, the rustling leaves and prattling rivulets brought repose to the agitated bosom, and bestowed a feeling akin to happiness on the apprehensive. Nor, strange to say, was the time without its pleasures. Young couples, who had loved long and hopelessly, suddenly found every impediment removed, and wealth pour in from the death of relatives. The very danger drew them closer. The immediate peril urged them to seize the immediate opportunity; wildly and passionately they sought to know what delights existence afforded, before they yielded to death, and

> *Snatching their pleasures with rough strife*
> *Thorough the iron gates of life,*[4]

they defied the conquering pestilence to destroy what had been, or to erase even from their death-bed thoughts the sentiment of happiness which had been theirs.

One instance of this kind came immediately under our notice, where a high-born girl had in early youth given her heart to one of meaner extraction. He was a schoolfellow and friend of her brother's, and usually spent a part of the holidays at the mansion of the duke her father. They had played together as children, been the confidants of each other's little secrets, mutual aids and consolers in difficulty and sorrow. Love had crept in, noiseless, terrorless at first, till each felt their life bound up in the other, and at the same time knew that they must part. Their extreme youth, and the purity of their attachment, made them yield with less resistance to the tyranny of circumstances. The father of the fair Juliet separated them; but not until the young lover had promised to remain absent only till he had rendered himself worthy of her, and she had vowed to preserve her virgin heart, his treasure, till he returned to claim and possess it.

Plague came, threatening to destroy at once the aim of the ambitious and the hopes of love. Long the Duke of L——derided the idea that there could be danger while he pursued his plans of cautious seclusion; and he so far succeeded, that it was not till this second summer, that the destroyer, at one fell stroke, overthrew his precautions, his security, and his life. Poor Juliet saw one by one, father, mother, brothers, and sisters, sicken and die. Most of the servants fled on the first appearance of disease, those who remained were infected mortally; no neighbour or rustic ventured within the verge of contagion. By a strange fatality Juliet alone escaped, and she to the last waited on her relatives, and smoothed the pillow of death. The moment at length came, when the last blow was given to the last of the house: the youthful survivor of her race sat alone among the dead. There was no living being near to soothe her, or withdraw her from this hideous company. With the declining heat of a September night, a whirlwind of storm, thunder, and hail, rattled round the house, and with ghastly harmony sung the dirge of her family. She sat upon the ground absorbed in wordless despair, when through the gusty wind and bickering rain she thought she heard her name called. Whose could that familiar voice be? Not one of her relations, for they lay glaring on her with stony eyes. Again her name was syllabled, and she shuddered as she asked herself, am I becoming mad, or am I dying, that I hear the voices of the departed? A second thought passed, swift as an arrow, into her brain; she rushed to the window; and a flash of lightning shewed to her the expected vision, her lover in the shrubbery beneath; joy lent her strength to descend the stairs, to open the door, and then she fainted in his supporting arms.

A thousand times she reproached herself, as with a crime, that she should revive to happiness with him. The natural clinging of the human mind to life and joy was in its full energy in her young heart; she gave herself impetuously up to the enchantment: they were married; and in their radiant features I saw incarnate, for the last time, the spirit of love, of rapturous sympathy, which once had been the life of the world.

I envied them, but felt how impossible it was to imbibe the same feeling, now that years had multiplied my ties in the world. Above all, the anxious mother, my own beloved and drooping Idris, claimed my earnest care; I could not reproach the anxiety that never for a moment slept in her heart, but I exerted myself to distract her attention from too keen an observation of the truth of things, of the near and nearer approaches of disease, misery, and death, of the wild look of our attendants as intelligence of another and yet another death reached us; for to the last something new occurred that seemed to transcend in horror all that had gone before. Wretched beings crawled to die under our succouring roof; the inhabitants of the Castle decreased daily, while the survivors huddled together in fear, and, as in a famine-struck boat, the sport of the wild, interminable waves, each looked in the other's face, to guess on whom the death-lot would next fall. All this I endeavoured to veil, so that it might least impress my Idris; yet, as I have said, my courage survived even despair: I might be vanquished, but I would not yield.

One day, it was the ninth of September, seemed devoted to every disaster, to every harrowing incident. Early in the day, I heard of the arrival of the aged grandmother of one of our servants at the Castle. This old woman had reached her hundredth year; her skin was shrivelled, her form was bent and lost in extreme decrepitude; but as still from year to year she continued in existence, out-living many younger and stronger, she began to feel as if she were to live for ever. The plague came, and the inhabitants of her village died. Clinging, with the dastard feeling of the aged, to the remnant of her spent life, she had, on hearing that the pestilence had come into her neighbourhood, barred her door, and closed her casement, refusing to communicate with any. She would wander out at night to get food, and returned home, pleased that she had met no one, that she was in no danger from the plague. As the earth became more desolate, her difficulty in acquiring sustenance increased; at first, her son, who lived near, had humoured her by placing articles of food in her way: at last he died. But, even though threatened by famine, her fear of the plague was paramount; and her greatest care was to avoid her fellow creatures. She grew weaker each day, and each day she had further to go. The night before, she had reached Datchet; and, prowling about, had found a baker's shop open and deserted. Laden with spoil, she hastened to return, and lost her way. The night was windless, hot, and cloudy; her load became too heavy for her; and one by one she threw away her loaves, still endeavouring to get along, though her hobbling fell into lameness, and her weakness at last into inability to move.

She lay down among the tall corn, and fell asleep. Deep in midnight, she was awaked by a rustling near her; she would have started up, but her stiff joints refused to obey her will. A low moan close to her ear followed, and the rustling increased; she heard a smothered voice breathe out, Water, Water! several times; and then again a sigh heaved from the heart of the sufferer. The old woman shuddered, she contrived at length to sit upright; but her teeth chattered, and her knees knocked together—close, very close, lay a half-naked figure, just discernible in the gloom, and the cry for water and the stifled moan were again uttered. Her motions at length attracted the attention of her unknown companion; her hand was seized with a convulsive violence that made the grasp feel like iron, the fingers like the keen teeth of a trap.—"At last you are come!" were the words given forth—but this exertion was the last effort of the dying— the joints relaxed, the figure fell prostrate, one low moan, the last, marked the moment of death. Morning broke; and the old woman saw the corpse, marked with the fatal disease, close to her; her wrist was livid with the hold loosened by death. She felt struck by the plague; her aged frame was unable to bear her away with sufficient speed; and now, believing herself infected, she no longer dreaded the association of others; but, as swiftly as she might, came to her grand-daughter, at Windsor Castle, there to lament and die. The sight was horrible; still she clung to life, and lamented her mischance with cries and hideous groans; while the swift advance of the disease shewed, what proved to be the fact, that she could not survive many hours.

While I was directing that the necessary care should be taken of her, Clara came in; she was trembling and pale; and, when I anxiously asked her the cause of her agitation, she threw herself into my arms weeping and exclaiming—"Uncle, dearest uncle, do not hate me for ever! I must tell you, for you must know, that Evelyn, poor little Evelyn"—her voice was choked by sobs. The fear of so mighty a calamity as the loss of our adored infant made the current of my blood pause with chilly horror; but the remembrance of the mother restored my presence of mind. I sought the little bed of my darling; he was oppressed by fever; but I trusted, I fondly and fearfully trusted, that there were no symptoms of the plague. He was not three years old, and his illness appeared only one of those attacks incident to infancy. I watched him long—his heavy half-closed lids, his burning cheeks and restless twining of his small fingers—the fever was violent, the torpor complete—enough, without the greater fear of pestilence, to awaken alarm. Idris must not see him in this state. Clara, though only twelve years old, was rendered, through extreme sensibility, so prudent and careful, that I felt secure in entrusting the charge of him to her, and it was my task to prevent Idris from observing their absence. I administered the fitting remedies, and left my sweet niece to watch beside him, and bring me notice of any change she should observe.

I then went to Idris, contriving in my way, plausible excuses for remaining all day in the Castle, and endeavouring to disperse the traces of care from my brow. Fortunately she was not alone. I found Merrival, the astronomer, with her. He was far too long sighted in his view of humanity to heed the casualties of the day, and lived in the midst of contagion unconscious of its existence. This poor man, learned as La Place, guileless and unforeseeing as a child, had often been on the point of starvation, he, his pale wife and numerous offspring, while he neither felt hunger, nor observed distress. His astronomical theories absorbed him; calculations were scrawled with coal on the bare walls of his garret: a hard-earned guinea, or an article of dress, was exchanged for a book without remorse; he neither heard his children cry, nor observed his companion's emaciated form, and the excess of calamity was merely to him as the occurrence of a cloudy night, when he would have given his right hand to observe a celestial phenomenon. His wife was one of those wondrous beings, to be found only among women, with affections not to be diminished by misfortune. Her mind was divided between boundless admiration for her husband, and tender anxiety for her children—she waited on him, worked for them, and never complained, though care rendered her life one long-drawn, melancholy dream.

He had introduced himself to Adrian, by a request he made to observe some planetary motions from his glass. His poverty was easily detected and relieved. He often thanked us for the books we lent him, and for the use of our instruments, but never spoke of his altered abode or change of circumstances. His wife assured us, that he had not observed any difference, except in the absence of the children from his study, and to her infinite surprise he complained of this unaccustomed quiet.

He came now to announce to us the completion of his Essay on the Pericyclical Motions of the Earth's Axis, and the precession of the equinoctial points. If an old Roman of the period of the Republic had returned to life, and talked of the impending election of some laurel-crowned consul, or of the last battle with Mithridates, his ideas would not have been more alien to the times, than the conversation of Merrival. Man, no longer with an appetite for sympathy, clothed his thoughts in visible signs; nor were there any readers left: while each one, having thrown away his sword with opposing shield alone, awaited the plague, Merrival talked of the state of mankind six thousand years hence. He might with equal interest to us, have added a commentary, to describe the unknown and unimaginable lineaments of the creatures, who would then occupy the vacated dwelling of mankind. We had not the heart to undeceive the poor old man; and at the moment I came in, he was reading parts of his book to Idris, asking what answer could be given to this or that position.

Idris could not refrain from a smile, as she listened; she had already gathered from him that his family was alive and in health; though not apt to forget the precipice of time on which she stood, yet I could perceive that she was amused for a moment, by the contrast between the contracted view we had so long taken of human life, and the seven league strides with which Merrival paced a coming eternity. I was glad to see her smile, because it assured me of her total ignorance of her infant's danger: but I shuddered to think of the revulsion that would be occasioned by a discovery of the truth. While Merrival was talking, Clara softly opened a door behind Idris, and beckoned me to come with a gesture and look of grief. A mirror betrayed the sign to Idris—she started up. To suspect evil, to perceive that, Alfred being with us, the danger must regard her youngest darling, to fly across the long chambers into his apartment, was the work but of a moment. There she beheld her Evelyn lying fever-stricken and motionless. I followed her, and strove to inspire more hope than I could myself entertain; but she shook her head mournfully. Anguish deprived her of presence of mind; she gave up to me and Clara the physician's and nurse's parts; she sat by the bed, holding one little burning hand, and, with glazed eyes fixed on her babe, passed the long day in one unvaried agony. It was not the plague that visited our little boy so roughly; but she could not listen to my assurances; apprehension deprived her of judgment and reflection; every slight convulsion of her child's features shook her frame —if he moved, she dreaded the instant crisis; if he remained still, she saw death in his torpor, and the cloud on her brow darkened.

The poor little thing's fever increased towards night. The sensation is most dreary, to use no stronger term, with which one looks forward to passing the long hours of night beside a sick bed, especially if the patient be an infant, who cannot explain its pain, and whose flickering life resembles the wasting flame of the watch-light,

> Whose narrow fire
> Is shaken by the wind, and on whose edge
> Devouring darkness hovers.[5]

With eagerness one turns toward the east, with angry impatience one marks the unchequered darkness; the crowing of a cock, that sound of glee during day-time, comes wailing and untuneable—the creaking of rafters, and slight stir of invisible insect is heard and felt as the signal and type of desolation. Clara, overcome by weariness, had seated herself at the foot of her cousin's bed, and in spite of her efforts slumber weighed down her lids; twice or thrice she shook it off; but at length she was conquered and slept. Idris sat at the bedside, holding Evelyn's hand; we were afraid to speak to each other; I watched the stars —I hung over my child—I felt his little pulse—I drew near the mother—again I receded. At the turn of morning a gentle sigh from the patient attracted me, the burning spot on his cheek faded—his pulse beat softly and regularly—torpor yielded to sleep. For a long time I dared not hope; but when his unobstructed breathing and the moisture that suffused his forehead, were tokens no longer to be mistaken of the departure of mortal malady, I ventured to whisper the news of the change to Idris, and at length succeeded in persuading her that I spoke truth.

But neither this assurance, nor the speedy convalescence of our child could restore her, even to the portion of peace she before enjoyed. Her fear had been too deep, too absorbing, too entire, to be changed to security. She felt as if during her past calm she had dreamed, but was now awake; she was

> As one
> In some lone watch-tower on the deep, awakened
> From soothing visions of the home he loves,
> Trembling to hear the wrathful billows roar;[6]

as one who has been cradled by a storm, and awakes to find the vessel sinking. Before, she had been visited by pangs of fear—now, she never enjoyed an interval of hope. No smile of the heart ever irradiated her fair countenance; sometimes she forced one, and then gushing tears would flow, and the sea of grief close above these wrecks of past happiness. Still while I was near her, she could not be in utter despair— she fully confided herself to me—she did not seem to fear my death, or revert to its possibility; to my guardianship she consigned the full freight of her anxieties, reposing on my love, as a wind-nipped fawn by the side of a doe, as a wounded nestling under its mother's wing, as a tiny, shattered boat, quivering still, beneath some protecting willow-tree. While I, not proudly as in days of joy, yet tenderly, and with glad consciousness of the comfort I afforded, drew my trembling girl close to my heart, and tried to ward every painful thought or rough circumstance from her sensitive nature.

One other incident occurred at the end of this summer. The Countess of Windsor, Ex-Queen of England, returned from Germany. She had at the beginning of the season quitted the vacant city of Vienna; and, unable to tame her haughty mind to anything like submission, she had delayed at Hamburgh, and, when at last she came to London, many weeks elapsed before she gave Adrian notice of her arrival. In spite of her coldness and long absence, he welcomed her with sensibility, displaying such affection as sought to heal the wounds of pride and sorrow, and was repulsed only by her total apparent want of sympathy. Idris heard of her mother's return with pleasure. Her own maternal feelings were so ardent, that she imagined her parent must now, in this waste world, have lost pride and harshness, and would receive with delight her filial attentions. The first check to her duteous demonstrations was a formal intimation from the fallen majesty of England, that I was in no manner to be intruded upon her. She consented, she said, to forgive her daughter, and acknowledge her grandchildren; larger concessions must not be expected.

To me this proceeding appeared (if so light a term may be permitted) extremely whimsical. Now that the race of man had lost in fact all distinction of rank, this pride was doubly fatuitous; now that we felt a kindred, fraternal nature with all who bore the stamp of humanity, this angry reminiscence of times for ever gone, was worse than foolish. Idris was too much taken up by her own dreadful fears, to be angry, hardly grieved; for she judged that insensibility must be the source of this continued rancour. This was not altogether the fact: but predominant self-will assumed the arms and masque of callous feeling; and the haughty lady disdained to exhibit any token of the struggle she endured; while the slave of pride, she fancied that she sacrificed her happiness to immutable principle.

False was all this—false all but the affections of our nature, and the links of sympathy with pleasure or pain. There was but one good and one evil in the world—life and death. The pomp of rank, the assumption of power, the possessions of wealth vanished like morning mist. One living beggar had become of more worth than a national peerage of dead lords— alas the day! —than of dead heroes, patriots, or men of genius. There was much of degradation in this: for even vice and virtue had lost their attributes—life—life—the continuation of our animal mechanism— was the Alpha and Omega of the desires, the prayers, the prostrate ambition of human race.

---

1. Calderon de la Barca.
2. Wordsworth.
3. Keats.
4. Andrew Marvell.
5. The Cenci.
6. The Brides' Tragedy, by T. L. Beddoes, Esq.

❧ 9 ❧

HALF ENGLAND WAS DESOLATE, when October came, and the equinoctial winds swept over the earth, chilling the ardours of the unhealthy season. The summer, which was uncommonly hot, had been protracted into the beginning of this month, when on the eighteenth a sudden change was brought about from summer temperature to winter frost. Pestilence then made a pause in her death-dealing career. Gasping, not daring to name our hopes, yet full even to the brim with intense expectation, we stood, as a ship-wrecked sailor stands on a barren rock islanded by the ocean, watching a distant vessel, fancying that now it nears, and then again that it is bearing from sight. This promise of a renewed lease of life turned rugged natures to melting tenderness, and by contrast filled the soft with harsh and unnatural sentiments. When it seemed destined that all were to die, we were reckless of the how and when—now that the virulence of the disease was mitigated, and it appeared willing to spare some, each was eager to be among the elect, and clung to life with dastard tenacity. Instances of desertion became more frequent; and even murders, which made the hearer sick with horror, where the fear of contagion had armed those nearest in blood against each other. But these smaller and separate tragedies were about to yield to a mightier interest—and, while we were promised calm from infectious influences, a tempest arose wilder than the winds, a tempest bred by the passions of man, nourished by his most violent impulses, unexampled and dire.

A number of people from North America, the relics of that populous continent, had set sail for the East with mad desire of change, leaving their native plains for lands not less afflicted than their own. Several hundreds landed in Ireland, about the first of November, and took possession of such vacant habitations as they could find; seizing upon the superabundant food, and the stray cattle. As they exhausted the produce of one spot, they went on to another. At length they began to interfere with the inhabitants, and strong in their concentrated numbers, ejected the natives from their dwellings, and robbed them of their winter store. A few events of this kind roused the fiery nature of the Irish; and they attacked the invaders. Some were destroyed; the major part escaped by quick and well ordered movements; and danger made them careful. Their numbers ably arranged; the very deaths among them concealed; moving on in good order, and apparently given up to enjoyment, they excited the envy of the Irish. The

Americans permitted a few to join their band, and presently the recruits outnumbered the strangers—nor did they join with them, nor imitate the admirable order which, preserved by the Trans-Atlantic chiefs, rendered them at once secure and formidable. The Irish followed their track in disorganized multitudes; each day increasing; each day becoming more lawless. The Americans were eager to escape from the spirit they had roused, and, reaching the eastern shores of the island, embarked for England. Their incursion would hardly have been felt had they come alone; but the Irish, collected in unnatural numbers, began to feel the inroads of famine, and they followed in the wake of the Americans for England also. The crossing of the sea could not arrest their progress. The harbours of the desolate sea-ports of the west of Ireland were filled with vessels of all sizes, from the man of war to the small fishers' boat, which lay sailorless, and rotting on the lazy deep. The emigrants embarked by hundreds, and unfurling their sails with rude hands, made strange havoc of buoy and cordage. Those who modestly betook themselves to the smaller craft, for the most part achieved their watery journey in safety. Some, in the true spirit of reckless enterprise, went on board a ship of an hundred and twenty guns; the vast hull drifted with the tide out of the bay, and after many hours its crew of landsmen contrived to spread a great part of her enormous canvass—the wind took it, and while a thousand mistakes of the helmsman made her present her head now to one point, and now to another, the vast fields of canvass that formed her sails flapped with a sound like that of a huge cataract; or such as a sea-like forest may give forth when buffeted by an equinoctial north-wind. The port-holes were open, and with every sea, which as she lurched, washed her decks, they received whole tons of water. The difficulties were increased by a fresh breeze which began to blow, whistling among the shrowds, dashing the sails this way and that, and rending them with horrid split, and such whir as may have visited the dreams of Milton, when he imagined the winnowing of the arch-fiend's van-like wings, which increased the uproar of wild chaos. These sounds were mingled with the roaring of the sea, the splash of the chafed billows round the vessel's sides, and the gurgling up of the water in the hold. The crew, many of whom had never seen the sea before, felt indeed as if heaven and earth came ruining together, as the vessel dipped her bows in the waves, or rose high upon them. Their yells were drowned in the clamour of elements, and the thunder rivings of their unwieldy habitation— they discovered at last that the water gained on them, and they betook themselves to their pumps; they might as well have laboured to empty the ocean by bucketfuls. As the sun went down, the gale increased; the ship seemed to feel her danger, she was now completely water- logged, and presented other indications of settling before she went down. The bay was crowded with vessels, whose crews, for the most part, were observing the uncouth sportings of this huge unwieldy machine—they saw her gradually sink; the waters now rising above her lower decks—they could hardly wink before she had utterly disappeared, nor could the place where the sea had closed over her be at all discerned. Some few of her crew were saved, but the greater part clinging to her cordage and masts went down with her, to rise only when death loosened their hold.

This event caused many of those who were about to sail, to put foot again on firm land, ready to encounter any evil rather than to rush into the yawning jaws of the pitiless ocean. But these were few, in comparison to the numbers who actually crossed. Many went up as high as Belfast to ensure a shorter passage, and then journeying south through Scotland, they were joined by the poorer natives of that country, and all poured with one consent into England.

Such incursions struck the English with affright, in all those towns where there was still sufficient population to feel the change. There was room enough indeed in our hapless country for twice the number of invaders; but their lawless spirit instigated them to violence; they took a delight in thrusting the possessors from their houses; in seizing on some mansion of luxury, where the noble dwellers secluded themselves in fear of the plague; in forcing these of either sex to become their servants and purveyors; till, the ruin complete in one place, they removed their locust visitation to another. When unopposed they spread their ravages wide; in cases of danger they clustered, and by dint of numbers overthrew their weak and despairing foes. They came from the east and the north, and directed their course without apparent motive, but unanimously towards our unhappy metropolis.

Communication had been to a great degree cut off through the paralyzing effects of pestilence, so that the van of our invaders had proceeded as far as Manchester and Derby, before we received notice of their arrival. They swept the country like a conquering army, burning—laying waste— murdering. The lower and vagabond English joined with them. Some few of the Lords Lieutenant who remained, endeavoured to collect the militia—but the ranks were vacant, panic seized on all, and the opposition that was made only served to increase the audacity and cruelty of the enemy. They talked of taking London, conquering England—calling to mind the long detail of injuries which had for many years been forgotten. Such vaunts displayed their weakness, rather than their strength—yet still they might do extreme mischief, which, ending in their destruction, would render them at last objects of compassion and remorse.

We were now taught how, in the beginning of the world, mankind clothed their enemies in impossible attributes—and how details proceeding from mouth to mouth, might, like Virgil's ever-growing Rumour, reach the heavens with her brow, and clasp Hesperus and Lucifer with her outstretched hands. Gorgon and Centaur, dragon and iron-hoofed lion, vast sea-monster and gigantic hydra, were but types of the strange and appalling accounts brought to London concerning our invaders. Their landing was long unknown, but having now advanced within an hundred miles of London, the country people flying before them arrived in successive troops, each exaggerating the numbers, fury, and cruelty of the assailants. Tumult filled the before quiet streets—women and children deserted their homes, escaping they knew not whither—fathers, husbands, and sons, stood trembling, not for themselves, but for their loved and defenceless relations. As the country people poured into London, the citizens fled southwards—they climbed the higher edifices of the town, fancying that they could discern the smoke and flames the enemy spread around them. As Windsor lay, to a great degree, in the line of march from the west, I removed my family to London, assigning the Tower for their sojourn, and joining Adrian, acted as his Lieutenant in the coming struggle.

We employed only two days in our preparations, and made good use of them. Artillery and arms were collected; the remnants of such regiments, as could be brought through many losses into any show of muster, were put under arms, with that appearance of military discipline which might encourage our own party, and seem most formidable to the disorganized multitude of our enemies. Even music was not wanting: banners floated in the air, and the shrill fife and loud trumpet breathed forth sounds of encouragement and victory. A practised ear might trace an undue faltering in the step of the soldiers; but this was not occasioned so much by fear of the adversary, as by disease, by sorrow, and by fatal prognostications, which often weighed most potently on the brave, and quelled the manly heart to abject subjection.

Adrian led the troops. He was full of care. It was small relief to him that our discipline should gain us success in such a conflict; while plague still hovered to equalize the conqueror and the conquered, it was not victory that he desired, but bloodless peace. As we advanced, we were met by bands of peasantry, whose almost naked condition, whose despair and horror, told at once the fierce nature of the coming enemy. The senseless spirit of conquest and thirst of spoil blinded them, while with insane fury they deluged the country in ruin. The sight of the military restored hope to those who fled, and revenge took place of fear. They inspired the soldiers with the same sentiment. Languor was changed to ardour, the slow step converted to a speedy pace, while the hollow murmur of the multitude, inspired by one feeling, and that deadly, filled the air, drowning the clang of arms and sound of music. Adrian perceived the change, and feared that it would be difficult to prevent them from wreaking their utmost fury on the Irish. He rode through the lines, charging the officers to restrain the troops, exhorting the soldiers, restoring order, and quieting in some degree the violent agitation that swelled every bosom.

We first came upon a few stragglers of the Irish at St. Albans. They retreated, and, joining others of their companions, still fell back, till they reached the main body. Tidings of an armed and regular opposition recalled them to a sort of order. They made Buckingham their head-quarters, and scouts were sent out to ascertain our situation. We remained for the night at Luton. In the morning a simultaneous movement caused us each to advance. It was early dawn, and the air, impregnated with freshest odour, seemed in idle mockery to play with our banners, and bore onwards towards the enemy the music of the bands, the neighings of the horses, and regular step of the infantry. The first sound of martial instruments that came upon our undisciplined foe, inspired surprise, not unmingled with dread. It spoke of other days, of days of concord and order; it was associated with times when plague was not, and man lived beyond the shadow of imminent fate. The pause was momentary. Soon we heard their disorderly clamour, the barbarian shouts, the untimed step of thousands coming on in disarray. Their troops now came pouring on us from the open country or narrow lanes; a large extent of unenclosed fields lay between us; we advanced to the middle of this, and then made a halt: being somewhat on superior ground, we could discern the space they covered. When their leaders perceived us drawn out in opposition, they also gave the word to halt, and endeavoured to form their men into some imitation of military discipline. The first ranks had muskets; some were mounted, but their arms were such as they had seized during their advance, their horses those they had taken from the peasantry; there was no uniformity, and little obedience, but their shouts and wild gestures showed the untamed spirit that inspired them. Our soldiers received the word, and advanced to quickest time, but in perfect order: their uniform dresses, the gleam of their polished arms, their silence, and looks of sullen hate, were more appalling than the savage clamour of our innumerous foe. Thus coming nearer and nearer each other, the howls and shouts of the Irish increased; the English proceeded in obedience to their officers, until they came near enough to distinguish the faces of their enemies; the sight inspired them with fury: with one cry, that rent heaven and was re-echoed by the furthest lines, they rushed on; they disdained the use of the bullet, but with fixed bayonet dashed among the opposing foe, while the ranks opening at intervals, the matchmen lighted the cannon, whose deafening roar and blinding smoke filled up the horror of the scene. I was beside Adrian; a moment before he had again given the word to halt, and had remained a few yards distant from us in deep meditation: he was forming swiftly his plan of action, to prevent the effusion of blood; the noise of cannon, the sudden rush of the troops, and yell of the foe, startled him: with flashing eyes he exclaimed, "Not one of these must perish!" and plunging the rowels into his horse's sides, he dashed between the conflicting bands. We, his staff, followed him to surround and protect him; obeying his signal, however, we fell back somewhat. The soldiery perceiving him, paused in their onset; he did not swerve from the bullets that passed near him, but rode immediately between the opposing lines. Silence succeeded to clamour; about fifty men lay on the ground dying or dead. Adrian raised his sword in act to speak: "By whose command," he cried, addressing his own troops, "do you advance? Who ordered your attack? Fall back; these misguided men shall not be slaughtered, while I am your general. Sheath your weapons; these are your brothers, commit not fratricide; soon the plague will not leave one for you to glut your revenge upon: will you be more pitiless than pestilence? As you honour me—as you worship God, in whose image those also are created—as your children and friends are dear to you,— shed not a drop of precious human blood."

He spoke with outstretched hand and winning voice, and then turning to our invaders, with a severe brow, he commanded them to lay down their arms: "Do you think," he said, "that because we are wasted by plague, you can overcome us; the plague is also among you, and when ye are vanquished by famine and disease, the ghosts of those you have murdered will arise to bid you not hope in death. Lay down your arms, barbarous and cruel men—men whose hands are stained with the blood of the innocent, whose souls are weighed down by the orphan's cry! We shall conquer, for the right is on our side; already your cheeks are pale—the weapons fall from your nerveless grasp. Lay down your arms, fellow men! brethren! Pardon, succour, and brotherly love await your repentance. You are dear to us, because you wear the frail shape of humanity; each one among you will find a friend and host among these forces. Shall man be the enemy of man, while plague, the foe to all, even now is above us, triumphing in our butchery, more cruel than her own?"

Each army paused. On our side the soldiers grasped their arms firmly, and looked with stern glances on the foe. These had not thrown down their weapons, more from fear than the spirit of contest; they looked at each other, each wishing to follow some example given him,— but they had no leader. Adrian threw himself from his horse, and approaching one of those just slain: "He was a man," he cried, "and he is dead. O quickly bind up the wounds of the fallen— let not one die; let not one more soul escape through your merciless gashes, to relate before the throne of God the tale of fratricide; bind up their wounds—restore them to their friends. Cast away the hearts of tigers that burn in your breasts; throw down those tools of cruelty and hate; in this pause of exterminating destiny, let each man be brother, guardian, and stay to the other. Away with those blood-stained arms, and hasten some of you to bind up these wounds."

As he spoke, he knelt on the ground, and raised in his arms a man from whose side the warm tide of life gushed—the poor wretch gasped—so still had either host become, that his moans were distinctly heard, and every heart, late fiercely bent on universal massacre, now beat anxiously in hope and fear for the fate of this one man. Adrian tore off his military scarf and bound it round the sufferer—it was too late—the man heaved a deep sigh, his head fell back, his limbs lost their sustaining power.— "He is dead!" said Adrian, as the corpse fell from his arms on the ground, and he bowed his head in sorrow and awe. The fate of the world seemed bound up in the death of this single man. On either side the bands threw down their arms, even the veterans wept, and our party held out their hands to their foes, while a gush of love and deepest amity filled every heart. The two forces mingling, unarmed and hand in hand, talking only how each might assist the other, the adversaries conjoined; each repenting, the one side their former cruelties, the other their late violence, they obeyed the orders of the General to proceed towards London.

Adrian was obliged to exert his utmost prudence, first to allay the discord, and then to provide for the multitude of the invaders. They were marched to various parts of the southern counties, quartered in deserted villages,—a part were sent back to their own island, while the season of winter so far revived our energy, that the passes of the country were defended, and any increase of numbers prohibited.

On this occasion Adrian and Idris met after a separation of nearly a year. Adrian had been occupied in fulfilling a laborious and painful task. He had been familiar with every species of human misery, and had for ever found his powers inadequate, his aid of small avail. Yet the purpose of his soul, his energy and ardent resolution, prevented any re-action of sorrow. He seemed born anew, and virtue, more potent than Medean alchemy, endued him with health and strength. Idris hardly recognized the fragile being, whose form had seemed to bend even to the summer breeze, in the energetic man, whose very excess of sensibility rendered him more capable of fulfilling his station of pilot in storm-tossed England.

It was not thus with Idris. She was uncomplaining; but the very soul of fear had taken its seat in her heart. She had grown thin and pale, her eyes filled with involuntary tears, her voice was broken and low. She tried to throw a veil over the change which she knew her brother must observe in her, but the effort was ineffectual; and when alone with him, with a burst of irrepressible grief she gave vent to her apprehensions and sorrow. She described in vivid terms the ceaseless care that with still renewing hunger ate into her soul; she compared this gnawing of sleepless expectation of evil, to the vulture that fed on the heart of Prometheus; under the influence of this eternal excitement, and of the interminable struggles she endured to combat and conceal it, she felt, she said, as if all the wheels and springs of the animal machine worked at double rate, and were fast consuming themselves. Sleep was not sleep, for her waking thoughts, bridled by some remains of reason, and by the sight of her children happy and in health, were then transformed to wild dreams, all her terrors were realized, all her fears received their dread fulfilment. To this state there was no hope, no alleviation, unless the grave should quickly receive its destined prey, and she be permitted to die, before she experienced a thousand living deaths in the loss of those she loved. Fearing to give me pain, she hid as best she could the excess of her wretchedness, but meeting thus her brother after a long absence, she could not restrain the expression of her woe, but with all the vividness of imagination with which misery is always replete, she poured out the emotions of her heart to her beloved and sympathizing Adrian.

Her present visit to London tended to augment her state of inquietude, by shewing in its utmost extent the ravages occasioned by pestilence. It hardly preserved the appearance of an inhabited city; grass sprung up thick in the streets; the squares were weed-grown, the houses were shut up, while silence and loneliness characterized the busiest parts of the town. Yet in the midst of desolation Adrian had preserved order; and each one continued to live according to law and custom—human institutions thus surviving as it were divine ones, and while the decree of population was abrogated, property continued sacred. It was a melancholy reflection; and in spite of the diminution of evil produced, it struck on the heart as a wretched mockery. All idea of resort for pleasure, of theatres and festivals had passed away. "Next summer," said Adrian as we parted on our return to Windsor, "will decide the fate of the human race. I shall not pause in my exertions until that time; but, if plague revives with the coming year, all contest with her must cease, and our only occupation be the choice of a grave."

I must not forget one incident that occurred during this visit to London. The visits of Merrival to Windsor, before frequent, had suddenly ceased. At this time where but a hair's line separated the living from the dead, I feared that our friend had become a victim to the all-embracing evil. On this occasion I went, dreading the worst, to his dwelling, to see if I could be of any service to those of his family who might have survived. The house was deserted, and had been one of those assigned to the invading strangers quartered in London. I saw his astronomical instruments put to strange uses, his globes defaced, his papers covered with abstruse calculations destroyed. The neighbours could tell me little, till I lighted on a poor woman who acted as nurse in these perilous times. She told me that all the family were dead, except Merrival himself, who had gone mad— mad, she called it, yet on questioning her further, it appeared that he was possessed only by the delirium of excessive grief. This old man, tottering on the edge of the grave, and prolonging his prospect through millions of calculated years,—this visionary who had not seen starvation in the wasted forms of his wife and children, or plague in the horrible sights and sounds that surrounded him—this astronomer, apparently dead on earth, and living only in the motion of the spheres—loved his family with unapparent but intense affection. Through long habit they had become a part of himself; his want of worldly knowledge, his absence of mind and infant guilelessness, made him utterly dependent on them. It was not till one of them died that he perceived their danger; one by one they were carried off by pestilence; and his wife, his helpmate and supporter, more necessary to him than his own limbs and frame, which had hardly been taught the lesson of self-preservation, the kind companion whose voice always spoke peace to him, closed her eyes in death. The old man felt the system of universal nature which he had so long studied and adored, slide from under him, and he stood among the dead, and lifted his voice in curses.—No wonder that the attendant should interpret as phrensy the harrowing maledictions of the grief-struck old man.

I had commenced my search late in the day, a November day, that closed in early with pattering rain and melancholy wind. As I turned from the door, I saw Merrival, or rather the shadow of Merrival, attenuated and wild, pass me, and sit on the steps of his home. The breeze scattered the grey locks on his temples, the rain drenched his uncovered head, he sat hiding his face in his withered hands. I pressed his shoulder to awaken his attention, but he did not alter his position. "Merrival," I said, "it is long since we have seen you—you must return to Windsor with me—Lady Idris desires to see you, you will not refuse her request—come home with me."

He replied in a hollow voice, "Why deceive a helpless old man, why talk hypocritically to one half crazed? Windsor is not my home; my true home I have found; the home that the Creator has prepared for me."

His accent of bitter scorn thrilled me—"Do not tempt me to speak," he continued, "my words would scare you—in an universe of cowards I dare think—among the church-yard tombs—among the victims of His merciless tyranny I dare reproach the Supreme Evil. How can he punish me? Let him bare his arm and transfix me with lightning—this is also one of his attributes"—and the old man laughed.

He rose, and I followed him through the rain to a neighbouring church-yard —he threw himself on the wet earth. "Here they are," he cried, "beautiful creatures—breathing, speaking, loving creatures. She who by day and night cherished the age-worn lover of her youth—they, parts of my flesh, my children—here they are: call them, scream their names through the night; they will not answer!" He clung to the little heaps that marked the graves. "I ask but one thing; I do not fear His hell, for I have it here; I do not desire His heaven, let me but die and be laid beside them; let me but, when I lie dead, feel my flesh as it moulders, mingle with theirs. Promise," and he raised himself painfully, and seized my arm, "promise to bury me with them."

"So God help me and mine as I promise," I replied, "on one condition: return with me to Windsor."

"To Windsor!" he cried with a shriek, "Never!—from this place I never go —my bones, my flesh, I myself, are already buried here, and what you see of me is corrupted clay like them. I will lie here, and cling here, till rain, and hail, and lightning and storm, ruining on me, make me one in substance with them below."

In a few words I must conclude this tragedy. I was obliged to leave London, and Adrian undertook to watch over him; the task was soon fulfilled; age, grief, and inclement weather, all united to hush his sorrows, and bring repose to his heart, whose beats were agony. He died embracing the sod, which was piled above his breast, when he was placed beside the beings whom he regretted with such wild despair.

I returned to Windsor at the wish of Idris, who seemed to think that there was greater safety for her children at that spot; and because, once having taken on me the guardianship of the district, I would not desert it while an inhabitant survived. I went also to act in conformity with Adrian's plans, which was to congregate in masses what remained of the population; for he possessed the conviction that it was only through the benevolent and social virtues that any safety was to be hoped for the remnant of mankind.

It was a melancholy thing to return to this spot so dear to us, as the scene of a happiness rarely before enjoyed, here to mark the extinction of our species, and trace the deep uneraseable footsteps of disease over the fertile and cherished soil. The aspect of the country had so far changed, that it had been impossible to enter on the task of sowing seed, and other autumnal labours. That season was now gone; and winter had set in with sudden and unusual severity. Alternate frosts and thaws succeeding to floods, rendered the country impassable. Heavy falls of snow gave an arctic appearance to the scenery; the roofs of the houses peeped from the white mass; the lowly cot and stately mansion, alike deserted, were blocked up, their thresholds uncleared; the windows were broken by the hail, while the prevalence of a north-east wind rendered out-door exertions extremely painful. The altered state of society made these accidents of nature, sources of real misery. The luxury of command and the attentions of servitude were lost. It is true that the necessaries of life were assembled in such quantities, as to supply to superfluity the wants of the diminished population; but still much labour was required to arrange these, as it were, raw materials; and depressed by sickness, and fearful of the future, we had not energy to enter boldly and decidedly on any system.

I can speak for myself—want of energy was not my failing. The intense life that quickened my pulses, and animated my frame, had the effect, not of drawing me into the mazes of active life, but of exalting my lowliness, and of bestowing majestic proportions on insignificant objects —I could have lived the life of a peasant in the same way—my trifling occupations were swelled into important pursuits; my affections were impetuous and engrossing passions, and nature with all her changes was invested in divine attributes. The very spirit of the Greek mythology inhabited my heart; I deified the uplands, glades, and streams, I

> Had sight of Proteus coming from the sea;
> And heard old Triton blow his wreathed horn.[1]

Strange, that while the earth preserved her monotonous course, I dwelt with ever-renewing wonder on her antique laws, and now that with excentric wheel she rushed into an untried path, I should feel this spirit fade; I struggled with despondency and weariness, but like a fog, they choked me. Perhaps, after the labours and stupendous excitement of the past summer, the calm of winter and the almost menial toils it brought with it, were by natural re-action doubly irksome. It was not the grasping passion of the preceding year, which gave life and individuality to each moment—it was not the aching pangs induced by the distresses of the times. The utter inutility that had attended all my exertions took from them their usual effects of exhilaration, and despair rendered abortive the balm of self applause—I longed to return to my old occupations, but of what use were they? To read were futile—to write, vanity indeed. The earth, late wide circus for the display of dignified exploits, vast theatre for a magnificent drama, now presented a vacant space, an empty stage—for actor or spectator there was no longer aught to say or hear.

Our little town of Windsor, in which the survivors from the neighbouring counties were chiefly assembled, wore a melancholy aspect. Its streets were blocked up with snow—the few passengers seemed palsied, and frozen by the ungenial visitation of winter. To escape these evils was the aim and scope of all our exertions. Families late devoted to exalting and refined pursuits, rich, blooming, and young, with diminished numbers and care-fraught hearts, huddled over a fire, grown selfish and grovelling through suffering. Without the aid of servants, it was necessary to discharge all household duties; hands unused to such labour must knead the bread, or in the absence of flour, the statesmen or perfumed courtier must undertake the butcher's office. Poor and rich were now equal, or rather the poor were the superior, since they entered on such tasks with alacrity and experience; while ignorance, inaptitude, and habits of repose, rendered them fatiguing to the luxurious, galling to the proud, disgustful to all whose minds, bent on intellectual improvement, held it their dearest privilege to be exempt from attending to mere animal wants.

But in every change goodness and affection can find field for exertion and display. Among some these changes produced a devotion and sacrifice of self at once graceful and heroic. It was a sight for the lovers of the human race to enjoy; to behold, as in ancient times, the patriarchal modes in which the variety of kindred and friendship fulfilled their duteous and kindly offices. Youths, nobles of the land, performed for the sake of mother or sister, the services of menials with amiable cheerfulness. They went to the river to break the ice, and draw water: they assembled on foraging expeditions, or axe in hand felled the trees for fuel. The females received them on their return with the simple and affectionate welcome known before only to the lowly cottage—a clean hearth and bright fire; the supper ready cooked by beloved hands; gratitude for the provision for to-morrow's meal: strange enjoyments for the high-born English, yet they were now their sole, hard earned, and dearly prized luxuries.

None was more conspicuous for this graceful submission to circumstances, noble humility, and ingenious fancy to adorn such acts with romantic colouring, than our own Clara. She saw my despondency, and the aching cares of Idris. Her perpetual study was to relieve us from labour and to spread ease and even elegance over our altered mode of life. We still had some attendants spared by disease, and warmly attached to us. But Clara was jealous of their services; she would be sole handmaid of Idris, sole minister to the wants of her little cousins; nothing gave her so much pleasure as our employing her in this way; she went beyond our desires, earnest, diligent, and unwearied,—

> Abra was ready ere we called her name,
> And though we called another, Abra came.[2]

It was my task each day to visit the various families assembled in our town, and when the weather permitted, I was glad to prolong my ride, and to muse in solitude over every changeful appearance of our destiny, endeavouring to gather lessons for the future from the experience of the past. The impatience with which, while in society, the ills that afflicted my species inspired me, were softened by loneliness, when individual suffering was merged in the general calamity, strange to say, less afflicting to contemplate. Thus often, pushing my way with difficulty through the narrow snow-blocked town, I crossed the bridge and passed through Eton. No youthful congregation of gallant-hearted boys thronged the portal of the college; sad silence pervaded the busy school-room and noisy playground. I extended my ride towards Salt Hill, on every side impeded by the snow. Were those the fertile fields I loved—was that the interchange of gentle upland and cultivated dale, once covered with waving corn, diversified by stately trees, watered by the meandering Thames? One sheet of white covered it, while bitter recollection told me that cold as the winter-clothed earth, were the hearts of the inhabitants. I met troops of horses, herds of cattle, flocks of sheep, wandering at will; here throwing down a hay-rick, and nestling from cold in its heart, which afforded them shelter and food—there having taken possession of a vacant cottage. Once on a frosty day, pushed on by restless unsatisfying reflections, I sought a favourite haunt, a little wood not far distant from Salt Hill. A bubbling spring prattles over stones on one side, and a plantation of a few elms and beeches, hardly deserve, and yet continue the name of wood. This spot had for me peculiar charms. It had been a favourite resort of Adrian; it was secluded; and he often said that in boyhood, his happiest hours were spent here; having escaped the stately bondage of his mother, he sat on the rough hewn steps that led to the spring, now reading a favourite book, now musing, with speculation beyond his years, on the still unravelled skein of morals or metaphysics. A melancholy foreboding assured me that I should never see this place more; so with careful thought, I noted each tree, every winding of the streamlet and irregularity of the soil, that I might better call up its idea in absence. A robin red-breast dropt from the frosty branches of the trees, upon the congealed rivulet; its panting breast and half-closed eyes shewed that it was dying: a hawk appeared in the air; sudden fear seized the little creature; it exerted its last strength, throwing itself on its back, raising its talons in impotent defence against its powerful enemy. I took it up and placed it in my breast. I fed it with a few crumbs from a biscuit; by degrees it revived; its warm fluttering heart beat against me; I cannot tell why I detail this trifling incident—but the scene is still before me; the snow-clad fields seen through the silvered trunks of the beeches,—the brook, in days of happiness alive with sparkling waters, now choked by ice—the leafless trees fantastically dressed in hoar frost—the shapes of summer leaves imaged by winter's frozen hand on the hard ground—the dusky sky, drear cold, and unbroken silence—while close in my bosom, my feathered nursling lay warm, and safe, speaking its content with a light chirp— painful reflections thronged, stirring my brain with wild commotion—cold and death-like as the snowy fields was all earth—misery-stricken the life-tide of the inhabitants—why should I oppose the cataract of destruction that swept us away?—why string my nerves and renew my wearied efforts—ah, why? But that my firm courage and cheerful exertions might shelter the dear mate, whom I chose in the spring of my life; though the throbbings of my heart be replete with pain, though my hopes for the future are chill, still while your dear head, my gentlest love, can repose in peace on that heart, and while you derive from its fostering care, comfort, and hope, my struggles shall not cease,—I will not call myself altogether vanquished.

One fine February day, when the sun had reassumed some of its genial power, I walked in the forest with my family. It was one of those lovely winter-days which assert the capacity of nature to bestow beauty on barrenness. The leafless trees spread their fibrous branches against the pure sky; their intricate and pervious tracery resembled delicate sea-weed; the deer were turning up the snow in search of the hidden grass; the white was made intensely dazzling by the sun, and trunks of the trees, rendered more conspicuous by the loss of preponderating foliage, gathered around like the labyrinthine columns of a vast temple; it was impossible not to receive pleasure from the sight of these things. Our children, freed from the bondage of winter, bounded before us; pursuing the deer, or rousing the pheasants and partridges from their coverts. Idris leant on my arm; her sadness yielded to the present sense of pleasure. We met other families on the Long Walk, enjoying like ourselves the return of the genial season. At once, I seemed to awake; I cast off the clinging sloth of the past months; earth assumed a new appearance, and my view of the future was suddenly made clear. I exclaimed, "I have now found out the secret!"

"What secret?"

In answer to this question, I described our gloomy winter-life, our sordid cares, our menial labours:—"This northern country," I said, "is no place for our diminished race. When mankind were few, it was not here that they battled with the powerful agents of nature, and were enabled to cover the globe with offspring. We must seek some natural Paradise, some garden of the earth, where our simple wants may be easily supplied, and the enjoyment of a delicious climate compensate for the social pleasures we have lost. If we survive this coming summer, I will not spend the ensuing winter in England; neither I nor any of us."

I spoke without much heed, and the very conclusion of what I said brought with it other thoughts. Should we, any of us, survive the coming summer? I saw the brow of Idris clouded; I again felt, that we were enchained to the car of fate, over whose coursers we had no control. We could no longer say, This we will do, and this we will leave undone. A mightier power than the human was at hand to destroy our plans or to achieve the work we avoided. It were madness to calculate upon another winter. This was our last. The coming summer was the extreme end of our vista; and, when we arrived there, instead of a continuation of the long road, a gulph yawned, into which we must of force be precipitated. The last blessing of humanity was wrested from us; we might no longer hope. Can the madman, as he clanks his chains, hope? Can the wretch, led to the scaffold, who when he lays his head on the block, marks the double shadow of himself and the executioner, whose uplifted arm bears the axe, hope? Can the ship-wrecked mariner, who spent with swimming, hears close behind the splashing waters divided by a shark which pursues him through the Atlantic, hope? Such hope as theirs, we also may entertain!

Old fable tells us, that this gentle spirit sprung from the box of Pandora, else crammed with evils; but these were unseen and null, while all admired the inspiriting loveliness of young Hope; each man's heart became her home; she was enthroned sovereign of our lives, here and here-after; she was deified and worshipped, declared incorruptible and everlasting. But like all other gifts of the Creator to Man, she is mortal; her life has attained its last hour. We have watched over her; nursed her flickering existence; now she has fallen at once from youth to decrepitude, from health to immedicinable disease; even as we spend ourselves in struggles for her recovery, she dies; to all nations the voice goes forth, Hope is dead! We are but mourners in the funeral train, and what immortal essence or perishable creation will refuse to make one in the sad procession that attends to its grave the dead comforter of humanity?

> Does not the sun call in his light? and day
> Like a thin exhalation melt away—
> Both wrapping up their beams in clouds to be
> Themselves close mourners at this obsequie.[3]

---

1. Wordsworth.
2. Prior's "Solomon."
3. Cleveland's Poems.

❧ III ❧

I

HEAR you not the rushing sound of the coming tempest? Do you not behold the clouds open, and destruction lurid and dire pour down on the blasted earth? See you not the thunderbolt fall, and are deafened by the shout of heaven that follows its descent? Feel you not the earth quake and open with agonizing groans, while the air is pregnant with shrieks and wailings,—all announcing the last days of man? No! none of these things accompanied our fall! The balmy air of spring, breathed from nature's ambrosial home, invested the lovely earth, which wakened as a young mother about to lead forth in pride her beauteous offspring to meet their sire who had been long absent. The buds decked the trees, the flowers adorned the land: the dark branches, swollen with seasonable juices, expanded into leaves, and the variegated foliage of spring, bending and singing in the breeze, rejoiced in the genial warmth of the unclouded empyrean: the brooks flowed murmuring, the sea was waveless, and the promontories that over-hung it were reflected in the placid waters; birds awoke in the woods, while abundant food for man and beast sprung up from the dark ground. Where was pain and evil? Not in the calm air or weltering ocean; not in the woods or fertile fields, nor among the birds that made the woods resonant with song, nor the animals that in the midst of plenty basked in the sunshine. Our enemy, like the Calamity of Homer, trod our hearts, and no sound was echoed from her steps—

> With ills the land is rife, with ills the sea,
> Diseases haunt our frail humanity,
> Through noon, through night, on casual wing they glide,
> Silent,—a voice the power all-wise denied.[1]

Once man was a favourite of the Creator, as the royal psalmist sang, "God had made him a little lower than the angels, and had crowned him with glory and honour. God made him to have dominion over the works of his hands, and put all things under his feet." Once it was so; now is man lord of the creation? Look at him—ha! I see plague! She has invested his form, is incarnate in his flesh, has entwined herself with his being, and blinds his heaven-seeking eyes.

Lie down, O man, on the flower-strown earth; give up all claim to your inheritance, all you can ever possess of it is the small cell which the dead require. Plague is the companion of spring, of sunshine, and plenty. We no longer struggle with her. We have forgotten what we did when she was not. Of old navies used to stem the giant ocean-waves betwixt Indus and the Pole for slight articles of luxury. Men made perilous journies to possess themselves of earth's splendid trifles, gems and gold. Human labour was wasted—human life set at nought. Now life is all that we covet; that this automaton of flesh should, with joints and springs in order, perform its functions, that this dwelling of the soul should be capable of containing its dweller. Our minds, late spread abroad through countless spheres and endless combinations of thought, now retrenched themselves behind this wall of flesh, eager to preserve its well-being only. We were surely sufficiently degraded.

At first the increase of sickness in spring brought increase of toil to such of us, who, as yet spared to life, bestowed our time and thoughts on our fellow creatures. We nerved ourselves to the task: "in the midst of despair we performed the tasks of hope." We went out with the resolution of disputing with our foe. We aided the sick, and comforted the sorrowing; turning from the multitudinous dead to the rare survivors, with an energy of desire that bore the resemblance of power, we bade them—live. Plague sat paramount the while, and laughed us to scorn.

Have any of you, my readers, observed the ruins of an anthill immediately after its destruction? At first it appears entirely deserted of its former inhabitants; in a little time you see an ant struggling through the upturned mould; they reappear by twos and threes, running hither and thither in search of their lost companions. Such were we upon earth, wondering aghast at the effects of pestilence. Our empty habitations remained, but the dwellers were gathered to the shades of the tomb.

As the rules of order and pressure of laws were lost, some began with hesitation and wonder to transgress the accustomed uses of society. Palaces were deserted, and the poor man dared at length, unreproved, intrude into the splendid apartments, whose very furniture and decorations were an unknown world to him. It was found, that, though at first the stop put to all circulation of property, had reduced those before supported by the factitious wants of society to sudden and hideous poverty, yet when the boundaries of private possession were thrown down, the products of human labour at present existing were more, far more, than the thinned generation could possibly consume. To some among the poor this was matter of exultation. We were all equal now; magnificent dwellings, luxurious carpets, and beds of down, were afforded to all. Carriages and horses, gardens, pictures, statues, and princely libraries, there were enough of these even to superfluity; and there was nothing to prevent each from assuming possession of his share. We were all equal now; but near at hand was an equality still more levelling, a state where beauty and strength, and wisdom, would be as vain as riches and birth. The grave yawned beneath us all, and its prospect prevented any of us from enjoying the ease and plenty which in so awful a manner was presented to us.

Still the bloom did not fade on the cheeks of my babes; and Clara sprung up in years and growth, unsullied by disease. We had no reason to think the site of Windsor Castle peculiarly healthy, for many other families had expired beneath its roof; we lived therefore without any particular precaution; but we lived, it seemed, in safety. If Idris became thin and pale, it was anxiety that occasioned the change; an anxiety I could in no way alleviate. She never complained, but sleep and appetite fled from her, a slow fever preyed on her veins, her colour was hectic, and she often wept in secret; gloomy prognostications, care, and agonizing dread, ate up the principle of life within her. I could not fail to perceive this change. I often wished that I had permitted her to take her own course, and engage herself in such labours for the welfare of others as might have distracted her thoughts. But it was too late now. Besides that, with the nearly extinct race of man, all our toils grew near a conclusion, she was too weak; consumption, if so it might be called, or rather the over active life within her, which, as with Adrian, spent the vital oil in the early morning hours, deprived her limbs of strength. At night, when she could leave me unperceived, she wandered through the house, or hung over the couches of her children; and in the day time would sink into a perturbed sleep, while her murmurs and starts betrayed the unquiet dreams that vexed her. As this state of wretchedness became more confirmed, and, in spite of her endeavours at concealment more apparent, I strove, though vainly, to awaken in her courage and hope. I could not wonder at the vehemence of her care; her very soul was tenderness; she trusted indeed that she should not outlive me if I became the prey of the vast calamity, and this thought sometimes relieved her. We had for many years trod the highway of life hand in hand, and still thus linked, we might step within the shades of death; but her children, her lovely, playful, animated children—beings sprung from her own dear side—portions of her own being—depositories of our loves—even if we died, it would be comfort to know that they ran man's accustomed course. But it would not be so; young and blooming as they were, they would die, and from the hopes of maturity, from the proud name of attained manhood, they were cut off for ever. Often with maternal affection she had figured their merits and talents exerted on life's wide stage. Alas for these latter days! The world had grown old, and all its inmates partook of the decrepitude. Why talk of infancy, manhood, and old age? We all stood equal sharers of the last throes of time-worn nature. Arrived at the same point of the world's age—there was no difference in us; the name of parent and child had lost their meaning; young boys and girls were level now with men. This was all true; but it was not less agonizing to take the admonition home.

Where could we turn, and not find a desolation pregnant with the dire lesson of example? The fields had been left uncultivated, weeds and gaudy flowers sprung up,—or where a few wheat-fields shewed signs of the living hopes of the husbandman, the work had been left halfway, the ploughman had died beside the plough; the horses had deserted the furrow, and no seedsman had approached the dead; the cattle unattended wandered over the fields and through the lanes; the tame inhabitants of the poultry yard, baulked of their daily food, had become wild—young lambs were dropt in flower-gardens, and the cow stalled in the hall of pleasure. Sickly and few, the country people neither went out to sow nor reap; but sauntered about the meadows, or lay under the hedges, when the inclement sky did not drive them to take shelter under the nearest roof. Many of those who remained, secluded themselves; some had laid up stores which should prevent the necessity of leaving their homes;—some deserted wife and child, and imagined that they secured their safety in utter solitude. Such had been Ryland's plan, and he was discovered dead and half-devoured by insects, in a house many miles from any other, with piles of food laid up in useless superfluity. Others made long journies to unite themselves to those they loved, and arrived to find them dead.

London did not contain above a thousand inhabitants; and this number was continually diminishing. Most of them were country people, come up for the sake of change; the Londoners had sought the country. The busy eastern part of the town was silent, or at most you saw only where, half from cupidity, half from curiosity, the warehouses had been more ransacked than pillaged: bales of rich India goods, shawls of price, jewels, and spices, unpacked, strewed the floors. In some places the possessor had to the last kept watch on his store, and died before the barred gates. The massy portals of the churches swung creaking on their hinges; and some few lay dead on the pavement. The wretched female, loveless victim of vulgar brutality, had wandered to the toilet of high-born beauty, and, arraying herself in the garb of splendour, had died before the mirror which reflected to herself alone her altered appearance. Women whose delicate feet had seldom touched the earth in their luxury, had fled in fright and horror from their homes, till, losing themselves in the squalid streets of the metropolis, they had died on the threshold of poverty. The heart sickened at the variety of misery presented; and, when I saw a specimen of this gloomy change, my soul ached with the fear of what might befall my beloved Idris and my babes. Were they, surviving Adrian and myself, to find themselves protectorless in the world? As yet the mind alone had suffered—could I for ever put off the time, when the delicate frame and shrinking nerves of my child of prosperity, the nursling of rank and wealth, who was my companion, should be invaded by famine, hardship, and disease? Better die at once—better plunge a poinard in her bosom, still untouched by drear adversity, and then again sheathe it in my own! But, no; in times of misery we must fight against our destinies, and strive not to be overcome by them. I would not yield, but to the last gasp resolutely defended my dear ones against sorrow and pain; and if I were vanquished at last, it should not be ingloriously. I stood in the gap, resisting the enemy—the impalpable, invisible foe, who had so long besieged us—as yet he had made no breach: it must be my care that he should not, secretly undermining, burst up within the very threshold of the temple of love, at whose altar I daily sacrificed. The hunger of Death was now stung more sharply by the diminution of his food: or was it that before, the survivors being many, the dead were less eagerly counted? Now each life was a gem, each human breathing form of far, O! far more worth than subtlest imagery of sculptured stone; and the daily, nay, hourly decrease visible in our numbers, visited the heart with sickening misery. This summer extinguished our hopes, the vessel of society was wrecked, and the shattered raft, which carried the few survivors over the sea of misery, was riven and tempest tost. Man existed by twos and threes; man, the individual who might sleep, and wake, and perform the animal functions; but man, in himself weak, yet more powerful in congregated numbers than wind or ocean; man, the queller of the elements, the lord of created nature, the peer of demi-gods, existed no longer.

Farewell to the patriotic scene, to the love of liberty and well earned mead of virtuous aspiration!—farewell to crowded senate, vocal with the councils of the wise, whose laws were keener than the sword blade tempered at Damascus!—farewell to kingly pomp and warlike pageantry; the crowns are in the dust, and the wearers are in their graves!—farewell to the desire of rule, and the hope of victory; to high vaulting ambition, to the appetite for praise, and the craving for the suffrage of their fellows! The nations are no longer! No senate sits in council for the dead; no scion of a time honoured dynasty pants to rule over the inhabitants of a charnel house; the general's hand is cold, and the soldier has his untimely grave dug in his native fields, unhonoured, though in youth. The market-place is empty, the candidate for popular favour finds none whom he can represent. To chambers of painted state farewell!—To midnight revelry, and the panting emulation of beauty, to costly dress and birth-day shew, to title and the gilded coronet, farewell!

Farewell to the giant powers of man,—to knowledge that could pilot the deep-drawing bark through the opposing waters of shoreless ocean,—to science that directed the silken balloon through the pathless air,—to the power that could put a barrier to mighty waters, and set in motion wheels, and beams, and vast machinery, that could divide rocks of granite or marble, and make the mountains plain!

Farewell to the arts,—to eloquence, which is to the human mind as the winds to the sea, stirring, and then allaying it;—farewell to poetry and deep philosophy, for man's imagination is cold, and his enquiring mind can no longer expatiate on the wonders of life, for "there is no work, nor device, nor knowledge, nor wisdom in the grave, whither thou goest!"—to the graceful building, which in its perfect proportion transcended the rude forms of nature, the fretted gothic and massy saracenic pile, to the stupendous arch and glorious dome, the fluted column with its capital, Corinthian, Ionic, or Doric, the peristyle and fair entablature, whose harmony of form is to the eye as musical concord to the ear!—farewell to sculpture, where the pure marble mocks human flesh, and in the plastic expression of the culled excellencies of the human shape, shines forth the god!—farewell to painting, the high wrought sentiment and deep knowledge of the artists's mind in pictured canvas—to paradisaical scenes, where trees are ever vernal, and the ambrosial air rests in perpetual glow:—to the stamped form of tempest, and wildest uproar of universal nature encaged in the narrow frame, O farewell! Farewell to music, and the sound of song; to the marriage of instruments, where the concord of soft and harsh unites in sweet harmony, and gives wings to the panting listeners, whereby to climb heaven, and learn the hidden pleasures of the eternals!—Farewell to the well-trod stage; a truer tragedy is enacted on the world's ample scene, that puts to shame mimic grief: to high-bred comedy, and the low buffoon, farewell!—Man may laugh no more. Alas! to enumerate the adornments of humanity, shews, by what we have lost, how supremely great man was. It is all over now. He is solitary; like our first parents expelled from Paradise, he looks back towards the scene he has quitted. The high walls of the tomb, and the flaming sword of plague, lie between it and him. Like to our first parents, the whole earth is before him, a wide desart. Unsupported and weak, let him wander through fields where the unreaped corn stands in barren plenty, through copses planted by his fathers, through towns built for his use. Posterity is no more; fame, and ambition, and love, are words void of meaning; even as the cattle that grazes in the field, do thou, O deserted one, lie down at evening-tide, unknowing of the past, careless of the future, for from such fond ignorance alone canst thou hope for ease!

Joy paints with its own colours every act and thought. The happy do not feel poverty—for delight is as a gold-tissued robe, and crowns them with priceless gems. Enjoyment plays the cook to their homely fare, and mingles intoxication with their simple drink. Joy strews the hard couch with roses, and makes labour ease.

Sorrow doubles the burthen to the bent-down back; plants thorns in the unyielding pillow; mingles gall with water; adds saltness to their bitter bread; cloathing them in rags, and strewing ashes on their bare heads. To our irremediable distress every small and pelting inconvenience came with added force; we had strung our frames to endure the Atlean weight thrown on us; we sank beneath the added feather chance threw on us, "the grasshopper was a burthen." Many of the survivors had been bred in luxury—their servants were gone, their powers of command vanished like unreal shadows: the poor even suffered various privations; and the idea of another winter like the last, brought affright to our minds. Was it not enough that we must die, but toil must be added?—must we prepare our funeral repast with labour, and with unseemly drudgery heap fuel on our deserted hearths —must we with servile hands fabricate the garments, soon to be our shroud?

Not so! We are presently to die, let us then enjoy to its full relish the remnant of our lives. Sordid care, avaunt! menial labours, and pains, slight in themselves, but too gigantic for our exhausted strength, shall make no part of our ephemeral existences. In the beginning of time, when, as now, man lived by families, and not by tribes or nations, they were placed in a genial clime, where earth fed them untilled, and the balmy air enwrapt their reposing limbs with warmth more pleasant than beds of down. The south is the native place of the human race; the land of fruits, more grateful to man than the hard-earned Ceres of the north,—of trees, whose boughs are as a palace-roof, of couches of roses, and of the thirst-appeasing grape. We need not there fear cold and hunger.

Look at England! the grass shoots up high in the meadows; but they are dank and cold, unfit bed for us. Corn we have none, and the crude fruits cannot support us. We must seek firing in the bowels of the earth, or the unkind atmosphere will fill us with rheums and aches.

The labour of hundreds of thousands alone could make this inclement nook fit habitation for one man. To the south then, to the sun!—where nature is kind, where Jove has showered forth the contents of Amalthea's horn, and earth is garden.

England, late birth-place of excellence and school of the wise, thy children are gone, thy glory faded! Thou, England, wert the triumph of man! Small favour was shewn thee by thy Creator, thou Isle of the North; a ragged canvas naturally, painted by man with alien colours; but the hues he gave are faded, never more to be renewed. So we must leave thee, thou marvel of the world; we must bid farewell to thy clouds, and cold, and scarcity for ever! Thy manly hearts are still; thy tale of power and liberty at its close! Bereft of man, O little isle! the ocean waves will buffet thee, and the raven flap his wings over thee; thy soil will be birth-place of weeds, thy sky will canopy barrenness. It was not for the rose of Persia thou wert famous, nor the banana of the east; not for the spicy gales of India, nor the sugar groves of America; not for thy vines nor thy double harvests, nor for thy vernal airs, nor solstitial sun—but for thy children, their unwearied industry and lofty aspiration. They are gone, and thou goest with them the oft trodden path that leads to oblivion, —

> Farewell, sad Isle, farewell, thy fatal glory
> Is summed, cast up, and cancelled in this story.[2]

---

1. Elton's translation of Hesiod.
2. Cleveland's Poems.

IN THE AUTUMN of this year 2096, the spirit of emigration crept in among the few survivors, who, congregating from various parts of England, met in London. This spirit existed as a breath, a wish, a far off thought, until communicated to Adrian, who imbibed it with ardour, and instantly engaged himself in plans for its execution. The fear of immediate death vanished with the heats of September. Another winter was before us, and we might elect our mode of passing it to the best advantage. Perhaps in rational philosophy none could be better chosen than this scheme of migration, which would draw us from the immediate scene of our woe, and, leading us through pleasant and picturesque countries, amuse for a time our despair. The idea once broached, all were impatient to put it in execution.

We were still at Windsor; our renewed hopes medicined the anguish we had suffered from the late tragedies. The death of many of our inmates had weaned us from the fond idea, that Windsor Castle was a spot sacred from the plague; but our lease of life was renewed for some months, and even Idris lifted her head, as a lily after a storm, when a last sunbeam tinges its silver cup. Just at this time Adrian came down to us; his eager looks shewed us that he was full of some scheme. He hastened to take me aside, and disclosed to me with rapidity his plan of emigration from England.

To leave England for ever! to turn from its polluted fields and groves, and, placing the sea between us, to quit it, as a sailor quits the rock on which he has been wrecked, when the saving ship rides by. Such was his plan.

To leave the country of our fathers, made holy by their graves!—We could not feel even as a voluntary exile of old, who might for pleasure or convenience forsake his native soil; though thousands of miles might divide him, England was still a part of him, as he of her. He heard of the passing events of the day; he knew that, if he returned, and resumed his place in society, the entrance was still open, and it required but the will, to surround himself at once with the associations and habits of boyhood. Not so with us, the remnant. We left none to represent us, none to repeople the desert land, and the name of England died, when we left her,

In vagabond pursuit of dreadful safety.

Yet let us go! England is in her shroud,—we may not enchain ourselves to a corpse. Let us go—the world is our country now, and we will choose for our residence its most fertile spot. Shall we, in these desart halls, under this wintry sky, sit with closed eyes and folded hands, expecting death? Let us rather go out to meet it gallantly: or perhaps—for all this pendulous orb, this fair gem in the sky's diadem, is not surely plague-striken—perhaps, in some secluded nook, amidst eternal spring, and waving trees, and purling streams, we may find Life. The world is vast, and England, though her many fields and wide spread woods seem interminable, is but a small part of her. At the close of a day's march over high mountains and through snowy vallies, we may come upon health, and committing our loved ones to its charge, replant the uprooted tree of humanity, and send to late posterity the tale of the ante-pestilential race, the heroes and sages of the lost state of things.

Hope beckons and sorrow urges us, the heart beats high with expectation, and this eager desire of change must be an omen of success. O come! Farewell to the dead! farewell to the tombs of those we loved!—farewell to giant London and the placid Thames, to river and mountain or fair district, birth-place of the wise and good, to Windsor Forest and its antique castle, farewell! themes for story alone are they,—we must live elsewhere.

Such were in part the arguments of Adrian, uttered with enthusiasm and unanswerable rapidity. Something more was in his heart, to which he dared not give words. He felt that the end of time was come; he knew that one by one we should dwindle into nothingness. It was not adviseable to wait this sad consummation in our native country; but travelling would give us our object for each day, that would distract our thoughts from the swift-approaching end of things. If we went to Italy, to sacred and eternal Rome, we might with greater patience submit to the decree, which had laid her mighty towers low. We might lose our selfish grief in the sublime aspect of its desolation. All this was in the mind of Adrian; but he thought of my children, and, instead of communicating to me these resources of despair, he called up the image of health and life to be found, where we knew not—when we knew not; but if never to be found, for ever and for ever to be sought. He won me over to his party, heart and soul.

It devolved on me to disclose our plan to Idris. The images of health and hope which I presented to her, made her with a smile consent. With a smile she agreed to leave her country, from which she had never before been absent, and the spot she had inhabited from infancy; the forest and its mighty trees, the woodland paths and green recesses, where she had played in childhood, and had lived so happily through youth; she would leave them without regret, for she hoped to purchase thus the lives of her children. They were her life; dearer than a spot consecrated to love, dearer than all else the earth contained. The boys heard with childish glee of our removal: Clara asked if we were to go to Athens. "It is possible," I replied; and her countenance became radiant with pleasure. There she would behold the tomb of her parents, and the territory filled with recollections of her father's glory. In silence, but without respite, she had brooded over these scenes. It was the recollection of them that had turned her infant gaiety to seriousness, and had impressed her with high and restless thoughts.

There were many dear friends whom we must not leave behind, humble though they were. There was the spirited and obedient steed which Lord Raymond had given his daughter; there was Alfred's dog and a pet eagle, whose sight was dimmed through age. But this catalogue of favourites to be taken with us, could not be made without grief to think of our heavy losses, and a deep sigh for the many things we must leave behind. The tears rushed into the eyes of Idris, while Alfred and Evelyn brought now a favourite rose tree, now a marble vase beautifully carved, insisting that these must go, and exclaiming on the pity that we could not take the castle and the forest, the deer and the birds, and all accustomed and cherished objects along with us. "Fond and foolish ones," I said, "we have lost for ever treasures far more precious than these; and we desert them, to preserve treasures to which in comparison they are nothing. Let us not for a moment forget our object and our hope; and they will form a resistless mound to stop the overflowing of our regret for trifles."

The children were easily distracted, and again returned to their prospect of future amusement. Idris had disappeared. She had gone to hide her weakness; escaping from the castle, she had descended to the little park, and sought solitude, that she might there indulge her tears; I found her clinging round an old oak, pressing its rough trunk with her roseate lips, as her tears fell plenteously, and her sobs and broken exclamations could not be suppressed; with surpassing grief I beheld this loved one of my heart thus lost in sorrow! I drew her towards me; and, as she felt my kisses on her eyelids, as she felt my arms press her, she revived to the knowledge of what remained to her. "You are very kind not to reproach me," she said: "I weep, and a bitter pang of intolerable sorrow tears my heart. And yet I am happy; mothers lament their children, wives lose their husbands, while you and my children are left to me. Yes, I am happy, most happy, that I can weep thus for imaginary sorrows, and that the slight loss of my adored country is not dwindled and annihilated in mightier misery. Take me where you will; where you and my children are, there shall be Windsor, and every country will be England to me. Let these tears flow not for myself, happy and ungrateful as I am, but for the dead world —for our lost country—for all of love, and life, and joy, now choked in the dusty chambers of death."

She spoke quickly, as if to convince herself; she turned her eyes from the trees and forest-paths she loved; she hid her face in my bosom, and we— yes, my masculine firmness dissolved —we wept together consolatory tears, and then calm—nay, almost cheerful, we returned to the castle.

The first cold weather of an English October, made us hasten our preparations. I persuaded Idris to go up to London, where she might better attend to necessary arrangements. I did not tell her, that to spare her the pang of parting from inanimate objects, now the only things left, I had resolved that we should none of us return to Windsor. For the last time we looked on the wide extent of country visible from the terrace, and saw the last rays of the sun tinge the dark masses of wood variegated by autumnal tints; the uncultivated fields and smokeless cottages lay in shadow below; the Thames wound through the wide plain, and the venerable pile of Eton college, stood in dark relief, a prominent object; the cawing of the myriad rooks which inhabited the trees of the little park, as in column or thick wedge they speeded to their nests, disturbed the silence of evening. Nature was the same, as when she was the kind mother of the human race; now, childless and forlorn, her fertility was a mockery; her loveliness a mask for deformity. Why should the breeze gently stir the trees, man felt not its refreshment? Why did dark night adorn herself with stars—man saw them not? Why are there fruits, or flowers, or streams, man is not here to enjoy them?

Idris stood beside me, her dear hand locked in mine. Her face was radiant with a smile. —"The sun is alone," she said, "but we are not. A strange star, my Lionel, ruled our birth; sadly and with dismay we may look upon the annihilation of man; but we remain for each other. Did I ever in the wide world seek other than thee? And since in the wide world thou remainest, why should I complain? Thou and nature are still true to me. Beneath the shades of night, and through the day, whose garish light displays our solitude, thou wilt still be at my side, and even Windsor will not be regretted."

I had chosen night time for our journey to London, that the change and desolation of the country might be the less observable. Our only surviving servant drove us. We past down the steep hill, and entered the dusky avenue of the Long Walk. At times like these, minute circumstances assume giant and majestic proportions; the very swinging open of the white gate that admitted us into the forest, arrested my thoughts as matter of interest; it was an every day act, never to occur again! The setting crescent of the moon glittered through the massy trees to our right, and when we entered the park, we scared a troop of deer, that fled bounding away in the forest shades. Our two boys quietly slept; once, before our road turned from the view, I looked back on the castle. Its windows glistened in the moonshine, and its heavy outline lay in a dark mass against the sky—the trees near us waved a solemn dirge to the midnight breeze. Idris leaned back in the carriage; her two hands pressed mine, her countenance was placid, she seemed to lose the sense of what she now left, in the memory of what she still possessed.

My thoughts were sad and solemn, yet not of unmingled pain. The very excess of our misery carried a relief with it, giving sublimity and elevation to sorrow. I felt that I carried with me those I best loved; I was pleased, after a long separation to rejoin Adrian; never again to part. I felt that I quitted what I loved, not what loved me. The castle walls, and long familiar trees, did not hear the parting sound of our carriage-wheels with regret. And, while I felt Idris to be near, and heard the regular breathing of my children, I could not be unhappy. Clara was greatly moved; with streaming eyes, suppressing her sobs, she leaned from the window, watching the last glimpse of her native Windsor.

Adrian welcomed us on our arrival. He was all animation; you could no longer trace in his look of health, the suffering valetudinarian; from his smile and sprightly tones you could not guess that he was about to lead forth from their native country, the numbered remnant of the English nation, into the tenantless realms of the south, there to die, one by one, till the LAST MAN should remain in a voiceless, empty world.

Adrian was impatient for our departure, and had advanced far in his preparations. His wisdom guided all. His care was the soul, to move the luckless crowd, who relied wholly on him. It was useless to provide many things, for we should find abundant provision in every town. It was Adrian's wish to prevent all labour; to bestow a festive appearance on this funeral train. Our numbers amounted to not quite two thousand persons. These were not all assembled in London, but each day witnessed the arrival of fresh numbers, and those who resided in the neighbouring towns, had received orders to assemble at one place, on the twentieth of November. Carriages and horses were provided for all; captains and under officers chosen, and the whole assemblage wisely organized. All obeyed the Lord Protector of dying England; all looked up to him. His council was chosen, it consisted of about fifty persons. Distinction and station were not the qualifications of their election. We had no station among us, but that which benevolence and prudence gave; no distinction save between the living and the dead. Although we were anxious to leave England before the depth of winter, yet we were detained. Small parties had been dispatched to various parts of England, in search of stragglers; we would not go, until we had assured ourselves that in all human probability we did not leave behind a single human being.

On our arrival in London, we found that the aged Countess of Windsor was residing with her son in the palace of the Protectorate; we repaired to our accustomed abode near Hyde Park. Idris now for the first time for many years saw her mother, anxious to assure herself that the childishness of old age did not mingle with unforgotten pride, to make this high-born dame still so inveterate against me. Age and care had furrowed her cheeks, and bent her form; but her eye was still bright, her manners authoritative and unchanged; she received her daughter coldly, but displayed more feeling as she folded her grand-children in her arms. It is our nature to wish to continue our systems and thoughts to posterity through our own offspring. The Countess had failed in this design with regard to her children; perhaps she hoped to find the next remove in birth more tractable. Once Idris named me casually—a frown, a convulsive gesture of anger, shook her mother, and, with voice trembling with hate, she said—"I am of little worth in this world; the young are impatient to push the old off the scene; but, Idris, if you do not wish to see your mother expire at your feet, never again name that person to me; all else I can bear; and now I am resigned to the destruction of my cherished hopes: but it is too much to require that I should love the instrument that providence gifted with murderous properties for my destruction."

This was a strange speech, now that, on the empty stage, each might play his part without impediment from the other. But the haughty Ex-Queen thought as Octavius Caesar and Mark Antony,

> We could not stall together
> In the whole world.

The period of our departure was fixed for the twenty-fifth of November. The weather was temperate; soft rains fell at night, and by day the wintry sun shone out. Our numbers were to move forward in separate parties, and to go by different routes, all to unite at last at Paris. Adrian and his division, consisting in all of five hundred persons, were to take the direction of Dover and Calais. On the twentieth of November, Adrian and I rode for the last time through the streets of London. They were grass-grown and desert. The open doors of the empty mansions creaked upon their hinges; rank herbage, and deforming dirt, had swiftly accumulated on the steps of the houses; the voiceless steeples of the churches pierced the smokeless air; the churches were open, but no prayer was offered at the altars; mildew and damp had already defaced their ornaments; birds, and tame animals, now homeless, had built nests, and made their lairs in consecrated spots. We passed St. Paul's. London, which had extended so far in suburbs in all direction, had been somewhat deserted in the midst, and much of what had in former days obscured this vast building was removed. Its ponderous mass, blackened stone, and high dome, made it look, not like a temple, but a tomb. Methought above the portico was engraved the Hic jacet of England. We passed on eastwards, engaged in such solemn talk as the times inspired. No human step was heard, nor human form discerned. Troops of dogs, deserted of their masters, passed us; and now and then a horse, unbridled and unsaddled, trotted towards us, and tried to attract the attention of those which we rode, as if to allure them to seek like liberty. An unwieldy ox, who had fed in an abandoned granary, suddenly lowed, and shewed his shapeless form in a narrow door-way; every thing was desert; but nothing was in ruin. And this medley of undamaged buildings, and luxurious accommodation, in trim and fresh youth, was contrasted with the lonely silence of the unpeopled streets.

Night closed in, and it began to rain. We were about to return homewards, when a voice, a human voice, strange now to hear, attracted our attention. It was a child singing a merry, lightsome air; there was no other sound. We had traversed London from Hyde Park even to where we now were in the Minories, and had met no person, heard no voice nor footstep. The singing was interrupted by laughing and talking; never was merry ditty so sadly timed, never laughter more akin to tears. The door of the house from which these sounds proceeded was open, the upper rooms were illuminated as for a feast. It was a large magnificent house, in which doubtless some rich merchant had lived. The singing again commenced, and rang through the high-roofed rooms, while we silently ascended the stair-case. Lights now appeared to guide us; and a long suite of splendid rooms illuminated, made us still more wonder. Their only inhabitant, a little girl, was dancing, waltzing, and singing about them, followed by a large Newfoundland dog, who boisterously jumping on her, and interrupting her, made her now scold, now laugh, now throw herself on the carpet to play with him. She was dressed grotesquely, in glittering robes and shawls fit for a woman; she appeared about ten years of age.

We stood at the door looking on this strange scene, till the dog perceiving us barked loudly; the child turned and saw us: her face, losing its gaiety, assumed a sullen expression: she slunk back, apparently meditating an escape. I came up to her, and held her hand; she did not resist, but with a stern brow, so strange in childhood, so different from her former hilarity, she stood still, her eyes fixed on the ground. "What do you do here?" I said gently; "Who are you?"—she was silent, but trembled violently.—"My poor child," asked Adrian, "are you alone?" There was a winning softness in his voice, that went to the heart of the little girl; she looked at him, then snatching her hand from me, threw herself into his arms, clinging round his neck, ejaculating —"Save me! save me!" while her unnatural sullenness dissolved in tears.

"I will save you," he replied, "of what are you afraid? you need not fear my friend, he will do you no harm. Are you alone?"

"No, Lion is with me."

"And your father and mother?—"

"I never had any; I am a charity girl. Every body is gone, gone for a great, great many days; but if they come back and find me out, they will beat me so!"

Her unhappy story was told in these few words: an orphan, taken on pretended charity, ill-treated and reviled, her oppressors had died: unknowing of what had passed around her, she found herself alone; she had not dared venture out, but by the continuance of her solitude her courage revived, her childish vivacity caused her to play a thousand freaks, and with her brute companion she passed a long holiday, fearing nothing but the return of the harsh voices and cruel usage of her protectors. She readily consented to go with Adrian.

In the mean time, while we descanted on alien sorrows, and on a solitude which struck our eyes and not our hearts, while we imagined all of change and suffering that had intervened in these once thronged streets, before, tenantless and abandoned, they became mere kennels for dogs, and stables for cattle:—while we read the death of the world upon the dark fane, and hugged ourselves in the remembrance that we possessed that which was all the world to us—in the meanwhile—

We had arrived from Windsor early in October, and had now been in London about six weeks. Day by day, during that time, the health of my Idris declined: her heart was broken; neither sleep nor appetite, the chosen servants of health, waited on her wasted form. To watch her children hour by hour, to sit by me, drinking deep the dear persuasion that I remained to her, was all her pastime. Her vivacity, so long assumed, her affectionate display of cheerfulness, her light-hearted tone and springy gait were gone. I could not disguise to myself, nor could she conceal, her life-consuming sorrow. Still change of scene, and reviving hopes might restore her; I feared the plague only, and she was untouched by that.

I had left her this evening, reposing after the fatigues of her preparations. Clara sat beside her, relating a story to the two boys. The eyes of Idris were closed: but Clara perceived a sudden change in the appearance of our eldest darling; his heavy lids veiled his eyes, an unnatural colour burnt in his cheeks, his breath became short. Clara looked at the mother; she slept, yet started at the pause the narrator made— Fear of awakening and alarming her, caused Clara to go on at the eager call of Evelyn, who was unaware of what was passing. Her eyes turned alternately from Alfred to Idris; with trembling accents she continued her tale, till she saw the child about to fall: starting forward she caught him, and her cry roused Idris. She looked on her son. She saw death stealing across his features; she laid him on a bed, she held drink to his parched lips.

Yet he might be saved. If I were there, he might be saved; perhaps it was not the plague. Without a counsellor, what could she do? stay and behold him die! Why at that moment was I away? "Look to him, Clara," she exclaimed, "I will return immediately."

She inquired among those who, selected as the companions of our journey, had taken up their residence in our house; she heard from them merely that I had gone out with Adrian. She entreated them to seek me: she returned to her child, he was plunged in a frightful state of torpor; again she rushed down stairs; all was dark, desert, and silent; she lost all self-possession; she ran into the street; she called on my name. The pattering rain and howling wind alone replied to her. Wild fear gave wings to her feet; she darted forward to seek me, she knew not where; but, putting all her thoughts, all her energy, all her being in speed only, most misdirected speed, she neither felt, nor feared, nor paused, but ran right on, till her strength suddenly deserted her so suddenly, that she had not thought to save herself. Her knees failed her, and she fell heavily on the pavement. She was stunned for a time; but at length rose, and though sorely hurt, still walked on, shedding a fountain of tears, stumbling at times, going she knew not whither, only now and then with feeble voice she called my name, adding with heart-piercing exclamations, that I was cruel and unkind. Human being there was none to reply; and the inclemency of the night had driven the wandering animals to the habitations they had usurped. Her thin dress was drenched with rain; her wet hair clung round her neck; she tottered through the dark streets; till, striking her foot against an unseen impediment, she again fell; she could not rise; she hardly strove; but, gathering up her limbs, she resigned herself to the fury of the elements, and the bitter grief of her own heart. She breathed an earnest prayer to die speedily, for there was no relief but death. While hopeless of safety for herself, she ceased to lament for her dying child, but shed kindly, bitter tears for the grief I should experience in losing her. While she lay, life almost suspended, she felt a warm, soft hand on her brow, and a gentle female voice asked her, with expressions of tender compassion, if she could not rise? That another human being, sympathetic and kind, should exist near, roused her; half rising, with clasped hands, and fresh springing tears, she entreated her companion to seek for me, to bid me hasten to my dying child, to save him, for the love of heaven, to save him!

The woman raised her; she led her under shelter, she entreated her to return to her home, whither perhaps I had already returned. Idris easily yielded to her persuasions, she leaned on the arm of her friend, she endeavoured to walk on, but irresistible faintness made her pause again and again.

Quickened by the increasing storm, we had hastened our return, our little charge was placed before Adrian on his horse. There was an assemblage of persons under the portico of our house, in whose gestures I instinctively read some heavy change, some new misfortune. With swift alarm, afraid to ask a single question, I leapt from my horse; the spectators saw me, knew me, and in awful silence divided to make way for me. I snatched a light, and rushing up stairs, and hearing a groan, without reflection I threw open the door of the first room that presented itself. It was quite dark; but, as I stepped within, a pernicious scent assailed my senses, producing sickening qualms, which made their way to my very heart, while I felt my leg clasped, and a groan repeated by the person that held me. I lowered my lamp, and saw a negro half clad, writhing under the agony of disease, while he held me with a convulsive grasp. With mixed horror and impatience I strove to disengage myself, and fell on the sufferer; he wound his naked festering arms round me, his face was close to mine, and his breath, death-laden, entered my vitals. For a moment I was overcome, my head was bowed by aching nausea; till, reflection returning, I sprung up, threw the wretch from me, and darting up the staircase, entered the chamber usually inhabited by my family. A dim light shewed me Alfred on a couch; Clara trembling, and paler than whitest snow, had raised him on her arm, holding a cup of water to his lips. I saw full well that no spark of life existed in that ruined form, his features were rigid, his eyes glazed, his head had fallen back. I took him from her, I laid him softly down, kissed his cold little mouth, and turned to speak in a vain whisper, when loudest sound of thunderlike cannon could not have reached him in his immaterial abode.

And where was Idris? That she had gone out to seek me, and had not returned, were fearful tidings, while the rain and driving wind clattered against the window, and roared round the house. Added to this, the sickening sensation of disease gained upon me; no time was to be lost, if ever I would see her again. I mounted my horse and rode out to seek her, fancying that I heard her voice in every gust, oppressed by fever and aching pain.

I rode in the dark and rain through the labyrinthine streets of unpeopled London. My child lay dead at home; the seeds of mortal disease had taken root in my bosom; I went to seek Idris, my adored, now wandering alone, while the waters were rushing from heaven like a cataract to bathe her dear head in chill damp, her fair limbs in numbing cold. A female stood on the step of a door, and called to me as I galloped past. It was not Idris; so I rode swiftly on, until a kind of second sight, a reflection back again on my senses of what I had seen but not marked, made me feel sure that another figure, thin, graceful and tall, stood clinging to the foremost person who supported her. In a minute I was beside the suppliant, in a minute I received the sinking Idris in my arms. Lifting her up, I placed her on the horse; she had not strength to support herself; so I mounted behind her, and held her close to my bosom, wrapping my riding-cloak round her, while her companion, whose well known, but changed countenance, (it was Juliet, daughter of the Duke of L——) could at this moment of horror obtain from me no more than a passing glance of compassion. She took the abandoned rein, and conducted our obedient steed homewards. Dare I avouch it? That was the last moment of my happiness; but I was happy. Idris must die, for her heart was broken: I must die, for I had caught the plague; earth was a scene of desolation; hope was madness; life had married death; they were one; but, thus supporting my fainting love, thus feeling that I must soon die, I revelled in the delight of possessing her once more; again and again I kissed her, and pressed her to my heart.

We arrived at our home. I assisted her to dismount, I carried her up stairs, and gave her into Clara's care, that her wet garments might be changed. Briefly I assured Adrian of her safety, and requested that we might be left to repose. As the miser, who with trembling caution visits his treasure to count it again and again, so I numbered each moment, and grudged every one that was not spent with Idris. I returned swiftly to the chamber where the life of my life reposed; before I entered the room I paused for a few seconds; for a few seconds I tried to examine my state; sickness and shuddering ever and anon came over me; my head was heavy, my chest oppressed, my legs bent under me; but I threw off resolutely the swift growing symptoms of my disorder, and met Idris with placid and even joyous looks. She was lying on a couch; carefully fastening the door to prevent all intrusion; I sat by her, we embraced, and our lips met in a kiss long drawn and breathless—would that moment had been my last!

Maternal feeling now awoke in my poor girl's bosom, and she asked: "And Alfred?"

"Idris," I replied, "we are spared to each other, we are together; do not let any other idea intrude. I am happy; even on this fatal night, I declare myself happy, beyond all name, all thought—what would you more, sweet one?"

Idris understood me: she bowed her head on my shoulder and wept. "Why," she again asked, "do you tremble, Lionel, what shakes you thus?"

"Well may I be shaken," I replied, "happy as I am. Our child is dead, and the present hour is dark and ominous. Well may I tremble! but, I am happy, mine own Idris, most happy."

"I understand thee, my kind love," said Idris, "thus—pale as thou art with sorrow at our loss; trembling and aghast, though wouldest assuage my grief by thy dear assurances. I am not happy," (and the tears flashed and fell from under her down-cast lids), "for we are inmates of a miserable prison, and there is no joy for us; but the true love I bear you will render this and every other loss endurable."

"We have been happy together, at least," I said; "no future misery can deprive us of the past. We have been true to each other for years, ever since my sweet princess-love came through the snow to the lowly cottage of the poverty-striken heir of the ruined Verney. Even now, that eternity is before us, we take hope only from the presence of each other. Idris, do you think, that when we die, we shall be divided?"

"Die! when we die! what mean you? What secret lies hid from me in those dreadful words?"

"Must we not all die, dearest?" I asked with a sad smile.

"Gracious God! are you ill, Lionel, that you speak of death? My only friend, heart of my heart, speak!"

"I do not think," replied I, "that we have any of us long to live; and when the curtain drops on this mortal scene, where, think you, we shall find ourselves?" Idris was calmed by my unembarrassed tone and look; she answered:—"You may easily believe that during this long progress of the plague, I have thought much on death, and asked myself, now that all mankind is dead to this life, to what other life they may have been borne. Hour after hour, I have dwelt on these thoughts, and strove to form a rational conclusion concerning the mystery of a future state. What a scare-crow, indeed, would death be, if we were merely to cast aside the shadow in which we now walk, and, stepping forth into the unclouded sunshine of knowledge and love, revived with the same companions, the same affections, and reached the fulfilment of our hopes, leaving our fears with our earthly vesture in the grave. Alas! the same strong feeling which makes me sure that I shall not wholly die, makes me refuse to believe that I shall live wholly as I do now. Yet, Lionel, never, never, can I love any but you; through eternity I must desire your society; and, as I am innocent of harm to others, and as relying and confident as my mortal nature permits, I trust that the Ruler of the world will never tear us asunder."

"Your remarks are like yourself, dear love," replied I, "gentle and good; let us cherish such a belief, and dismiss anxiety from our minds. But, sweet, we are so formed, (and there is no sin, if God made our nature, to yield to what he ordains), we are so formed, that we must love life, and cling to it; we must love the living smile, the sympathetic touch, and thrilling voice, peculiar to our mortal mechanism. Let us not, through security in hereafter, neglect the present. This present moment, short as it is, is a part of eternity, and the dearest part, since it is our own unalienably. Thou, the hope of my futurity, art my present joy. Let me then look on thy dear eyes, and, reading love in them, drink intoxicating pleasure."

Timidly, for my vehemence somewhat terrified her, Idris looked on me. My eyes were bloodshot, starting from my head; every artery beat, methought, audibly, every muscle throbbed, each single nerve felt. Her look of wild affright told me, that I could no longer keep my secret:—"So it is, mine own beloved," I said, "the last hour of many happy ones is arrived, nor can we shun any longer the inevitable destiny. I cannot live long—but, again and again, I say, this moment is ours!"

Paler than marble, with white lips and convulsed features, Idris became aware of my situation. My arm, as I sat, encircled her waist. She felt the palm burn with fever, even on the heart it pressed:—"One moment," she murmured, scarce audibly, "only one moment."—

She kneeled, and hiding her face in her hands, uttered a brief, but earnest prayer, that she might fulfil her duty, and watch over me to the last. While there was hope, the agony had been unendurable;—all was now concluded; her feelings became solemn and calm. Even as Epicharis, unperturbed and firm, submitted to the instruments of torture, did Idris, suppressing every sigh and sign of grief, enter upon the endurance of torments, of which the rack and the wheel are but faint and metaphysical symbols.

I was changed; the tight-drawn cord that sounded so harshly was loosened, the moment that Idris participated in my knowledge of our real situation. The perturbed and passion-tossed waves of thought subsided, leaving only the heavy swell that kept right on without any outward manifestation of its disturbance, till it should break on the remote shore towards which I rapidly advanced:—"It is true that I am sick," I said, "and your society, my Idris is my only medicine; come, and sit beside me."

She made me lie down on the couch, and, drawing a low ottoman near, sat close to my pillow, pressing my burning hands in her cold palms. She yielded to my feverish restlessness, and let me talk, and talked to me, on subjects strange indeed to beings, who thus looked the last, and heard the last, of what they loved alone in the world. We talked of times gone by; of the happy period of our early love; of Raymond, Perdita, and Evadne. We talked of what might arise on this desert earth, if, two or three being saved, it were slowly re-peopled.—We talked of what was beyond the tomb; and, man in his human shape being nearly extinct, we felt with certainty of faith, that other spirits, other minds, other perceptive beings, sightless to us, must people with thought and love this beauteous and imperishable universe.

We talked—I know not how long—but, in the morning I awoke from a painful heavy slumber; the pale cheek of Idris rested on my pillow; the large orbs of her eyes half raised the lids, and shewed the deep blue lights beneath; her lips were unclosed, and the slight murmurs they formed told that, even while asleep, she suffered. "If she were dead," I thought, "what difference? now that form is the temple of a residing deity; those eyes are the windows of her soul; all grace, love, and intelligence are throned on that lovely bosom—were she dead, where would this mind, the dearer half of mine, be? For quickly the fair proportion of this edifice would be more defaced, than are the sand-choked ruins of the desert temples of Palmyra."

IDRIS STIRRED AND AWOKE; alas! she awoke to misery. She saw the signs of disease on my countenance, and wondered how she could permit the long night to pass without her having sought, not cure, that was impossible, but alleviation to my sufferings. She called Adrian; my couch was quickly surrounded by friends and assistants, and such medicines as were judged fitting were administered. It was the peculiar and dreadful distinction of our visitation, that none who had been attacked by the pestilence had recovered. The first symptom of the disease was the death-warrant, which in no single instance had been followed by pardon or reprieve. No gleam of hope therefore cheered my friends.

While fever producing torpor, heavy pains, sitting like lead on my limbs, and making my breast heave, were upon me; I continued insensible to every thing but pain, and at last even to that. I awoke on the fourth morning as from a dreamless sleep. An irritating sense of thirst, and, when I strove to speak or move, an entire dereliction of power, was all I felt.

For three days and nights Idris had not moved from my side. She administered to all my wants, and never slept nor rested. She did not hope; and therefore she neither endeavoured to read the physician's countenance, nor to watch for symptoms of recovery. All her thought was to attend on me to the last, and then to lie down and die beside me. On the third night animation was suspended; to the eye and touch of all I was dead. With earnest prayer, almost with force, Adrian tried to draw Idris from me. He exhausted every adjuration, her child's welfare and his own. She shook her head, and wiped a stealing tear from her sunk cheek, but would not yield; she entreated to be allowed to watch me that one night only, with such affliction and meek earnestness, that she gained her point, and sat silent and motionless, except when, stung by intolerable remembrance, she kissed my closed eyes and pallid lips, and pressed my stiffening hands to her beating heart.

At dead of night, when, though it was mid winter, the cock crowed at three o'clock, as herald of the morning change, while hanging over me, and mourning in silent, bitter thought for the loss of all of love towards her that had been enshrined in my heart; her dishevelled hair hung over her face, and the long tresses fell on the bed; she saw one ringlet in motion, and the scattered hair slightly stirred, as by a breath. It is not so, she thought, for he will never breathe more. Several times the same thing occurred, and she only marked it by the same reflection; till the whole ringlet waved back, and she thought she saw my breast heave. Her first emotion was deadly fear, cold dew stood on her brow; my eyes half opened; and, re-assured, she would have exclaimed, "He lives!" but the words were choked by a spasm, and she fell with a groan on the floor.

Adrian was in the chamber. After long watching, he had unwillingly fallen into a sleep. He started up, and beheld his sister senseless on the earth, weltering in a stream of blood that gushed from her mouth. Encreasing signs of life in me in some degree explained her state; the surprise, the burst of joy, the revulsion of every sentiment, had been too much for her frame, worn by long months of care, late shattered by every species of woe and toil. She was now in far greater danger than I, the wheels and springs of my life, once again set in motion, acquired elasticity from their short suspension. For a long time, no one believed that I should indeed continue to live; during the reign of the plague upon earth, not one person, attacked by the grim disease, had recovered. My restoration was looked on as a deception; every moment it was expected that the evil symptoms would recur with redoubled violence, until confirmed convalescence, absence of all fever or pain, and increasing strength, brought slow conviction that I had recovered from the plague.

The restoration of Idris was more problematical. When I had been attacked by illness, her cheeks were sunk, her form emaciated; but now, the vessel, which had broken from the effects of extreme agitation, did not entirely heal, but was as a channel that drop by drop drew from her the ruddy stream that vivified her heart. Her hollow eyes and worn countenance had a ghastly appearance; her cheek-bones, her open fair brow, the projection of the mouth, stood fearfully prominent; you might tell each bone in the thin anatomy of her frame. Her hand hung powerless; each joint lay bare, so that the light penetrated through and through. It was strange that life could exist in what was wasted and worn into a very type of death.

To take her from these heart-breaking scenes, to lead her to forget the world's desolation in the variety of objects presented by travelling, and to nurse her failing strength in the mild climate towards which we had resolved to journey, was my last hope for her preservation. The preparations for our departure, which had been suspended during my illness, were renewed. I did not revive to doubtful convalescence; health spent her treasures upon me; as the tree in spring may feel from its wrinkled limbs the fresh green break forth, and the living sap rise and circulate, so did the renewed vigour of my frame, the cheerful current of my blood, the new-born elasticity of my limbs, influence my mind to cheerful endurance and pleasurable thoughts. My body, late the heavy weight that bound me to the tomb, was exuberant with health; mere common exercises were insufficient for my reviving strength; methought I could emulate the speed of the race-horse, discern through the air objects at a blinding distance, hear the operations of nature in her mute abodes; my senses had become so refined and susceptible after my recovery from mortal disease.

Hope, among my other blessings, was not denied to me; and I did fondly trust that my unwearied attentions would restore my adored girl. I was therefore eager to forward our preparations. According to the plan first laid down, we were to have quitted London on the twenty-fifth of November; and, in pursuance of this scheme, two-thirds of our people—the people— all that remained of England, had gone forward, and had already been some weeks in Paris. First my illness, and subsequently that of Idris, had detained Adrian with his division, which consisted of three hundred persons, so that we now departed on the first of January, 2098. It was my wish to keep Idris as distant as possible from the hurry and clamour of the crowd, and to hide from her those appearances that would remind her most forcibly of our real situation. We separated ourselves to a great degree from Adrian, who was obliged to give his whole time to public business. The Countess of Windsor travelled with her son. Clara, Evelyn, and a female who acted as our attendant, were the only persons with whom we had contact. We occupied a commodious carriage, our servant officiated as coachman. A party of about twenty persons preceded us at a small distance. They had it in charge to prepare our halting places and our nightly abode. They had been selected for this service out of a great number that offered, on account of the superior sagacity of the man who had been appointed their leader.

Immediately on our departure, I was delighted to find a change in Idris, which I fondly hoped prognosticated the happiest results. All the cheerfulness and gentle gaiety natural to her revived. She was weak, and this alteration was rather displayed in looks and voice than in acts; but it was permanent and real. My recovery from the plague and confirmed health instilled into her a firm belief that I was now secure from this dread enemy. She told me that she was sure she should recover. That she had a presentiment, that the tide of calamity which deluged our unhappy race had now turned. That the remnant would be preserved, and among them the dear objects of her tender affection; and that in some selected spot we should wear out our lives together in pleasant society. "Do not let my state of feebleness deceive you," she said; "I feel that I am better; there is a quick life within me, and a spirit of anticipation that assures me, that I shall continue long to make a part of this world. I shall throw off this degrading weakness of body, which infects even my mind with debility, and I shall enter again on the performance of my duties. I was sorry to leave Windsor: but now I am weaned from this local attachment; I am content to remove to a mild climate, which will complete my recovery. Trust me, dearest, I shall neither leave you, nor my brother, nor these dear children; my firm determination to remain with you to the last, and to continue to contribute to your happiness and welfare, would keep me alive, even if grim death were nearer at hand than he really is."

I was only half re-assured by these expressions; I could not believe that the over-quick flow of her blood was a sign of health, or that her burning cheeks denoted convalescence. But I had no fears of an immediate catastrophe; nay, I persuaded myself that she would ultimately recover. And thus cheerfulness reigned in our little society. Idris conversed with animation on a thousand topics. Her chief desire was to lead our thoughts from melancholy reflections; so she drew charming pictures of a tranquil solitude, of a beauteous retreat, of the simple manners of our little tribe, and of the patriarchal brotherhood of love, which would survive the ruins of the populous nations which had lately existed. We shut out from our thoughts the present, and withdrew our eyes from the dreary landscape we traversed. Winter reigned in all its gloom. The leafless trees lay without motion against the dun sky; the forms of frost, mimicking the foliage of summer, strewed the ground; the paths were overgrown; the unploughed cornfields were patched with grass and weeds; the sheep congregated at the threshold of the cottage, the horned ox thrust his head from the window. The wind was bleak, and frequent sleet or snow-storms, added to the melancholy appearance wintry nature assumed.

We arrived at Rochester, and an accident caused us to be detained there a day. During that time, a circumstance occurred that changed our plans, and which, alas! in its result changed the eternal course of events, turning me from the pleasant new sprung hope I enjoyed, to an obscure and gloomy desert. But I must give some little explanation before I proceed with the final cause of our temporary alteration of plan, and refer again to those times when man walked the earth fearless, before Plague had become Queen of the World.

There resided a family in the neighbourhood of Windsor, of very humble pretensions, but which had been an object of interest to us on account of one of the persons of whom it was composed. The family of the Claytons had known better days; but, after a series of reverses, the father died a bankrupt, and the mother heartbroken, and a confirmed invalid, retired with her five children to a little cottage between Eton and Salt Hill. The eldest of these children, who was thirteen years old, seemed at once from the influence of adversity, to acquire the sagacity and principle belonging to a more mature age. Her mother grew worse and worse in health, but Lucy attended on her, and was as a tender parent to her younger brothers and sisters, and in the meantime shewed herself so good-humoured, social, and benevolent, that she was beloved as well as honoured, in her little neighbourhood.

Lucy was besides extremely pretty; so when she grew to be sixteen, it was to be supposed, notwithstanding her poverty, that she should have admirers. One of these was the son of a country-curate; he was a generous, frank-hearted youth, with an ardent love of knowledge, and no mean acquirements. Though Lucy was untaught, her mother's conversation and manners gave her a taste for refinements superior to her present situation. She loved the youth even without knowing it, except that in any difficulty she naturally turned to him for aid, and awoke with a lighter heart every Sunday, because she knew that she would be met and accompanied by him in her evening walk with her sisters. She had another admirer, one of the head-waiters at the inn at Salt Hill. He also was not without pretensions to urbane superiority, such as he learnt from gentlemen's servants and waiting-maids, who initiating him in all the slang of high life below stairs, rendered his arrogant temper ten times more intrusive. Lucy did not disclaim him—she was incapable of that feeling; but she was sorry when she saw him approach, and quietly resisted all his endeavours to establish an intimacy. The fellow soon discovered that his rival was preferred to him; and this changed what was at first a chance admiration into a passion, whose main springs were envy, and a base desire to deprive his competitor of the advantage he enjoyed over himself.

Poor Lucy's sad story was but a common one. Her lover's father died; and he was left destitute. He accepted the offer of a gentleman to go to India with him, feeling secure that he should soon acquire an independence, and return to claim the hand of his beloved. He became involved in the war carried on there, was taken prisoner, and years elapsed before tidings of his existence were received in his native land. In the meantime disastrous poverty came on Lucy. Her little cottage, which stood looking from its trellice, covered with woodbine and jessamine, was burnt down; and the whole of their little property was included in the destruction. Whither betake them? By what exertion of industry could Lucy procure them another abode? Her mother nearly bed-rid, could not survive any extreme of famine-struck poverty. At this time her other admirer stept forward, and renewed his offer of marriage. He had saved money, and was going to set up a little inn at Datchet. There was nothing alluring to Lucy in this offer, except the home it secured to her mother; and she felt more sure of this, since she was struck by the apparent generosity which occasioned the present offer. She accepted it; thus sacrificing herself for the comfort and welfare of her parent.

It was some years after her marriage that we became acquainted with her. The accident of a storm caused us to take refuge in the inn, where we witnessed the brutal and quarrelsome behaviour of her husband, and her patient endurance. Her lot was not a fortunate one. Her first lover had returned with the hope of making her his own, and met her by accident, for the first time, as the mistress of his country inn, and the wife of another. He withdrew despairingly to foreign parts; nothing went well with him; at last he enlisted, and came back again wounded and sick, and yet Lucy was debarred from nursing him. Her husband's brutal disposition was aggravated by his yielding to the many temptations held out by his situation, and the consequent disarrangement of his affairs. Fortunately she had no children; but her heart was bound up in her brothers and sisters, and these his avarice and ill temper soon drove from the house; they were dispersed about the country, earning their livelihood with toil and care. He even shewed an inclination to get rid of her mother—but Lucy was firm here—she had sacrificed herself for her; she lived for her —she would not part with her—if the mother went, she would also go beg bread for her, die with her, but never desert her. The presence of Lucy was too necessary in keeping up the order of the house, and in preventing the whole establishment from going to wreck, for him to permit her to leave him. He yielded the point; but in all accesses of anger, or in his drunken fits, he recurred to the old topic, and stung poor Lucy's heart by opprobrious epithets bestowed on her parent.

A passion however, if it be wholly pure, entire, and reciprocal, brings with it its own solace. Lucy was truly, and from the depth of heart, devoted to her mother; the sole end she proposed to herself in life, was the comfort and preservation of this parent. Though she grieved for the result, yet she did not repent of her marriage, even when her lover returned to bestow competence on her. Three years had intervened, and how, in their pennyless state, could her mother have existed during this time? This excellent woman was worthy of her child's devotion. A perfect confidence and friendship existed between them; besides, she was by no means illiterate; and Lucy, whose mind had been in some degree cultivated by her former lover, now found in her the only person who could understand and appreciate her. Thus, though suffering, she was by no means desolate, and when, during fine summer days, she led her mother into the flowery and shady lanes near their abode, a gleam of unmixed joy enlightened her countenance; she saw that her parent was happy, and she knew that this happiness was of her sole creating.

Meanwhile her husband's affairs grew more and more involved; ruin was near at hand, and she was about to lose the fruit of all her labours, when pestilence came to change the aspect of the world. Her husband reaped benefit from the universal misery; but, as the disaster increased, the spirit of lawlessness seized him; he deserted his home to revel in the luxuries promised him in London, and found there a grave. Her former lover had been one of the first victims of the disease. But Lucy continued to live for and in her mother. Her courage only failed when she dreaded peril for her parent, or feared that death might prevent her from performing those duties to which she was unalterably devoted.

When we had quitted Windsor for London, as the previous step to our final emigration, we visited Lucy, and arranged with her the plan of her own and her mother's removal. Lucy was sorry at the necessity which forced her to quit her native lanes and village, and to drag an infirm parent from her comforts at home, to the homeless waste of depopulate earth; but she was too well disciplined by adversity, and of too sweet a temper, to indulge in repinings at what was inevitable.

Subsequent circumstances, my illness and that of Idris, drove her from our remembrance; and we called her to mind at last, only to conclude that she made one of the few who came from Windsor to join the emigrants, and that she was already in Paris. When we arrived at Rochester therefore, we were surprised to receive, by a man just come from Slough, a letter from this exemplary sufferer. His account was, that, journeying from his home, and passing through Datchet, he was surprised to see smoke issue from the chimney of the inn, and supposing that he should find comrades for his journey assembled there, he knocked and was admitted. There was no one in the house but Lucy, and her mother; the latter had been deprived of the use of her limbs by an attack of rheumatism, and so, one by one, all the remaining inhabitants of the country set forward, leaving them alone. Lucy intreated the man to stay with her; in a week or two her mother would be better, and they would then set out; but they must perish, if they were left thus helpless and forlorn. The man said, that his wife and children were already among the emigrants, and it was therefore, according to his notion, impossible for him to remain. Lucy, as a last resource, gave him a letter for Idris, to be delivered to her wherever he should meet us. This commission at least he fulfilled, and Idris received with emotion the following letter:—

"HONOURED LADY,

"I am sure that you will remember and pity me, and I dare hope that you will assist me; what other hope have I? Pardon my manner of writing, I am so bewildered. A month ago my dear mother was deprived of the use of her limbs. She is already better, and in another month would I am sure be able to travel, in the way you were so kind as to say you would arrange for us. But now everybody is gone—everybody—as they went away, each said, that perhaps my mother would be better, before we were quite deserted. But three days ago I went to Samuel Woods, who, on account of his new-born child, remained to the last; and there being a large family of them, I thought I could persuade them to wait a little longer for us; but I found the house deserted. I have not seen a soul since, till this good man came. —What will become of us? My mother does not know our state; she is so ill, that I have hidden it from her.

"Will you not send some one to us? I am sure we must perish miserably as we are. If I were to try to move my mother now, she would die on the road; and if, when she gets better, I were able, I cannot guess how, to find out the roads, and get on so many many miles to the sea, you would all be in France, and the great ocean would be between us, which is so terrible even to sailors. What would it be to me, a woman, who never saw it? We should be imprisoned by it in this country, all, all alone, with no help; better die where we are. I can hardly write—I cannot stop my tears—it is not for myself; I could put my trust in God; and let the worst come, I think I could bear it, if I were alone. But my mother, my sick, my dear, dear mother, who never, since I was born, spoke a harsh word to me, who has been patient in many sufferings; pity her, dear Lady, she must die a miserable death if you do not pity her. People speak carelessly of her, because she is old and infirm, as if we must not all, if we are spared, become so; and then, when the young are old themselves, they will think that they ought to be taken care of. It is very silly of me to write in this way to you; but, when I hear her trying not to groan, and see her look smiling on me to comfort me, when I know she is in pain; and when I think that she does not know the worst, but she soon must; and then she will not complain; but I shall sit guessing at all that she is dwelling upon, of famine and misery—I feel as if my heart must break, and I do not know what I say or do; my mother—mother for whom I have borne much, God preserve you from this fate! Preserve her, Lady, and He will bless you; and I, poor miserable creature as I am, will thank you and pray for you while I live.

"Your unhappy and dutiful servant,

"Dec. 30th, 2097. LUCY MARTIN."

This letter deeply affected Idris, and she instantly proposed, that we should return to Datchet, to assist Lucy and her mother. I said that I would without delay set out for that place, but entreated her to join her brother, and there await my return with the children. But Idris was in high spirits, and full of hope. She declared that she could not consent even to a temporary separation from me, but that there was no need of this, the motion of the carriage did her good, and the distance was too trifling to be considered. We could dispatch messengers to Adrian, to inform him of our deviation from the original plan. She spoke with vivacity, and drew a picture after her own dear heart, of the pleasure we should bestow upon Lucy, and declared, if I went, she must accompany me, and that she should very much dislike to entrust the charge of rescuing them to others, who might fulfil it with coldness or inhumanity. Lucy's life had been one act of devotion and virtue; let her now reap the small reward of finding her excellence appreciated, and her necessity assisted, by those whom she respected and honoured.

These, and many other arguments, were urged with gentle pertinacity, and the ardour of a wish to do all the good in her power, by her whose simple expression of a desire and slightest request had ever been a law with me. I, of course, consented, the moment that I saw that she had set her heart upon this step. We sent half our attendant troop on to Adrian; and with the other half our carriage took a retrograde course back to Windsor.

I wonder now how I could be so blind and senseless, as thus to risk the safety of Idris; for, if I had eyes, surely I could see the sure, though deceitful, advance of death in her burning cheek and increasing weakness. But she said she was better; and I believed her. Extinction could not be near a being, whose vivacity and intelligence hourly increased, and whose frame was endowed with an intense, and I fondly thought, a strong and permanent spirit of life. Who, after a great disaster, has not looked back with wonder at his inconceivable obtuseness of understanding, that could not perceive the many minute threads with which fate weaves the inextricable net of our destinies, until he is inmeshed completely in it?

The cross roads which we now entered upon, were even in a worse state than the long neglected high-ways; and the inconvenience seemed to menace the perishing frame of Idris with destruction. Passing through Dartford, we arrived at Hampton on the second day. Even in this short interval my beloved companion grew sensibly worse in health, though her spirits were still light, and she cheered my growing anxiety with gay sallies; sometimes the thought pierced my brain—Is she dying?—as I saw her fair fleshless hand rest on mine, or observed the feebleness with which she performed the accustomed acts of life. I drove away the idea, as if it had been suggested by insanity; but it occurred again and again, only to be dispelled by the continued liveliness of her manner.

About mid-day, after quitting Hampton, our carriage broke down: the shock caused Idris to faint, but on her reviving no other ill consequence ensued; our party of attendants had as usual gone on before us, and our coachman went in search of another vehicle, our former one being rendered by this accident unfit for service. The only place near us was a poor village, in which he found a kind of caravan, able to hold four people, but it was clumsy and ill hung; besides this he found a very excellent cabriolet: our plan was soon arranged; I would drive Idris in the latter; while the children were conveyed by the servant in the former. But these arrangements cost time; we had agreed to proceed that night to Windsor, and thither our purveyors had gone: we should find considerable difficulty in getting accommodation, before we reached this place; after all, the distance was only ten miles; my horse was a good one; I would go forward at a good pace with Idris, leaving the children to follow at a rate more consonant to the uses of their cumberous machine.

Evening closed in quickly, far more quickly than I was prepared to expect. At the going down of the sun it began to snow heavily. I attempted in vain to defend my beloved companion from the storm; the wind drove the snow in our faces; and it lay so high on the ground, that we made but small way; while the night was so dark, that but for the white covering on the ground we should not have been able to see a yard before us. We had left our accompanying caravan far behind us; and now I perceived that the storm had made me unconsciously deviate from my intended route. I had gone some miles out of my way. My knowledge of the country enabled me to regain the right road; but, instead of going, as at first agreed upon, by a cross road through Stanwell to Datchet, I was obliged to take the way of Egham and Bishopgate. It was certain therefore that I should not be rejoined by the other vehicle, that I should not meet a single fellow-creature till we arrived at Windsor.

The back of our carriage was drawn up, and I hung a pelisse before it, thus to curtain the beloved sufferer from the pelting sleet. She leaned on my shoulder, growing every moment more languid and feeble; at first she replied to my words of cheer with affectionate thanks; but by degrees she sunk into silence; her head lay heavily upon me; I only knew that she lived by her irregular breathing and frequent sighs. For a moment I resolved to stop, and, opposing the back of the cabriolet to the force of the tempest, to expect morning as well as I might. But the wind was bleak and piercing, while the occasional shudderings of my poor Idris, and the intense cold I felt myself, demonstrated that this would be a dangerous experiment. At length methought she slept—fatal sleep, induced by frost: at this moment I saw the heavy outline of a cottage traced on the dark horizon close to us: "Dearest love," I said, "support yourself but one moment, and we shall have shelter; let us stop here, that I may open the door of this blessed dwelling."

As I spoke, my heart was transported, and my senses swam with excessive delight and thankfulness; I placed the head of Idris against the carriage, and, leaping out, scrambled through the snow to the cottage, whose door was open. I had apparatus about me for procuring light, and that shewed me a comfortable room, with a pile of wood in one corner, and no appearance of disorder, except that, the door having been left partly open, the snow, drifting in, had blocked up the threshold. I returned to the carriage, and the sudden change from light to darkness at first blinded me. When I recovered my sight—eternal God of this lawless world! O supreme Death! I will not disturb thy silent reign, or mar my tale with fruitless exclamations of horror—I saw Idris, who had fallen from the seat to the bottom of the carriage; her head, its long hair pendent, with one arm, hung over the side.—Struck by a spasm of horror, I lifted her up; her heart was pulseless, her faded lips unfanned by the slightest breath.

I carried her into the cottage; I placed her on the bed. Lighting a fire, I chafed her stiffening limbs; for two long hours I sought to restore departed life; and, when hope was as dead as my beloved, I closed with trembling hands her glazed eyes. I did not doubt what I should now do. In the confusion attendant on my illness, the task of interring our darling Alfred had devolved on his grandmother, the Ex-Queen, and she, true to her ruling passion, had caused him to be carried to Windsor, and buried in the family vault, in St. George's Chapel. I must proceed to Windsor, to calm the anxiety of Clara, who would wait anxiously for us—yet I would fain spare her the heart-breaking spectacle of Idris, brought in by me lifeless from the journey. So first I would place my beloved beside her child in the vault, and then seek the poor children who would be expecting me.

I lighted the lamps of my carriage; I wrapt her in furs, and placed her along the seat; then taking the reins, made the horses go forward. We proceeded through the snow, which lay in masses impeding the way, while the descending flakes, driving against me with redoubled fury, blinded me. The pain occasioned by the angry elements, and the cold iron of the shafts of frost which buffetted me, and entered my aching flesh, were a relief to me; blunting my mental suffering. The horses staggered on, and the reins hung loosely in my hands. I often thought I would lay my head close to the sweet, cold face of my lost angel, and thus resign myself to conquering torpor. Yet I must not leave her a prey to the fowls of the air; but, in pursuance of my determination place her in the tomb of her forefathers, where a merciful God might permit me to rest also.

The road we passed through Egham was familiar to me; but the wind and snow caused the horses to drag their load slowly and heavily. Suddenly the wind veered from south-west to west, and then again to north-west. As Sampson with tug and strain stirred from their bases the columns that supported the Philistine temple, so did the gale shake the dense vapours propped on the horizon, while the massy dome of clouds fell to the south, disclosing through the scattered web the clear empyrean, and the little stars, which were set at an immeasurable distance in the crystalline fields, showered their small rays on the glittering snow. Even the horses were cheered, and moved on with renovated strength. We entered the forest at Bishopgate, and at the end of the Long Walk I saw the Castle, "the proud Keep of Windsor, rising in the majesty of proportion, girt with the double belt of its kindred and coeval towers." I looked with reverence on a structure, ancient almost as the rock on which it stood, abode of kings, theme of admiration for the wise. With greater reverence and, tearful affection I beheld it as the asylum of the long lease of love I had enjoyed there with the perishable, unmatchable treasure of dust, which now lay cold beside me. Now indeed, I could have yielded to all the softness of my nature, and wept; and, womanlike, have uttered bitter plaints; while the familiar trees, the herds of living deer, the sward oft prest by her fairy-feet, one by one with sad association presented themselves. The white gate at the end of the Long Walk was wide open, and I rode up the empty town through the first gate of the feudal tower; and now St. George's Chapel, with its blackened fretted sides, was right before me. I halted at its door, which was open; I entered, and placed my lighted lamp on the altar; then I returned, and with tender caution I bore Idris up the aisle into the chancel, and laid her softly down on the carpet which covered the step leading to the communion table. The banners of the knights of the garter, and their half drawn swords, were hung in vain emblazonry above the stalls. The banner of her family hung there, still surmounted by its regal crown. Farewell to the glory and heraldry of England!—I turned from such vanity with a slight feeling of wonder, at how mankind could have ever been interested in such things. I bent over the lifeless corpse of my beloved; and, while looking on her uncovered face, the features already contracted by the rigidity of death, I felt as if all the visible universe had grown as soulless, inane, and comfortless as the clay-cold image beneath me. I felt for a moment the intolerable sense of struggle with, and detestation for, the laws which govern the world; till the calm still visible on the face of my dead love recalled me to a more soothing tone of mind, and I proceeded to fulfil the last office that could now be paid her. For her I could not lament, so much I envied her enjoyment of "the sad immunities of the grave."

The vault had been lately opened to place our Alfred therein. The ceremony customary in these latter days had been cursorily performed, and the pavement of the chapel, which was its entrance, having been removed, had not been replaced. I descended the steps, and walked through the long passage to the large vault which contained the kindred dust of my Idris. I distinguished the small coffin of my babe. With hasty, trembling hands I constructed a bier beside it, spreading it with the furs and Indian shawls, which had wrapt Idris in her journey thither. I lighted the glimmering lamp, which flickered in this damp abode of the dead; then I bore my lost one to her last bed, decently composing her limbs, and covering them with a mantle, veiling all except her face, which remained lovely and placid. She appeared to rest like one over-wearied, her beauteous eyes steeped in sweet slumber. Yet, so it was not—she was dead! How intensely I then longed to lie down beside her, to gaze till death should gather me to the same repose.

But death does not come at the bidding of the miserable. I had lately recovered from mortal illness, and my blood had never flowed with such an even current, nor had my limbs ever been so instinct with quick life, as now. I felt that my death must be voluntary. Yet what more natural than famine, as I watched in this chamber of mortality, placed in a world of the dead, beside the lost hope of my life? Meanwhile as I looked on her, the features, which bore a sisterly resemblance to Adrian, brought my thoughts back again to the living, to this dear friend, to Clara, and to Evelyn, who were probably now in Windsor, waiting anxiously for our arrival.

Methought I heard a noise, a step in the far chapel, which was re-echoed by its vaulted roof, and borne to me through the hollow passages. Had Clara seen my carriage pass up the town, and did she seek me here? I must save her at least from the horrible scene the vault presented. I sprung up the steps, and then saw a female figure, bent with age, and clad in long mourning robes, advance through the dusky chapel, supported by a slender cane, yet tottering even with this support. She heard me, and looked up; the lamp I held illuminated my figure, and the moon-beams, struggling through the painted glass, fell upon her face, wrinkled and gaunt, yet with a piercing eye and commanding brow—I recognized the Countess of Windsor. With a hollow voice she asked, "Where is the princess?"

I pointed to the torn up pavement: she walked to the spot, and looked down into the palpable darkness; for the vault was too distant for the rays of the small lamp I had left there to be discernible.

"Your light," she said. I gave it her; and she regarded the now visible, but precipitous steps, as if calculating her capacity to descend. Instinctively I made a silent offer of my assistance. She motioned me away with a look of scorn, saying in an harsh voice, as she pointed downwards, "There at least I may have her undisturbed."

She walked deliberately down, while I, overcome, miserable beyond words, or tears, or groans, threw myself on the pavement near—the stiffening form of Idris was before me, the death-struck countenance hushed in eternal repose beneath. That was to me the end of all! The day before, I had figured to my self various adventures, and communion with my friends in after time—now I had leapt the interval, and reached the utmost edge and bourne of life. Thus wrapt in gloom, enclosed, walled up, vaulted over by the omnipotent present, I was startled by the sound of feet on the steps of the tomb, and I remembered her whom I had utterly forgotten, my angry visitant; her tall form slowly rose upwards from the vault, a living statue, instinct with hate, and human, passionate strife: she seemed to me as having reached the pavement of the aisle; she stood motionless, seeking with her eyes alone, some desired object—till, perceiving me close to her, she placed her wrinkled hand on my arm, exclaiming with tremulous accents, "Lionel Verney, my son!" This name, applied at such a moment by my angel's mother, instilled into me more respect than I had ever before felt for this disdainful lady. I bowed my head, and kissed her shrivelled hand, and, remarking that she trembled violently, supported her to the end of the chancel, where she sat on the steps that led to the regal stall. She suffered herself to be led, and still holding my hand, she leaned her head back against the stall, while the moon beams, tinged with various colours by the painted glass, fell on her glistening eyes; aware of her weakness, again calling to mind her long cherished dignity, she dashed the tears away; yet they fell fast, as she said, for excuse, "She is so beautiful and placid, even in death. No harsh feeling ever clouded her serene brow; how did I treat her? wounding her gentle heart with savage coldness; I had no compassion on her in past years, does she forgive me now? Little, little does it boot to talk of repentance and forgiveness to the dead, had I during her life once consulted her gentle wishes, and curbed my rugged nature to do her pleasure, I should not feel thus."

Idris and her mother were unlike in person. The dark hair, deep-set black eyes, and prominent features of the Ex-Queen were in entire contrast to the golden tresses, the full blue orbs, and the soft lines and contour of her daughter's countenance. Yet, in latter days, illness had taken from my poor girl the full outline of her face, and reduced it to the inflexible shape of the bone beneath. In the form of her brow, in her oval chin, there was to be found a resemblance to her mother; nay in some moods, their gestures were not unlike; nor, having lived so long together, was this wonderful.

There is a magic power in resemblance. When one we love dies, we hope to see them in another state, and half expect that the agency of mind will inform its new garb in imitation of its decayed earthly vesture. But these are ideas of the mind only. We know that the instrument is shivered, the sensible image lies in miserable fragments, dissolved to dusty nothingness; a look, a gesture, or a fashioning of the limbs similar to the dead in a living person, touches a thrilling chord, whose sacred harmony is felt in the heart's dearest recess. Strangely moved, prostrate before this spectral image, and enslaved by the force of blood manifested in likeness of look and movement, I remained trembling in the presence of the harsh, proud, and till now unloved mother of Idris.

Poor, mistaken woman! in her tenderest mood before, she had cherished the idea, that a word, a look of reconciliation from her, would be received with joy, and repay long years of severity. Now that the time was gone for the exercise of such power, she fell at once upon the thorny truth of things, and felt that neither smile nor caress could penetrate to the unconscious state, or influence the happiness of her who lay in the vault beneath. This conviction, together with the remembrance of soft replies to bitter speeches, of gentle looks repaying angry glances; the perception of the falsehood, paltryness and futility of her cherished dreams of birth and power; the overpowering knowledge, that love and life were the true emperors of our mortal state; all, as a tide, rose, and filled her soul with stormy and bewildering confusion. It fell to my lot, to come as the influential power, to allay the fierce tossing of these tumultuous waves. I spoke to her; I led her to reflect how happy Idris had really been, and how her virtues and numerous excellencies had found scope and estimation in her past career. I praised her, the idol of my heart's dear worship, the admired type of feminine perfection. With ardent and overflowing eloquence, I relieved my heart from its burthen, and awoke to the sense of a new pleasure in life, as I poured forth the funeral eulogy. Then I referred to Adrian, her loved brother, and to her surviving child. I declared, which I had before almost forgotten, what my duties were with regard to these valued portions of herself, and bade the melancholy repentant mother reflect, how she could best expiate unkindness towards the dead, by redoubled love of the survivors. Consoling her, my own sorrows were assuaged; my sincerity won her entire conviction.

She turned to me. The hard, inflexible, persecuting woman, turned with a mild expression of face, and said, "If our beloved angel sees us now, it will delight her to find that I do you even tardy justice. You were worthy of her; and from my heart I am glad that you won her away from me. Pardon, my son, the many wrongs I have done you; forget my bitter words and unkind treatment—take me, and govern me as you will."

I seized this docile moment to propose our departure from the church.

"First," she said, "let us replace the pavement above the vault."

We drew near to it; "Shall we look on her again?" I asked.

"I cannot," she replied, "and, I pray you, neither do you. We need not torture ourselves by gazing on the soulless body, while her living spirit is buried quick in our hearts, and her surpassing loveliness is so deeply carved there, that sleeping or waking she must ever be present to us."

For a few moments, we bent in solemn silence over the open vault. I consecrated my future life, to the embalming of her dear memory; I vowed to serve her brother and her child till death. The convulsive sob of my companion made me break off my internal orisons. I next dragged the stones over the entrance of the tomb, and closed the gulph that contained the life of my life. Then, supporting my decrepid fellow-mourner, we slowly left the chapel. I felt, as I stepped into the open air, as if I had quitted an happy nest of repose, for a dreary wilderness, a tortuous path, a bitter, joyless, hopeless pilgrimage.

4

Our escort had been directed to prepare our abode for the night at the inn, opposite the ascent to the Castle. We could not again visit the halls and familiar chambers of our home, on a mere visit. We had already left for ever the glades of Windsor, and all of coppice, flowery hedgerow, and murmuring stream, which gave shape and intensity to the love of our country, and the almost superstitious attachment with which we regarded native England. It had been our intention to have called at Lucy's dwelling in Datchet, and to have re-assured her with promises of aid and protection before we repaired to our quarters for the night. Now, as the Countess of Windsor and I turned down the steep hill that led from the Castle, we saw the children, who had just stopped in their caravan, at the inn-door. They had passed through Datchet without halting. I dreaded to meet them, and to be the bearer of my tragic story, so while they were still occupied in the hurry of arrival, I suddenly left them, and through the snow and clear moon-light air, hastened along the well known road to Datchet.

Well known indeed it was. Each cottage stood on its accustomed site, each tree wore its familiar appearance. Habit had graven uneraseably on my memory, every turn and change of object on the road. At a short distance beyond the Little Park, was an elm half blown down by a storm, some ten years ago; and still, with leafless snow-laden branches, it stretched across the pathway, which wound through a meadow, beside a shallow brook, whose brawling was silenced by frost—that stile, that white gate, that hollow oak tree, which doubtless once belonged to the forest, and which now shewed in the moonlight its gaping rent; to whose fanciful appearance, tricked out by the dusk into a resemblance of the human form, the children had given the name of Falstaff;—all these objects were as well known to me as the cold hearth of my deserted home, and every moss-grown wall and plot of orchard ground, alike as twin lambs are to each other in a stranger's eye, yet to my accustomed gaze bore differences, distinction, and a name. England remained, though England was dead—it was the ghost of merry England that I beheld, under those greenwood shade passing generations had sported in security and ease. To this painful recognition of familiar places, was added a feeling experienced by all, understood by none—a feeling as if in some state, less visionary than a dream, in some past real existence, I had seen all I saw, with precisely the same feelings as I now beheld them—as if all my sensations were a duplex mirror of a former revelation. To get rid of this oppressive sense I strove to imagine change in this tranquil spot—this augmented my mood, by causing me to bestow more attention on the objects which occasioned me pain.

I reached Datchet and Lucy's humble abode—once noisy with Saturday night revellers, or trim and neat on Sunday morning it had borne testimony to the labours and orderly habits of the housewife. The snow lay high about the door, as if it had remained unclosed for many days. "What scene of death hath Roscius now to act?" I muttered to myself as I looked at the dark casements. At first I thought I saw a light in one of them, but it proved to be merely the refraction of the moon-beams, while the only sound was the crackling branches as the breeze whirred the snow flakes from them—the moon sailed high and unclouded in the interminable ether, while the shadow of the cottage lay black on the garden behind. I entered this by the open wicket, and anxiously examined each window. At length I detected a ray of light struggling through a closed shutter in one of the upper rooms—it was a novel feeling, alas! to look at any house and say there dwells its usual inmate—the door of the house was merely on the latch: so I entered and ascended the moon-lit staircase. The door of the inhabited room was ajar: looking in, I saw Lucy sitting as at work at the table on which the light stood; the implements of needlework were about her, but her hand had fallen on her lap, and her eyes, fixed on the ground, shewed by their vacancy that her thoughts wandered. Traces of care and watching had diminished her former attractions—but her simple dress and cap, her desponding attitude, and the single candle that cast its light upon her, gave for a moment a picturesque grouping to the whole. A fearful reality recalled me from the thought—a figure lay stretched on the bed covered by a sheet—her mother was dead, and Lucy, apart from all the world, deserted and alone, watched beside the corpse during the weary night. I entered the room, and my unexpected appearance at first drew a scream from the lone survivor of a dead nation; but she recognised me, and recovered herself, with the quick exercise of self-control habitual to her. "Did you not expect me?" I asked, in that low voice which the presence of the dead makes us as it were instinctively assume.

"You are very good," replied she, "to have come yourself; I can never thank you sufficiently; but it is too late."

"Too late," cried I, "what do you mean? It is not too late to take you from this deserted place, and conduct you to—"

My own loss, which I had forgotten as I spoke, now made me turn away, while choking grief impeded my speech. I threw open the window, and looked on the cold, waning, ghastly, misshaped circle on high, and the chill white earth beneath—did the spirit of sweet Idris sail along the moon-frozen crystal air?—No, no, a more genial atmosphere, a lovelier habitation was surely hers!

I indulged in this meditation for a moment, and then again addressed the mourner, who stood leaning against the bed with that expression of resigned despair, of complete misery, and a patient sufferance of it, which is far more touching than any of the insane ravings or wild gesticulation of untamed sorrow. I desired to draw her from this spot; but she opposed my wish. That class of persons whose imagination and sensibility have never been taken out of the narrow circle immediately in view, if they possess these qualities to any extent, are apt to pour their influence into the very realities which appear to destroy them, and to cling to these with double tenacity from not being able to comprehend any thing beyond. Thus Lucy, in desert England, in a dead world, wished to fulfil the usual ceremonies of the dead, such as were customary to the English country people, when death was a rare visitant, and gave us time to receive his dreaded usurpation with pomp and circumstance—going forth in procession to deliver the keys of the tomb into his conquering hand. She had already, alone as she was, accomplished some of these, and the work on which I found her employed, was her mother's shroud. My heart sickened at such detail of woe, which a female can endure, but which is more painful to the masculine spirit than deadliest struggle, or throes of unutterable but transient agony.

This must not be, I told her; and then, as further inducement, I communicated to her my recent loss, and gave her the idea that she must come with me to take charge of the orphan children, whom the death of Idris had deprived of a mother's care. Lucy never resisted the call of a duty, so she yielded, and closing the casements and doors with care, she accompanied me back to Windsor. As we went she communicated to me the occasion of her mother's death. Either by some mischance she had got sight of Lucy's letter to Idris, or she had overheard her conversation with the countryman who bore it; however it might be, she obtained a knowledge of the appalling situation of herself and her daughter, her aged frame could not sustain the anxiety and horror this discovery instilled—she concealed her knowledge from Lucy, but brooded over it through sleepless nights, till fever and delirium, swift forerunners of death, disclosed the secret. Her life, which had long been hovering on its extinction, now yielded at once to the united effects of misery and sickness, and that same morning she had died.

After the tumultuous emotions of the day, I was glad to find on my arrival at the inn that my companions had retired to rest. I gave Lucy in charge to the Countess's attendant, and then sought repose from my various struggles and impatient regrets. For a few moments the events of the day floated in disastrous pageant through my brain, till sleep bathed it in forgetfulness; when morning dawned and I awoke, it seemed as if my slumber had endured for years.

My companions had not shared my oblivion. Clara's swollen eyes shewed that she has passed the night in weeping. The Countess looked haggard and wan. Her firm spirit had not found relief in tears, and she suffered the more from all the painful retrospect and agonizing regret that now occupied her. We departed from Windsor, as soon as the burial rites had been performed for Lucy's mother, and, urged on by an impatient desire to change the scene, went forward towards Dover with speed, our escort having gone before to provide horses; finding them either in the warm stables they instinctively sought during the cold weather, or standing shivering in the bleak fields ready to surrender their liberty in exchange for offered corn.

During our ride the Countess recounted to me the extraordinary circumstances which had brought her so strangely to my side in the chancel of St. George's chapel. When last she had taken leave of Idris, as she looked anxiously on her faded person and pallid countenance, she had suddenly been visited by a conviction that she saw her for the last time. It was hard to part with her while under the dominion of this sentiment, and for the last time she endeavoured to persuade her daughter to commit herself to her nursing, permitting me to join Adrian. Idris mildly refused, and thus they separated. The idea that they should never again meet grew on the Countess's mind, and haunted her perpetually; a thousand times she had resolved to turn back and join us, and was again and again restrained by the pride and anger of which she was the slave. Proud of heart as she was, she bathed her pillow with nightly tears, and through the day was subdued by nervous agitation and expectation of the dreaded event, which she was wholly incapable of curbing. She confessed that at this period her hatred of me knew no bounds, since she considered me as the sole obstacle to the fulfilment of her dearest wish, that of attending upon her daughter in her last moments. She desired to express her fears to her son, and to seek consolation from his sympathy with, or courage from his rejection of, her auguries.

On the first day of her arrival at Dover she walked with him on the sea beach, and with the timidity characteristic of passionate and exaggerated feeling was by degrees bringing the conversation to the desired point, when she could communicate her fears to him, when the messenger who bore my letter announcing our temporary return to Windsor, came riding down to them. He gave some oral account of how he had left us, and added, that notwithstanding the cheerfulness and good courage of Lady Idris, he was afraid that she would hardly reach Windsor alive. "True," said the Countess, "your fears are just, she is about to expire!"

As she spoke, her eyes were fixed on a tomblike hollow of the cliff, and she saw, she averred the same to me with solemnity, Idris pacing slowly towards this cave. She was turned from her, her head was bent down, her white dress was such as she was accustomed to wear, except that a thin crape-like veil covered her golden tresses, and concealed her as a dim transparent mist. She looked dejected, as docilely yielding to a commanding power; she submissively entered, and was lost in the dark recess.

"Were I subject to visionary moods," said the venerable lady, as she continued her narrative, "I might doubt my eyes, and condemn my credulity; but reality is the world I live in, and what I saw I doubt not had existence beyond myself. From that moment I could not rest; it was worth my existence to see her once again before she died; I knew that I should not accomplish this, yet I must endeavour. I immediately departed for Windsor; and, though I was assured that we travelled speedily, it seemed to me that our progress was snail-like, and that delays were created solely for my annoyance. Still I accused you, and heaped on your head the fiery ashes of my burning impatience. It was no disappointment, though an agonizing pang, when you pointed to her last abode; and words would ill express the abhorrence I that moment felt towards you, the triumphant impediment to my dearest wishes. I saw her, and anger, and hate, and injustice died at her bier, giving place at their departure to a remorse (Great God, that I should feel it!) which must last while memory and feeling endure."

To medicine such remorse, to prevent awakening love and new-born mildness from producing the same bitter fruit that hate and harshness had done, I devoted all my endeavours to soothe the venerable penitent. Our party was a melancholy one; each was possessed by regret for what was remediless; for the absence of his mother shadowed even the infant gaiety of Evelyn. Added to this was the prospect of the uncertain future. Before the final accomplishment of any great voluntary change the mind vacillates, now soothing itself by fervent expectation, now recoiling from obstacles which seem never to have presented themselves before with so frightful an aspect. An involuntary tremor ran through me when I thought that in another day we might have crossed the watery barrier, and have set forward on that hopeless, interminable, sad wandering, which but a short time before I regarded as the only relief to sorrow that our situation afforded.

Our approach to Dover was announced by the loud roarings of the wintry sea. They were borne miles inland by the sound-laden blast, and by their unaccustomed uproar, imparted a feeling of insecurity and peril to our stable abode. At first we hardly permitted ourselves to think that any unusual eruption of nature caused this tremendous war of air and water, but rather fancied that we merely listened to what we had heard a thousand times before, when we had watched the flocks of fleece-crowned waves, driven by the winds, come to lament and die on the barren sands and pointed rocks. But we found upon advancing farther, that Dover was overflowed— many of the houses were overthrown by the surges which filled the streets, and with hideous brawlings sometimes retreated leaving the pavement of the town bare, till again hurried forward by the influx of ocean, they returned with thunder-sound to their usurped station.

Hardly less disturbed than the tempestuous world of waters was the assembly of human beings, that from the cliff fearfully watched its ravings. On the morning of the arrival of the emigrants under the conduct of Adrian, the sea had been serene and glassy, the slight ripples refracted the sunbeams, which shed their radiance through the clear blue frosty air. This placid appearance of nature was hailed as a good augury for the voyage, and the chief immediately repaired to the harbour to examine two steamboats which were moored there. On the following midnight, when all were at rest, a frightful storm of wind and clattering rain and hail first disturbed them, and the voice of one shrieking in the streets, that the sleepers must awake or they would be drowned; and when they rushed out, half clothed, to discover the meaning of this alarm, they found that the tide, rising above every mark, was rushing into the town. They ascended the cliff, but the darkness permitted only the white crest of waves to be seen, while the roaring wind mingled its howlings in dire accord with the wild surges. The awful hour of night, the utter inexperience of many who had never seen the sea before, the wailing of women and cries of children added to the horror of the tumult. All the following day the same scene continued. When the tide ebbed, the town was left dry; but on its flow, it rose even higher than on the preceding night. The vast ships that lay rotting in the roads were whirled from their anchorage, and driven and jammed against the cliff, the vessels in the harbour were flung on land like sea-weed, and there battered to pieces by the breakers. The waves dashed against the cliff, which if in any place it had been before loosened, now gave way, and the affrighted crowd saw vast fragments of the near earth fall with crash and roar into the deep. This sight operated differently on different persons. The greater part thought it a judgment of God, to prevent or punish our emigration from our native land. Many were doubly eager to quit a nook of ground now become their prison, which appeared unable to resist the inroads of ocean's giant waves.

When we arrived at Dover, after a fatiguing day's journey, we all required rest and sleep; but the scene acting around us soon drove away such ideas. We were drawn, along with the greater part of our companions, to the edge of the cliff, there to listen to and make a thousand conjectures. A fog narrowed our horizon to about a quarter of a mile, and the misty veil, cold and dense, enveloped sky and sea in equal obscurity. What added to our inquietude was the circumstance that two-thirds of our original number were now waiting for us in Paris, and clinging, as we now did most painfully, to any addition to our melancholy remnant, this division, with the tameless impassable ocean between, struck us with affright. At length, after loitering for several hours on the cliff, we retired to Dover Castle, whose roof sheltered all who breathed the English air, and sought the sleep necessary to restore strength and courage to our worn frames and languid spirits.

Early in the morning Adrian brought me the welcome intelligence that the wind had changed: it had been south-west; it was now north-east. The sky was stripped bare of clouds by the increasing gale, while the tide at its ebb seceded entirely from the town. The change of wind rather increased the fury of the sea, but it altered its late dusky hue to a bright green; and in spite of its unmitigated clamour, its more cheerful appearance instilled hope and pleasure. All day we watched the ranging of the mountainous waves, and towards sunset a desire to decypher the promise for the morrow at its setting, made us all gather with one accord on the edge of the cliff. When the mighty luminary approached within a few degrees of the tempest-tossed horizon, suddenly, a wonder! three other suns, alike burning and brilliant, rushed from various quarters of the heavens towards the great orb; they whirled round it. The glare of light was intense to our dazzled eyes; the sun itself seemed to join in the dance, while the sea burned like a furnace, like all Vesuvius a-light, with flowing lava beneath. The horses broke loose from their stalls in terror—a herd of cattle, panic struck, raced down to the brink of the cliff, and blinded by light, plunged down with frightful yells in the waves below. The time occupied by the apparition of these meteors was comparatively short; suddenly the three mock suns united in one, and plunged into the sea. A few seconds afterwards, a deafening watery sound came up with awful peal from the spot where they had disappeared.

Meanwhile the sun, disencumbered from his strange satellites, paced with its accustomed majesty towards its western home. When—we dared not trust our eyes late dazzled, but it seemed that—the sea rose to meet it—it mounted higher and higher, till the fiery globe was obscured, and the wall of water still ascended the horizon; it appeared as if suddenly the motion of earth was revealed to us—as if no longer we were ruled by ancient laws, but were turned adrift in an unknown region of space. Many cried aloud, that these were no meteors, but globes of burning matter, which had set fire to the earth, and caused the vast cauldron at our feet to bubble up with its measureless waves; the day of judgment was come they averred, and a few moments would transport us before the awful countenance of the omnipotent judge; while those less given to visionary terrors, declared that two conflicting gales had occasioned the last phaenomenon. In support of this opinion they pointed out the fact that the east wind died away, while the rushing of the coming west mingled its wild howl with the roar of the advancing waters. Would the cliff resist this new battery? Was not the giant wave far higher than the precipice? Would not our little island be deluged by its approach? The crowd of spectators fled. They were dispersed over the fields, stopping now and then, and looking back in terror. A sublime sense of awe calmed the swift pulsations of my heart—I awaited the approach of the destruction menaced, with that solemn resignation which an unavoidable necessity instils. The ocean every moment assumed a more terrific aspect, while the twilight was dimmed by the rack which the west wind spread over the sky. By slow degrees however, as the wave advanced, it took a more mild appearance; some under current of air, or obstruction in the bed of the waters, checked its progress, and it sank gradually; while the surface of the sea became uniformly higher as it dissolved into it. This change took from us the fear of an immediate catastrophe, although we were still anxious as to the final result. We continued during the whole night to watch the fury of the sea and the pace of the driving clouds, through whose openings the rare stars rushed impetuously; the thunder of conflicting elements deprived us of all power to sleep.

This endured ceaselessly for three days and nights. The stoutest hearts quailed before the savage enmity of nature; provisions began to fail us, though every day foraging parties were dispersed to the nearer towns. In vain we schooled ourselves into the belief, that there was nothing out of the common order of nature in the strife we witnessed; our disasterous and overwhelming destiny turned the best of us to cowards. Death had hunted us through the course of many months, even to the narrow strip of time on which we now stood; narrow indeed, and buffeted by storms, was our footway overhanging the great sea of calamity—

> As an unsheltered northern shore
> Is shaken by the wintry wave —
> And frequent storms for evermore,
> (While from the west the loud winds rave,
> Or from the east, or mountains hoar)
> The struck and tott'ring sand-bank lave.[1]

It required more than human energy to bear up against the menaces of destruction that every where surrounded us.

After the lapse of three days, the gale died away, the sea-gull sailed upon the calm bosom of the windless atmosphere, and the last yellow leaf on the topmost branch of the oak hung without motion. The sea no longer broke with fury; but a swell setting in steadily for shore, with long sweep and sullen burst replaced the roar of the breakers. Yet we derived hope from the change, and we did not doubt that after the interval of a few days the sea would resume its tranquility. The sunset of the fourth day favoured this idea; it was clear and golden. As we gazed on the purple sea, radiant beneath, we were attracted by a novel spectacle; a dark speck

—as it neared, visibly a boat—rode on the top of the waves, every now and then lost in the steep vallies between. We marked its course with eager questionings; and, when we saw that it evidently made for shore, we descended to the only practicable landing place, and hoisted a signal to direct them. By the help of glasses we distinguished her crew; it consisted of nine men, Englishmen, belonging in truth to the two divisions of our people, who had preceded us, and had been for several weeks at Paris. As countryman was wont to meet countryman in distant lands, did we greet our visitors on their landing, with outstretched hands and gladsome welcome. They were slow to reciprocate our gratulations. They looked angry and resentful; not less than the chafed sea which they had traversed with imminent peril, though apparently more displeased with each other than with us. It was strange to see these human beings, who appeared to be given forth by the earth like rare and inestimable plants, full of towering passion, and the spirit of angry contest. Their first demand was to be conducted to the Lord Protector of England, so they called Adrian, though he had long discarded the empty title, as a bitter mockery of the shadow to which the Protectorship was now reduced. They were speedily led to Dover Castle, from whose keep Adrian had watched the movements of the boat. He received them with the interest and wonder so strange a visitation created. In the confusion occasioned by their angry demands for precedence, it was long before we could discover the secret meaning of this strange scene. By degrees, from the furious declamations of one, the fierce interruptions of another, and the bitter scoffs of a third, we found that they were deputies from our colony at Paris, from three parties there formed, who, each with angry rivalry, tried to attain a superiority over the other two. These deputies had been dispatched by them to Adrian, who had been selected arbiter; and they had journied from Paris to Calais, through the vacant towns and desolate country, indulging the while violent hatred against each other; and now they pleaded their several causes with unmitigated party-spirit.

By examining the deputies apart, and after much investigation, we learnt the true state of things at Paris. Since parliament had elected him Ryland's deputy, all the surviving English had submitted to Adrian. He was our captain to lead us from our native soil to unknown lands, our lawgiver and our preserver. On the first arrangement of our scheme of emigration, no continued separation of our members was contemplated, and the command of the whole body in gradual ascent of power had its apex in the Earl of Windsor. But unforeseen circumstances changed our plans for us, and occasioned the greater part of our numbers to be divided for the space of nearly two months, from the supreme chief. They had gone over in two distinct bodies; and on their arrival at Paris dissension arose between them.

They had found Paris a desert. When first the plague had appeared, the return of travellers and merchants, and communications by letter, informed us regularly of the ravages made by disease on the continent. But with the increased mortality this intercourse declined and ceased. Even in England itself communication from one part of the island to the other became slow and rare. No vessel stemmed the flood that divided Calais from Dover; or if some melancholy voyager, wishing to assure himself of the life or death of his relatives, put from the French shore to return among us, often the greedy ocean swallowed his little craft, or after a day or two he was infected by the disorder, and died before he could tell the tale of the desolation of France. We were therefore to a great degree ignorant of the state of things on the continent, and were not without some vague hope of finding numerous companions in its wide track. But the same causes that had so fearfully diminished the English nation had had even greater scope for mischief in the sister land. France was a blank; during the long line of road from Calais to Paris not one human being was found. In Paris there were a few, perhaps a hundred, who, resigned to their coming fate, flitted about the streets of the capital and assembled to converse of past times, with that vivacity and even gaiety that seldom deserts the individuals of this nation.

The English took uncontested possession of Paris. Its high houses and narrow streets were lifeless. A few pale figures were to be distinguished at the accustomed resort at the Tuileries; they wondered wherefore the islanders should approach their ill-fated city—for in the excess of wretchedness, the sufferers always imagine, that their part of the calamity is the bitterest, as, when enduring intense pain, we would exchange the particular torture we writhe under, for any other which should visit a different part of the frame. They listened to the account the emigrants gave of their motives for leaving their native land, with a shrug almost of disdain —"Return," they said, "return to your island, whose sea breezes, and division from the continent gives some promise of health; if Pestilence among you has slain its hundreds, with us it has slain its thousands. Are you not even now more numerous than we are?—A year ago you would have found only the sick burying the dead; now we are happier; for the pang of struggle has passed away, and the few you find here are patiently waiting the final blow. But you, who are not content to die, breathe no longer the air of France, or soon you will only be a part of her soil."

Thus, by menaces of the sword, they would have driven back those who had escaped from fire. But the peril left behind was deemed imminent by my countrymen; that before them doubtful and distant; and soon other feelings arose to obliterate fear, or to replace it by passions, that ought to have had no place among a brotherhood of unhappy survivors of the expiring world.

The more numerous division of emigrants, which arrived first at Paris, assumed a superiority of rank and power; the second party asserted their independence. A third was formed by a sectarian, a self-erected prophet, who, while he attributed all power and rule to God, strove to get the real command of his comrades into his own hands. This third division consisted of fewest individuals, but their purpose was more one, their obedience to their leader more entire, their fortitude and courage more unyielding and active.

During the whole progress of the plague, the teachers of religion were in possession of great power; a power of good, if rightly directed, or of incalculable mischief, if fanaticism or intolerance guided their efforts. In the present instance, a worse feeling than either of these actuated the leader. He was an impostor in the most determined sense of the term. A man who had in early life lost, through the indulgence of vicious propensities, all sense of rectitude or self-esteem; and who, when ambition was awakened in him, gave himself up to its influence unbridled by any scruple. His father had been a methodist preacher, an enthusiastic man with simple intentions; but whose pernicious doctrines of election and special grace had contributed to destroy all conscientious feeling in his son. During the progress of the pestilence he had entered upon various schemes, by which to acquire adherents and power. Adrian had discovered and defeated these attempts; but Adrian was absent; the wolf assumed the shepherd's garb, and the flock admitted the deception: he had formed a party during the few weeks he had been in Paris, who zealously propagated the creed of his divine mission, and believed that safety and salvation were to be afforded only to those who put their trust in him.

When once the spirit of dissension had arisen, the most frivolous causes gave it activity. The first party, on arriving at Paris, had taken possession of the Tuileries; chance and friendly feeling had induced the second to lodge near to them. A contest arose concerning the distribution of the pillage; the chiefs of the first division demanded that the whole should be placed at their disposal; with this assumption the opposite party refused to comply. When next the latter went to forage, the gates of Paris were shut on them. After overcoming this difficulty, they marched in a body to the Tuileries. They found that their enemies had been already expelled thence by the Elect, as the fanatical party designated themselves, who refused to admit any into the palace who did not first abjure obedience to all except God, and his delegate on earth, their chief. Such was the beginning of the strife, which at length proceeded so far, that the three divisions, armed, met in the Place Vendome, each resolved to subdue by force the resistance of its adversaries. They assembled, their muskets were loaded, and even pointed at the breasts of their so called enemies. One word had been sufficient; and there the last of mankind would have burthened their souls with the crime of murder, and dipt their hands in each other's blood. A sense of shame, a recollection that not only their cause, but the existence of the whole human race was at stake, entered the breast of the leader of the more numerous party. He was aware, that if the ranks were thinned, no other recruits could fill them up; that each man was as a priceless gem in a kingly crown, which if destroyed, the earth's deep entrails could yield no paragon. He was a young man, and had been hurried on by presumption, and the notion of his high rank and superiority to all other pretenders; now he repented his work, he felt that all the blood about to be shed would be on his head; with sudden impulse therefore he spurred his horse between the bands, and, having fixed a white handkerchief on the point of his uplifted sword, thus demanded parley; the opposite leaders obeyed the signal. He spoke with warmth; he reminded them of the oath all the chiefs had taken to submit to the Lord Protector; he declared their present meeting to be an act of treason and mutiny; he allowed that he had been hurried away by passion, but that a cooler moment had arrived; and he proposed that each party should send deputies to the Earl of Windsor, inviting his interference and offering submission to his decision. His offer was accepted so far, that each leader consented to command a retreat, and moreover agreed, that after the approbation of their several parties had been consulted, they should meet that night on some neutral spot to ratify the truce. At the meeting of the chiefs, this plan was finally concluded upon. The leader of the fanatics indeed refused to admit the arbitration of Adrian; he sent ambassadors, rather than deputies, to assert his claim, not plead his cause.

The truce was to continue until the first of February, when the bands were again to assemble on the Place Vendome; it was of the utmost consequence therefore that Adrian should arrive in Paris by that day, since an hair might turn the scale, and peace, scared away by intestine broils, might only return to watch by the silent dead. It was now the twenty-eighth of January; every vessel stationed near Dover had been beaten to pieces and destroyed by the furious storms I have commemorated. Our journey however would admit of no delay. That very night, Adrian, and I, and twelve others, either friends or attendants, put off from the English shore, in the boat that had brought over the deputies. We all took our turn at the oar; and the immediate occasion of our departure affording us abundant matter for conjecture and discourse, prevented the feeling that we left our native country, depopulate England, for the last time, to enter deeply into the minds of the greater part of our number. It was a serene starlight night, and the dark line of the English coast continued for some time visible at intervals, as we rose on the broad back of the waves. I exerted myself with my long oar to give swift impulse to our skiff; and, while the waters splashed with melancholy sound against its sides, I looked with sad affection on this last glimpse of sea-girt England, and strained my eyes not too soon to lose sight of the castellated cliff, which rose to protect the land of heroism and beauty from the inroads of ocean, that, turbulent as I had lately seen it, required such cyclopean walls for its repulsion. A solitary sea-gull winged its flight over our heads, to seek its nest in a cleft of the precipice. Yes, thou shalt revisit the land of thy birth, I thought, as I looked invidiously on the airy voyager; but we shall, never more! Tomb of Idris, farewell! Grave, in which my heart lies sepultured, farewell for ever!

We were twelve hours at sea, and the heavy swell obliged us to exert all our strength. At length, by mere dint of rowing, we reached the French coast. The stars faded, and the grey morning cast a dim veil over the silver horns of the waning moon—the sun rose broad and red from the sea, as we walked over the sands to Calais. Our first care was to procure horses, and although wearied by our night of watching and toil, some of our party immediately went in quest of these in the wide fields of the unenclosed and now barren plain round Calais. We divided ourselves, like seamen, into watches, and some reposed, while others prepared the morning's repast. Our foragers returned at noon with only six horses—on these, Adrian and I, and four others, proceeded on our journey towards the great city, which its inhabitants had fondly named the capital of the civilized world. Our horses had become, through their long holiday, almost wild, and we crossed the plain round Calais with impetuous speed. From the height near Boulogne, I turned again to look on England; nature had cast a misty pall over her, her cliff was hidden—there was spread the watery barrier that divided us, never again to be crossed; she lay on the ocean plain,

In the great pool a swan's nest.

Ruined the nest, alas! the swans of Albion had passed away for ever—an uninhabited rock in the wide Pacific, which had remained since the creation uninhabited, unnamed, unmarked, would be of as much account in the world's future history, as desert England.

Our journey was impeded by a thousand obstacles. As our horses grew tired, we had to seek for others; and hours were wasted, while we exhausted our artifices to allure some of these enfranchised slaves of man to resume the yoke; or as we went from stable to stable through the towns, hoping to find some who had not forgotten the shelter of their native stalls. Our ill success in procuring them, obliged us continually to leave some one of our companions behind; and on the first of February, Adrian and I entered Paris, wholly unaccompanied. The serene morning had dawned when we arrived at Saint Denis, and the sun was high, when the clamour of voices, and the clash, as we feared, of weapons, guided us to where our countrymen had assembled on the Place Vendome. We passed a knot of Frenchmen, who were talking earnestly of the madness of the insular invaders, and then coming by a sudden turn upon the Place, we saw the sun glitter on drawn swords and fixed bayonets, while yells and clamours rent the air. It was a scene of unaccustomed confusion in these days of depopulation. Roused by fancied wrongs, and insulting scoffs, the opposite parties had rushed to attack each other; while the elect, drawn up apart, seemed to wait an opportunity to fall with better advantage on their foes, when they should have mutually weakened each other. A merciful power interposed, and no blood was shed; for, while the insane mob were in the very act of attack, the females, wives, mothers and daughters, rushed between; they seized the bridles; they embraced the knees of the horsemen, and hung on the necks, or enweaponed arms of their enraged relatives; the shrill female scream was mingled with the manly shout, and formed the wild clamour that welcomed us on our arrival.

Our voices could not be heard in the tumult; Adrian however was eminent for the white charger he rode; spurring him, he dashed into the midst of the throng: he was recognized, and a loud cry raised for England and the Protector. The late adversaries, warmed to affection at the sight of him, joined in heedless confusion, and surrounded him; the women kissed his hands, and the edges of his garments; nay, his horse received tribute of their embraces; some wept their welcome; he appeared an angel of peace descended among them; and the only danger was, that his mortal nature would be demonstrated, by his suffocation from the kindness of his friends. His voice was at length heard, and obeyed; the crowd fell back; the chiefs alone rallied round him. I had seen Lord Raymond ride through his lines; his look of victory, and majestic mien obtained the respect and obedience of all: such was not the appearance or influence of Adrian. His slight figure, his fervent look, his gesture, more of deprecation than rule, were proofs that love, unmingled with fear, gave him dominion over the hearts of a multitude, who knew that he never flinched from danger, nor was actuated by other motives than care for the general welfare. No distinction was now visible between the two parties, late ready to shed each other's blood, for, though neither would submit to the other, they both yielded ready obedience to the Earl of Windsor.

One party however remained, cut off from the rest, which did not sympathize in the joy exhibited on Adrian's arrival, or imbibe the spirit of peace, which fell like dew upon the softened hearts of their countrymen. At the head of this assembly was a ponderous, dark-looking man, whose malign eye surveyed with gloating delight the stern looks of his followers. They had hitherto been inactive, but now, perceiving themselves to be forgotten in the universal jubilee, they advanced with threatening gestures: our friends had, as it were in wanton contention, attacked each other; they wanted but to be told that their cause was one, for it to become so: their mutual anger had been a fire of straw, compared to the slow-burning hatred they both entertained for these seceders, who seized a portion of the world to come, there to entrench and incastellate themselves, and to issue with fearful sally, and appalling denunciations, on the mere common children of the earth. The first advance of the little army of the elect reawakened their rage; they grasped their arms, and waited but their leader's signal to commence the attack, when the clear tones of Adrian's voice were heard, commanding them to fall back; with confused murmur and hurried retreat, as the wave ebbs clamorously from the sands it lately covered, our friends obeyed. Adrian rode singly into the space between the opposing bands; he approached the hostile leader, as requesting him to imitate his example, but his look was not obeyed, and the chief advanced, followed by his whole troop. There were many women among them, who seemed more eager and resolute than their male companions. They pressed round their leader, as if to shield him, while they loudly bestowed on him every sacred denomination and epithet of worship. Adrian met them half way; they halted: "What," he said, "do you seek? Do you require any thing of us that we refuse to give, and that you are forced to acquire by arms and warfare?"

His questions were answered by a general cry, in which the words election, sin, and red right arm of God, could alone be heard.

Adrian looked expressly at their leader, saying, "Can you not silence your followers? Mine, you perceive, obey me."

The fellow answered by a scowl; and then, perhaps fearful that his people should become auditors of the debate he expected to ensue, he commanded them to fall back, and advanced by himself. "What, I again ask," said Adrian, "do you require of us?"

"Repentance," replied the man, whose sinister brow gathered clouds as he spoke. "Obedience to the will of the Most High, made manifest to these his Elected People. Do we not all die through your sins, O generation of unbelief, and have we not a right to demand of you repentance and obedience?"

"And if we refuse them, what then?" his opponent inquired mildly.

"Beware," cried the man, "God hears you, and will smite your stony heart in his wrath; his poisoned arrows fly, his dogs of death are unleashed! We will not perish unrevenged—and mighty will our avenger be, when he descends in visible majesty, and scatters destruction among you."

"My good fellow," said Adrian, with quiet scorn, "I wish that you were ignorant only, and I think it would be no difficult task to prove to you, that you speak of what you do not understand. On the present occasion however, it is enough for me to know that you seek nothing of us; and, heaven is our witness, we seek nothing of you. I should be sorry to embitter by strife the few days that we any of us may have here to live; when there," he pointed downwards, "we shall not be able to contend, while here we need not. Go home, or stay; pray to your God in your own mode; your friends may do the like. My orisons consist in peace and good will, in resignation and hope. Farewell!"

He bowed slightly to the angry disputant who was about to reply; and, turning his horse down Rue Saint Honore, called on his friends to follow him. He rode slowly, to give time to all to join him at the Barrier, and then issued his orders that those who yielded obedience to him, should rendezvous at Versailles. In the meantime he remained within the walls of Paris, until he had secured the safe retreat of all. In about a fortnight the remainder of the emigrants arrived from England, and they all repaired to Versailles; apartments were prepared for the family of the Protector in the Grand Trianon, and there, after the excitement of these events, we reposed amidst the luxuries of the departed Bourbons.

-----

1. Chorus in Oedipus Coloneus.

5

AFTER THE REPOSE of a few days, we held a council, to decide on our future movements. Our first plan had been to quit our wintry native latitude, and seek for our diminished numbers the luxuries and delights of a southern climate. We had not fixed on any precise spot as the termination of our wanderings; but a vague picture of perpetual spring, fragrant groves, and sparkling streams, floated in our imagination to entice us on. A variety of causes had detained us in England, and we had now arrived at the middle of February; if we pursued our original project, we should find ourselves in a worse situation than before, having exchanged our temperate climate for the intolerable heats of a summer in Egypt or Persia. We were therefore obliged to modify our plan, as the season continued to be inclement; and it was determined that we should await the arrival of spring in our present abode, and so order our future movements as to pass the hot months in the icy vallies of Switzerland, deferring our southern progress until the ensuing autumn, if such a season was ever again to be beheld by us.

The castle and town of Versailles afforded our numbers ample accommodation, and foraging parties took it by turns to supply our wants. There was a strange and appalling motley in the situation of these the last of the race. At first I likened it to a colony, which borne over the far seas, struck root for the first time in a new country. But where was the bustle and industry characteristic of such an assemblage; the rudely constructed dwelling, which was to suffice till a more commodious mansion could be built; the marking out of fields; the attempt at cultivation; the eager curiosity to discover unknown animals and herbs; the excursions for the sake of exploring the country? Our habitations were palaces our food was ready stored in granaries— there was no need of labour, no inquisitiveness, no restless desire to get on. If we had been assured that we should secure the lives of our present numbers, there would have been more vivacity and hope in our councils. We should have discussed as to the period when the existing produce for man's sustenance would no longer suffice for us, and what mode of life we should then adopt. We should have considered more carefully our future plans, and debated concerning the spot where we should in future dwell. But summer and the plague were near, and we dared not look forward. Every heart sickened at the thought of amusement; if the younger part of our community were ever impelled, by youthful and untamed hilarity, to enter on any dance or song, to cheer the melancholy time, they would suddenly break off, checked by a mournful look or agonizing sigh from any one among them, who was prevented by sorrows and losses from mingling in the festivity. If laughter echoed under our roof, yet the heart was vacant of joy; and, when ever it chanced that I witnessed such attempts at pastime, they increased instead of diminishing my sense of woe. In the midst of the pleasure-hunting throng, I would close my eyes, and see before me the obscure cavern, where was garnered the mortality of Idris, and the dead lay around, mouldering in hushed repose. When I again became aware of the present hour, softest melody of Lydian flute, or harmonious maze of graceful dance, was but as the demoniac chorus in the Wolf's Glen, and the caperings of the reptiles that surrounded the magic circle.

My dearest interval of peace occurred, when, released from the obligation of associating with the crowd, I could repose in the dear home where my children lived. Children I say, for the tenderest emotions of paternity bound me to Clara. She was now fourteen; sorrow, and deep insight into the scenes around her, calmed the restless spirit of girlhood; while the remembrance of her father whom she idolized, and respect for me and Adrian, implanted an high sense of duty in her young heart. Though serious she was not sad; the eager desire that makes us all, when young, plume our wings, and stretch our necks, that we may more swiftly alight tiptoe on the height of maturity, was subdued in her by early experience. All that she could spare of overflowing love from her parents' memory, and attention to her living relatives, was spent upon religion. This was the hidden law of her heart, which she concealed with childish reserve, and cherished the more because it was secret. What faith so entire, what charity so pure, what hope so fervent, as that of early youth? and she, all love, all tenderness and trust, who from infancy had been tossed on the wide sea of passion and misfortune, saw the finger of apparent divinity in all, and her best hope was to make herself acceptable to the power she worshipped. Evelyn was only five years old; his joyous heart was incapable of sorrow, and he enlivened our house with the innocent mirth incident to his years.

The aged Countess of Windsor had fallen from her dream of power, rank and grandeur; she had been suddenly seized with the conviction, that love was the only good of life, virtue the only ennobling distinction and enriching wealth. Such a lesson had been taught her by the dead lips of her neglected daughter; and she devoted herself, with all the fiery violence of her character, to the obtaining the affection of the remnants of her family. In early years the heart of Adrian had been chilled towards her; and, though he observed a due respect, her coldness, mixed with the recollection of disappointment and madness, caused him to feel even pain in her society. She saw this, and yet determined to win his love; the obstacle served the rather to excite her ambition. As Henry, Emperor of Germany, lay in the snow before Pope Leo's gate for three winter days and nights, so did she in humility wait before the icy barriers of his closed heart, till he, the servant of love, and prince of tender courtesy, opened it wide for her admittance, bestowing, with fervency and gratitude, the tribute of filial affection she merited. Her understanding, courage, and presence of mind, became powerful auxiliaries to him in the difficult task of ruling the tumultuous crowd, which were subjected to his control, in truth by a single hair.

The principal circumstances that disturbed our tranquility during this interval, originated in the vicinity of the impostor-prophet and his followers. They continued to reside at Paris; but missionaries from among them often visited Versailles—and such was the power of assertions, however false, yet vehemently iterated, over the ready credulity of the ignorant and fearful, that they seldom failed in drawing over to their party some from among our numbers. An instance of this nature coming immediately under our notice, we were led to consider the miserable state in which we should leave our countrymen, when we should, at the approach of summer, move on towards Switzerland, and leave a deluded crew behind us in the hands of their miscreant leader. The sense of the smallness of our numbers, and expectation of decrease, pressed upon us; and, while it would be a subject of congratulation to ourselves to add one to our party, it would be doubly gratifying to rescue from the pernicious influence of superstition and unrelenting tyranny, the victims that now, though voluntarily enchained, groaned beneath it. If we had considered the preacher as sincere in a belief of his own denunciations, or only moderately actuated by kind feeling in the exercise of his assumed powers, we should have immediately addressed ourselves to him, and endeavoured with our best arguments to soften and humanize his views. But he was instigated by ambition, he desired to rule over these last stragglers from the fold of death; his projects went so far, as to cause him to calculate that, if, from these crushed remains, a few survived, so that a new race should spring up, he, by holding tight the reins of belief, might be remembered by the post-pestilential race as a patriarch, a prophet, nay a deity; such as of old among the post-diluvians were Jupiter the conqueror, Serapis the lawgiver, and Vishnou the preserver. These ideas made him inflexible in his rule, and violent in his hate of any who presumed to share with him his usurped empire.

It is a strange fact, but incontestible, that the philanthropist, who ardent in his desire to do good, who patient, reasonable and gentle, yet disdains to use other argument than truth, has less influence over men's minds, than he who, grasping and selfish, refuses not to adopt any means, nor awaken any passion, nor diffuse any falsehood, for the advancement of his cause. If this from time immemorial has been the case, the contrast was infinitely greater, now that the one could bring harrowing fears and transcendent hopes into play; while the other had few hopes to hold forth, nor could influence the imagination to diminish the fears which he himself was the first to entertain. The preacher had persuaded his followers, that their escape from the plague, the salvation of their children, and the rise of a new race of men from their seed, depended on their faith in, and their submission to him. They greedily imbibed this belief; and their over-weening credulity even rendered them eager to make converts to the same faith.

How to seduce any individuals from such an alliance of fraud, was a frequent subject of Adrian's meditations and discourse. He formed many plans for the purpose; but his own troop kept him in full occupation to ensure their fidelity and safety; beside which the preacher was as cautious and prudent, as he was cruel. His victims lived under the strictest rules and laws, which either entirely imprisoned them within the Tuileries, or let them out in such numbers, and under such leaders, as precluded the possibility of controversy. There was one among them however whom I resolved to save; she had been known to us in happier days; Idris had loved her; and her excellent nature made it peculiarly lamentable that she should be sacrificed by this merciless cannibal of souls.

This man had between two and three hundred persons enlisted under his banners. More than half of them were women; there were about fifty children of all ages; and not more than eighty men. They were mostly drawn from that which, when such distinctions existed, was denominated the lower rank of society. The exceptions consisted of a few high-born females, who, panic-struck, and tamed by sorrow, had joined him. Among these was one, young, lovely, and enthusiastic, whose very goodness made her a more easy victim. I have mentioned her before: Juliet, the youngest daughter, and now sole relic of the ducal house of L——. There are some beings, whom fate seems to select on whom to pour, in unmeasured portion, the vials of her wrath, and whom she bathes even to the lips in misery. Such a one was the ill-starred Juliet. She had lost her indulgent parents, her brothers and sisters, companions of her youth; in one fell swoop they had been carried off from her. Yet she had again dared to call herself happy; united to her admirer, to him who possessed and filled her whole heart, she yielded to the lethean powers of love, and knew and felt only his life and presence. At the very time when with keen delight she welcomed the tokens of maternity, this sole prop of her life failed, her husband died of the plague. For a time she had been lulled in insanity; the birth of her child restored her to the cruel reality of things, but gave her at the same time an object for whom to preserve at once life and reason. Every friend and relative had died off, and she was reduced to solitude and penury; deep melancholy and angry impatience distorted her judgment, so that she could not persuade herself to disclose her distress to us. When she heard of the plan of universal emigration, she resolved to remain behind with her child, and alone in wide England to live or die, as fate might decree, beside the grave of her beloved. She had hidden herself in one of the many empty habitations of London; it was she who rescued my Idris on the fatal twentieth of November, though my immediate danger, and the subsequent illness of Idris, caused us to forget our hapless friend. This circumstance had however brought her again in contact with her fellow-creatures; a slight illness of her infant, proved to her that she was still bound to humanity by an indestructible tie; to preserve this little creature's life became the object of her being, and she joined the first division of migrants who went over to Paris.

She became an easy prey to the methodist; her sensibility and acute fears rendered her accessible to every impulse; her love for her child made her eager to cling to the merest straw held out to save him. Her mind, once unstrung, and now tuned by roughest inharmonious hands, made her credulous: beautiful as fabled goddess, with voice of unrivalled sweetness, burning with new lighted enthusiasm, she became a stedfast proselyte, and powerful auxiliary to the leader of the elect. I had remarked her in the crowd, on the day we met on the Place Vendome; and, recollecting suddenly her providential rescue of my lost one, on the night of the twentieth of November, I reproached myself for my neglect and ingratitude, and felt impelled to leave no means that I could adopt untried, to recall her to her better self, and rescue her from the fangs of the hypocrite destroyer.

I will not, at this period of my story, record the artifices I used to penetrate the asylum of the Tuileries, or give what would be a tedious account of my stratagems, disappointments, and perseverance. I at last succeeded in entering these walls, and roamed its halls and corridors in eager hope to find my selected convert. In the evening I contrived to mingle unobserved with the congregation, which assembled in the chapel to listen to the crafty and eloquent harangue of their prophet. I saw Juliet near him. Her dark eyes, fearfully impressed with the restless glare of madness, were fixed on him; she held her infant, not yet a year old, in her arms; and care of it alone could distract her attention from the words to which she eagerly listened. After the sermon was over, the congregation dispersed; all quitted the chapel except she whom I sought; her babe had fallen asleep; so she placed it on a cushion, and sat on the floor beside, watching its tranquil slumber.

I presented myself to her; for a moment natural feeling produced a sentiment of gladness, which disappeared again, when with ardent and affectionate exhortation I besought her to accompany me in flight from this den of superstition and misery. In a moment she relapsed into the delirium of fanaticism, and, but that her gentle nature forbade, would have loaded me with execrations. She conjured me, she commanded me to leave her— "Beware, O beware," she cried, "fly while yet your escape is practicable. Now you are safe; but strange sounds and inspirations come on me at times, and if the Eternal should in awful whisper reveal to me his will, that to save my child you must be sacrificed, I would call in the satellites of him you call the tyrant; they would tear you limb from limb; nor would I hallow the death of him whom Idris loved, by a single tear."

She spoke hurriedly, with tuneless voice, and wild look; her child awoke, and, frightened, began to cry; each sob went to the ill-fated mother's heart, and she mingled the epithets of endearment she addressed to her infant, with angry commands that I should leave her. Had I had the means, I would have risked all, have torn her by force from the murderer's den, and trusted to the healing balm of reason and affection. But I had no choice, no power even of longer struggle; steps were heard along the gallery, and the voice of the preacher drew near. Juliet, straining her child in a close embrace, fled by another passage. Even then I would have followed her; but my foe and his satellites entered; I was surrounded, and taken prisoner.

I remembered the menace of the unhappy Juliet, and expected the full tempest of the man's vengeance, and the awakened wrath of his followers, to fall instantly upon me. I was questioned. My answers were simple and sincere. "His own mouth condemns him," exclaimed the impostor; "he confesses that his intention was to seduce from the way of salvation our well-beloved sister in God; away with him to the dungeon; to-morrow he dies the death; we are manifestly called upon to make an example, tremendous and appalling, to scare the children of sin from our asylum of the saved."

My heart revolted from his hypocritical jargon: but it was unworthy of me to combat in words with the ruffian; and my answer was cool; while, far from being possessed with fear, methought, even at the worst, a man true to himself, courageous and determined, could fight his way, even from the boards of the scaffold, through the herd of these misguided maniacs. "Remember," I said, "who I am; and be well assured that I shall not die unavenged. Your legal magistrate, the Lord Protector, knew of my design, and is aware that I am here; the cry of blood will reach him, and you and your miserable victims will long lament the tragedy you are about to act."

My antagonist did not deign to reply, even by a look;—"You know your duty," he said to his comrades,—"obey."

In a moment I was thrown on the earth, bound, blindfolded, and hurried away —liberty of limb and sight was only restored to me, when, surrounded by dungeon-walls, dark and impervious, I found myself a prisoner and alone.

Such was the result of my attempt to gain over the proselyte of this man of crime; I could not conceive that he would dare put me to death.—Yet I was in his hands; the path of his ambition had ever been dark and cruel; his power was founded upon fear; the one word which might cause me to die, unheard, unseen, in the obscurity of my dungeon, might be easier to speak than the deed of mercy to act. He would not risk probably a public execution; but a private assassination would at once terrify any of my companions from attempting a like feat, at the same time that a cautious line of conduct might enable him to avoid the enquiries and the vengeance of Adrian.

Two months ago, in a vault more obscure than the one I now inhabited, I had revolved the design of quietly laying me down to die; now I shuddered at the approach of fate. My imagination was busied in shaping forth the kind of death he would inflict. Would he allow me to wear out life with famine; or was the food administered to me to be medicined with death? Would he steal on me in my sleep; or should I contend to the last with my murderers, knowing, even while I struggled, that I must be overcome? I lived upon an earth whose diminished population a child's arithmetic might number; I had lived through long months with death stalking close at my side, while at intervals the shadow of his skeleton-shape darkened my path. I had believed that I despised the grim phantom, and laughed his power to scorn.

Any other fate I should have met with courage, nay, have gone out gallantly to encounter. But to be murdered thus at the midnight hour by cold-blooded assassins, no friendly hand to close my eyes, or receive my parting blessing—to die in combat, hate and execration—ah, why, my angel love, didst thou restore me to life, when already I had stepped within the portals of the tomb, now that so soon again I was to be flung back a mangled corpse!

Hours passed—centuries. Could I give words to the many thoughts which occupied me in endless succession during this interval, I should fill volumes. The air was dank, the dungeon-floor mildewed and icy cold; hunger came upon me too, and no sound reached me from without. To-morrow the ruffian had declared that I should die. When would to-morrow come? Was it not already here?

My door was about to be opened. I heard the key turn, and the bars and bolts slowly removed. The opening of intervening passages permitted sounds from the interior of the palace to reach me; and I heard the clock strike one. They come to murder me, I thought; this hour does not befit a public execution. I drew myself up against the wall opposite the entrance; I collected my forces, I rallied my courage, I would not fall a tame prey. Slowly the door receded on its hinges—I was ready to spring forward to seize and grapple with the intruder, till the sight of who it was changed at once the temper of my mind. It was Juliet herself; pale and trembling she stood, a lamp in her hand, on the threshold of the dungeon, looking at me with wistful countenance. But in a moment she re-assumed her self-possession; and her languid eyes recovered their brilliancy. She said, "I am come to save you, Verney."

"And yourself also," I cried: "dearest friend, can we indeed be saved?"

"Not a word," she replied, "follow me!"

I obeyed instantly. We threaded with light steps many corridors, ascended several flights of stairs, and passed through long galleries; at the end of one she unlocked a low portal; a rush of wind extinguished our lamp; but, in lieu of it, we had the blessed moon-beams and the open face of heaven. Then first Juliet spoke:—"You are safe," she said, "God bless you!— farewell!"

I seized her reluctant hand—"Dear friend," I cried, "misguided victim, do you not intend to escape with me? Have you not risked all in facilitating my flight? and do you think, that I will permit you to return, and suffer alone the effects of that miscreant's rage? Never!"

"Do not fear for me," replied the lovely girl mournfully, "and do not imagine that without the consent of our chief you could be without these walls. It is he that has saved you; he assigned to me the part of leading you hither, because I am best acquainted with your motives for coming here, and can best appreciate his mercy in permitting you to depart."

"And are you," I cried, "the dupe of this man? He dreads me alive as an enemy, and dead he fears my avengers. By favouring this clandestine escape he preserves a shew of consistency to his followers; but mercy is far from his heart. Do you forget his artifices, his cruelty, and fraud? As I am free, so are you. Come, Juliet, the mother of our lost Idris will welcome you, the noble Adrian will rejoice to receive you; you will find peace and love, and better hopes than fanaticism can afford. Come, and fear not; long before day we shall be at Versailles; close the door on this abode of crime —come, sweet Juliet, from hypocrisy and guilt to the society of the affectionate and good."

I spoke hurriedly, but with fervour: and while with gentle violence I drew her from the portal, some thought, some recollection of past scenes of youth and happiness, made her listen and yield to me; suddenly she broke away with a piercing shriek:—"My child, my child! he has my child; my darling girl is my hostage."

She darted from me into the passage; the gate closed between us—she was left in the fangs of this man of crime, a prisoner, still to inhale the pestilential atmosphere which adhered to his demoniac nature; the unimpeded breeze played on my cheek, the moon shone graciously upon me, my path was free. Glad to have escaped, yet melancholy in my very joy, I retrod my steps to Versailles.

6

EVENTFUL WINTER PASSED; winter, the respite of our ills. By degrees the sun, which with slant beams had before yielded the more extended reign to night, lengthened his diurnal journey, and mounted his highest throne, at once the fosterer of earth's new beauty, and her lover. We who, like flies that congregate upon a dry rock at the ebbing of the tide, had played wantonly with time, allowing our passions, our hopes, and our mad desires to rule us, now heard the approaching roar of the ocean of destruction, and would have fled to some sheltered crevice, before the first wave broke over us. We resolved without delay, to commence our journey to Switzerland; we became eager to leave France. Under the icy vaults of the glaciers, beneath the shadow of the pines, the swinging of whose mighty branches was arrested by a load of snow; beside the streams whose intense cold proclaimed their origin to be from the slow-melting piles of congelated waters, amidst frequent storms which might purify the air, we should find health, if in truth health were not herself diseased.

We began our preparations at first with alacrity. We did not now bid adieu to our native country, to the graves of those we loved, to the flowers, and streams, and trees, which had lived beside us from infancy. Small sorrow would be ours on leaving Paris. A scene of shame, when we remembered our late contentions, and thought that we left behind a flock of miserable, deluded victims, bending under the tyranny of a selfish impostor. Small pangs should we feel in leaving the gardens, woods, and halls of the palaces of the Bourbons at Versailles, which we feared would soon be tainted by the dead, when we looked forward to vallies lovelier than any garden, to mighty forests and halls, built not for mortal majesty, but palaces of nature's own, with the Alp of marmoreal whiteness for their walls, the sky for their roof.

Yet our spirits flagged, as the day drew near which we had fixed for our departure. Dire visions and evil auguries, if such things were, thickened around us, so that in vain might men say—

These are their reasons, they are natural,[1]

we felt them to be ominous, and dreaded the future event enchained to them. That the night owl should screech before the noon-day sun, that the hard-winged bat should wheel around the bed of beauty, that muttering thunder should in early spring startle the cloudless air, that sudden and exterminating blight should fall on the tree and shrub, were unaccustomed, but physical events, less horrible than the mental creations of almighty fear. Some had sight of funeral processions, and faces all begrimed with tears, which flitted through the long avenues of the gardens, and drew aside the curtains of the sleepers at dead of night. Some heard wailing and cries in the air; a mournful chaunt would stream through the dark atmosphere, as if spirits above sang the requiem of the human race. What was there in all this, but that fear created other senses within our frames, making us see, hear, and feel what was not? What was this, but the action of diseased imaginations and childish credulity? So might it be; but what was most real, was the existence of these very fears; the staring looks of horror, the faces pale even to ghastliness, the voices struck dumb with harrowing dread, of those among us who saw and heard these things. Of this number was Adrian, who knew the delusion, yet could not cast off the clinging terror. Even ignorant infancy appeared with timorous shrieks and convulsions to acknowledge the presence of unseen powers. We must go: in change of scene, in occupation, and such security as we still hoped to find, we should discover a cure for these gathering horrors.

On mustering our company, we found them to consist of fourteen hundred souls, men, women, and children. Until now therefore, we were undiminished in numbers, except by the desertion of those who had attached themselves to the impostor-prophet, and remained behind in Paris. About fifty French joined us. Our order of march was easily arranged; the ill success which had attended our division, determined Adrian to keep all in one body. I, with an hundred men, went forward first as purveyor, taking the road of the Cote d'Or, through Auxerre, Dijon, Dole, over the Jura to Geneva. I was to make arrangements, at every ten miles, for the accommodation of such numbers as I found the town or village would receive, leaving behind a messenger with a written order, signifying how many were to be quartered there. The remainder of our tribe was then divided into bands of fifty each, every division containing eighteen men, and the remainder, consisting of women and children. Each of these was headed by an officer, who carried the roll of names, by which they were each day to be mustered. If the numbers were divided at night, in the morning those in the van waited for those in the rear. At each of the large towns before mentioned, we were all to assemble; and a conclave of the principal officers would hold council for the general weal. I went first, as I said; Adrian last. His mother, with Clara and Evelyn under her protection, remained also with him. Thus our order being determined, I departed. My plan was to go at first no further than Fontainebleau, where in a few days I should be joined by Adrian, before I took flight again further eastward.

My friend accompanied me a few miles from Versailles. He was sad; and, in a tone of unaccustomed despondency, uttered a prayer for our speedy arrival among the Alps, accompanied with an expression of vain regret that we were not already there. "In that case," I observed, "we can quicken our march; why adhere to a plan whose dilatory proceeding you already disapprove?"

"Nay," replied he, "it is too late now. A month ago, and we were masters of ourselves; now, —" he turned his face from me; though gathering twilight had already veiled its expression, he turned it yet more away, as he added —"a man died of the plague last night!"

He spoke in a smothered voice, then suddenly clasping his hands, he exclaimed, "Swiftly, most swiftly advances the last hour for us all; as the stars vanish before the sun, so will his near approach destroy us. I have done my best; with grasping hands and impotent strength, I have hung on the wheel of the chariot of plague; but she drags me along with it, while, like

Juggernaut, she proceeds crushing out the being of all who strew the high road of life. Would that it were over—would that her procession achieved, we had all entered the tomb together!"

Tears streamed from his eyes. "Again and again," he continued, "will the tragedy be acted; again I must hear the groans of the dying, the wailing of the survivors; again witness the pangs, which, consummating all, envelope an eternity in their evanescent existence. Why am I reserved for this? Why the tainted wether of the flock, am I not struck to earth among the first? It is hard, very hard, for one of woman born to endure all that I endure!"

Hitherto, with an undaunted spirit, and an high feeling of duty and worth, Adrian had fulfilled his self-imposed task. I had contemplated him with reverence, and a fruitless desire of imitation. I now offered a few words of encouragement and sympathy. He hid his face in his hands, and while he strove to calm himself, he ejaculated, "For a few months, yet for a few months more, let not, O God, my heart fail, or my courage be bowed down; let not sights of intolerable misery madden this half-crazed brain, or cause this frail heart to beat against its prison-bound, so that it burst. I have believed it to be my destiny to guide and rule the last of the race of man, till death extinguish my government; and to this destiny I submit.

"Pardon me, Verney, I pain you, but I will no longer complain. Now I am myself again, or rather I am better than myself. You have known how from my childhood aspiring thoughts and high desires have warred with inherent disease and overstrained sensitiveness, till the latter became victors. You know how I placed this wasted feeble hand on the abandoned helm of human government. I have been visited at times by intervals of fluctuation; yet, until now, I have felt as if a superior and indefatigable spirit had taken up its abode within me or rather incorporated itself with my weaker being. The holy visitant has for a time slept, perhaps to show me how powerless I am without its inspiration. Yet, stay for a while, O Power of goodness and strength; disdain not yet this rent shrine of fleshly mortality, O immortal Capability! While one fellow creature remains to whom aid can be afforded, stay by and prop your shattered, falling engine!"

His vehemence, and voice broken by irrepressible sighs, sunk to my heart; his eyes gleamed in the gloom of night like two earthly stars; and, his form dilating, his countenance beaming, truly it almost seemed as if at his eloquent appeal a more than mortal spirit entered his frame, exalting him above humanity. He turned quickly towards me, and held out his hand. "Farewell, Verney," he cried, "brother of my love, farewell; no other weak expression must cross these lips, I am alive again: to our tasks, to our combats with our unvanquishable foe, for to the last I will struggle against her."

He grasped my hand, and bent a look on me, more fervent and animated than any smile; then turning his horse's head, he touched the animal with the spur, and was out of sight in a moment.

A man last night had died of the plague. The quiver was not emptied, nor the bow unstrung. We stood as marks, while Parthian Pestilence aimed and shot, insatiated by conquest, unobstructed by the heaps of slain. A sickness of the soul, contagious even to my physical mechanism, came over me. My knees knocked together, my teeth chattered, the current of my blood, clotted by sudden cold, painfully forced its way from my heavy heart. I did not fear for myself, but it was misery to think that we could not even save this remnant. That those I loved might in a few days be as clay-cold as Idris in her antique tomb; nor could strength of body or energy of mind ward off the blow. A sense of degradation came over me. Did God create man, merely in the end to become dead earth in the midst of healthful vegetating nature? Was he of no more account to his Maker, than a field of corn blighted in the ear? Were our proud dreams thus to fade? Our name was written "a little lower than the angels;" and, behold, we were no better than ephemera. We had called ourselves the "paragon of animals," and, lo! we were a "quint-essence of dust." We repined that the pyramids had outlasted the embalmed body of their builder. Alas! the mere shepherd's hut of straw we passed on the road, contained in its structure the principle of greater longevity than the whole race of man. How reconcile this sad change to our past aspirations, to our apparent powers!

Sudden an internal voice, articulate and clear, seemed to say:—Thus from eternity, it was decreed: the steeds that bear Time onwards had this hour and this fulfilment enchained to them, since the void brought forth its burthen. Would you read backwards the unchangeable laws of Necessity?

Mother of the world! Servant of the Omnipotent! eternal, changeless Necessity! who with busy fingers sittest ever weaving the indissoluble chain of events!—I will not murmur at thy acts. If my human mind cannot acknowledge that all that is, is right; yet since what is, must be, I will sit amidst the ruins and smile. Truly we were not born to enjoy, but to submit, and to hope.

Will not the reader tire, if I should minutely describe our long-drawn journey from Paris to Geneva? If, day by day, I should record, in the form of a journal, the thronging miseries of our lot, could my hand write, or language afford words to express, the variety of our woe; the hustling and crowding of one deplorable event upon another? Patience, oh reader! whoever thou art, wherever thou dwellest, whether of race spiritual, or, sprung from some surviving pair, thy nature will be human, thy habitation the earth; thou wilt here read of the acts of the extinct race, and wilt ask wonderingly, if they, who suffered what thou findest recorded, were of frail flesh and soft organization like thyself. Most true, they were— weep therefore; for surely, solitary being, thou wilt be of gentle disposition; shed compassionate tears; but the while lend thy attention to the tale, and learn the deeds and sufferings of thy predecessors.

Yet the last events that marked our progress through France were so full of strange horror and gloomy misery, that I dare not pause too long in the narration. If I were to dissect each incident, every small fragment of a second would contain an harrowing tale, whose minutest word would curdle the blood in thy young veins. It is right that I should erect for thy instruction this monument of the foregone race; but not that I should drag thee through the wards of an hospital, nor the secret chambers of the charnel-house. This tale, therefore, shall be rapidly unfolded. Images of destruction, pictures of despair, the procession of the last triumph of death, shall be drawn before thee, swift as the rack driven by the north wind along the blotted splendour of the sky.

Weed-grown fields, desolate towns, the wild approach of riderless horses had now become habitual to my eyes; nay, sights far worse, of the unburied dead, and human forms which were strewed on the road side, and on the steps of once frequented habitations, where,

> Through the flesh that wastes away
> Beneath the parching sun, the whitening bones
> Start forth, and moulder in the sable dust.[2]

Sights like these had become—ah, woe the while! so familiar, that we had ceased to shudder, or spur our stung horses to sudden speed, as we passed them. France in its best days, at least that part of France through which we travelled, had been a cultivated desert, and the absence of enclosures, of cottages, and even of peasantry, was saddening to a traveler from sunny Italy, or busy England. Yet the towns were frequent and lively, and the cordial politeness and ready smile of the wooden-shoed peasant restored good humour to the splenetic. Now, the old woman sat no more at the door with her distaff—the lank beggar no longer asked charity in courtier-like phrase; nor on holidays did the peasantry thread with slow grace the mazes of the dance. Silence, melancholy bride of death, went in procession with him from town to town through the spacious region.

We arrived at Fontainebleau, and speedily prepared for the reception of our friends. On mustering our numbers for the night, three were found missing. When I enquired for them, the man to whom I spoke, uttered the word "plague," and fell at my feet in convulsions; he also was infected. There were hard faces around me; for among my troop were sailors who had crossed the line times unnumbered, soldiers who, in Russia and far America, had suffered famine, cold and danger, and men still sterner-featured, once nightly depredators in our over-grown metropolis; men bred from their cradle to see the whole machine of society at work for their destruction. I looked round, and saw upon the faces of all horror and despair written in glaring characters.

We passed four days at Fontainebleau. Several sickened and died, and in the mean time neither Adrian nor any of our friends appeared. My own troop was in commotion; to reach Switzerland, to plunge into rivers of snow, and to dwell in caves of ice, became the mad desire of all. Yet we had promised to wait for the Earl; and he came not. My people demanded to be led forward— rebellion, if so we might call what was the mere casting away of straw-formed shackles, appeared manifestly among them. They would away on the word without a leader. The only chance of safety, the only hope of preservation from every form of indescribable suffering, was our keeping together. I told them this; while the most determined among them answered with sullenness, that they could take care of themselves, and replied to my entreaties with scoffs and menaces.

At length, on the fifth day, a messenger arrived from Adrian, bearing letters, which directed us to proceed to Auxerre, and there await his arrival, which would only be deferred for a few days. Such was the tenor of his public letters. Those privately delivered to me, detailed at length the difficulties of his situation, and left the arrangement of my future plans to my own discretion. His account of the state of affairs at Versailles was brief, but the oral communications of his messenger filled up his omissions, and shewed me that perils of the most frightful nature were gathering around him. At first the re-awakening of the plague had been concealed; but the number of deaths increasing, the secret was divulged, and the destruction already achieved, was exaggerated by the fears of the survivors. Some emissaries of the enemy of mankind, the accursed Impostors, were among them instilling their doctrine that safety and life could only be ensured by submission to their chief; and they succeeded so well, that soon, instead of desiring to proceed to Switzerland, the major part of the multitude, weak-minded women, and dastardly men, desired to return to Paris, and, by ranging themselves under the banners of the so called prophet, and by a cowardly worship of the principle of evil, to purchase respite, as they hoped, from impending death. The discord and tumult induced by these conflicting fears and passions, detained Adrian. It required all his ardour in pursuit of an object, and his patience under difficulties, to calm and animate such a number of his followers, as might counterbalance the panic of the rest, and lead them back to the means from which alone safety could be derived. He had hoped immediately to follow me; but, being defeated in this intention, he sent his messenger urging me to secure my own troop at such a distance from Versailles, as to prevent the contagion of rebellion from reaching them; promising, at the same time, to join me the moment a favourable occasion should occur, by means of which he could withdraw the main body of the emigrants from the evil influence at present exercised over them.

I was thrown into a most painful state of uncertainty by these communications. My first impulse was that we should all return to Versailles, there to assist in extricating our chief from his perils. I accordingly assembled my troop, and proposed to them this retrograde movement, instead of the continuation of our journey to Auxerre. With one voice they refused to comply. The notion circulated among them was, that the ravages of the plague alone detained the Protector; they opposed his order to my request; they came to a resolve to proceed without me, should I refuse to accompany them. Argument and adjuration were lost on these dastards. The continual diminution of their own numbers, effected by pestilence, added a sting to their dislike of delay; and my opposition only served to bring their resolution to a crisis. That same evening they departed towards Auxerre. Oaths, as from soldiers to their general, had been taken by them: these they broke. I also had engaged myself not to desert them; it appeared to me inhuman to ground any infraction of my word on theirs. The same spirit that caused them to rebel against me, would impel them to desert each other; and the most dreadful sufferings would be the consequence of their journey in their present unordered and chiefless array. These feelings for a time were paramount; and, in obedience to them, I accompanied the rest towards Auxerre. We arrived the same night at Villeneuve-la-Guiard, a town at the distance of four posts from Fontainebleau. When my companions had retired to rest, and I was left alone to revolve and ruminate upon the intelligence I received of Adrian's situation, another view of the subject presented itself to me. What was I doing, and what was the object of my present movements? Apparently I was to lead this troop of selfish and lawless men towards Switzerland, leaving behind my family and my selected friend, which, subject as they were hourly to the death that threatened to all, I might never see again. Was it not my first duty to assist the Protector, setting an example of attachment and duty? At a crisis, such as the one I had reached, it is very difficult to balance nicely opposing interests, and that towards which our inclinations lead us, obstinately assumes the appearance of selfishness, even when we meditate a sacrifice. We are easily led at such times to make a compromise of the question; and this was my present resource. I resolved that very night to ride to Versailles; if I found affairs less desperate than I now deemed them, I would return without delay to my troop; I had a vague idea that my arrival at that town, would occasion some sensation more or less strong, of which we might profit, for the purpose of leading forward the vacillating multitude—at least no time was to be lost—I visited the stables, I saddled my favourite horse, and vaulting on his back, without giving myself time for further reflection or hesitation, quitted Villeneuve-la-Guiard on my return to Versailles.

I was glad to escape from my rebellious troop, and to lose sight for a time, of the strife of evil with good, where the former for ever remained triumphant. I was stung almost to madness by my uncertainty concerning the fate of Adrian, and grew reckless of any event, except what might lose or preserve my unequalled friend. With an heavy heart, that sought relief in the rapidity of my course, I rode through the night to Versailles. I spurred my horse, who addressed his free limbs to speed, and tossed his gallant head in pride. The constellations reeled swiftly by, swiftly each tree and stone and landmark fled past my onward career. I bared my head to the rushing wind, which bathed my brow in delightful coolness. As I lost sight of Villeneuve-la-Guiard, I forgot the sad drama of human misery; methought it was happiness enough to live, sensitive the while of the beauty of the verdure-clad earth, the star-bespangled sky, and the tameless wind that lent animation to the whole. My horse grew tired—and I, forgetful of his fatigue, still as he lagged, cheered him with my voice, and urged him with the spur. He was a gallant animal, and I did not wish to exchange him for any chance beast I might light on, leaving him never to be refound. All night we went forward; in the morning he became sensible that we approached Versailles, to reach which as his home, he mustered his flagging strength. The distance we had come was not less than fifty miles, yet he shot down the long Boulevards swift as an arrow; poor fellow, as I dismounted at the gate of the castle, he sunk on his knees, his eyes were covered with a film, he fell on his side, a few gasps inflated his noble chest, and he died. I saw him expire with an anguish, unaccountable even to myself, the spasm was as the wrenching of some limb in agonizing torture, but it was brief as it was intolerable. I forgot him, as I swiftly darted through the open portal, and up the majestic stairs of this castle of victories—heard Adrian's voice—O fool! O woman nurtured, effeminate and contemptible being—I heard his voice, and answered it with convulsive shrieks; I rushed into the Hall of Hercules, where he stood surrounded by a crowd, whose eyes, turned in wonder on me, reminded me that on the stage of the world, a man must repress such girlish extacies. I would have given worlds to have embraced him; I dared not—Half in exhaustion, half voluntarily, I threw myself at my length on the ground— dare I disclose the truth to the gentle offspring of solitude? I did so, that I might kiss the dear and sacred earth he trod.

I found everything in a state of tumult. An emissary of the leader of the elect, had been so worked up by his chief, and by his own fanatical creed, as to make an attempt on the life of the Protector and preserver of lost mankind. His hand was arrested while in the act of poignarding the Earl; this circumstance had caused the clamour I heard on my arrival at the castle, and the confused assembly of persons that I found assembled in the Salle d'Hercule. Although superstition and demoniac fury had crept among the emigrants, yet several adhered with fidelity to their noble chieftain; and many, whose faith and love had been unhinged by fear, felt all their latent affection rekindled by this detestable attempt. A phalanx of faithful breasts closed round him; the wretch, who, although a prisoner and in bonds, vaunted his design, and madly claimed the crown of martyrdom, would have been torn to pieces, had not his intended victim interposed. Adrian, springing forward, shielded him with his own person, and commanded with energy the submission of his infuriate friends—at this moment I had entered.

Discipline and peace were at length restored in the castle; and then Adrian went from house to house, from troop to troop, to soothe the disturbed minds of his followers, and recall them to their ancient obedience. But the fear of immediate death was still rife amongst these survivors of a world's destruction; the horror occasioned by the attempted assassination, past away; each eye turned towards Paris. Men love a prop so well, that they will lean on a pointed poisoned spear; and such was he, the impostor, who, with fear of hell for his scourge, most ravenous wolf, played the driver to a credulous flock.

It was a moment of suspense, that shook even the resolution of the unyielding friend of man. Adrian for one moment was about to give in, to cease the struggle, and quit, with a few adherents, the deluded crowd, leaving them a miserable prey to their passions, and to the worse tyrant who excited them. But again, after a brief fluctuation of purpose, he resumed his courage and resolves, sustained by the singleness of his purpose, and the untried spirit of benevolence which animated him. At this moment, as an omen of excellent import, his wretched enemy pulled destruction on his head, destroying with his own hands the dominion he had erected.

His grand hold upon the minds of men, took its rise from the doctrine inculcated by him, that those who believed in, and followed him, were the remnant to be saved, while all the rest of mankind were marked out for death. Now, at the time of the Flood, the omnipotent repented him that he had created man, and as then with water, now with the arrows of pestilence, was about to annihilate all, except those who obeyed his decrees, promulgated by the ipse dixit prophet. It is impossible to say on what foundations this man built his hopes of being able to carry on such an imposture. It is likely that he was fully aware of the lie which murderous nature might give to his assertions, and believed it to be the cast of a die, whether he should in future ages be reverenced as an inspired delegate from heaven, or be recognized as an impostor by the present dying generation. At any rate he resolved to keep up the drama to the last act. When, on the first approach of summer, the fatal disease again made its ravages among the followers of Adrian, the impostor exultingly proclaimed the exemption of his own congregation from the universal calamity. He was believed; his followers, hitherto shut up in Paris, now came to Versailles. Mingling with the coward band there assembled, they reviled their admirable leader, and asserted their own superiority and exemption. At length the plague, slow-footed, but sure in her noiseless advance, destroyed the illusion, invading the congregation of the elect, and showering promiscuous death among them. Their leader endeavoured to conceal this event; he had a few followers, who, admitted into the arcana of his wickedness, could help him in the execution of his nefarious designs. Those who sickened were immediately and quietly withdrawn, the cord and a midnight-grave disposed of them for ever; while some plausible excuse was given for their absence. At last a female, whose maternal vigilance subdued even the effects of the narcotics administered to her, became a witness of their murderous designs on her only child. Mad with horror, she would have burst among her deluded fellow-victims, and, wildly shrieking, have awaked the dull ear of night with the history of the fiend-like crime; when the Impostor, in his last act of rage and desperation, plunged a poignard in her bosom. Thus wounded to death, her garments dripping with her own life-blood, bearing her strangled infant in her arms, beautiful and young as she was, Juliet, (for it was she) denounced to the host of deceived believers, the wickedness of their leader. He saw the aghast looks of her auditors, changing from horror to fury—the names of those already sacrificed were echoed by their relatives, now assured of their loss. The wretch with that energy of purpose, which had borne him thus far in his guilty career, saw his danger, and resolved to evade the worst forms of it—he rushed on one of the foremost, seized a pistol from his girdle, and his loud laugh of derision mingled with the report of the weapon with which he destroyed himself.

They left his miserable remains even where they lay; they placed the corpse of poor Juliet and her babe upon a bier, and all, with hearts subdued to saddest regret, in long procession walked towards Versailles. They met troops of those who had quitted the kindly protection of Adrian, and were journeying to join the fanatics. The tale of horror was recounted—all turned back; and thus at last, accompanied by the undiminished numbers of surviving humanity, and preceded by the mournful emblem of their recovered reason, they appeared before Adrian, and again and for ever vowed obedience to his commands, and fidelity to his cause.

---

1. Shakespeare—Julius Caesar.
2. Elton's Translation of Hesiod's "Shield of Hercules."

7

THESE EVENTS OCCUPIED SO much time, that June had numbered more than half its days, before we again commenced our long-protracted journey. The day after my return to Versailles, six men, from among those I had left at Villeneuve-la-Guiard, arrived, with intelligence, that the rest of the troop had already proceeded towards Switzerland. We went forward in the same track.

It is strange, after an interval of time, to look back on a period, which, though short in itself, appeared, when in actual progress, to be drawn out interminably. By the end of July we entered Dijon; by the end of July those hours, days, and weeks had mingled with the ocean of forgotten time, which in their passage teemed with fatal events and agonizing sorrow. By the end of July, little more than a month had gone by, if man's life were measured by the rising and setting of the sun: but, alas! in that interval ardent youth had become grey-haired; furrows deep and uneraseable were trenched in the blooming cheek of the young mother; the elastic limbs of early manhood, paralyzed as by the burthen of years, assumed the decrepitude of age. Nights passed, during whose fatal darkness the sun grew old before it rose; and burning days, to cool whose baleful heat the balmy eve, lingering far in eastern climes, came lagging and ineffectual; days, in which the dial, radiant in its noon-day station, moved not its shadow the space of a little hour, until a whole life of sorrow had brought the sufferer to an untimely grave.

We departed from Versailles fifteen hundred souls. We set out on the eighteenth of June. We made a long procession, in which was contained every dear relationship, or tie of love, that existed in human society. Fathers and husbands, with guardian care, gathered their dear relatives around them; wives and mothers looked for support to the manly form beside them, and then with tender anxiety bent their eyes on the infant troop around. They were sad, but not hopeless. Each thought that someone would be saved; each, with that pertinacious optimism, which to the last characterized our human nature, trusted that their beloved family would be the one preserved.

We passed through France, and found it empty of inhabitants. Some one or two natives survived in the larger towns, which they roamed through like ghosts; we received therefore small increase to our numbers, and such decrease through death, that at last it became easier to count the scanty list of survivors. As we never deserted any of the sick, until their death permitted us to commit their remains to the shelter of a grave, our journey was long, while every day a frightful gap was made in our troop—they died by tens, by fifties, by hundreds. No mercy was shewn by death; we ceased to expect it, and every day welcomed the sun with the feeling that we might never see it rise again.

The nervous terrors and fearful visions which had scared us during the spring, continued to visit our coward troop during this sad journey. Every evening brought its fresh creation of spectres; a ghost was depicted by every blighted tree; and appalling shapes were manufactured from each shaggy bush. By degrees these common marvels palled on us, and then other wonders were called into being. Once it was confidently asserted, that the sun rose an hour later than its seasonable time; again it was discovered that he grew paler and paler; that shadows took an uncommon appearance. It was impossible to have imagined, during the usual calm routine of life men had before experienced, the terrible effects produced by these extravagant delusions: in truth, of such little worth are our senses, when unsupported by concurring testimony, that it was with the utmost difficulty I kept myself free from the belief in supernatural events, to which the major part of our people readily gave credit. Being one sane amidst a crowd of the mad, I hardly dared assert to my own mind, that the vast luminary had undergone no change—that the shadows of night were unthickened by innumerable shapes of awe and terror; or that the wind, as it sung in the trees, or whistled round an empty building, was not pregnant with sounds of wailing and despair. Sometimes realities took ghostly shapes; and it was impossible for one's blood not to curdle at the perception of an evident mixture of what we knew to be true, with the visionary semblance of all that we feared.

Once, at the dusk of the evening, we saw a figure all in white, apparently of more than human stature, flourishing about the road, now throwing up its arms, now leaping to an astonishing height in the air, then turning round several times successively, then raising itself to its full height and gesticulating violently. Our troop, on the alert to discover and believe in the supernatural, made a halt at some distance from this shape; and, as it became darker, there was something appalling even to the incredulous, in the lonely spectre, whose gambols, if they hardly accorded with spiritual dignity, were beyond human powers. Now it leapt right up in the air, now sheer over a high hedge, and was again the moment after in the road before us. By the time I came up, the fright experienced by the spectators of this ghostly exhibition, began to manifest itself in the flight of some, and the close huddling together of the rest. Our goblin now perceived us; he approached, and, as we drew reverentially back, made a low bow. The sight was irresistibly ludicrous even to our hapless band, and his politeness was hailed by a shout of laughter;—then, again springing up, as a last effort, it sunk to the ground, and became almost invisible through the dusky night. This circumstance again spread silence and fear through the troop; the more courageous at length advanced, and, raising the dying wretch, discovered the tragic explanation of this wild scene. It was an opera-dancer, and had been one of the troop which deserted from Villeneuve-la-Guiard: falling sick, he had been deserted by his companions; in an access of delirium he had fancied himself on the stage, and, poor fellow, his dying sense eagerly accepted the last human applause that could ever be bestowed on his grace and agility.

At another time we were haunted for several days by an apparition, to which our people gave the appellation of the Black Spectre. We never saw it except at evening, when his coal black steed, his mourning dress, and plume of black feathers, had a majestic and awe-striking appearance; his face, one said, who had seen it for a moment, was ashy pale; he had lingered far behind the rest of his troop, and suddenly at a turn in the road, saw the Black Spectre coming towards him; he hid himself in fear, and the horse and his rider slowly past, while the moonbeams fell on the face of the latter, displaying its unearthly hue. Sometimes at dead of night, as we watched the sick, we heard one galloping through the town; it was the Black Spectre come in token of inevitable death. He grew giant tall to vulgar eyes; an icy atmosphere, they said, surrounded him; when he was heard, all animals shuddered, and the dying knew that their last hour was come. It was Death himself, they declared, come visibly to seize on subject earth, and quell at once our decreasing numbers, sole rebels to his law. One day at noon, we saw a dark mass on the road before us, and, coming up, beheld the Black Spectre fallen from his horse, lying in the agonies of disease upon the ground. He did not survive many hours; and his last words disclosed the secret of his mysterious conduct. He was a French noble of distinction, who, from the effects of plague, had been left alone in his district; during many months, he had wandered from town to town, from province to province, seeking some survivor for a companion, and abhorring the loneliness to which he was condemned. When he discovered our troop, fear of contagion conquered his love of society. He dared not join us, yet he could not resolve to lose sight of us, sole human beings who besides himself existed in wide and fertile France; so he accompanied us in the spectral guise I have described, till pestilence gathered him to a larger congregation, even that of Dead Mankind.

It had been well, if such vain terrors could have distracted our thoughts from more tangible evils. But these were too dreadful and too many not to force themselves into every thought, every moment, of our lives. We were obliged to halt at different periods for days together, till another and yet another was consigned as a clod to the vast clod which had been once our living mother. Thus we continued travelling during the hottest season; and it was not till the first of August, that we, the emigrants,—reader, there were just eighty of us in number,— entered the gates of Dijon.

We had expected this moment with eagerness, for now we had accomplished the worst part of our drear journey, and Switzerland was near at hand. Yet how could we congratulate ourselves on any event thus imperfectly fulfilled? Were these miserable beings, who, worn and wretched, passed in sorrowful procession, the sole remnants of the race of man, which, like a flood, had once spread over and possessed the whole earth? It had come down clear and unimpeded from its primal mountain source in Ararat, and grew from a puny streamlet to a vast perennial river, generation after generation flowing on ceaselessly. The same, but diversified, it grew, and swept onwards towards the absorbing ocean, whose dim shores we now reached. It had been the mere plaything of nature, when first it crept out of uncreative void into light; but thought brought forth power and knowledge; and, clad with these, the race of man assumed dignity and authority. It was then no longer the mere gardener of earth, or the shepherd of her flocks; "it carried with it an imposing and majestic aspect; it had a pedigree and illustrious ancestors; it had its gallery of portraits, its monumental inscriptions, its records and titles."[1]

This was all over, now that the ocean of death had sucked in the slackening tide, and its source was dried up. We first had bidden adieu to the state of things which having existed many thousand years, seemed eternal; such a state of government, obedience, traffic, and domestic intercourse, as had moulded our hearts and capacities, as far back as memory could reach. Then to patriotic zeal, to the arts, to reputation, to enduring fame, to the name of country, we had bidden farewell. We saw depart all hope of retrieving our ancient state—all expectation, except the feeble one of saving our individual lives from the wreck of the past. To preserve these we had quitted England—England, no more; for without her children, what name could that barren island claim? With tenacious grasp we clung to such rule and order as could best save us; trusting that, if a little colony could be preserved, that would suffice at some remoter period to restore the lost community of mankind.

But the game is up! We must all die; nor leave survivor nor heir to the wide inheritance of earth. We must all die! The species of man must perish; his frame of exquisite workmanship; the wondrous mechanism of his senses; the noble proportion of his godlike limbs; his mind, the throned king of these; must perish. Will the earth still keep her place among the planets; will she still journey with unmarked regularity round the sun; will the seasons change, the trees adorn themselves with leaves, and flowers shed their fragrance, in solitude? Will the mountains remain unmoved, and streams still keep a downward course towards the vast abyss; will the tides rise and fall, and the winds fan universal nature; will beasts pasture, birds fly, and fishes swim, when man, the lord, possessor, perceiver, and recorder of all these things, has passed away, as though he had never been? O, what mockery is this! Surely death is not death, and humanity is not extinct; but merely passed into other shapes, unsubjected to our perceptions. Death is a vast portal, an high road to life: let us hasten to pass; let us exist no more in this living death, but die that we may live!

We had longed with inexpressible earnestness to reach Dijon, since we had fixed on it, as a kind of station in our progress. But now we entered it with a torpor more painful than acute suffering. We had come slowly but irrevocably to the opinion, that our utmost efforts would not preserve one human being alive. We took our hands therefore away from the long grasped rudder; and the frail vessel on which we floated, seemed, the government over her suspended, to rush, prow foremost, into the dark abyss of the billows. A gush of grief, a wanton profusion of tears, and vain laments, and overflowing tenderness, and passionate but fruitless clinging to the priceless few that remained, was followed by languor and recklessness.

During this disastrous journey we lost all those, not of our own family, to whom we had particularly attached ourselves among the survivors. It were not well to fill these pages with a mere catalogue of losses; yet I cannot refrain from this last mention of those principally dear to us. The little girl whom Adrian had rescued from utter desertion, during our ride through London on the twentieth of November, died at Auxerre. The poor child had attached herself greatly to us; and the suddenness of her death added to our sorrow. In the morning we had seen her apparently in health—in the evening, Lucy, before we retired to rest, visited our quarters to say that she was dead. Poor Lucy herself only survived, till we arrived at Dijon. She had devoted herself throughout to the nursing the sick, and attending the friendless. Her excessive exertions brought on a slow fever, which ended in the dread disease whose approach soon released her from her sufferings. She had throughout been endeared to us by her good qualities, by her ready and cheerful execution of every duty, and mild acquiescence in every turn of adversity. When we consigned her to the tomb, we seemed at the same time to bid a final adieu to those peculiarly feminine virtues conspicuous in her; uneducated and unpretending as she was, she was distinguished for patience, forbearance, and sweetness. These, with all their train of qualities peculiarly English, would never again be revived for us. This type of all that was most worthy of admiration in her class among my countrywomen, was placed under the sod of desert France; and it was as a second separation from our country to have lost sight of her for ever.

The Countess of Windsor died during our abode at Dijon. One morning I was informed that she wished to see me. Her message made me remember, that several days had elapsed since I had last seen her. Such a circumstance had often occurred during our journey, when I remained behind to watch to their close the last moments of some one of our hapless comrades, and the rest of the troop past on before me. But there was something in the manner of her messenger, that made me suspect that all was not right. A caprice of the imagination caused me to conjecture that some ill had occurred to Clara or Evelyn, rather than to this aged lady. Our fears, for ever on the stretch, demanded a nourishment of horror; and it seemed too natural an occurrence, too like past times, for the old to die before the young. I found the venerable mother of my Idris lying on a couch, her tall emaciated figure stretched out; her face fallen away, from which the nose stood out in sharp profile, and her large dark eyes, hollow and deep, gleamed with such light as may edge a thunder cloud at sun-set. All was shrivelled and dried up, except these lights; her voice too was fearfully changed, as she spoke to me at intervals. "I am afraid," said she, "that it is selfish in me to have asked you to visit the old woman again, before she dies: yet perhaps it would have been a greater shock to hear suddenly that I was dead, than to see me first thus."

I clasped her shrivelled hand: "Are you indeed so ill?" I asked.

"Do you not perceive death in my face," replied she, "it is strange; I ought to have expected this, and yet I confess it has taken me unaware. I never clung to life, or enjoyed it, till these last months, while among those I senselessly deserted: and it is hard to be snatched immediately away. I am glad, however, that I am not a victim of the plague; probably I should have died at this hour, though the world had continued as it was in my youth."

She spoke with difficulty, and I perceived that she regretted the necessity of death, even more than she cared to confess. Yet she had not to complain of an undue shortening of existence; her faded person shewed that life had naturally spent itself. We had been alone at first; now Clara entered; the Countess turned to her with a smile, and took the hand of this lovely child; her roseate palm and snowy fingers, contrasted with relaxed fibres and yellow hue of those of her aged friend; she bent to kiss her, touching her withered mouth with the warm, full lips of youth. "Verney," said the Countess, "I need not recommend this dear girl to you, for your own sake you will preserve her. Were the world as it was, I should have a thousand sage precautions to impress, that one so sensitive, good, and beauteous, might escape the dangers that used to lurk for the destruction of the fair and excellent. This is all nothing now.

"I commit you, my kind nurse, to your uncle's care; to yours I entrust the dearest relic of my better self. Be to Adrian, sweet one, what you have been to me—enliven his sadness with your sprightly sallies; sooth his anguish by your sober and inspired converse, when he is dying; nurse him as you have done me."

Clara burst into tears; "Kind girl," said the Countess, "do not weep for me. Many dear friends are left to you."

"And yet," cried Clara, "you talk of their dying also. This is indeed cruel —how could I live, if they were gone? If it were possible for my beloved protector to die before me, I could not nurse him; I could only die too."

The venerable lady survived this scene only twenty-four hours. She was the last tie binding us to the ancient state of things. It was impossible to look on her, and not call to mind in their wonted guise, events and persons, as alien to our present situation as the disputes of Themistocles and Aristides, or the wars of the two roses in our native land. The crown of England had pressed her brow; the memory of my father and his misfortunes, the vain struggles of the late king, the images of Raymond, Evadne, and Perdita, who had lived in the world's prime, were brought vividly before us. We consigned her to the oblivious tomb with reluctance; and when I turned from her grave, Janus veiled his retrospective face; that which gazed on future generations had long lost its faculty.

After remaining a week at Dijon, until thirty of our number deserted the vacant ranks of life, we continued our way towards Geneva. At noon on the second day we arrived at the foot of Jura. We halted here during the heat of the day. Here fifty human beings—fifty, the only human beings that survived of the food-teeming earth, assembled to read in the looks of each other ghastly plague, or wasting sorrow, desperation, or worse, carelessness of future or present evil. Here we assembled at the foot of this mighty wall of mountain, under a spreading walnut tree; a brawling stream refreshed the green sward by its sprinkling; and the busy grasshopper chirped among the thyme. We clustered together a group of wretched sufferers. A mother cradled in her enfeebled arms the child, last of many, whose glazed eye was about to close for ever. Here beauty, late glowing in youthful lustre and consciousness, now wan and neglected, knelt fanning with uncertain motion the beloved, who lay striving to paint his features, distorted by illness, with a thankful smile. There an hard-featured, weather-worn veteran, having prepared his meal, sat, his head dropped on his breast, the useless knife falling from his grasp, his limbs utterly relaxed, as thought of wife and child, and dearest relative, all lost, passed across his recollection. There sat a man who for forty years had basked in fortune's tranquil sunshine; he held the hand of his last hope, his beloved daughter, who had just attained womanhood; and he gazed on her with anxious eyes, while she tried to rally her fainting spirit to comfort him. Here a servant, faithful to the last, though dying, waited on one, who, though still erect with health, gazed with gasping fear on the variety of woe around.

Adrian stood leaning against a tree; he held a book in his hand, but his eye wandered from the pages, and sought mine; they mingled a sympathetic glance; his looks confessed that his thoughts had quitted the inanimate print, for pages more pregnant with meaning, more absorbing, spread out before him. By the margin of the stream, apart from all, in a tranquil nook, where the purling brook kissed the green sward gently, Clara and Evelyn were at play, sometimes beating the water with large boughs, sometimes watching the summer-flies that sported upon it. Evelyn now chased a butterfly—now gathered a flower for his cousin; and his laughing cherub-face and clear brow told of the light heart that beat in his bosom. Clara, though she endeavoured to give herself up to his amusement, often forgot him, as she turned to observe Adrian and me. She was now fourteen, and retained her childish appearance, though in height a woman; she acted the part of the tenderest mother to my little orphan boy; to see her playing with him, or attending silently and submissively on our wants, you thought only of her admirable docility and patience; but, in her soft eyes, and the veined curtains that veiled them, in the clearness of her marmoreal brow, and the tender expression of her lips, there was an intelligence and beauty that at once excited admiration and love.

When the sun had sunk towards the precipitate west, and the evening shadows grew long, we prepared to ascend the mountain. The attention that we were obliged to pay to the sick, made our progress slow. The winding road, though steep, presented a confined view of rocky fields and hills, each hiding the other, till our farther ascent disclosed them in succession. We were seldom shaded from the declining sun, whose slant beams were instinct with exhausting heat. There are times when minor difficulties grow gigantic —times, when as the Hebrew poet expressively terms it, "the grasshopper is a burthen;" so was it with our ill fated party this evening. Adrian, usually the first to rally his spirits, and dash foremost into fatigue and hardship, with relaxed limbs and declined head, the reins hanging loosely in his grasp, left the choice of the path to the instinct of his horse, now and then painfully rousing himself, when the steepness of the ascent required that he should keep his seat with better care. Fear and horror encompassed me. Did his languid air attest that he also was struck with contagion? How long, when I look on this matchless specimen of mortality, may I perceive that his thought answers mine? how long will those limbs obey the kindly spirit within? how long will light and life dwell in the eyes of this my sole remaining friend? Thus pacing slowly, each hill surmounted, only presented another to be ascended; each jutting corner only discovered another, sister to the last, endlessly. Sometimes the pressure of sickness in one among us, caused the whole cavalcade to halt; the call for water, the eagerly expressed wish to repose; the cry of pain, and suppressed sob of the mourner—such were the sorrowful attendants of our passage of the Jura.

Adrian had gone first. I saw him, while I was detained by the loosening of a girth, struggling with the upward path, seemingly more difficult than any we had yet passed. He reached the top, and the dark outline of his figure stood in relief against the sky. He seemed to behold something unexpected and wonderful; for, pausing, his head stretched out, his arms for a moment extended, he seemed to give an All Hail! to some new vision. Urged by curiosity, I hurried to join him. After battling for many tedious minutes with the precipice, the same scene presented itself to me, which had wrapt him in extatic wonder.

Nature, or nature's favourite, this lovely earth, presented her most unrivalled beauties in resplendent and sudden exhibition. Below, far, far below, even as it were in the yawning abyss of the ponderous globe, lay the placid and azure expanse of lake Leman; vine-covered hills hedged it in, and behind dark mountains in cone-like shape, or irregular cyclopean wall, served for further defence. But beyond, and high above all, as if the spirits of the air had suddenly unveiled their bright abodes, placed in scaleless altitude in the stainless sky, heaven-kissing, companions of the unattainable ether, were the glorious Alps, clothed in dazzling robes of light by the setting sun. And, as if the world's wonders were never to be exhausted, their vast immensities, their jagged crags, and roseate painting, appeared again in the lake below, dipping their proud heights beneath the unruffled waves—palaces for the Naiads of the placid waters. Towns and villages lay scattered at the foot of Jura, which, with dark ravine, and black promontories, stretched its roots into the watery expanse beneath. Carried away by wonder, I forgot the death of man, and the living and beloved friend near me. When I turned, I saw tears streaming from his eyes; his thin hands pressed one against the other, his animated countenance beaming with admiration; "Why," cried he, at last, "Why, oh heart, whisperest thou of grief to me? Drink in the beauty of that scene, and possess delight beyond what a fabled paradise could afford."

By degrees, our whole party surmounting the steep, joined us, not one among them, but gave visible tokens of admiration, surpassing any before experienced. One cried, "God reveals his heaven to us; we may die blessed." Another and another, with broken exclamations, and extravagant phrases, endeavoured to express the intoxicating effect of this wonder of nature. So we remained awhile, lightened of the pressing burthen of fate, forgetful of death, into whose night we were about to plunge; no longer reflecting that our eyes now and for ever were and would be the only ones which might perceive the divine magnificence of this terrestrial exhibition. An enthusiastic transport, akin to happiness, burst, like a sudden ray from the sun, on our darkened life. Precious attribute of woe-worn humanity! that can snatch extatic emotion, even from under the very share and harrow, that ruthlessly ploughs up and lays waste every hope.

This evening was marked by another event. Passing through Ferney in our way to Geneva, unaccustomed sounds of music arose from the rural church which stood embosomed in trees, surrounded by smokeless, vacant cottages. The peal of an organ with rich swell awoke the mute air, lingering along, and mingling with the intense beauty that clothed the rocks and woods, and waves around. Music—the language of the immortals, disclosed to us as testimony of their existence—music, "silver key of the fountain of tears," child of love, soother of grief, inspirer of heroism and radiant thoughts, O music, in this our desolation, we had forgotten thee! Nor pipe at eve cheered us, nor harmony of voice, nor linked thrill of string; thou camest upon us now, like the revealing of other forms of being; and transported as we had been by the loveliness of nature, fancying that we beheld the abode of spirits, now we might well imagine that we heard their melodious communings. We paused in such awe as would seize on a pale votarist, visiting some holy shrine at midnight; if she beheld animated and smiling, the image which she worshipped. We all stood mute; many knelt. In a few minutes however, we were recalled to human wonder and sympathy by a familiar strain. The air was Haydn's "New-Created World," and, old and drooping as humanity had become, the world yet fresh as at creation's day, might still be worthily celebrated by such an hymn of praise. Adrian and I entered the church; the nave was empty, though the smoke of incense rose from the altar, bringing with it the recollection of vast congregations, in once thronged cathedrals; we went into the loft. A blind old man sat at the bellows; his whole soul was ear; and as he sat in the attitude of attentive listening, a bright glow of pleasure was diffused over his countenance; for, though his lack-lustre eye could not reflect the beam, yet his parted lips, and every line of his face and venerable brow spoke delight. A young woman sat at the keys, perhaps twenty years of age. Her auburn hair hung on her neck, and her fair brow shone in its own beauty; but her drooping eyes let fall fast-flowing tears, while the constraint she exercised to suppress her sobs, and still her trembling, flushed her else pale cheek; she was thin; languor, and alas! sickness, bent her form. We stood looking at the pair, forgetting what we heard in the absorbing sight; till, the last chord struck, the peal died away in lessening reverberations. The mighty voice, inorganic we might call it, for we could in no way associate it with mechanism of pipe or key, stilled its sonorous tone, and the girl, turning to lend her assistance to her aged companion, at length perceived us.

It was her father; and she, since childhood, had been the guide of his darkened steps. They were Germans from Saxony, and, emigrating thither but a few years before, had formed new ties with the surrounding villagers. About the time that the pestilence had broken out, a young German student had joined them. Their simple history was easily divined. He, a noble, loved the fair daughter of the poor musician, and followed them in their flight from the persecutions of his friends; but soon the mighty leveller came with unblunted scythe to mow, together with the grass, the tall flowers of the field. The youth was an early victim. She preserved herself for her father's sake. His blindness permitted her to continue a delusion, at first the child of accident—and now solitary beings, sole survivors in the land, he remained unacquainted with the change, nor was aware that when he listened to his child's music, the mute mountains, senseless lake, and unconscious trees, were, himself excepted, her sole auditors.

The very day that we arrived she had been attacked by symptomatic illness. She was paralyzed with horror at the idea of leaving her aged, sightless father alone on the empty earth; but she had not courage to disclose the truth, and the very excess of her desperation animated her to surpassing exertions. At the accustomed vesper hour, she led him to the chapel; and, though trembling and weeping on his account, she played, without fault in time, or error in note, the hymn written to celebrate the creation of the adorned earth, soon to be her tomb.

We came to her like visitors from heaven itself; her high-wrought courage; her hardly sustained firmness, fled with the appearance of relief. With a shriek she rushed towards us, embraced the knees of Adrian, and uttering but the words, "O save my father!" with sobs and hysterical cries, opened the long-shut floodgates of her woe.

Poor girl!—she and her father now lie side by side, beneath the high walnut-tree where her lover reposes, and which in her dying moments she had pointed out to us. Her father, at length aware of his daughter's danger, unable to see the changes of her dear countenance, obstinately held her hand, till it was chilled and stiffened by death. Nor did he then move or speak, till, twelve hours after, kindly death took him to his breakless repose. They rest beneath the sod, the tree their monument;—the hallowed spot is distinct in my memory, paled in by craggy Jura, and the far, immeasurable Alps; the spire of the church they frequented still points from out the embosoming trees; and though her hand be cold, still methinks the sounds of divine music which they loved wander about, solacing their gentle ghosts.

----

1. Burke's Reflections on the French Revolution.

❧ 8 ❧

WE HAD NOW REACHED SWITZERLAND, so long the final mark and aim of our exertions. We had looked, I know not wherefore, with hope and pleasing expectation on her congregation of hills and snowy crags, and opened our bosoms with renewed spirits to the icy Biz, which even at Midsummer used to come from the northern glacier laden with cold. Yet how could we nourish expectation of relief? Like our native England, and the vast extent of fertile France, this mountain-embowered land was desolate of its inhabitants. Nor bleak mountain-top, nor snow-nourished rivulet; not the ice-laden Biz, nor thunder, the tamer of contagion, had preserved them— why therefore should we claim exemption?

Who was there indeed to save? What troop had we brought fit to stand at bay, and combat with the conqueror? We were a failing remnant, tamed to mere submission to the coming blow. A train half dead, through fear of death—a hopeless, unresisting, almost reckless crew, which, in the tossed bark of life, had given up all pilotage, and resigned themselves to the destructive force of ungoverned winds. Like a few furrows of unreaped corn, which, left standing on a wide field after the rest is gathered to the garner, are swiftly borne down by the winter storm. Like a few straggling swallows, which, remaining after their fellows had, on the first unkind breath of passing autumn, migrated to genial climes, were struck to earth by the first frost of November. Like a stray sheep that wanders over the sleet-beaten hill-side, while the flock is in the pen, and dies before morning-dawn. Like a cloud, like one of many that were spread in impenetrable woof over the sky, which, when the shepherd north has driven its companions "to drink Antipodean noon," fades and dissolves in the clear ether—Such were we!

We left the fair margin of the beauteous lake of Geneva, and entered the Alpine ravines; tracing to its source the brawling Arve, through the rock-bound valley of Servox, beside the mighty waterfalls, and under the shadow of the inaccessible mountains, we travelled on; while the luxuriant walnut-tree gave place to the dark pine, whose musical branches swung in the wind, and whose upright forms had braved a thousand storms—till the verdant sod, the flowery dell, and shrubbery hill were exchanged for the sky-piercing, untrodden, seedless rock, "the bones of the world, waiting to be clothed with every thing necessary to give life and beauty."[1] Strange that we should seek shelter here! Surely, if, in those countries where earth was wont, like a tender mother, to nourish her children, we had found her a destroyer, we need not seek it here, where stricken by keen penury she seems to shudder through her stony veins. Nor were we mistaken in our conjecture. We vainly sought the vast and ever moving glaciers of Chamounix, rifts of pendant ice, seas of congelated waters, the leafless groves of tempest-battered pines, dells, mere paths for the loud avalanche, and hill-tops, the resort of thunder-storms. Pestilence reigned paramount even here. By the time that day and night, like twin sisters of equal growth, shared equally their dominion over the hours, one by one, beneath the ice-caves, beside the waters springing from the thawed snows of a thousand winters, another and yet another of the remnant of the race of Man, closed their eyes for ever to the light.

Yet we were not quite wrong in seeking a scene like this, whereon to close the drama. Nature, true to the last, consoled us in the very heart of misery. Sublime grandeur of outward objects soothed our hapless hearts, and were in harmony with our desolation. Many sorrows have befallen man during his chequered course; and many a woe-stricken mourner has found himself sole survivor among many. Our misery took its majestic shape and colouring from the vast ruin, that accompanied and made one with it. Thus on lovely earth, many a dark ravine contains a brawling stream, shadowed by romantic rocks, threaded by mossy paths—but all, except this, wanted the mighty back-ground, the towering Alps, whose snowy capes, or bared ridges, lifted us from our dull mortal abode, to the palaces of Nature's own.

This solemn harmony of event and situation regulated our feelings, and gave as it were fitting costume to our last act. Majestic gloom and tragic pomp attended the decease of wretched humanity. The funeral procession of monarchs of old, was transcended by our splendid shews. Near the sources of the Arveiron we performed the rites for, four only excepted, the last of the species. Adrian and I, leaving Clara and Evelyn wrapt in peaceful unobserving slumber, carried the body to this desolate spot, and placed it in those caves of ice beneath the glacier, which rive and split with the slightest sound, and bring destruction on those within the clefts—no bird or beast of prey could here profane the frozen form. So, with hushed steps and in silence, we placed the dead on a bier of ice, and then, departing, stood on the rocky platform beside the river springs. All hushed as we had been, the very striking of the air with our persons had sufficed to disturb the repose of this thawless region; and we had hardly left the cavern, before vast blocks of ice, detaching themselves from the roof, fell, and covered the human image we had deposited within. We had chosen a fair moonlight night, but our journey thither had been long, and the crescent sank behind the western heights by the time we had accomplished our purpose. The snowy mountains and blue glaciers shone in their own light. The rugged and abrupt ravine, which formed one side of Mont Anvert, was opposite to us, the glacier at our side; at our feet Arveiron, white and foaming, dashed over the pointed rocks that jutted into it, and, with whirring spray and ceaseless roar, disturbed the stilly night. Yellow lightnings played around the vast dome of Mont Blanc, silent as the snow-clad rock they illuminated; all was bare, wild, and sublime, while the singing of the pines in melodious murmurings added a gentle interest to the rough magnificence. Now the riving and fall of icy rocks clave the air; now the thunder of the avalanche burst on our ears. In countries whose features are of less magnitude, nature betrays her living powers in the foliage of the trees, in the growth of herbage, in the soft purling of meandering streams; here, endowed with giant attributes, the torrent, the thunder-storm, and the flow of massive waters, display her activity. Such the church-yard, such the requiem, such the eternal congregation, that waited on our companion's funeral!

Nor was it the human form alone which we had placed in this eternal sepulchre, whose obsequies we now celebrated. With this last victim Plague vanished from the earth. Death had never wanted weapons wherewith to destroy life, and we, few and weak as we had become, were still exposed to every other shaft with which his full quiver teemed. But pestilence was absent from among them. For seven years it had had full sway upon earth; she had trod every nook of our spacious globe; she had mingled with the atmosphere, which as a cloak enwraps all our fellow-creatures—the inhabitants of native Europe—the luxurious Asiatic—the swarthy African and free American had been vanquished and destroyed by her. Her barbarous tyranny came to its close here in the rocky vale of Chamounix.

Still recurring scenes of misery and pain, the fruits of this distemper, made no more a part of our lives—the word plague no longer rung in our ears—the aspect of plague incarnate in the human countenance no longer appeared before our eyes. From this moment I saw plague no more. She abdicated her throne, and despoiled herself of her imperial sceptre among the ice rocks that surrounded us. She left solitude and silence co-heirs of her kingdom.

My present feelings are so mingled with the past, that I cannot say whether the knowledge of this change visited us, as we stood on this sterile spot. It seems to me that it did; that a cloud seemed to pass from over us, that a weight was taken from the air; that henceforth we breathed more freely, and raised our heads with some portion of former liberty. Yet we did not hope. We were impressed by the sentiment, that our race was run, but that plague would not be our destroyer. The coming time was as a mighty river, down which a charmed boat is driven, whose mortal steersman knows, that the obvious peril is not the one he needs fear, yet that danger is nigh; and who floats awe-struck under beetling precipices, through the dark and turbid waters—seeing in the distance yet stranger and ruder shapes, towards which he is irresistibly impelled. What would become of us? O for some Delphic oracle, or Pythian maid, to utter the secrets of futurity! O for some Oedipus to solve the riddle of the cruel Sphynx! Such Oedipus was I to be—not divining a word's juggle, but whose agonizing pangs, and sorrow-tainted life were to be the engines, wherewith to lay bare the secrets of destiny, and reveal the meaning of the enigma, whose explanation closed the history of the human race.

Dim fancies, akin to these, haunted our minds, and instilled feelings not unallied to pleasure, as we stood beside this silent tomb of nature, reared by these lifeless mountains, above her living veins, choking her vital principle. "Thus are we left," said Adrian, "two melancholy blasted trees, where once a forest waved. We are left to mourn, and pine, and die. Yet even now we have our duties, which we must string ourselves to fulfil: the duty of bestowing pleasure where we can, and by force of love, irradiating with rainbow hues the tempest of grief. Nor will I repine if in this extremity we preserve what we now possess. Something tells me, Verney, that we need no longer dread our cruel enemy, and I cling with delight to the oracular voice. Though strange, it will be sweet to mark the growth of your little boy, and the development of Clara's young heart. In the midst of a desert world, we are everything to them; and, if we live, it must be our task to make this new mode of life happy to them. At present this is easy, for their childish ideas do not wander into futurity, and the stinging craving for sympathy, and all of love of which our nature is susceptible, is not yet awake within them: we cannot guess what will happen then, when nature asserts her indefeasible and sacred powers; but, long before that time, we may all be cold, as he who lies in yonder tomb of ice. We need only provide for the present, and endeavour to fill with pleasant images the inexperienced fancy of your lovely niece. The scenes which now surround us, vast and sublime as they are, are not such as can best contribute to this work. Nature is here like our fortunes, grand, but too destructive, bare, and rude, to be able to afford delight to her young imagination. Let us descend to the sunny plains of Italy. Winter will soon be here, to clothe this wilderness in double desolation; but we will cross the bleak hill-tops, and lead her to scenes of fertility and beauty, where her path will be adorned with flowers, and the cheery atmosphere inspire pleasure and hope."

In pursuance of this plan we quitted Chamounix on the following day. We had no cause to hasten our steps; no event was transacted beyond our actual sphere to enchain our resolves, so we yielded to every idle whim, and deemed our time well spent, when we could behold the passage of the hours without dismay. We loitered along the lovely Vale of Servox; passed long hours on the bridge, which, crossing the ravine of Arve, commands a prospect of its pine-clothed depths, and the snowy mountains that wall it in. We rambled through romantic Switzerland; till, fear of coming winter leading us forward, the first days of October found us in the valley of La Maurienne, which leads to Cenis. I cannot explain the reluctance we felt at leaving this land of mountains; perhaps it was, that we regarded the Alps as boundaries between our former and our future state of existence, and so clung fondly to what of old we had loved. Perhaps, because we had now so few impulses urging to a choice between two modes of action, we were pleased to preserve the existence of one, and preferred the prospect of what we were to do, to the recollection of what had been done. We felt that for this year danger was past; and we believed that, for some months, we were secured to each other. There was a thrilling, agonizing delight in the thought—it filled the eyes with misty tears, it tore the heart with tumultuous heavings; frailer than the "snow fall in the river," were we each and all—but we strove to give life and individuality to the meteoric course of our several existences, and to feel that no moment escaped us unenjoyed. Thus tottering on the dizzy brink, we were happy. Yes! as we sat beneath the toppling rocks, beside the waterfalls, near

> —Forests, ancient as the hills,

And folding sunny spots of greenery, where the chamois grazed, and the timid squirrel laid up its hoard—descanting on the charms of nature, drinking in the while her unalienable beauties—we were, in an empty world, happy.

Yet, O days of joy—days, when eye spoke to eye, and voices, sweeter than the music of the swinging branches of the pines, or rivulet's gentle murmur, answered mine—yet, O days replete with beatitude, days of loved society—days unutterably dear to me forlorn—pass, O pass before me, making me in your memory forget what I am. Behold, how my streaming eyes blot this senseless paper—behold, how my features are convulsed by agonizing throes, at your mere recollection, now that, alone, my tears flow, my lips quiver, my cries fill the air, unseen, unmarked, unheard! Yet, O yet, days of delight! let me dwell on your long-drawn hours!

As the cold increased upon us, we passed the Alps, and descended into Italy. At the uprising of morn, we sat at our repast, and cheated our regrets by gay sallies or learned disquisitions. The live-long day we sauntered on, still keeping in view the end of our journey, but careless of the hour of its completion. As the evening star shone out, and the orange sunset, far in the west, marked the position of the dear land we had for ever left, talk, thought enchaining, made the hours fly—O that we had lived thus for ever and for ever! Of what consequence was it to our four hearts, that they alone were the fountains of life in the wide world? As far as mere individual sentiment was concerned, we had rather be left thus united together, than if, each alone in a populous desert of unknown men, we had wandered truly companionless till life's last term. In this manner, we endeavoured to console each other; in this manner, true philosophy taught us to reason.

It was the delight of Adrian and myself to wait on Clara, naming her the little queen of the world, ourselves her humblest servitors. When we arrived at a town, our first care was to select for her its most choice abode; to make sure that no harrowing relic remained of its former inhabitants; to seek food for her, and minister to her wants with assiduous tenderness. Clara entered into our scheme with childish gaiety. Her chief business was to attend on Evelyn; but it was her sport to array herself in splendid robes, adorn herself with sunny gems, and ape a princely state. Her religion, deep and pure, did not teach her to refuse to blunt thus the keen sting of regret; her youthful vivacity made her enter, heart and soul, into these strange masquerades.

We had resolved to pass the ensuing winter at Milan, which, as being a large and luxurious city, would afford us choice of homes. We had descended the Alps, and left far behind their vast forests and mighty crags. We entered smiling Italy. Mingled grass and corn grew in her plains, the unpruned vines threw their luxuriant branches around the elms. The grapes, overripe, had fallen on the ground, or hung purple, or burnished green, among the red and yellow leaves. The ears of standing corn winnowed to emptiness by the spendthrift winds; the fallen foliage of the trees, the weed-grown brooks, the dusky olive, now spotted with its blackened fruit; the chestnuts, to which the squirrel only was harvest-man; all plenty, and yet, alas! all poverty, painted in wondrous hues and fantastic groupings this land of beauty. In the towns, in the voiceless towns, we visited the churches, adorned by pictures, master-pieces of art, or galleries of statues—while in this genial clime the animals, in new found liberty, rambled through the gorgeous palaces, and hardly feared our forgotten aspect. The dove-coloured oxen turned their full eyes on us, and paced slowly by; a startling throng of silly sheep, with pattering feet, would start up in some chamber, formerly dedicated to the repose of beauty, and rush, huddling past us, down the marble staircase into the street, and again in at the first open door, taking unrebuked possession of hallowed sanctuary, or kingly council-chamber. We no longer started at these occurrences, nor at worse exhibition of change—when the palace had become a mere tomb, pregnant with fetid stench, strewn with the dead; and we could perceive how pestilence and fear had played strange antics, chasing the luxurious dame to the dank fields and bare cottage; gathering, among carpets of Indian woof, and beds of silk, the rough peasant, or the deformed half-human shape of the wretched beggar.

We arrived at Milan, and stationed ourselves in the Vice-Roy's palace. Here we made laws for ourselves, dividing our day, and fixing distinct occupations for each hour. In the morning we rode in the adjoining country, or wandered through the palaces, in search of pictures or antiquities. In the evening we assembled to read or to converse. There were few books that we dared read; few, that did not cruelly deface the painting we bestowed on our solitude, by recalling combinations and emotions never more to be experienced by us. Metaphysical disquisition; fiction, which wandering from all reality, lost itself in self-created errors; poets of times so far gone by, that to read of them was as to read of Atlantis and Utopia; or such as referred to nature only, and the workings of one particular mind; but most of all, talk, varied and ever new, beguiled our hours.

While we paused thus in our onward career towards death, time held on its accustomed course. Still and for ever did the earth roll on, enthroned in her atmospheric car, speeded by the force of the invisible coursers of never-erring necessity. And now, this dew-drop in the sky, this ball, ponderous with mountains, lucent with waves, passing from the short tyranny of watery Pisces and the frigid Ram, entered the radiant demesne of Taurus and the Twins. There, fanned by vernal airs, the Spirit of Beauty sprung from her cold repose; and, with winnowing wings and soft pacing feet, set a girdle of verdure around the earth, sporting among the violets, hiding within the springing foliage of the trees, tripping lightly down the radiant streams into the sunny deep. "For lo! winter is past, the rain is over and gone; the flowers appear on the earth, the time of the singing of birds is come, and the voice of the turtle is heard in our land; the fig tree putteth forth her green figs, and the vines, with the tender grape, give a good smell."[2] Thus was it in the time of the ancient regal poet; thus was it now.

Yet how could we miserable hail the approach of this delightful season? We hoped indeed that death did not now as heretofore walk in its shadow; yet, left as we were alone to each other, we looked in each other's faces with enquiring eyes, not daring altogether to trust to our presentiments, and endeavouring to divine which would be the hapless survivor to the other three. We were to pass the summer at the lake of Como, and thither we removed as soon as spring grew to her maturity, and the snow disappeared from the hill tops. Ten miles from Como, under the steep heights of the eastern mountains, by the margin of the lake, was a villa called the Pliniana, from its being built on the site of a fountain, whose periodical ebb and flow is described by the younger Pliny in his letters. The house had nearly fallen into ruin, till in the year 2090, an English nobleman had bought it, and fitted it up with every luxury. Two large halls, hung with splendid tapestry, and paved with marble, opened on each side of a court, of whose two other sides one overlooked the deep dark lake, and the other was bounded by a mountain, from whose stony side gushed, with roar and splash, the celebrated fountain. Above, underwood of myrtle and tufts of odorous plants crowned the rock, while the star-pointing giant cypresses reared themselves in the blue air, and the recesses of the hills were adorned with the luxuriant growth of chestnut-trees. Here we fixed our summer residence. We had a lovely skiff, in which we sailed, now stemming the midmost waves, now coasting the over-hanging and craggy banks, thick sown with evergreens, which dipped their shining leaves in the waters, and were mirrored in many a little bay and creek of waters of translucent darkness. Here orange plants bloomed, here birds poured forth melodious hymns; and here, during spring, the cold snake emerged from the clefts, and basked on the sunny terraces of rock.

Were we not happy in this paradisiacal retreat? If some kind spirit had whispered forgetfulness to us, methinks we should have been happy here, where the precipitous mountains, nearly pathless, shut from our view the far fields of desolate earth, and with small exertion of the imagination, we might fancy that the cities were still resonant with popular hum, and the peasant still guided his plough through the furrow, and that we, the world's free denizens, enjoyed a voluntary exile, and not a remediless cutting off from our extinct species.

Not one among us enjoyed the beauty of this scenery so much as Clara. Before we quitted Milan, a change had taken place in her habits and manners. She lost her gaiety, she laid aside her sports, and assumed an almost vestal plainness of attire. She shunned us, retiring with Evelyn to some distant chamber or silent nook; nor did she enter into his pastimes with the same zest as she was wont, but would sit and watch him with sadly tender smiles, and eyes bright with tears, yet without a word of complaint. She approached us timidly, avoided our caresses, nor shook off her embarrassment till some serious discussion or lofty theme called her for awhile out of herself. Her beauty grew as a rose, which, opening to the summer wind, discloses leaf after leaf till the sense aches with its excess of loveliness. A slight and variable colour tinged her cheeks, and her motions seemed attuned by some hidden harmony of surpassing sweetness. We redoubled our tenderness and earnest attentions. She received them with grateful smiles, that fled swift as sunny beam from a glittering wave on an April day.

Our only acknowledged point of sympathy with her, appeared to be Evelyn. This dear little fellow was a comforter and delight to us beyond all words. His buoyant spirit, and his innocent ignorance of our vast calamity, were balm to us, whose thoughts and feelings were over-wrought and spun out in the immensity of speculative sorrow. To cherish, to caress, to amuse him was the common task of all. Clara, who felt towards him in some degree like a young mother, gratefully acknowledged our kindness towards him. To me, O! to me, who saw the clear brows and soft eyes of the beloved of my heart, my lost and ever dear Idris, re-born in his gentle face, to me he was dear even to pain; if I pressed him to my heart, methought I clasped a real and living part of her, who had lain there through long years of youthful happiness.

It was the custom of Adrian and myself to go out each day in our skiff to forage in the adjacent country. In these expeditions we were seldom accompanied by Clara or her little charge, but our return was an hour of hilarity. Evelyn ransacked our stores with childish eagerness, and we always brought some new found gift for our fair companion. Then too we made discoveries of lovely scenes or gay palaces, whither in the evening we all proceeded. Our sailing expeditions were most divine, and with a fair wind or transverse course we cut the liquid waves; and, if talk failed under the pressure of thought, I had my clarionet with me, which awoke the echoes, and gave the change to our careful minds. Clara at such times often returned to her former habits of free converse and gay sally; and though our four hearts alone beat in the world, those four hearts were happy.

One day, on our return from the town of Como, with a laden boat, we expected as usual to be met at the port by Clara and Evelyn, and we were somewhat surprised to see the beach vacant. I, as my nature prompted, would not prognosticate evil, but explained it away as a mere casual incident. Not so Adrian. He was seized with sudden trembling and apprehension, and he called to me with vehemence to steer quickly for land, and, when near, leapt from the boat, half falling into the water; and, scrambling up the steep bank, hastened along the narrow strip of garden, the only level space between the lake and the mountain. I followed without delay; the garden and inner court were empty, so was the house, whose every room we visited. Adrian called loudly upon Clara's name, and was about to rush up the near mountain-path, when the door of a summer-house at the end of the garden slowly opened, and Clara appeared, not advancing towards us, but leaning against a column of the building with blanched cheeks, in a posture of utter despondency. Adrian sprang towards her with a cry of joy, and folded her delightedly in his arms. She withdrew from his embrace, and, without a word, again entered the summer-house. Her quivering lips, her despairing heart refused to afford her voice to express our misfortune. Poor little Evelyn had, while playing with her, been seized with sudden fever, and now lay torpid and speechless on a little couch in the summer-house.

For a whole fortnight we unceasingly watched beside the poor child, as his life declined under the ravages of a virulent typhus. His little form and tiny lineaments encaged the embryo of the world-spanning mind of man. Man's nature, brimful of passions and affections, would have had an home in that little heart, whose swift pulsations hurried towards their close. His small hand's fine mechanism, now flaccid and unbent, would in the growth of sinew and muscle, have achieved works of beauty or of strength. His tender rosy feet would have trod in firm manhood the bowers and glades of earth— these reflections were now of little use: he lay, thought and strength suspended, waiting unresisting the final blow.

We watched at his bedside, and when the access of fever was on him, we neither spoke nor looked at each other, marking only his obstructed breath and the mortal glow that tinged his sunken cheek, the heavy death that weighed on his eyelids. It is a trite evasion to say, that words could not express our long drawn agony; yet how can words image sensations, whose tormenting keenness throw us back, as it were, on the deep roots and hidden foundations of our nature, which shake our being with earth-quake-throe, so that we leave to confide in accustomed feelings which like mother-earth support us, and cling to some vain imagination or deceitful hope, which will soon be buried in the ruins occasioned by the final shock. I have called that period a fortnight, which we passed watching the changes of the sweet child's malady—and such it might have been—at night, we wondered to find another day gone, while each particular hour seemed endless. Day and night were exchanged for one another uncounted; we slept hardly at all, nor did we even quit his room, except when a pang of grief seized us, and we retired from each other for a short period to conceal our sobs and tears. We endeavoured in vain to abstract Clara from this deplorable scene. She sat, hour after hour, looking at him, now softly arranging his pillow, and, while he had power to swallow, administered his drink. At length the moment of his death came: the blood paused in its flow —his eyes opened, and then closed again: without convulsion or sigh, the frail tenement was left vacant of its spiritual inhabitant.

I have heard that the sight of the dead has confirmed materialists in their belief. I ever felt otherwise. Was that my child—that moveless decaying inanimation? My child was enraptured by my caresses; his dear voice cloathed with meaning articulations his thoughts, otherwise inaccessible; his smile was a ray of the soul, and the same soul sat upon its throne in his eyes. I turn from this mockery of what he was. Take, O earth, thy debt! freely and for ever I consign to thee the garb thou didst afford. But thou, sweet child, amiable and beloved boy, either thy spirit has sought a fitter dwelling, or, shrined in my heart, thou livest while it lives.

We placed his remains under a cypress, the upright mountain being scooped out to receive them. And then Clara said, "If you wish me to live, take me from hence. There is something in this scene of transcendent beauty, in these trees, and hills and waves, that for ever whisper to me, leave thy cumbrous flesh, and make a part of us. I earnestly entreat you to take me away."

So on the fifteenth of August we bade adieu to our villa, and the embowering shades of this abode of beauty; to calm bay and noisy waterfall; to Evelyn's little grave we bade farewell! and then, with heavy hearts, we departed on our pilgrimage towards Rome.

---

1. Mary Wollstonecraft's Letters from Norway.
2. Solomon's Song.

✳ *9* ✳

Now—soft awhile—have I arrived so near the end? Yes! it is all over now—a step or two over those new made graves, and the wearisome way is done. Can I accomplish my task? Can I streak my paper with words capacious of the grand conclusion? Arise, black Melancholy! quit thy Cimmerian solitude! Bring with thee murky fogs from hell, which may drink up the day; bring blight and pestiferous exhalations, which, entering the hollow caverns and breathing places of earth, may fill her stony veins with corruption, so that not only herbage may no longer flourish, the trees may rot, and the rivers run with gall—but the everlasting mountains be decomposed, and the mighty deep putrify, and the genial atmosphere which clips the globe, lose all powers of generation and sustenance. Do this, sad visaged power, while I write, while eyes read these pages.

And who will read them? Beware, tender offspring of the re-born world— beware, fair being, with human heart, yet untamed by care, and human brow, yet unploughed by time— beware, lest the cheerful current of thy blood be checked, thy golden locks turn grey, thy sweet dimpling smiles be changed to fixed, harsh wrinkles! Let not day look on these lines, lest garish day waste, turn pale, and die. Seek a cypress grove, whose moaning boughs will be harmony befitting; seek some cave, deep embowered in earth's dark entrails, where no light will penetrate, save that which struggles, red and flickering, through a single fissure, staining thy page with grimmest livery of death.

There is a painful confusion in my brain, which refuses to delineate distinctly succeeding events. Sometimes the irradiation of my friend's gentle smile comes before me; and methinks its light spans and fills eternity—then, again, I feel the gasping throes—

We quitted Como, and in compliance with Adrian's earnest desire, we took Venice in our way to Rome. There was something to the English peculiarly attractive in the idea of this wave-encircled, island-enthroned city. Adrian had never seen it. We went down the Po and the Brenta in a boat; and, the days proving intolerably hot, we rested in the bordering palaces during the day, travelling through the night, when darkness made the bordering banks indistinct, and our solitude less remarkable; when the wandering moon lit the waves that divided before our prow, and the night-wind filled our sails, and the murmuring stream, waving trees, and swelling canvass, accorded in harmonious strain. Clara, long overcome by excessive grief, had to a great degree cast aside her timid, cold reserve, and received our attentions with grateful tenderness. While Adrian with poetic fervour discoursed of the glorious nations of the dead, of the beauteous earth and the fate of man, she crept near him, drinking in his speech with silent pleasure. We banished from our talk, and as much as possible from our thoughts, the knowledge of our desolation. And it would be incredible to an inhabitant of cities, to one among a busy throng, to what extent we succeeded. It was as a man confined in a dungeon, whose small and grated rift at first renders the doubtful light more sensibly obscure, till, the visual orb having drunk in the beam, and adapted itself to its scantiness, he finds that clear noon inhabits his cell. So we, a simple triad on empty earth, were multiplied to each other, till we became all in all. We stood like trees, whose roots are loosened by the wind, which support one another, leaning and clinging with increased fervour while the wintry storms howl. Thus we floated down the widening stream of the Po, sleeping when the cicale sang, awake with the stars. We entered the narrower banks of the Brenta, and arrived at the shore of the Laguna at sunrise on the sixth of September. The bright orb slowly rose from behind its cupolas and towers, and shed its penetrating light upon the glassy waters. Wrecks of gondolas, and some few uninjured ones, were strewed on the beach at Fusina. We embarked in one of these for the widowed daughter of ocean, who, abandoned and fallen, sat forlorn on her propping isles, looking towards the far mountains of Greece. We rowed lightly over the Laguna, and entered Canale Grande. The tide ebbed sullenly from out the broken portals and violated halls of Venice: sea weed and sea monsters were left on the blackened marble, while the salt ooze defaced the matchless works of art that adorned their walls, and the sea gull flew out from the shattered window. In the midst of this appalling ruin of the monuments of man's power, nature asserted her ascendancy, and shone more beauteous from the contrast. The radiant waters hardly trembled, while the rippling waves made many sided mirrors to the sun; the blue immensity, seen beyond Lido, stretched far, unspecked by boat, so tranquil, so lovely, that it seemed to invite us to quit the land strewn with ruins, and to seek refuge from sorrow and fear on its placid extent.

We saw the ruins of this hapless city from the height of the tower of San Marco, immediately under us, and turned with sickening hearts to the sea, which, though it be a grave, rears no monument, discloses no ruin. Evening had come apace. The sun set in calm majesty behind the misty summits of the Apennines, and its golden and roseate hues painted the mountains of the opposite shore. "That land," said Adrian, "tinged with the last glories of the day, is Greece." Greece! The sound had a responsive chord in the bosom of Clara. She vehemently reminded us that we had promised to take her once again to Greece, to the tomb of her parents. Why go to Rome? what should we do at Rome? We might take one of the many vessels to be found here, embark in it, and steer right for Albania.

I objected the dangers of ocean, and the distance of the mountains we saw, from Athens; a distance which, from the savage uncultivation of the country, was almost impassable. Adrian, who was delighted with Clara's proposal, obviated these objections. The season was favourable; the north-west that blew would take us transversely across the gulph; and then we might find, in some abandoned port, a light Greek caique, adapted for such navigation, and run down the coast of the Morea, and, passing over the Isthmus of Corinth, without much land-travelling or fatigue, find ourselves at Athens. This appeared to me wild talk; but the sea, glowing with a thousand purple hues, looked so brilliant and safe; my beloved companions were so earnest, so determined, that, when Adrian said, "Well, though it is not exactly what you wish, yet consent, to please me"—I could no longer refuse. That evening we selected a vessel, whose size just seemed fitted for our enterprise; we bent the sails and put the rigging in order, and reposing that night in one of the city's thousand palaces, agreed to embark at sunrise the following morning.

> When winds that move not its calm surface, sweep
> The azure sea, I love the land no more;
> The smiles of the serene and tranquil deep
> Tempt my unquiet mind—

Thus said Adrian, quoting a translation of Moschus's poem, as in the clear morning light, we rowed over the Laguna, past Lido, into the open sea—I would have added in continuation,

> But when the roar
> Of ocean's gray abyss resounds, and foam
> Gathers upon the sea, and vast waves burst—

But my friends declared that such verses were evil augury; so in cheerful mood we left the shallow waters, and, when out at sea, unfurled our sails to catch the favourable breeze. The laughing morning air filled them, while sun-light bathed earth, sky and ocean—the placid waves divided to receive our keel, and playfully kissed the dark sides of our little skiff, murmuring a welcome; as land receded, still the blue expanse, most waveless, twin sister to the azure empyrean, afforded smooth conduct to our bark. As the air and waters were tranquil and balmy, so were our minds steeped in quiet. In comparison with the unstained deep, funereal earth appeared a grave, its high rocks and stately mountains were but monuments, its trees the plumes of a herse, the brooks and rivers brackish with tears for departed man. Farewell to desolate towns —to fields with their savage intermixture of corn and weeds—to ever multiplying relics of our lost species. Ocean, we commit ourselves to thee —even as the patriarch of old floated above the drowned world, let us be saved, as thus we betake ourselves to thy perennial flood.

Adrian sat at the helm; I attended to the rigging, the breeze right aft filled our swelling canvas, and we ran before it over the untroubled deep. The wind died away at noon; its idle breath just permitted us to hold our course. As lazy, fair-weather sailors, careless of the coming hour, we talked gaily of our coasting voyage, of our arrival at Athens. We would make our home of one of the Cyclades, and there in myrtle-groves, amidst perpetual spring, fanned by the wholesome sea-breezes—we would live long years in beatific union—Was there such a thing as death in the world?—

The sun passed its zenith, and lingered down the stainless floor of heaven. Lying in the boat, my face turned up to the sky, I thought I saw on its blue white, marbled streaks, so slight, so immaterial, that now I said— They are there—and now, It is a mere imagination. A sudden fear stung me while I gazed; and, starting up, and running to the prow,—as I stood, my hair was gently lifted on my brow—a dark line of ripples appeared to the east, gaining rapidly on us— my breathless remark to Adrian, was followed by the flapping of the canvas, as the adverse wind struck it, and our boat lurched—swift as speech, the web of the storm thickened over head, the sun went down red, the dark sea was strewed with foam, and our skiff rose and fell in its increasing furrows.

Behold us now in our frail tenement, hemmed in by hungry, roaring waves, buffeted by winds. In the inky east two vast clouds, sailing contrary ways, met; the lightning leapt forth, and the hoarse thunder muttered. Again in the south, the clouds replied, and the forked stream of fire running along the black sky, shewed us the appalling piles of clouds, now met and obliterated by the heaving waves. Great God! And we alone—we three— alone—alone—sole dwellers on the sea and on the earth, we three must perish! The vast universe, its myriad worlds, and the plains of boundless earth which we had left—the extent of shoreless sea around —contracted to my view—they and all that they contained, shrunk up to one point, even to our tossing bark, freighted with glorious humanity.

A convulsion of despair crossed the love-beaming face of Adrian, while with set teeth he murmured, "Yet they shall be saved!" Clara, visited by an human pang, pale and trembling, crept near him—he looked on her with an encouraging smile—"Do you fear, sweet girl? O, do not fear, we shall soon be on shore!"

The darkness prevented me from seeing the changes of her countenance; but her voice was clear and sweet, as she replied, "Why should I fear? neither sea nor storm can harm us, if mighty destiny or the ruler of destiny does not permit. And then the stinging fear of surviving either of you, is not here—one death will clasp us undivided."

Meanwhile we took in all our sails, save a gib; and, as soon as we might without danger, changed our course, running with the wind for the Italian shore. Dark night mixed everything; we hardly discerned the white crests of the murderous surges, except when lightning made brief noon, and drank the darkness, shewing us our danger, and restoring us to double night. We were all silent, except when Adrian, as steersman, made an encouraging observation. Our little shell obeyed the rudder miraculously well, and ran along on the top of the waves, as if she had been an offspring of the sea, and the angry mother sheltered her endangered child.

I sat at the prow, watching our course; when suddenly I heard the waters break with redoubled fury. We were certainly near the shore—at the same time I cried, "About there!" and a broad lightning filling the concave, shewed us for one moment the level beach a-head, disclosing even the sands, and stunted, ooze-sprinkled beds of reeds, that grew at high water mark. Again it was dark, and we drew in our breath with such content as one may, who, while fragments of volcano-hurled rock darken the air, sees a vast mass ploughing the ground immediately at his feet. What to do we knew not —the breakers here, there, everywhere, encompassed us—they roared, and dashed, and flung their hated spray in our faces. With considerable difficulty and danger we succeeded at length in altering our course, and stretched out from shore. I urged my companions to prepare for the wreck of our little skiff, and to bind themselves to some oar or spar which might suffice to float them. I was myself an excellent swimmer—the very sight of the sea was wont to raise in me such sensations, as a huntsman experiences, when he hears a pack of hounds in full cry; I loved to feel the waves wrap me and strive to overpower me; while I, lord of myself, moved this way or that, in spite of their angry buffetings. Adrian also could swim—but the weakness of his frame prevented him from feeling pleasure in the exercise, or acquiring any great expertness. But what power could the strongest swimmer oppose to the overpowering violence of ocean in its fury? My efforts to prepare my companions were rendered nearly futile —for the roaring breakers prevented our hearing one another speak, and the waves, that broke continually over our boat, obliged me to exert all my strength in lading the water out, as fast as it came in. The while darkness, palpable and rayless, hemmed us round, dissipated only by the lightning; sometimes we beheld thunderbolts, fiery red, fall into the sea, and at intervals vast spouts stooped from the clouds, churning the wild ocean, which rose to meet them; while the fierce gale bore the rack onwards, and they were lost in the chaotic mingling of sky and sea. Our gunwales had been torn away, our single sail had been rent to ribbands, and borne down the stream of the wind. We had cut away our mast, and lightened the boat of all she contained—Clara attempted to assist me in heaving the water from the hold, and, as she turned her eyes to look on the lightning, I could discern by that momentary gleam, that resignation had conquered every fear. We have a power given us in any worst extremity, which props the else feeble mind of man, and enables us to endure the most savage tortures with a stillness of soul which in hours of happiness we could not have imagined. A calm, more dreadful in truth than the tempest, allayed the wild beatings of my heart—a calm like that of the gamester, the suicide, and the murderer, when the last die is on the point of being cast—while the poisoned cup is at the lips,—as the death-blow is about to be given.

Hours passed thus—hours which might write old age on the face of beardless youth, and grizzle the silky hair of infancy—-hours, while the chaotic uproar continued, while each dread gust transcended in fury the one before, and our skiff hung on the breaking wave, and then rushed into the valley below, and trembled and spun between the watery precipices that seemed most to meet above her. For a moment the gale paused, and ocean sank to comparative silence—it was a breathless interval; the wind which, as a practised leaper, had gathered itself up before it sprung, now with terrific roar rushed over the sea, and the waves struck our stern. Adrian exclaimed that the rudder was gone;—"We are lost," cried Clara, "Save yourselves—O save yourselves!" The lightning shewed me the poor girl half buried in the water at the bottom of the boat; as she was sinking in it Adrian caught her up, and sustained her in his arms. We were without a rudder—we rushed prow foremost into the vast billows piled up a-head— they broke over and filled the tiny skiff; one scream I heard—one cry that we were gone, I uttered; I found myself in the waters; darkness was around. When the light of the tempest flashed, I saw the keel of our upset boat close to me—I clung to this, grasping it with clenched hand and nails, while I endeavoured during each flash to discover any appearance of my companions. I thought I saw Adrian at no great distance from me, clinging to an oar; I sprung from my hold, and with energy beyond my human strength, I dashed aside the waters as I strove to lay hold of him. As that hope failed, instinctive love of life animated me, and feelings of contention, as if a hostile will combated with mine. I breasted the surges, and flung them from me, as I would the opposing front and sharpened claws of a lion about to enfang my bosom. When I had been beaten down by one wave, I rose on another, while I felt bitter pride curl my lip.

Ever since the storm had carried us near the shore, we had never attained any great distance from it. With every flash I saw the bordering coast; yet the progress I made was small, while each wave, as it receded, carried me back into ocean's far abysses. At one moment I felt my foot touch the sand, and then again I was in deep water; my arms began to lose their power of motion; my breath failed me under the influence of the strangling waters— a thousand wild and delirious thoughts crossed me: as well as I can now recall them, my chief feeling was, how sweet it would be to lay my head on the quiet earth, where the surges would no longer strike my weakened frame, nor the sound of waters ring in my ears—to attain this repose, not to save my life, I made a last effort—the shelving shore suddenly presented a footing for me. I rose, and was again thrown down by the breakers—a point of rock to which I was enabled to cling, gave me a moment's respite; and then, taking advantage of the ebbing of the waves, I ran forwards— gained the dry sands, and fell senseless on the oozy reeds that sprinkled them.

I must have lain long deprived of life; for when first, with a sickening feeling, I unclosed my eyes, the light of morning met them. Great change had taken place meanwhile: grey dawn dappled the flying clouds, which sped onwards, leaving visible at intervals vast lakes of pure ether. A fountain of light arose in an increasing stream from the east, behind the waves of the Adriatic, changing the grey to a roseate hue, and then flooding sky and sea with aerial gold.

A kind of stupor followed my fainting; my senses were alive, but memory was extinct. The blessed respite was short—a snake lurked near me to sting me into life—on the first retrospective emotion I would have started up, but my limbs refused to obey me; my knees trembled, the muscles had lost all power. I still believed that I might find one of my beloved companions cast like me, half alive, on the beach; and I strove in every way to restore my frame to the use of its animal functions. I wrung the brine from my hair; and the rays of the risen sun soon visited me with genial warmth. With the restoration of my bodily powers, my mind became in some degree aware of the universe of misery, henceforth to be its dwelling. I ran to the water's edge, calling on the beloved names. Ocean drank in, and absorbed my feeble voice, replying with pitiless roar. I climbed a near tree: the level sands bounded by a pine forest, and the sea clipped round by the horizon, was all that I could discern. In vain I extended my researches along the beach; the mast we had thrown overboard, with tangled cordage, and remnants of a sail, was the sole relic land received of our wreck. Sometimes I stood still, and wrung my hands. I accused earth and sky —the universal machine and the Almighty power that misdirected it. Again I threw myself on the sands, and then the sighing wind, mimicking a human cry, roused me to bitter, fallacious hope. Assuredly if any little bark or smallest canoe had been near, I should have sought the savage plains of ocean, found the dear remains of my lost ones, and clinging round them, have shared their grave.

The day passed thus; each moment contained eternity; although when hour after hour had gone by, I wondered at the quick flight of time. Yet even now I had not drunk the bitter potion to the dregs; I was not yet persuaded of my loss; I did not yet feel in every pulsation, in every nerve, in every thought, that I remained alone of my race,—that I was the LAST MAN.

The day had clouded over, and a drizzling rain set in at sunset. Even the eternal skies weep, I thought; is there any shame then, that mortal man should spend himself in tears? I remembered the ancient fables, in which human beings are described as dissolving away through weeping into ever-gushing fountains. Ah! that so it were; and then my destiny would be in some sort akin to the watery death of Adrian and Clara. Oh! grief is fantastic; it weaves a web on which to trace the history of its woe from every form and change around; it incorporates itself with all living nature; it finds sustenance in every object; as light, it fills all things, and, like light, it gives its own colours to all.

I had wandered in my search to some distance from the spot on which I had been cast, and came to one of those watch-towers, which at stated distances line the Italian shore. I was glad of shelter, glad to find a work of human hands, after I had gazed so long on nature's drear barrenness; so I entered, and ascended the rough winding staircase into the guard-room. So far was fate kind, that no harrowing vestige remained of its former inhabitants; a few planks laid across two iron tressels, and strewed with the dried leaves of Indian corn, was the bed presented to me; and an open chest, containing some half mouldered biscuit, awakened an appetite, which perhaps existed before, but of which, until now, I was not aware. Thirst also, violent and parching, the result of the sea-water I had drank, and of the exhaustion of my frame, tormented me. Kind nature had gifted the supply of these wants with pleasurable sensations, so that I—even I!—was refreshed and calmed, as I ate of this sorry fare, and drank a little of the sour wine which half filled a flask left in this abandoned dwelling. Then I stretched myself on the bed, not to be disdained by the victim of shipwreck. The earthy smell of the dried leaves was balm to my sense after the hateful odour of sea-weed. I forgot my state of loneliness. I neither looked backward nor forward; my senses were hushed to repose; I fell asleep and dreamed of all dear inland scenes, of hay-makers, of the shepherd's whistle to his dog, when he demanded his help to drive the flock to fold; of sights and sounds peculiar to my boyhood's mountain life, which I had long forgotten.

I awoke in a painful agony—for I fancied that ocean, breaking its bounds, carried away the fixed continent and deep rooted mountains, together with the streams I loved, the woods, and the flocks—it raged around, with that continued and dreadful roar which had accompanied the last wreck of surviving humanity. As my waking sense returned, the bare walls of the guard room closed round me, and the rain pattered against the single window. How dreadful it is, to emerge from the oblivion of slumber, and to receive as a good morrow the mute wailing of one's own hapless heart —to return from the land of deceptive dreams, to the heavy knowledge of unchanged disaster!—Thus was it with me, now, and for ever! The sting of other griefs might be blunted by time; and even mine yielded sometimes during the day, to the pleasure inspired by the imagination or the senses; but I never look first upon the morning-light but with my fingers pressed tight on my bursting heart, and my soul deluged with the interminable flood of hopeless misery. Now I awoke for the first time in the dead world—I awoke alone—and the dull dirge of the sea, heard even amidst the rain, recalled me to the reflection of the wretch I had become. The sound came like a reproach, a scoff—like the sting of remorse in the soul—I gasped—the veins and muscles of my throat swelled, suffocating me. I put my fingers to my ears, I buried my head in the leaves of my couch, I would have dived to the centre to lose hearing of that hideous moan.

But another task must be mine—again I visited the detested beach— again I vainly looked far and wide—again I raised my unanswered cry, lifting up the only voice that could ever again force the mute air to syllable the human thought.

What a pitiable, forlorn, disconsolate being I was! My very aspect and garb told the tale of my despair. My hair was matted and wild—my limbs soiled with salt ooze; while at sea, I had thrown off those of my garments that encumbered me, and the rain drenched the thin summer-clothing I had retained—my feet were bare, and the stunted reeds and broken shells made them bleed—the while, I hurried to and fro, now looking earnestly on some distant rock which, islanded in the sands, bore for a moment a deceptive appearance—now with flashing eyes reproaching the murderous ocean for its unutterable cruelty.

For a moment I compared myself to that monarch of the waste—Robinson Crusoe. We had been both thrown companionless—he on the shore of a desolate island: I on that of a desolate world. I was rich in the so called goods of life. If I turned my steps from the near barren scene, and entered any of the earth's million cities, I should find their wealth stored up for my accommodation—clothes, food, books, and a choice of dwelling beyond the command of the princes of former times—every climate was subject to my selection, while he was obliged to toil in the acquirement of every necessary, and was the inhabitant of a tropical island, against whose heats and storms he could obtain small shelter.—Viewing the question thus, who would not have preferred the Sybarite enjoyments I could command, the philosophic leisure, and ample intellectual resources, to his life of labour and peril? Yet he was far happier than I: for he could hope, nor hope in vain—the destined vessel at last arrived, to bear him to countrymen and kindred, where the events of his solitude became a fire-side tale. To none could I ever relate the story of my adversity; no hope had I. He knew that, beyond the ocean which begirt his lonely island, thousands lived whom the sun enlightened when it shone also on him: beneath the meridian sun and visiting moon, I alone bore human features; I alone could give articulation to thought; and, when I slept, both day and night were unbeheld of any. He had fled from his fellows, and was transported with terror at the print of a human foot. I would have knelt down and worshipped the same. The wild and cruel Caribbee, the merciless Cannibal—or worse than these, the uncouth, brute, and remorseless veteran in the vices of civilization, would have been to me a beloved companion, a treasure dearly prized—his nature would be kin to mine; his form cast in the same mould; human blood would flow in his veins; a human sympathy must link us for ever. It cannot be that I shall never behold a fellow being more!—never! —never!—not in the course of years!—Shall I wake, and speak to none, pass the interminable hours, my soul, islanded in the world, a solitary point, surrounded by vacuum? Will day follow day endlessly thus? —No! no! a God rules the world—providence has not exchanged its golden sceptre for an aspic's sting. Away! let me fly from the ocean-grave, let me depart from this barren nook, paled in, as it is, from access by its own desolateness; let me tread once again the paved towns; step over the threshold of man's dwellings, and most certainly I shall find this thought a horrible vision—a maddening, but evanescent dream.

I entered Ravenna, (the town nearest to the spot whereon I had been cast), before the second sun had set on the empty world; I saw many living creatures; oxen, and horses, and dogs, but there was no man among them; I entered a cottage, it was vacant; I ascended the marble stairs of a palace, the bats and the owls were nestled in the tapestry; I stepped softly, not to awaken the sleeping town: I rebuked a dog, that by yelping disturbed the sacred stillness; I would not believe that all was as it seemed—The world was not dead, but I was mad; I was deprived of sight, hearing, and sense of touch; I was labouring under the force of a spell, which permitted me to behold all sights of earth, except its human inhabitants; they were pursuing their ordinary labours. Every house had its inmate; but I could not perceive them. If I could have deluded myself into a belief of this kind, I should have been far more satisfied. But my brain, tenacious of its reason, refused to lend itself to such imaginations—and though I endeavoured to play the antic to myself, I knew that I, the offspring of man, during long years one among many—now remained sole survivor of my species.

The sun sank behind the western hills; I had fasted since the preceding evening, but, though faint and weary, I loathed food, nor ceased, while yet a ray of light remained, to pace the lonely streets. Night came on, and sent every living creature but me to the bosom of its mate. It was my solace, to blunt my mental agony by personal hardship—of the thousand beds around, I would not seek the luxury of one; I lay down on the pavement,—a cold marble step served me for a pillow—midnight came; and then, though not before, did my wearied lids shut out the sight of the twinkling stars, and their reflex on the pavement near. Thus I passed the second night of my desolation.

I AWOKE IN THE MORNING, just as the higher windows of the lofty houses received the first beams of the rising sun. The birds were chirping, perched on the windows sills and deserted thresholds of the doors. I awoke, and my first thought was, Adrian and Clara are dead. I no longer shall be hailed by their good-morrow—or pass the long day in their society. I shall never see them more. The ocean has robbed me of them—stolen their hearts of love from their breasts, and given over to corruption what was dearer to me than light, or life, or hope.

I was an untaught shepherd-boy, when Adrian deigned to confer on me his friendship. The best years of my life had been passed with him. All I had possessed of this world's goods, of happiness, knowledge, or virtue—I owed to him. He had, in his person, his intellect, and rare qualities, given a glory to my life, which without him it had never known. Beyond all other beings he had taught me, that goodness, pure and single, can be an attribute of man. It was a sight for angels to congregate to behold, to view him lead, govern, and solace, the last days of the human race.

My lovely Clara also was lost to me—she who last of the daughters of man, exhibited all those feminine and maiden virtues, which poets, painters, and sculptors, have in their various languages strove to express. Yet, as far as she was concerned, could I lament that she was removed in early youth from the certain advent of misery? Pure she was of soul, and all her intents were holy. But her heart was the throne of love, and the sensibility her lovely countenance expressed, was the prophet of many woes, not the less deep and drear, because she would have for ever concealed them.

These two wondrously endowed beings had been spared from the universal wreck, to be my companions during the last year of solitude. I had felt, while they were with me, all their worth. I was conscious that every other sentiment, regret, or passion had by degrees merged into a yearning, clinging affection for them. I had not forgotten the sweet partner of my youth, mother of my children, my adored Idris; but I saw at least a part of her spirit alive again in her brother; and after, that by Evelyn's death I had lost what most dearly recalled her to me; I enshrined her memory in Adrian's form, and endeavoured to confound the two dear ideas. I sound the depths of my heart, and try in vain to draw thence the expressions that can typify my love for these remnants of my race. If regret and sorrow came athwart me, as well it might in our solitary and uncertain state, the clear tones of Adrian's voice, and his fervent look, dissipated the gloom; or I was cheered unaware by the mild content and sweet resignation Clara's cloudless brow and deep blue eyes expressed. They were all to me—the suns of my benighted soul—repose in my weariness—slumber in my sleepless woe. Ill, most ill, with disjointed words, bare and weak, have I expressed the feeling with which I clung to them. I would have wound myself like ivy inextricably round them, so that the same blow might destroy us. I would have entered and been a part of them—so that

If the dull substance of my flesh were thought,

even now I had accompanied them to their new and incommunicable abode.

Never shall I see them more. I am bereft of their dear converse—bereft of sight of them. I am a tree rent by lightning; never will the bark close over the bared fibres—never will their quivering life, torn by the winds, receive the opiate of a moment's balm. I am alone in the world— but that expression as yet was less pregnant with misery, than that Adrian and Clara are dead.

The tide of thought and feeling rolls on for ever the same, though the banks and shapes around, which govern its course, and the reflection in the wave, vary. Thus the sentiment of immediate loss in some sort decayed, while that of utter, irremediable loneliness grew on me with time. Three days I wandered through Ravenna—now thinking only of the beloved beings who slept in the oozy caves of ocean—now looking forward on the dread blank before me; shuddering to make an onward step—writhing at each change that marked the progress of the hours.

For three days I wandered to and fro in this melancholy town. I passed whole hours in going from house to house, listening whether I could detect some lurking sign of human existence. Sometimes I rang at a bell; it tinkled through the vaulted rooms, and silence succeeded to the sound. I called myself hopeless, yet still I hoped; and still disappointment ushered in the hours, intruding the cold, sharp steel which first pierced me, into the aching festering wound. I fed like a wild beast, which seizes its food only when stung by intolerable hunger. I did not change my garb, or seek the shelter of a roof, during all those days. Burning heats, nervous irritation, a ceaseless, but confused flow of thought, sleepless nights, and days instinct with a frenzy of agitation, possessed me during that time.

As the fever of my blood increased, a desire of wandering came upon me. I remember, that the sun had set on the fifth day after my wreck, when, without purpose or aim, I quitted the town of Ravenna. I must have been very ill. Had I been possessed by more or less of delirium, that night had surely been my last; for, as I continued to walk on the banks of the Mantone, whose upward course I followed, I looked wistfully on the stream, acknowledging to myself that its pellucid waves could medicine my woes for ever, and was unable to account to myself for my tardiness in seeking their shelter from the poisoned arrows of thought, that were piercing me through and through. I walked a considerable part of the night, and excessive weariness at length conquered my repugnance to the availing myself of the deserted habitations of my species. The waning moon, which had just risen, shewed me a cottage, whose neat entrance and trim garden reminded me of my own England. I lifted up the latch of the door and entered. A kitchen first presented itself, where, guided by the moon beams, I found materials for striking a light. Within this was a bed room; the couch was furnished with sheets of snowy whiteness; the wood piled on the hearth, and an array as for a meal, might almost have deceived me into the dear belief that I had here found what I had so long sought—one survivor, a companion for my loneliness, a solace to my despair. I steeled myself against the delusion; the room itself was vacant: it was only prudent, I repeated to myself, to examine the rest of the house. I fancied that I was proof against the expectation; yet my heart beat audibly, as I laid my hand on the lock of each door, and it sunk again, when I perceived in each the same vacancy. Dark and silent they were as vaults; so I returned to the first chamber, wondering what sightless host had spread the materials for my repast, and my repose. I drew a chair to the table, and examined what the viands were of which I was to partake. In truth it was a death feast! The bread was blue and mouldy; the cheese lay a heap of dust. I did not dare examine the other dishes; a troop of ants passed in a double line across the table cloth; every utensil was covered with dust, with cobwebs, and myriads of dead flies: these were objects each and all betokening the fallaciousness of my expectations. Tears rushed into my eyes; surely this was a wanton display of the power of the destroyer. What had I done, that each sensitive nerve was thus to be anatomized? Yet why complain more now than ever? This vacant cottage revealed no new sorrow— the world was empty; mankind was dead—I knew it well—why quarrel therefore with an acknowledged and stale truth? Yet, as I said, I had hoped in the very heart of despair, so that every new impression of the hard-cut reality on my soul brought with it a fresh pang, telling me the yet unstudied lesson, that neither change of place nor time could bring alleviation to my misery, but that, as I now was, I must continue, day after day, month after month, year after year, while I lived. I hardly dared conjecture what space of time that expression implied. It is true, I was no longer in the first blush of manhood; neither had I declined far in the vale of years—men have accounted mine the prime of life: I had just entered my thirty-seventh year; every limb was as well knit, every articulation as true, as when I had acted the shepherd on the hills of Cumberland; and with these advantages I was to commence the train of solitary life. Such were the reflections that ushered in my slumber on that night.

The shelter, however, and less disturbed repose which I enjoyed, restored me the following morning to a greater portion of health and strength, than I had experienced since my fatal shipwreck. Among the stores I had discovered on searching the cottage the preceding night, was a quantity of dried grapes; these refreshed me in the morning, as I left my lodging and proceeded towards a town which I discerned at no great distance. As far as I could divine, it must have been Forli. I entered with pleasure its wide and grassy streets. All, it is true, pictured the excess of desolation; yet I loved to find myself in those spots which had been the abode of my fellow creatures. I delighted to traverse street after street, to look up at the tall houses, and repeat to myself, once they contained beings similar to myself—I was not always the wretch I am now. The wide square of Forli, the arcade around it, its light and pleasant aspect cheered me. I was pleased with the idea, that, if the earth should be again peopled, we, the lost race, would, in the relics left behind, present no contemptible exhibition of our powers to the new comers.

I entered one of the palaces, and opened the door of a magnificent saloon. I started—I looked again with renewed wonder. What wild-looking, unkempt, half-naked savage was that before me? The surprise was momentary.

I perceived that it was I myself whom I beheld in a large mirror at the end of the hall. No wonder that the lover of the princely Idris should fail to recognize himself in the miserable object there portrayed. My tattered dress was that in which I had crawled half alive from the tempestuous sea. My long and tangled hair hung in elf locks on my brow—my dark eyes, now hollow and wild, gleamed from under them—my cheeks were discoloured by the jaundice, which (the effect of misery and neglect) suffused my skin, and were half hid by a beard of many days' growth.

Yet why should I not remain thus, I thought; the world is dead, and this squalid attire is a fitter mourning garb than the foppery of a black suit. And thus, methinks, I should have remained, had not hope, without which I do not believe man could exist, whispered to me, that, in such a plight, I should be an object of fear and aversion to the being, preserved I knew not where, but I fondly trusted, at length, to be found by me. Will my readers scorn the vanity, that made me attire myself with some care, for the sake of this visionary being? Or will they forgive the freaks of a half crazed imagination? I can easily forgive myself—for hope, however vague, was so dear to me, and a sentiment of pleasure of so rare occurrence, that I yielded readily to any idea, that cherished the one, or promised any recurrence of the former to my sorrowing heart. After such occupation, I visited every street, alley, and nook of Forli. These Italian towns presented an appearance of still greater desolation, than those of England or France. Plague had appeared here earlier—it had finished its course, and achieved its work much sooner than with us. Probably the last summer had found no human being alive, in all the track included between the shores of Calabria and the northern Alps. My search was utterly vain, yet I did not despond. Reason methought was on my side; and the chances were by no means contemptible, that there should exist in some part of Italy a survivor like myself—of a wasted, depopulate land. As therefore I rambled through the empty town, I formed my plan for future operations. I would continue to journey on towards Rome. After I should have satisfied myself, by a narrow search, that I left behind no human being in the towns through which I passed, I would write up in a conspicuous part of each, with white paint, in three languages, that "Verney, the last of the race of Englishmen, had taken up his abode in Rome."

In pursuance of this scheme, I entered a painter's shop, and procured myself the paint. It is strange that so trivial an occupation should have consoled, and even enlivened me. But grief renders one childish, despair fantastic. To this simple inscription, I merely added the adjuration, "Friend, come! I wait for thee!—Deh, vieni! ti aspetto!" On the following morning, with something like hope for my companion, I quitted Forli on my way to Rome. Until now, agonizing retrospect, and dreary prospects for the future, had stung me when awake, and cradled me to my repose. Many times I had delivered myself up to the tyranny of anguish— many times I resolved a speedy end to my woes; and death by my own hands was a remedy, whose practicability was even cheering to me. What could I fear in the other world? If there were an hell, and I were doomed to it, I should come an adept to the sufferance of its tortures— the act were easy, the speedy and certain end of my deplorable tragedy. But now these thoughts faded before the new born expectation. I went on my way, not as before, feeling each hour, each minute, to be an age instinct with incalculable pain.

As I wandered along the plain, at the foot of the Appennines—through their vallies, and over their bleak summits, my path led me through a country which had been trodden by heroes, visited and admired by thousands. They had, as a tide, receded, leaving me blank and bare in the midst. But why complain? Did I not hope?—so I schooled myself, even after the enlivening spirit had really deserted me, and thus I was obliged to call up all the fortitude I could command, and that was not much, to prevent a recurrence of that chaotic and intolerable despair, that had succeeded to the miserable shipwreck, that had consummated every fear, and dashed to annihilation every joy.

I rose each day with the morning sun, and left my desolate inn. As my feet strayed through the unpeopled country, my thoughts rambled through the universe, and I was least miserable when I could, absorbed in reverie, forget the passage of the hours. Each evening, in spite of weariness, I detested to enter any dwelling, there to take up my nightly abode—I have sat, hour after hour, at the door of the cottage I had selected, unable to lift the latch, and meet face to face blank desertion within. Many nights, though autumnal mists were spread around, I passed under an ilex—many times I have supped on arbutus berries and chestnuts, making a fire, gypsy-like, on the ground—because wild natural scenery reminded me less acutely of my hopeless state of loneliness. I counted the days, and bore with me a peeled willow-wand, on which, as well as I could remember, I had notched the days that had elapsed since my wreck, and each night I added another unit to the melancholy sum.

I had toiled up a hill which led to Spoleto. Around was spread a plain, encircled by the chestnut-covered Appennines. A dark ravine was on one side, spanned by an aqueduct, whose tall arches were rooted in the dell below, and attested that man had once deigned to bestow labour and thought here, to adorn and civilize nature. Savage, ungrateful nature, which in wild sport defaced his remains, protruding her easily renewed, and fragile growth of wild flowers and parasite plants around his eternal edifices. I sat on a fragment of rock, and looked round. The sun had bathed in gold the western atmosphere, and in the east the clouds caught the radiance, and budded into transient loveliness. It set on a world that contained me alone for its inhabitant. I took out my wand—I counted the marks. Twenty-five were already traced—twenty-five days had already elapsed, since human voice had gladdened my ears, or human countenance met my gaze. Twenty-five long, weary days, succeeded by dark and lonesome nights, had mingled with foregone years, and had become a part of the past—the never to be recalled—a real, undeniable portion of my life—twenty-five long, long days.

Why this was not a month!—Why talk of days—or weeks—or months—I must grasp years in my imagination, if I would truly picture the future to myself—three, five, ten, twenty, fifty anniversaries of that fatal epoch might elapse—every year containing twelve months, each of more numerous calculation in a diary, than the twenty-five days gone by—Can it be? Will it be? —We had been used to look forward to death tremulously— wherefore, but because its place was obscure? But more terrible, and far more obscure, was the unveiled course of my lone futurity. I broke my wand; I threw it from me. I needed no recorder of the inch and barley-corn growth of my life, while my unquiet thoughts created other divisions, than those ruled over by the planets—and, in looking back on the age that had elapsed since I had been alone, I disdained to give the name of days and hours to the throes of agony which had in truth portioned it out.

I hid my face in my hands. The twitter of the young birds going to rest, and their rustling among the trees, disturbed the still evening-air—the crickets chirped—the aziolo cooed at intervals. My thoughts had been of death—these sounds spoke to me of life. I lifted up my eyes —a bat wheeled round—the sun had sunk behind the jagged line of mountains, and the paly, crescent moon was visible, silver white, amidst the orange sunset, and accompanied by one bright star, prolonged thus the twilight. A herd of cattle passed along in the dell below, untended, towards their watering place—the grass was rustled by a gentle breeze, and the olive-woods, mellowed into soft masses by the moonlight, contrasted their sea-green with the dark chestnut foliage. Yes, this is the earth; there is no change—no ruin—no rent made in her verdurous expanse; she continues to wheel round and round, with alternate night and day, through the sky, though man is not her adorner or inhabitant. Why could I not forget myself like one of those animals, and no longer suffer the wild tumult of misery that I endure? Yet, ah! what a deadly breach yawns between their state and mine! Have not they companions? Have not they each their mate—their cherished young, their home, which, though unexpressed to us, is, I doubt not, endeared and enriched, even in their eyes, by the society which kind nature has created for them? It is I only that am alone—I, on this little hill top, gazing on plain and mountain recess—on sky, and its starry population, listening to every sound of earth, and air, and murmuring wave,—I only cannot express to any companion my many thoughts, nor lay my throbbing head on any loved bosom, nor drink from meeting eyes an intoxicating dew, that transcends the fabulous nectar of the gods. Shall I not then complain? Shall I not curse the murderous engine which has mowed down the children of men, my brethren? Shall I not bestow a malediction on every other of nature's offspring, which dares live and enjoy, while I live and suffer?

Ah, no! I will discipline my sorrowing heart to sympathy in your joys; I will be happy, because ye are so. Live on, ye innocents, nature's selected darlings; I am not much unlike to you. Nerves, pulse, brain, joint, and flesh, of such am I composed, and ye are organized by the same laws. I have something beyond this, but I will call it a defect, not an endowment, if it leads me to misery, while ye are happy. Just then, there emerged from a near copse two goats and a little kid, by the mother's side; they began to browze the herbage of the hill. I approached near to them, without their perceiving me; I gathered a handful of fresh grass, and held it out; the little one nestled close to its mother, while she timidly withdrew. The male stepped forward, fixing his eyes on me: I drew near, still holding out my lure, while he, depressing his head, rushed at me with his horns. I was a very fool; I knew it, yet I yielded to my rage. I snatched up a huge fragment of rock; it would have crushed my rash foe. I poized it—aimed it—then my heart failed me. I hurled it wide of the mark; it rolled clattering among the bushes into dell. My little visitants, all aghast, galloped back into the covert of the wood; while I, my very heart bleeding and torn, rushed down the hill, and by the violence of bodily exertion, sought to escape from my miserable self.

No, no, I will not live among the wild scenes of nature, the enemy of all that lives. I will seek the towns—Rome, the capital of the world, the crown of man's achievements. Among its storied streets, hallowed ruins, and stupendous remains of human exertion, I shall not, as here, find every thing forgetful of man; trampling on his memory, defacing his works, proclaiming from hill to hill, and vale to vale,—by the torrents freed from the boundaries which he imposed —by the vegetation liberated from the laws which he enforced—by his habitation abandoned to mildew and weeds, that his power is lost, his race annihilated for ever.

I hailed the Tiber, for that was as it were an unalienable possession of humanity. I hailed the wild Campagna, for every rood had been trod by man; and its savage uncultivation, of no recent date, only proclaimed more distinctly his power, since he had given an honourable name and sacred title to what else would have been a worthless, barren track. I entered Eternal Rome by the Porta del Popolo, and saluted with awe its time-honoured space. The wide square, the churches near, the long extent of the Corso, the near eminence of Trinita de' Monti appeared like fairy work, they were so silent, so peaceful, and so very fair. It was evening; and the population of animals which still existed in this mighty city, had gone to rest; there was no sound, save the murmur of its many fountains, whose soft monotony was harmony to my soul. The knowledge that I was in Rome, soothed me; that wondrous city, hardly more illustrious for its heroes and sages, than for the power it exercised over the imaginations of men. I went to rest that night; the eternal burning of my heart quenched,—my senses tranquil.

The next morning I eagerly began my rambles in search of oblivion. I ascended the many terraces of the garden of the Colonna Palace, under whose roof I had been sleeping; and passing out from it at its summit, I found myself on Monte Cavallo. The fountain sparkled in the sun; the obelisk above pierced the clear dark-blue air. The statues on each side, the works, as they are inscribed, of Phidias and Praxiteles, stood in undiminished grandeur, representing Castor and Pollux, who with majestic power tamed the rearing animal at their side. If those illustrious artists had in truth chiselled these forms, how many passing generations had their giant proportions outlived! and now they were viewed by the last of the species they were sculptured to represent and deify. I had shrunk into insignificance in my own eyes, as I considered the multitudinous beings these stone demigods had outlived, but this after-thought restored me to dignity in my own conception. The sight of the poetry eternized in these statues, took the sting from the thought, arraying it only in poetic ideality.

I repeated to myself,—I am in Rome! I behold, and as it were, familiarly converse with the wonder of the world, sovereign mistress of the imagination, majestic and eternal survivor of millions of generations of extinct men. I endeavoured to quiet the sorrows of my aching heart, by even now taking an interest in what in my youth I had ardently longed to see. Every part of Rome is replete with relics of ancient times. The meanest streets are strewed with truncated columns, broken capitals—Corinthian and Ionic, and sparkling fragments of granite or porphyry. The walls of the most penurious dwellings enclose a fluted pillar or ponderous stone, which once made part of the palace of the Caesars; and the voice of dead time, in still vibrations, is breathed from these dumb things, animated and glorified as they were by man.

I embraced the vast columns of the temple of Jupiter Stator, which survives in the open space that was the Forum, and leaning my burning cheek against its cold durability, I tried to lose the sense of present misery and present desertion, by recalling to the haunted cell of my brain vivid memories of times gone by. I rejoiced at my success, as I figured Camillus, the Gracchi, Cato, and last the heroes of Tacitus, which shine meteors of surpassing brightness during the murky night of the empire;—as the verses of Horace and Virgil, or the glowing periods of Cicero thronged into the opened gates of my mind, I felt myself exalted by long forgotten enthusiasm. I was delighted to know that I beheld the scene which they beheld—the scene which their wives and mothers, and crowds of the unnamed witnessed, while at the same time they honoured, applauded, or wept for these matchless specimens of humanity. At length, then, I had found a consolation. I had not vainly sought the storied precincts of Rome—I had discovered a medicine for my many and vital wounds.

I sat at the foot of these vast columns. The Coliseum, whose naked ruin is robed by nature in a verdurous and glowing veil, lay in the sunlight on my right. Not far off, to the left, was the Tower of the Capitol. Triumphal arches, the falling walls of many temples, strewed the ground at my feet. I strove, I resolved, to force myself to see the Plebeian multitude and lofty Patrician forms congregated around; and, as the Diorama of ages passed across my subdued fancy, they were replaced by the modern Roman; the Pope, in his white stole, distributing benedictions to the kneeling worshippers; the friar in his cowl; the dark-eyed girl, veiled by her mezzera; the noisy, sun-burnt rustic, leading his herd of buffaloes and oxen to the Campo Vaccino. The romance with which, dipping our pencils in the rainbow hues of sky and transcendent nature, we to a degree gratuitously endow the Italians, replaced the solemn grandeur of antiquity. I remembered the dark monk, and floating figures of "The Italian," and how my boyish blood had thrilled at the description. I called to mind Corinna ascending the Capitol to be crowned, and, passing from the heroine to the author, reflected how the Enchantress Spirit of Rome held sovereign sway over the minds of the imaginative, until it rested on me—sole remaining spectator of its wonders.

I was long wrapt by such ideas; but the soul wearies of a pauseless flight; and, stooping from its wheeling circuits round and round this spot, suddenly it fell ten thousand fathom deep, into the abyss of the present— into self-knowledge—into tenfold sadness. I roused myself —I cast off my waking dreams; and I, who just now could almost hear the shouts of the Roman throng, and was hustled by countless multitudes, now beheld the desart ruins of Rome sleeping under its own blue sky; the shadows lay tranquilly on the ground; sheep were grazing untended on the Palatine, and a buffalo stalked down the Sacred Way that led to the Capitol. I was alone in the Forum; alone in Rome; alone in the world. Would not one living man —one companion in my weary solitude, be worth all the glory and remembered power of this time-honoured city? Double sorrow—sadness, bred in Cimmerian caves, robed my soul in a mourning garb. The generations I had conjured up to my fancy, contrasted more strongly with the end of all —the single point in which, as a pyramid, the mighty fabric of society had ended, while I, on the giddy height, saw vacant space around me.

From such vague laments I turned to the contemplation of the minutiae of my situation. So far, I had not succeeded in the sole object of my desires, the finding a companion for my desolation. Yet I did not despair. It is true that my inscriptions were set up for the most part, in insignificant towns and villages; yet, even without these memorials, it was possible that the person, who like me should find himself alone in a depopulate land, should, like me, come to Rome. The more slender my expectation was, the more I chose to build on it, and to accommodate my actions to this vague possibility.

It became necessary therefore, that for a time I should domesticate myself at Rome. It became necessary, that I should look my disaster in the face— not playing the school-boy's part of obedience without submission; enduring life, and yet rebelling against the laws by which I lived.

Yet how could I resign myself? Without love, without sympathy, without communion with any, how could I meet the morning sun, and with it trace its oft repeated journey to the evening shades? Why did I continue to live— why not throw off the weary weight of time, and with my own hand, let out the fluttering prisoner from my agonized breast?—It was not cowardice that withheld me; for the true fortitude was to endure; and death had a soothing sound accompanying it, that would easily entice me to enter its demesne. But this I would not do. I had, from the moment I had reasoned on the subject, instituted myself the subject to fate, and the servant of necessity, the visible laws of the invisible God—I believed that my obedience was the result of sound reasoning, pure feeling, and an exalted sense of the true excellence and nobility of my nature. Could I have seen in this empty earth, in the seasons and their change, the hand of a blind power only, most willingly would I have placed my head on the sod, and closed my eyes on its loveliness for ever. But fate had administered life to me, when the plague had already seized on its prey—she had dragged me by the hair from out the strangling waves —By such miracles she had bought me for her own; I admitted her authority, and bowed to her decrees. If, after mature consideration, such was my resolve, it was doubly necessary that I should not lose the end of life, the improvement of my faculties, and poison its flow by repinings without end. Yet how cease to repine, since there was no hand near to extract the barbed spear that had entered my heart of hearts? I stretched out my hand, and it touched none whose sensations were responsive to mine. I was girded, walled in, vaulted over, by seven-fold barriers of loneliness. Occupation alone, if I could deliver myself up to it, would be capable of affording an opiate to my sleepless sense of woe. Having determined to make Rome my abode, at least for some months, I made arrangements for my accommodation—I selected my home. The Colonna Palace was well adapted for my purpose. Its grandeur— its treasure of paintings, its magnificent halls were objects soothing and even exhilarating.

I found the granaries of Rome well stored with grain, and particularly with Indian corn; this product requiring less art in its preparation for food, I selected as my principal support. I now found the hardships and lawlessness of my youth turn to account. A man cannot throw off the habits of sixteen years. Since that age, it is true, I had lived luxuriously, or at least surrounded by all the conveniences civilization afforded. But before that time, I had been "as uncouth a savage, as the wolf-bred founder of old Rome"—and now, in Rome itself, robber and shepherd propensities, similar to those of its founder, were of advantage to its sole inhabitant. I spent the morning riding and shooting in the Campagna—I passed long hours in the various galleries—I gazed at each statue, and lost myself in a reverie before many a fair Madonna or beauteous nymph. I haunted the Vatican, and stood surrounded by marble forms of divine beauty. Each stone deity was possessed by sacred gladness, and the eternal fruition of love. They looked on me with unsympathizing complacency, and often in wild accents I reproached them for their supreme indifference—for they were human shapes, the human form divine was manifest in each fairest limb and lineament. The perfect moulding brought with it the idea of colour and motion; often, half in bitter mockery, half in self-delusion, I clasped their icy proportions, and, coming between Cupid and his Psyche's lips, pressed the unconceiving marble.

I endeavoured to read. I visited the libraries of Rome. I selected a volume, and, choosing some sequestered, shady nook, on the banks of the Tiber, or opposite the fair temple in the Borghese Gardens, or under the old pyramid of Cestius, I endeavoured to conceal me from myself, and immerse myself in the subject traced on the pages before me. As if in the same soil you plant nightshade and a myrtle tree, they will each appropriate the mould, moisture, and air administered, for the fostering their several properties—so did my grief find sustenance, and power of existence, and growth, in what else had been divine manna, to feed radiant meditation. Ah! while I streak this paper with the tale of what my so named occupations were —while I shape the skeleton of my days—my hand trembles—my heart pants, and my brain refuses to lend expression, or phrase, or idea, by which to image forth the veil of unutterable woe that clothed these bare realities. O, worn and beating heart, may I dissect thy fibres, and tell how in each unmitigable misery, sadness dire, repinings, and despair, existed? May I record my many ravings—the wild curses I hurled at torturing nature—and how I have passed days shut out from light and food—from all except the burning hell alive in my own bosom?

I was presented, meantime, with one other occupation, the one best fitted to discipline my melancholy thoughts, which strayed backwards, over many a ruin, and through many a flowery glade, even to the mountain recess, from which in early youth I had first emerged.

During one of my rambles through the habitations of Rome, I found writing materials on a table in an author's study. Parts of a manuscript lay scattered about. It contained a learned disquisition on the Italian language; one page an unfinished dedication to posterity, for whose profit the writer had sifted and selected the niceties of this harmonious language —to whose everlasting benefit he bequeathed his labours.

I also will write a book, I cried—for whom to read?—to whom dedicated? And then with silly flourish (what so capricious and childish as despair?) I wrote, DEDICATION TO THE ILLUSTRIOUS DEAD. SHADOWS, ARISE, AND READ YOUR FALL! BEHOLD THE HISTORY OF THE LAST MAN.

Yet, will not this world be re-peopled, and the children of a saved pair of lovers, in some to me unknown and unattainable seclusion, wandering to these prodigious relics of the ante-pestilential race, seek to learn how beings so wondrous in their achievements, with imaginations infinite, and powers godlike, had departed from their home to an unknown country?

I will write and leave in this most ancient city, this "world's sole monument," a record of these things. I will leave a monument of the existence of Verney, the Last Man. At first I thought only to speak of plague, of death, and last, of desertion; but I lingered fondly on my early years, and recorded with sacred zeal the virtues of my companions. They have been with me during the fulfilment of my task. I have brought it to an end—I lift my eyes from my paper—again they are lost to me. Again I feel that I am alone.

A year has passed since I have been thus occupied. The seasons have made their wonted round, and decked this eternal city in a changeful robe of surpassing beauty. A year has passed; and I no longer guess at my state or my prospects—loneliness is my familiar, sorrow my inseparable companion. I have endeavoured to brave the storm—I have endeavoured to school myself to fortitude—I have sought to imbue myself with the lessons of wisdom. It will not do. My hair has become nearly grey—my voice, unused now to utter sound, comes strangely on my ears. My person, with its human powers and features, seem to me a monstrous excrescence of nature. How express in human language a woe human being until this hour never knew! How give intelligible expression to a pang none but I could ever understand!— No one has entered Rome. None will ever come. I smile bitterly at the delusion I have so long nourished, and still more, when I reflect that I have exchanged it for another as delusive, as false, but to which I now cling with the same fond trust.

Winter has come again; and the gardens of Rome have lost their leaves— the sharp air comes over the Campagna, and has driven its brute inhabitants to take up their abode in the many dwellings of the deserted city—frost has suspended the gushing fountains—and Trevi has stilled her eternal music. I had made a rough calculation, aided by the stars, by which I endeavoured to ascertain the first day of the new year. In the old out-worn age, the Sovereign Pontiff was used to go in solemn pomp, and mark the renewal of the year by driving a nail in the gate of the temple of Janus. On that day I ascended St. Peter's, and carved on its topmost stone the aera 2100, last year of the world!

My only companion was a dog, a shaggy fellow, half water and half shepherd's dog, whom I found tending sheep in the Campagna. His master was dead, but nevertheless he continued fulfilling his duties in expectation of his return. If a sheep strayed from the rest, he forced it to return to the flock, and sedulously kept off every intruder. Riding in the Campagna I had come upon his sheep-walk, and for some time observed his repetition of lessons learned from man, now useless, though unforgotten. His delight was excessive when he saw me. He sprung up to my knees; he capered round and round, wagging his tail, with the short, quick bark of pleasure: he left his fold to follow me, and from that day has never neglected to watch by and attend on me, shewing boisterous gratitude whenever I caressed or talked to him. His pattering steps and mine alone were heard, when we entered the magnificent extent of nave and aisle of St. Peter's. We ascended the myriad steps together, when on the summit I achieved my design, and in rough figures noted the date of the last year. I then turned to gaze on the country, and to take leave of Rome. I had long determined to quit it, and I now formed the plan I would adopt for my future career, after I had left this magnificent abode.

A solitary being is by instinct a wanderer, and that I would become. A hope of amelioration always attends on change of place, which would even lighten the burthen of my life. I had been a fool to remain in Rome all this time: Rome noted for Malaria, the famous caterer for death. But it was still possible, that, could I visit the whole extent of earth, I should find in some part of the wide extent a survivor. Methought the sea-side was the most probable retreat to be chosen by such a one. If left alone in an inland district, still they could not continue in the spot where their last hopes had been extinguished; they would journey on, like me, in search of a partner for their solitude, till the watery barrier stopped their further progress.

To that water—cause of my woes, perhaps now to be their cure, I would betake myself. Farewell, Italy!—farewell, thou ornament of the world, matchless Rome, the retreat of the solitary one during long months!—to civilized life—to the settled home and succession of monotonous days, farewell! Peril will now be mine; and I hail her as a friend—death will perpetually cross my path, and I will meet him as a benefactor; hardship, inclement weather, and dangerous tempests will be my sworn mates. Ye spirits of storm, receive me! ye powers of destruction, open wide your arms, and clasp me for ever! if a kinder power have not decreed another end, so that after long endurance I may reap my reward, and again feel my heart beat near the heart of another like to me.

Tiber, the road which is spread by nature's own hand, threading her continent, was at my feet, and many a boat was tethered to the banks. I would with a few books, provisions, and my dog, embark in one of these and float down the current of the stream into the sea; and then, keeping near land, I would coast the beauteous shores and sunny promontories of the blue Mediterranean, pass Naples, along Calabria, and would dare the twin perils of Scylla and Charybdis; then, with fearless aim, (for what had I to lose?) skim ocean's surface towards Malta and the further Cyclades. I would avoid Constantinople, the sight of whose well-known towers and inlets belonged to another state of existence from my present one; I would coast Asia Minor, and Syria, and, passing the seven-mouthed Nile, steer northward again, till losing sight of forgotten Carthage and deserted Lybia, I should reach the pillars of Hercules. And then—no matter where—the oozy caves, and soundless depths of ocean may be my dwelling, before I accomplish this long-drawn voyage, or the arrow of disease find my heart as I float singly on the weltering Mediterranean; or, in some place I touch at, I may find what I seek—a companion; or if this may not be—to endless time, decrepid and grey headed—youth already in the grave with those I love— the lone wanderer will still unfurl his sail, and clasp the tiller—and, still obeying the breezes of heaven, for ever round another and another promontory, anchoring in another and another bay, still ploughing seedless ocean, leaving behind the verdant land of native Europe, adown the tawny shore of Africa, having weathered the fierce seas of the Cape, I may moor my worn skiff in a creek, shaded by spicy groves of the odorous islands of the far Indian ocean.

These are wild dreams. Yet since, now a week ago, they came on me, as I stood on the height of St. Peter's, they have ruled my imagination. I have chosen my boat, and laid in my scant stores. I have selected a few books; the principal are Homer and Shakespeare—But the libraries of the world are thrown open to me—and in any port I can renew my stock. I form no expectation of alteration for the better; but the monotonous present is intolerable to me. Neither hope nor joy are my pilots—restless despair and fierce desire of change lead me on. I long to grapple with danger, to be excited by fear, to have some task, however slight or voluntary, for each day's fulfilment. I shall witness all the variety of appearance, that the elements can assume —I shall read fair augury in the rainbow— menace in the cloud—some lesson or record dear to my heart in everything. Thus around the shores of deserted earth, while the sun is high, and the moon waxes or wanes, angels, the spirits of the dead, and the ever-open eye of the Supreme, will behold the tiny bark, freighted with Verney—the LAST MAN.

THE SCARLET PLAGUE

JACK LONDON

THE WAY LED along upon what had once been the embankment of a railroad. But no train had run upon it for many years. The forest on either side swelled up the slopes of the embankment and crested across it in a green wave of trees and bushes. The trail was as narrow as a man's body, and was no more than a wild-animal runway. Occasionally, a piece of rusty iron, showing through the forest-mould, advertised that the rail and the ties still remained. In one place, a ten-inch tree, bursting through at a connection, had lifted the end of a rail clearly into view. The tie had evidently followed the rail, held to it by the spike long enough for its bed to be filled with gravel and rotten leaves, so that now the crumbling, rotten timber thrust itself up at a curious slant. Old as the road was, it was manifest that it had been of the mono-rail type.

An old man and a boy travelled along this runway. They moved slowly, for the old man was very old, a touch of palsy made his movements tremulous, and he leaned heavily upon his staff. A rude skull-cap of goat-skin protected his head from the sun. From beneath this fell a scant fringe of stained and dirty-white hair. A visor, ingeniously made from a large leaf, shielded his eyes, and from under this he peered at the way of his feet on the trail. His beard, which should have been snow-white but which showed the same weather-wear and camp-stain as his hair, fell nearly to his waist in a great tangled mass. About his chest and shoulders hung a single, mangy garment of goat-skin. His arms and legs, withered and skinny, betokened extreme age, as well as did their sunburn and scars and scratches betoken long years of exposure to the elements.

The boy, who led the way, checking the eagerness of his muscles to the slow progress of the elder, likewise wore a single garment—a ragged-edged piece of bear-skin, with a hole in the middle through which he had thrust his head. He could not have been more than twelve years old. Tucked coquettishly over one ear was the freshly severed tail of a pig. In one hand he carried a medium-sized bow and an arrow.

On his back was a quiverful of arrows. From a sheath hanging about his neck on a thong, projected the battered handle of a hunting knife. He was as brown as a berry, and walked softly, with almost a catlike tread. In marked contrast with his sunburned skin were his eyes—blue, deep blue, but keen and sharp as a pair of gimlets. They seemed to bore into aft about him in a

way that was habitual. As he went along he smelled things, as well, his distended, quivering
nostrils carrying to his brain an endless series of messages from the outside world. Also, his
hearing was acute, and had been so trained that it operated automatically. Without conscious
effort, he heard all the slight sounds in the apparent quiet—heard, and differentiated, and
classified these sounds—whether they were of the wind rustling the leaves, of the humming of
bees and gnats, of the distant rumble of the sea that drifted to him only in lulls, or of the
gopher, just under his foot, shoving a pouchful of earth into the entrance of his hole.

Suddenly he became alertly tense. Sound, sight, and odor had given him a simultaneous
warning. His hand went back to the old man, touching him, and the pair stood still. Ahead, at
one side of the top of the embankment, arose a crackling sound, and the boy's gaze was fixed
on the tops of the agitated bushes. Then a large bear, a grizzly, crashed into view, and likewise
stopped abruptly, at sight of the humans. He did not like them, and growled querulously.
Slowly the boy fitted the arrow to the bow, and slowly he pulled the bowstring taut. But he
never removed his eyes from the bear.

The old man peered from under his green leaf at the danger, and stood as quietly as the boy.
For a few seconds this mutual scrutinizing went on; then, the bear betraying a growing
irritability, the boy, with a movement of his head, indicated that the old man must step aside
from the trail and go down the embankment. The boy followed, going backward, still holding
the bow taut and ready. They waited till a crashing among the bushes from the opposite side of
the embankment told them the bear had gone on. The boy grinned as he led back to the trail.

"A big un, Granser," he chuckled.

The old man shook his head.

"They get thicker every day," he complained in a thin, undependable falsetto. "Who'd have
thought I'd live to see the time when a man would be afraid of his life on the way to the Cliff
House. When I was a boy, Edwin, men and women and little babies used to come out here from
San Francisco by tens of thousands on a nice day. And there weren't any bears then. No, sir.
They used to pay money to look at them in cages, they were that rare."

"What is money, Granser?"

Before the old man could answer, the boy recollected and triumphantly shoved his hand
into a pouch under his bear-skin and pulled forth a battered and tarnished silver dollar. The old
man's eyes glistened, as he held the coin close to them.

"I can't see," he muttered. "You look and see if you can make out the date, Edwin."

The boy laughed.

"You're a great Granser," he cried delightedly, "always making believe them little marks
mean something."

The old man manifested an accustomed chagrin as he brought the coin back again close to
his own eyes.

"2012," he shrilled, and then fell to cackling grotesquely. "That was the year Morgan the
Fifth was appointed President of the United States by the Board of Magnates. It must have been
one of the last coins minted, for the Scarlet Death came in 2013. Lord! Lord!—think of it! Sixty
years ago, and I am the only person alive to-day that lived in those times. Where did you find
it, Edwin?"

The boy, who had been regarding him with the tolerant curiousness one accords to the
prattlings of the feeble-minded, answered promptly.

"I got it off of Hoo-Hoo. He found it when we was herdin' goats down near San José last
spring. Hoo-Hoo said it was *money*. Ain't you hungry, Granser?"

The ancient caught his staff in a tighter grip and urged along the trail, his old eyes shining
greedily.

"I hope Har-Lip 's found a crab... or two," he mumbled. "They're good eating, crabs, mighty good eating when you've no more teeth and you've got grandsons that love their old grandsire and make a point of catching crabs for him. When I was a boy—"

But Edwin, suddenly stopped by what he saw, was drawing the bowstring on a fitted arrow. He had paused on the brink of a crevasse in the embankment. An ancient culvert had here washed out, and the stream, no longer confined, had cut a passage through the fill. On the opposite side, the end of a rail projected and overhung. It showed rustily through the creeping vines which overran it. Beyond, crouching by a bush, a rabbit looked across at him in trembling hesitancy. Fully fifty feet was the distance, but the arrow flashed true; and the transfixed rabbit, crying out in sudden fright and hurt, struggled painfully away into the brush. The boy himself was a flash of brown skin and flying fur as he bounded down the steep wall of the gap and up the other side. His lean muscles were springs of steel that released into graceful and efficient action. A hundred feet beyond, in a tangle of bushes, he overtook the wounded creature, knocked its head on a convenient tree-trunk, and turned it over to Granser to carry.

"Rabbit is good, very good," the ancient quavered, "but when it comes to a toothsome delicacy I prefer crab. When I was a boy—"

"Why do you say so much that ain't got no sense?" Edwin impatiently interrupted the other's threatened garrulousness.

The boy did not exactly utter these words, but something that remotely resembled them and that was more guttural and explosive and economical of qualifying phrases. His speech showed distant kinship with that of the old man, and the latter's speech was approximately an English that had gone through a bath of corrupt usage.

"What I want to know," Edwin continued, "is why you call crab 'toothsome delicacy'? Crab is crab, ain't it? No one I never heard calls it such funny things."

The old man sighed but did not answer, and they moved on in silence. The surf grew suddenly louder, as they emerged from the forest upon a stretch of sand dunes bordering the sea. A few goats were browsing among the sandy hillocks, and a skin-clad boy, aided by a wolfish-looking dog that was only faintly reminiscent of a collie, was watching them. Mingled with the roar of the surf was a continuous, deep-throated barking or bellowing, which came from a cluster of jagged rocks a hundred yards out from shore. Here huge sea-lions hauled themselves up to lie in the sun or battle with one another. In the immediate foreground arose the smoke of a fire, tended by a third savage-looking boy. Crouched near him were several wolfish dogs similar to the one that guarded the goats.

The old man accelerated his pace, sniffing eagerly as he neared the fire.

"Mussels!" he muttered ecstatically. "Mussels! And ain't that a crab, Hoo-Hoo? Ain't that a crab? My, my, you boys are good to your old grandsire."

Hoo-Hoo, who was apparently of the same age as Edwin, grinned.

"All you want, Granser. I got four."

The old man's palsied eagerness was pitiful. Sitting down in the sand as quickly as his stiff limbs would let him, he poked a large rock-mussel from out of the coals. The heat had forced its shells apart, and the meat, salmon-colored, was thoroughly cooked. Between thumb and forefinger, in trembling haste, he caught the morsel and carried it to his mouth. But it was too hot, and the next moment was violently ejected. The old man spluttered with the pain, and tears ran out of his eyes and down his cheeks.

The boys were true savages, possessing only the cruel humor of the savage. To them the incident was excruciatingly funny, and they burst into loud laughter. Hoo-Hoo danced up and down, while Edwin rolled gleefully on the ground. The boy with the goats came running to join in the fun.

"Set 'em to cool, Edwin, set 'em to cool," the old man besought, in the midst of his grief, making no attempt to wipe away the tears that still flowed from his eyes. "And cool a crab, Edwin, too. You know your grandsire likes crabs."

From the coals arose a great sizzling, which proceeded from the many mussels bursting open their shells and exuding their moisture. They were large shellfish, running from three to six inches in length. The boys raked them out with sticks and placed them on a large piece of driftwood to cool.

"When I was a boy, we did not laugh at our elders; we respected them."

The boys took no notice, and Granser continued to babble an incoherent flow of complaint and censure. But this time he was more careful, and did not burn his mouth. All began to eat, using nothing but their hands and making loud mouth-noises and lip-smackings. The third boy, who was called Hare-Lip, slyly deposited a pinch of sand on a mussel the ancient was carrying to his mouth; and when the grit of it bit into the old fellow's mucous membrane and gums, the laughter was again uproarious. He was unaware that a joke had been played on him, and spluttered and spat until Edwin, relenting, gave him a gourd of fresh water with which to wash out his mouth.

"Where's them crabs, Hoo-Hoo?" Edwin demanded. "Granser's set upon having a snack."

Again Granser's eyes burned with greediness as a large crab was handed to him. It was a shell with legs and all complete, but the meat had long since departed. With shaky fingers and babblings of anticipation, the old man broke off a leg and found it filled with emptiness.

"The crabs, Hoo-Hoo?" he wailed. "The crabs?"

"I was fooling Granser. They ain't no crabs! I never found one."

The boys were overwhelmed with delight at sight of the tears of senile disappointment that dribbled down the old man's cheeks. Then, unnoticed, Hoo-Hoo replaced the empty shell with a fresh-cooked crab. Already dismembered, from the cracked legs the white meat sent forth a small cloud of savory steam. This attracted the old man's nostrils, and he looked down in amazement.

The change of his mood to one of joy was immediate. He snuffled and muttered and mumbled, making almost a croon of delight, as he began to eat. Of this the boys took little notice, for it was an accustomed spectacle. Nor did they notice his occasional exclamations and utterances of phrases which meant nothing to them, as, for instance, when he smacked his lips and champed his gums while muttering: "Mayonnaise! Just think—mayonnaise! And it's sixty years since the last was ever made! Two generations and never a smell of it! Why, in those days it was served in every restaurant with crab."

When he could eat no more, the old man sighed, wiped his hands on his naked legs, and gazed out over the sea. With the content of a full stomach, he waxed reminiscent.

"To think of it! I've seen this beach alive with men, women, and children on a pleasant Sunday. And there weren't any bears to eat them up, either. And right up there on the cliff was a big restaurant where you could get anything you wanted to eat. Four million people lived in San Francisco then. And now, in the whole city and county there aren't forty all told. And out there on the sea were ships and ships always to be seen, going in for the Golden Gate or coming out. And airships in the air—dirigibles and flying machines. They could travel two hundred miles an hour. The mail contracts with the New York and San Francisco Limited demanded that for the minimum. There was a chap, a Frenchman, I forget his name, who succeeded in making three hundred; but the thing was risky, too risky for conservative persons. But he was on the right clew, and he would have managed it if it hadn't been for the Great Plague. When I was a boy, there were men alive who remembered the coming of the first aeroplanes, and now I have lived to see the last of them, and that sixty years ago."

The old man babbled on, unheeded by the boys, who were long accustomed to his garrulousness, and whose vocabularies, besides, lacked the greater portion of the words he used. It was noticeable that in these rambling soliloquies his English seemed to recrudesce into better construction and phraseology. But when he talked directly with the boys it lapsed, largely, into their own uncouth and simpler forms.

"But there weren't many crabs in those days," the old man wandered on. "They were fished out, and they were great delicacies. The open season was only a month long, too. And now crabs are accessible the whole year around. Think of it—catching all the crabs you want, any time you want, in the surf of the Cliff House beach!"

A sudden commotion among the goats brought the boys to their feet. The dogs about the fire rushed to join their snarling fellow who guarded the goats, while the goats themselves stampeded in the direction of their human protectors. A half dozen forms, lean and gray, glided about on the sand hillocks and faced the bristling dogs. Edwin arched an arrow that fell short. But Hare-Lip, with a sling such as David carried into battle against Goliath, hurled a stone through the air that whistled from the speed of its flight. It fell squarely among the wolves and caused them to slink away toward the dark depths of the eucalyptus forest.

The boys laughed and lay down again in the sand, while Granser sighed ponderously. He had eaten too much, and, with hands clasped on his paunch, the fingers interlaced, he resumed his maunderings.

"'The fleeting systems lapse like foam,'" he mumbled what was evidently a quotation. "That's it—foam, and fleeting. All man's toil upon the planet was just so much foam. He domesticated the serviceable animals, destroyed the hostile ones, and cleared the land of its wild vegetation. And then he passed, and the flood of primordial life rolled back again, sweeping his handiwork away—the weeds and the forest inundated his fields, the beasts of prey swept over his flocks, and now there are wolves on the Cliff House beach." He was appalled by the thought. "Where four million people disported themselves, the wild wolves roam to-day, and the savage progeny of our loins, with prehistoric weapons, defend themselves against the fanged despoilers. Think of it! And all because of the Scarlet Death—"

The adjective had caught Hare-Lip's ear.

"He's always saying that," he said to Edwin. "What is scarlet?"

"'The scarlet of the maples can shake me like the cry of bugles going by,'" the old man quoted.

"It's red," Edwin answered the question. "And you don't know it because you come from the Chauffeur Tribe. They never did know nothing, none of them. Scarlet is red—I know that."

"Red is red, ain't it?" Hare-Lip grumbled. "Then what's the good of gettin' cocky and calling it scarlet?"

"Granser, what for do you always say so much what nobody knows?" he asked. "Scarlet ain't anything, but red is red. Why don't you say red, then?"

"Red is not the right word," was the reply. "The plague was scarlet. The whole face and body turned scarlet in an hour's time. Don't I know? Didn't I see enough of it? And I am telling you it was scarlet because—well, because it was scarlet. There is no other word for it."

"Red is good enough for me," Hare-Lip muttered obstinately. "My dad calls red red, and he ought to know. He says everybody died of the Red Death."

"Your dad is a common fellow, descended from a common fellow," Granser retorted heatedly. "Don't I know the beginnings of the Chauffeurs? Your grandsire was a chauffeur, a servant, and without education. He worked for other persons. But your grandmother was of good stock, only the children did not take after her. Don't I remember when I first met them, catching fish at Lake Temescal?"

"What is *education?*" Edwin asked.

"Calling red scarlet," Hare-Lip sneered, then returned to the attack on Granser. "My dad told me, an' he got it from his dad afore he croaked, that your wife was a Santa Rosan, an' that she was sure no account. He said she was a *hash-slinger* before the Red Death, though I don't know what a *hash-slinger* is. You can tell me, Edwin."

But Edwin shook his head in token of ignorance.

"It is true, she was a waitress," Granser acknowledged. "But she was a good woman, and your mother was her daughter. Women were very scarce in the days after the Plague. She was the only wife I could find, even if she was a *hash-slinger*, as your father calls it. But it is not nice to talk about our progenitors that way."

"Dad says that the wife of the first Chauffeur was a *lady*—"

"What's a *lady?*" Hoo-Hoo demanded.

"A *lady*'s a Chauffeur squaw," was the quick reply of Hare-Lip.

"The first Chauffeur was Bill, a common fellow, as I said before," the old man expounded; "but his wife was a lady, a great lady. Before the Scarlet Death she was the wife of Van Worden. He was President of the Board of Industrial Magnates, and was one of the dozen men who ruled America. He was worth one billion, eight hundred millions of dollars—coins like you have there in your pouch, Edwin. And then came the Scarlet Death, and his wife became the wife of Bill, the first Chauffeur. He used to beat her, too. I have seen it myself."

Hoo-Hoo, lying on his stomach and idly digging his toes in the sand, cried out and investigated, first, his toe-nail, and next, the small hole he had dug. The other two boys joined him, excavating the sand rapidly with their hands till there lay three skeletons exposed. Two were of adults, the third being that of a part-grown child. The old man hudged along on the ground and peered at the find.

"Plague victims," he announced. "That's the way they died everywhere in the last days. This must have been a family, running away from the contagion and perishing here on the Cliff House beach. They—what are you doing, Edwin?"

This question was asked in sudden dismay, as Edwin, using the back of his hunting knife, began to knock out the teeth from the jaws of one of the skulls.

"Going to string 'em," was the response.

The three boys were now hard at it; and quite a knocking and hammering arose, in which Granser babbled on unnoticed.

"You are true savages. Already has begun the custom of wearing human teeth. In another generation you will be perforating your noses and ears and wearing ornaments of bone and shell. I know. The human race is doomed to sink back farther and farther into the primitive night ere again it begins its bloody climb upward to civilization. When we increase and feel the lack of room, we will proceed to kill one another. And then I suppose you will wear human scalp-locks at your waist, as well—as you, Edwin, who are the gentlest of my grandsons, have already begun with that vile pigtail. Throw it away, Edwin, boy; throw it away."

"What a gabble the old geezer makes," Hare-Lip remarked, when, the teeth all extracted, they began an attempt at equal division.

They were very quick and abrupt in their actions, and their speech, in moments of hot discussion over the allotment of the choicer teeth, was truly a gabble. They spoke in monosyllables and short jerky sentences that was more a gibberish than a language. And yet, through it ran hints of grammatical construction, and appeared vestiges of the conjugation of some superior culture. Even the speech of Granser was so corrupt that were it put down literally it would be almost so much nonsense to the reader. This, however, was when he talked with the boys.

When he got into the full swing of babbling to himself, it slowly purged itself into pure English. The sentences grew longer and were enunciated with a rhythm and ease that was reminiscent of the lecture platform.

"Tell us about the Red Death, Granser," Hare-Lip demanded, when the teeth affair had been satisfactorily concluded.

"The Scarlet Death," Edwin corrected.

"An' don't work all that funny lingo on us," Hare-Lip went on. "Talk sensible, Granser, like a Santa Rosan ought to talk. Other Santa Rosans don't talk like you."

2

THE OLD MAN showed pleasure in being thus called upon. He cleared his throat and began.

"Twenty or thirty years ago my story was in great demand. But in these days nobody seems interested—"

"There you go!" Hare-Lip cried hotly. "Cut out the funny stuff and talk sensible. What's *interested*? You talk like a baby that don't know how."

"Let him alone," Edwin urged, "or he'll get mad and won't talk at all. Skip the funny places. We'll catch on to some of what he tells us."

"Let her go, Granser," Hoo-Hoo encouraged; for the old man was already maundering about the disrespect for elders and the reversion to cruelty of all humans that fell from high culture to primitive conditions.

The tale began.

"There were very many people in the world in those days. San Francisco alone held four millions—"

"What is millions?" Edwin interrupted.

Granser looked at him kindly.

"I know you cannot count beyond ten, so I will tell you. Hold up your two hands. On both of them you have altogether ten fingers and thumbs. Very well. I now take this grain of sand—you hold it, Hoo-Hoo." He dropped the grain of sand into the lad's palm and went on. "Now that grain of sand stands for the ten fingers of Edwin. I add another grain. That's ten more fingers. And I add another, and another, and another, until I have added as many grains as Edwin has fingers and thumbs. That makes what I call one hundred. Remember that word— one hundred. Now I put this pebble in Hare-Lip's hand. It stands for ten grains of sand, or ten tens of fingers, or one hundred fingers. I put in ten pebbles. They stand for a thousand fingers. I take a mussel-shell, and it stands for ten pebbles, or one hundred grains of sand, or one thousand fingers...." And so on, laboriously, and with much reiteration, he strove to build up in their minds a crude conception of numbers. As the quantities increased, he had the boys holding different magnitudes in each of their hands. For still higher sums, he laid the symbols on the log of driftwood; and for symbols he was hard put, being compelled to use the teeth from the skulls for millions, and the crab-shells for billions. It was here that he stopped, for the boys were showing signs of becoming tired.

"There were four million people in San Francisco—four teeth."

The boys' eyes ranged along from the teeth and from hand to hand, down through the pebbles and sand-grains to Edwin's fingers. And back again they ranged along the ascending series in the effort to grasp such inconceivable numbers.

"That was a lot of folks, Granser," Edwin at last hazarded.

"Like sand on the beach here, like sand on the beach, each grain of sand a man, or woman, or child. Yes, my boy, all those people lived right here in San Francisco. And at one time or another all those people came out on this very beach—more people than there are grains of sand. More—more—more. And San Francisco was a noble city. And across the bay—where we camped last year, even more people lived, clear from Point Richmond, on the level ground and on the hills, all the way around to San Leandro—one great city of seven million people.—Seven teeth... there, that's it, seven millions."

Again the boys' eyes ranged up and down from Edwin's fingers to the teeth on the log.

"The world was full of people. The census of 2010 gave eight billions for the whole world—eight crab-shells, yes, eight billions. It was not like to-day. Mankind knew a great deal more about getting food. And the more food there was, the more people there were. In the year 1800, there were one hundred and seventy millions in Europe alone. One hundred years later—a grain of sand, Hoo-Hoo—one hundred years later, at 1900, there were five hundred millions in Europe—five grains of sand, Hoo-Hoo, and this one tooth. This shows how easy was the getting of food, and how men increased. And in the year 2000 there were fifteen hundred millions in Europe. And it was the same all over the rest of the world. Eight crab-shells there, yes, eight billion people were alive on the earth when the Scarlet Death began.

"I was a young man when the Plague came—twenty-seven years old; and I lived on the other side of San Francisco Bay, in Berkeley. You remember those great stone houses, Edwin, when we came down the hills from Contra Costa? That was where I lived, in those stone houses. I was a professor of English literature."

Much of this was over the heads of the boys, but they strove to comprehend dimly this tale of the past.

"What was them stone houses for?" Hare-Lip queried.

"You remember when your dad taught you to swim?" The boy nodded. "Well, in the University of California—that is the name we had for the houses—we taught young men and women how to think, just as I have taught you now, by sand and pebbles and shells, to know how many people lived in those days. There was very much to teach. The young men and women we taught were called students. We had large rooms in which we taught. I talked to them, forty or fifty at a time, just as I am talking to you now. I told them about the books other men had written before their time, and even, sometimes, in their time—"

"Was that all you did?—just talk, talk, talk?" Hoo-Hoo demanded. "Who hunted your meat for you? and milked the goats? and caught the fish?"

"A sensible question, Hoo-Hoo, a sensible question. As I have told you, in those days food-getting was easy. We were very wise. A few men got the food for many men. The other men did other things. As you say, I talked. I talked all the time, and for this food was given me—much food, fine food, beautiful food, food that I have not tasted in sixty years and shall never taste again. I sometimes think the most wonderful achievement of our tremendous civilization was food—its inconceivable abundance, its infinite variety, its marvellous delicacy. O my grandsons, life was life in those days, when we had such wonderful things to eat."

This was beyond the boys, and they let it slip by, words and thoughts, as a mere senile wandering in the narrative.

"Our food-getters were called *freemen*. This was a joke. We of the ruling classes owned all the land, all the machines, everything. These food-getters were our slaves. We took almost all the food they got, and left them a little so that they might eat, and work, and get us more food—"

"I'd have gone into the forest and got food for myself," Hare-Lip announced; "and if any man tried to take it away from me, I'd have killed him."

The old man laughed.

"Did I not tell you that we of the ruling class owned all the land, all the forest, everything? Any food-getter who would not get food for us, him we punished or compelled to starve to death. And very few did that. They preferred to get food for us, and make clothes for us, and prepare and administer to us a thousand—a mussel-shell, Hoo-Hoo—a thousand satisfactions and delights. And I was Professor Smith in those days—Professor James Howard Smith. And my lecture courses were very popular—that is, very many of the young men and women liked to hear me talk about the books other men had written.

"And I was very happy, and I had beautiful things to eat. And my hands were soft, because I did no work with them, and my body was clean all over and dressed in the softest garments—"

"He surveyed his mangy goat-skin with disgust.

"We did not wear such things in those days. Even the slaves had better garments. And we were most clean. We washed our faces and hands often every day. You boys never wash unless you fall into the water or go swimming."

"Neither do you Granzer," Hoo-Hoo retorted.

"I know, I know, I am a filthy old man, but times have changed. Nobody washes these days, there are no conveniences. It is sixty years since I have seen a piece of soap.

"You do not know what soap is, and I shall not tell you, for I am telling the story of the Scarlet Death. You know what sickness is. We called it a disease. Very many of the diseases came from what we called germs. Remember that word—germs. A germ is a very small thing. It is like a woodtick, such as you find on the dogs in the spring of the year when they run in the forest. Only the germ is very small. It is so small that you cannot see it—"

Hoo-Hoo began to laugh.

"You're a queer un, Granser, talking about things you can't see. If you can't see 'em, how do you know they are? That's what I want to know. How do you know anything you can't see?"

"A good question, a very good question, Hoo-Hoo. But we did see—some of them. We had what we called microscopes and ultramicroscopes, and we put them to our eyes and looked through them, so that we saw things larger than they really were, and many things we could not see without the microscopes at all. Our best ultramicroscopes could make a germ look forty thousand times larger. A mussel-shell is a thousand fingers like Edwin's. Take forty mussel-shells, and by as many times larger was the germ when we looked at it through a microscope. And after that, we had other ways, by using what we called moving pictures, of making the forty-thousand-times germ many, many thousand times larger still. And thus we saw all these things which our eyes of themselves could not see. Take a grain of sand. Break it into ten pieces. Take one piece and break it into ten. Break one of those pieces into ten, and one of those into ten, and one of those into ten, and one of those into ten, and do it all day, and maybe, by sunset, you will have a piece as small as one of the germs." The boys were openly incredulous. Hare-Lip sniffed and sneered and Hoo-Hoo snickered, until Edwin nudged them to be silent.

"The woodtick sucks the blood of the dog, but the germ, being so very small, goes right into the blood of the body, and there it has many children. In those days there would be as many as a billion—a crab-shell, please—as many as that crab-shell in one man's body. We called germs micro-organisms. When a few million, or a billion, of them were in a man, in all the blood of a man, he was sick. These germs were a disease. There were many different kinds of them—more different kinds than there are grains of sand on this beach. We knew only a few of the kinds. The micro-organic world was an invisible world, a world we could not see, and we knew very little about it. Yet we did know something. There was the *bacillus anthracis*; there was the *micrococcus*; there was the *Bacterium termo*, and the *Bacterium lactis*—that's what turns the goat milk sour even to this day, Hare-Lip; and there were *Schizomycetes* without end. And there were many others...."

Here the old man launched into a disquisition on germs and their natures, using words and phrases of such extraordinary length and meaninglessness, that the boys grinned at one another and looked out over the deserted ocean till they forgot the old man was babbling on.

"But the Scarlet Death, Granser," Edwin at last suggested.

Granser recollected himself, and with a start tore himself away from the rostrum of the lecture-hall, where, to another world audience, he had been expounding the latest theory, sixty years gone, of germs and germ-diseases.

"Yes, yes, Edwin; I had forgotten. Sometimes the memory of the past is very strong upon me, and I forget that I am a dirty old man, clad in goat-skin, wandering with my savage grandsons who are goatherds in the primeval wilderness. 'The fleeting systems lapse like foam,' and so lapsed our glorious, colossal civilization. I am Granser, a tired old man. I belong to the tribe of Santa Rosans. I married into that tribe. My sons and daughters married into the Chauffeurs, the Sacramen-tos, and the Palo-Altos. You, Hare-Lip, are of the Chauffeurs. You, Edwin, are of the Sacramentos. And you, Hoo-Hoo, are of the Palo-Altos. Your tribe takes its name from a town that was near the seat of another great institution of learning. It was called Stanford University. Yes, I remember now. It is perfectly clear. I was telling you of the Scarlet Death. Where was I in my story?"

"You was telling about germs, the things you can't see but which make men sick," Edwin prompted.

"Yes, that's where I was. A man did not notice at first when only a few of these germs got into his body. But each germ broke in half and became two germs, and they kept doing this very rapidly so that in a short time there were many millions of them in the body. Then the man was sick. He had a disease, and the disease was named after the kind of a germ that was in him. It might be measles, it might be influenza, it might be yellow fever; it might be any of thousands and thousands of kinds of diseases.

"Now this is the strange thing about these germs. There were always new ones coming to live in men's bodies. Long and long and long ago, when there were only a few men in the world, there were few diseases. But as men increased and lived closely together in great cities and civilizations, new diseases arose, new kinds of germs entered their bodies. Thus were countless millions and billions of human beings killed. And the more thickly men packed together, the more terrible were the new diseases that came to be. Long before my time, in the middle ages, there was the Black Plague that swept across Europe. It swept across Europe many times. There was tuberculosis, that entered into men wherever they were thickly packed. A hundred years before my time there was the bubonic plague. And in Africa was the sleeping sickness. The bacteriologists fought all these sicknesses and destroyed them, just as you boys fight the wolves away from your goats, or squash the mosquitoes that light on you. The bacteriologists—"

"But, Granser, what is a what-you-call-it?" Edwin interrupted.

"You, Edwin, are a goatherd. Your task is to watch the goats. You know a great deal about goats. A bacteriologist watches germs. That's his task, and he knows a great deal about them. So, as I was saying, the bacteriologists fought with the germs and destroyed them—sometimes. There was leprosy, a horrible disease. A hundred years before I was born, the bacteriologists discovered the germ of leprosy. They knew all about it. They made pictures of it. I have seen those pictures. But they never found a way to kill it. But in 1984, there was the Pantoblast Plague, a disease that broke out in a country called Brazil and that killed millions of people. But the bacteriologists found it out, and found the way to kill it, so that the Pantoblast Plague went no farther. They made what they called a serum, which they put into a man's body and which killed the pantoblast germs without killing the man. And in 1910, there was Pellagra, and also the hookworm. These were easily killed by the bacteriologists. But in 1947 there arose a new disease that had never been seen before. It got into the bodies of babies of only ten months old or less, and it made them unable to move their hands and feet, or to eat, or anything; and the bacteriologists were eleven years in discovering how to kill that particular germ and save the babies.

"In spite of all these diseases, and of all the new ones that continued to arise, there were more and more men in the world. This was because it was easy to get food. The easier it was to get food, the more men there were; the more men there were, the more thickly were they packed together on the earth; and the more thickly they were packed, the more new kinds of germs became diseases. There were warnings. Soldervetzsky, as early as 1929, told the bacteriologists that they had no guaranty against some new disease, a thousand times more deadly than any they knew, arising and killing by the hundreds of millions and even by the billion. You see, the micro-organic world remained a mystery to the end. They knew there was such a world, and that from time to time armies of new germs emerged from it to kill men.

"And that was all they knew about it. For all they knew, in that invisible micro-organic world there might be as many different kinds of germs as there are grains of sand on this beach. And also, in that same invisible world it might well be that new kinds of germs came to be. It might be there that life originated—the 'abysmal fecundity,' Soldervetzsky called it, applying the words of other men who had written before him...."

It was at this point that Hare-Lip rose to his feet, an expression of huge contempt on his face.

"Granser," he announced, "you make me sick with your gabble. Why don't you tell about the Red Death? If you ain't going to, say so, an' we'll start back for camp."

The old man looked at him and silently began to cry. The weak tears of age rolled down his cheeks and all the feebleness of his eighty-seven years showed in his grief-stricken countenance.

"Sit down," Edwin counselled soothingly. "Granser's all right. He's just gettin' to the Scarlet Death, ain't you, Granser? He's just goin' to tell us about it right now. Sit down, Hare-Lip. Go ahead, Granser."

3

THE OLD MAN wiped the tears away on his grimy knuckles and took up the tale in a tremulous, piping voice that soon strengthened as he got the swing of the narrative.

"It was in the summer of 2013 that the Plague came. I was twenty-seven years old, and well do I remember it. Wireless despatches—"

Hare-Lip spat loudly his disgust, and Granser hastened to make amends.

"We talked through the air in those days, thousands and thousands of miles. And the word came of a strange disease that had broken out in New York. There were seventeen millions of people living then in that noblest city of America. Nobody thought anything about the news. It was only a small thing. There had been only a few deaths. It seemed, though, that they had died very quickly, and that one of the first signs of the disease was the turning red of the face and all the body. Within twenty-four hours came the report of the first case in Chicago. And on the same day, it was made public that London, the greatest city in the world, next to Chicago, had been secretly fighting the plague for two weeks and censoring the news despatches—that is, not permitting the word to go forth to the rest of the world that London had the plague.

"It looked serious, but we in California, like everywhere else, were not alarmed. We were sure that the bacteriologists would find a way to overcome this new germ, just as they had overcome other germs in the past. But the trouble was the astonishing quickness with which this germ destroyed human beings, and the fact that it inevitably killed any human body it entered. No one ever recovered. There was the old Asiatic cholera, when you might eat dinner with a well man in the evening, and the next morning, if you got up early enough, you would see him being hauled by your window in the death-cart. But this new plague was quicker than that—much quicker.

"From the moment of the first signs of it, a man would be dead in an hour. Some lasted for several hours. Many died within ten or fifteen minutes of the appearance of the first signs.

"The heart began to beat faster and the heat of the body to increase. Then came the scarlet rash, spreading like wildfire over the face and body. Most persons never noticed the increase in heat and heart-beat, and the first they knew was when the scarlet rash came out. Usually, they had convulsions at the time of the appearance of the rash. But these convulsions did not last long and were not very severe. If one lived through them, he became perfectly quiet, and only did he feel a numbness swiftly creeping up his body from the feet. The heels became numb first, then the legs, and hips, and when the numbness reached as high as his heart he died. They did not rave or sleep. Their minds always remained cool and calm up to the moment their heart numbed and stopped. And another strange thing was the rapidity of decomposition. No sooner was a person dead than the body seemed to fall to pieces, to fly apart, to melt away even as you looked at it. That was one of the reasons the plague spread so rapidly. All the billions of germs in a corpse were so immediately released.

"And it was because of all this that the bacteriologists had so little chance in fighting the germs. They were killed in their laboratories even as they studied the germ of the Scarlet Death. They were heroes. As fast as they perished, others stepped forth and took their places. It was in London that they first isolated it. The news was telegraphed everywhere. Trask was the name of the man who succeeded in this, but within thirty hours he was dead. Then came the struggle in all the laboratories to find something that would kill the plague germs. All drugs failed. You see, the problem was to get a drug, or serum, that would kill the germs in the body and not kill the body. They tried to fight it with other germs, to put into the body of a sick man germs that were the enemies of the plague germs—"

"And you can't see these germ-things, Granser," Hare-Lip objected, "and here you gabble, gabble, gabble about them as if they was anything, when they're nothing at all. Anything you can't see, ain't, that's what. Fighting things that ain't with things that ain't! They must have been all fools in them days. That's why they croaked. I ain't goin' to believe in such rot, I tell you that."

Granser promptly began to weep, while Edwin hotly took up his defence.

"Look here, Hare-Lip, you believe in lots of things you can't see."

Hare-Lip shook his head.

"You believe in dead men walking about. You never seen one dead man walk about."

"I tell you I seen 'em, last winter, when I was wolf-hunting with dad."

"Well, you always spit when you cross running water," Edwin challenged.

"That's to keep off bad luck," was Hare-Lip's defence.

"You believe in bad luck?"

"Sure."

"An' you ain't never seen bad luck," Edwin concluded triumphantly. "You're just as bad as Granser and his germs. You believe in what you don't see. Go on, Granser."

Hare-Lip, crushed by this metaphysical defeat, remained silent, and the old man went on. Often and often, though this narrative must not be clogged by the details, was Granser's tale interrupted while the boys squabbled among themselves. Also, among themselves they kept up a constant, low-voiced exchange of explanation and conjecture, as they strove to follow the old man into his unknown and vanished world.

"The Scarlet Death broke out in San Francisco. The first death came on a Monday morning. By Thursday they were dying like flies in Oakland and San Francisco. They died everywhere— in their beds, at their work, walking along the street. It was on Tuesday that I saw my first death—Miss Collbran, one of my students, sitting right there before my eyes, in my lecture-room. I noticed her face while I was talking. It had suddenly turned scarlet. I ceased speaking and could only look at her, for the first fear of the plague was already on all of us and we knew that it had come. The young women screamed and ran out of the room. So did the young men run out, all but two. Miss Collbran's convulsions were very mild and lasted less than a minute. One of the young men fetched her a glass of water. She drank only a little of it, and cried out:

"'My feet! All sensation has left them.'

"After a minute she said, 'I have no feet. I am unaware that I have any feet. And my knees are cold. I can scarcely feel that I have knees.'

"She lay on the floor, a bundle of notebooks under her head. And we could do nothing. The coldness and the numbness crept up past her hips to her heart, and when it reached her heart she was dead. In fifteen minutes, by the clock—I timed it—she was dead, there, in my own classroom, dead. And she was a very beautiful, strong, healthy young woman. And from the first sign of the plague to her death only fifteen minutes elapsed. That will show you how swift was the Scarlet Death.

"Yet in those few minutes I remained with the dying woman in my classroom, the alarm had spread over the university; and the students, by thousands, all of them, had deserted the lecture-room and laboratories. When I emerged, on my way to make report to the President of the Faculty, I found the university deserted. Across the campus were several stragglers hurrying for their homes. Two of them were running.

"President Hoag, I found in his office, all alone, looking very old and very gray, with a multitude of wrinkles in his face that I had never seen before. At the sight of me, he pulled himself to his feet and tottered away to the inner office, banging the door after him and locking it. You see, he knew I had been exposed, and he was afraid. He shouted to me through the door to go away. I shall never forget my feelings as I walked down the silent corridors and out across that deserted campus. I was not afraid. I had been exposed, and I looked upon myself as already dead. It was not that, but a feeling of awful depression that impressed me. Everything had stopped. It was like the end of the world to me—my world. I had been born within sight and sound of the university. It had been my predestined career. My father had been a professor there before me, and his father before him. For a century and a half had this university, like a splendid machine, been running steadily on. And now, in an instant, it had stopped. It was like seeing the sacred flame die down on some thrice-sacred altar. I was shocked, unutterably shocked.

"When I arrived home, my housekeeper screamed as I entered, and fled away. And when I rang, I found the housemaid had likewise fled. I investigated. In the kitchen I found the cook on the point of departure. But she screamed, too, and in her haste dropped a suitcase of her personal belongings and ran out of the house and across the grounds, still screaming. I can hear her scream to this day. You see, we did not act in this way when ordinary diseases smote us. We were always calm over such things, and sent for the doctors and nurses who knew just what to do. But this was different. It struck so suddenly, and killed so swiftly, and never missed a stroke. When the scarlet rash appeared on a person's face, that person was marked by death. There was never a known case of a recovery.

"I was alone in my big house. As I have told you often before, in those days we could talk with one another over wires or through the air. The telephone bell rang, and I found my brother talking to me. He told me that he was not coming home for fear of catching the plague from me, and that he had taken our two sisters to stop at Professor Bacon's home. He advised me to remain where I was, and wait to find out whether or not I had caught the plague.

"To all of this I agreed, staying in my house and for the first time in my life attempting to cook. And the plague did not come out on me. By means of the telephone I could talk with whomsoever I pleased and get the news. Also, there were the newspapers, and I ordered all of them to be thrown up to my door so that I could know what was happening with the rest of the world.

"New York City and Chicago were in chaos. And what happened with them was happening in all the large cities. A third of the New York police were dead. Their chief was also dead, likewise the mayor. All law and order had ceased. The bodies were lying in the streets unburied. All railroads and vessels carrying food and such things into the great city had ceased runnings and mobs of the hungry poor were pillaging the stores and warehouses. Murder and robbery and drunkenness were everywhere. Already the people had fled from the city by millions—at first the rich, in their private motor-cars and dirigibles, and then the great mass of the population, on foot, carrying the plague with them, themselves starving and pillaging the farmers and all the towns and villages on the way.

"The man who sent this news, the wireless operator, was alone with his instrument on the top of a lofty building. The people remaining in the city—he estimated them at several hundred thousand—had gone mad from fear and drink, and on all sides of him great fires were raging. He was a hero, that man who staid by his post—an obscure newspaperman, most likely.

"For twenty-four hours, he said, no transatlantic airships had arrived, and no more messages were coming from England. He did state, though, that a message from Berlin—that's in Germany—announced that Hoffmeyer, a bacteriologist of the Metchnikoff School, had discovered the serum for the plague. That was the last word, to this day, that we of America ever received from Europe. If Hoffmeyer discovered the serum, it was too late, or otherwise, long ere this, explorers from Europe would have come looking for us. We can only conclude that what happened in America happened in Europe, and that, at the best, some several score may have survived the Scarlet Death on that whole continent.

"For one day longer the despatches continued to come from New York. Then they, too, ceased. The man who had sent them, perched in his lofty building, had either died of the plague or been consumed in the great conflagrations he had described as raging around him. And what had occurred in New York had been duplicated in all the other cities. It was the same in San Francisco, and Oakland, and Berkeley. By Thursday the people were dying so rapidly that their corpses could not be handled, and dead bodies lay everywhere. Thursday night the panic outrush for the country began. Imagine, my grandsons, people, thicker than the salmon-run you have seen on the Sacramento river, pouring out of the cities by millions, madly over the country, in vain attempt to escape the ubiquitous death. You see, they carried the germs with them. Even the airships of the rich, fleeing for mountain and desert fastnesses, carried the germs.

"Hundreds of these airships escaped to Hawaii, and not only did they bring the plague with them, but they found the plague already there before them. This we learned, by the despatches, until all order in San Francisco vanished, and there were no operators left at their posts to receive or send. It was amazing, astounding, this loss of communication with the world. It was exactly as if the world had ceased, been blotted out. For sixty years that world has no longer existed for me. I know there must be such places as New York, Europe, Asia, and Africa; but not one word has been heard of them—not in sixty years. With the coming of the Scarlet Death the world fell apart, absolutely, irretrievably. Ten thousand years of culture and civilization passed in the twinkling of an eye, 'lapsed like foam.'

"I was telling about the airships of the rich. They carried the plague with them and no matter where they fled, they died. I never encountered but one survivor of any of them— Mungerson. He was afterwards a Santa Rosan, and he married my eldest daughter. He came into the tribe eight years after the plague. He was then nineteen years old, and he was compelled to wait twelve years more before he could marry. You see, there were no unmarried women, and some of the older daughters of the Santa Rosans were already bespoken. So he was forced to wait until my Mary had grown to sixteen years. It was his son, Gimp-Leg, who was killed last year by the mountain lion.

"Mungerson was eleven years old at the time of the plague. His father was one of the Industrial Magnates, a very wealthy, powerful man. It was on his airship, the Condor, that they were fleeing, with all the family, for the wilds of British Columbia, which is far to the north of here. But there was some accident, and they were wrecked near Mount Shasta. You have heard of that mountain. It is far to the north. The plague broke out amongst them, and this boy of eleven was the only survivor. For eight years he was alone, wandering over a deserted land and looking vainly for his own kind. And at last, travelling south, he picked up with us, the Santa Rosans.

"But I am ahead of my story. When the great exodus from the cities around San Francisco Bay began, and while the telephones were still working, I talked with my brother. I told him this flight from the cities was insanity, that there were no symptoms of the plague in me, and that the thing for us to do was to isolate ourselves and our relatives in some safe place. We decided on the Chemistry Building, at the university, and we planned to lay in a supply of provisions, and by force of arms to prevent any other persons from forcing their presence upon us after we had retired to our refuge.

"All this being arranged, my brother begged me to stay in my own house for at least twenty-four hours more, on the chance of the plague developing in me. To this I agreed, and he promised to come for me next day. We talked on over the details of the provisioning and the defending of the Chemistry Building until the telephone died. It died in the midst of our conversation. That evening there were no electric lights, and I was alone in my house in the darkness. No more newspapers were being printed, so I had no knowledge of what was taking place outside.

"I heard sounds of rioting and of pistol shots, and from my windows I could see the glare of the sky of some conflagration in the direction of Oakland. It was a night of terror. I did not sleep a wink. A man—why and how I do not know—was killed on the sidewalk in front of the house. I heard the rapid reports of an automatic pistol, and a few minutes later the wounded wretch crawled up to my door, moaning and crying out for help. Arming myself with two automatics, I went to him. By the light of a match I ascertained that while he was dying of the bullet wounds, at the same time the plague was on him. I fled indoors, whence I heard him moan and cry out for half an hour longer.

"In the morning, my brother came to me. I had gathered into a handbag what things of value I purposed taking, but when I saw his face I knew that he would never accompany me to the Chemistry Building. The plague was on him. He intended shaking my hand, but I went back hurriedly before him.

"'Look at yourself in the mirror,' I commanded.

"He did so, and at sight of his scarlet face, the color deepening as he looked at it, he sank down nervelessly in a chair.

"'My God!' he said. 'I've got it. Don't come near me. I am a dead man.'

"Then the convulsions seized him. He was two hours in dying, and he was conscious to the last, complaining about the coldness and loss of sensation in his feet, his calves, his thighs, until at last it was his heart and he was dead.

"That was the way the Scarlet Death slew. I caught up my handbag and fled. The sights in the streets were terrible. One stumbled on bodies everywhere. Some were not yet dead. And even as you looked, you saw men sink down with the death fastened upon them. There were numerous fires burning in Berkeley, while Oakland and San Francisco were apparently being swept by vast conflagrations. The smoke of the burning filled the heavens, so that the midday was as a gloomy twilight, and, in the shifts of wind, sometimes the sun shone through dimly, a dull red orb. Truly, my grandsons, it was like the last days of the end of the world.

"There were numerous stalled motor cars, showing that the gasoline and the engine supplies of the garages had given out. I remember one such car. A man and a woman lay back dead in the seats, and on the pavement near it were two more women and a child. Strange and terrible sights there were on every hand. People slipped by silently, furtively, like ghosts—white-faced women carrying infants in their arms; fathers leading children by the hand; singly, and in couples, and in families—all fleeing out of the city of death. Some carried supplies of food, others blankets and valuables, and there were many who carried nothing.

"There was a grocery store—a place where food was sold. The man to whom it belonged—I knew him well—a quiet, sober, but stupid and obstinate fellow, was defending it. The windows and doors had been broken in, but he, inside, hiding behind a counter, was discharging his pistol at a number of men on the sidewalk who were breaking in. In the entrance were several bodies—of men, I decided, whom he had killed earlier in the day. Even as I looked on from a distance, I saw one of the robbers break the windows of the adjoining store, a place where shoes were sold, and deliberately set fire to it. I did not go to the groceryman's assistance. The time for such acts had already passed. Civilization was crumbling, and it was each for himself."

❦ 4 ❧

I WENT AWAY HASTILY, down a cross-street, and at the first corner I saw another tragedy. Two men of the working class had caught a man and a woman with two children, and were robbing them. I knew the man by sight, though I had never been introduced to him. He was a poet whose verses I had long admired. Yet I did not go to his help, for at the moment I came upon the scene there was a pistol shot, and I saw him sinking to the ground. The woman screamed, and she was felled with a fist-blow by one of the brutes. I cried out threateningly, whereupon they discharged their pistols at me and I ran away around the corner. Here I was blocked by an advancing conflagration. The buildings on both sides were burning, and the street was filled with smoke and flame. From somewhere in that murk came a woman's voice calling shrilly for help. But I did not go to her. A man's heart turned to iron amid such scenes, and one heard all too many appeals for help.

"Returning to the corner, I found the two robbers were gone. The poet and his wife lay dead on the pavement. It was a shocking sight. The two children had vanished—whither I could not tell. And I knew, now, why it was that the fleeing persons I encountered slipped along so furtively and with such white faces. In the midst of our civilization, down in our slums and labor-ghettos, we had bred a race of barbarians, of savages; and now, in the time of our calamity, they turned upon us like the wild beasts they were and destroyed us. And they destroyed themselves as well.

"They inflamed themselves with strong drink and committed a thousand atrocities, quarreling and killing one another in the general madness. One group of workingmen I saw, of the better sort, who had banded together, and, with their women and children in their midst, the sick and aged in litters and being carried, and with a number of horses pulling a truck-load of provisions, they were fighting their way out of the city. They made a fine spectacle as they came down the street through the drifting smoke, though they nearly shot me when I first appeared in their path. As they went by, one of their leaders shouted out to me in apologetic explanation. He said they were killing the robbers and looters on sight, and that they had thus banded together as the only-means by which to escape the prowlers.

"It was here that I saw for the first time what I was soon to see so often. One of the marching men had suddenly shown the unmistakable mark of the plague. Immediately those about him drew away, and he, without a remonstrance, stepped out of his place to let them pass on. A woman, most probably his wife, attempted to follow him. She was leading a little boy by the hand. But the husband commanded her sternly to go on, while others laid hands on her and restrained her from following him. This I saw, and I saw the man also, with his scarlet blaze of face, step into a doorway on the opposite side of the street. I heard the report of his pistol, and saw him sink lifeless to the ground.

"After being turned aside twice again by advancing fires, I succeeded in getting through to the university. On the edge of the campus I came upon a party of university folk who were going in the direction of the Chemistry Building. They were all family men, and their families were with them, including the nurses and the servants. Professor Badminton greeted me, I had difficulty in recognizing him. Somewhere he had gone through flames, and his beard was singed off. About his head was a bloody bandage, and his clothes were filthy.

"He told me he had prowlers, and that his brother had been killed the previous night, in the defence of their dwelling.

"Midway across the campus, he pointed suddenly to Mrs. Swinton's face. The unmistakable scarlet was there. Immediately all the other women set up a screaming and began to run away from her. Her two children were with a nurse, and these also ran with the women. But her husband, Doctor Swinton, remained with her.

"'Go on, Smith,' he told me. 'Keep an eye on the children. As for me, I shall stay with my wife. I know she is as already dead, but I can't leave her. Afterwards, if I escape, I shall come to the Chemistry Building, and do you watch for me and let me in.'

"I left him bending over his wife and soothing her last moments, while I ran to overtake the party. We were the last to be admitted to the Chemistry Building. After that, with our automatic rifles we maintained our isolation. By our plans, we had arranged for a company of sixty to be in this refuge. Instead, every one of the number originally planned had added relatives and friends and whole families until there were over four hundred souls. But the Chemistry Building was large, and, standing by itself, was in no danger of being burned by the great fires that raged everywhere in the city.

"A large quantity of provisions had been gathered, and a food committee took charge of it, issuing rations daily to the various families and groups that arranged themselves into messes. A number of committees were appointed, and we developed a very efficient organization. I was on the committee of defence, though for the first day no prowlers came near. We could see them in the distance, however, and by the smoke of their fires knew that several camps of them were occupying the far edge of the campus. Drunkenness was rife, and often we heard them singing ribald songs or insanely shouting. While the world crashed to ruin about them and all the air was filled with the smoke of its burning, these low creatures gave rein to their bestiality and fought and drank and died. And after all, what did it matter? Everybody died anyway, the good and the bad, the efficients and the weaklings, those that loved to live and those that scorned to live. They passed. Everything passed.

"When twenty-four hours had gone by and no signs of the plague were apparent, we congratulated ourselves and set about digging a well. You have seen the great iron pipes which in those days carried water to all the city-dwellers. We feared that the fires in the city would burst the pipes and empty the reservoirs. So we tore up the cement floor of the central court of the Chemistry Building and dug a well. There were many young men, undergraduates, with us, and we worked night and day on the well. And our fears were confirmed. Three hours before we reached water, the pipes went dry.

"A second twenty-four hours passed, and still the plague did not appear among us. We thought we were saved. But we did not know what I afterwards decided to be true, namely, that the period of the incubation of the plague germs in a human's body was a matter of a number of days. It slew so swiftly when once it manifested itself, that we were led to believe that the period of incubation was equally swift. So, when two days had left us unscathed, we were elated with the idea that we were free of the contagion.

"But the third day disillusioned us. I can never forget the night preceding it. I had charge of the night guards from eight to twelve, and from the roof of the building I watched the passing of all man's glorious works. So terrible were the local conflagrations that all the sky was lighted up. One could read the finest print in the red glare. All the world seemed wrapped in flames. San Francisco spouted smoke and fire from a score of vast conflagrations that were like so many active volcanoes. Oakland, San Leandro, Haywards—all were burning; and to the northward, clear to Point Richmond, other fires were at work. It was an awe-inspiring spectacle. Civilization, my grandsons, civilization was passing in a sheet of flame and a breath of death. At ten o'clock that night, the great powder magazines at Point Pinole exploded in rapid succession. So terrific were the concussions that the strong building rocked as in an earthquake, while every pane of glass was broken. It was then that I left the roof and went down the long corridors, from room to room, quieting the alarmed women and telling them what had happened.

"An hour later, at a window on the ground floor, I heard pandemonium break out in the camps of the prowlers. There were cries and screams, and shots from many pistols. As we afterward conjectured, this fight had been precipitated by an attempt on the part of those that were well to drive out those that were sick. At any rate, a number of the plague-stricken prowlers escaped across the campus and drifted against our doors. We warned them back, but they cursed us and discharged a fusillade from their pistols. Professor Merryweather, at one of the windows, was instantly killed, the bullet striking him squarely between the eyes. We opened fire in turn, and all the prowlers fled away with the exception of three. One was a woman. The plague was on them and they were reckless. Like foul fiends, there in the red glare from the skies, with faces blazing, they continued to curse us and fire at us. One of the men I shot with my own hand. After that the other man and the woman, still cursing us, lay down under our windows, where we were compelled to watch them die of the plague.

"The situation was critical. The explosions of the powder magazines had broken all the windows of the Chemistry Building, so that we were exposed to the germs from the corpses. The sanitary committee was called upon to act, and it responded nobly. Two men were required to go out and remove the corpses, and this meant the probable sacrifice of their own lives, for, having performed the task, they were not to be permitted to reenter the building. One of the professors, who was a bachelor, and one of the undergraduates volunteered. They bade good-bye to us and went forth. They were heroes. They gave up their lives that four hundred others might live. After they had performed their work, they stood for a moment, at a distance, looking at us wistfully. Then they waved their hands in farewell and went away slowly across the campus toward the burning city.

"And yet it was all useless. The next morning the first one of us was smitten with the plague —a little nurse-girl in the family of Professor Stout. It was no time for weak-kneed, sentimental policies. On the chance that she might be the only one, we thrust her forth from the building and commanded her to be gone.

"She went away slowly across the campus, wringing her hands and crying pitifully. We felt like brutes, but what were we to do? There were four hundred of us, and individuals had to be sacrificed.

"In one of the laboratories three families had domiciled themselves, and that afternoon we found among them no less than four corpses and seven cases of the plague in all its different stages.

"Then it was that the horror began. Leaving the dead lie, we forced the living ones to segregate themselves in another room. The plague began to break out among the rest of us, and as fast as the symptoms appeared, we sent the stricken ones to these segregated rooms. We compelled them to walk there by themselves, so as to avoid laying hands on them. It was heartrending. But still the plague raged among us, and room after room was filled with the dead and dying. And so we who were yet clean retreated to the next floor and to the next, before this sea of the dead, that, room by room and floor by floor, inundated the building.

"The place became a charnel house, and in the middle of the night the survivors fled forth, taking nothing with them except arms and ammunition and a heavy store of tinned foods. We camped on the opposite side of the campus from the prowlers, and, while some stood guard, others of us volunteered to scout into the city in quest of horses, motor cars, carts, and wagons, or anything that would carry our provisions and enable us to emulate the banded workingmen I had seen fighting their way out to the open country.

"I was one of these scouts; and Doctor Hoyle, remembering that his motor car had been left behind in his home garage, told me to look for it. We scouted in pairs, and Dombey, a young undergraduate, accompanied me. We had to cross half a mile of the residence portion of the city to get to Doctor Hoyle's home. Here the buildings stood apart, in the midst of trees and grassy lawns, and here the fires had played freaks, burning whole blocks, skipping blocks and often skipping a single house in a block. And here, too, the prowlers were still at their work. We carried our automatic pistols openly in our hands, and looked desperate enough, forsooth, to keep them from attacking us. But at Doctor Hoyle's house the thing happened. Untouched by fire, even as we came to it the smoke of flames burst forth.

"The miscreant who had set fire to it staggered down the steps and out along the driveway. Sticking out of his coat pockets were bottles of whiskey, and he was very drunk. My first impulse was to shoot him, and I have never ceased regretting that I did not. Staggering and maundering to himself, with bloodshot eyes, and a raw and bleeding slash down one side of his bewhiskered face, he was altogether the most nauseating specimen of degradation and filth I had ever encountered. I did not shoot him, and he leaned against a tree on the lawn to let us go by. It was the most absolute, wanton act. Just as we were opposite him, he suddenly drew a pistol and shot Dombey through the head. The next instant I shot him. But it was too late. Dombey expired without a groan, immediately. I doubt if he even knew what had happened to him.

"Leaving the two corpses, I hurried on past the burning house to the garage, and there found Doctor Hoyle's motor car. The tanks were filled with gasoline, and it was ready for use. And it was in this car that I threaded the streets of the ruined city and came back to the survivors on the campus. The other scouts returned, but none had been so fortunate. Professor Fairmead had found a Shetland pony, but the poor creature, tied in a stable and abandoned for days, was so weak from want of food and water that it could carry no burden at all. Some of the men were for turning it loose, but I insisted that we should lead it along with us, so that, if we got out of food, we would have it to eat.

"There were forty-seven of us when we started, many being women and children. The President of the Faculty, an old man to begin with, and now hopelessly broken by the awful happenings of the past week, rode in the motor car with several young children and the aged mother of Professor Fairmead. Wathope, a young professor of English, who had a grievous bullet-wound in his leg, drove the car. The rest of us walked, Professor Fairmead leading the pony.

"It was what should have been a bright summer day, but the smoke from the burning world filled the sky, through which the sun shone murkily, a dull and lifeless orb, blood-red and ominous. But we had grown accustomed to that blood-red sun. With the smoke it was different. It bit into our nostrils and eyes, and there was not one of us whose eyes were not bloodshot. We directed our course to the southeast through the endless miles of suburban residences, travelling along where the first swells of low hills rose from the flat of the central city. It was by this way, only, that we could expect to gain the country.

"Our progress was painfully slow. The women and children could not walk fast. They did not dream of walking, my grandsons, in the way all people walk to-day. In truth, none of us knew how to walk. It was not until after the plague that I learned really to walk. So it was that the pace of the slowest was the pace of all, for we dared not separate on account of the prowlers. There were not so many now of these human beasts of prey. The plague had already well diminished their numbers, but enough still lived to be a constant menace to us. Many of the beautiful residences were untouched by fire, yet smoking ruins were everywhere. The prowlers, too, seemed to have got over their insensate desire to burn, and it was more rarely that we saw houses freshly on fire.

"Several of us scouted among the private garages in search of motor cars and gasoline. But in this we were unsuccessful. The first great flights from the cities had swept all such utilities away. Calgan, a fine young man, was lost in this work. He was shot by prowlers while crossing a lawn. Yet this was our only casualty, though, once, a drunken brute deliberately opened fire on all of us. Luckily, he fired wildly, and we shot him before he had done any hurt.

"At Fruitvale, still in the heart of the magnificent residence section of the city, the plague again smote us. Professor Fair-mead was the victim. Making signs to us that his mother was not to know, he turned aside into the grounds of a beautiful mansion. He sat down forlornly on the steps of the front veranda, and I, having lingered, waved him a last farewell. That night, several miles beyond Fruitvale and still in the city, we made camp. And that night we shifted camp twice to get away from our dead. In the morning there were thirty of us. I shall never forget the President of the Faculty. During the morning's march his wife, who was walking, betrayed the fatal symptoms, and when she drew aside to let us go on, he insisted on leaving the motor car and remaining with her. There was quite a discussion about this, but in the end we gave in. It was just as well, for we knew not which ones of us, if any, might ultimately escape.

"That night, the second of our march, we camped beyond Haywards in the first stretches of country. And in the morning there were eleven of us that lived. Also, during the night, Wathope, the professor with the wounded leg, deserted us in the motor car. He took with him his sister and his mother and most of our tinned provisions. It was that day, in the afternoon, while resting by the wayside, that I saw the last airship I shall ever see. The smoke was much thinner here in the country, and I first sighted the ship drifting and veering helplessly at an elevation of two thousand feet. What had happened I could not conjecture, but even as we looked we saw her bow dip down lower and lower. Then the bulkheads of the various gas-chambers must have burst, for, quite perpendicular, she fell like a plummet to the earth.

"And from that day to this I have not seen another airship. Often and often, during the next few years, I scanned the sky for them, hoping against hope that somewhere in the world civilization had survived. But it was not to be. What happened with us in California must have happened with everybody everywhere.

"Another day, and at Niles there were three of us. Beyond Niles, in the middle of the highway, we found Wathope. The motor car had broken down, and there, on the rugs which they had spread on the ground, lay the bodies of his sister, his mother, and himself.

"Wearied by the unusual exercise of continual walking, that night I slept heavily. In the morning I was alone in the world. Canfield and Parsons, my last companions, were dead of the plague. Of the four hundred that sought shelter in the Chemistry Building, and of the forty-seven that began the march, I alone remained—I and the Shetland pony. Why this should be so there is no explaining. I did not catch the plague, that is all. I was immune. I was merely the one lucky man in a million—just as every survivor was one in a million, or, rather, in several millions, for the proportion was at least that."

"For two days I sheltered in a pleasant grove where there had been no deaths. In those two days, while badly depressed and believing that my turn would come at any moment, nevertheless I rested and recuperated. So did the pony. And on the third day, putting what small store of tinned provisions I possessed on the pony's back, I started on across a very lonely land. Not a live man, woman, or child, did I encounter, though the dead were everywhere. Food, however, was abundant. The land then was not as it is now. It was all cleared of trees and brush, and it was cultivated. The food for millions of mouths was growing, ripening, and going to waste. From the fields and orchards I gathered vegetables, fruits, and berries. Around the deserted farmhouses I got eggs and caught chickens. And frequently I found supplies of tinned provisions in the store-rooms.

"A strange thing was what was taking place with all the domestic animals. Everywhere they were going wild and preying on one another. The chickens and ducks were the first to be destroyed, while the pigs were the first to go wild, followed by the cats. Nor were the dogs long in adapting themselves to the changed conditions. There was a veritable plague of dogs. They devoured the corpses, barked and howled during the nights, and in the daytime slunk about in the distance. As the time went by, I noticed a change in their behavior. At first they were apart from one another, very suspicious and very prone to fight. But after a not very long while they began to come together and run in packs. The dog, you see, always was a social animal, and this was true before ever he came to be domesticated by man. In the last days of the world before the plague, there were many many very different kinds of dogs—dogs without hair and dogs with warm fur, dogs so small that they would make scarcely a mouthful for other dogs that were as large as mountain lions. Well, all the small dogs, and the weak types, were killed by their fellows. Also, the very large ones were not adapted for the wild life and bred out. As a result, the many different kinds of dogs disappeared, and there remained, running in packs, the medium-sized wolfish dogs that you know to-day."

"But the cats don't run in packs, Granser," Hoo-Hoo objected.

"The cat was never a social animal. As one writer in the nineteenth century said, the cat walks by himself. He always walked by himself, from before the time he was tamed by man, down through the long ages of domestication, to to-day when once more he is wild.

"The horses also went wild, and all the fine breeds we had degenerated into the small mustang horse you know to-day. The cows likewise went wild, as did the pigeons and the sheep. And that a few of the chickens survived you know yourself. But the wild chicken of to-day is quite a different thing from the chickens we had in those days.

"But I must go on with my story. I travelled through a deserted land. As the time went by I began to yearn more and more for human beings. But I never found one, and I grew lonelier and lonelier. I crossed Livermore Valley and the mountains between it and the great valley of the San Joaquin. You have never seen that valley, but it is very large and it is the home of the wild horse. There are great droves there, thousands and tens of thousands. I revisited it thirty years after, so I know. You think there are lots of wild horses down here in the coast valleys, but they are as nothing compared with those of the San Joaquin. Strange to say, the cows, when they went wild, went back into the lower mountains. Evidently they were better able to protect themselves there.

"In the country districts the ghouls and prowlers had been less in evidence, for I found many villages and towns untouched by fire. But they were filled by the pestilential dead, and I passed by without exploring them. It was near Lathrop that, out of my loneliness, I picked up a pair of collie dogs that were so newly free that they were urgently willing to return to their allegiance to man. These collies accompanied me for many years, and the strains of them are in those very dogs there that you boys have to-day. But in sixty years the collie strain has worked out. These brutes are more like domesticated wolves than anything else."

Hare-Lip rose to his feet, glanced to see that the goats were safe, and looked at the sun's position in the afternoon sky, advertising impatience at the prolixity of the old man's tale. Urged to hurry by Edwin, Granser went on.

"There is little more to tell. With my two dogs and my pony, and riding a horse I had managed to capture, I crossed the San Joaquin and went on to a wonderful valley in the Sierras called Yosemite. In the great hotel there I found a prodigious supply of tinned provisions. The pasture was abundant, as was the game, and the river that ran through the valley was full of trout. I remained there three years in an utter loneliness that none but a man who has once been highly civilized can understand. Then I could stand it no more. I felt that I was going crazy. Like the dog, I was a social animal and I needed my kind. I reasoned that since I had survived the plague, there was a possibility that others had survived. Also, I reasoned that after three years the plague germs must all be gone and the land be clean again.

"With my horse and dogs and pony, I set out. Again I crossed the San Joaquin Valley, the mountains beyond, and came down into Livermore Valley. The change in those three years was amazing. All the land had been splendidly tilled, and now I could scarcely recognize it, 'such was the sea of rank vegetation that had overrun the agricultural handiwork of man. You see, the wheat, the vegetables, and orchard trees had always been cared for and nursed by man, so that they were soft and tender. The weeds and wild bushes and such things, on the contrary, had always been fought by man, so that they were tough and resistant. As a result, when the hand of man was removed, the wild vegetation smothered and destroyed practically all the domesticated vegetation. The coyotes were greatly increased, and it was at this time that I first encountered wolves, straying in twos and threes and small packs down from the regions where they had always persisted.

"It was at Lake Temescal, not far from the one-time city of Oakland, that I came upon the first live human beings. Oh, my grandsons, how can I describe to you my emotion, when, astride my horse and dropping down the hillside to the lake, I saw the smoke of a campfire rising through the trees. Almost did my heart stop beating. I felt that I was going crazy. Then I heard the cry of a babe—a human babe. And dogs barked, and my dogs answered. I did not know but what I was the one human alive in the whole world. It could not be true that here were others—smoke, and the cry of a babe.

"Emerging on the lake, there, before my eyes, not a hundred yards away, I saw a man, a large man. He was standing on an outjutting rock and fishing. I was overcome. I stopped my horse. I tried to call out but could not. I waved my hand. It seemed to me that the man looked at me, but he did not appear to wave. Then I laid my head on my arms there in the saddle. I was afraid to look again, for I knew it was an hallucination, and I knew that if I looked the man would be gone. And so precious was the hallucination, that I wanted it to persist yet a little while. I knew, too, that as long as I did not look it would persist.

"Thus I remained, until I heard my dogs snarling, and a man's voice. What do you think the voice said? I will tell you. It said: *'Where in hell did you come from??'*

"Those were the words, the exact words. That was what your other grandfather said to me, Hare-Lip, when he greeted me there on the shore of Lake Temescal fifty-seven years ago. And they were the most ineffable words I have ever heard. I opened my eyes, and there he stood before me, a large, dark, hairy man, heavy-jawed, slant-browed, fierce-eyed. How I got off my horse I do not know. But it seemed that the next I knew I was clasping his hand with both of mine and crying. I would have embraced him, but he was ever a narrow-minded, suspicious man, and he drew away from me. Yet did I cling to his hand and cry."

Granser's voice faltered and broke at the recollection, and the weak tears streamed down his cheeks while the boys looked on and giggled.

"Yet did I cry," he continued, "and desire to embrace him, though the Chauffeur was a brute, a perfect brute—the most abhorrent man I have ever known. His name was... strange, how I have forgotten his name. Everybody called him Chauffeur—it was the name of his occupation, and it stuck. That is how, to this day, the tribe he founded is called the Chauffeur Tribe.

"He was a violent, unjust man. Why the plague germs spared him I can never understand. It would seem, in spite of our old metaphysical notions about absolute justice, that there is no justice in the universe. Why did he live?—an iniquitous, moral monster, a blot on the face of nature, a cruel, relentless, bestial cheat as well. All he could talk about was motor cars, machinery, gasoline, and garages—and especially, and with huge delight, of his mean pilferings and sordid swindlings of the persons who had employed him in the days before the coming of the plague. And yet he was spared, while hundreds of millions, yea, billions, of better men were destroyed.

"I went on with him to his camp, and there I saw her, Vesta, the one woman. It was glorious and... pitiful. There she was, Vesta Van Warden, the young wife of John Van Warden, clad in rags, with marred and scarred and toil-calloused hands, bending over the campfire and doing scullion work—she, Vesta, who had been born to the purple of the greatest baronage of wealth the world had ever known. John Van Warden, her husband, worth one billion, eight hundred millions and President of the Board of Industrial Magnates, had been the ruler of America. Also, sitting on the International Board of Control, he had been one of the seven men who ruled the world. And she herself had come of equally noble stock. Her father, Philip Saxon, had been President of the Board of Industrial Magnates up to the time of his death. This office was in process of becoming hereditary, and had Philip Saxon had a son that son would have succeeded him. But his only child was Vesta, the perfect flower of generations of the highest culture this planet has ever produced. It was not until the engagement between Vesta and Van Warden took place, that Saxon indicated the latter as his successor. It was, I am sure, a political marriage. I have reason to believe that Vesta never really loved her husband in the mad passionate way of which the poets used to sing. It was more like the marriages that obtained among crowned heads in the days before they were displaced by the Magnates.

"And there she was, boiling fish-chowder in a soot-covered pot, her glorious eyes inflamed by the acrid smoke of the open fire. Hers was a sad story. She was the one survivor in a million, as I had been, as the Chauffeur had been. On a crowning eminence of the Alameda Hills, overlooking San Francisco Bay, Van Warden had built a vast summer palace. It was surrounded by a park of a thousand acres. When the plague broke out, Van Warden sent her there. Armed guards patrolled the boundaries of the park, and nothing entered in the way of provisions or even mail matter that was not first fumigated. And yet did the plague enter, killing the guards at their posts, the servants at their tasks, sweeping away the whole army of retainers—or, at least, all of them who did not flee to die elsewhere. So it was that Vesta found herself the sole living person in the palace that had become a charnel house.

"Now the Chauffeur had been one of the servants that ran away. Returning, two months afterward, he discovered Vesta in a little summer pavilion where there had been no deaths and where she had established herself. He was a brute. She was afraid, and she ran away and hid among the trees. That night, on foot, she fled into the mountains—she, whose tender feet and delicate body had never known the bruise of stones nor the scratch of briars. He followed, and that night he caught her. He struck her. Do you understand? He beat her with those terrible fists of his and made her his slave. It was she who had to gather the firewood, build the fires, cook, and do all the degrading camp-labor—she, who had never performed a menial act in her life. These things he compelled her to do, while he, a proper savage, elected to lie around camp and look on. He did nothing, absolutely nothing, except on occasion to hunt meat or catch fish."

"Good for Chauffeur," Hare-Lip commented in an undertone to the other boys. "I remember him before he died. He was a corker. But he did things, and he made things go. You know, Dad married his daughter, an' you ought to see the way he knocked the spots outa Dad. The Chauffeur was a son-of-a-gun. He made us kids stand around. Even when he was croaking he reached out for me, once, an' laid my head open with that long stick he kept always beside him."

Hare-Lip rubbed his bullet head reminiscently, and the boys returned to the old man, who was maundering ecstatically about Vesta, the squaw of the founder of the Chauffeur Tribe.

"And so I say to you that you cannot understand the awfulness of the situation. The Chauffeur was a servant, understand, a servant. And he cringed, with bowed head, to such as she. She was a lord of life, both by birth and by marriage. The destinies of millions, such as he, she carried in the hollow of her pink-white hand. And, in the days before the plague, the slightest contact with such as he would have been pollution. Oh, I have seen it. Once, I remember, there was Mrs. Goldwin, wife of one of the great magnates. It was on a landing stage, just as she was embarking in her private dirigible, that she dropped her parasol. A servant picked it up and made the mistake of handing it to her—to her, one of the greatest royal ladies of the land! She shrank back, as though he were a leper, and indicated her secretary to receive it. Also, she ordered her secretary to ascertain the creature's name and to see that he was immediately discharged from service. And such a woman was Vesta Van Warden. And her the Chauffeur beat and made his slave.

"—Bill—that was it; Bill, the Chauffeur. That was his name. He was a wretched, primitive man, wholly devoid of the finer instincts and chivalrous promptings of a cultured soul. No, there is no absolute justice, for to him fell that wonder of womanhood, Vesta Van Warden. The grievous-ness of this you will never understand, my grandsons; for you are yourselves primitive little savages, unaware of aught else but savagery. Why should Vesta not have been mine? I was a man of culture and refinement, a professor in a great university. Even so, in the time before the plague, such was her exalted position, she would not have deigned to know that I existed. Mark, then, the abysmal degradation to which she fell at the hands of the Chauffeur. Nothing less than the destruction of all mankind had made it possible that I should know her, look in her eyes, converse with her, touch her hand—ay, and love her and know that her feelings toward me were very kindly. I have reason to believe that she, even she, would have loved me, there being no other man in the world except the Chauffeur. Why, when it destroyed eight billions of souls, did not the plague destroy just one more man, and that man the Chauffeur?

"Once, when the Chauffeur was away fishing, she begged me to kill him. With tears in her eyes she begged me to kill him. But he was a strong and violent man, and I was afraid. Afterwards, I talked with him. I offered him my horse, my pony, my dogs, all that I possessed, if he would give Vesta to me. And he grinned in my face and shook his head. He was very insulting. He said that in the old days he had been a servant, had been dirt under the feet of men like me and of women like Vesta, and that now he had the greatest lady in the land to be servant to him and cook his food and nurse his brats. 'You had your day before the plague,' he said; 'but this is my day, and a damned good day it is. I wouldn't trade back to the old times for anything.' Such words he spoke, but they are not his words. He was a vulgar, low-minded man, and vile oaths fell continually from his lips.

"Also, he told me that if he caught me making eyes at his woman he'd wring my neck and give her a beating as well. What was I to do? I was afraid. He was a brute. That first night, when I discovered the camp, Vesta and I had great talk about the things of our vanished world. We talked of art, and books, and poetry; and the Chauffeur listened and grinned and sneered. He was bored and angered by our way of speech which he did not comprehend, and finally he spoke up and said: 'And this is Vesta Van Warden, one-time wife of Van Warden the Magnate— a high and stuck-up beauty, who is now my squaw. Eh, Professor Smith, times is changed, times is changed. Here, you, woman, take off my moccasins, and lively about it. I want Professor Smith to see how well I have you trained.'

"I saw her clench her teeth, and the flame of revolt rise in her face. He drew back his gnarled fist to strike, and I was afraid, and sick at heart. I could do nothing to prevail against him. So I got up to go, and not be witness to such indignity. But the Chauffeur laughed and threatened me with a beating if I did not stay and behold. And I sat there, perforce, by the campfire on the shore of Lake Temescal, and saw Vesta, Vesta Van Warden, kneel and remove the moccasins of that grinning, hairy, apelike human brute.

"—Oh, you do not understand, my grandsons. You have never known anything else, and you do not understand.

"'Halter-broke and bridle-wise,' the Chauffeur gloated, while she performed that dreadful, menial task. 'A trifle balky at times, Professor, a trifle balky; but a clout alongside the jaw makes her as meek and gentle as a lamb.'

"And another time he said: 'We've got to start all over and replenish the earth and multiply. You're handicapped, Professor. You ain't got no wife, and we're up against a regular Garden-of-Eden proposition. But I ain't proud. I'll tell you what, Professor.' He pointed at their little infant, barely a year old. 'There's your wife, though you'll have to wait till she grows up. It's rich, ain't it? We're all equals here, and I'm the biggest toad in the splash. But I ain't stuck up— not I. I do you the honor, Professor Smith, the very great honor of betrothing to you my and Vesta Van Warden's daughter. Ain't it cussed bad that Van Warden ain't here to see?'"

🕉 6 🕉

"I LIVED three weeks of infinite torment there in the Chauffeur's camp. And then, one day, tiring of me, or of what to him was my bad effect on Vesta, he told me that the year before, wandering through the Contra Costa Hills to the Straits of Carquinez, across the Straits he had seen a smoke. This meant that there were still other human beings, and that for three weeks he had kept this inestimably precious information from me. I departed at once, with my dogs and horses, and journeyed across the Contra Costa Hills to the Straits. I saw no smoke on the other side, but at Port Costa discovered a small steel barge on which I was able to embark my animals. Old canvas which I found served me for a sail, and a southerly breeze fanned me across the Straits and up to the ruins of Vallejo. Here, on the outskirts of the city, I found evidences of a recently occupied camp.

"Many clam-shells showed me why these humans had come to the shores of the Bay. This was the Santa Rosa Tribe, and I followed its track along the old railroad right of way across the salt marshes to Sonoma Valley. Here, at the old brickyard at Glen Ellen, I came upon the camp. There were eighteen souls all told. Two were old men, one of whom was Jones, a banker. The other was Harrison, a retired pawnbroker, who had taken for wife the matron of the State Hospital for the Insane at Napa. Of all the persons of the city of Napa, and of all the other towns and villages in that rich and populous valley, she had been the only-survivor. Next, there were the three young men—Cardiff and Hale, who had been farmers, and Wainwright, a common day-laborer. All three had found wives. To Hale, a crude, illiterate farmer, had fallen Isadore, the greatest prize, next to Vesta, of the women who came through the plague. She was one of the world's most noted singers, and the plague had caught her at San Francisco. She has talked with me for hours at a time, telling me of her adventures, until, at last, rescued by Hale in the Mendocino Forest Reserve, there had remained nothing for her to do but become his wife. But Hale was a good fellow, in spite of his illiteracy. He had a keen sense of justice and right-dealing, and she was far happier with him than was Vesta with the Chauffeur.

"The wives of Cardiff and Wainwright were ordinary women, accustomed to toil with strong constitutions—just the type for the wild new life which they were compelled to live. In addition were two adult idiots from the feeble-minded home at El-dredge, and five or six young children and infants born after the formation of the Santa Rosa Tribe. Also, there was Bertha. She was a good woman, Hare-Lip, in spite of the sneers of your father. Her I took for wife. She was the mother of your father, Edwin, and of yours, Hoo-Hoo. And it was our daughter, Vera, who married your father, Hare-Lip—your father, Sandow, who was the oldest son of Vesta Van Warden and the Chauffeur.

"And so it was that I became the nineteenth member of the Santa Rosa Tribe. There were only two outsiders added after me. One was Mungerson, descended from the Magnates, who wandered alone in the wilds of Northern California for eight years before he came south and joined us. He it was who waited twelve years more before he married my daughter, Mary. The other was Johnson, the man who founded the Utah Tribe. That was where he came from, Utah, a country that lies very far away from here, across the great deserts, to the east. It was not until twenty-seven years after the plague that Johnson reached California. In all that Utah region he reported but three survivors, himself one, and all men. For many years these three men lived and hunted together, until, at last, desperate, fearing that with them the human race would perish utterly from the planet, they headed westward on the possibility of finding women survivors in California. Johnson alone came through the great desert, where his two companions died. He was forty-six years old when he joined us, and he married the fourth daughter of Isadore and Hale, and his eldest son married your aunt, Hare-Lip, who was the third daughter of Vesta and the Chauffeur. Johnson was a strong man, with a will of his own. And it was because of this that he seceded from the Santa Rosans and formed the Utah Tribe at San José. It is a small tribe—there are only nine in it; but, though he is dead, such was his influence and the strength of his breed, that it will grow into a strong tribe and play a leading part in the recivilization of the planet.

"There are only two other tribes that we know of—the Los Angelitos and the Carmelitos. The latter started from one man and woman. He was called Lopez, and he was descended from the ancient Mexicans and was very black. He was a cowherd in the ranges beyond Carmel, and his wife was a maidservant in the great Del Monte Hotel. It was seven years before we first got in touch with the Los Ange-litos. They have a good country down there, but it is too warm. I estimate the present population of the world at between three hundred and fifty and four hundred—provided, of course, that there are no scattered little tribes elsewhere in the world. If there be such, we have not heard from them. Since Johnson crossed the desert from Utah, no word nor sign has come from the East or anywhere else. The great world which I knew in my boyhood and early manhood is gone. It has ceased to be. I am the last man who was alive in the days of the plague and who knows the wonders of that far-off time. We, who mastered the planet—its earth, and sea, and sky—and who were as very gods, now live in primitive savagery along the water courses of this California country.

"But we are increasing rapidly—your sister, Hare-Lip, already has four children. We are increasing rapidly and making ready for a new climb toward civilization. In time, pressure of population will compel us to spread out, and a hundred generations from now we may expect our descendants to start across the Sierras, oozing slowly along, generation by generation, over the great continent to the colonization of the East—a new Aryan drift around the world.

"But it will be slow, very slow; we have so far to climb. We fell so hopelessly far. If only one physicist or one chemist had survived! But it was not to be, and we have forgotten everything. The Chauffeur started working in iron. He made the forge which we use to this day. But he was a lazy man, and when he died he took with him all he knew of metals and machinery. What was I to know of such things? I was a classical scholar, not a chemist.. The other men who survived were not educated. Only two things did the Chauffeur accomplish—the brewing of strong drink and the growing of tobacco. It was while he was drunk, once, that he killed Vesta. I firmly believe that he killed Vesta in a fit of drunken cruelty though he always maintained that she fell into the lake and was drowned.

"And, my grandsons, let me warn you against the medicine-men. They call themselves *doctors*, travestying what was once a noble profession, but in reality they are medicine-men, devil-devil men, and they make for superstition and darkness. They are cheats and liars. But so debased and degraded are we, that we believe their lies. They, too, will increase in numbers as we increase, and they will strive to rule us. Yet are they liars and charlatans. Look at young Cross-Eyes, posing as a doctor, selling charms against sickness, giving good hunting, exchanging promises of fair weather for good meat and skins, sending the death-stick, performing a thousand abominations. Yet I say to you, that when he says he can do these things, he lies. I, Professor Smith, Professor James Howard Smith, say that he lies. I have told him so to his teeth. Why has he not sent me the death-stick? Because he knows that with me it is without avail. But you, Hare-Lip, so deeply are you sunk in black superstition that did you awake this night and find the death-stick beside you, you would surely die. And you would die, not because of any virtues in the stick, but because you are a savage with the dark and clouded mind of a savage.

"The doctors must be destroyed, and all that was lost must be discovered over again. Wherefore, earnestly, I repeat unto you certain things which you must remember and tell to your children after you. You must tell them that when water is made hot by fire, there resides in it a wonderful thing called steam, which is stronger than ten thousand men and which can do all man's work for him. There are other very useful things. In the lightning flash resides a similarly strong servant of man, which was of old his slave and which some day will be his slave again.

"Quite a different thing is the alphabet. It is what enables me to know the meaning of fine markings, whereas you boys know only rude picture-writing. In that dry cave on Telegraph Hill, where you see me often go when the tribe is down by the sea, I have stored many books. In them is great wisdom. Also, with them, I have placed a key to the alphabet, so that one who knows picture-writing may also know print. Some day men will read again; and then, if no accident has befallen my cave, they will know that Professor James Howard Smith once lived and saved for them the knowledge of the ancients.

"There is another little device that men inevitably will rediscover. It is called gunpowder. It was what enabled us to kill surely and at long distances. Certain things which are found in the ground, when combined in the right proportions, will make this gunpowder. What these things are, I have forgotten, or else I never knew. But I wish I did know. Then would I make powder, and then would I certainly kill Cross-Eyes and rid the land of superstition—"

"After I am man-grown I am going to give Cross-Eyes all the goats, and meat, and skins I can get, so that he'll teach me to be a doctor," Hoo-Hoo asserted. "And when I know, I'll make everybody else sit up and take notice. They'll get down in the dirt to me, you bet."

The old man nodded his head solemnly, and murmured:

"Strange it is to hear the vestiges and remnants of the complicated Aryan speech falling from the lips of a filthy little skin-clad savage. All the world is topsy-turvy. And it has been topsy-turvy ever since the plague."

"You won't make me sit up," Hare-Lip boasted to the would-be medicine-man. "If I paid you for a sending of the death-stick and it didn't work, I'd bust in your head—understand, you Hoo-Hoo, you?"

"I'm going to get Granser to remember this here gunpowder stuff," Edwin said softly, "and then I'll have you all on the run. You, Hare-Lip, will do my fighting for me and get my meat for me, and you, Hoo-Hoo, will send the death-stick for me and make everybody afraid. And if I catch Hare-Lip trying to bust your head, Hoo-Hoo, I'll fix him with that same gunpowder. Granser ain't such a fool as you think, and I'm going to listen to him and some day I'll be boss over the whole bunch of you."

The old man shook his head sadly, and said:

"The gunpowder will come. Nothing can stop it—the same old story over and over. Man will increase, and men will fight. The gunpowder will enable men to kill millions of men, and in this way only, by fire and blood, will a new civilization, in some remote day, be evolved. And of what profit will it be? Just as the old civilization passed, so will the new. It may take fifty thousand years to build, but it will pass. All things pass. Only remain cosmic force and matter, ever in flux, ever acting and reacting and realizing the eternal types—the priest, the soldier, and the king. Out of the mouths of babes comes the wisdom of all the ages. Some will fight, some will rule, some will pray; and all the rest will toil and suffer sore while on their bleeding carcasses is reared again, and yet again, without end, the amazing beauty and surpassing wonder of the civilized state. It were just as well that I destroyed those cave-stored books— whether they remain or perish, all their old truths will be discovered, their old lies lived and handed down. What is the profit—"

Hare-Lip leaped to his feet, giving a quick glance at the pasturing goats and the afternoon sun.

"Gee!" he muttered to Edwin, "The old geezer gets more long-winded every day. Let's pull for camp."

While the other two, aided by the dogs, assembled the goats and started them for the trail through the forest, Edwin stayed by the old man and guided him in the same direction. When they reached the old right of way, Edwin stopped suddenly and looked back. Hare-Lip and Hoo-Hoo and the dogs and the goats passed on. Edwin was looking at a small herd of wild horses which had come down on the hard sand. There were at least twenty of them, young colts and yearlings and mares, led by a beautiful stallion which stood in the foam at the edge of the surf, with arched neck and bright wild eyes, sniffing the salt air from off the sea.

"What is it?" Granser queried.

"Horses," was the answer. "First time I ever seen 'em on the beach. It's the mountain lions getting thicker and thicker and driving 'em down."

The low sun shot red shafts of light, fan-shaped, up from a cloud-tumbled horizon. And close at hand, in the white waste of shore-lashed waters, the sea-lions, bellowing their old primeval chant, hauled up out of the sea on the black rocks and fought and loved.

"Come on, Granser," Edwin prompted. And old man and boy, skin-clad and barbaric, turned and went along the right of way into the forest in the wake of the goats.

Printed in Great Britain
by Amazon

39410456R00272